Archie

MODERN CLASSICS

MANIA

Publisher / Co-CEO: Jon Goldwater
President / Editor-In-Chief: Mike Pellerito
Chief Creative Officer: Roberto Aguirre-Sacasa
Chief Operating Officer: William Mooar
Chief Financial Officer: Robert Wintle
Director: Jonathan Betancourt
Senior Director of Editorial: Jamie Lee Rotante
Art Director: Vincent Lovallo
Production Manager: Stephen Oswald
Lead Designer: Kari McLachlan
Associate Editor: Carlos Antunes
Co-CEO: Nancy Silberkleit

Published by Archie Comic Publications, Inc. 629 Fifth Avenue, Pelham, NY 10803-1242

ISBN: 978-1-64576-881-4

STORIES

FRANCIS BONNET, DAN PARENT, RON ROBBINS, ANGELO DECESARE, CRAIG BOLDMAN, BILL GOLLIHER, TOM DEFALCO, TANIA DEL RIO & TEE FRANKLIN

ART

BILL GOLLIHER, DAN PARENT, REX LINDSEY, JEFF SHULTZ, BILL GALVAN, PAT KENNEDY, TIM KENNEDY, JIM AMASH, BOB SMITH, BEN GALVAN, GLENN WHITMORE, JACK MORELLI & ROSARIO "TITO" PEÑA

CONTENTS

CHAPTER

01

ARCHIE COMICS

P. 007

CHAPTER

02

BETTY & VERONICA

P. 068

CHAPTER

03

WORLD OF
ARCHIE

P. 124

CHAPTER

04

WORLD OF
B&V

P. 180

CHAPTER

05

ARCHIE
MILESTONES

P. 231

2022 was a banner year for classic-style Archie stories, and one that also marks the start of a new era of classic Archie. Archie and his best friends, Jughead, Betty, Veronica, and, yes, even Reggie, said hello to quite a few new faces in Riverdale. Comic series like *Archie & Friends* and *B&V Friends Forever* expanded the ever-growing roster with brand new faces like Stacy Banks, Eliza Han, Amber Nightstone, and the lovable Halloween sprites Trick 'n' Treat, who would also make notable appearances in digest stories as well.

The Archie digest line also started featuring classic characters like Cosmo the Merry Martian, Jughead's Uncle Herman, Veronica's mischievous cousin Leroy, pop singing superstar Bingo Wilkin and his girlfriend Samantha Smythe, the nefarious Mad Doctor Doom and his lackey Chester Plunkett, and even the Power Pets! Expect even more of these new and returning characters to come throughout 2023 and beyond!

The *Archie Milestones Jumbo Comics Series* also got a facelift this year, as we continue our 80th anniversary festivities. Each issue featured a brand new story, set in a different notable decade from Archie's history. Speaking of notable dates and celebrations, it was also a landmark year for Archie Editor-in-Chief Mike Pellerito, who celebrated his 22nd anniversary at Archie Comics!

The Archie classic line is stronger than ever, and only continuing to grow. Now, turn the page to experience these fun, heartwarming, and action-packed stories from 2022!

01

ARCHIE COMICS

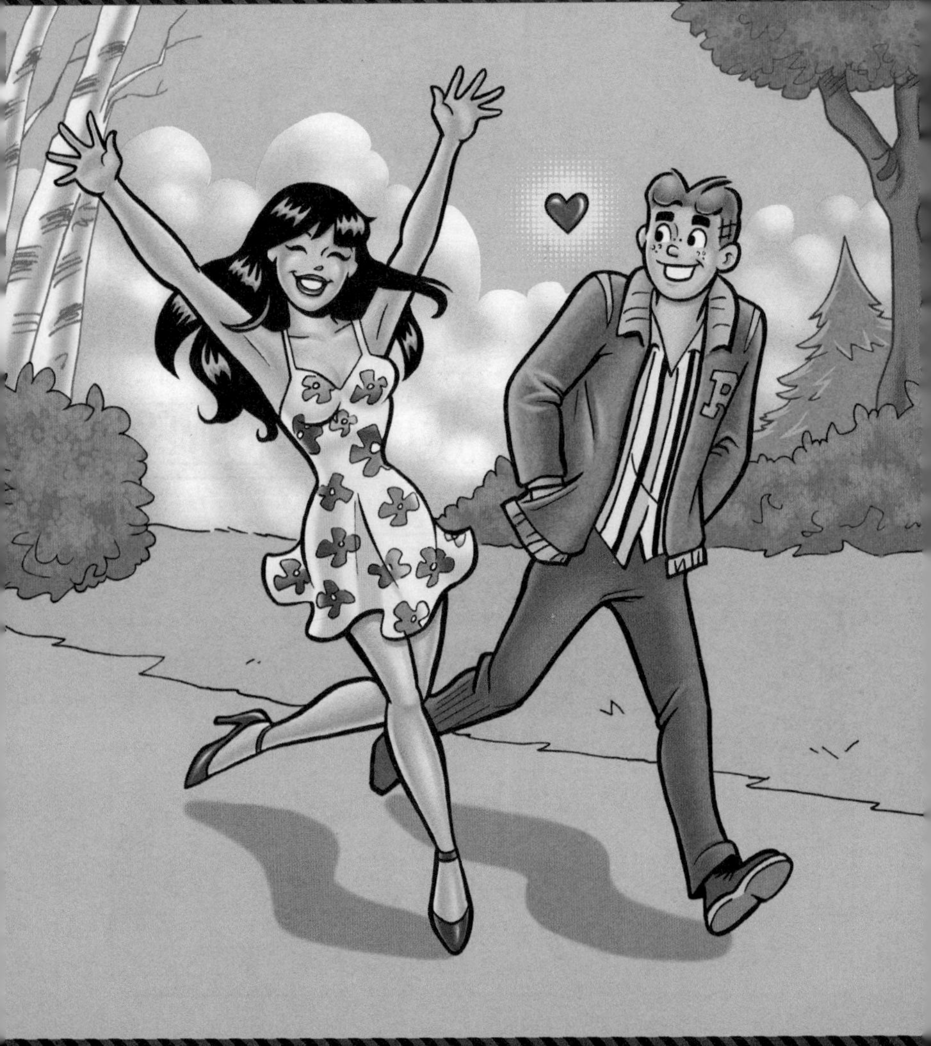

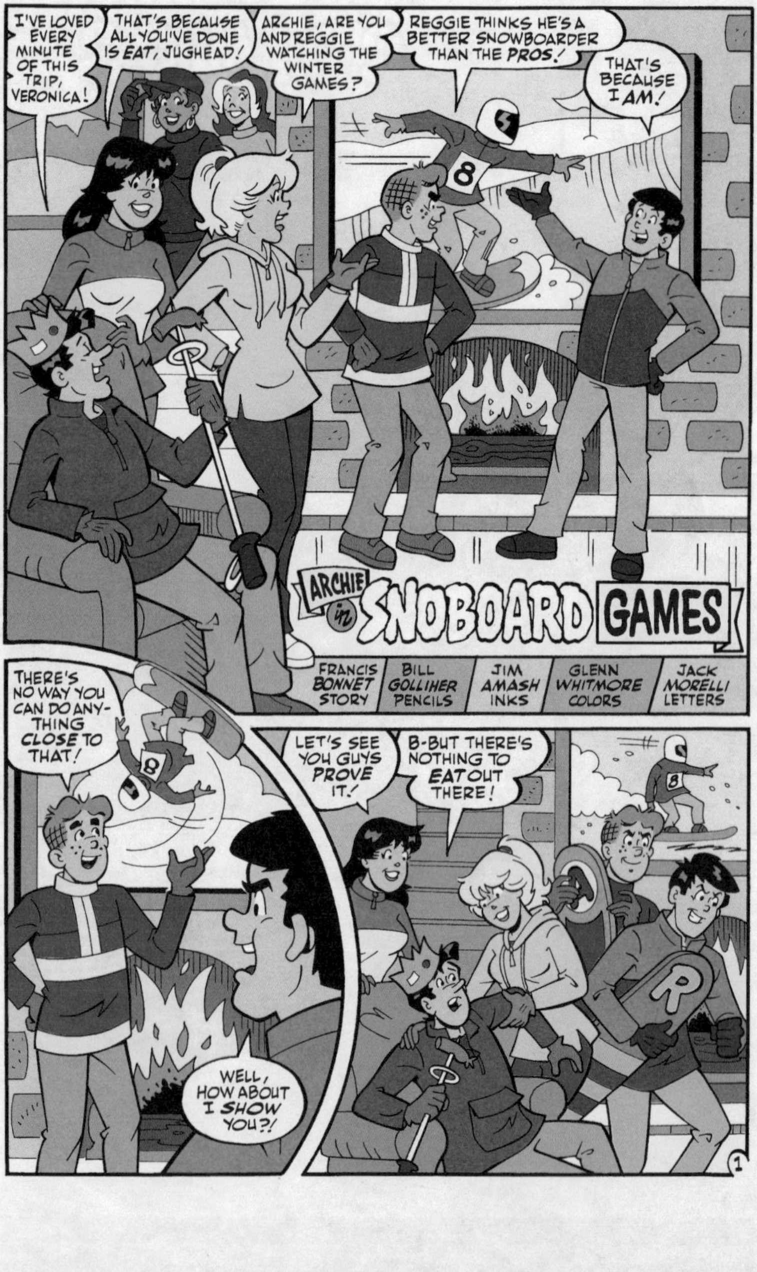
I'VE LOVED EVERY MINUTE OF THIS TRIP, VERONICA!
THAT'S BECAUSE ALL YOU'VE DONE IS EAT, JUGHEAD!
ARCHIE, ARE YOU AND REGGIE WATCHING THE WINTER GAMES?
REGGIE THINKS HE'S A BETTER SNOWBOARDER THAN THE PROS!
THAT'S BECAUSE I AM!
8
ARCHIE in SNOBOARD GAMES
FRANCIS BONNET STORY
BILL GOLLIHER PENCILS
JIM AMASH INKS
GLENN WHITMORE COLORS
JACK MORELLI LETTERS
THERE'S NO WAY YOU CAN DO ANYTHING CLOSE TO THAT!
WELL, HOW ABOUT I SHOW YOU?!
LET'S SEE YOU GUYS PROVE IT!
B-BUT THERE'S NOTHING TO EAT OUT THERE!
R
1

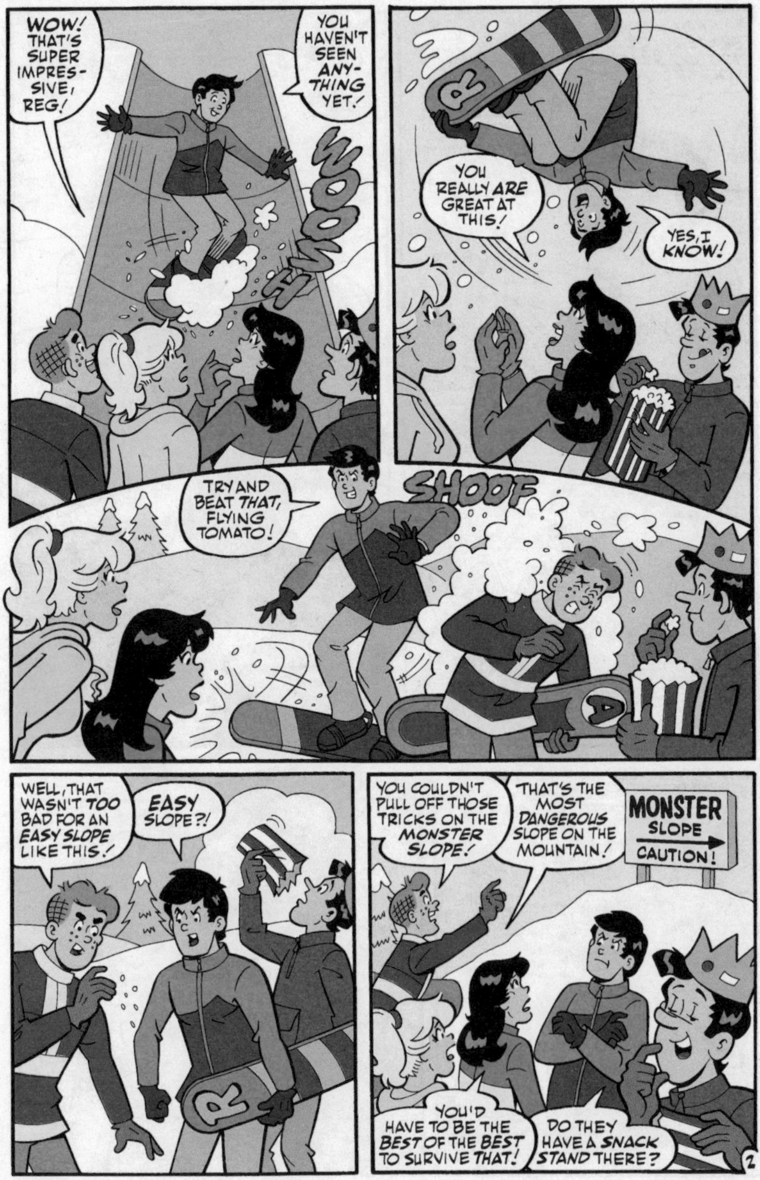
WOW! THAT'S SUPER IMPRES-SIVE, REG!
YOU HAVEN'T SEEN ANY-THING YET!
WOOSH
YOU REALLY ARE GREAT AT THIS!
YES, I KNOW!
TRY AND BEAT THAT, FLYING TOMATO!
SHOOF
WELL, THAT WASN'T TOO BAD FOR AN EASY SLOPE LIKE THIS!
EASY SLOPE?!
YOU COULDN'T PULL OFF THOSE TRICKS ON THE MONSTER SLOPE!
THAT'S THE MOST DANGEROUS SLOPE ON THE MOUNTAIN!
MONSTER SLOPE CAUTION!
YOU'D HAVE TO BE THE BEST OF THE BEST TO SURVIVE THAT!
DO THEY HAVE A SNACK STAND THERE?
2

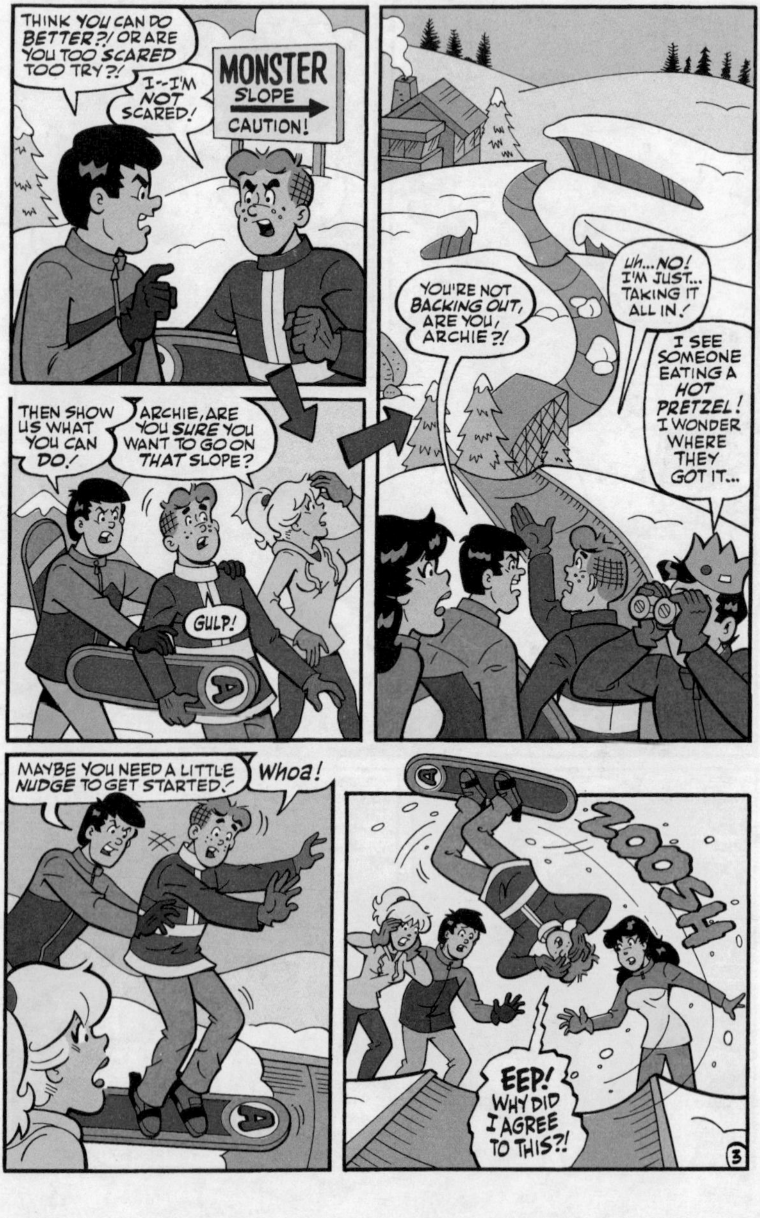
THINK YOU CAN DO BETTER?! OR ARE YOU TOO SCARED TOO TRY?!
I--I'M NOT SCARED!
MONSTER SLOPE
CAUTION!
YOU'RE NOT BACKING OUT, ARE YOU, ARCHIE?!
UH...NO! I'M JUST... TAKING IT ALL IN!
I SEE SOMEONE EATING A HOT PRETZEL! I WONDER WHERE THEY GOT IT...
THEN SHOW US WHAT YOU CAN DO!
ARCHIE, ARE YOU SURE YOU WANT TO GO ON THAT SLOPE?
GULP!
MAYBE YOU NEED A LITTLE NUDGE TO GET STARTED!
Whoa!
ZOOOSH
EEP! WHY DID I AGREE TO THIS?!
3

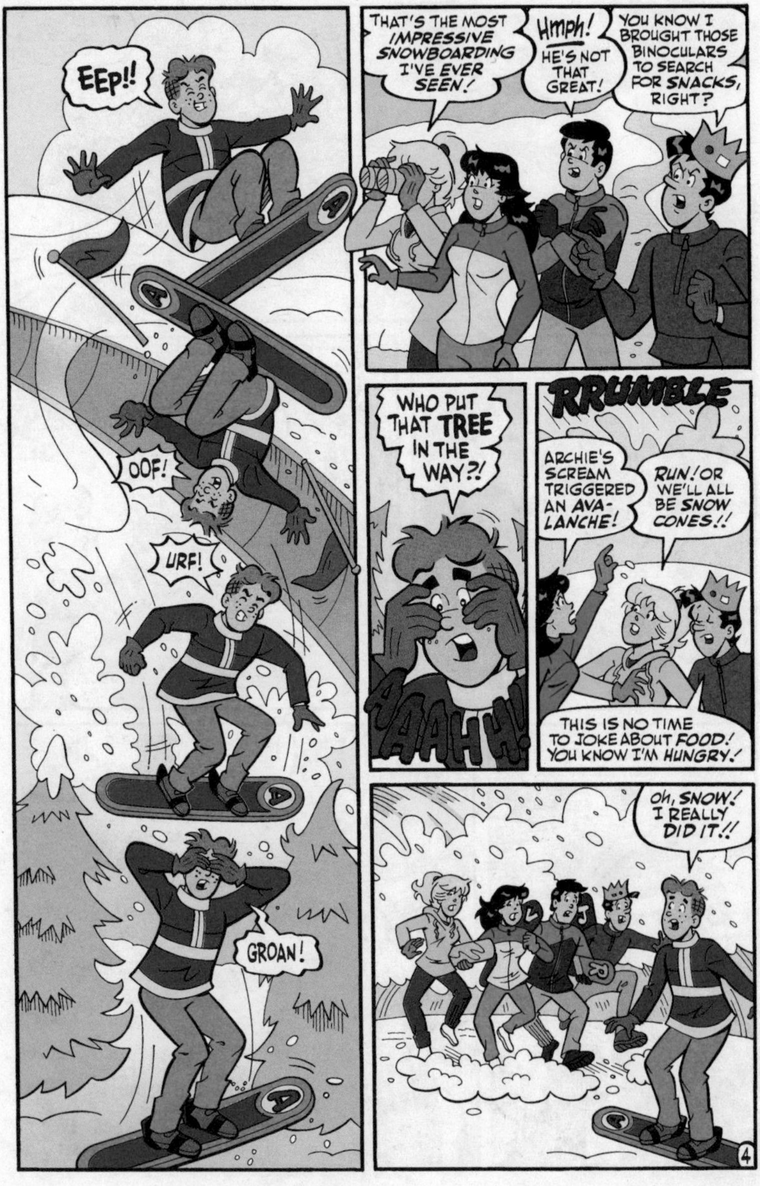
EEP!!
OOF!
URF!
GROAN!
THAT'S THE MOST IMPRESSIVE SNOWBOARDING I'VE EVER SEEN!
Hmph! HE'S NOT THAT GREAT!
YOU KNOW I BROUGHT THOSE BINOCULARS TO SEARCH FOR SNACKS, RIGHT?
WHO PUT THAT TREE IN THE WAY?!
AAAHH!
RRUMBLE
ARCHIE'S SCREAM TRIGGERED AN AVA-LANCHE!
RUN! OR WE'LL ALL BE SNOW CONES!!
THIS IS NO TIME TO JOKE ABOUT FOOD! YOU KNOW I'M HUNGRY!
Oh, SNOW! I REALLY DID IT!!
4

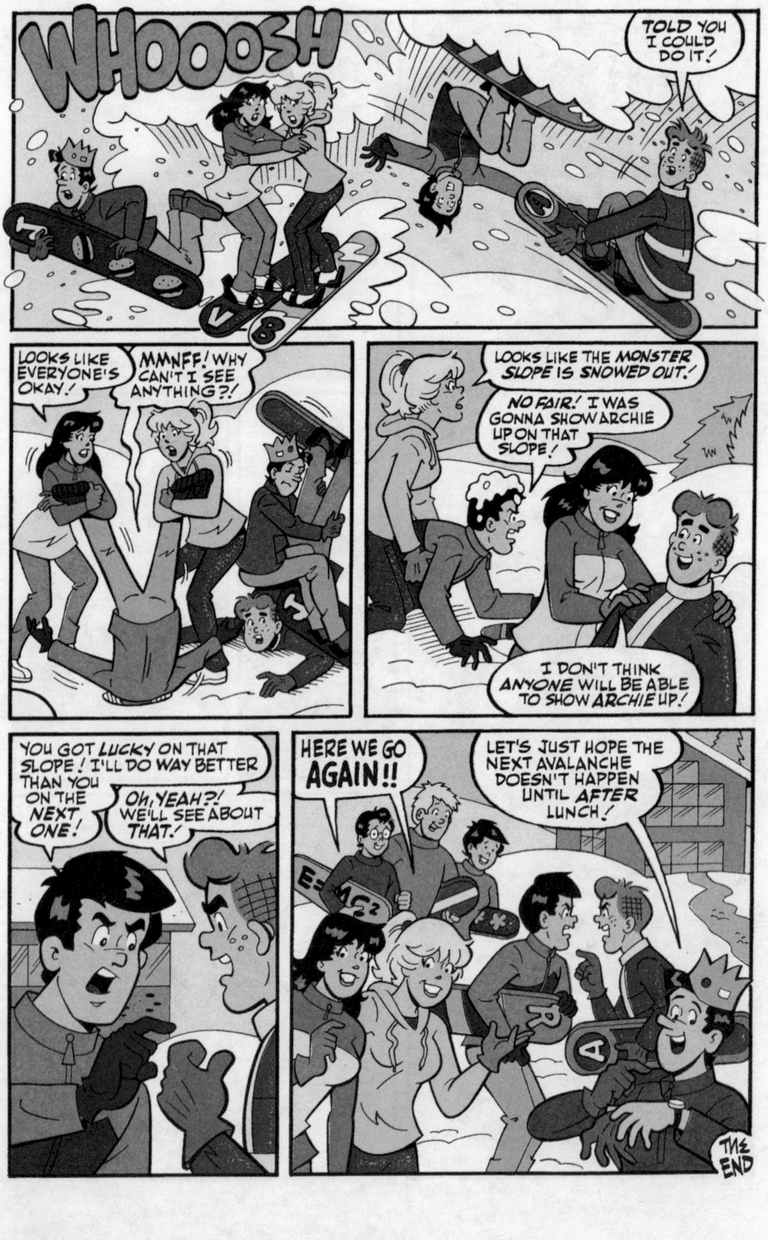
WHOOOSH
TOLD YOU I COULD DO IT!
LOOKS LIKE EVERYONE'S OKAY!
MMNFF! WHY CAN'T I SEE ANYTHING?!
LOOKS LIKE THE MONSTER SLOPE IS SNOWED OUT!
NO FAIR! I WAS GONNA SHOW ARCHIE UP ON THAT SLOPE!
I DON'T THINK ANYONE WILL BE ABLE TO SHOW ARCHIE UP!
YOU GOT LUCKY ON THAT SLOPE! I'LL DO WAY BETTER THAN YOU ON THE NEXT ONE!
OH, YEAH?! WE'LL SEE ABOUT THAT!
HERE WE GO AGAIN!!
LET'S JUST HOPE THE NEXT AVALANCHE DOESN'T HAPPEN UNTIL AFTER LUNCH!
THE END

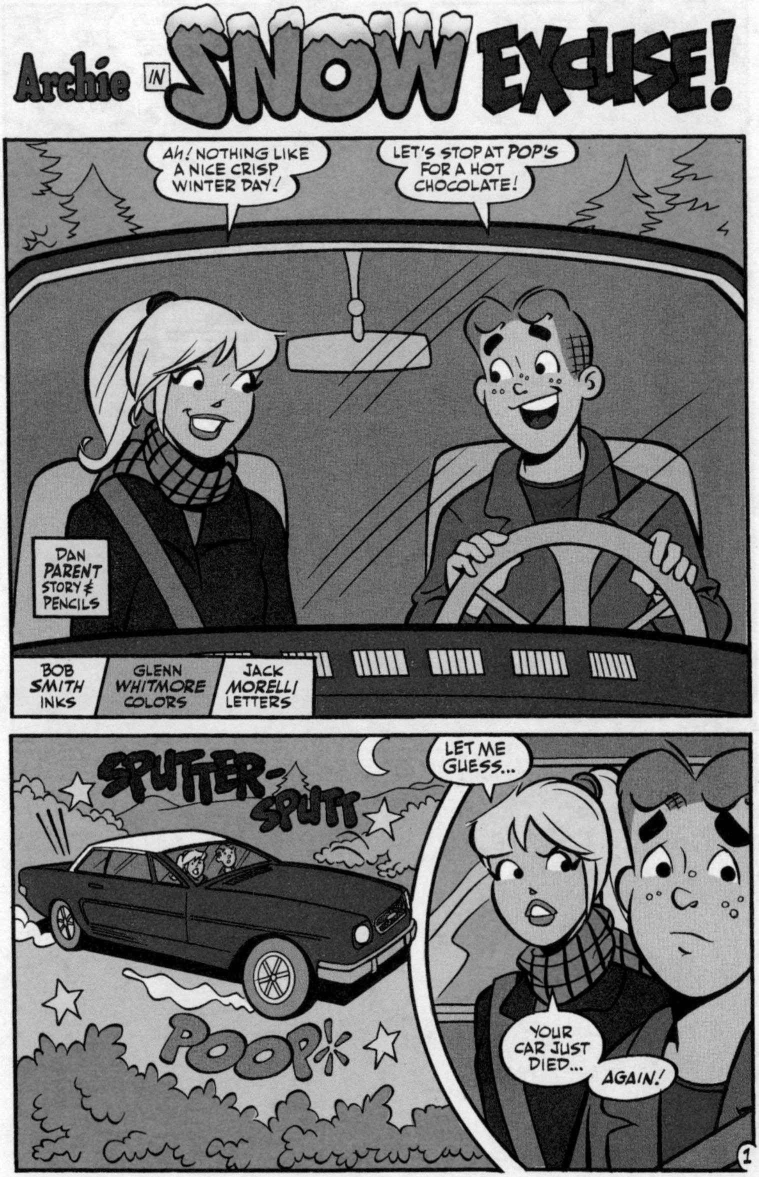
Archie IN SNOW EXCUSE!
AH! NOTHING LIKE A NICE CRISP WINTER DAY!
LET'S STOP AT POP'S FOR A HOT CHOCOLATE!
DAN PARENT STORY & PENCILS
BOB SMITH INKS
GLENN WHITMORE COLORS
JACK MORELLI LETTERS
SPUTTER-SPUTT
POOP!
LET ME GUESS...
YOUR CAR JUST DIED...
AGAIN!
1

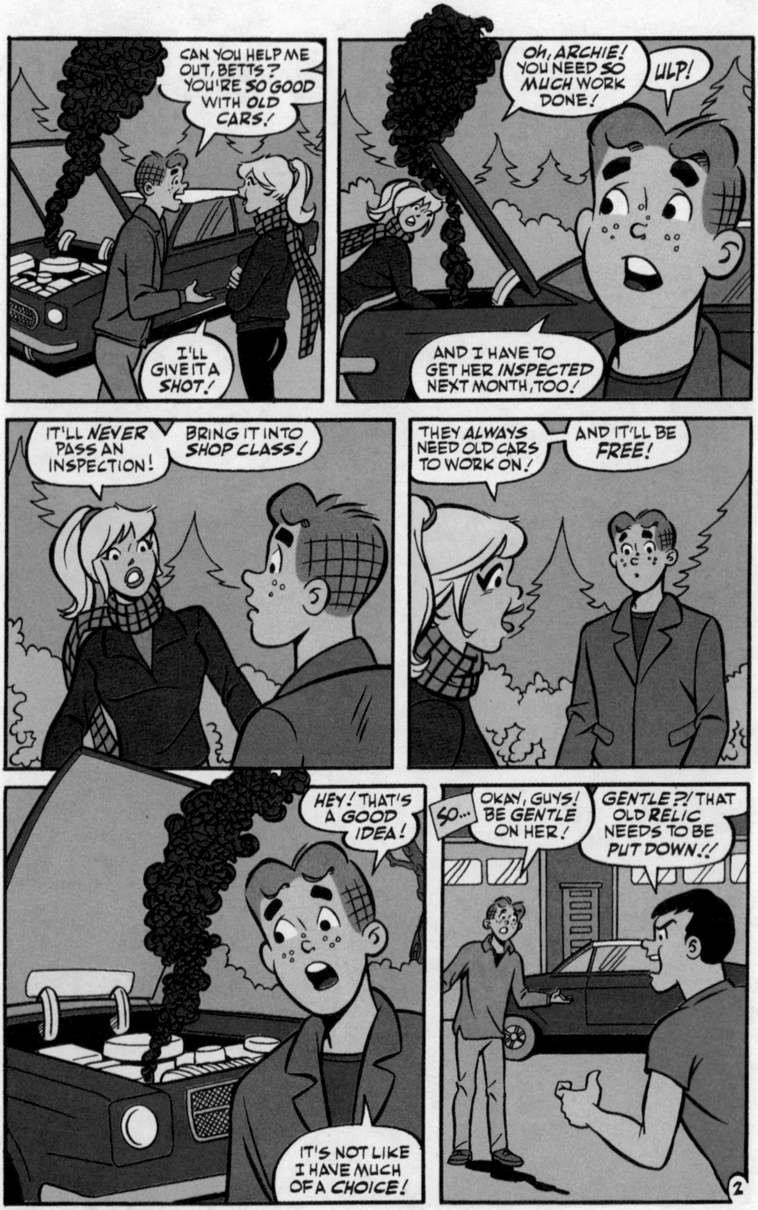
CAN YOU HELP ME OUT, BETTS? YOU'RE SO GOOD WITH OLD CARS!
I'LL GIVE IT A SHOT!
OH, ARCHIE! YOU NEED SO MUCH WORK DONE!
ULP!
AND I HAVE TO GET HER INSPECTED NEXT MONTH, TOO!
IT'LL NEVER PASS AN INSPECTION!
BRING IT INTO SHOP CLASS!
THEY ALWAYS NEED OLD CARS TO WORK ON!
AND IT'LL BE FREE!
HEY! THAT'S A GOOD IDEA!
IT'S NOT LIKE I HAVE MUCH OF A CHOICE!
SO...
OKAY, GUYS! BE GENTLE ON HER!
GENTLE?! THAT OLD RELIC NEEDS TO BE PUT DOWN!!
2

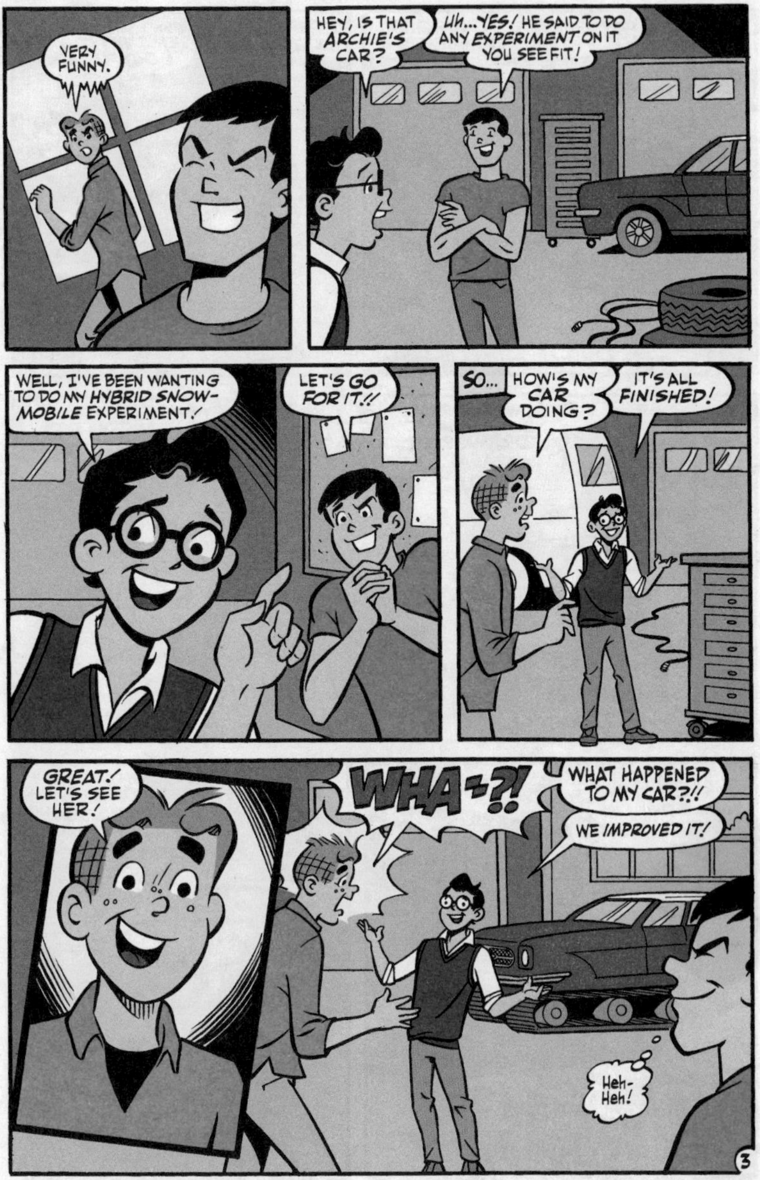
VERY FUNNY.
HEY, IS THAT ARCHIE'S CAR?
Uh...YES! HE SAID TO DO ANY EXPERIMENT ON IT YOU SEE FIT!
WELL, I'VE BEEN WANTING TO DO MY HYBRID SNOW-MOBILE EXPERIMENT!
LET'S GO FOR IT!!
SO...
HOW'S MY CAR DOING?
IT'S ALL FINISHED!
GREAT! LET'S SEE HER!
WHA-?!
WHAT HAPPENED TO MY CAR?!!
WE IMPROVED IT!
Heh-Heh!
3

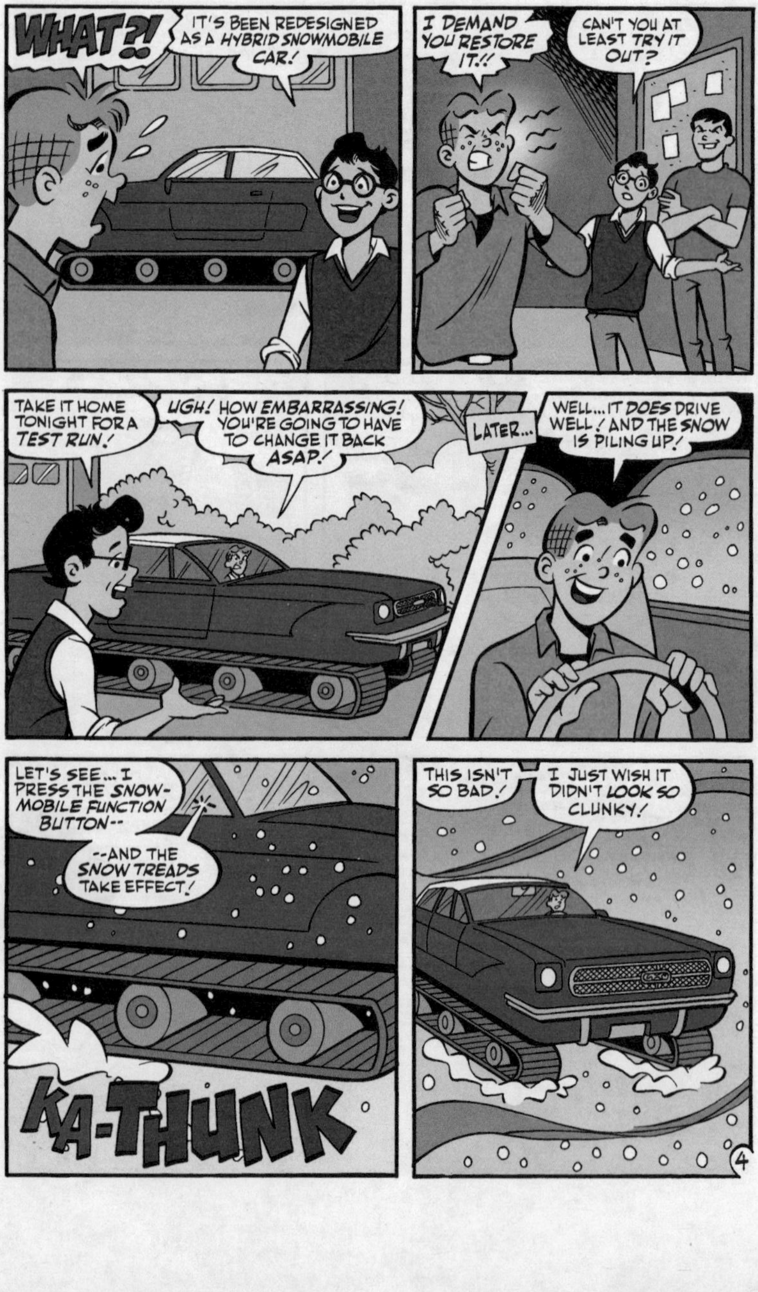
WHAT?!
IT'S BEEN REDESIGNED AS A HYBRID SNOWMOBILE CAR!
I DEMAND YOU RESTORE IT!!
CAN'T YOU AT LEAST TRY IT OUT?
TAKE IT HOME TONIGHT FOR A TEST RUN!
UGH! HOW EMBARRASSING! YOU'RE GOING TO HAVE TO CHANGE IT BACK ASAP!
LATER...
WELL... IT DOES DRIVE WELL! AND THE SNOW IS PILING UP!
LET'S SEE... I PRESS THE SNOW-MOBILE FUNCTION BUTTON--
--AND THE SNOW TREADS TAKE EFFECT!
KA-THUNK
THIS ISN'T SO BAD!
I JUST WISH IT DIDN'T LOOK SO CLUNKY!
4

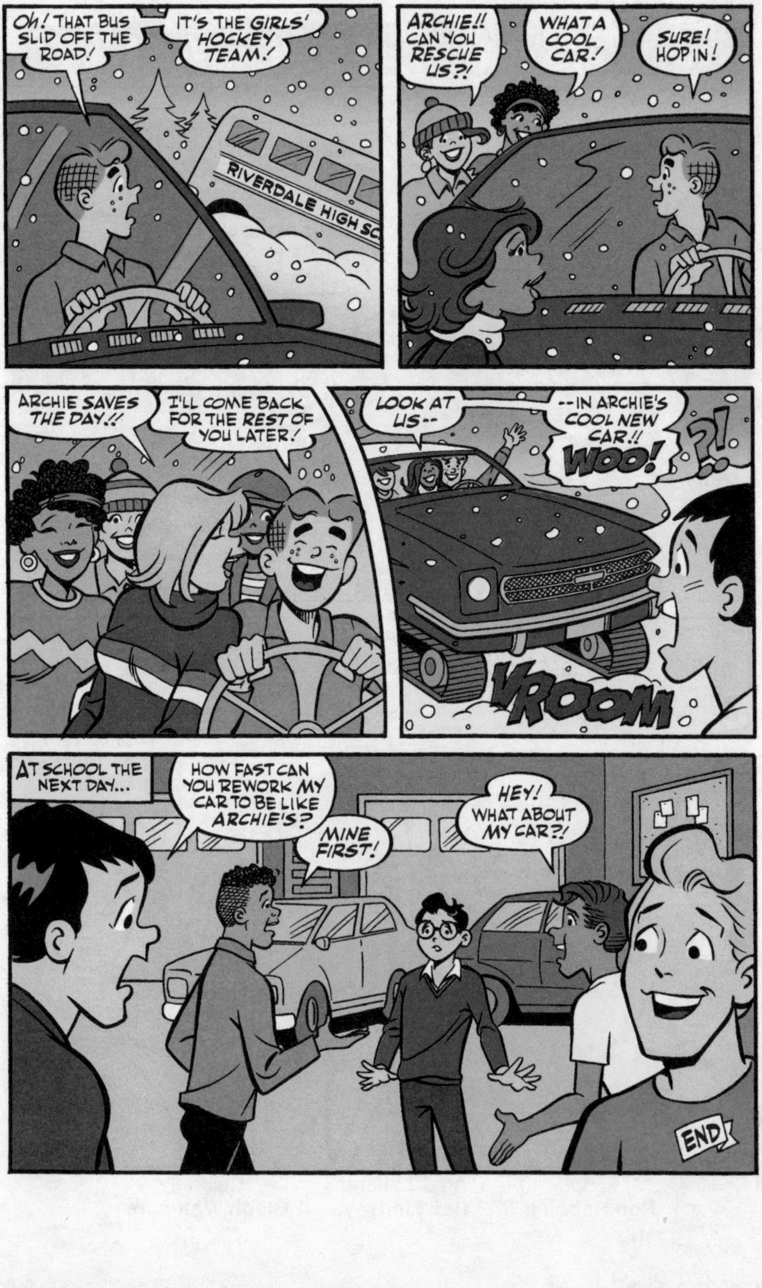
Oh! THAT BUS SLID OFF THE ROAD!
IT'S THE GIRLS' HOCKEY TEAM.!
RIVERDALE HIGH SC
ARCHIE!! CAN YOU RESCUE US?!
WHAT A COOL CAR.!
SURE! HOP IN!
ARCHIE SAVES THE DAY.!!
I'LL COME BACK FOR THE REST OF YOU LATER.!
LOOK AT US--
--IN ARCHIE'S COOL NEW CAR.!!
WOO!
?!
VROOM
AT SCHOOL THE NEXT DAY...
HOW FAST CAN YOU REWORK MY CAR TO BE LIKE ARCHIE'S?
MINE FIRST!
HEY! WHAT ABOUT MY CAR?!
END

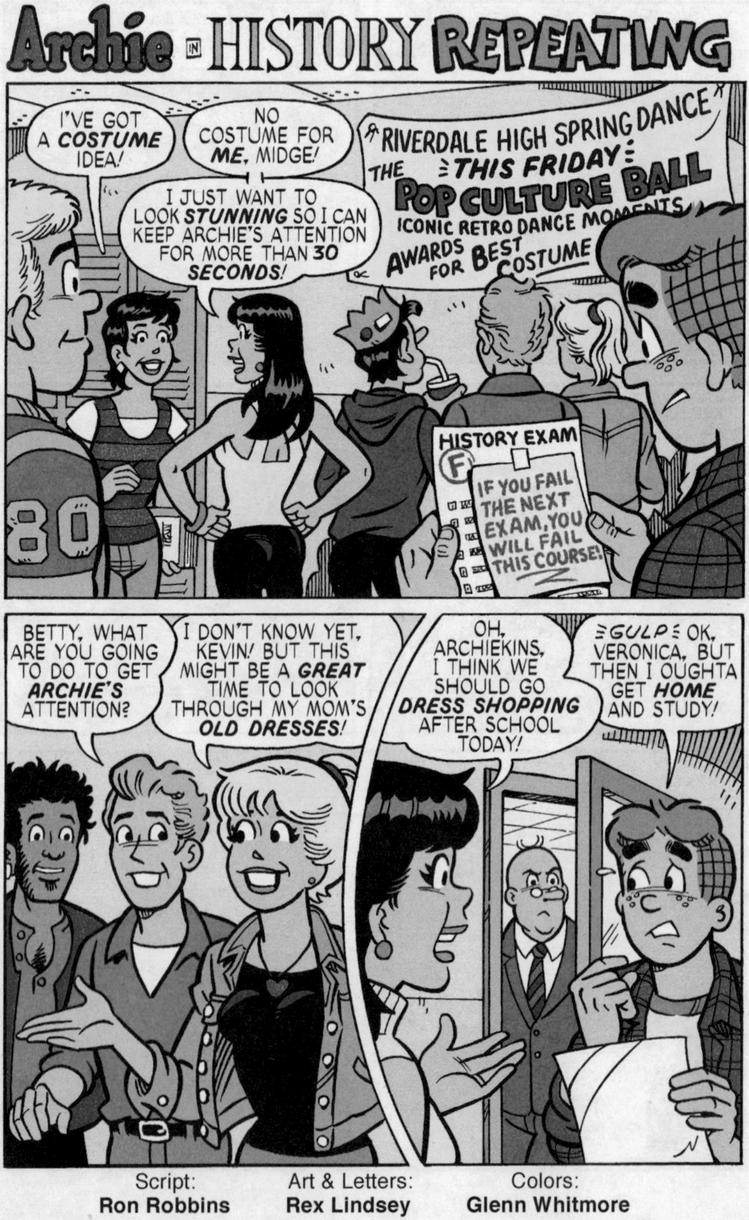
Archie IN HISTORY REPEATING
I'VE GOT A COSTUME IDEA!
NO COSTUME FOR ME, MIDGE!
I JUST WANT TO LOOK STUNNING SO I CAN KEEP ARCHIE'S ATTENTION FOR MORE THAN 30 SECONDS!
RIVERDALE HIGH SPRING DANCE
THE THIS FRIDAY POP CULTURE BALL
ICONIC RETRO DANCE MOMENTS
AWARDS FOR BEST COSTUME
HISTORY EXAM
F
IF YOU FAIL THE NEXT EXAM, YOU WILL FAIL THIS COURSE!
80
BETTY, WHAT ARE YOU GOING TO DO TO GET ARCHIE'S ATTENTION?
I DON'T KNOW YET, KEVIN! BUT THIS MIGHT BE A GREAT TIME TO LOOK THROUGH MY MOM'S OLD DRESSES!
OH, ARCHIEKINS, I THINK WE SHOULD GO DRESS SHOPPING AFTER SCHOOL TODAY!
GULP OK, VERONICA, BUT THEN I OUGHTA GET HOME AND STUDY!

Script: **Ron Robbins** | Art & Letters: **Rex Lindsey** | Colors: **Glenn Whitmore**

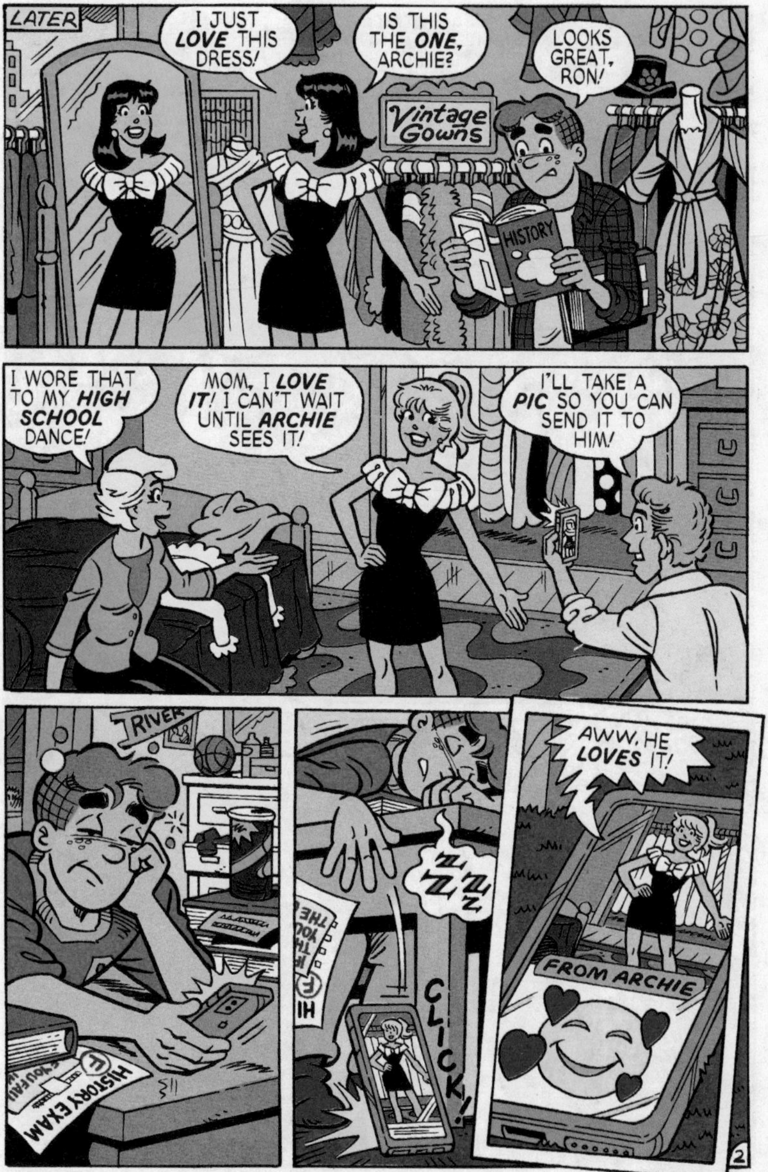
LATER
I JUST LOVE THIS DRESS!
IS THIS THE ONE, ARCHIE?
LOOKS GREAT, RON!
Vintage Gowns
HISTORY
I WORE THAT TO MY HIGH SCHOOL DANCE!
MOM, I LOVE IT! I CAN'T WAIT UNTIL ARCHIE SEES IT!
I'LL TAKE A PIC SO YOU CAN SEND IT TO HIM!
RIVER
HISTORY EXAM
ZZZ
CLICK!
AWW, HE LOVES IT!
FROM ARCHIE
2

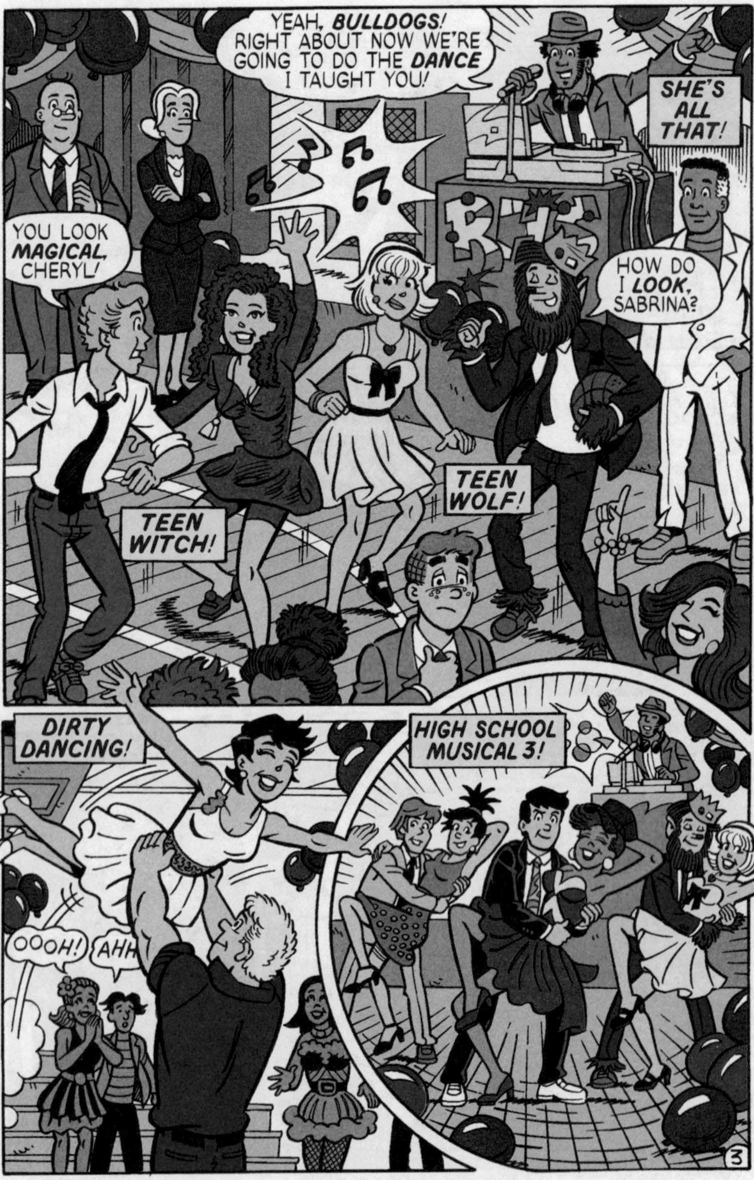
YEAH, BULLDOGS! RIGHT ABOUT NOW WE'RE GOING TO DO THE DANCE I TAUGHT YOU!
SHE'S ALL THAT!
YOU LOOK MAGICAL, CHERYL!
HOW DO I LOOK, SABRINA?
TEEN WOLF!
TEEN WITCH!
DIRTY DANCING!
HIGH SCHOOL MUSICAL 3!
OOOH!
AHH
3

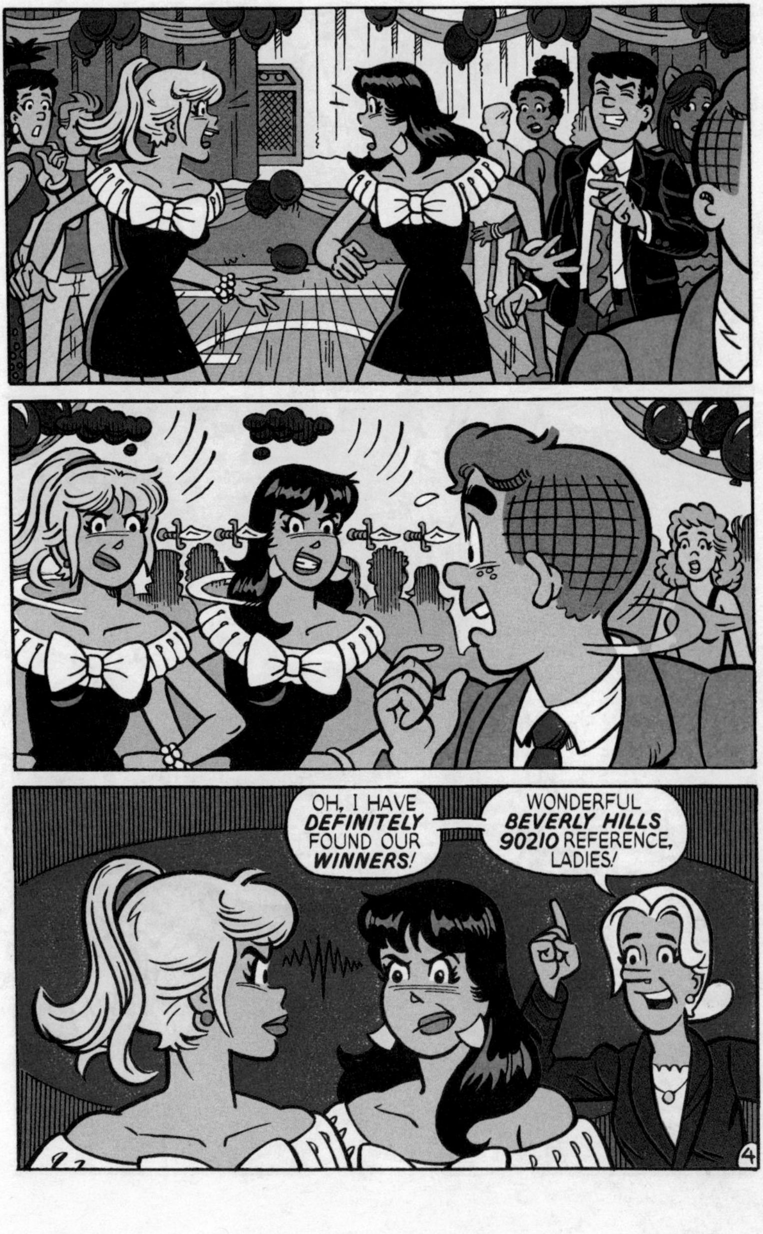
OH, I HAVE DEFINITELY FOUND OUR WINNERS!
WONDERFUL BEVERLY HILLS 90210 REFERENCE, LADIES!
4

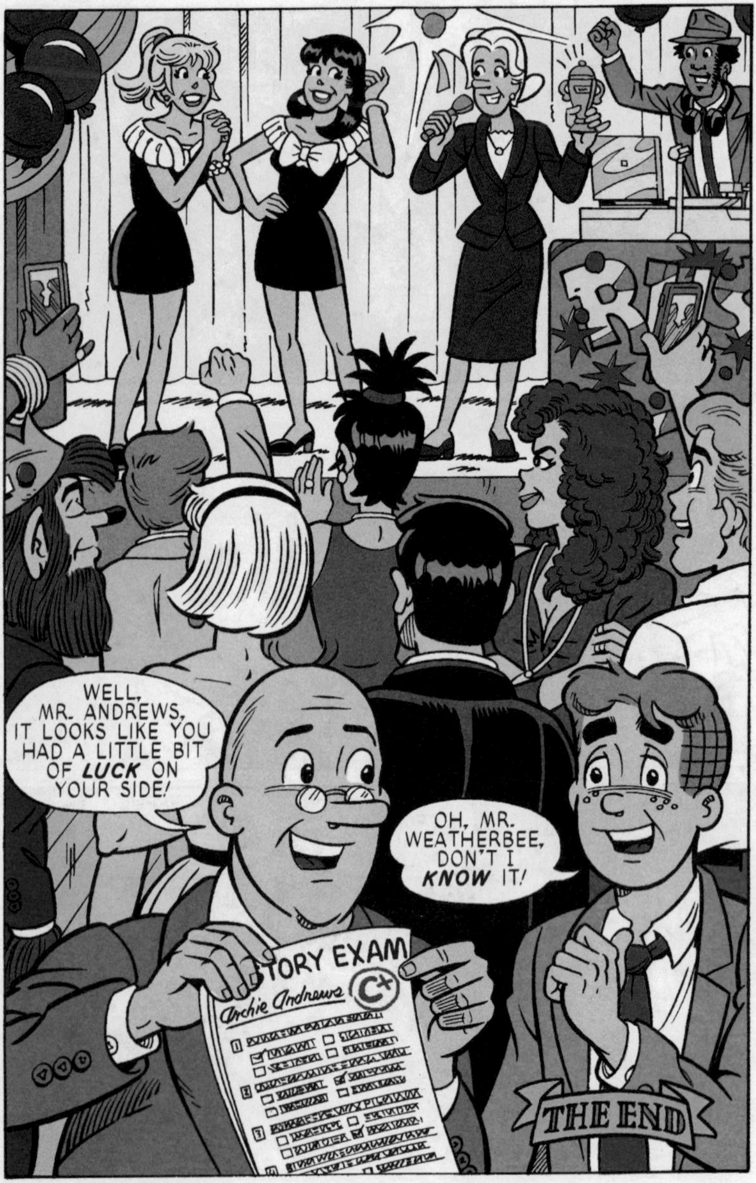
WELL, MR. ANDREWS, IT LOOKS LIKE YOU HAD A LITTLE BIT OF **LUCK** ON YOUR SIDE!
OH, MR. WEATHERBEE, DON'T I **KNOW** IT!
STORY EXAM
Archie Andrews
C+
THE END

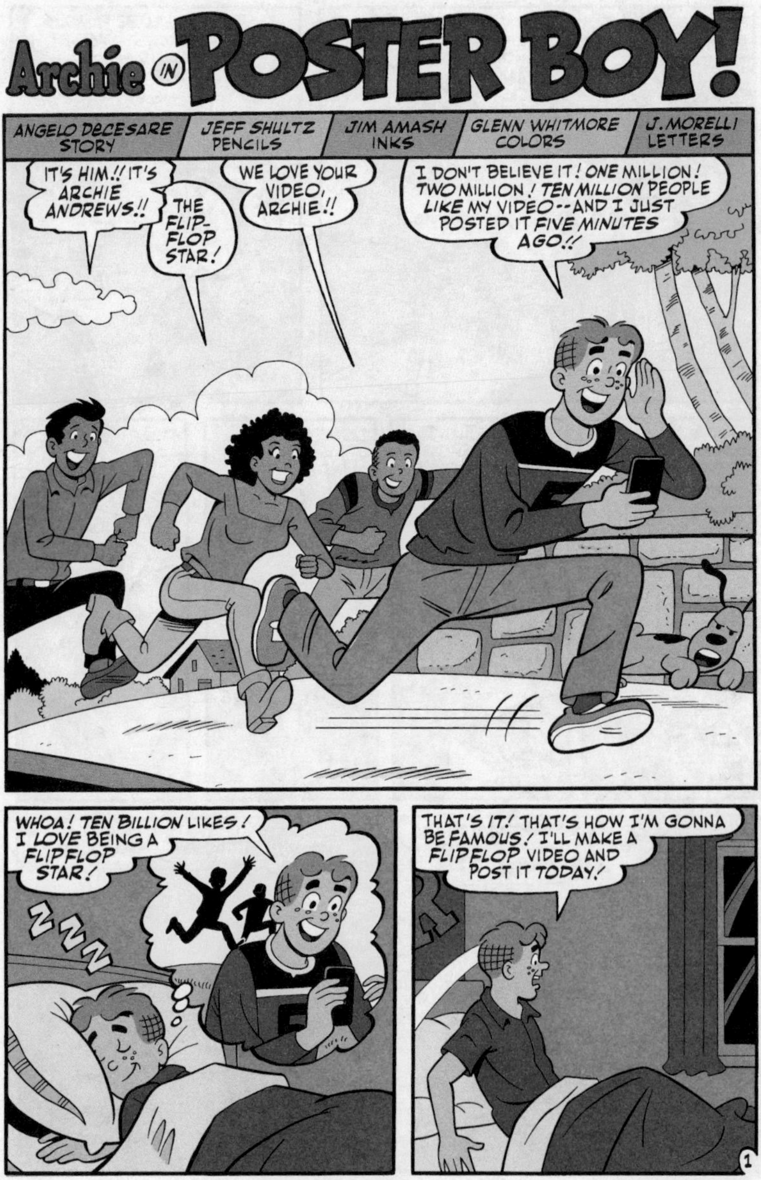
Archie IN POSTER BOY!
ANGELO DECESARE STORY
JEFF SHULTZ PENCILS
JIM AMASH INKS
GLENN WHITMORE COLORS
J. MORELLI LETTERS
IT'S HIM!! IT'S ARCHIE ANDREWS!!
THE FLIP-FLOP STAR!
WE LOVE YOUR VIDEO, ARCHIE!!
I DON'T BELIEVE IT! ONE MILLION! TWO MILLION! TEN MILLION PEOPLE LIKE MY VIDEO--AND I JUST POSTED IT FIVE MINUTES AGO!!
WHOA! TEN BILLION LIKES! I LOVE BEING A FLIPFLOP STAR!
Z Z Z
THAT'S IT! THAT'S HOW I'M GONNA BE FAMOUS! I'LL MAKE A FLIPFLOP VIDEO AND POST IT TODAY!
1

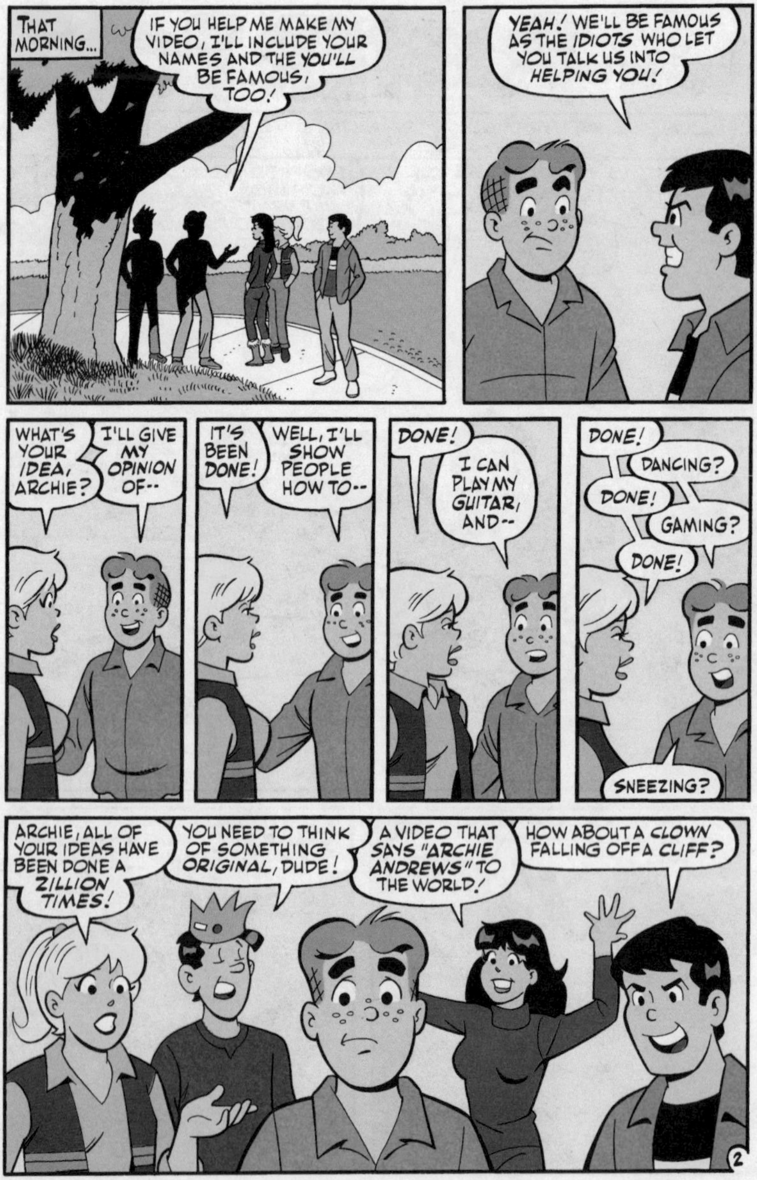
THAT MORNING...
IF YOU HELP ME MAKE MY VIDEO, I'LL INCLUDE YOUR NAMES AND THE YOU'LL BE FAMOUS, TOO!
YEAH! WE'LL BE FAMOUS AS THE IDIOTS WHO LET YOU TALK US INTO HELPING YOU!
WHAT'S YOUR IDEA, ARCHIE?
I'LL GIVE MY OPINION OF--
IT'S BEEN DONE!
WELL, I'LL SHOW PEOPLE HOW TO--
DONE!
I CAN PLAY MY GUITAR, AND--
DONE!
DANCING?
DONE!
GAMING?
DONE!
SNEEZING?
ARCHIE, ALL OF YOUR IDEAS HAVE BEEN DONE A ZILLION TIMES!
YOU NEED TO THINK OF SOMETHING ORIGINAL, DUDE!
A VIDEO THAT SAYS "ARCHIE ANDREWS" TO THE WORLD!
HOW ABOUT A CLOWN FALLING OFF A CLIFF?
2

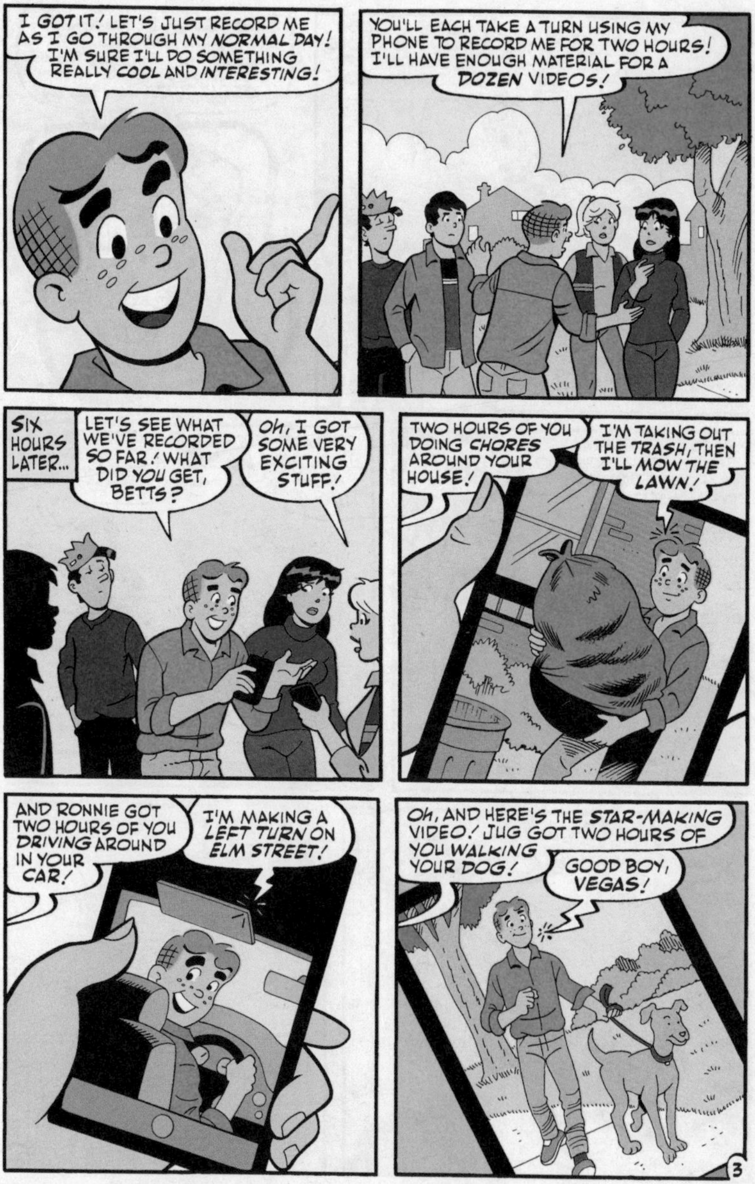

I GOT IT! LET'S JUST RECORD ME AS I GO THROUGH MY NORMAL DAY! I'M SURE I'LL DO SOMETHING REALLY COOL AND INTERESTING!
YOU'LL EACH TAKE A TURN USING MY PHONE TO RECORD ME FOR TWO HOURS! I'LL HAVE ENOUGH MATERIAL FOR A DOZEN VIDEOS!
SIX HOURS LATER...
LET'S SEE WHAT WE'VE RECORDED SO FAR! WHAT DID YOU GET, BETTS?
Oh, I GOT SOME VERY EXCITING STUFF!
TWO HOURS OF YOU DOING CHORES AROUND YOUR HOUSE!
I'M TAKING OUT THE TRASH, THEN I'LL MOW THE LAWN!
AND RONNIE GOT TWO HOURS OF YOU DRIVING AROUND IN YOUR CAR!
I'M MAKING A LEFT TURN ON ELM STREET!
Oh, AND HERE'S THE STAR-MAKING VIDEO! JUG GOT TWO HOURS OF YOU WALKING YOUR DOG!
GOOD BOY, VEGAS!
3

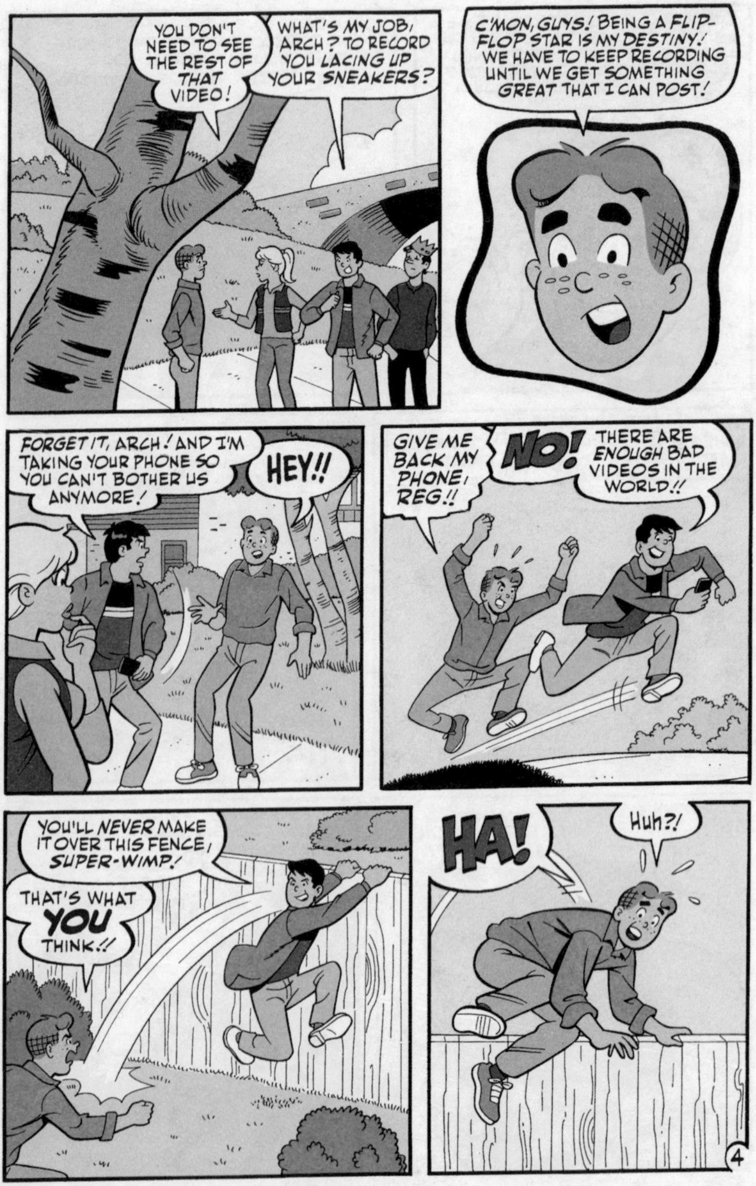
YOU DON'T NEED TO SEE THE REST OF THAT VIDEO!
WHAT'S MY JOB, ARCH? TO RECORD YOU LACING UP YOUR SNEAKERS?
C'MON, GUYS! BEING A FLIP-FLOP STAR IS MY DESTINY! WE HAVE TO KEEP RECORDING UNTIL WE GET SOMETHING GREAT THAT I CAN POST!
FORGET IT, ARCH! AND I'M TAKING YOUR PHONE SO YOU CAN'T BOTHER US ANYMORE!
HEY!!
GIVE ME BACK MY PHONE, REG!!
NO! THERE ARE ENOUGH BAD VIDEOS IN THE WORLD!!
YOU'LL NEVER MAKE IT OVER THIS FENCE, SUPER-WIMP!
THAT'S WHAT YOU THINK!!
HA!
Huh?!
4

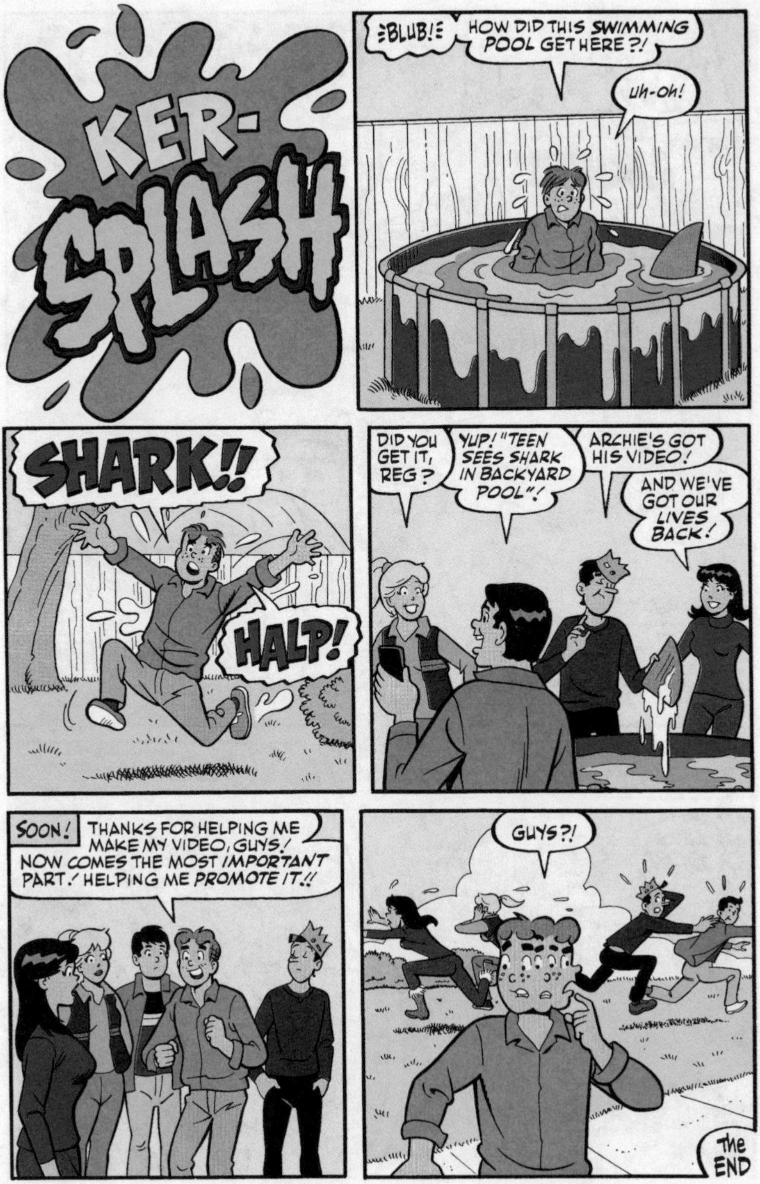
KER-SPLASH
BLUB!
HOW DID THIS SWIMMING POOL GET HERE ?!
uh-oh!
SHARK!!
HALP!
DID YOU GET IT, REG ?
YUP! "TEEN SEES SHARK IN BACKYARD POOL"!
ARCHIE'S GOT HIS VIDEO!
AND WE'VE GOT OUR LIVES BACK!
SOON!
THANKS FOR HELPING ME MAKE MY VIDEO, GUYS! NOW COMES THE MOST IMPORTANT PART! HELPING ME PROMOTE IT!!
GUYS?!
The END

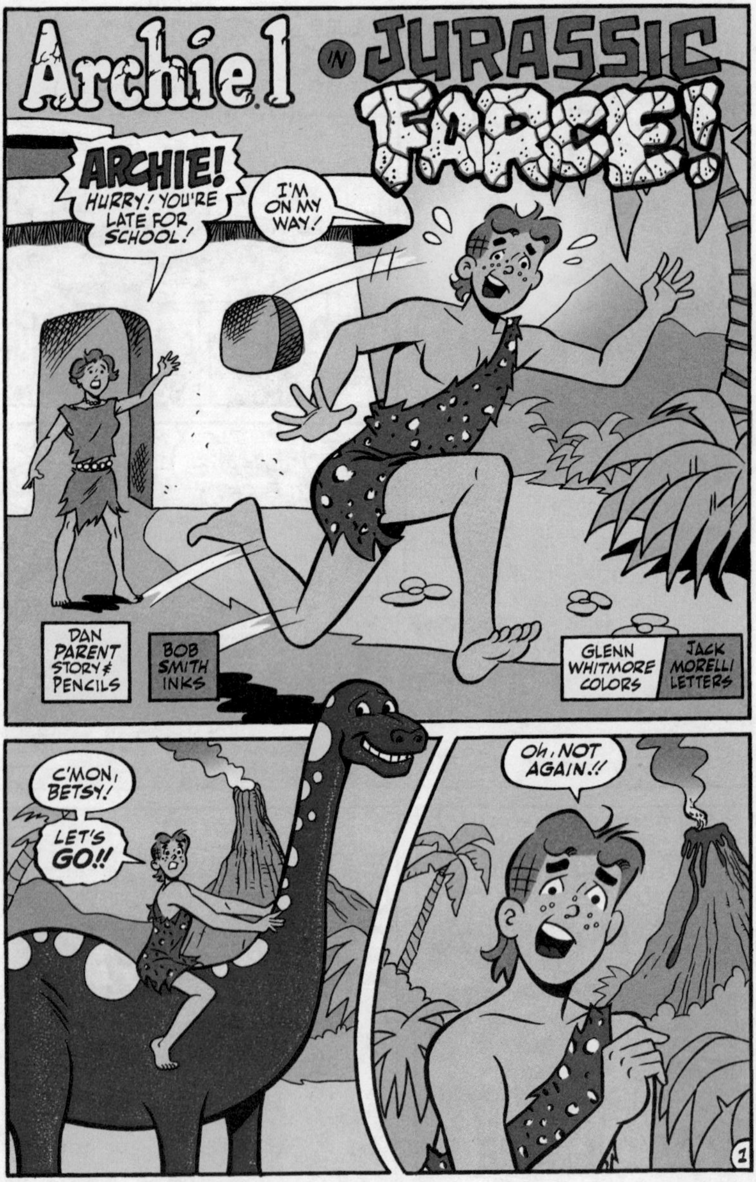
Archie
in
JURASSIC FARCE!
ARCHIE! HURRY! YOU'RE LATE FOR SCHOOL!
I'M ON MY WAY!
DAN PARENT STORY & PENCILS
BOB SMITH INKS
GLENN WHITMORE COLORS
JACK MORELLI LETTERS
C'MON, BETSY!
LET'S GO!!
Oh, NOT AGAIN!!
1

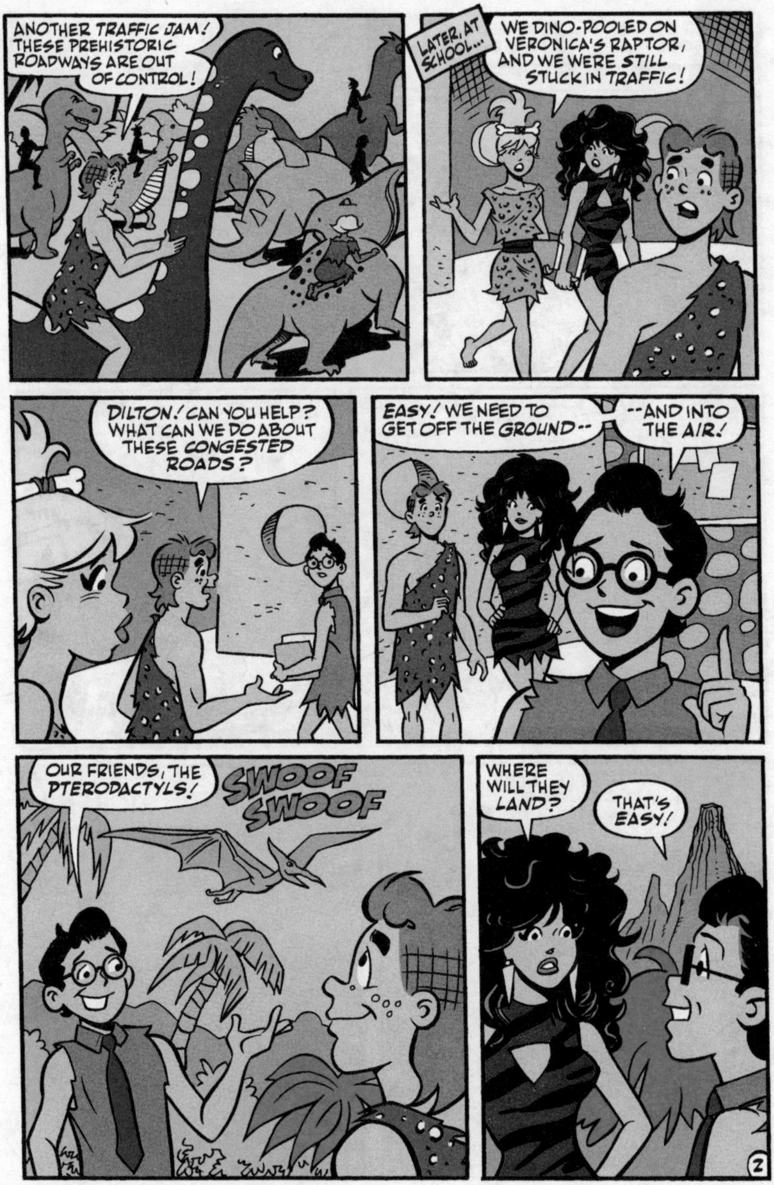
ANOTHER TRAFFIC JAM! THESE PREHISTORIC ROADWAYS ARE OUT OF CONTROL!
LATER, AT SCHOOL...
WE DINO-POOLED ON VERONICA'S RAPTOR, AND WE WERE STILL STUCK IN TRAFFIC!
DILTON! CAN YOU HELP? WHAT CAN WE DO ABOUT THESE CONGESTED ROADS?
EASY! WE NEED TO GET OFF THE GROUND--
--AND INTO THE AIR!
OUR FRIENDS, THE PTERODACTYLS!
SWOOF SWOOF
WHERE WILL THEY LAND?
THAT'S EASY!
2

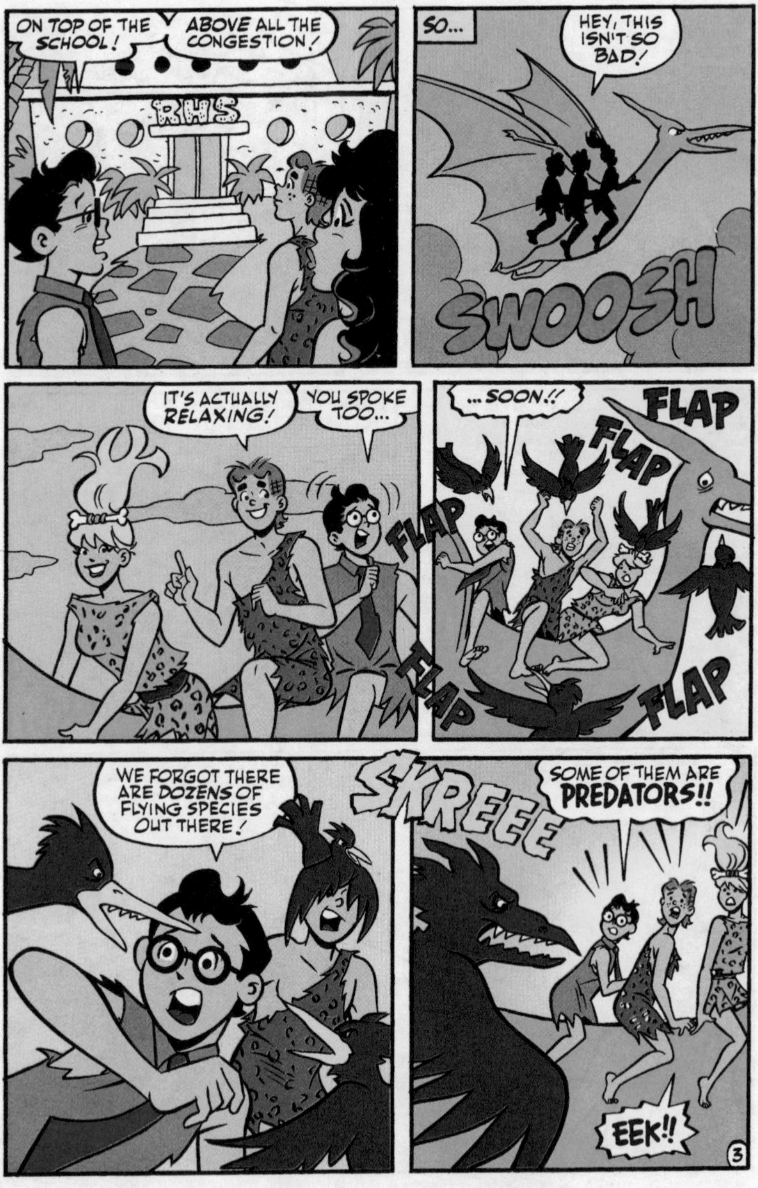
ON TOP OF THE SCHOOL!
ABOVE ALL THE CONGESTION!
RHS
SO...
HEY, THIS ISN'T SO BAD!
SWOOSH
IT'S ACTUALLY RELAXING!
YOU SPOKE TOO...
FLAP
FLAP
...SOON!!
FLAP
FLAP
FLAP
FLAP
WE FORGOT THERE ARE DOZENS OF FLYING SPECIES OUT THERE!
SKREEEE
SOME OF THEM ARE PREDATORS!!
EEK!!
3

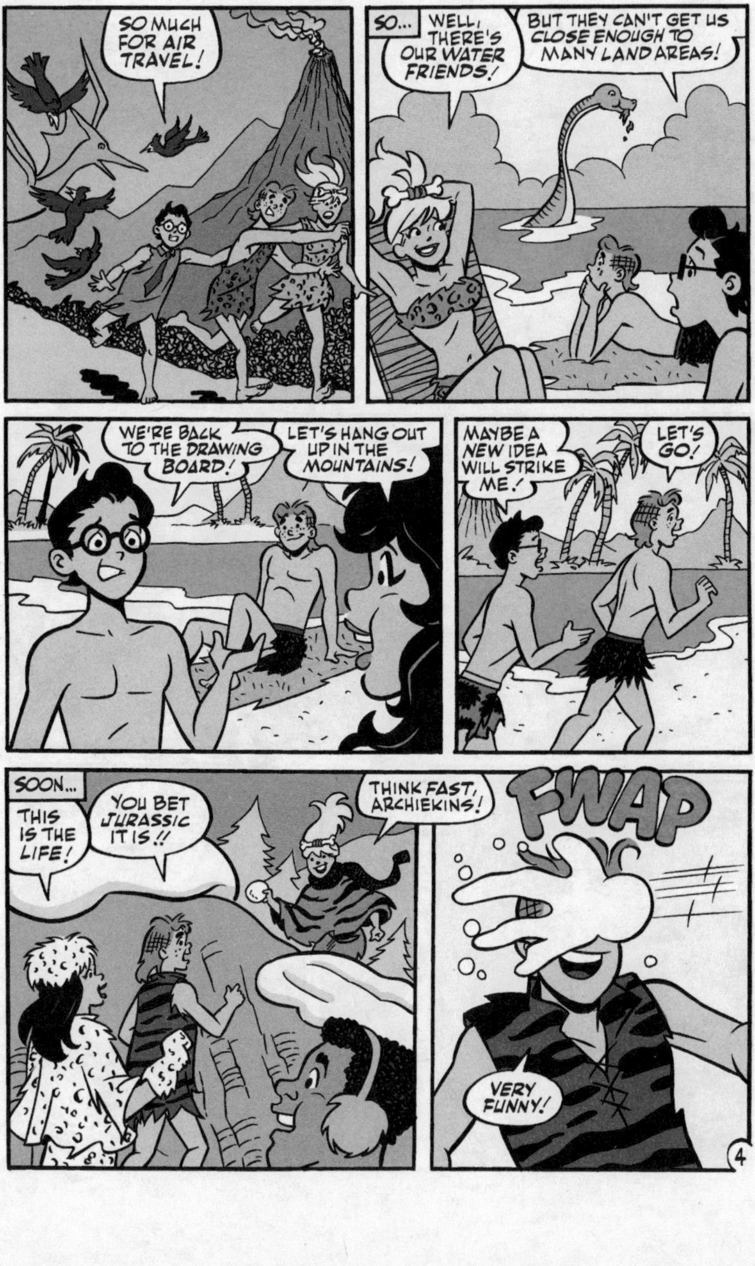
SO MUCH FOR AIR TRAVEL!
SO...
WELL, THERE'S OUR WATER FRIENDS!
BUT THEY CAN'T GET US CLOSE ENOUGH TO MANY LAND AREAS!
WE'RE BACK TO THE DRAWING BOARD!
LET'S HANG OUT UP IN THE MOUNTAINS!
MAYBE A NEW IDEA WILL STRIKE ME!
LET'S GO!
SOON...
THIS IS THE LIFE!
YOU BET JURASSIC IT IS!!
THINK FAST, ARCHIEKINS!
FWAP
VERY FUNNY!
4

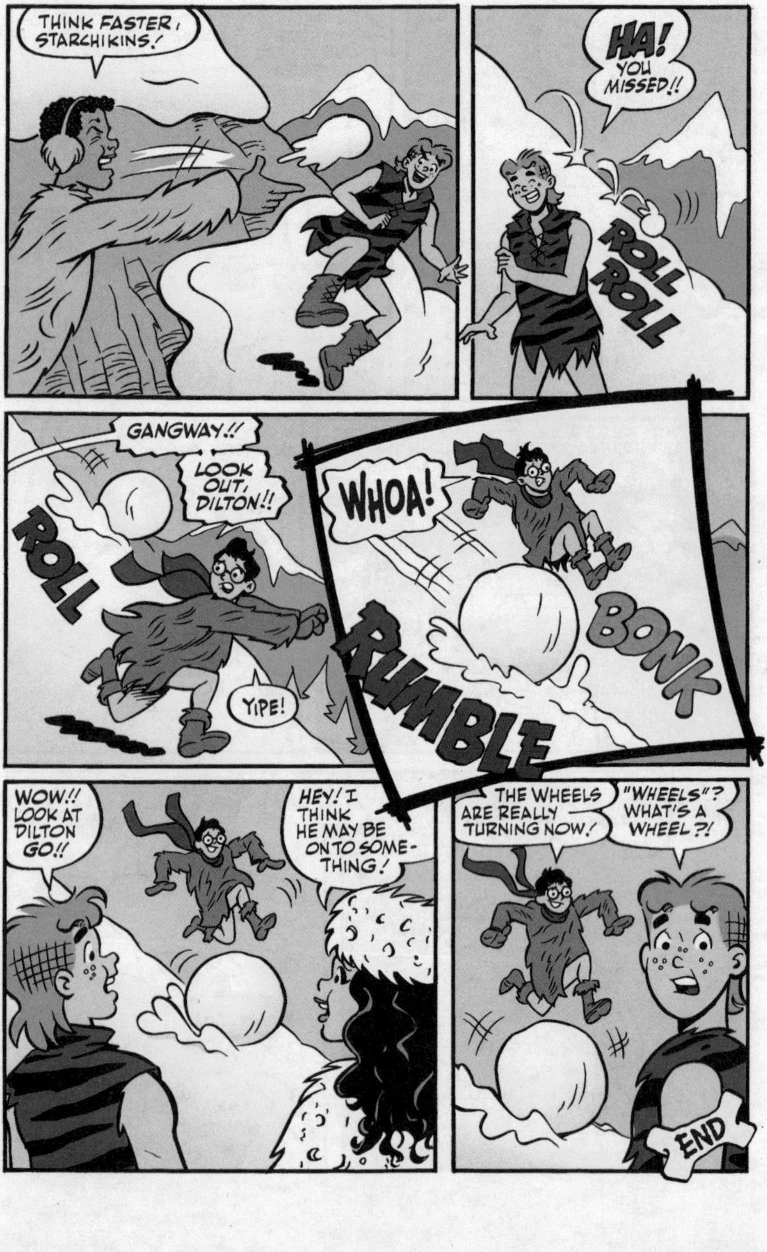
THINK FASTER, STARCHIKINS!
HA! YOU MISSED!!
ROLL ROLL
GANGWAY!!
LOOK OUT, DILTON!!
ROLL
YIPE!
WHOA!
BONK
RUMBLE
WOW!! LOOK AT DILTON GO!!
HEY! I THINK HE MAY BE ON TO SOME-THING!
THE WHEELS ARE REALLY TURNING NOW!
"WHEELS"? WHAT'S A WHEEL?!
END

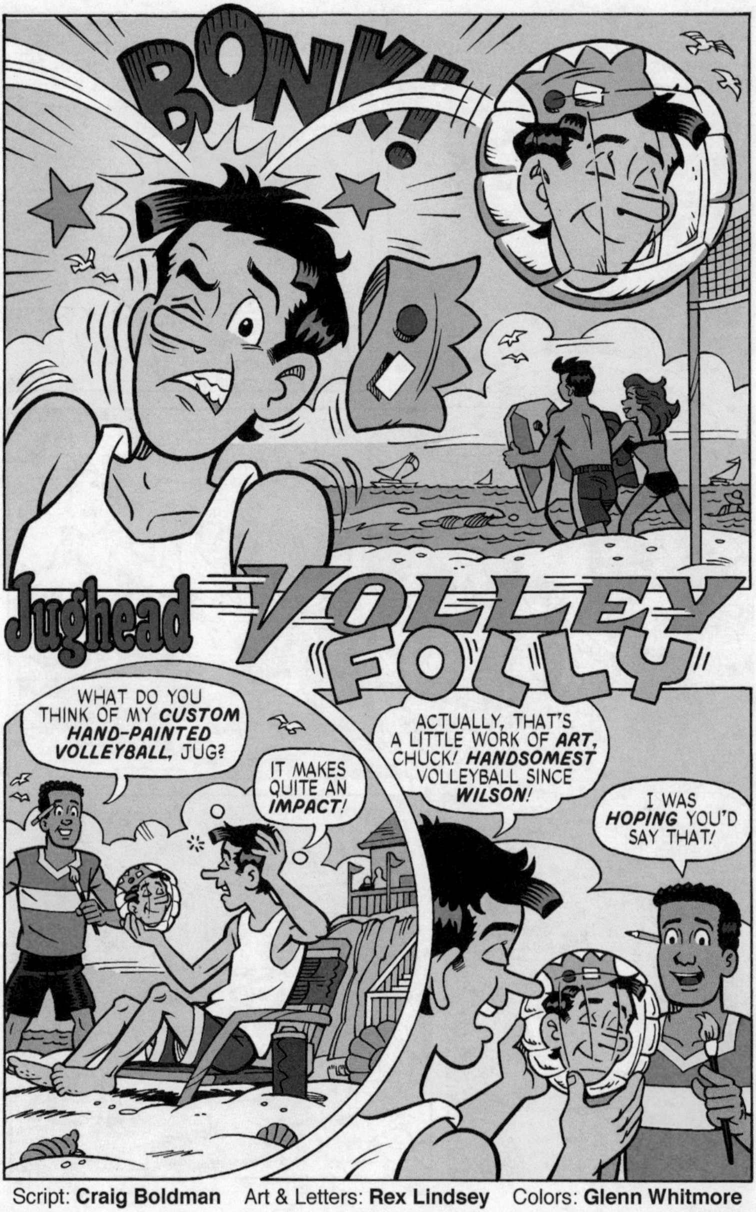
BONK!
Jughead
VOLLEY FOLLY
WHAT DO YOU THINK OF MY CUSTOM HAND-PAINTED VOLLEYBALL, JUG?
IT MAKES QUITE AN IMPACT!
ACTUALLY, THAT'S A LITTLE WORK OF ART, CHUCK! HANDSOMEST VOLLEYBALL SINCE WILSON!
I WAS HOPING YOU'D SAY THAT!

Script: **Craig Boldman** Art & Letters: **Rex Lindsey** Colors: **Glenn Whitmore**

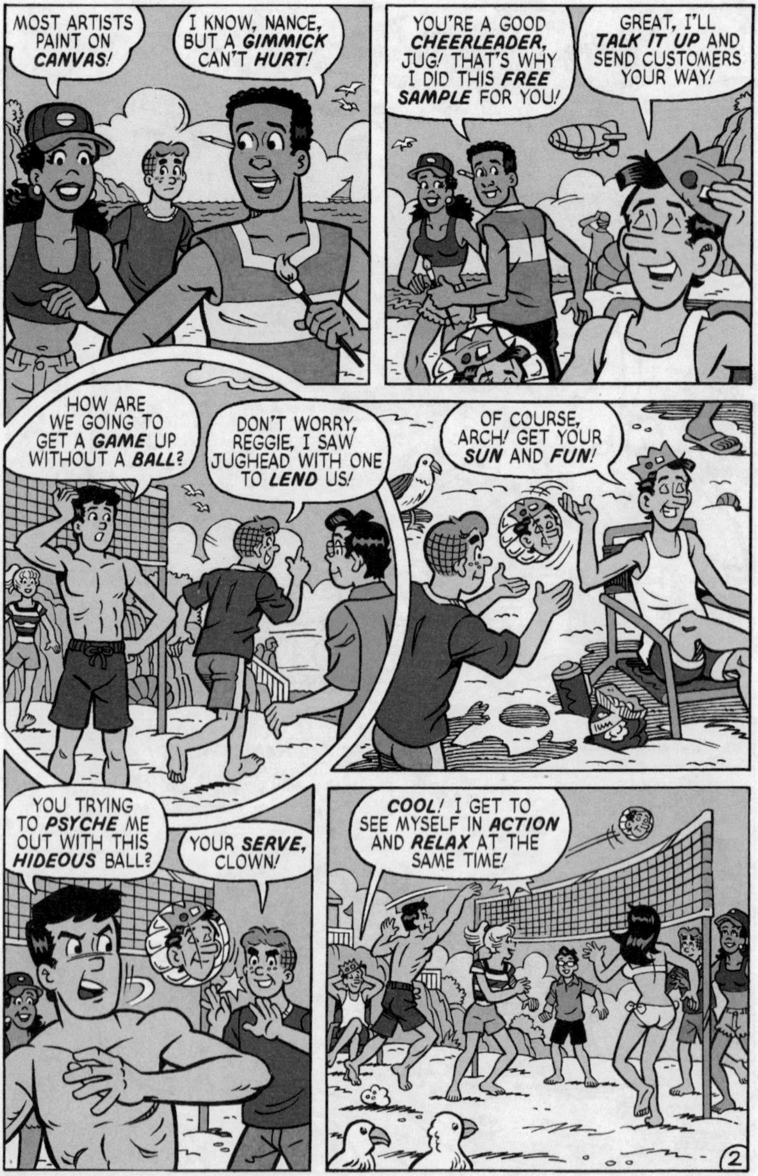
MOST ARTISTS PAINT ON CANVAS!
I KNOW, NANCE, BUT A GIMMICK CAN'T HURT!
YOU'RE A GOOD CHEERLEADER, JUG! THAT'S WHY I DID THIS FREE SAMPLE FOR YOU!
GREAT, I'LL TALK IT UP AND SEND CUSTOMERS YOUR WAY!
HOW ARE WE GOING TO GET A GAME UP WITHOUT A BALL?
DON'T WORRY, REGGIE, I SAW JUGHEAD WITH ONE TO LEND US!
OF COURSE, ARCH! GET YOUR SUN AND FUN!
YOU TRYING TO PSYCHE ME OUT WITH THIS HIDEOUS BALL?
YOUR SERVE, CLOWN!
COOL! I GET TO SEE MYSELF IN ACTION AND RELAX AT THE SAME TIME!
2

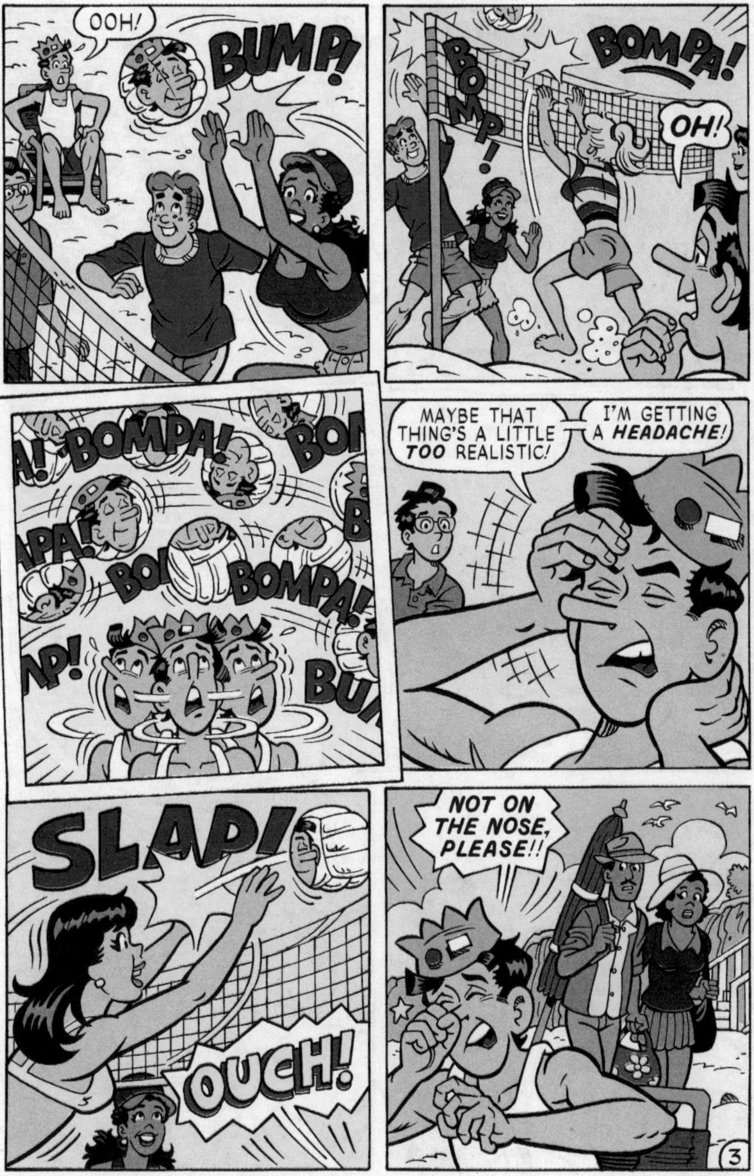
OOH!
BUMP!
BOMP!
BOMPA!
OH!
BOMPA!
BOMPA!
MAYBE THAT THING'S A LITTLE TOO REALISTIC!
I'M GETTING A HEADACHE!
SLAP!
OUCH!
NOT ON THE NOSE, PLEASE!!
3

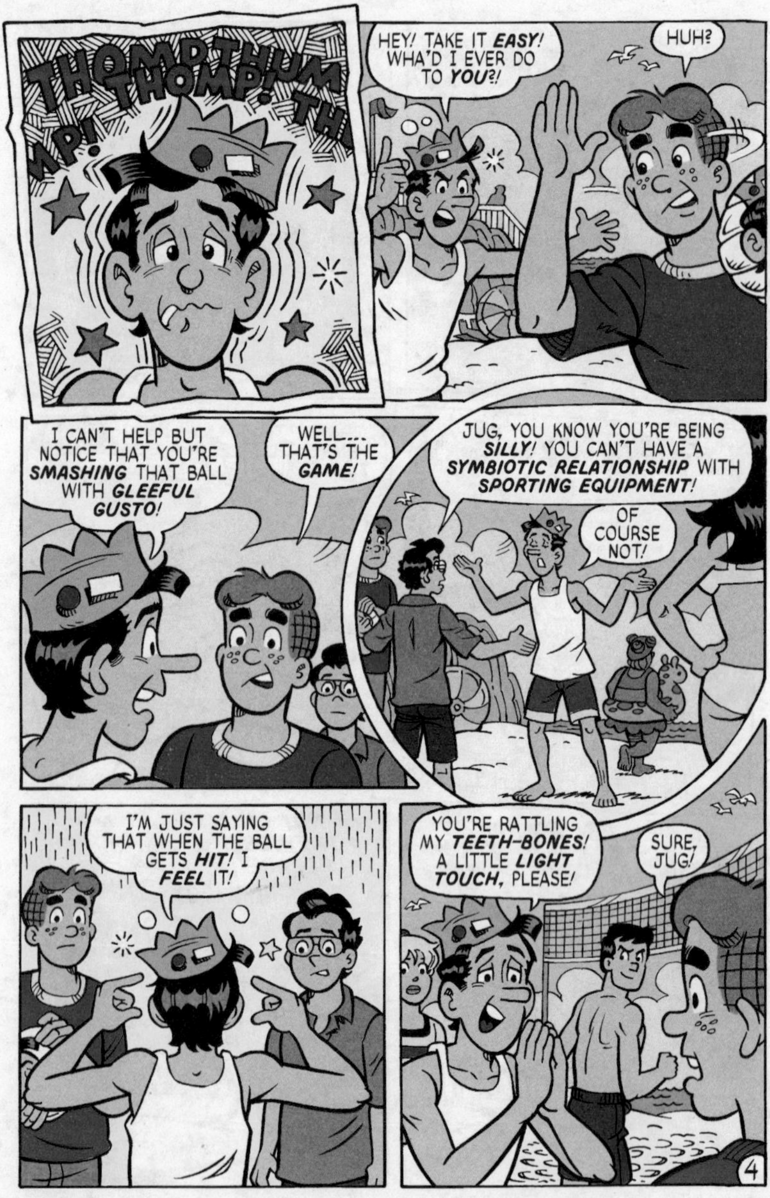
THOMP! THUMP! THOMP! THUMP!
HEY! TAKE IT EASY! WHA'D I EVER DO TO YOU?!
HUH?
I CAN'T HELP BUT NOTICE THAT YOU'RE SMASHING THAT BALL WITH GLEEFUL GUSTO!
WELL... THAT'S THE GAME!
JUG, YOU KNOW YOU'RE BEING SILLY! YOU CAN'T HAVE A SYMBIOTIC RELATIONSHIP WITH SPORTING EQUIPMENT!
OF COURSE NOT!
I'M JUST SAYING THAT WHEN THE BALL GETS HIT! I FEEL IT!
YOU'RE RATTLING MY TEETH-BONES! A LITTLE LIGHT TOUCH, PLEASE!
SURE, JUG!
4

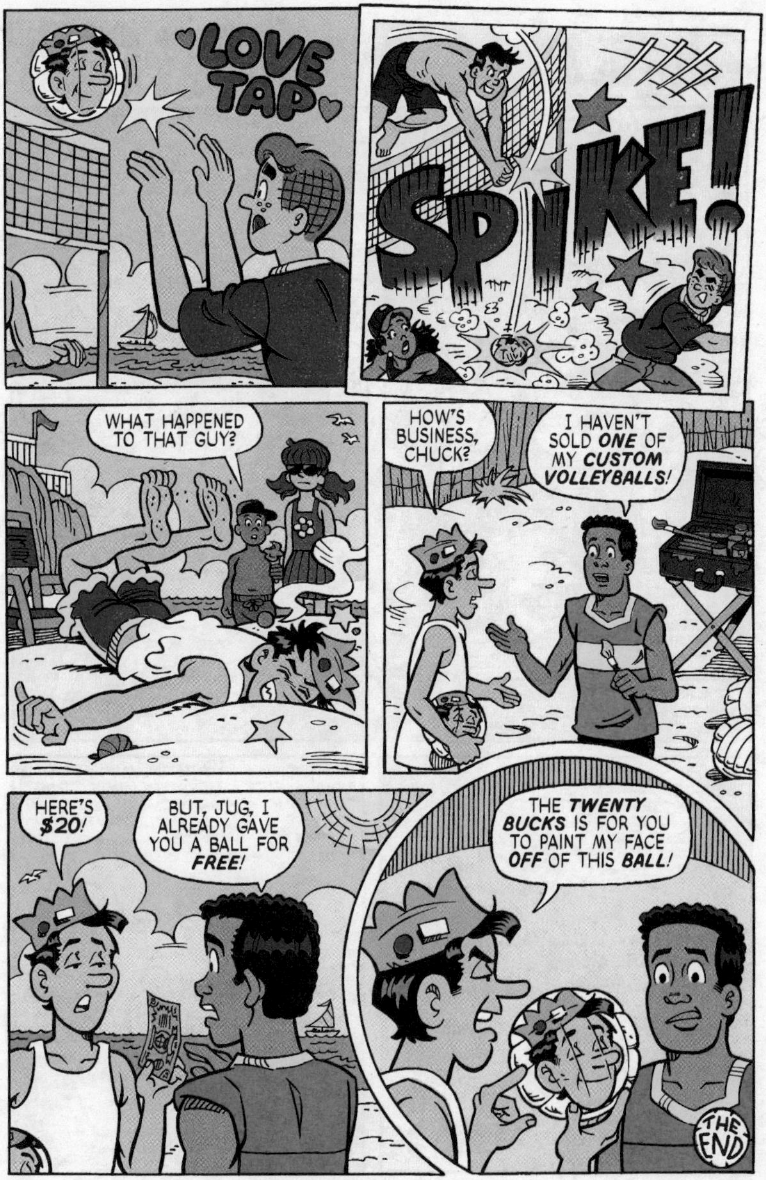
LOVE TAP
SPIKE!
WHAT HAPPENED TO THAT GUY?
HOW'S BUSINESS, CHUCK?
I HAVEN'T SOLD ONE OF MY CUSTOM VOLLEYBALLS!
HERE'S $20!
BUT, JUG, I ALREADY GAVE YOU A BALL FOR FREE!
THE TWENTY BUCKS IS FOR YOU TO PAINT MY FACE OFF OF THIS BALL!
THE END

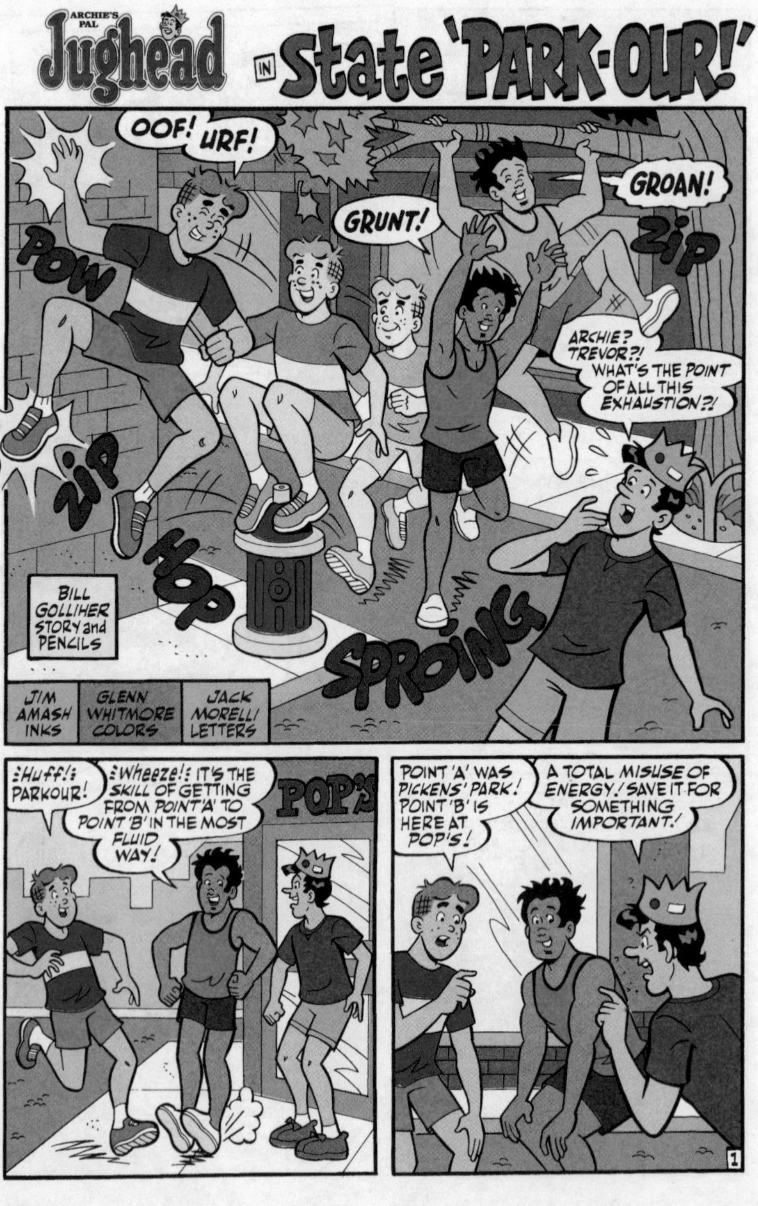

ARCHIE'S PAL
Jughead
IN
State 'PARK-OUR!'
OOF!
URF!
GRUNT!
GROAN!
POW
ZIP
ZIP
HOP
SPROING
ARCHIE? TREVOR?! WHAT'S THE POINT OF ALL THIS EXHAUSTION?!
BILL GOLLIHER STORY and PENCILS
JIM AMASH INKS
GLENN WHITMORE COLORS
JACK MORELLI LETTERS
Huff! PARKOUR!
Wheeze! IT'S THE SKILL OF GETTING FROM POINT 'A' TO POINT 'B' IN THE MOST FLUID WAY!
POP'S
POINT 'A' WAS PICKENS' PARK! POINT 'B' IS HERE AT POP'S!
A TOTAL MISUSE OF ENERGY! SAVE IT FOR SOMETHING IMPORTANT!
1

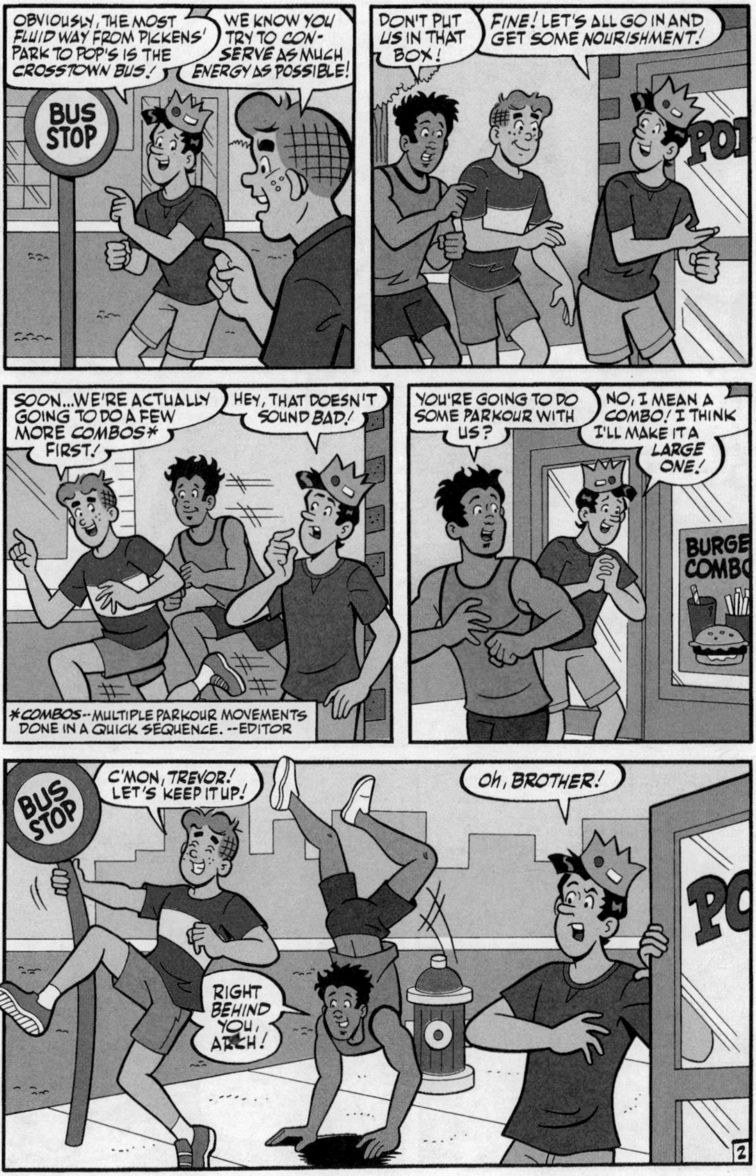
OBVIOUSLY, THE MOST FLUID WAY FROM PICKENS' PARK TO POP'S IS THE CROSSTOWN BUS!
WE KNOW YOU TRY TO CONSERVE AS MUCH ENERGY AS POSSIBLE!
BUS STOP
DON'T PUT US IN THAT BOX!
FINE! LET'S ALL GO IN AND GET SOME NOURISHMENT!
SOON...WE'RE ACTUALLY GOING TO DO A FEW MORE COMBOS* FIRST!
HEY, THAT DOESN'T SOUND BAD!
*COMBOS--MULTIPLE PARKOUR MOVEMENTS DONE IN A QUICK SEQUENCE. --EDITOR
YOU'RE GOING TO DO SOME PARKOUR WITH US?
NO, I MEAN A COMBO! I THINK I'LL MAKE IT A LARGE ONE!
BUS STOP
C'MON, TREVOR! LET'S KEEP IT UP!
RIGHT BEHIND YOU, ARCH!
Oh, BROTHER!
2

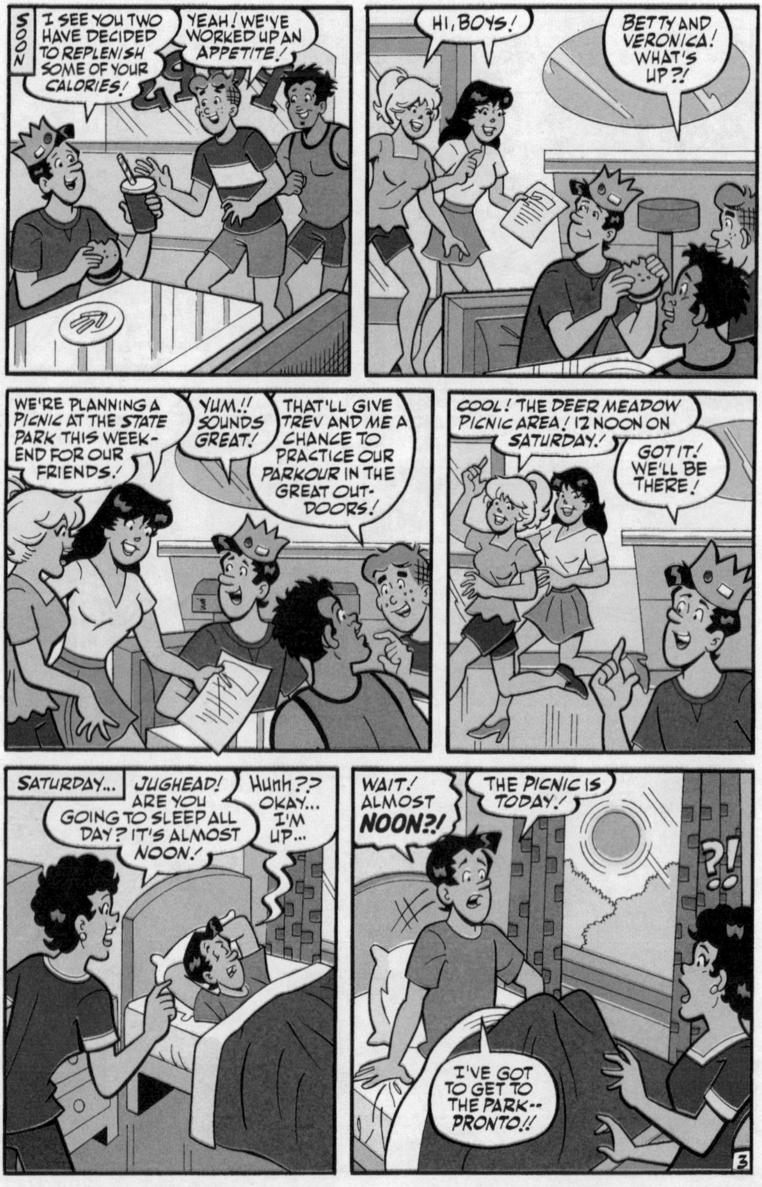
SOON
I SEE YOU TWO HAVE DECIDED TO REPLENISH SOME OF YOUR CALORIES!
YEAH! WE'VE WORKED UP AN APPETITE!
HI, BOYS!
BETTY AND VERONICA! WHAT'S UP?!
WE'RE PLANNING A PICNIC AT THE STATE PARK THIS WEEK-END FOR OUR FRIENDS!
YUM!! SOUNDS GREAT!
THAT'LL GIVE TREV AND ME A CHANCE TO PRACTICE OUR PARKOUR IN THE GREAT OUT-DOORS!
COOL! THE DEER MEADOW PICNIC AREA! 12 NOON ON SATURDAY!
GOT IT! WE'LL BE THERE!
SATURDAY...
JUGHEAD! ARE YOU GOING TO SLEEP ALL DAY? IT'S ALMOST NOON!
Hunh?? OKAY... I'M UP...
WAIT! ALMOST NOON?!
THE PICNIC IS TODAY!
?!
I'VE GOT TO GET TO THE PARK-- PRONTO!!
3

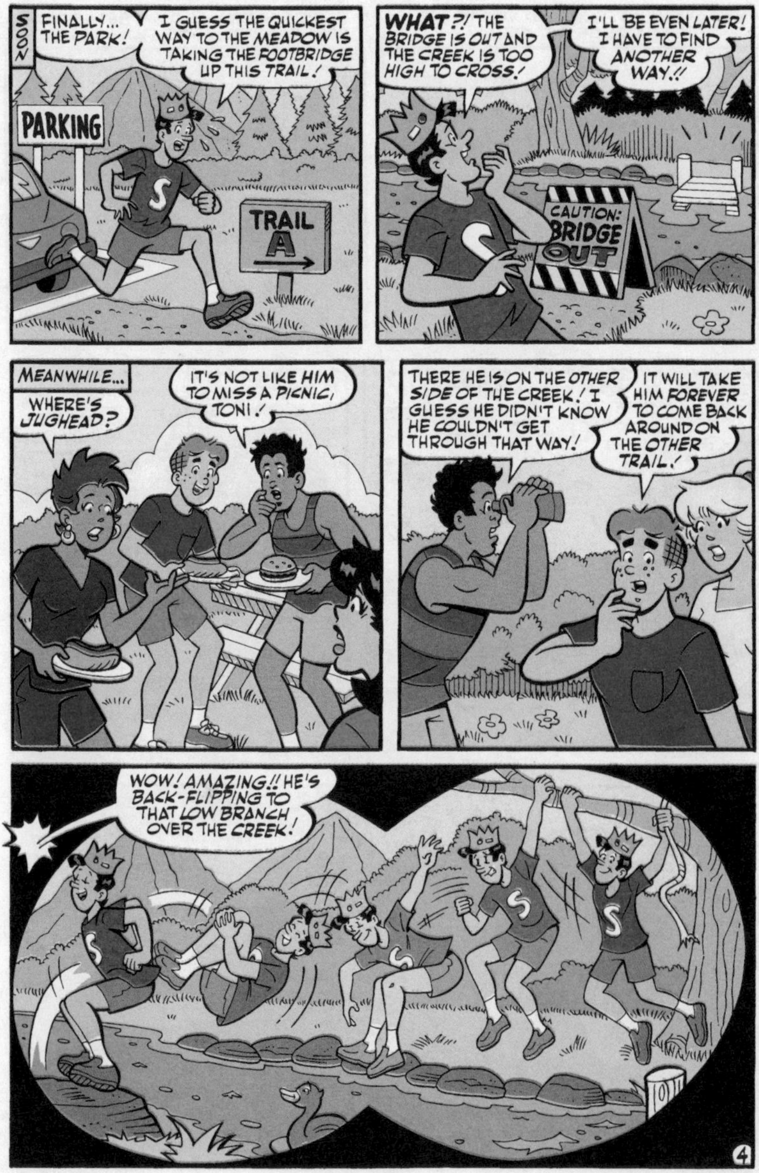
SOON
FINALLY... THE PARK!
I GUESS THE QUICKEST WAY TO THE MEADOW IS TAKING THE FOOTBRIDGE UP THIS TRAIL!
PARKING
TRAIL A
WHAT?! THE BRIDGE IS OUT AND THE CREEK IS TOO HIGH TO CROSS!
I'LL BE EVEN LATER! I HAVE TO FIND ANOTHER WAY.!!
CAUTION: BRIDGE OUT
MEANWHILE...
WHERE'S JUGHEAD?
IT'S NOT LIKE HIM TO MISS A PICNIC, TONI!
THERE HE IS ON THE OTHER SIDE OF THE CREEK! I GUESS HE DIDN'T KNOW HE COULDN'T GET THROUGH THAT WAY!
IT WILL TAKE HIM FOREVER TO COME BACK AROUND ON THE OTHER TRAIL!
WOW! AMAZING!! HE'S BACK-FLIPPING TO THAT LOW BRANCH OVER THE CREEK!
4

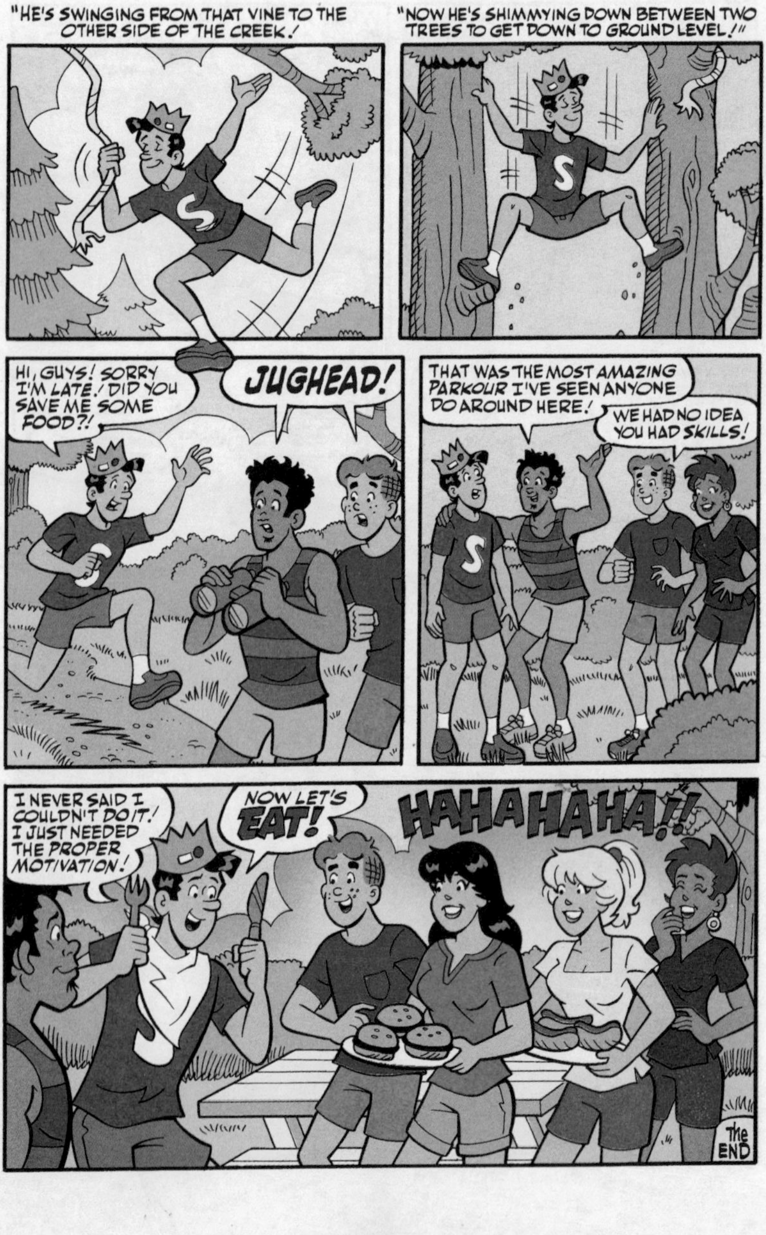
"HE'S SWINGING FROM THAT VINE TO THE OTHER SIDE OF THE CREEK!
"NOW HE'S SHIMMYING DOWN BETWEEN TWO TREES TO GET DOWN TO GROUND LEVEL!"
HI, GUYS! SORRY I'M LATE! DID YOU SAVE ME SOME FOOD?!
JUGHEAD!
THAT WAS THE MOST AMAZING PARKOUR I'VE SEEN ANYONE DO AROUND HERE!
WE HAD NO IDEA YOU HAD SKILLS!
I NEVER SAID I COULDN'T DO IT! I JUST NEEDED THE PROPER MOTIVATION!
NOW LET'S EAT!
HAHAHAHAHA!!
THE END

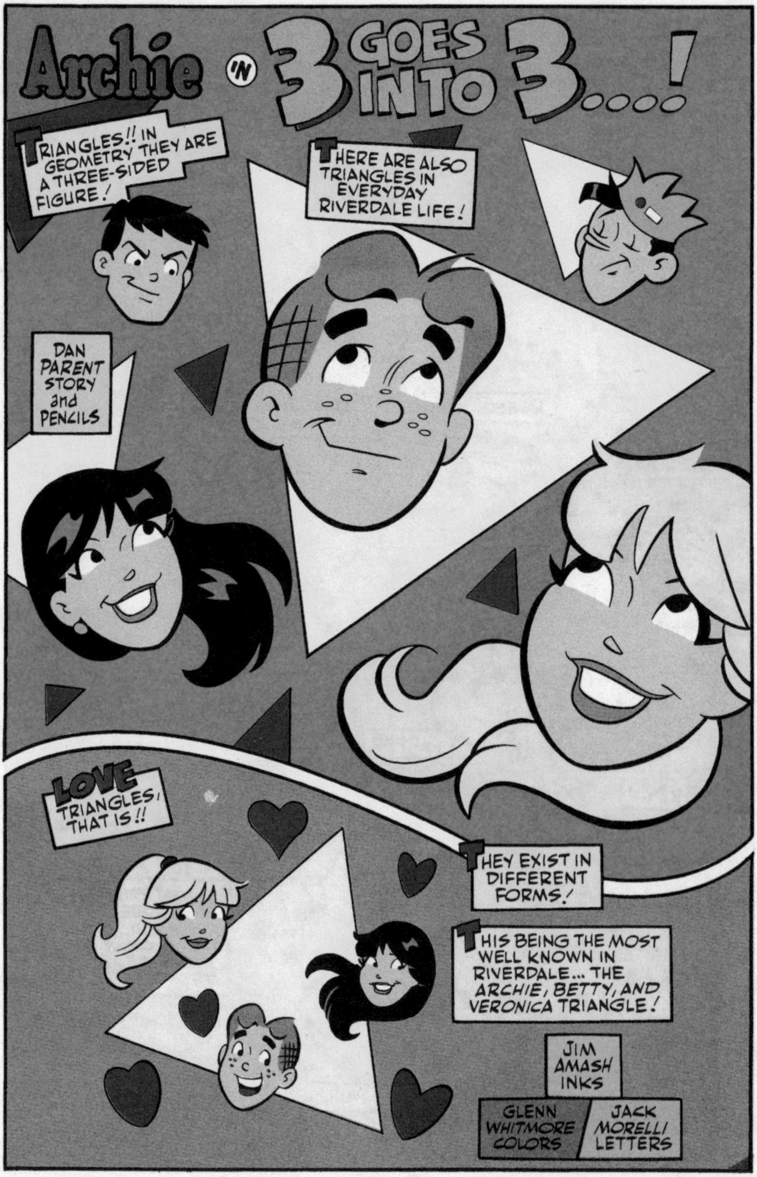
Archie in 3 GOES INTO 3....!
TRIANGLES!! IN GEOMETRY THEY ARE A THREE-SIDED FIGURE!
THERE ARE ALSO TRIANGLES IN EVERYDAY RIVERDALE LIFE!
DAN PARENT STORY and PENCILS
LOVE TRIANGLES, THAT IS!!
THEY EXIST IN DIFFERENT FORMS!
THIS BEING THE MOST WELL KNOWN IN RIVERDALE... THE ARCHIE, BETTY, AND VERONICA TRIANGLE!
JIM AMASH INKS
GLENN WHITMORE COLORS
JACK MORELLI LETTERS

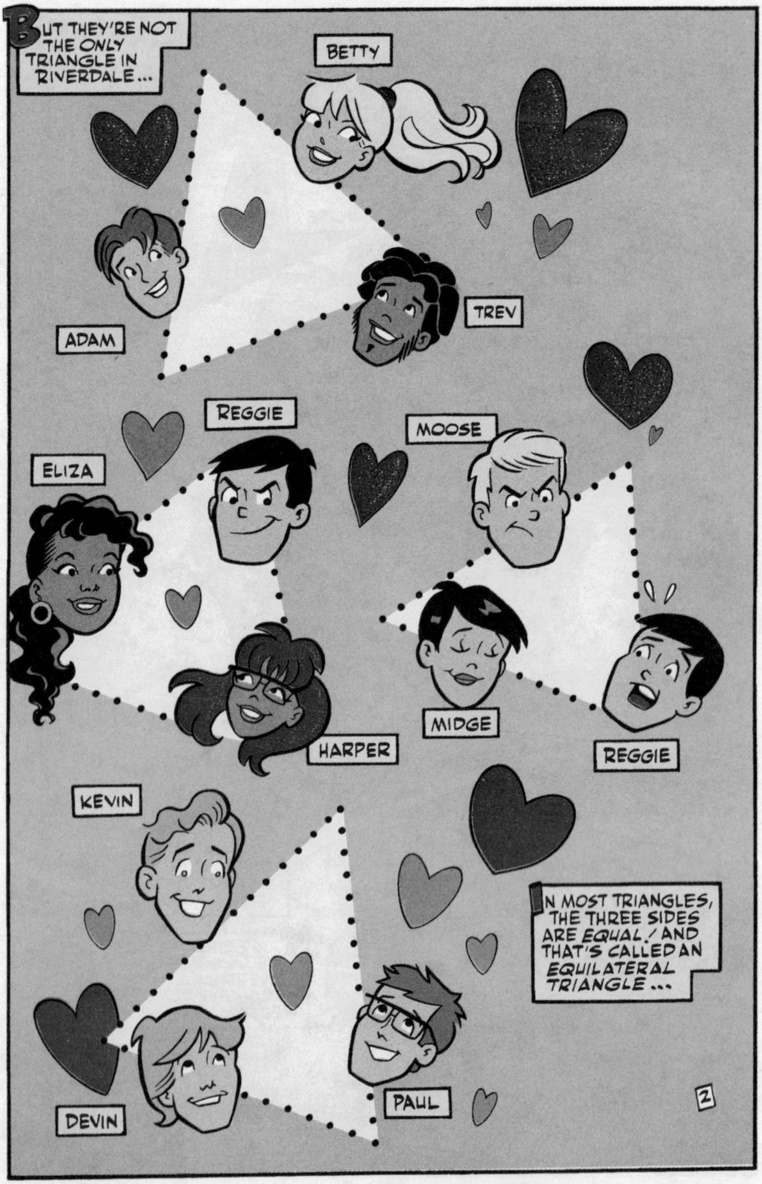
BUT THEY'RE NOT THE ONLY TRIANGLE IN RIVERDALE...
BETTY
ADAM
TREV
REGGIE
MOOSE
ELIZA
HARPER
MIDGE
REGGIE
KEVIN
IN MOST TRIANGLES, THE THREE SIDES ARE EQUAL! AND THAT'S CALLED AN EQUILATERAL TRIANGLE...
DEVIN
PAUL
2

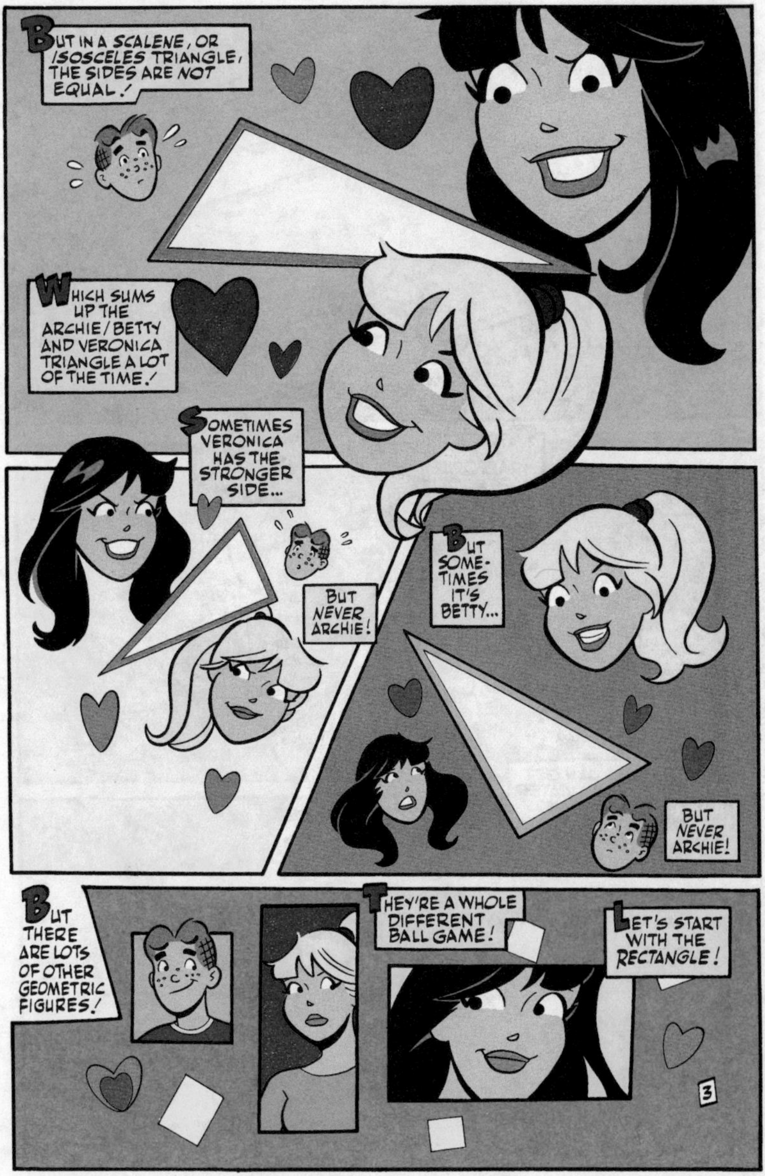
BUT IN A SCALENE, OR ISOSCELES TRIANGLE, THE SIDES ARE NOT EQUAL!
WHICH SUMS UP THE ARCHIE/BETTY AND VERONICA TRIANGLE A LOT OF THE TIME!
SOMETIMES VERONICA HAS THE STRONGER SIDE...
BUT NEVER ARCHIE!
BUT SOMETIMES IT'S BETTY...
BUT NEVER ARCHIE!
BUT THERE ARE LOTS OF OTHER GEOMETRIC FIGURES!
THEY'RE A WHOLE DIFFERENT BALL GAME!
LET'S START WITH THE RECTANGLE!
3

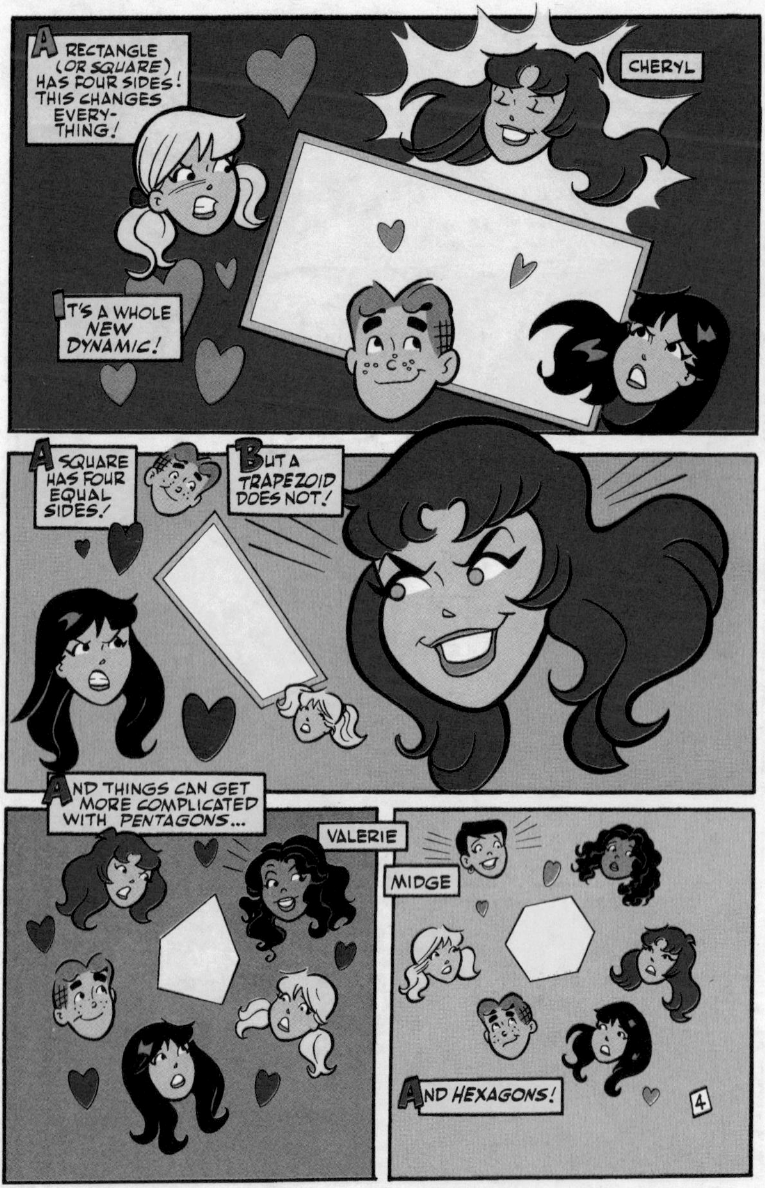
A RECTANGLE (OR SQUARE) HAS FOUR SIDES! THIS CHANGES EVERY-THING!
CHERYL
IT'S A WHOLE NEW DYNAMIC!
A SQUARE HAS FOUR EQUAL SIDES!
BUT A TRAPEZOID DOES NOT!
AND THINGS CAN GET MORE COMPLICATED WITH PENTAGONS...
VALERIE
MIDGE
AND HEXAGONS!
4

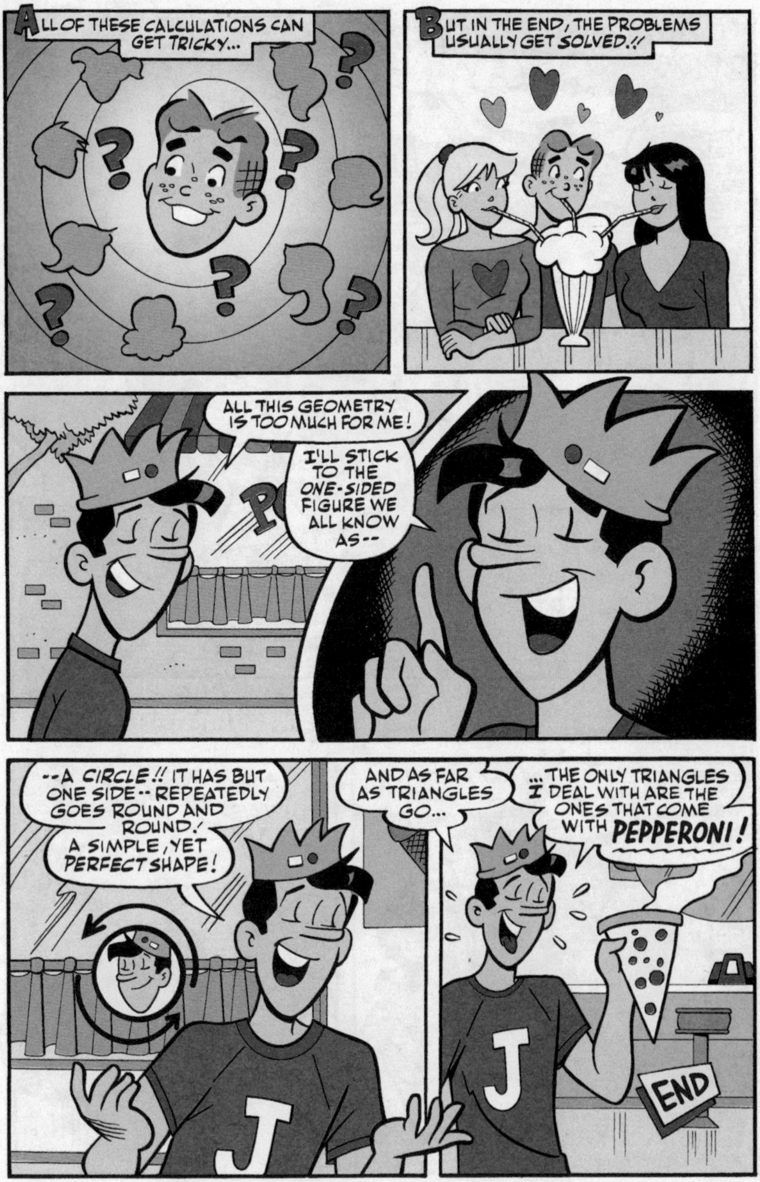
ALL OF THESE CALCULATIONS CAN GET TRICKY...
BUT IN THE END, THE PROBLEMS USUALLY GET SOLVED.!!
ALL THIS GEOMETRY IS TOO MUCH FOR ME!
I'LL STICK TO THE ONE-SIDED FIGURE WE ALL KNOW AS--
--A CIRCLE!! IT HAS BUT ONE SIDE-- REPEATEDLY GOES ROUND AND ROUND! A SIMPLE, YET PERFECT SHAPE!
AND AS FAR AS TRIANGLES GO...
...THE ONLY TRIANGLES I DEAL WITH ARE THE ONES THAT COME WITH PEPPERONI!
END

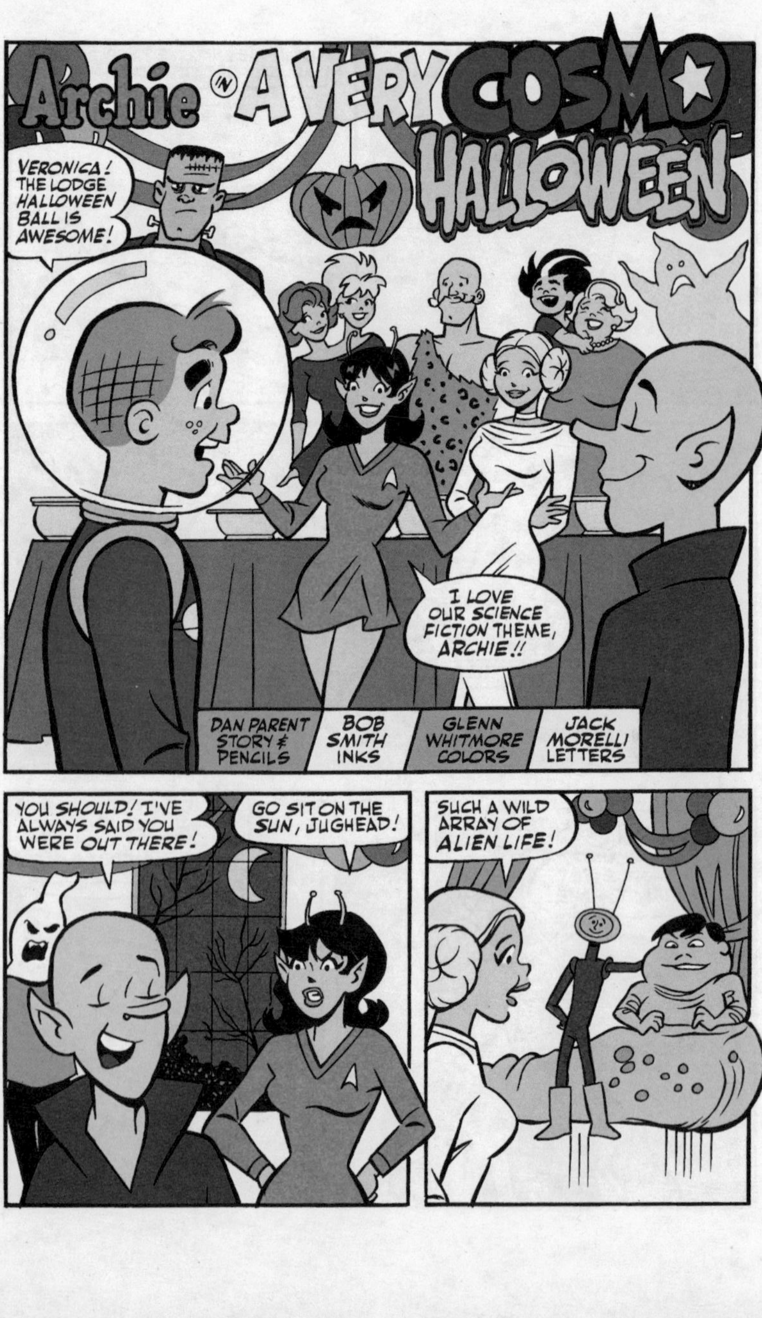
Archie in A VERY COSMO HALLOWEEN
VERONICA! THE LODGE HALLOWEEN BALL IS AWESOME!
I LOVE OUR SCIENCE FICTION THEME, ARCHIE!!
DAN PARENT STORY & PENCILS
BOB SMITH INKS
GLENN WHITMORE COLORS
JACK MORELLI LETTERS
YOU SHOULD! I'VE ALWAYS SAID YOU WERE OUT THERE!
GO SIT ON THE SUN, JUGHEAD!
SUCH A WILD ARRAY OF ALIEN LIFE!

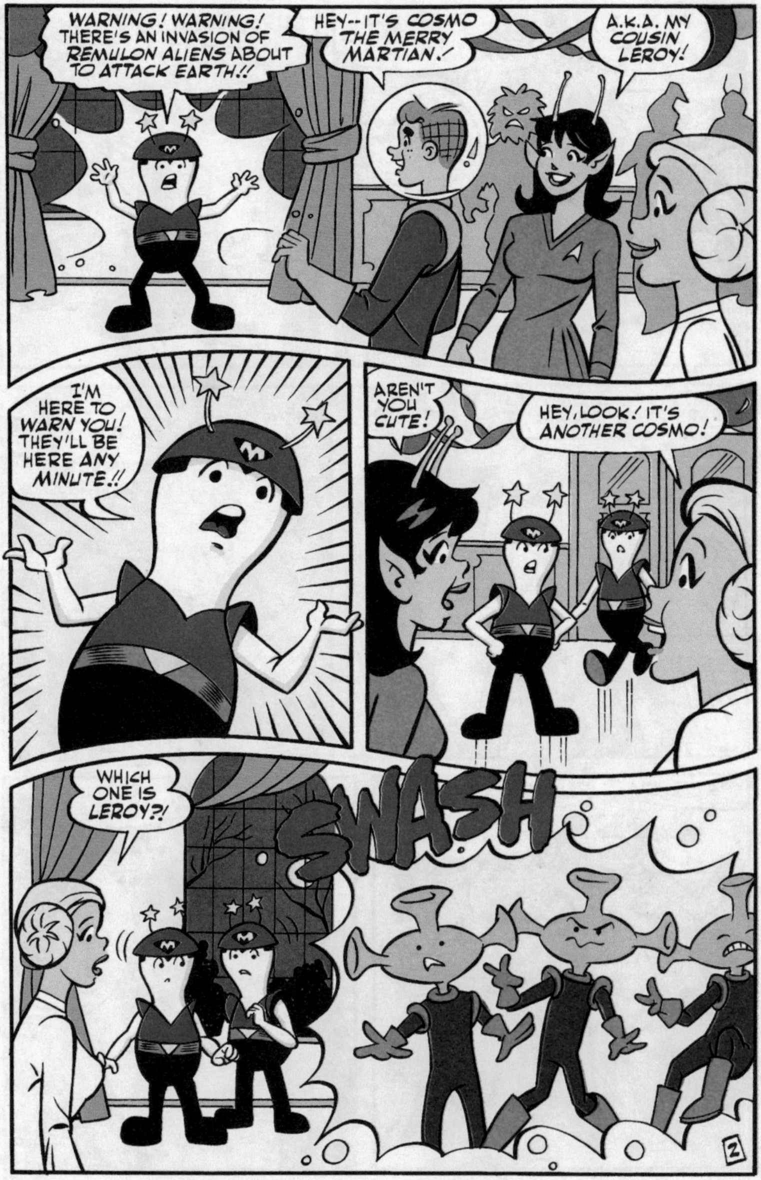
WARNING! WARNING! THERE'S AN INVASION OF REMULON ALIENS ABOUT TO ATTACK EARTH!!
HEY--IT'S COSMO THE MERRY MARTIAN!
A.K.A. MY COUSIN LEROY!
I'M HERE TO WARN YOU! THEY'LL BE HERE ANY MINUTE!!
AREN'T YOU CUTE!
HEY, LOOK! IT'S ANOTHER COSMO!
WHICH ONE IS LEROY?!
SWASH
2

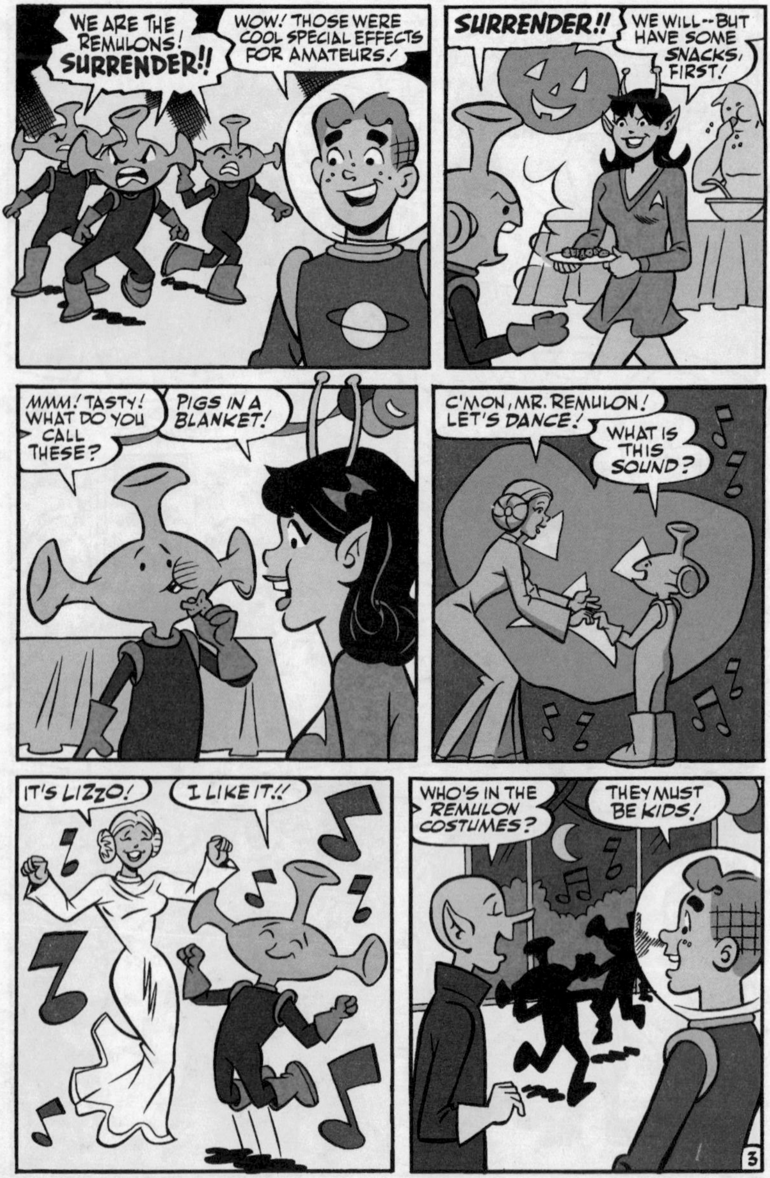
WE ARE THE REMULONS! SURRENDER!!
WOW! THOSE WERE COOL SPECIAL EFFECTS FOR AMATEURS!
SURRENDER!!
WE WILL--BUT HAVE SOME SNACKS, FIRST!
MMM! TASTY! WHAT DO YOU CALL THESE?
PIGS IN A BLANKET!
C'MON, MR. REMULON! LET'S DANCE!
WHAT IS THIS SOUND?
IT'S LIZZO!
I LIKE IT!!
WHO'S IN THE REMULON COSTUMES?
THEY MUST BE KIDS!
3

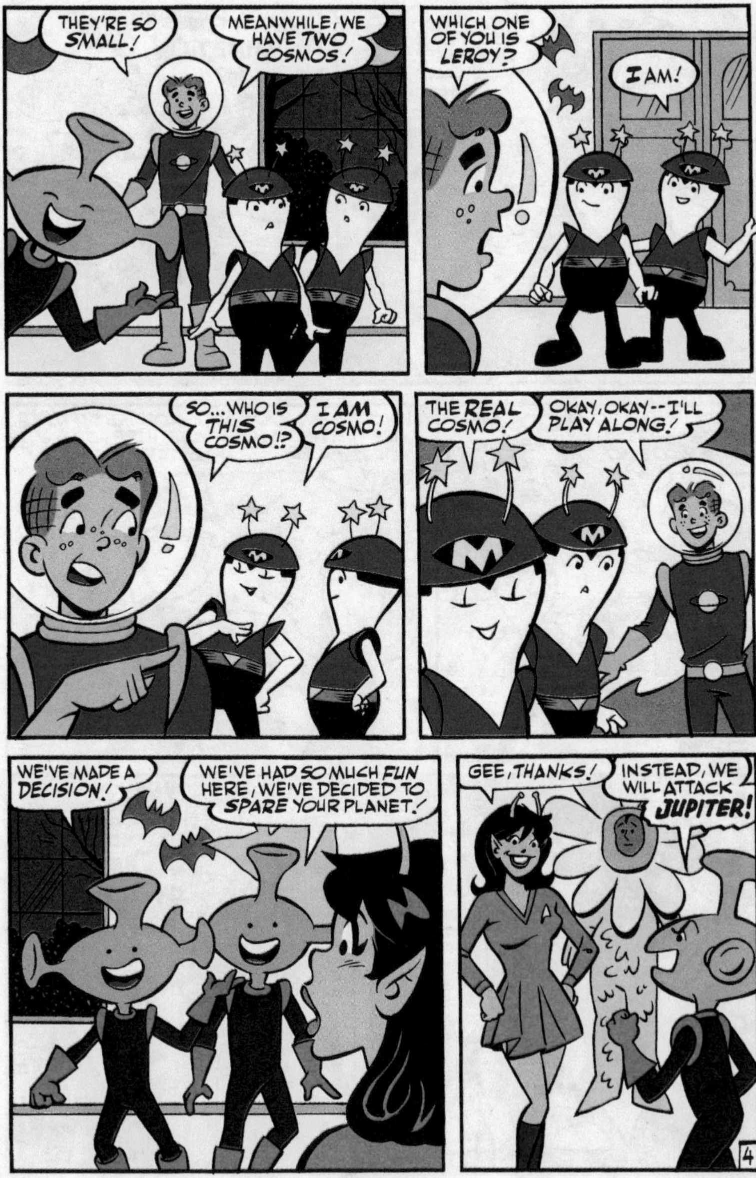
THEY'RE SO SMALL!
MEANWHILE, WE HAVE TWO COSMOS!
WHICH ONE OF YOU IS LEROY?
I AM!
SO... WHO IS THIS COSMO!?
I AM COSMO!
THE REAL COSMO!
OKAY, OKAY-- I'LL PLAY ALONG!
WE'VE MADE A DECISION!
WE'VE HAD SO MUCH FUN HERE, WE'VE DECIDED TO SPARE YOUR PLANET!
GEE, THANKS!
INSTEAD, WE WILL ATTACK JUPITER!
4

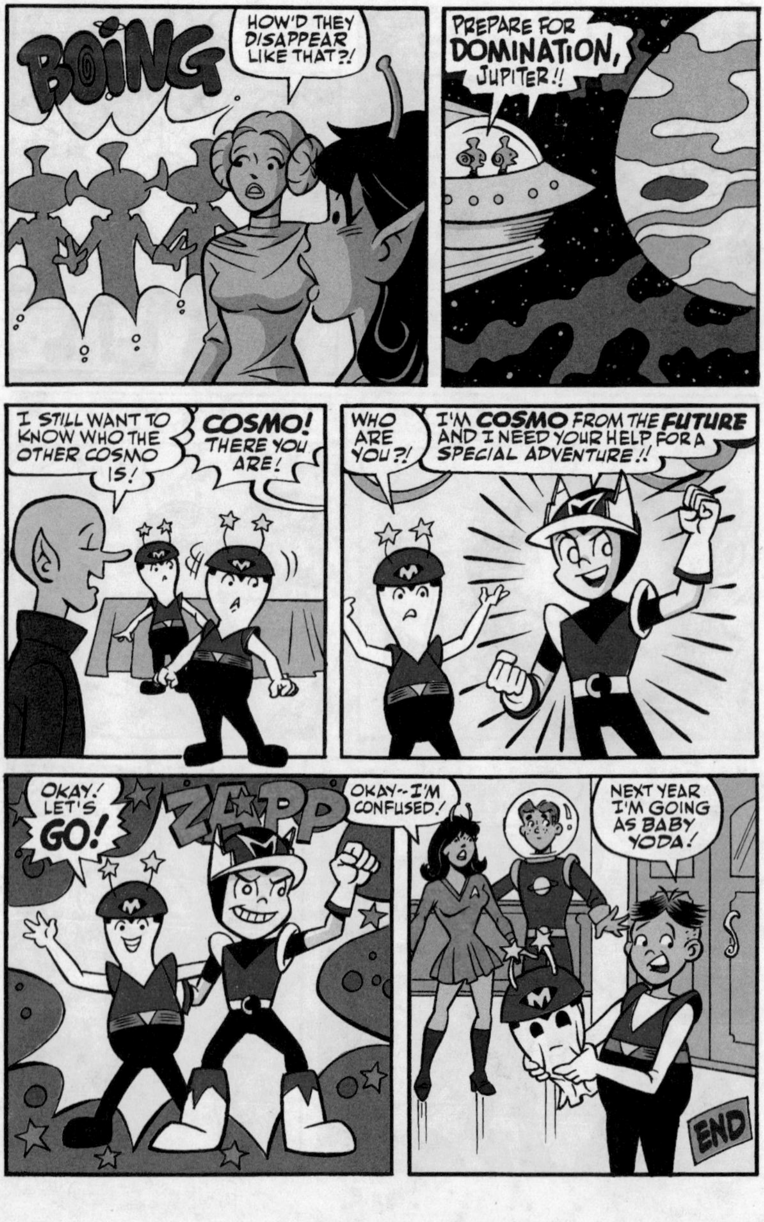
BOING
HOW'D THEY DISAPPEAR LIKE THAT?!
PREPARE FOR DOMINATION, JUPITER!!
I STILL WANT TO KNOW WHO THE OTHER COSMO IS!
COSMO! THERE YOU ARE!
WHO ARE YOU?!
I'M COSMO FROM THE FUTURE AND I NEED YOUR HELP FOR A SPECIAL ADVENTURE!!
OKAY! LET'S GO!
ZAPP
OKAY-- I'M CONFUSED!
NEXT YEAR I'M GOING AS BABY YODA!
END

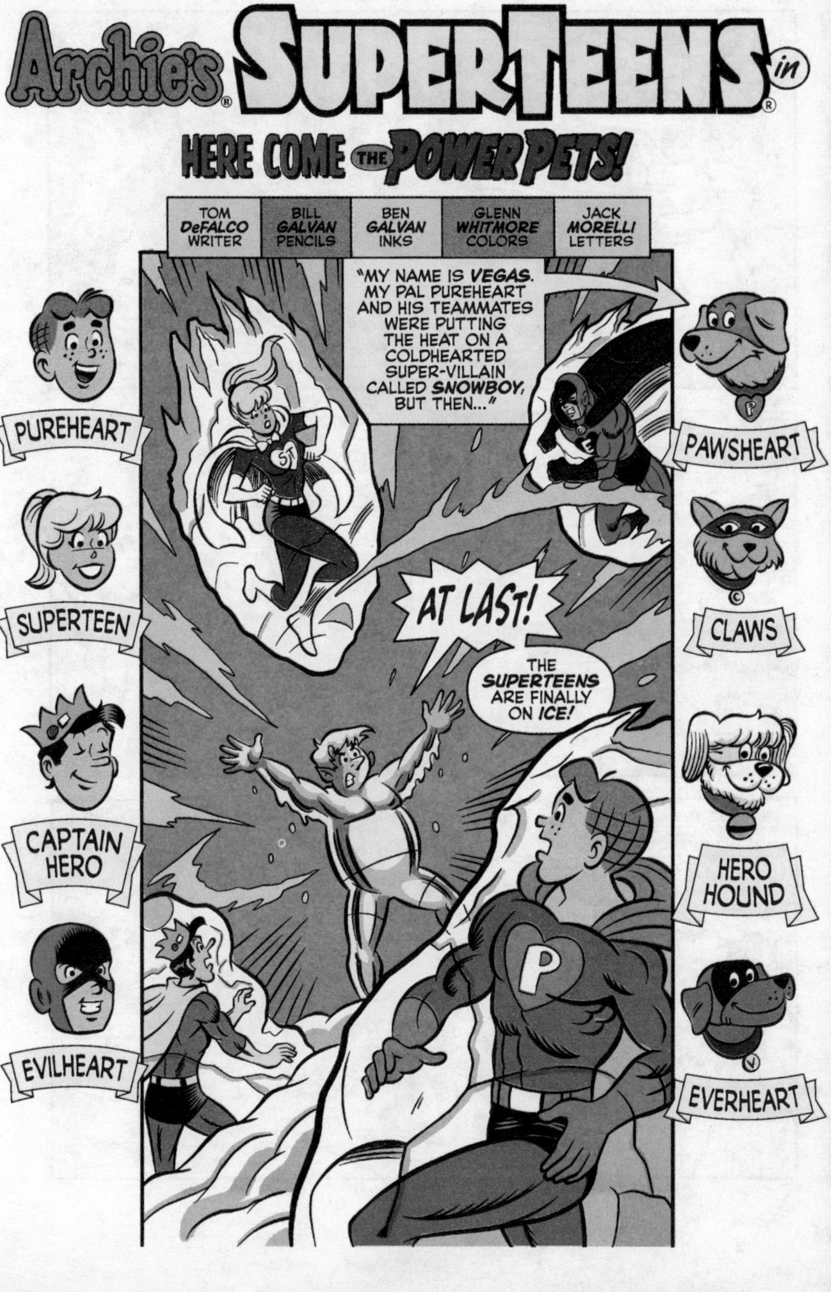

Archie's SUPERTEENS in
HERE COME THE POWER PETS!
TOM DeFALCO WRITER
BILL GALVAN PENCILS
BEN GALVAN INKS
GLENN WHITMORE COLORS
JACK MORELLI LETTERS
"MY NAME IS VEGAS. MY PAL PUREHEART AND HIS TEAMMATES WERE PUTTING THE HEAT ON A COLDHEARTED SUPER-VILLAIN CALLED SNOWBOY, BUT THEN..."
AT LAST!
THE SUPERTEENS ARE FINALLY ON ICE!
PUREHEART
SUPERTEEN
CAPTAIN HERO
EVILHEART
PAWSHEART
CLAWS
HERO HOUND
EVERHEART

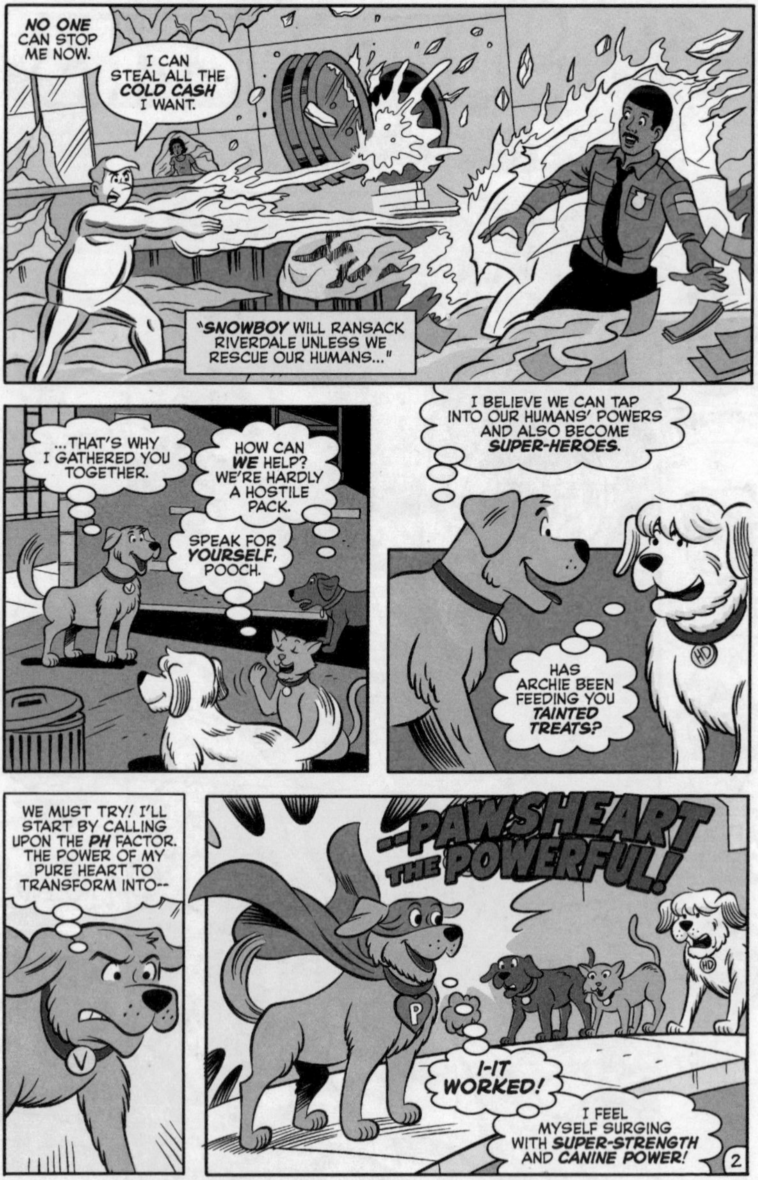
NO ONE CAN STOP ME NOW.
I CAN STEAL ALL THE COLD CASH I WANT.
"SNOWBOY WILL RANSACK RIVERDALE UNLESS WE RESCUE OUR HUMANS..."
...THAT'S WHY I GATHERED YOU TOGETHER.
HOW CAN WE HELP? WE'RE HARDLY A HOSTILE PACK.
SPEAK FOR YOURSELF, POOCH.
I BELIEVE WE CAN TAP INTO OUR HUMANS' POWERS AND ALSO BECOME SUPER-HEROES.
HAS ARCHIE BEEN FEEDING YOU TAINTED TREATS?
WE MUST TRY! I'LL START BY CALLING UPON THE PH FACTOR. THE POWER OF MY PURE HEART TO TRANSFORM INTO--
--PAWSHEART THE POWERFUL!
I-IT WORKED!
I FEEL MYSELF SURGING WITH SUPER-STRENGTH AND CANINE POWER!
2

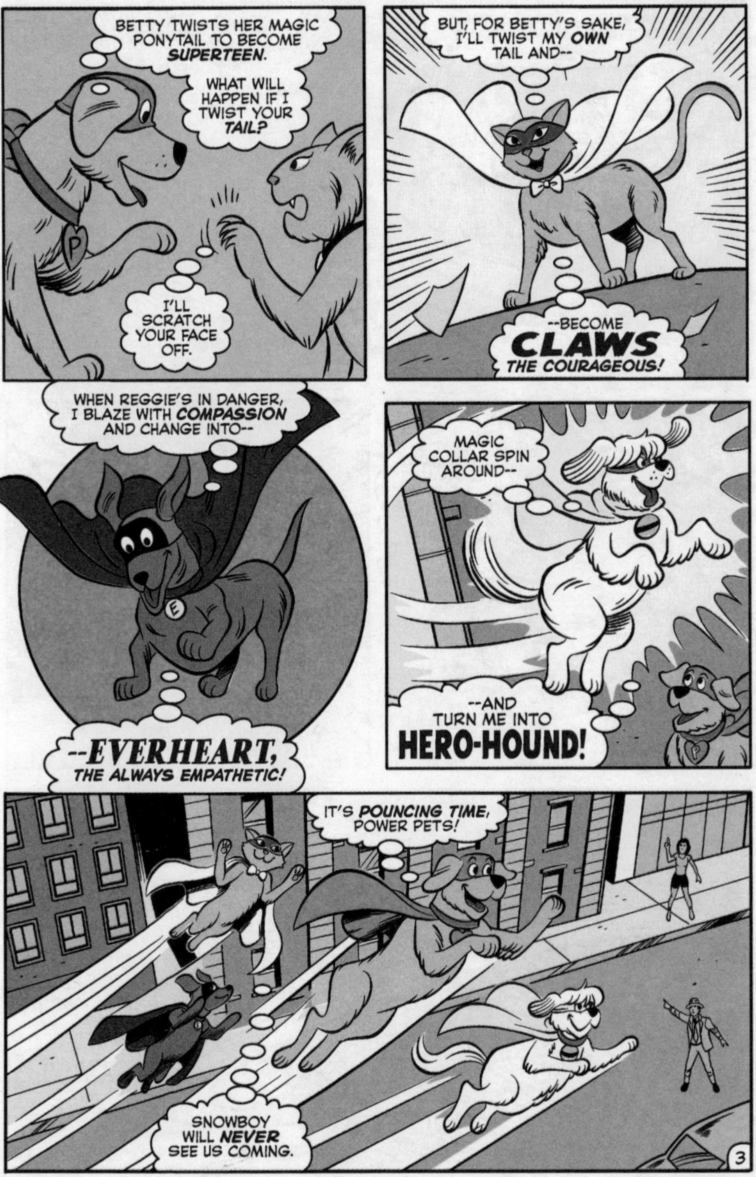

BETTY TWISTS HER MAGIC PONYTAIL TO BECOME SUPERTEEN.
WHAT WILL HAPPEN IF I TWIST YOUR TAIL?
I'LL SCRATCH YOUR FACE OFF.
BUT, FOR BETTY'S SAKE, I'LL TWIST MY OWN TAIL AND--
--BECOME CLAWS THE COURAGEOUS!
WHEN REGGIE'S IN DANGER, I BLAZE WITH COMPASSION AND CHANGE INTO--
--EVERHEART, THE ALWAYS EMPATHETIC!
MAGIC COLLAR SPIN AROUND--
--AND TURN ME INTO HERO-HOUND!
IT'S POUNCING TIME, POWER PETS!
SNOWBOY WILL NEVER SEE US COMING.
3

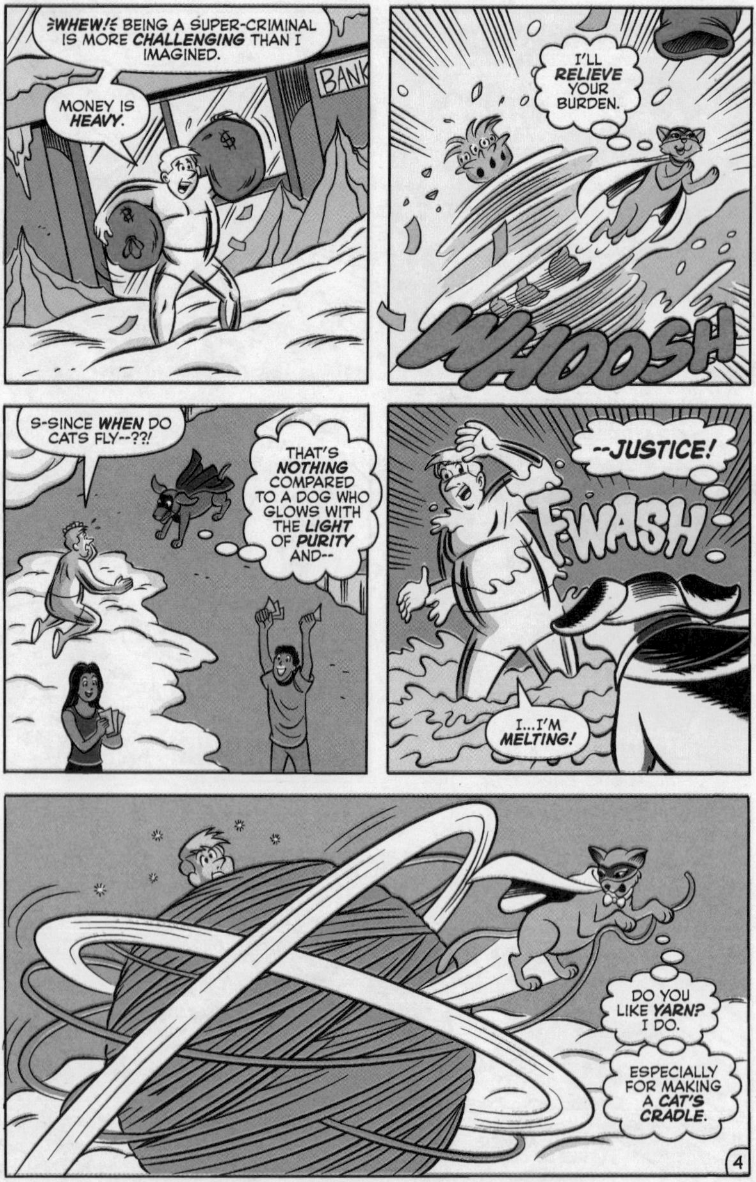
WHEW! BEING A SUPER-CRIMINAL IS MORE CHALLENGING THAN I IMAGINED.
MONEY IS HEAVY.
BANK
I'LL RELIEVE YOUR BURDEN.
WHOOSH
S-SINCE WHEN DO CATS FLY--??!
THAT'S NOTHING COMPARED TO A DOG WHO GLOWS WITH THE LIGHT OF PURITY AND--
--JUSTICE!
FWASH
I...I'M MELTING!
DO YOU LIKE YARN? I DO.
ESPECIALLY FOR MAKING A CAT'S CRADLE.
4

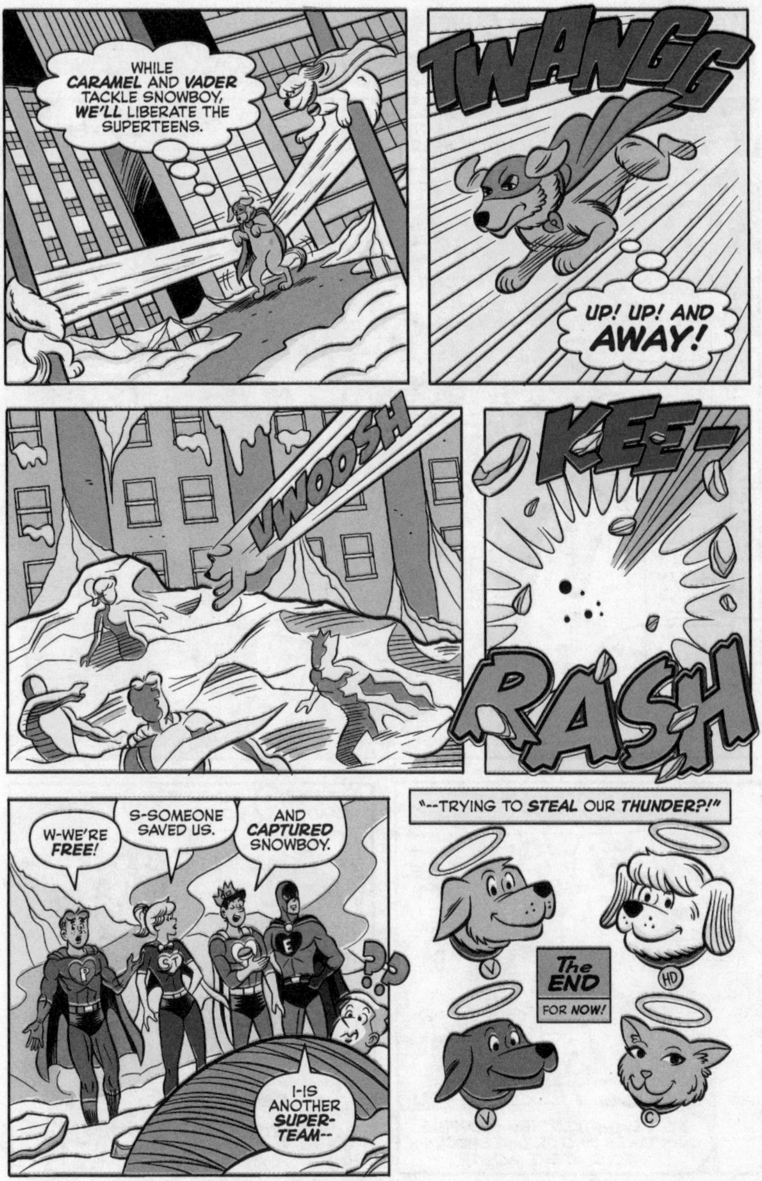
WHILE CARAMEL AND VADER TACKLE SNOWBOY, WE'LL LIBERATE THE SUPERTEENS.
TWANGG
UP! UP! AND AWAY!
VWOOSH
KEE-RASH
W-WE'RE FREE!
S-SOMEONE SAVED US.
AND CAPTURED SNOWBOY.
I-IS ANOTHER SUPER-TEAM--
"--TRYING TO STEAL OUR THUNDER?!"
The END FOR NOW!

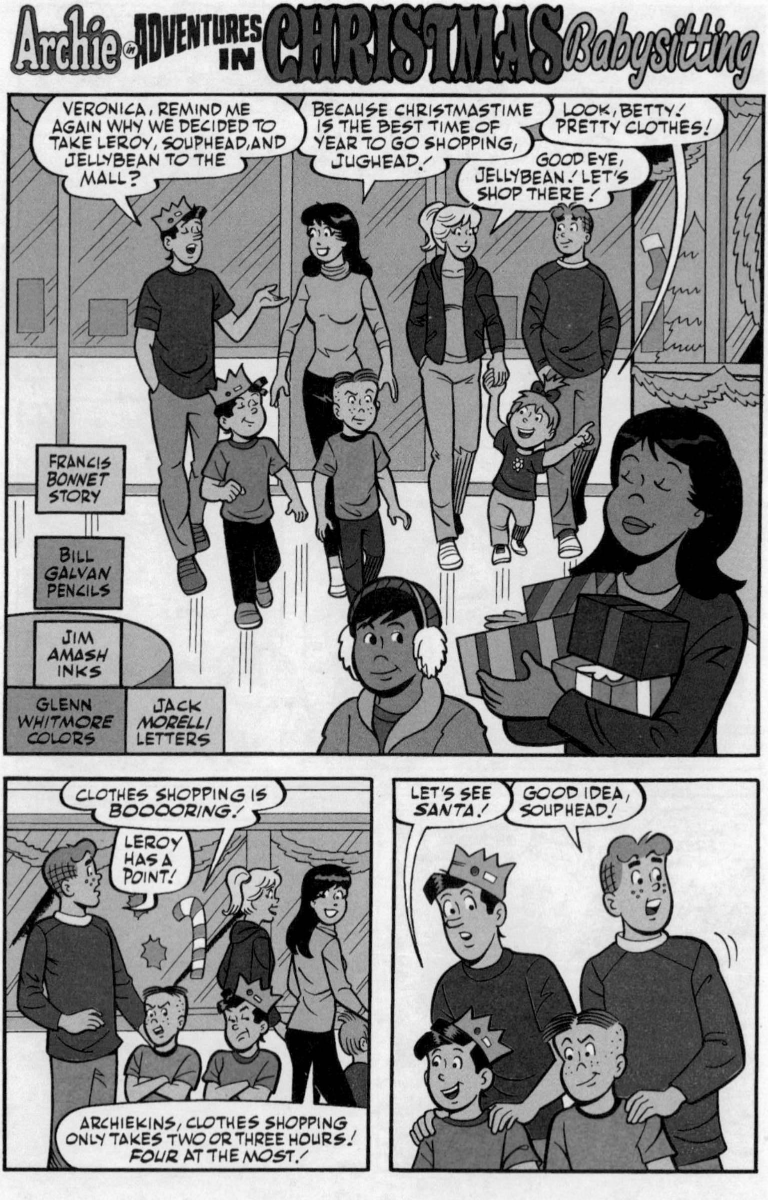
Archie in ADVENTURES IN CHRISTMAS Babysitting
VERONICA, REMIND ME AGAIN WHY WE DECIDED TO TAKE LEROY, SOUPHEAD, AND JELLYBEAN TO THE MALL?
BECAUSE CHRISTMASTIME IS THE BEST TIME OF YEAR TO GO SHOPPING, JUGHEAD!
LOOK, BETTY! PRETTY CLOTHES!
GOOD EYE, JELLYBEAN! LET'S SHOP THERE!
FRANCIS BONNET STORY
BILL GALVAN PENCILS
JIM AMASH INKS
GLENN WHITMORE COLORS
JACK MORELLI LETTERS
CLOTHES SHOPPING IS BOOOORING!
LEROY HAS A POINT!
ARCHIEKINS, CLOTHES SHOPPING ONLY TAKES TWO OR THREE HOURS! FOUR AT THE MOST!
LET'S SEE SANTA!
GOOD IDEA, SOUPHEAD!

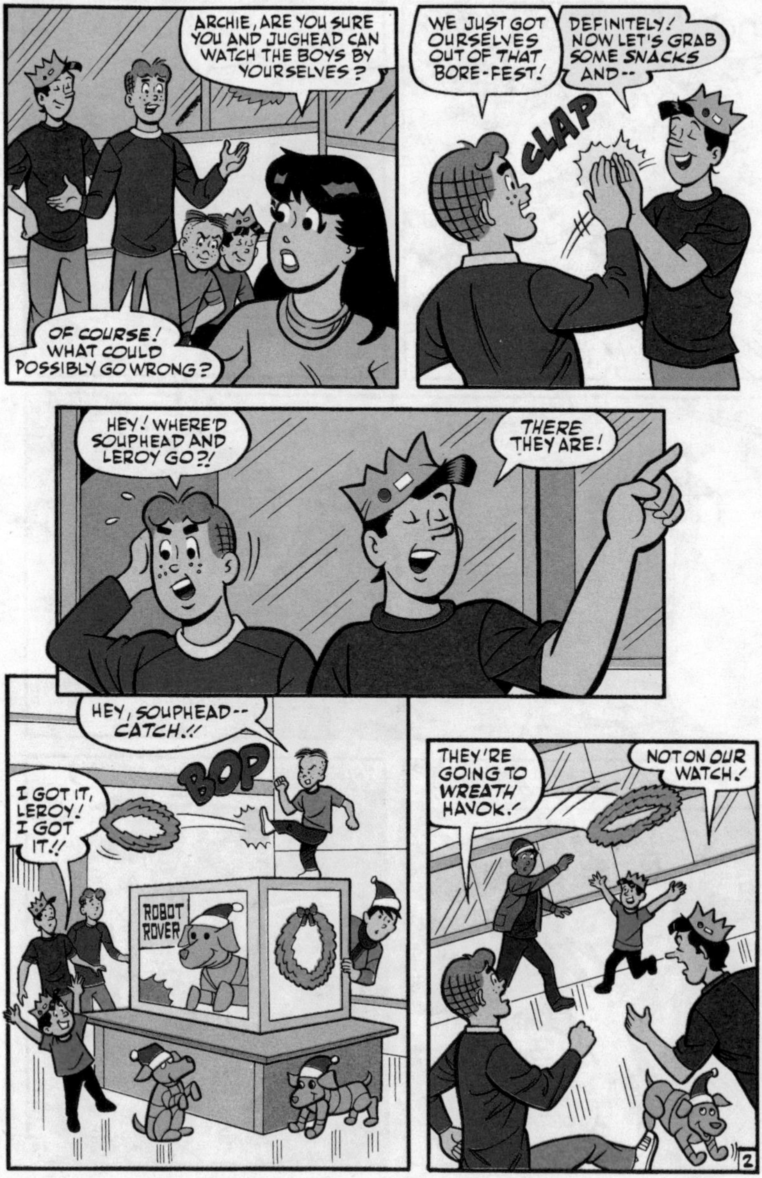
ARCHIE, ARE YOU SURE YOU AND JUGHEAD CAN WATCH THE BOYS BY YOURSELVES?
OF COURSE! WHAT COULD POSSIBLY GO WRONG?
WE JUST GOT OURSELVES OUT OF THAT BORE-FEST!
DEFINITELY! NOW LET'S GRAB SOME SNACKS AND--
CLAP
HEY! WHERE'D SOUPHEAD AND LEROY GO?!
THERE THEY ARE!
HEY, SOUPHEAD-- CATCH!!
BOP
I GOT IT, LEROY! I GOT IT!!
ROBOT ROVER
THEY'RE GOING TO WREATH HAVOK!
NOT ON OUR WATCH!
2

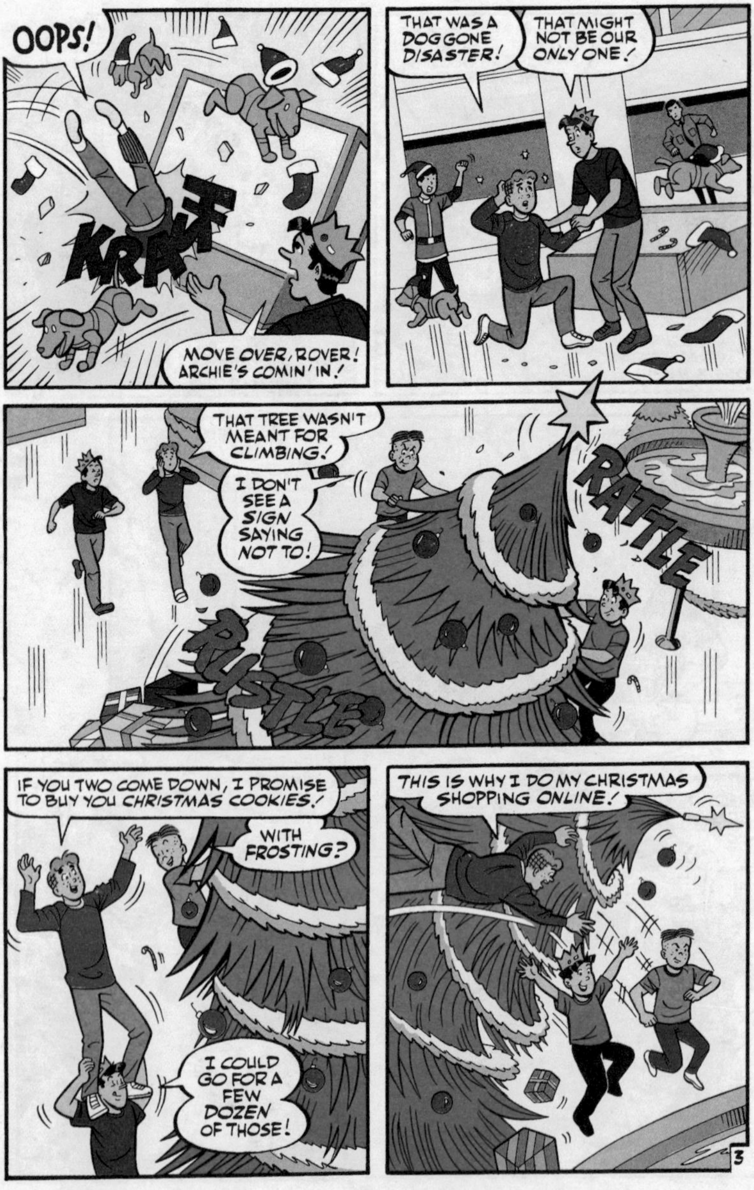
OOPS!
KRAK
MOVE OVER, ROVER! ARCHIE'S COMIN' IN!
THAT WAS A DOGGONE DISASTER!
THAT MIGHT NOT BE OUR ONLY ONE!
THAT TREE WASN'T MEANT FOR CLIMBING!
I DON'T SEE A SIGN SAYING NOT TO!
RATTLE
RUSTLE
IF YOU TWO COME DOWN, I PROMISE TO BUY YOU CHRISTMAS COOKIES!
WITH FROSTING?
I COULD GO FOR A FEW DOZEN OF THOSE!
THIS IS WHY I DO MY CHRISTMAS SHOPPING ONLINE!
3

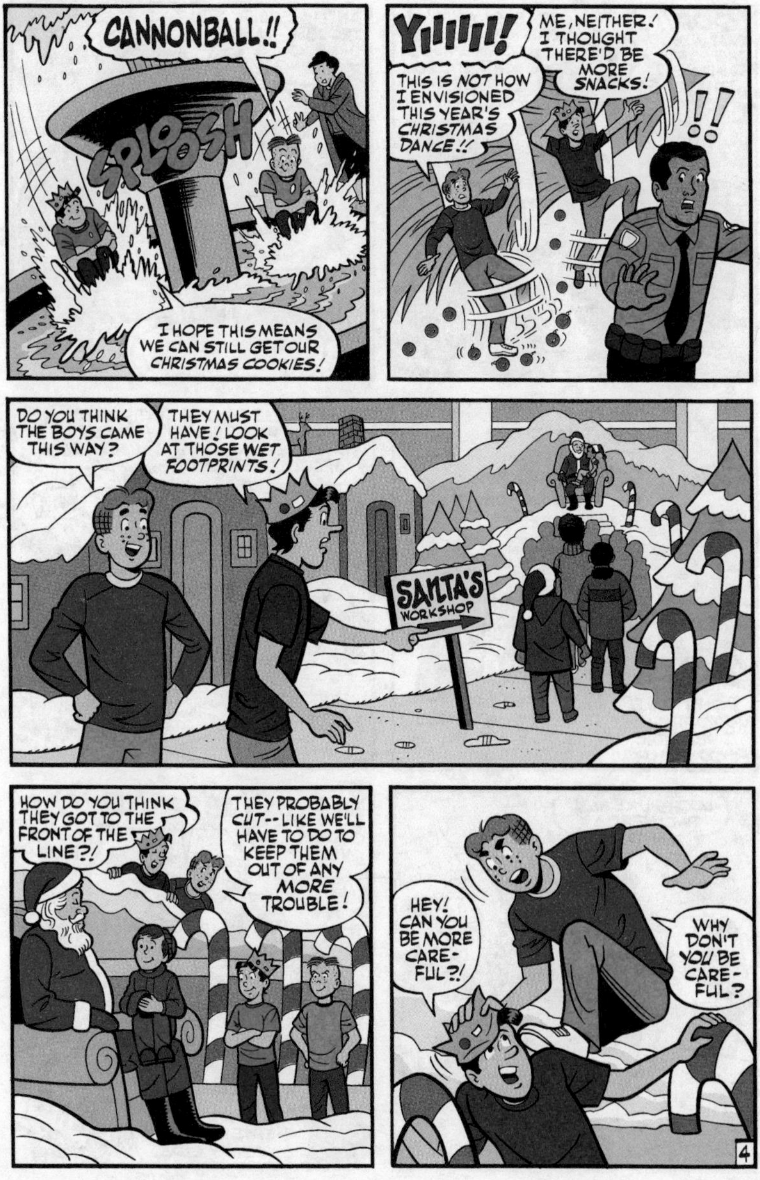
CANNONBALL!!
SPLOOSH
I HOPE THIS MEANS WE CAN STILL GET OUR CHRISTMAS COOKIES!
YIIIIII!
THIS IS NOT HOW I ENVISIONED THIS YEAR'S CHRISTMAS DANCE!!
ME, NEITHER! I THOUGHT THERE'D BE MORE SNACKS!
!!
DO YOU THINK THE BOYS CAME THIS WAY?
THEY MUST HAVE! LOOK AT THOSE WET FOOTPRINTS!
SANTA'S WORKSHOP
HOW DO YOU THINK THEY GOT TO THE FRONT OF THE LINE?!
THEY PROBABLY CUT-- LIKE WE'LL HAVE TO DO TO KEEP THEM OUT OF ANY MORE TROUBLE!
HEY! CAN YOU BE MORE CARE-FUL?!
WHY DON'T YOU BE CARE-FUL?
4

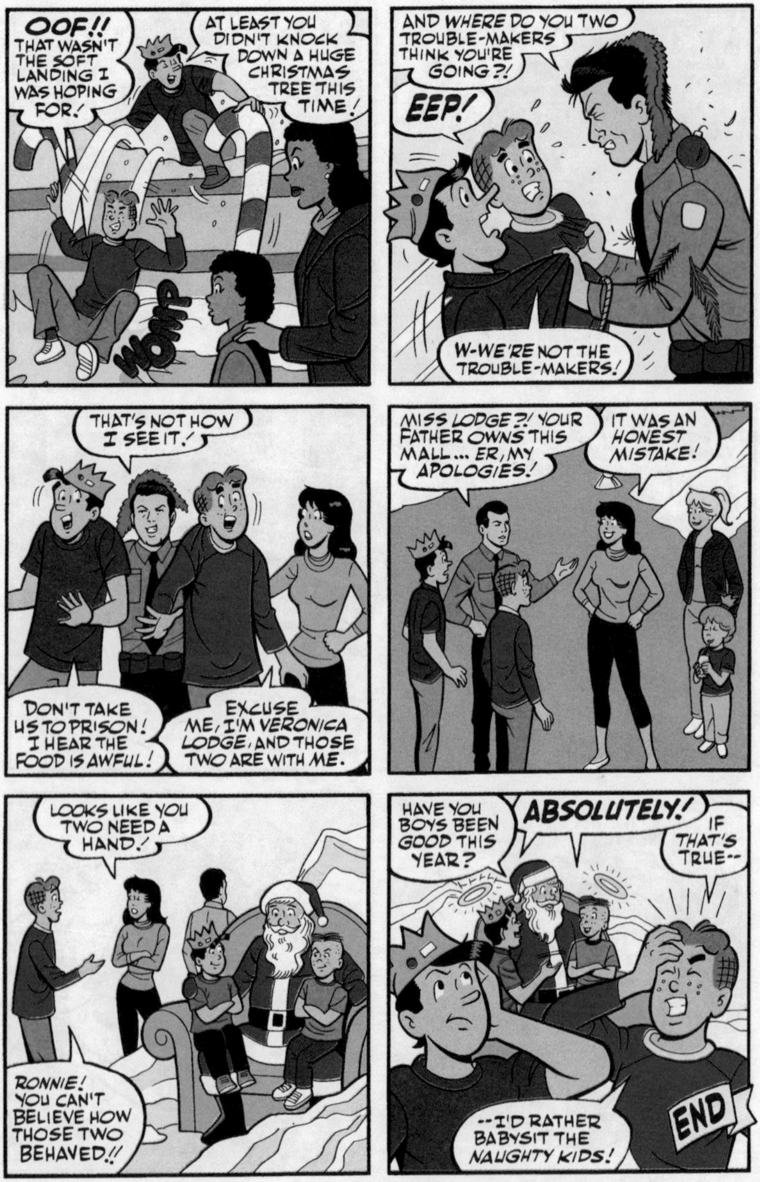
OOF!! THAT WASN'T THE SOFT LANDING I WAS HOPING FOR!
AT LEAST YOU DIDN'T KNOCK DOWN A HUGE CHRISTMAS TREE THIS TIME!
WOMP
AND WHERE DO YOU TWO TROUBLE-MAKERS THINK YOU'RE GOING?!
EEP!
W-WE'RE NOT THE TROUBLE-MAKERS!
THAT'S NOT HOW I SEE IT!
DON'T TAKE US TO PRISON! I HEAR THE FOOD IS AWFUL!
EXCUSE ME, I'M VERONICA LODGE, AND THOSE TWO ARE WITH ME.
MISS LODGE?! YOUR FATHER OWNS THIS MALL... ER, MY APOLOGIES!
IT WAS AN HONEST MISTAKE!
LOOKS LIKE YOU TWO NEED A HAND!
RONNIE! YOU CAN'T BELIEVE HOW THOSE TWO BEHAVED!!
HAVE YOU BOYS BEEN GOOD THIS YEAR?
ABSOLUTELY!
IF THAT'S TRUE--
--I'D RATHER BABYSIT THE NAUGHTY KIDS!
END

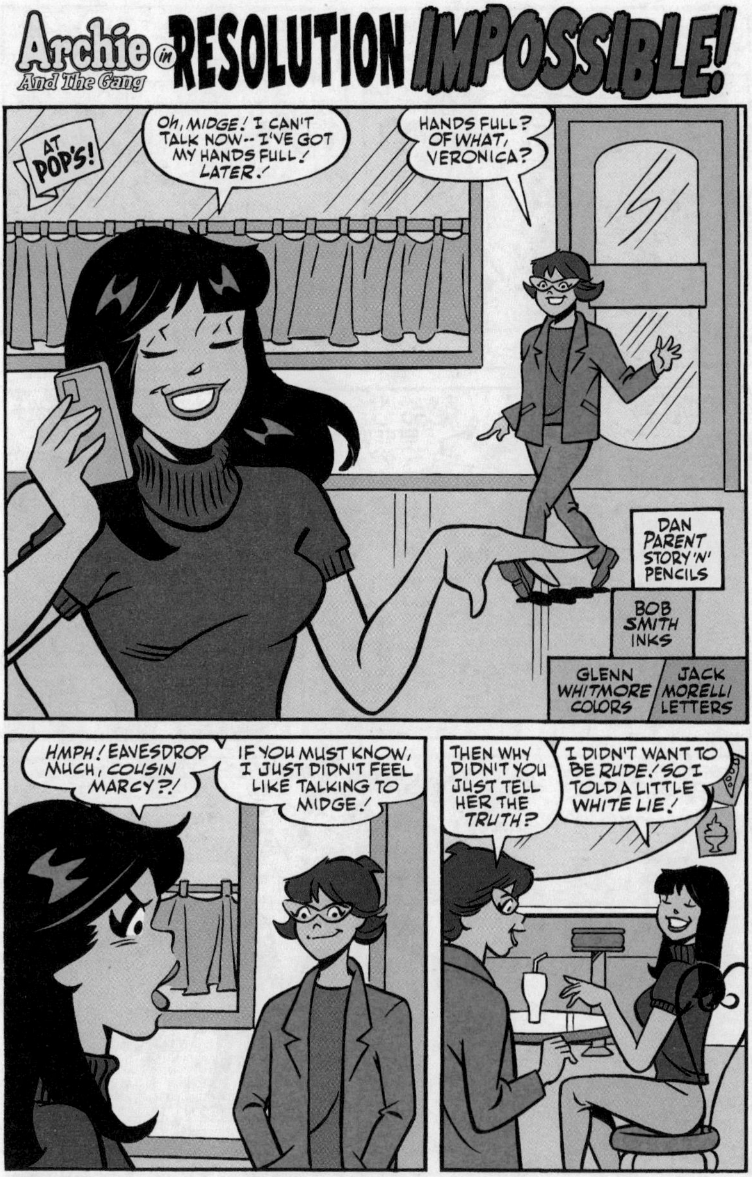

Archie And The Gang in RESOLUTION IMPOSSIBLE!
AT POP'S!
Oh, MIDGE! I CAN'T TALK NOW-- I'VE GOT MY HANDS FULL! LATER!
HANDS FULL? OF WHAT, VERONICA?
DAN PARENT STORY 'N' PENCILS
BOB SMITH INKS
GLENN WHITMORE COLORS
JACK MORELLI LETTERS
HMPH! EAVESDROP MUCH, COUSIN MARCY?!
IF YOU MUST KNOW, I JUST DIDN'T FEEL LIKE TALKING TO MIDGE!
THEN WHY DIDN'T YOU JUST TELL HER THE TRUTH?
I DIDN'T WANT TO BE RUDE! SO I TOLD A LITTLE WHITE LIE!

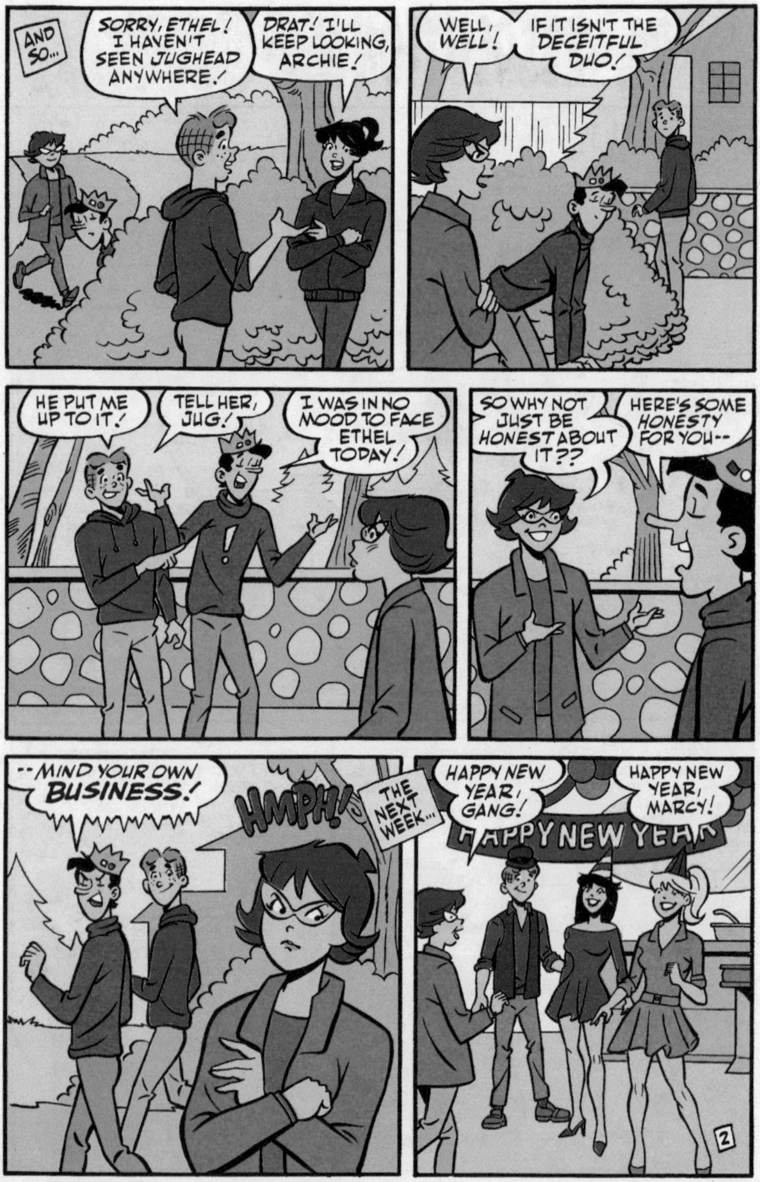
AND SO...
SORRY, ETHEL! I HAVEN'T SEEN JUGHEAD ANYWHERE!
DRAT! I'LL KEEP LOOKING, ARCHIE!
WELL, WELL!
IF IT ISN'T THE DECEITFUL DUO!
HE PUT ME UP TO IT!
TELL HER, JUG!
I WAS IN NO MOOD TO FACE ETHEL TODAY!
SO WHY NOT JUST BE HONEST ABOUT IT??
HERE'S SOME HONESTY FOR YOU--
--MIND YOUR OWN BUSINESS!
HMPH!
THE NEXT WEEK...
HAPPY NEW YEAR, GANG!
HAPPY NEW YEAR, MARCY!
HAPPY NEW YEAR
2

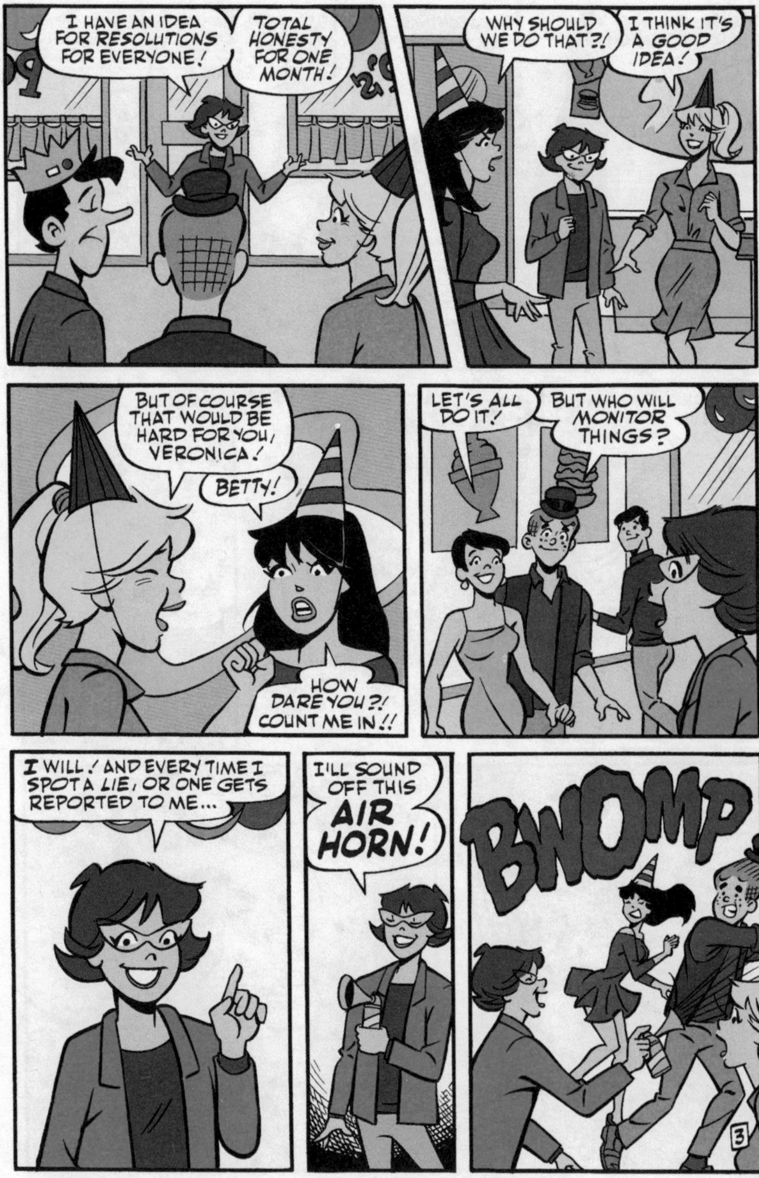
I HAVE AN IDEA FOR RESOLUTIONS FOR EVERYONE!
TOTAL HONESTY FOR ONE MONTH!
WHY SHOULD WE DO THAT?!
I THINK IT'S A GOOD IDEA!
BUT OF COURSE THAT WOULD BE HARD FOR YOU, VERONICA!
BETTY!
HOW DARE YOU?! COUNT ME IN!!
LET'S ALL DO IT!
BUT WHO WILL MONITOR THINGS?
I WILL! AND EVERY TIME I SPOT A LIE, OR ONE GETS REPORTED TO ME...
I'LL SOUND OFF THIS AIR HORN!
BWOMP
3

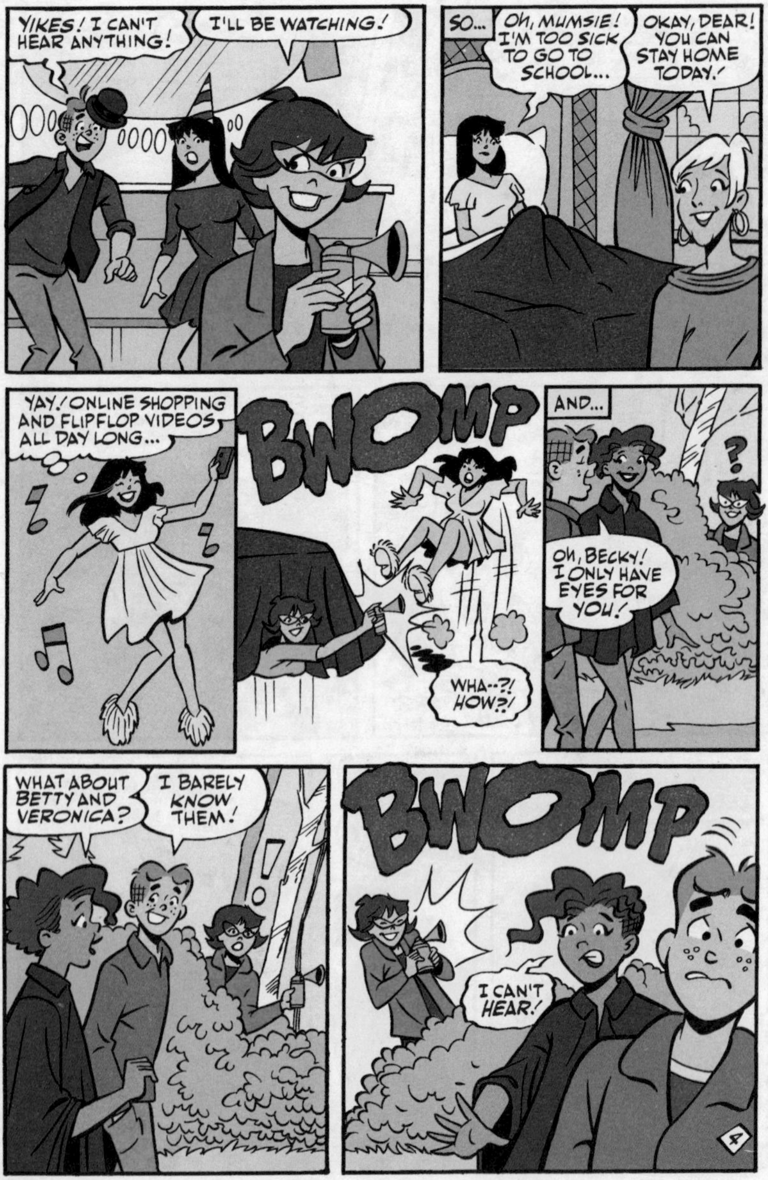
YIKES! I CAN'T HEAR ANYTHING!
I'LL BE WATCHING!
SO...
OH, MUMSIE! I'M TOO SICK TO GO TO SCHOOL...
OKAY, DEAR! YOU CAN STAY HOME TODAY!
YAY! ONLINE SHOPPING AND FLIPFLOP VIDEOS ALL DAY LONG...
BWOMP
WHA--?! HOW?!
AND...
?
OH, BECKY! I ONLY HAVE EYES FOR YOU!
WHAT ABOUT BETTY AND VERONICA?
I BARELY KNOW THEM!
!
BWOMP
I CAN'T HEAR!
4

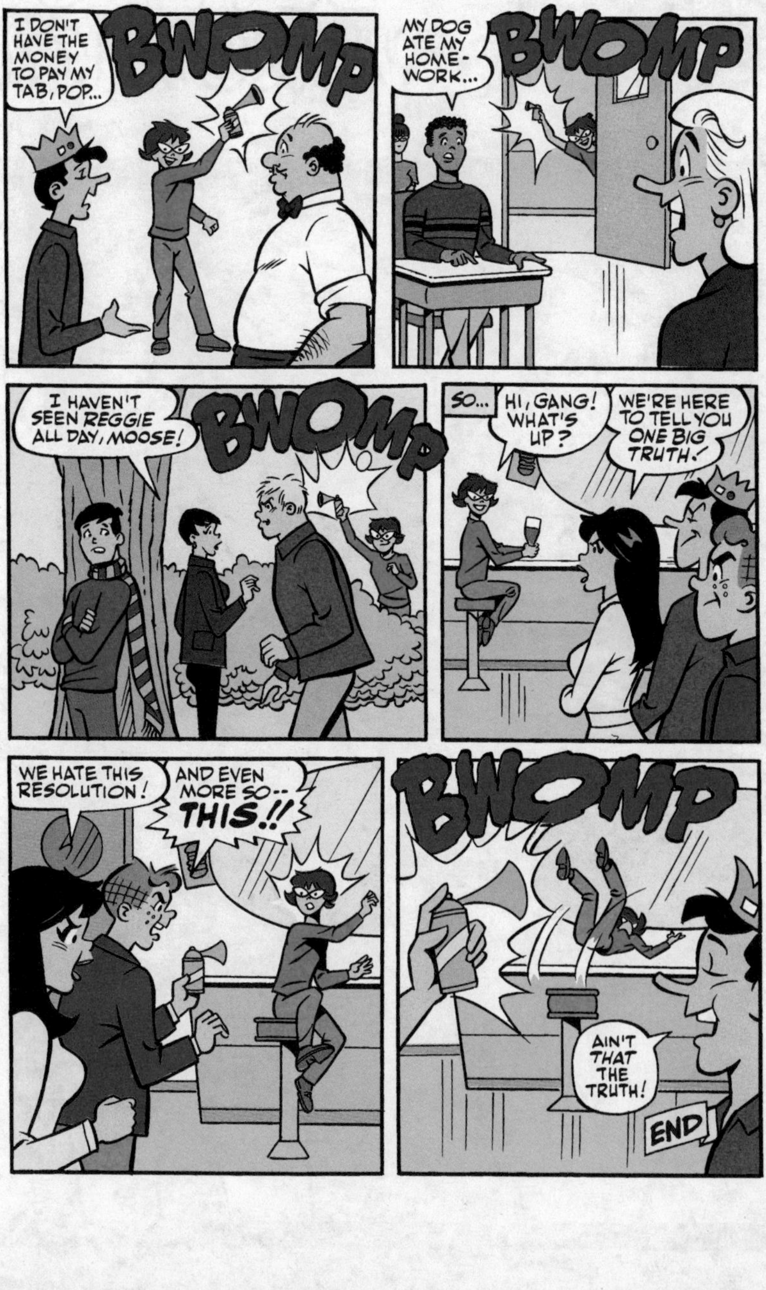
I DON'T HAVE THE MONEY TO PAY MY TAB, POP...
BWOMP
MY DOG ATE MY HOME-WORK...
BWOMP
I HAVEN'T SEEN REGGIE ALL DAY, MOOSE!
BWOMP
SO...
HI, GANG! WHAT'S UP?
WE'RE HERE TO TELL YOU ONE BIG TRUTH!
WE HATE THIS RESOLUTION!
AND EVEN MORE SO-- THIS!!
BWOMP
AIN'T THAT THE TRUTH!
END

02 BETTY & VERONICA

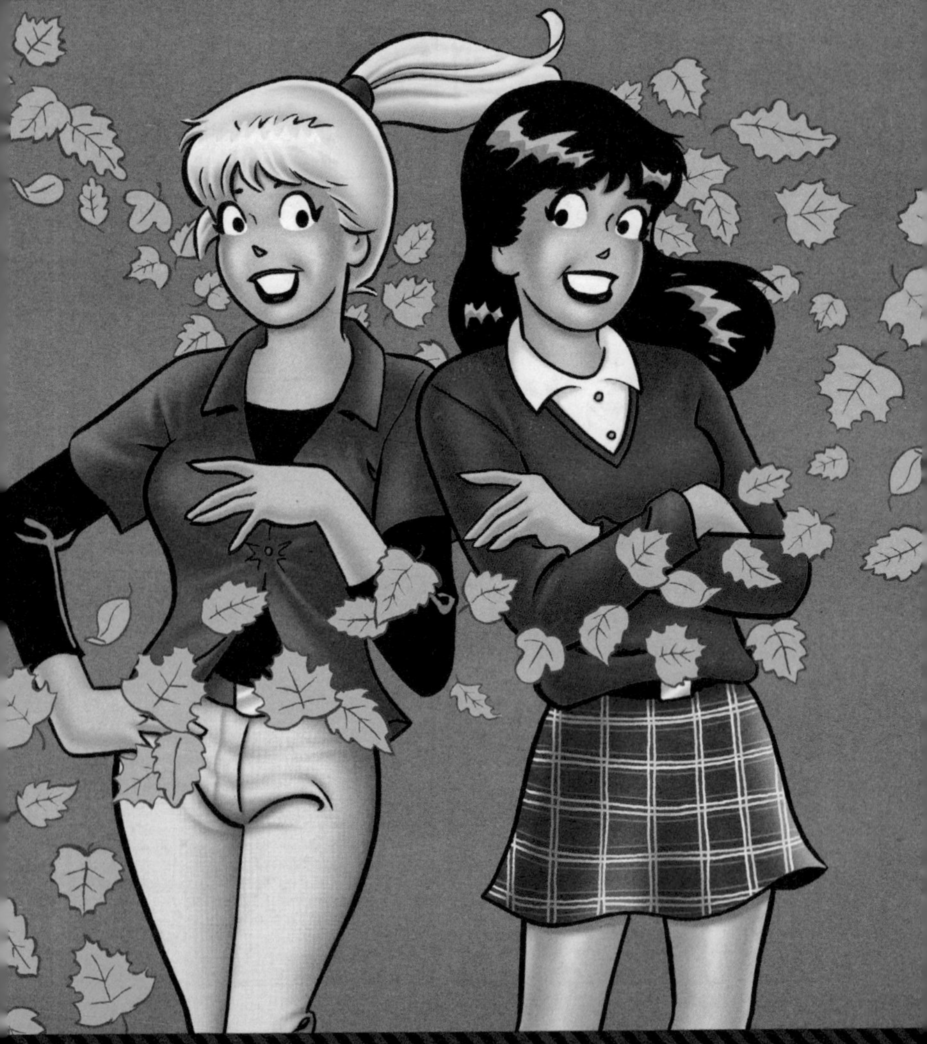

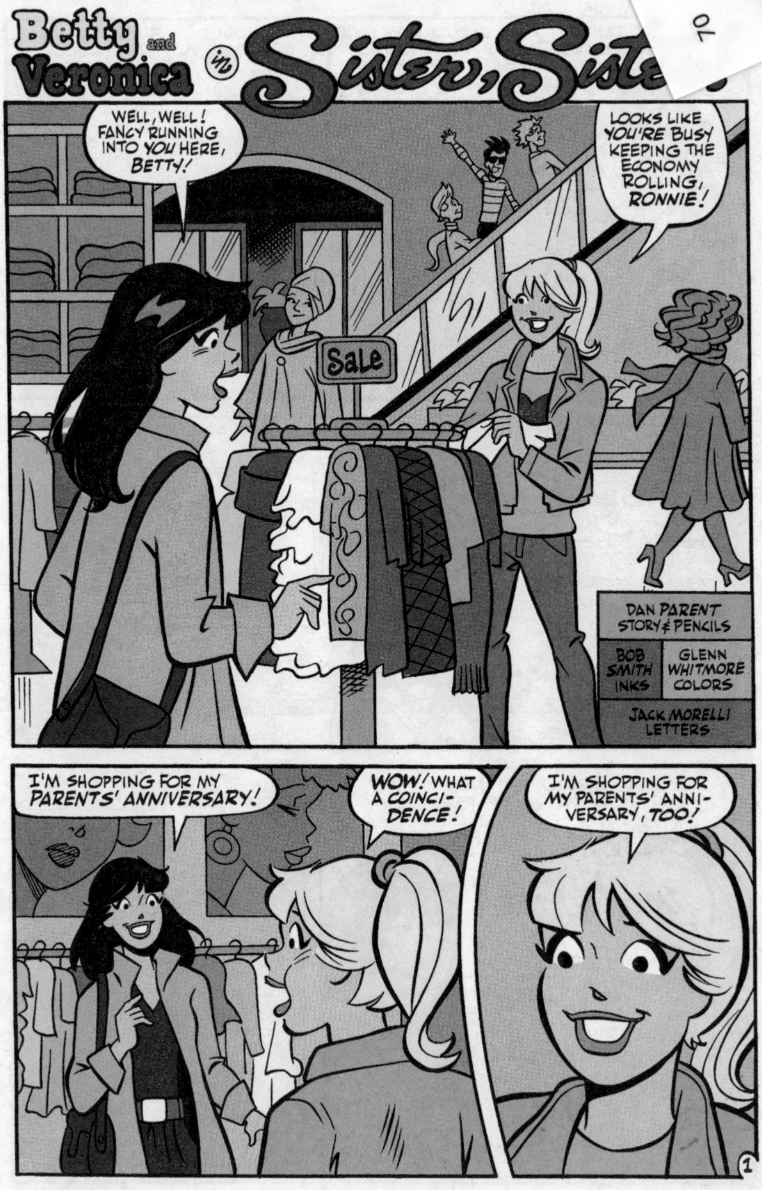
Betty and Veronica in Sister, Siste
WELL, WELL! FANCY RUNNING INTO YOU HERE, BETTY!
LOOKS LIKE YOU'RE BUSY KEEPING THE ECONOMY ROLLING, RONNIE!
Sale
DAN PARENT STORY & PENCILS
BOB SMITH INKS
GLENN WHITMORE COLORS
JACK MORELLI LETTERS
I'M SHOPPING FOR MY PARENTS' ANNIVERSARY!
WOW! WHAT A COINCI- DENCE!
I'M SHOPPING FOR MY PARENTS' ANNI- VERSARY, TOO!
1

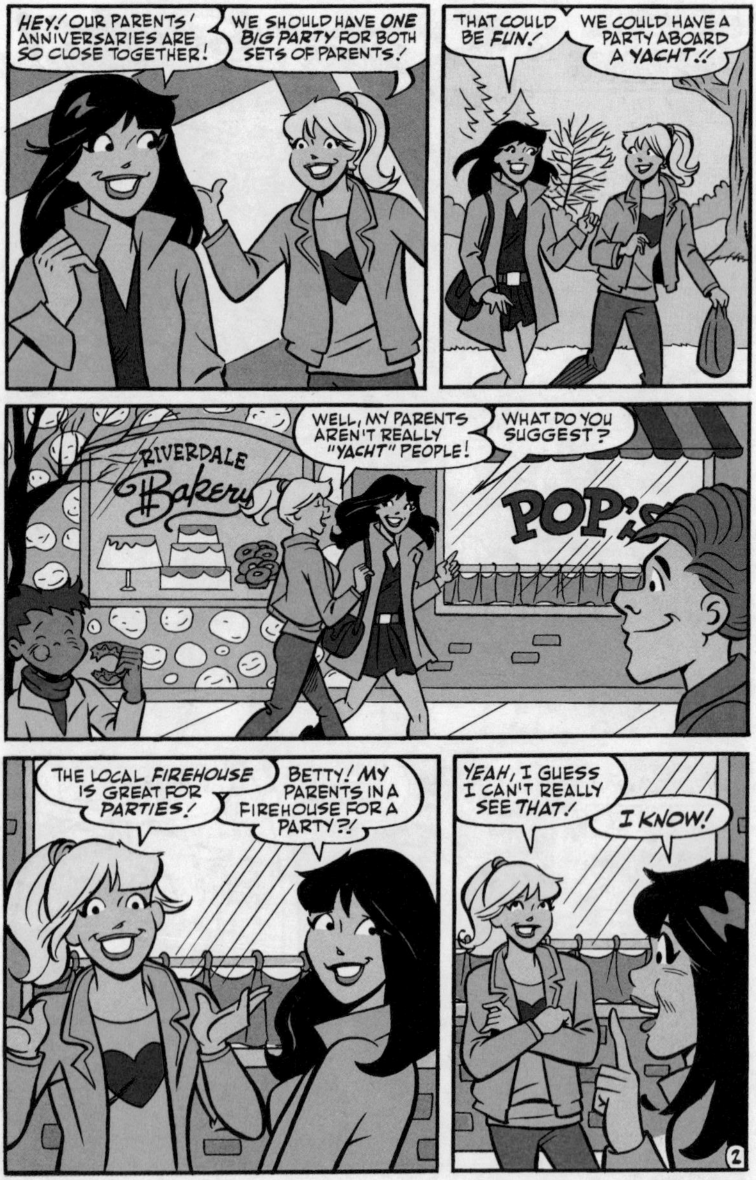
HEY! OUR PARENTS' ANNIVERSARIES ARE SO CLOSE TOGETHER!
WE SHOULD HAVE ONE BIG PARTY FOR BOTH SETS OF PARENTS!
THAT COULD BE FUN!
WE COULD HAVE A PARTY ABOARD A YACHT!!
RIVERDALE Bakery
WELL, MY PARENTS AREN'T REALLY "YACHT" PEOPLE!
WHAT DO YOU SUGGEST?
POP'S
THE LOCAL FIREHOUSE IS GREAT FOR PARTIES!
BETTY! MY PARENTS IN A FIREHOUSE FOR A PARTY?!
YEAH, I GUESS I CAN'T REALLY SEE THAT!
I KNOW!
2

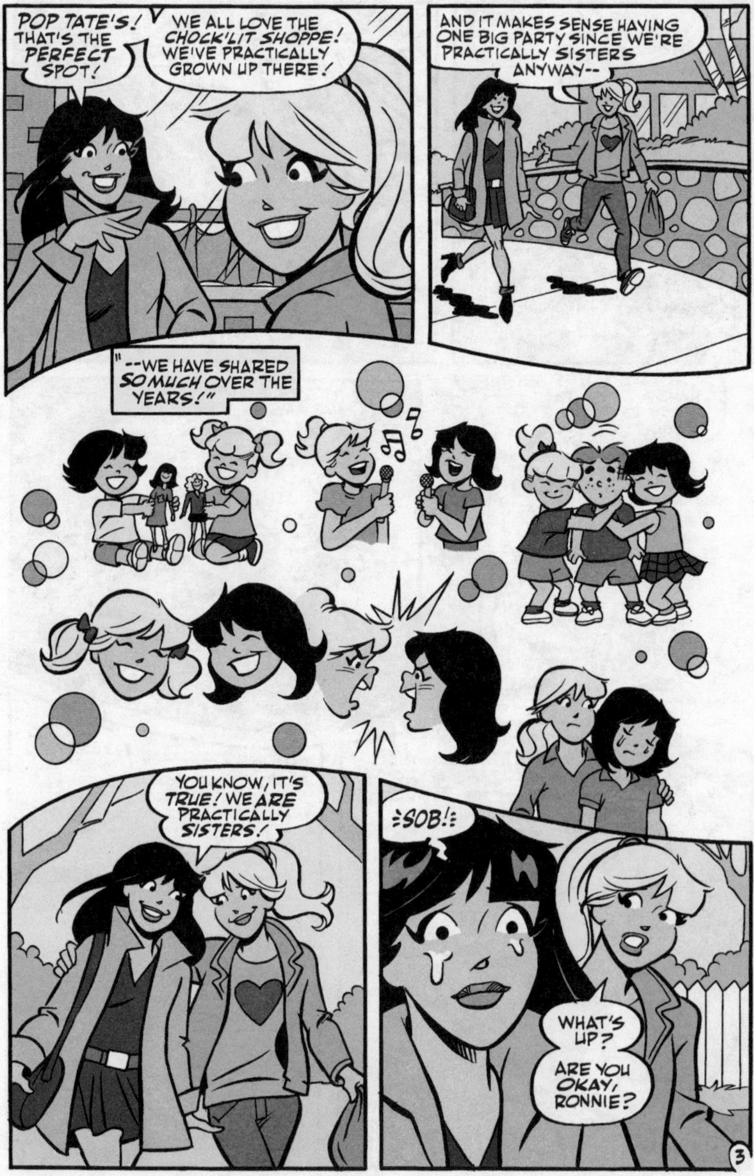
POP TATE'S! THAT'S THE PERFECT SPOT!
WE ALL LOVE THE CHOCK'LIT SHOPPE! WE'VE PRACTICALLY GROWN UP THERE!
AND IT MAKES SENSE HAVING ONE BIG PARTY SINCE WE'RE PRACTICALLY SISTERS ANYWAY--
"--WE HAVE SHARED SO MUCH OVER THE YEARS!"
YOU KNOW, IT'S TRUE! WE ARE PRACTICALLY SISTERS!
SOB!
WHAT'S UP?
ARE YOU OKAY, RONNIE?
3

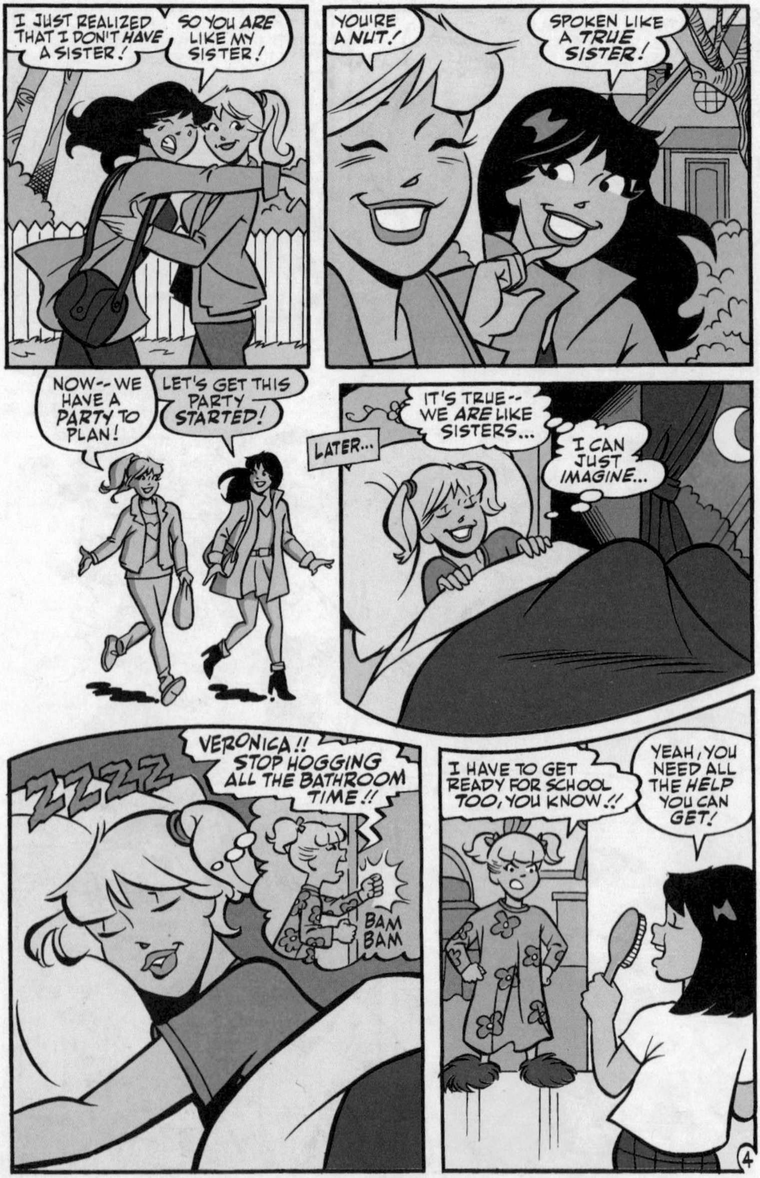
I JUST REALIZED THAT I DON'T HAVE A SISTER!
SO YOU ARE LIKE MY SISTER!
YOU'RE A NUT!
SPOKEN LIKE A TRUE SISTER!
NOW-- WE HAVE A PARTY TO PLAN!
LET'S GET THIS PARTY STARTED!
LATER...
IT'S TRUE-- WE ARE LIKE SISTERS...
I CAN JUST IMAGINE...
ZZZZ
VERONICA!! STOP HOGGING ALL THE BATHROOM TIME!!
BAM BAM
I HAVE TO GET READY FOR SCHOOL TOO, YOU KNOW!!
YEAH, YOU NEED ALL THE HELP YOU CAN GET!
4

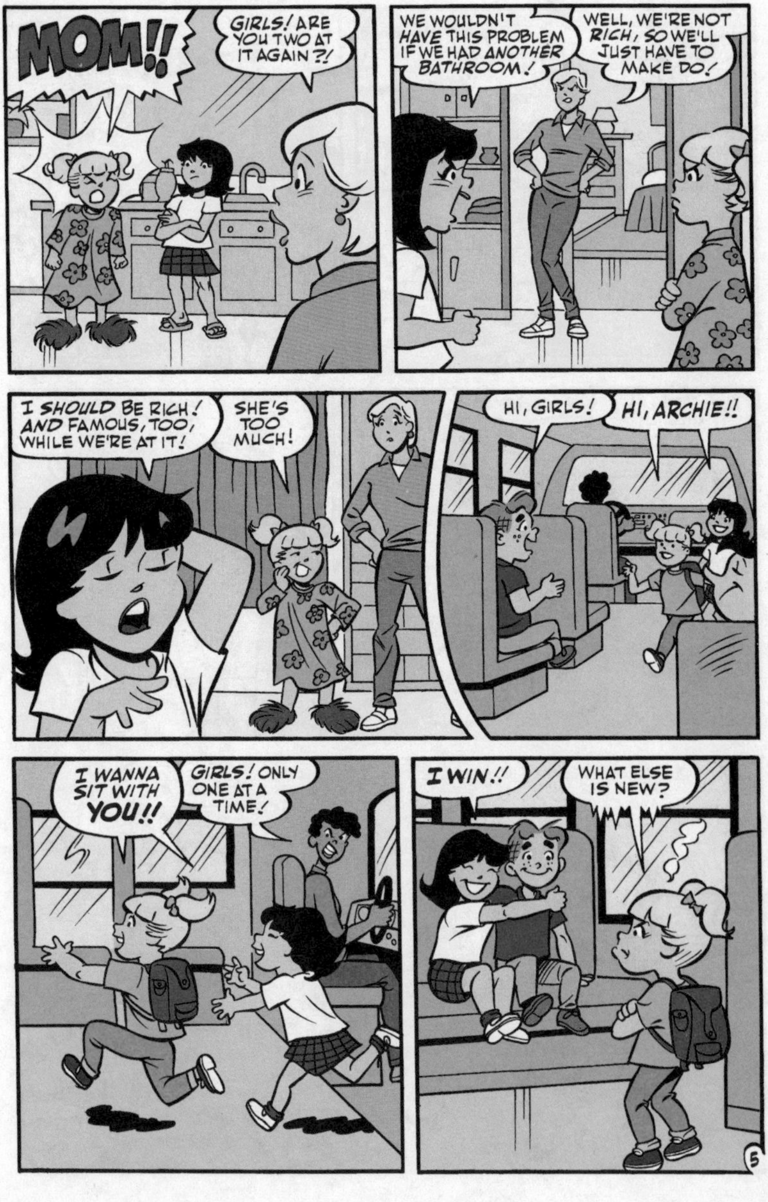
MOM!!
GIRLS! ARE YOU TWO AT IT AGAIN?!
WE WOULDN'T HAVE THIS PROBLEM IF WE HAD ANOTHER BATHROOM!
WELL, WE'RE NOT RICH, SO WE'LL JUST HAVE TO MAKE DO!
I SHOULD BE RICH! AND FAMOUS, TOO, WHILE WE'RE AT IT!
SHE'S TOO MUCH!
HI, GIRLS!
HI, ARCHIE!!
I WANNA SIT WITH YOU!!
GIRLS! ONLY ONE AT A TIME!
I WIN!!
WHAT ELSE IS NEW?
5

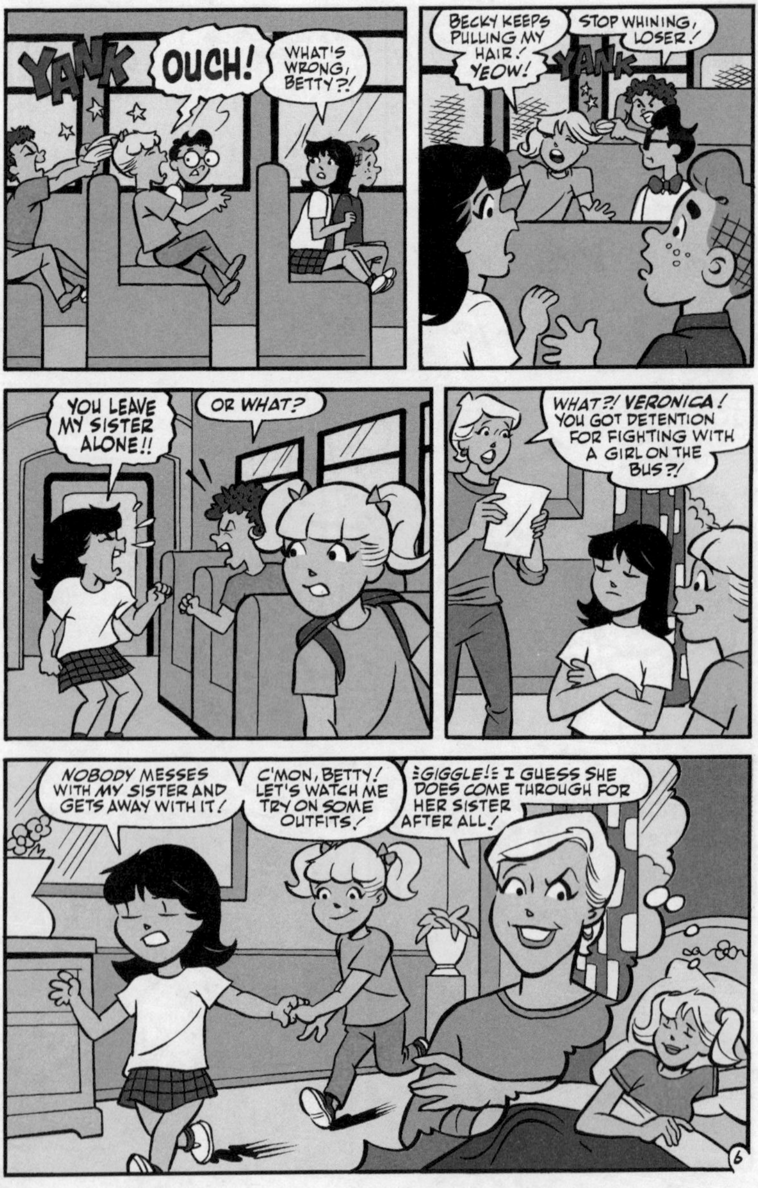
YANK
OUCH!
WHAT'S WRONG, BETTY?!
BECKY KEEPS PULLING MY HAIR! YEOW!
YANK
STOP WHINING, LOSER!
YOU LEAVE MY SISTER ALONE!!
OR WHAT?
WHAT?! VERONICA! YOU GOT DETENTION FOR FIGHTING WITH A GIRL ON THE BUS?!
NOBODY MESSES WITH MY SISTER AND GETS AWAY WITH IT!
C'MON, BETTY! LET'S WATCH ME TRY ON SOME OUTFITS!
GIGGLE! I GUESS SHE DOES COME THROUGH FOR HER SISTER AFTER ALL!
6

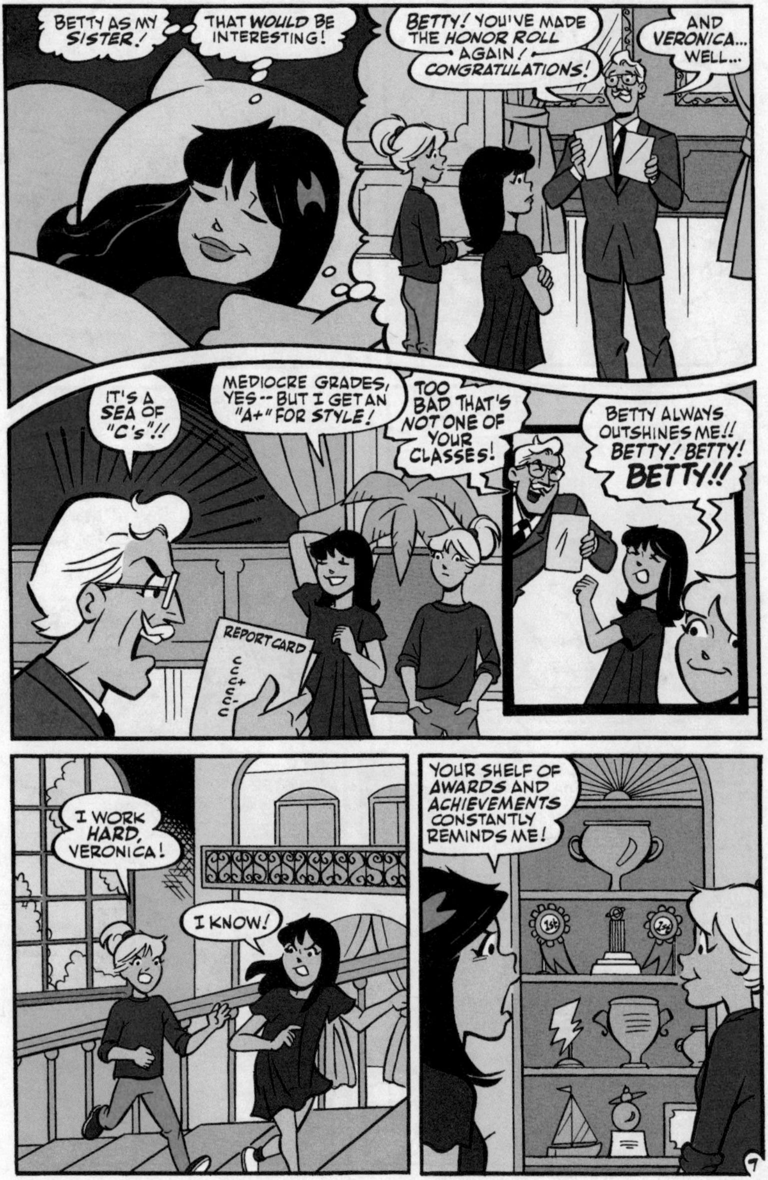
BETTY AS MY SISTER!
THAT WOULD BE INTERESTING!
BETTY! YOU'VE MADE THE HONOR ROLL AGAIN! CONGRATULATIONS!
AND VERONICA... WELL...
IT'S A SEA OF "C's"!!
MEDIOCRE GRADES, YES -- BUT I GET AN "A+" FOR STYLE!
TOO BAD THAT'S NOT ONE OF YOUR CLASSES!
BETTY ALWAYS OUTSHINES ME!! BETTY! BETTY! BETTY!!
REPORT CARD
I WORK HARD, VERONICA!
I KNOW!
YOUR SHELF OF AWARDS AND ACHIEVEMENTS CONSTANTLY REMINDS ME!
1st
1st
7

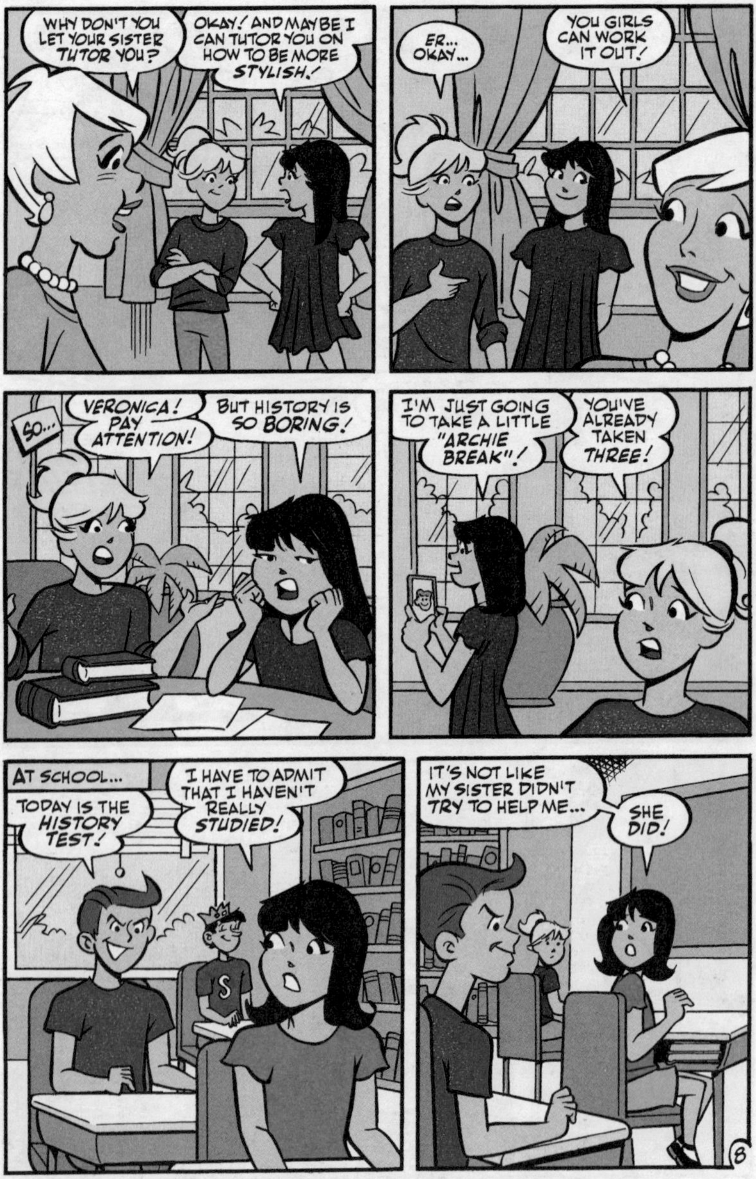
WHY DON'T YOU LET YOUR SISTER TUTOR YOU?
OKAY! AND MAYBE I CAN TUTOR YOU ON HOW TO BE MORE STYLISH!
ER... OKAY...
YOU GIRLS CAN WORK IT OUT!
SO...
VERONICA! PAY ATTENTION!
BUT HISTORY IS SO BORING!
I'M JUST GOING TO TAKE A LITTLE "ARCHIE BREAK"!
YOU'VE ALREADY TAKEN THREE!
AT SCHOOL...
TODAY IS THE HISTORY TEST!
I HAVE TO ADMIT THAT I HAVEN'T REALLY STUDIED!
IT'S NOT LIKE MY SISTER DIDN'T TRY TO HELP ME...
SHE DID!
8

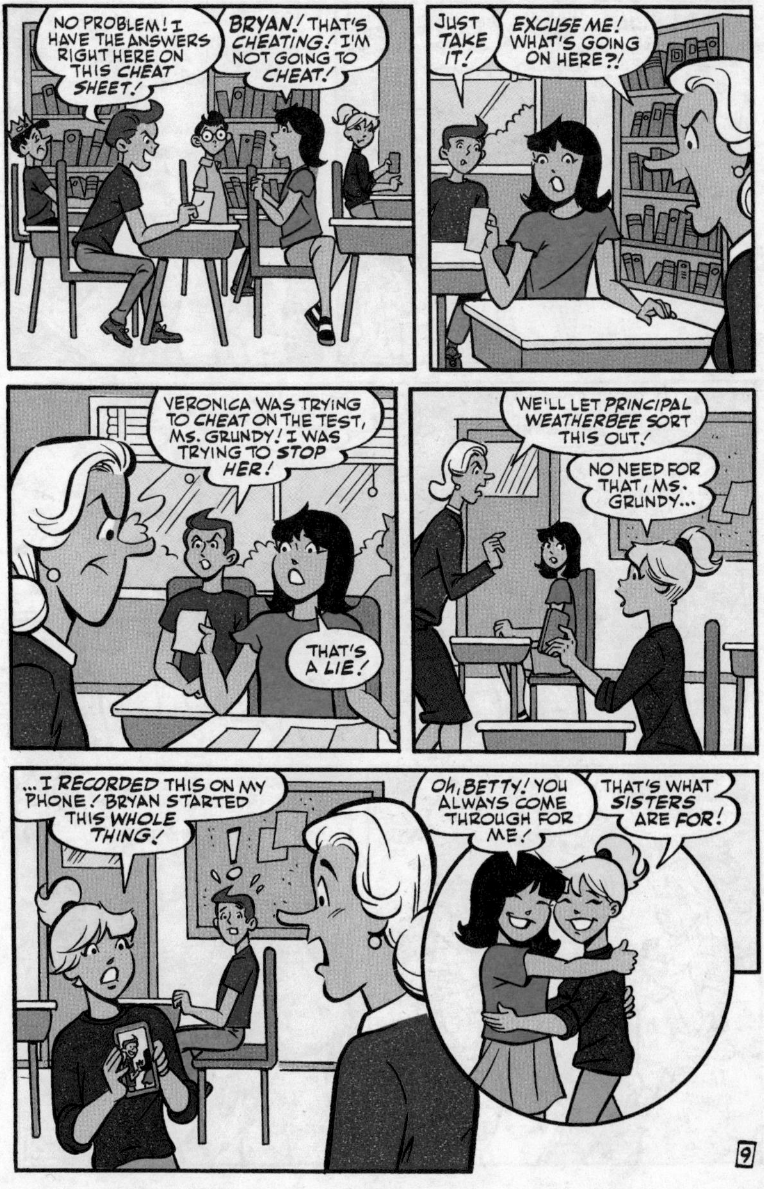
NO PROBLEM! I HAVE THE ANSWERS RIGHT HERE ON THIS CHEAT SHEET!
BRYAN! THAT'S CHEATING! I'M NOT GOING TO CHEAT!
JUST TAKE IT!
EXCUSE ME! WHAT'S GOING ON HERE?!
VERONICA WAS TRYING TO CHEAT ON THE TEST, MS. GRUNDY! I WAS TRYING TO STOP HER!
THAT'S A LIE!
WE'LL LET PRINCIPAL WEATHERBEE SORT THIS OUT!
NO NEED FOR THAT, MS. GRUNDY...
...I RECORDED THIS ON MY PHONE! BRYAN STARTED THIS WHOLE THING!
!
Oh, BETTY! YOU ALWAYS COME THROUGH FOR ME!
THAT'S WHAT SISTERS ARE FOR!
9

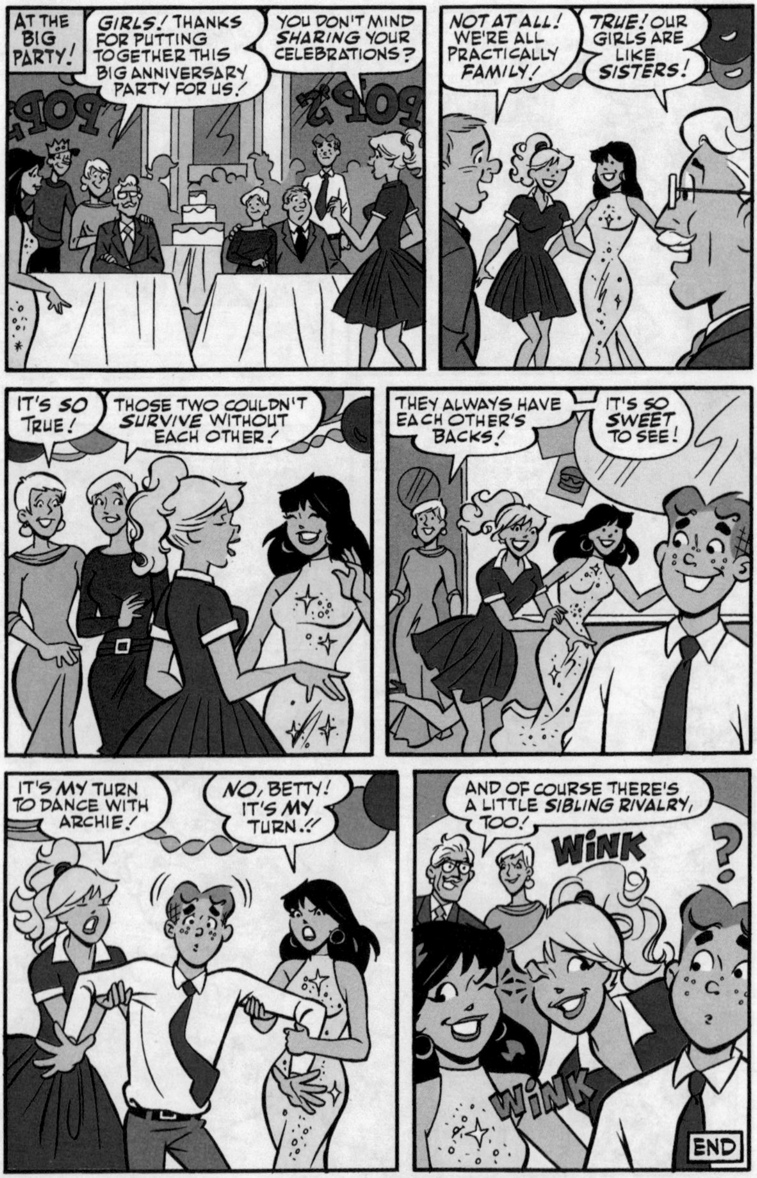
AT THE BIG PARTY!
GIRLS! THANKS FOR PUTTING TOGETHER THIS BIG ANNIVERSARY PARTY FOR US!
YOU DON'T MIND SHARING YOUR CELEBRATIONS?
POP'S
NOT AT ALL! WE'RE ALL PRACTICALLY FAMILY!
TRUE! OUR GIRLS ARE LIKE SISTERS!
IT'S SO TRUE!
THOSE TWO COULDN'T SURVIVE WITHOUT EACH OTHER!
THEY ALWAYS HAVE EACH OTHER'S BACKS!
IT'S SO SWEET TO SEE!
IT'S MY TURN TO DANCE WITH ARCHIE!
NO, BETTY! IT'S MY TURN.!!
AND OF COURSE THERE'S A LITTLE SIBLING RIVALRY, TOO!
WINK
?
WINK
END

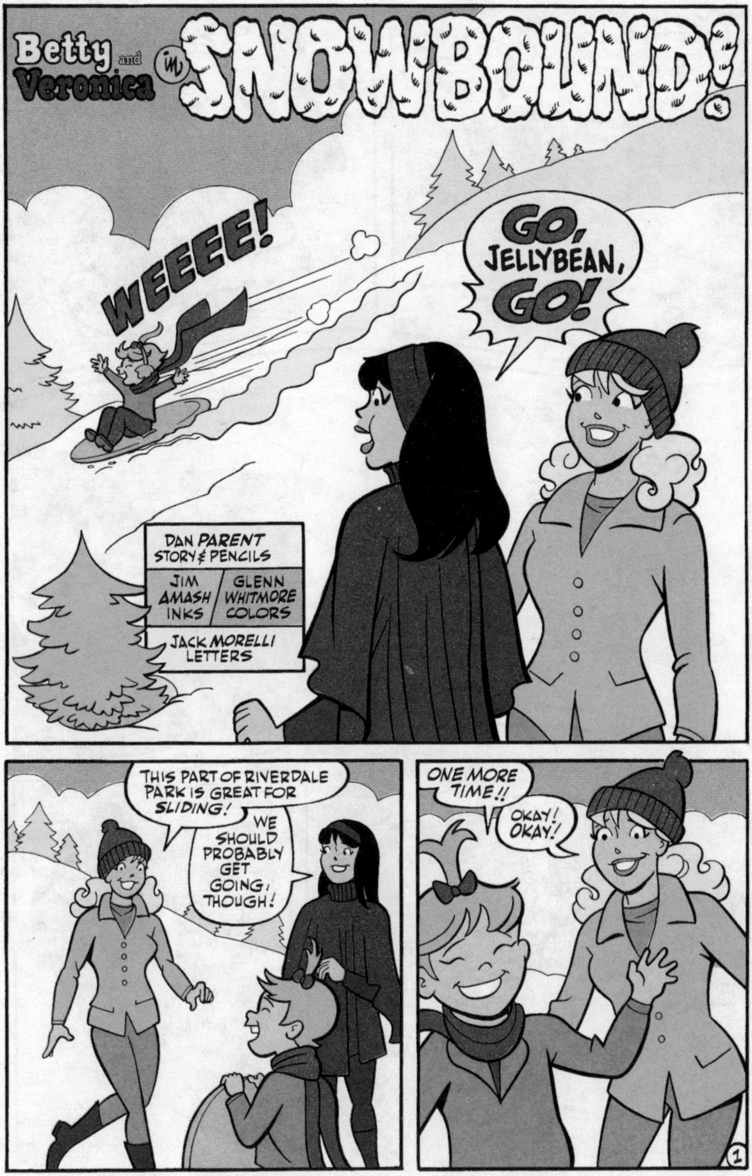
Betty and Veronica in SNOWBOUND!
WEEEEE!
GO, JELLYBEAN, GO!
DAN PARENT STORY & PENCILS
JIM AMASH INKS
GLENN WHITMORE COLORS
JACK MORELLI LETTERS
THIS PART OF RIVERDALE PARK IS GREAT FOR SLIDING!
WE SHOULD PROBABLY GET GOING, THOUGH!
ONE MORE TIME!!
OKAY! OKAY!
1

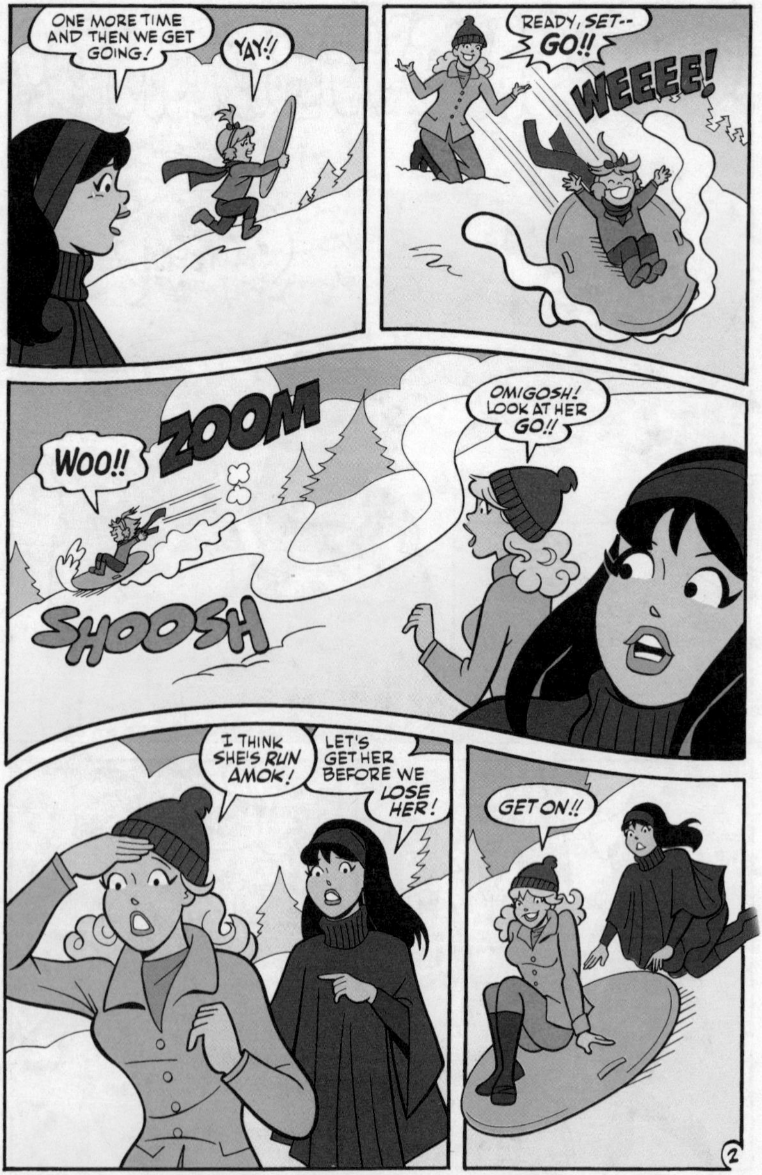
ONE MORE TIME AND THEN WE GET GOING!
YAY!!
READY, SET-- GO!!
WEEEEE!
WOO!!
ZOOM
SHOOSH
OMIGOSH! LOOK AT HER GO!!
I THINK SHE'S RUN AMOK!
LET'S GET HER BEFORE WE LOSE HER!
GET ON!!
2

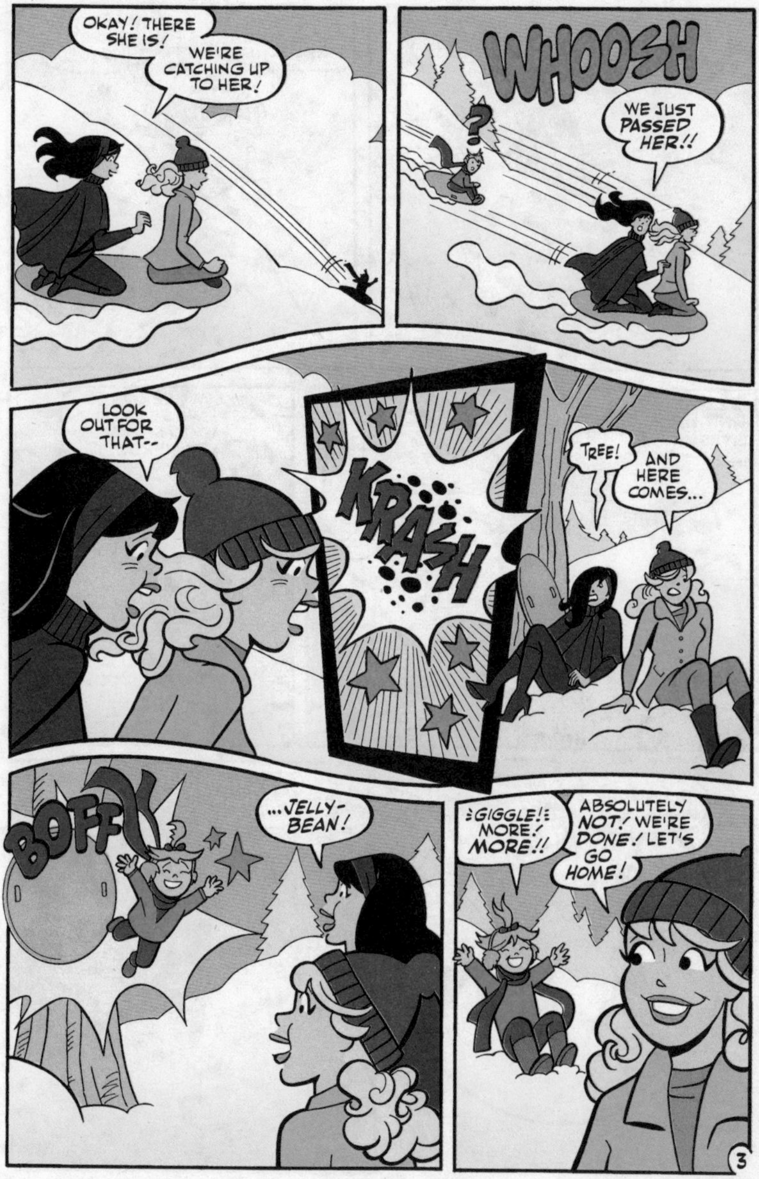
OKAY! THERE SHE IS!
WE'RE CATCHING UP TO HER!
WHOOSH
?
WE JUST PASSED HER!!
LOOK OUT FOR THAT--
KRASH
TREE!
AND HERE COMES...
BOFF
...JELLY-BEAN!
:GIGGLE!: MORE! MORE!!
ABSOLUTELY NOT! WE'RE DONE! LET'S GO HOME!
3

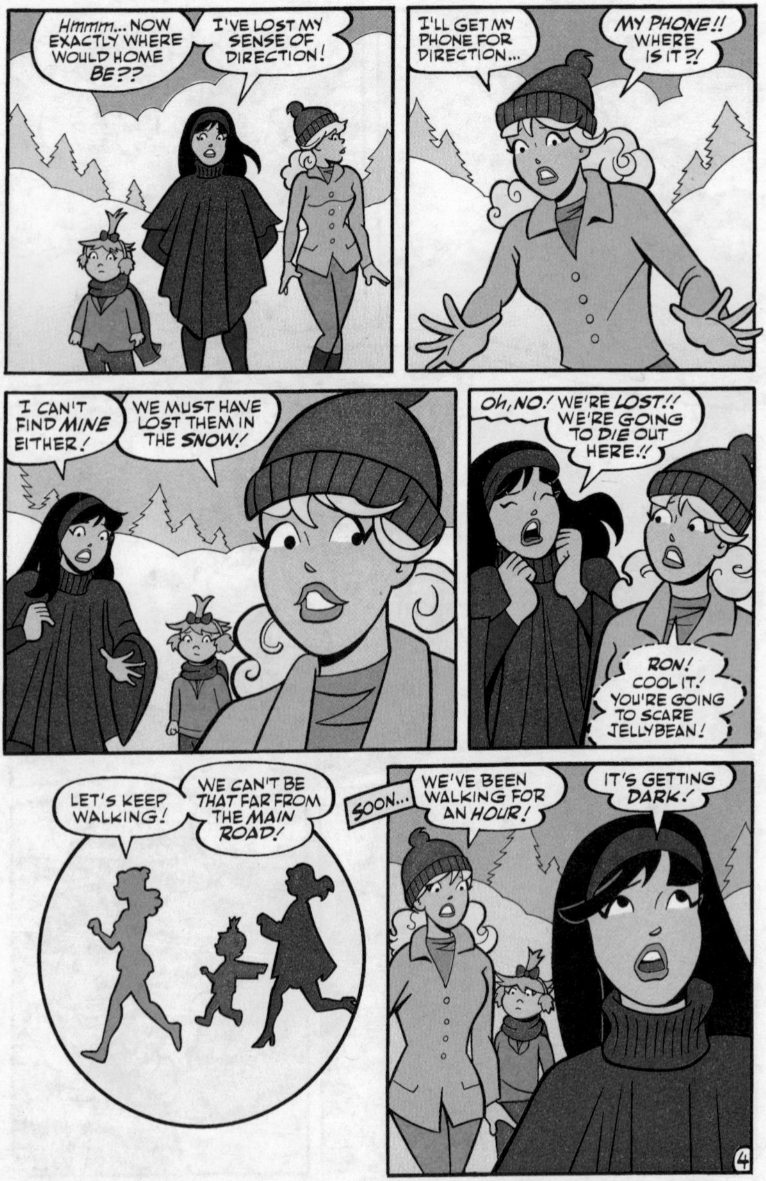
Hmmm... NOW EXACTLY WHERE WOULD HOME BE??
I'VE LOST MY SENSE OF DIRECTION!
I'LL GET MY PHONE FOR DIRECTION...
MY PHONE!! WHERE IS IT?!
I CAN'T FIND MINE EITHER!
WE MUST HAVE LOST THEM IN THE SNOW!
Oh, NO! WE'RE LOST!! WE'RE GOING TO DIE OUT HERE!!
RON! COOL IT! YOU'RE GOING TO SCARE JELLYBEAN!
LET'S KEEP WALKING!
WE CAN'T BE THAT FAR FROM THE MAIN ROAD!
SOON...
WE'VE BEEN WALKING FOR AN HOUR!
IT'S GETTING DARK!
4

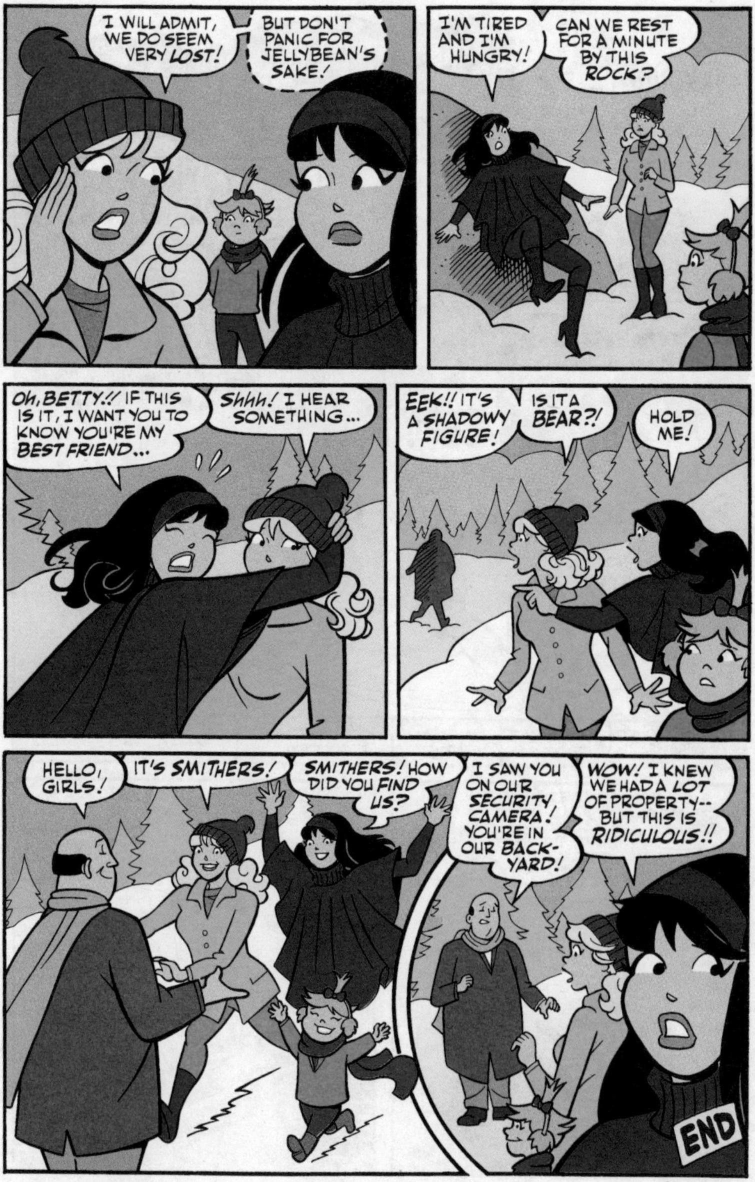
I WILL ADMIT, WE DO SEEM VERY LOST!
BUT DON'T PANIC FOR JELLYBEAN'S SAKE!
I'M TIRED AND I'M HUNGRY!
CAN WE REST FOR A MINUTE BY THIS ROCK?
Oh, BETTY!! IF THIS IS IT, I WANT YOU TO KNOW YOU'RE MY BEST FRIEND...
Shhh! I HEAR SOMETHING...
EEK!! IT'S A SHADOWY FIGURE!
IS IT A BEAR?!
HOLD ME!
HELLO, GIRLS!
IT'S SMITHERS!
SMITHERS! HOW DID YOU FIND US?
I SAW YOU ON OUR SECURITY CAMERA! YOU'RE IN OUR BACK-YARD!
WOW! I KNEW WE HAD A LOT OF PROPERTY-- BUT THIS IS RIDICULOUS!!
END

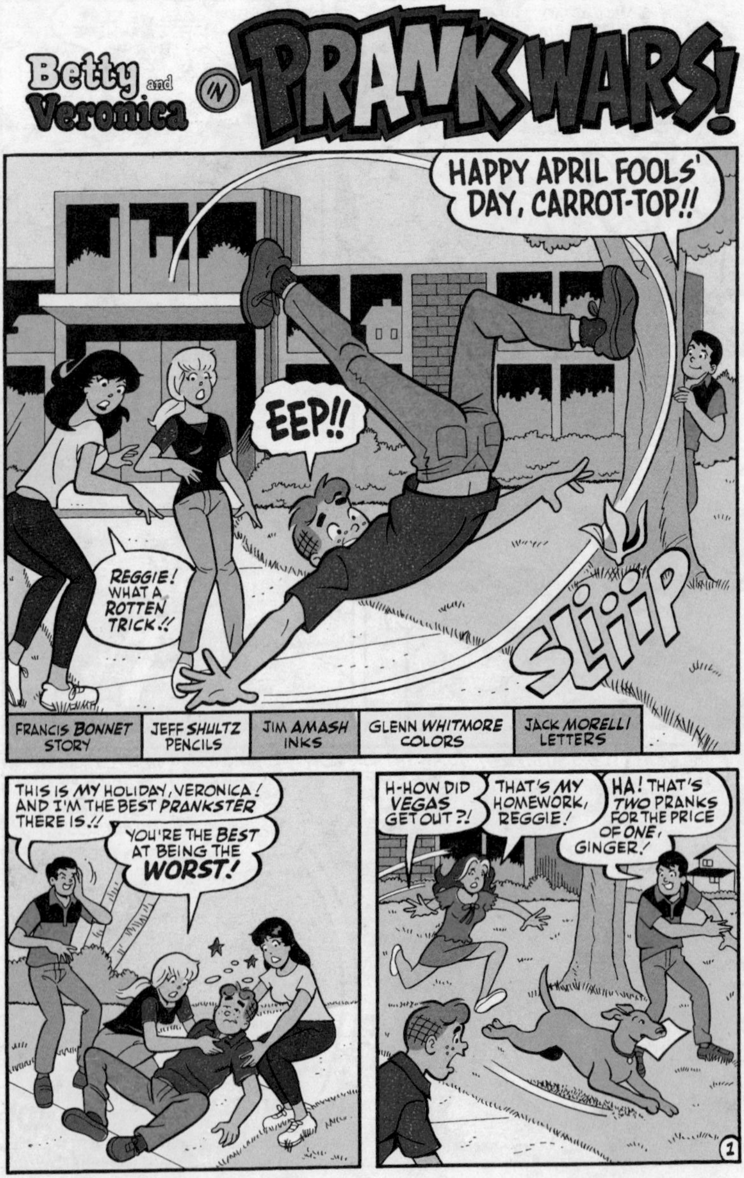
Betty and Veronica in PRANK WARS!
HAPPY APRIL FOOLS' DAY, CARROT-TOP!!
EEP!!
REGGIE! WHAT A ROTTEN TRICK!!
SLIIIP
FRANCIS BONNET STORY
JEFF SHULTZ PENCILS
JIM AMASH INKS
GLENN WHITMORE COLORS
JACK MORELLI LETTERS
THIS IS MY HOLIDAY, VERONICA! AND I'M THE BEST PRANKSTER THERE IS!!
YOU'RE THE BEST AT BEING THE WORST!
H-HOW DID VEGAS GET OUT?!
THAT'S MY HOMEWORK, REGGIE!
HA! THAT'S TWO PRANKS FOR THE PRICE OF ONE, GINGER!
1

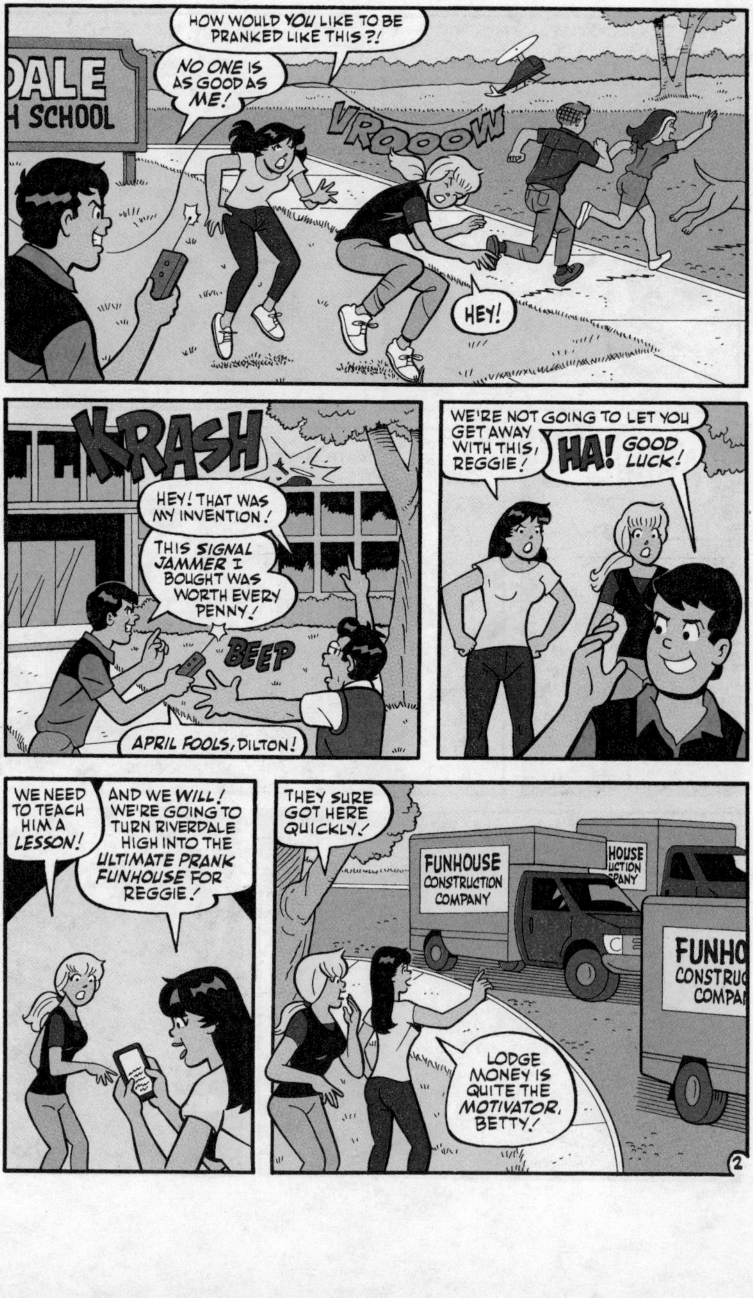

DALE
H SCHOOL
HOW WOULD YOU LIKE TO BE PRANKED LIKE THIS?!
NO ONE IS AS GOOD AS ME!
VROOOOW
HEY!
KRASH
HEY! THAT WAS MY INVENTION!
THIS SIGNAL JAMMER I BOUGHT WAS WORTH EVERY PENNY!
BEEP
APRIL FOOLS, DILTON!
WE'RE NOT GOING TO LET YOU GET AWAY WITH THIS, REGGIE!
HA! GOOD LUCK!
WE NEED TO TEACH HIM A LESSON!
AND WE WILL! WE'RE GOING TO TURN RIVERDALE HIGH INTO THE ULTIMATE PRANK FUNHOUSE FOR REGGIE!
THEY SURE GOT HERE QUICKLY!
FUNHOUSE CONSTRUCTION COMPANY
LODGE MONEY IS QUITE THE MOTIVATOR, BETTY!
2

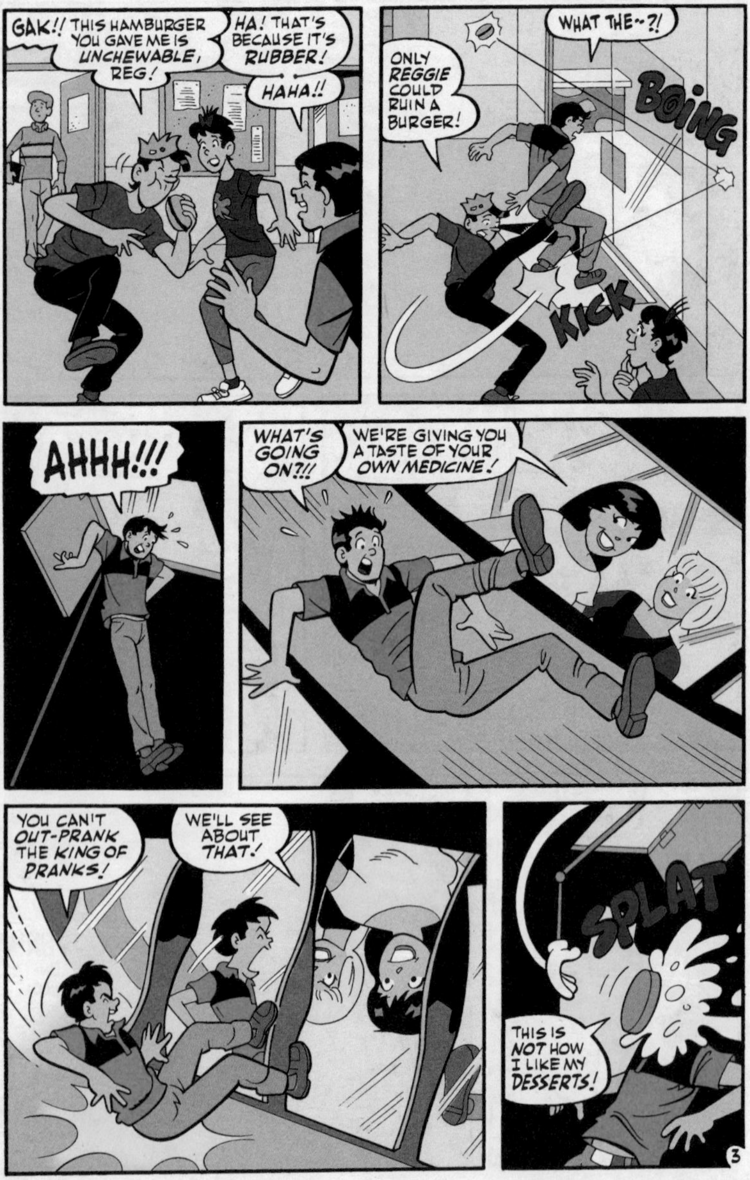
GAK!! THIS HAMBURGER YOU GAVE ME IS UNCHEWABLE, REG!
HA! THAT'S BECAUSE IT'S RUBBER!
HAHA!!
ONLY REGGIE COULD RUIN A BURGER!
WHAT THE--?!
BOING
KICK
AHHH!!!
WHAT'S GOING ON?!!
WE'RE GIVING YOU A TASTE OF YOUR OWN MEDICINE!
YOU CAN'T OUT-PRANK THE KING OF PRANKS!
WE'LL SEE ABOUT THAT!
SPLAT
THIS IS NOT HOW I LIKE MY DESSERTS!
3

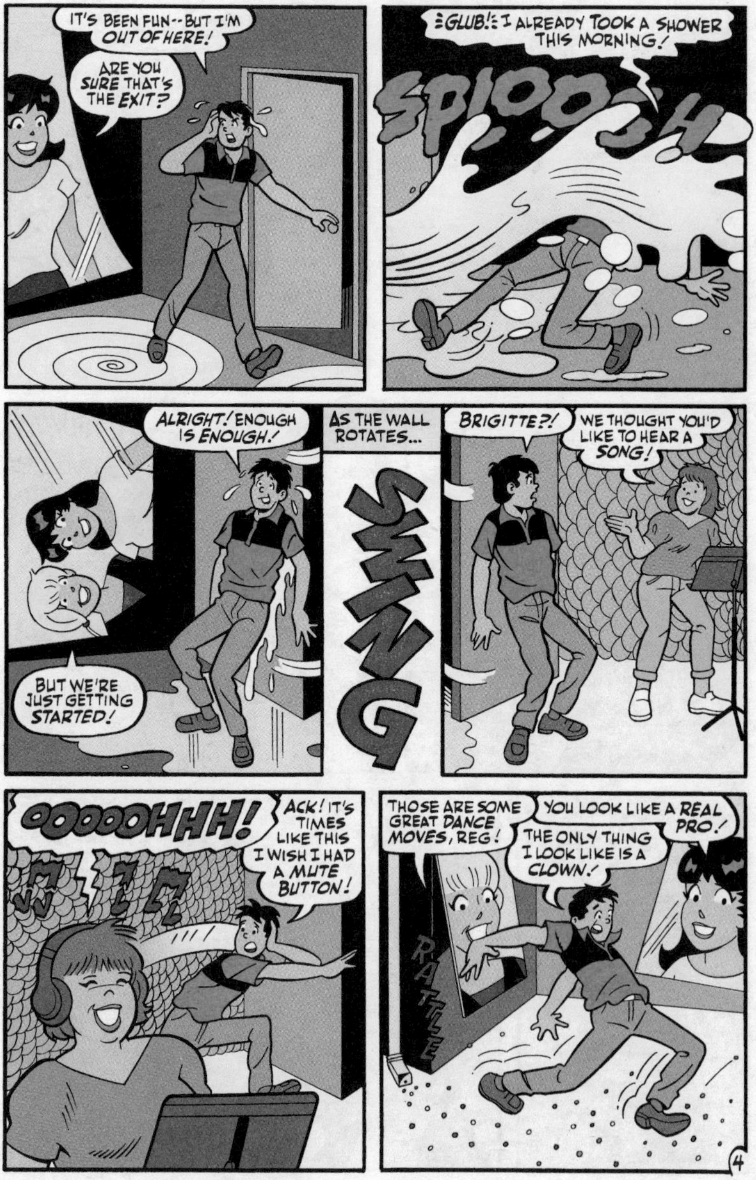
IT'S BEEN FUN--BUT I'M OUT OF HERE!
ARE YOU SURE THAT'S THE EXIT?
GLUB! I ALREADY TOOK A SHOWER THIS MORNING!
SPLOOSH
ALRIGHT! ENOUGH IS ENOUGH!
BUT WE'RE JUST GETTING STARTED!
AS THE WALL ROTATES...
SWING
BRIGITTE?!
WE THOUGHT YOU'D LIKE TO HEAR A SONG!
OOOOOOHHH!
ACK! IT'S TIMES LIKE THIS I WISH I HAD A MUTE BUTTON!
THOSE ARE SOME GREAT DANCE MOVES, REG!
YOU LOOK LIKE A REAL PRO!
THE ONLY THING I LOOK LIKE IS A CLOWN!
RATTLE
4

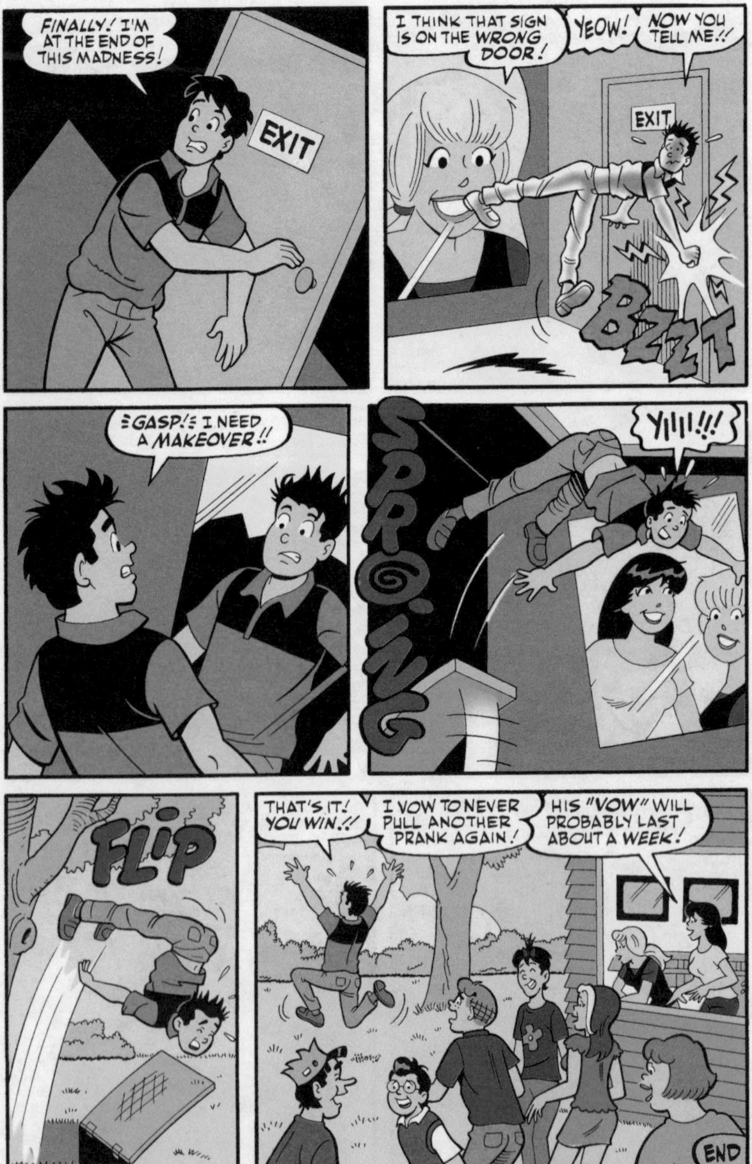
FINALLY! I'M AT THE END OF THIS MADNESS!
EXIT
I THINK THAT SIGN IS ON THE WRONG DOOR!
YEOW!
NOW YOU TELL ME!!
EXIT
BZZT
GASP! I NEED A MAKEOVER!!
SPROING
YIII!!!
FLIP
THAT'S IT! YOU WIN!!
I VOW TO NEVER PULL ANOTHER PRANK AGAIN!
HIS "VOW" WILL PROBABLY LAST ABOUT A WEEK!
END

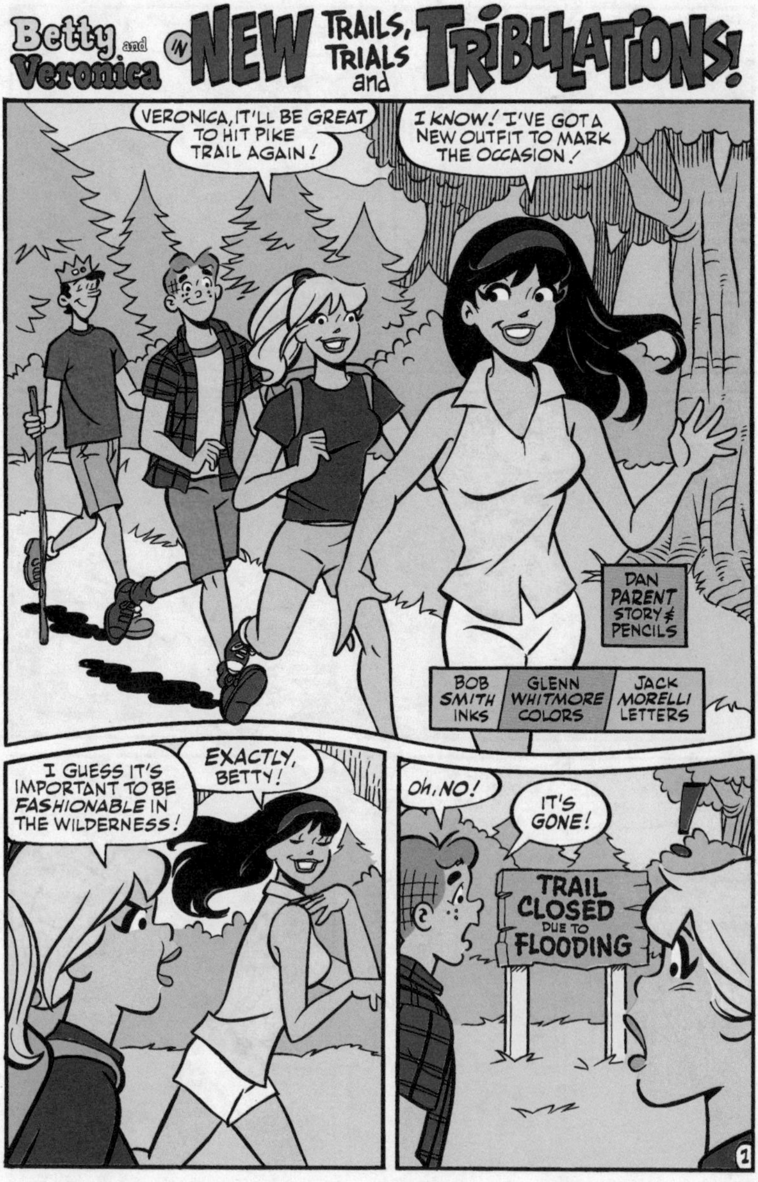
Betty and Veronica
IN NEW TRAILS, TRIALS and TRIBULATIONS!
VERONICA, IT'LL BE GREAT TO HIT PIKE TRAIL AGAIN!
I KNOW! I'VE GOT A NEW OUTFIT TO MARK THE OCCASION!
DAN PARENT STORY & PENCILS
BOB SMITH INKS
GLENN WHITMORE COLORS
JACK MORELLI LETTERS
I GUESS IT'S IMPORTANT TO BE FASHIONABLE IN THE WILDERNESS!
EXACTLY, BETTY!
Oh, NO!
IT'S GONE!
!
TRAIL CLOSED DUE TO FLOODING
1

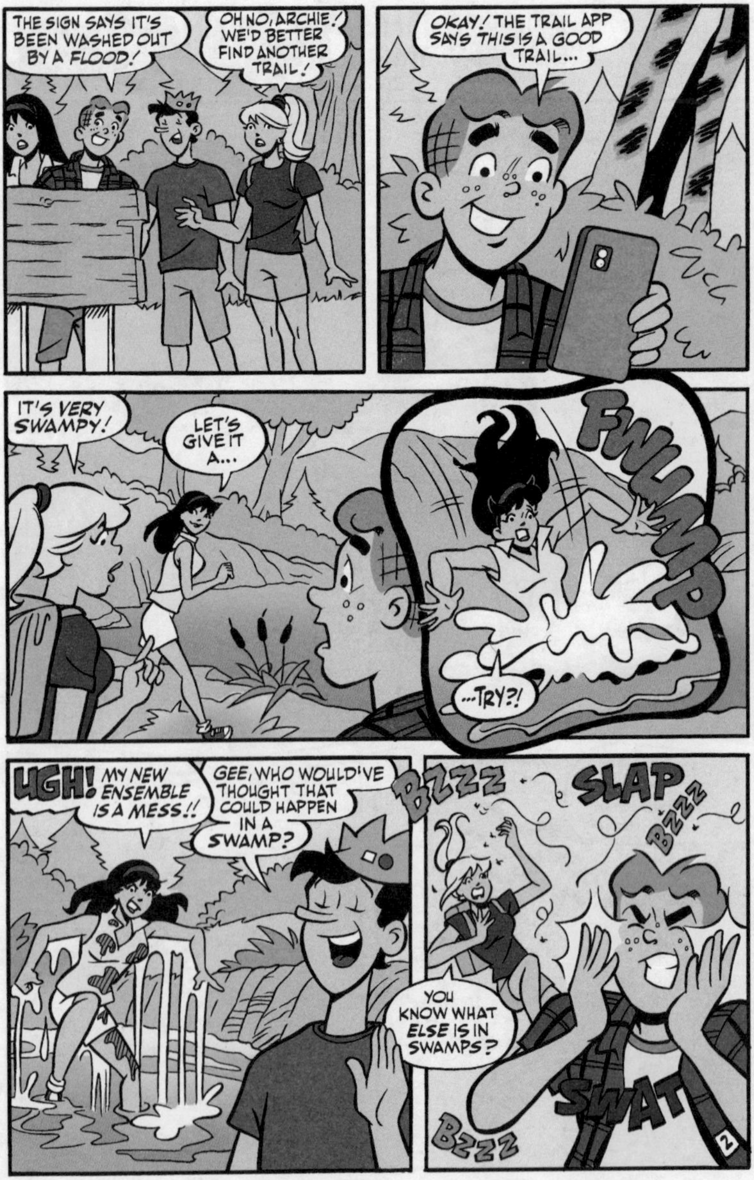
THE SIGN SAYS IT'S BEEN WASHED OUT BY A FLOOD!
OH NO, ARCHIE! WE'D BETTER FIND ANOTHER TRAIL!
OKAY! THE TRAIL APP SAYS THIS IS A GOOD TRAIL...
IT'S VERY SWAMPY!
LET'S GIVE IT A...
FWUMP
...TRY?!
UGH! MY NEW ENSEMBLE IS A MESS!!
GEE, WHO WOULD'VE THOUGHT THAT COULD HAPPEN IN A SWAMP?
BZZZ
SLAP
BZZZ
YOU KNOW WHAT ELSE IS IN SWAMPS?
SWAT
BZZZ
2

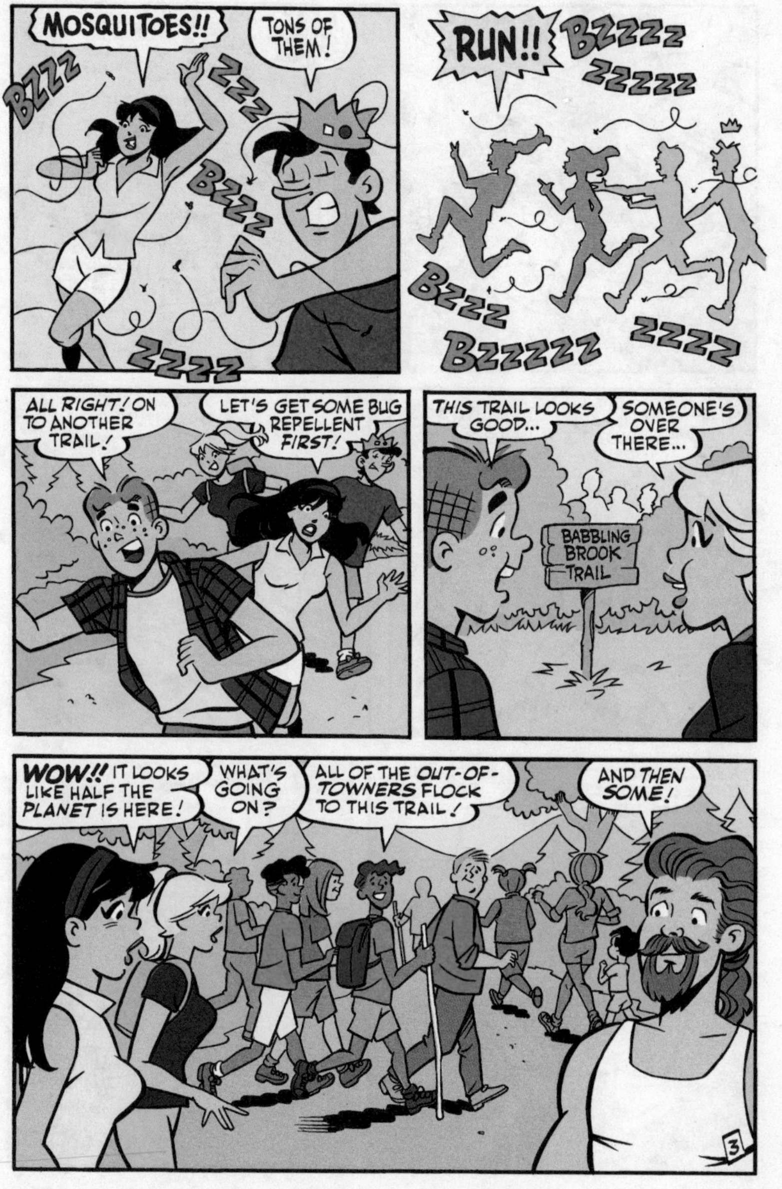
MOSQUITOES!!
TONS OF THEM!
BZZZ
ZZZZ
BZZZZ
ZZZZ
RUN!!
BZZZZ
ZZZZZ
BZZZ
BZZZZZ
ZZZZ
ALL RIGHT! ON TO ANOTHER TRAIL!
LET'S GET SOME BUG REPELLENT FIRST!
THIS TRAIL LOOKS GOOD...
SOMEONE'S OVER THERE...
BABBLING BROOK TRAIL
WOW!! IT LOOKS LIKE HALF THE PLANET IS HERE!
WHAT'S GOING ON?
ALL OF THE OUT-OF-TOWNERS FLOCK TO THIS TRAIL!
AND THEN SOME!
3

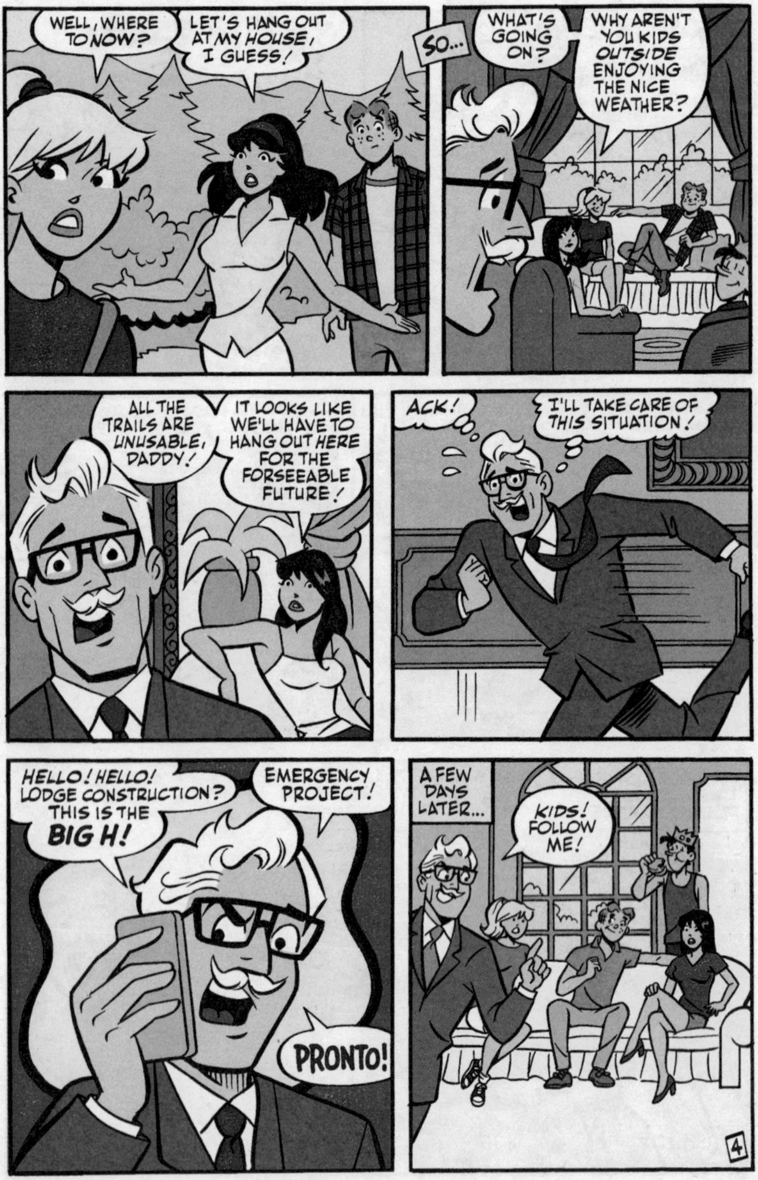
WELL, WHERE TO NOW?
LET'S HANG OUT AT MY HOUSE, I GUESS!
SO...
WHAT'S GOING ON?
WHY AREN'T YOU KIDS OUTSIDE ENJOYING THE NICE WEATHER?
ALL THE TRAILS ARE UNUSABLE, DADDY!
IT LOOKS LIKE WE'LL HAVE TO HANG OUT HERE FOR THE FORSEEABLE FUTURE!
ACK!
I'LL TAKE CARE OF THIS SITUATION!
HELLO! HELLO! LODGE CONSTRUCTION? THIS IS THE BIG H!
EMERGENCY PROJECT!
PRONTO!
A FEW DAYS LATER...
KIDS! FOLLOW ME!
4

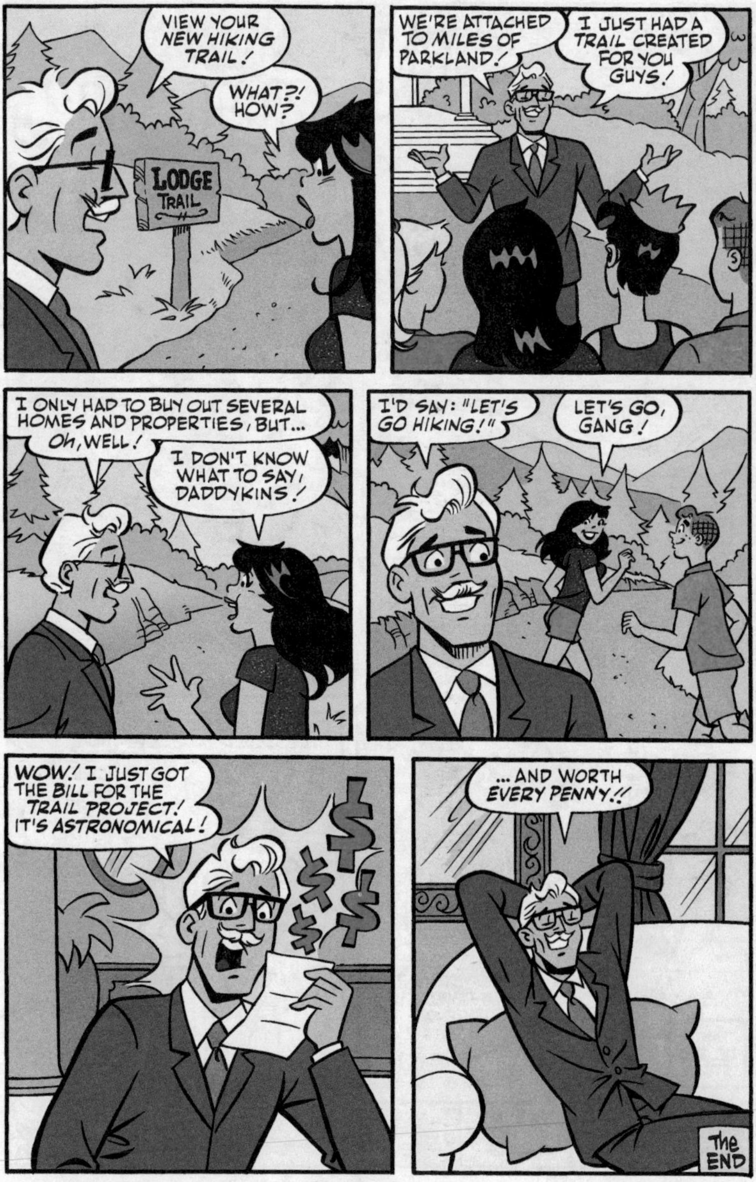
VIEW YOUR NEW HIKING TRAIL!
WHAT?! HOW?
LODGE TRAIL
WE'RE ATTACHED TO MILES OF PARKLAND!
I JUST HAD A TRAIL CREATED FOR YOU GUYS!
I ONLY HAD TO BUY OUT SEVERAL HOMES AND PROPERTIES, BUT... Oh, WELL!
I DON'T KNOW WHAT TO SAY, DADDYKINS!
I'D SAY: "LET'S GO HIKING!"
LET'S GO, GANG!
WOW! I JUST GOT THE BILL FOR THE TRAIL PROJECT! IT'S ASTRONOMICAL!
... AND WORTH EVERY PENNY!!
The END

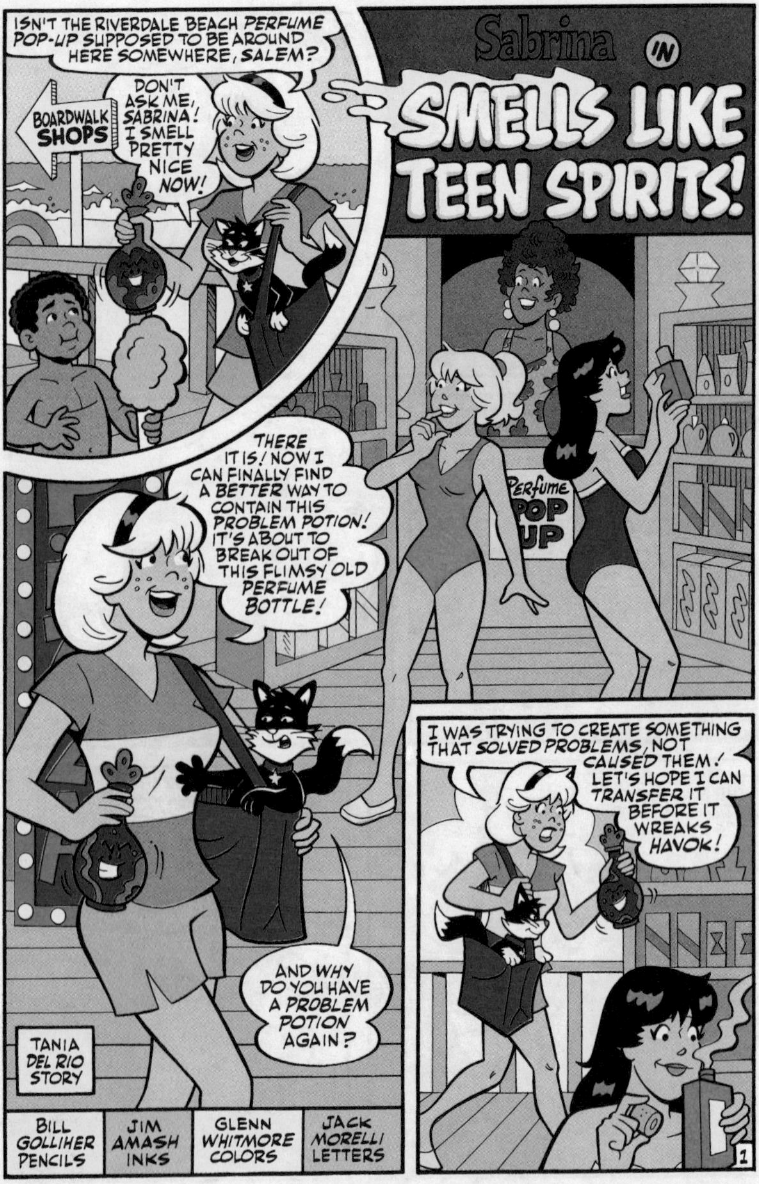
ISN'T THE RIVERDALE BEACH PERFUME POP-UP SUPPOSED TO BE AROUND HERE SOMEWHERE, SALEM?
BOARDWALK SHOPS
DON'T ASK ME, SABRINA! I SMELL PRETTY NICE NOW!
Sabrina IN
SMELLS LIKE TEEN SPIRITS!
THERE IT IS! NOW I CAN FINALLY FIND A BETTER WAY TO CONTAIN THIS PROBLEM POTION! IT'S ABOUT TO BREAK OUT OF THIS FLIMSY OLD PERFUME BOTTLE!
Perfume POP UP
AND WHY DO YOU HAVE A PROBLEM POTION AGAIN?
TANIA DEL RIO STORY
BILL GOLLIHER PENCILS
JIM AMASH INKS
GLENN WHITMORE COLORS
JACK MORELLI LETTERS
I WAS TRYING TO CREATE SOMETHING THAT SOLVED PROBLEMS, NOT CAUSED THEM! LET'S HOPE I CAN TRANSFER IT BEFORE IT WREAKS HAVOK!
1

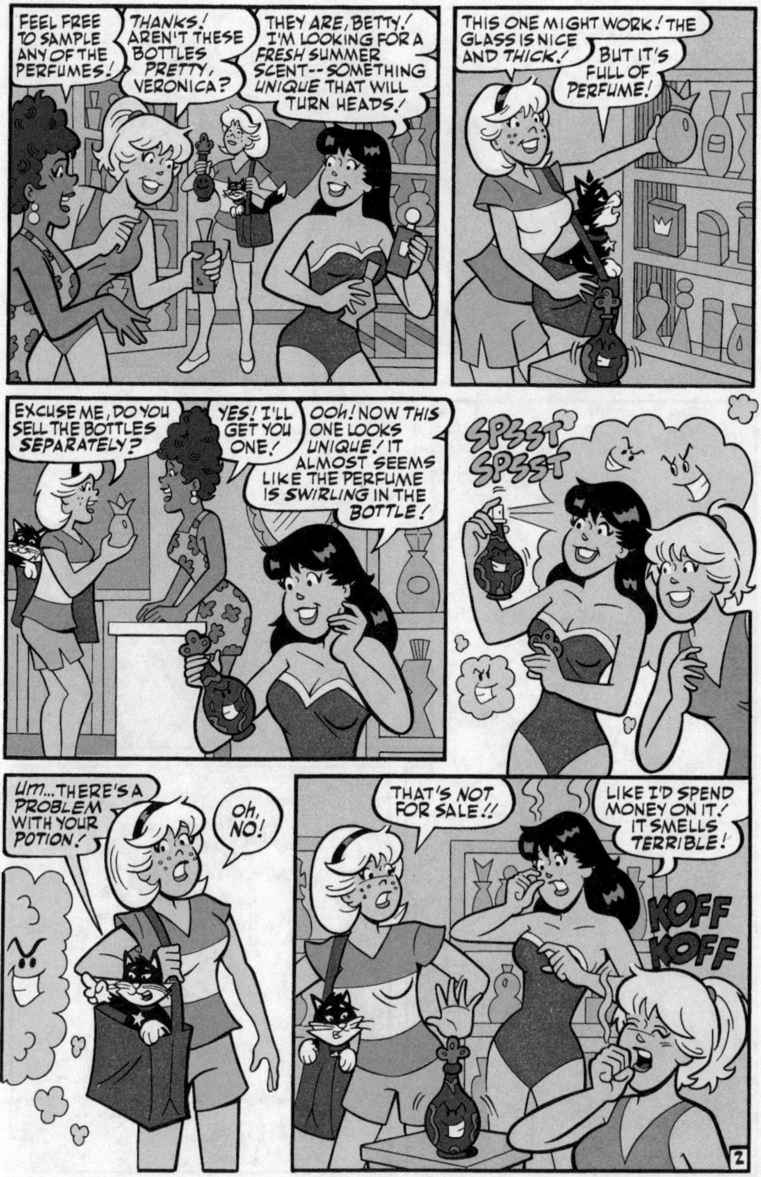
FEEL FREE TO SAMPLE ANY OF THE PERFUMES!
THANKS! AREN'T THESE BOTTLES PRETTY, VERONICA?
THEY ARE, BETTY! I'M LOOKING FOR A FRESH SUMMER SCENT-- SOMETHING UNIQUE THAT WILL TURN HEADS!
THIS ONE MIGHT WORK! THE GLASS IS NICE AND THICK!
BUT IT'S FULL OF PERFUME!
EXCUSE ME, DO YOU SELL THE BOTTLES SEPARATELY?
YES! I'LL GET YOU ONE!
OOH! NOW THIS ONE LOOKS UNIQUE! IT ALMOST SEEMS LIKE THE PERFUME IS SWIRLING IN THE BOTTLE!
SPSST SPSST
UM... THERE'S A PROBLEM WITH YOUR POTION!
OH, NO!
THAT'S NOT FOR SALE!!
LIKE I'D SPEND MONEY ON IT! IT SMELLS TERRIBLE!
KOFF KOFF
2

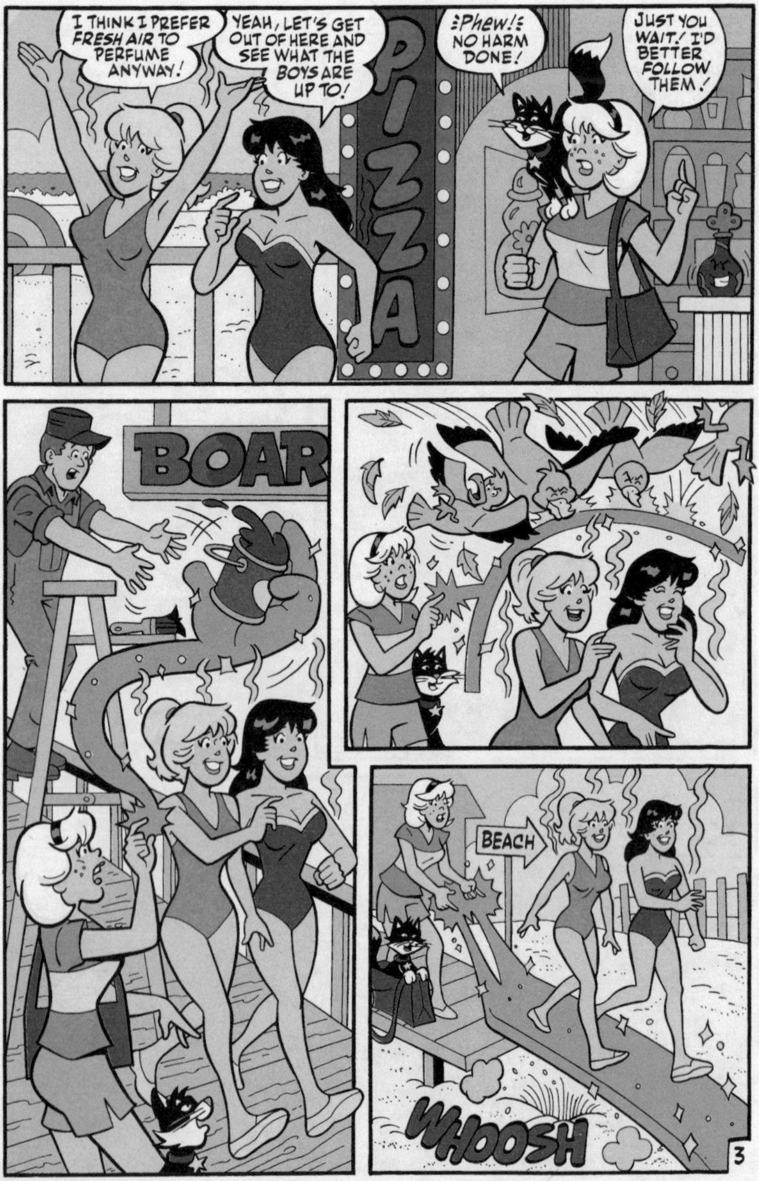
I THINK I PREFER FRESH AIR TO PERFUME ANYWAY!
YEAH, LET'S GET OUT OF HERE AND SEE WHAT THE BOYS ARE UP TO!
PIZZA
Phew! NO HARM DONE!
JUST YOU WAIT! I'D BETTER FOLLOW THEM!
BOAR
BEACH
WHOOSH
3

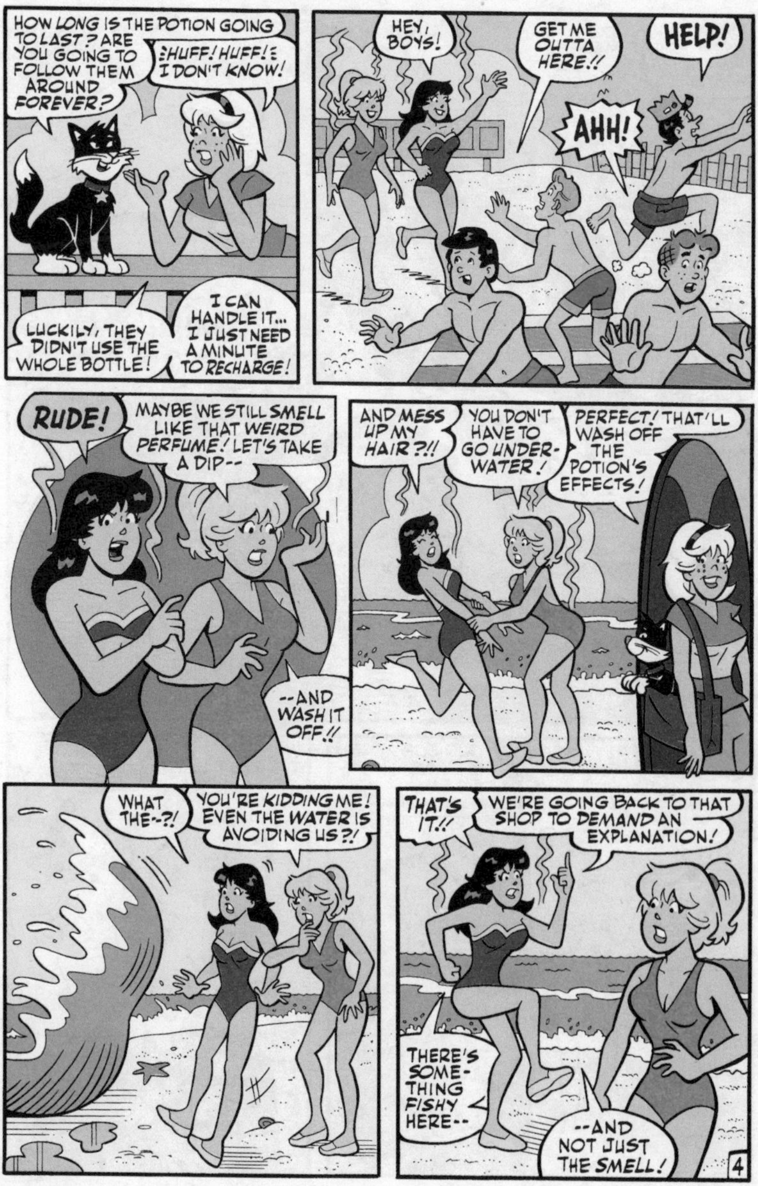
HOW LONG IS THE POTION GOING TO LAST? ARE YOU GOING TO FOLLOW THEM AROUND FOREVER?
HUFF! HUFF! I DON'T KNOW!
LUCKILY, THEY DIDN'T USE THE WHOLE BOTTLE!
I CAN HANDLE IT... I JUST NEED A MINUTE TO RECHARGE!
HEY, BOYS!
GET ME OUTTA HERE!!
HELP!
AHH!
RUDE!
MAYBE WE STILL SMELL LIKE THAT WEIRD PERFUME! LET'S TAKE A DIP--
--AND WASH IT OFF!!
AND MESS UP MY HAIR?!!
YOU DON'T HAVE TO GO UNDER-WATER!
PERFECT! THAT'LL WASH OFF THE POTION'S EFFECTS!
WHAT THE--?!
YOU'RE KIDDING ME! EVEN THE WATER IS AVOIDING US?!
THAT'S IT!!
WE'RE GOING BACK TO THAT SHOP TO DEMAND AN EXPLANATION!
THERE'S SOME-THING FISHY HERE--
--AND NOT JUST THE SMELL!
4

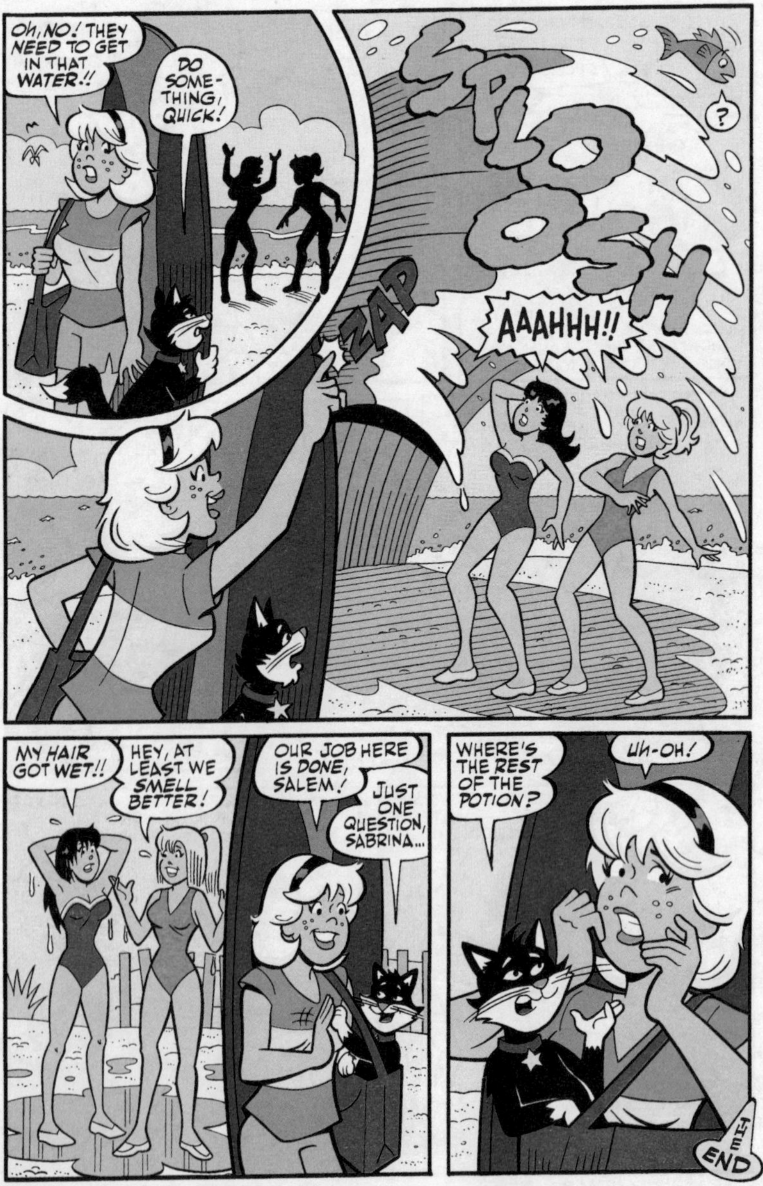
OH, NO! THEY NEED TO GET IN THAT WATER!!
DO SOME-THING, QUICK!
SPLOOSH
?
ZAP
AAAHHH!!
MY HAIR GOT WET!!
HEY, AT LEAST WE SMELL BETTER!
OUR JOB HERE IS DONE, SALEM!
JUST ONE QUESTION, SABRINA...
WHERE'S THE REST OF THE POTION?
UH-OH!
THE END

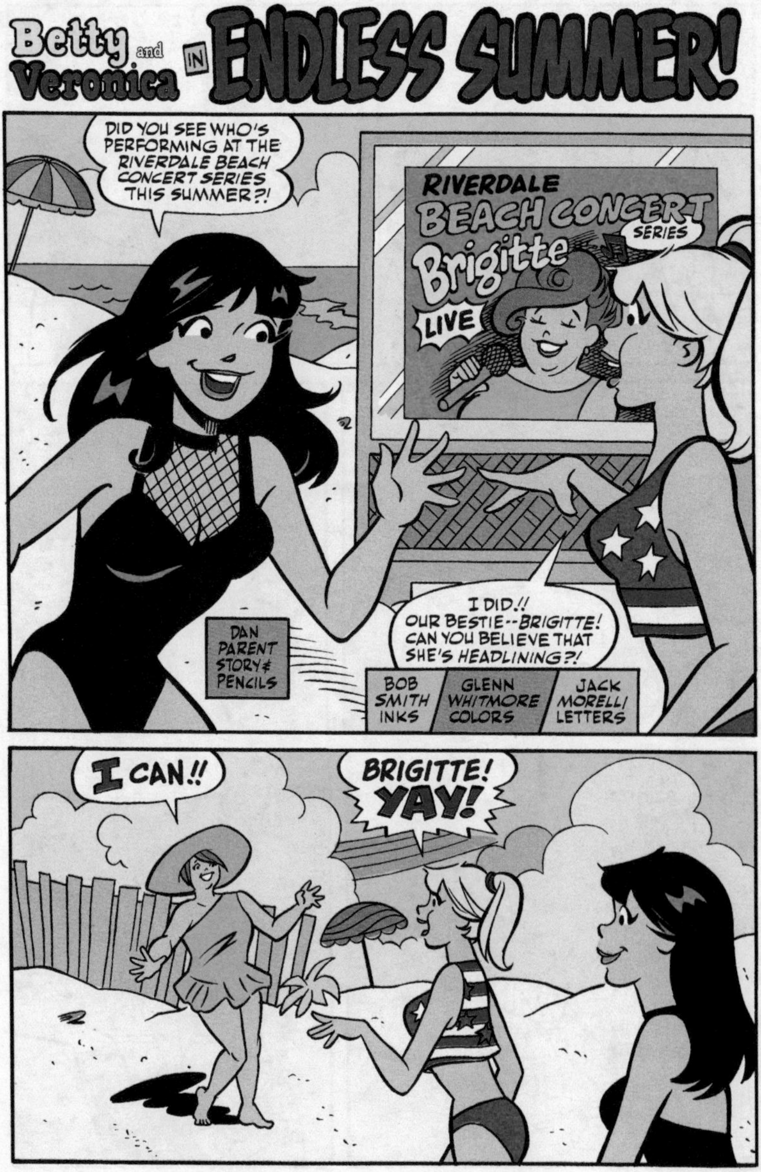
Betty and Veronica IN ENDLESS SUMMER!
DID YOU SEE WHO'S PERFORMING AT THE RIVERDALE BEACH CONCERT SERIES THIS SUMMER?!
RIVERDALE BEACH CONCERT SERIES
Brigitte
LIVE
I DID!! OUR BESTIE--BRIGITTE! CAN YOU BELIEVE THAT SHE'S HEADLINING?!
DAN PARENT STORY & PENCILS
BOB SMITH INKS
GLENN WHITMORE COLORS
JACK MORELLI LETTERS
I CAN!!
BRIGITTE! YAY!

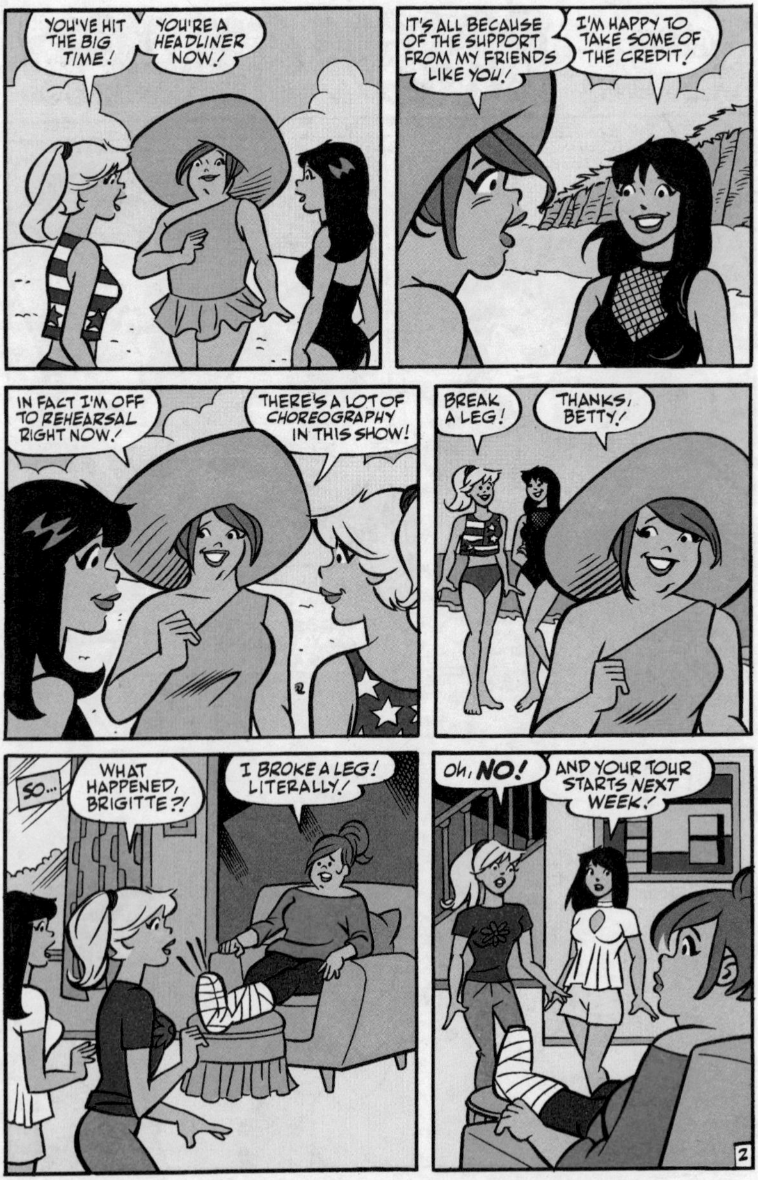
YOU'VE HIT THE BIG TIME!
YOU'RE A HEADLINER NOW!
IT'S ALL BECAUSE OF THE SUPPORT FROM MY FRIENDS LIKE YOU!
I'M HAPPY TO TAKE SOME OF THE CREDIT!
IN FACT I'M OFF TO REHEARSAL RIGHT NOW!
THERE'S A LOT OF CHOREOGRAPHY IN THIS SHOW!
BREAK A LEG!
THANKS, BETTY!
SO...
WHAT HAPPENED, BRIGITTE?!
I BROKE A LEG! LITERALLY!
Oh, NO!
AND YOUR TOUR STARTS NEXT WEEK!
2

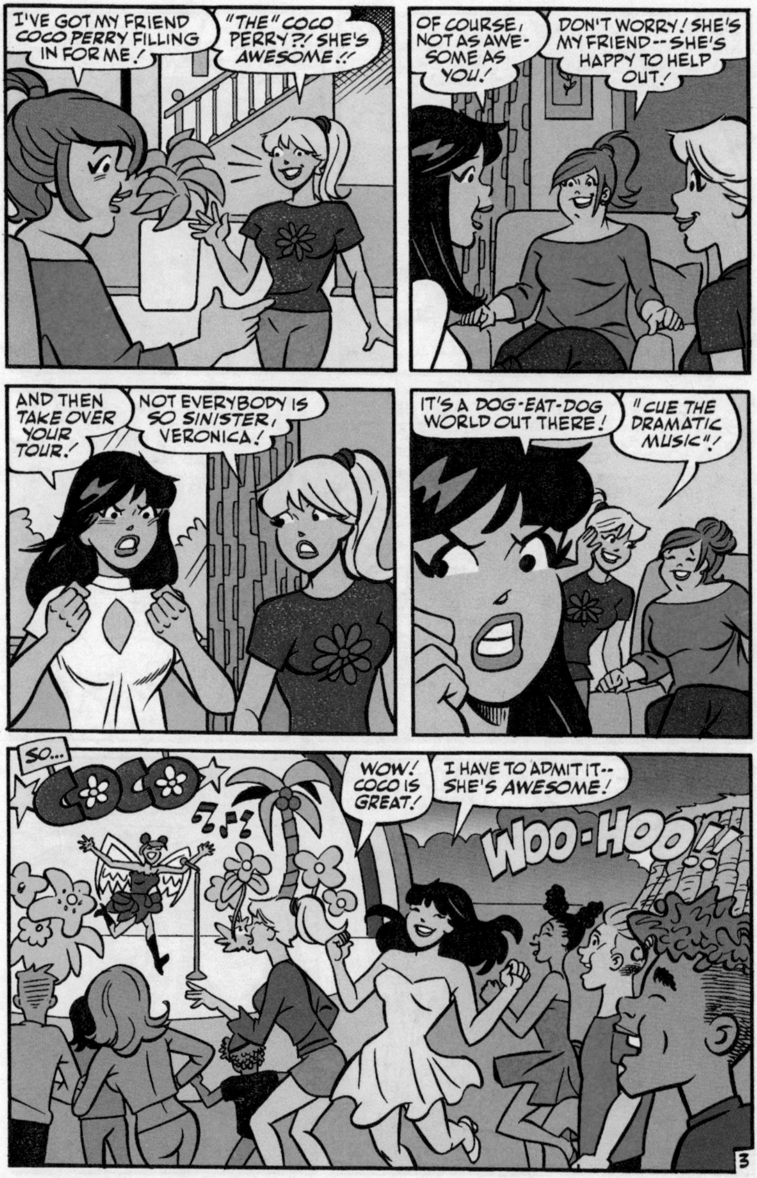
I'VE GOT MY FRIEND COCO PERRY FILLING IN FOR ME!
"THE" COCO PERRY?! SHE'S AWESOME!!
OF COURSE, NOT AS AWE-SOME AS YOU!
DON'T WORRY! SHE'S MY FRIEND--SHE'S HAPPY TO HELP OUT!
AND THEN TAKE OVER YOUR TOUR!
NOT EVERYBODY IS SO SINISTER, VERONICA!
IT'S A DOG-EAT-DOG WORLD OUT THERE!
"CUE THE DRAMATIC MUSIC"!
SO...
COCO
WOW! COCO IS GREAT!
I HAVE TO ADMIT IT--SHE'S AWESOME!
WOO-HOO!!
3

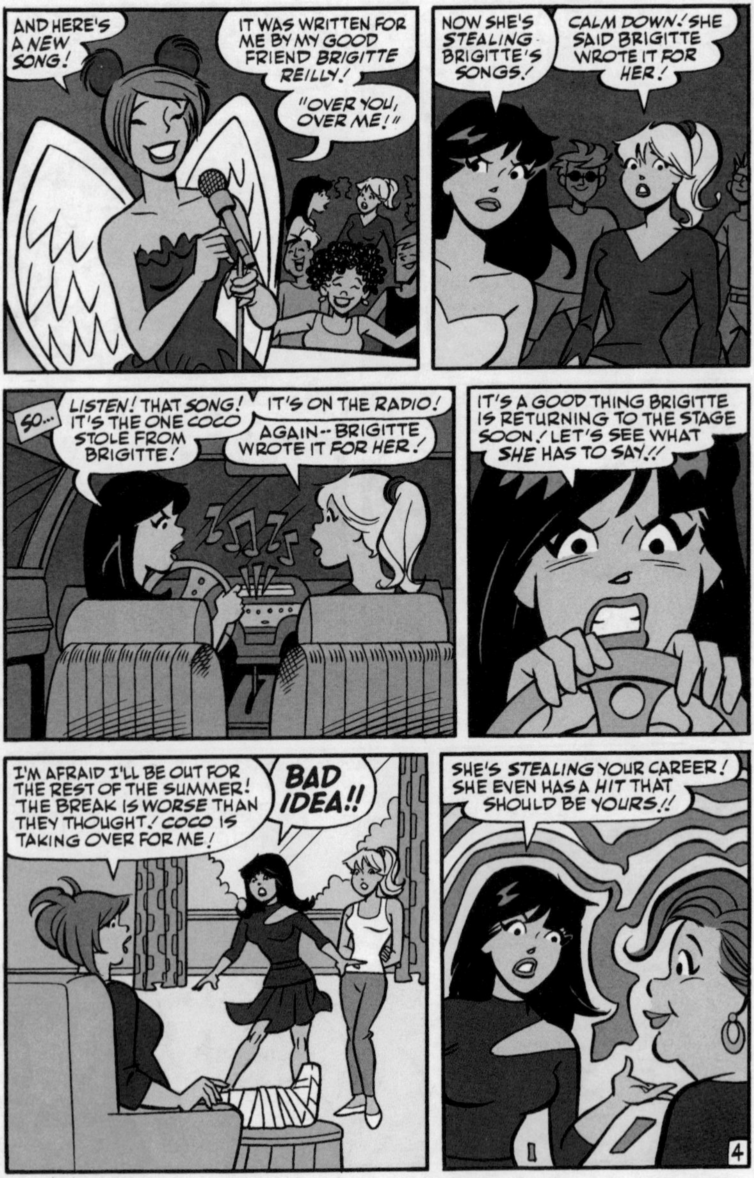
AND HERE'S A NEW SONG!
IT WAS WRITTEN FOR ME BY MY GOOD FRIEND BRIGITTE REILLY!
"OVER YOU, OVER ME!"
NOW SHE'S STEALING BRIGITTE'S SONGS!
CALM DOWN! SHE SAID BRIGITTE WROTE IT FOR HER!
SO...
LISTEN! THAT SONG! IT'S THE ONE COCO STOLE FROM BRIGITTE!
IT'S ON THE RADIO!
AGAIN-- BRIGITTE WROTE IT FOR HER!
IT'S A GOOD THING BRIGITTE IS RETURNING TO THE STAGE SOON! LET'S SEE WHAT SHE HAS TO SAY!!
I'M AFRAID I'LL BE OUT FOR THE REST OF THE SUMMER! THE BREAK IS WORSE THAN THEY THOUGHT! COCO IS TAKING OVER FOR ME!
BAD IDEA!!
SHE'S STEALING YOUR CAREER! SHE EVEN HAS A HIT THAT SHOULD BE YOURS!!
4

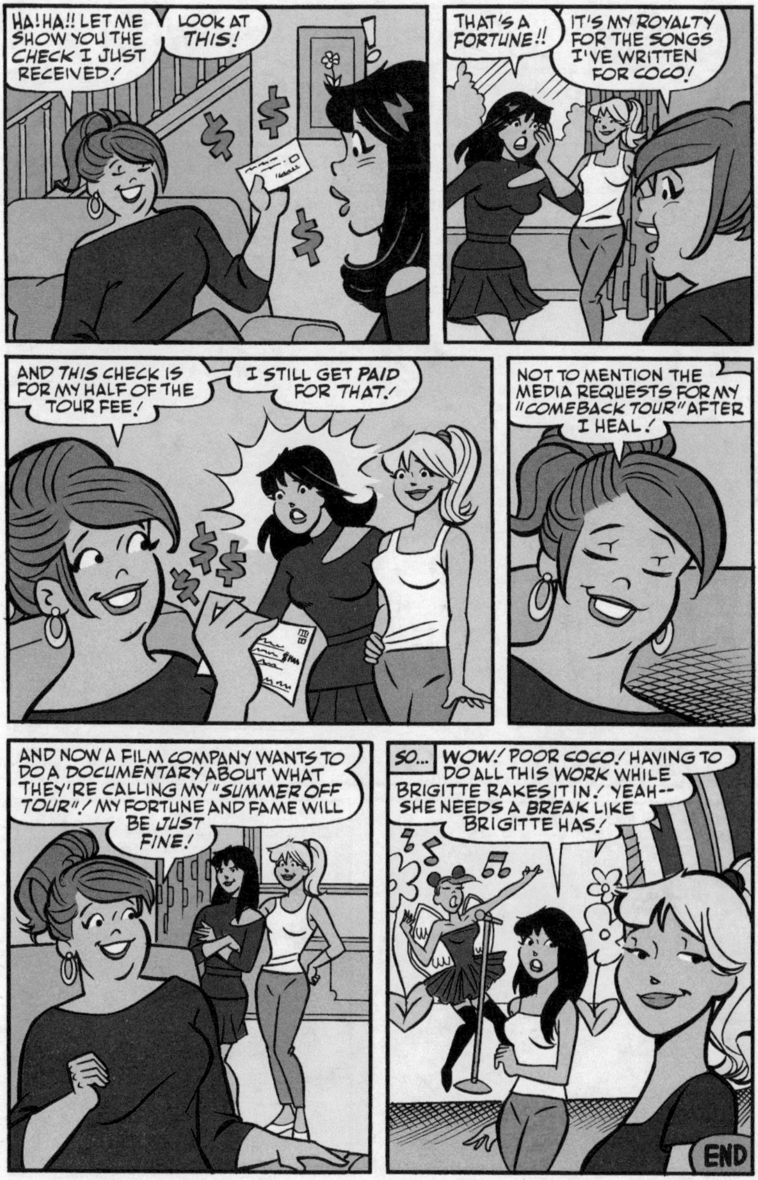
HA! HA!! LET ME SHOW YOU THE CHECK I JUST RECEIVED!
LOOK AT THIS!
!
THAT'S A FORTUNE!!
IT'S MY ROYALTY FOR THE SONGS I'VE WRITTEN FOR COCO!
AND THIS CHECK IS FOR MY HALF OF THE TOUR FEE!
I STILL GET PAID FOR THAT!
NOT TO MENTION THE MEDIA REQUESTS FOR MY "COMEBACK TOUR" AFTER I HEAL!
AND NOW A FILM COMPANY WANTS TO DO A DOCUMENTARY ABOUT WHAT THEY'RE CALLING MY "SUMMER OFF TOUR"! MY FORTUNE AND FAME WILL BE JUST FINE!
SO...
WOW! POOR COCO! HAVING TO DO ALL THIS WORK WHILE BRIGITTE RAKES IT IN! YEAH-- SHE NEEDS A BREAK LIKE BRIGITTE HAS!
END

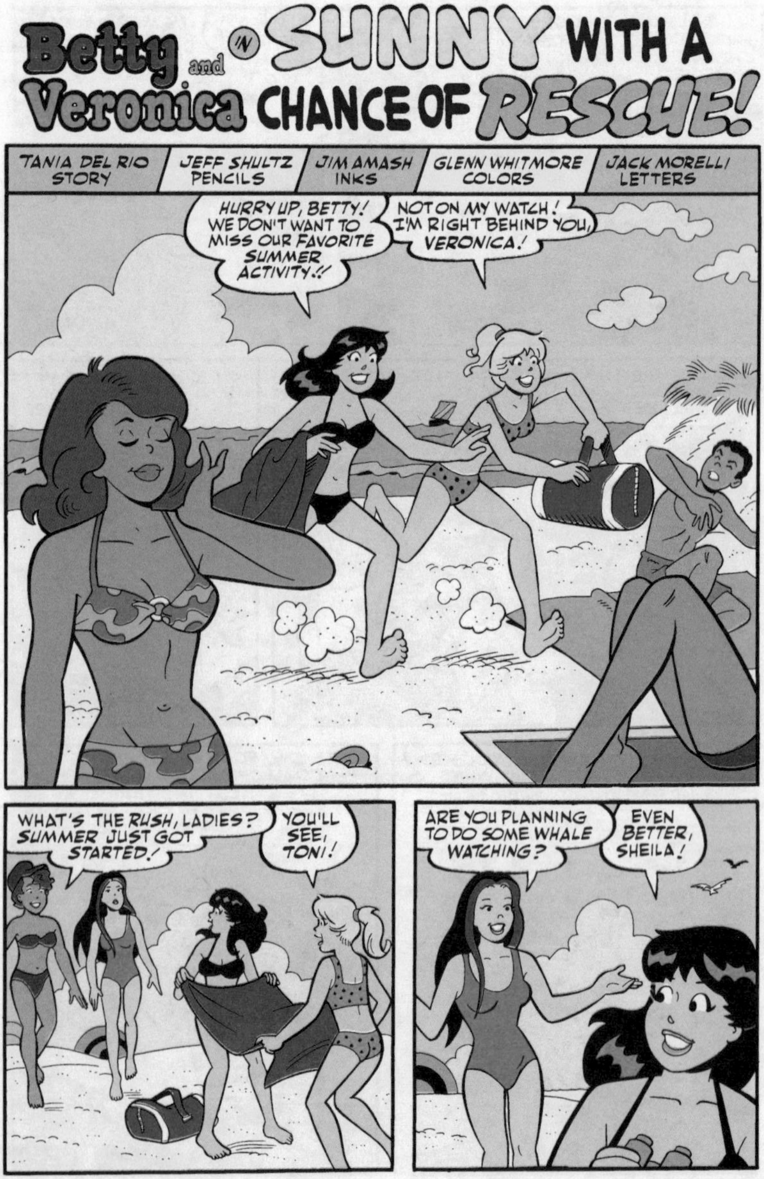
Betty and Veronica
IN
SUNNY WITH A CHANCE OF RESCUE!
TANIA DEL RIO STORY
JEFF SHULTZ PENCILS
JIM AMASH INKS
GLENN WHITMORE COLORS
JACK MORELLI LETTERS
HURRY UP, BETTY! WE DON'T WANT TO MISS OUR FAVORITE SUMMER ACTIVITY!?!
NOT ON MY WATCH! I'M RIGHT BEHIND YOU, VERONICA!
WHAT'S THE RUSH, LADIES? SUMMER JUST GOT STARTED!
YOU'LL SEE, TONI!
ARE YOU PLANNING TO DO SOME WHALE WATCHING?
EVEN BETTER, SHEILA!

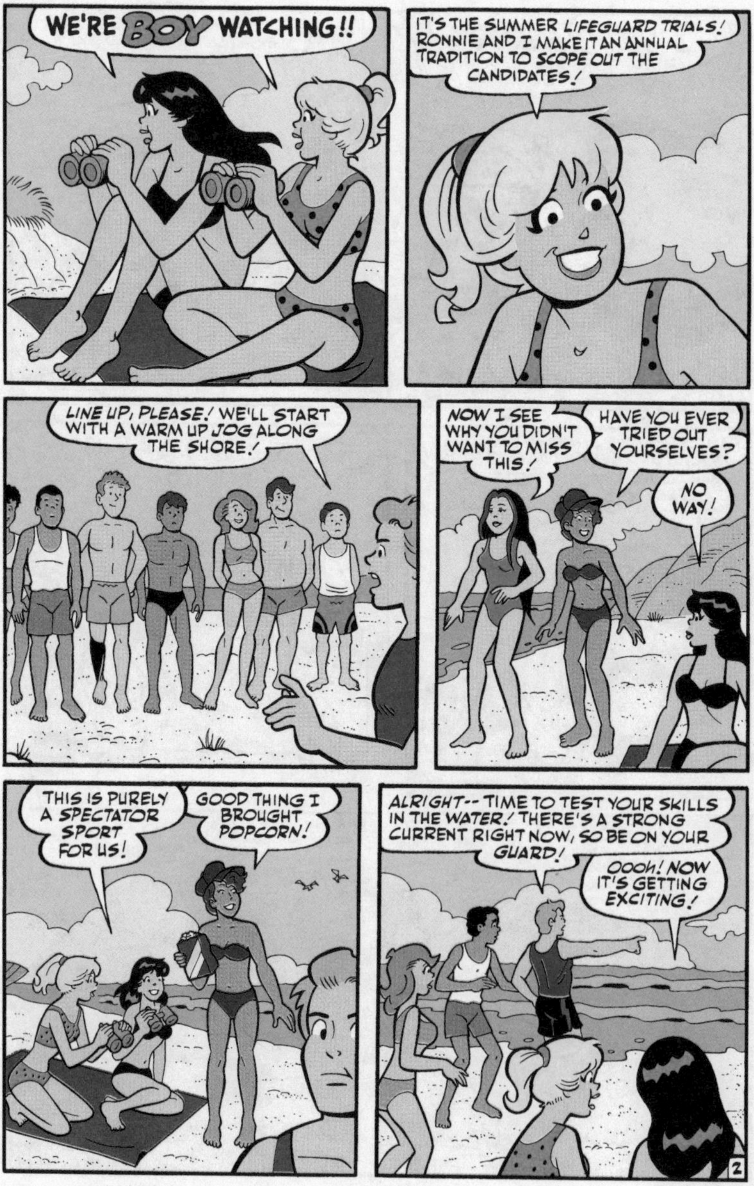
WE'RE BOY WATCHING!!
IT'S THE SUMMER LIFEGUARD TRIALS! RONNIE AND I MAKE IT AN ANNUAL TRADITION TO SCOPE OUT THE CANDIDATES!
LINE UP, PLEASE! WE'LL START WITH A WARM UP JOG ALONG THE SHORE!
NOW I SEE WHY YOU DIDN'T WANT TO MISS THIS!
HAVE YOU EVER TRIED OUT YOURSELVES?
NO WAY!
THIS IS PURELY A SPECTATOR SPORT FOR US!
GOOD THING I BROUGHT POPCORN!
ALRIGHT-- TIME TO TEST YOUR SKILLS IN THE WATER! THERE'S A STRONG CURRENT RIGHT NOW, SO BE ON YOUR GUARD!
Oooh! NOW IT'S GETTING EXCITING!
2

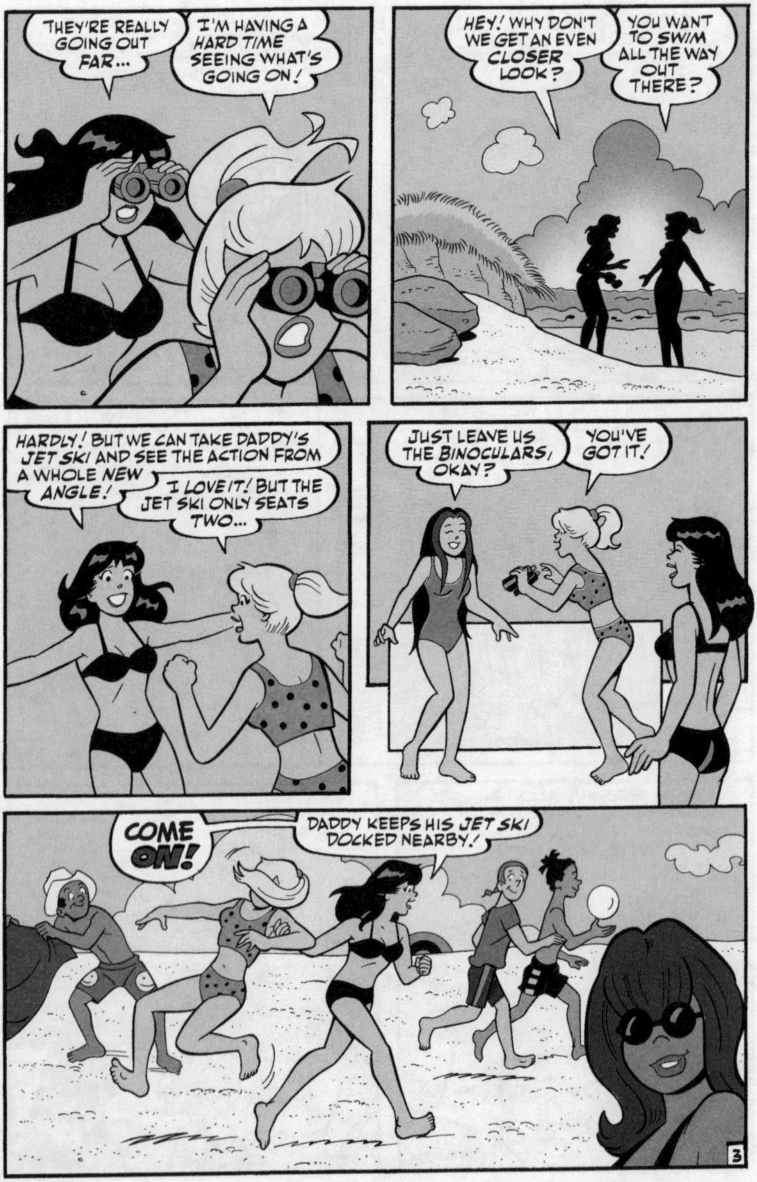
THEY'RE REALLY GOING OUT FAR...
I'M HAVING A HARD TIME SEEING WHAT'S GOING ON!
HEY! WHY DON'T WE GET AN EVEN CLOSER LOOK?
YOU WANT TO SWIM ALL THE WAY OUT THERE?
HARDLY! BUT WE CAN TAKE DADDY'S JET SKI AND SEE THE ACTION FROM A WHOLE NEW ANGLE!
I LOVE IT! BUT THE JET SKI ONLY SEATS TWO...
JUST LEAVE US THE BINOCULARS, OKAY?
YOU'VE GOT IT!
COME ON!
DADDY KEEPS HIS JET SKI DOCKED NEARBY!
3

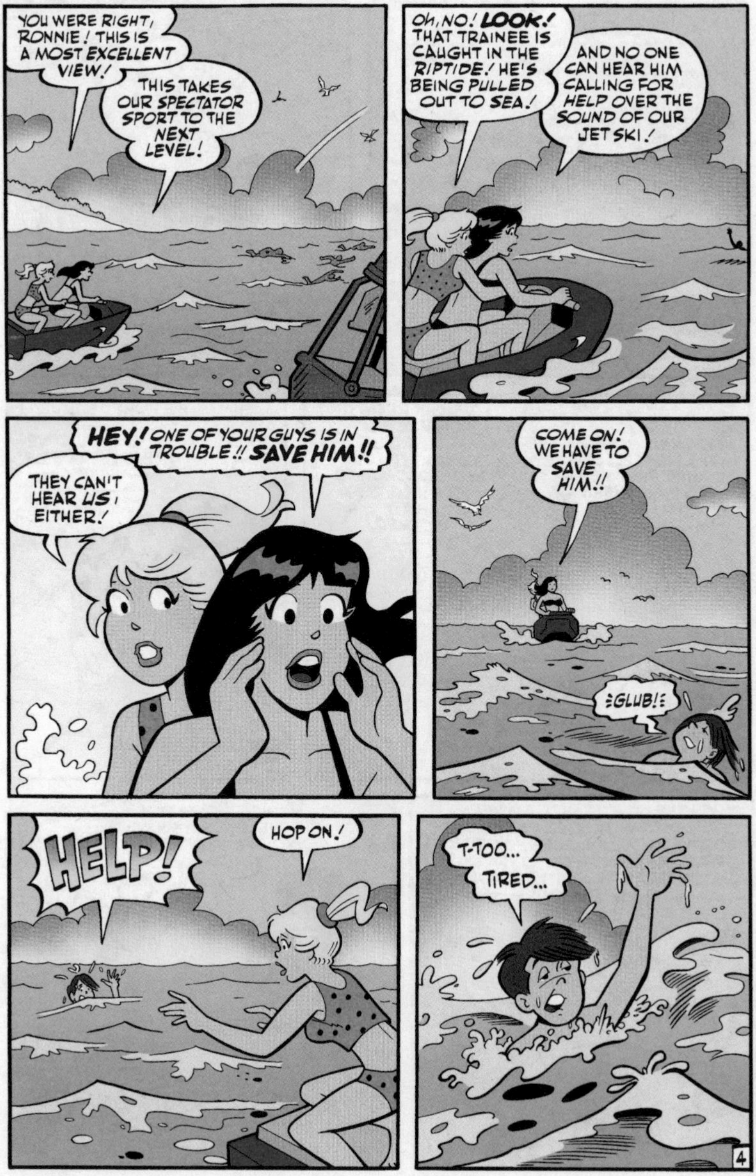
YOU WERE RIGHT, RONNIE! THIS IS A MOST EXCELLENT VIEW!
THIS TAKES OUR SPECTATOR SPORT TO THE NEXT LEVEL!
OH, NO! LOOK! THAT TRAINEE IS CAUGHT IN THE RIPTIDE! HE'S BEING PULLED OUT TO SEA!
AND NO ONE CAN HEAR HIM CALLING FOR HELP OVER THE SOUND OF OUR JET SKI!
HEY! ONE OF YOUR GUYS IS IN TROUBLE!! SAVE HIM!!
THEY CAN'T HEAR US, EITHER!
COME ON! WE HAVE TO SAVE HIM!!
GLUB!
HELP!
HOP ON!
T-TOO... TIRED...
4

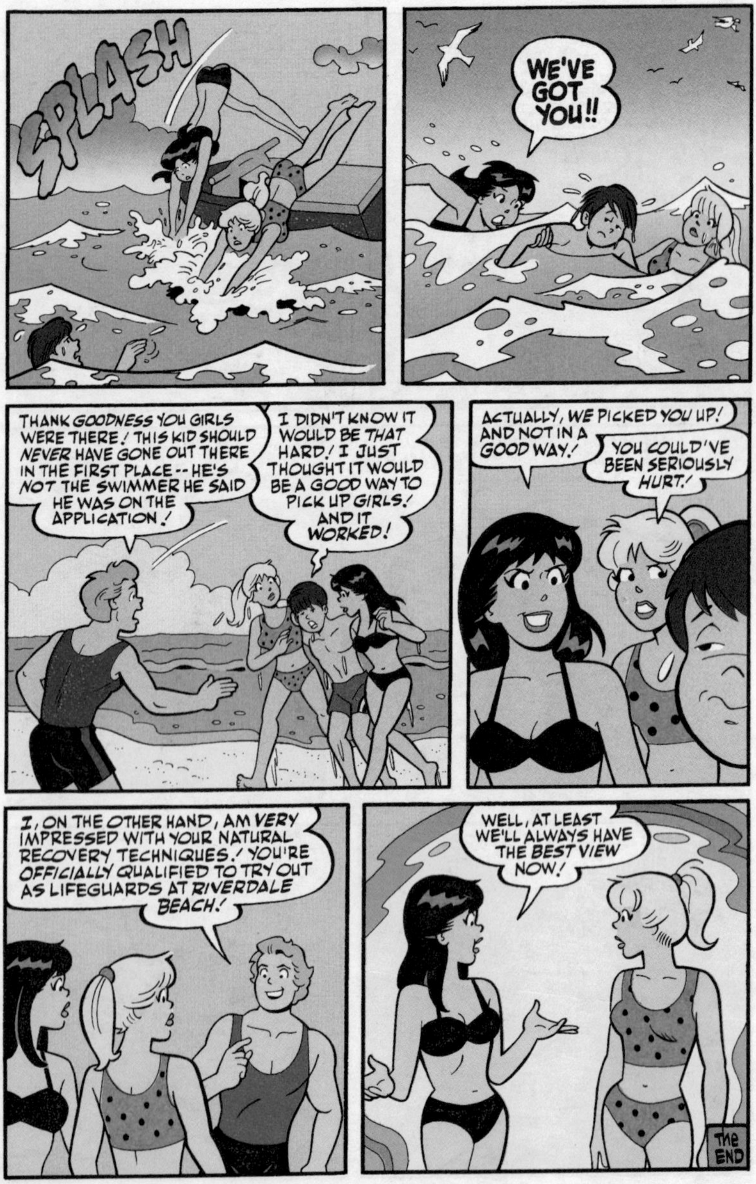
SPLASH
WE'VE GOT YOU!!
THANK GOODNESS YOU GIRLS WERE THERE! THIS KID SHOULD NEVER HAVE GONE OUT THERE IN THE FIRST PLACE -- HE'S NOT THE SWIMMER HE SAID HE WAS ON THE APPLICATION!
I DIDN'T KNOW IT WOULD BE THAT HARD! I JUST THOUGHT IT WOULD BE A GOOD WAY TO PICK UP GIRLS! AND IT WORKED!
ACTUALLY, WE PICKED YOU UP! AND NOT IN A GOOD WAY!
YOU COULD'VE BEEN SERIOUSLY HURT!
I, ON THE OTHER HAND, AM VERY IMPRESSED WITH YOUR NATURAL RECOVERY TECHNIQUES! YOU'RE OFFICIALLY QUALIFIED TO TRY OUT AS LIFEGUARDS AT RIVERDALE BEACH!
WELL, AT LEAST WE'LL ALWAYS HAVE THE BEST VIEW NOW!
THE END

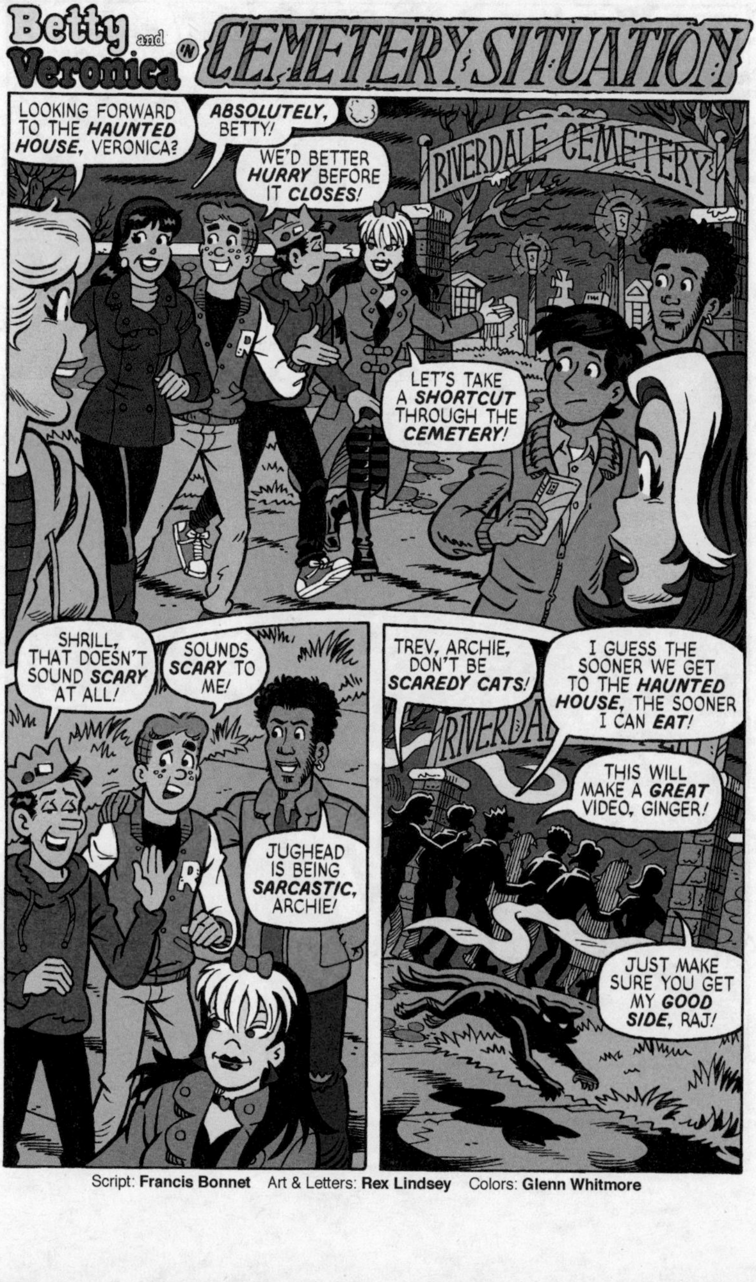
Betty and Veronica in
CEMETERY SITUATION
LOOKING FORWARD TO THE HAUNTED HOUSE, VERONICA?
ABSOLUTELY, BETTY!
WE'D BETTER HURRY BEFORE IT CLOSES!
RIVERDALE CEMETERY
LET'S TAKE A SHORTCUT THROUGH THE CEMETERY!
SHRILL, THAT DOESN'T SOUND SCARY AT ALL!
SOUNDS SCARY TO ME!
JUGHEAD IS BEING SARCASTIC, ARCHIE!
TREV, ARCHIE, DON'T BE SCAREDY CATS!
I GUESS THE SOONER WE GET TO THE HAUNTED HOUSE, THE SOONER I CAN EAT!
THIS WILL MAKE A GREAT VIDEO, GINGER!
JUST MAKE SURE YOU GET MY GOOD SIDE, RAJ!

Script: **Francis Bonnet** Art & Letters: **Rex Lindsey** Colors: **Glenn Whitmore**

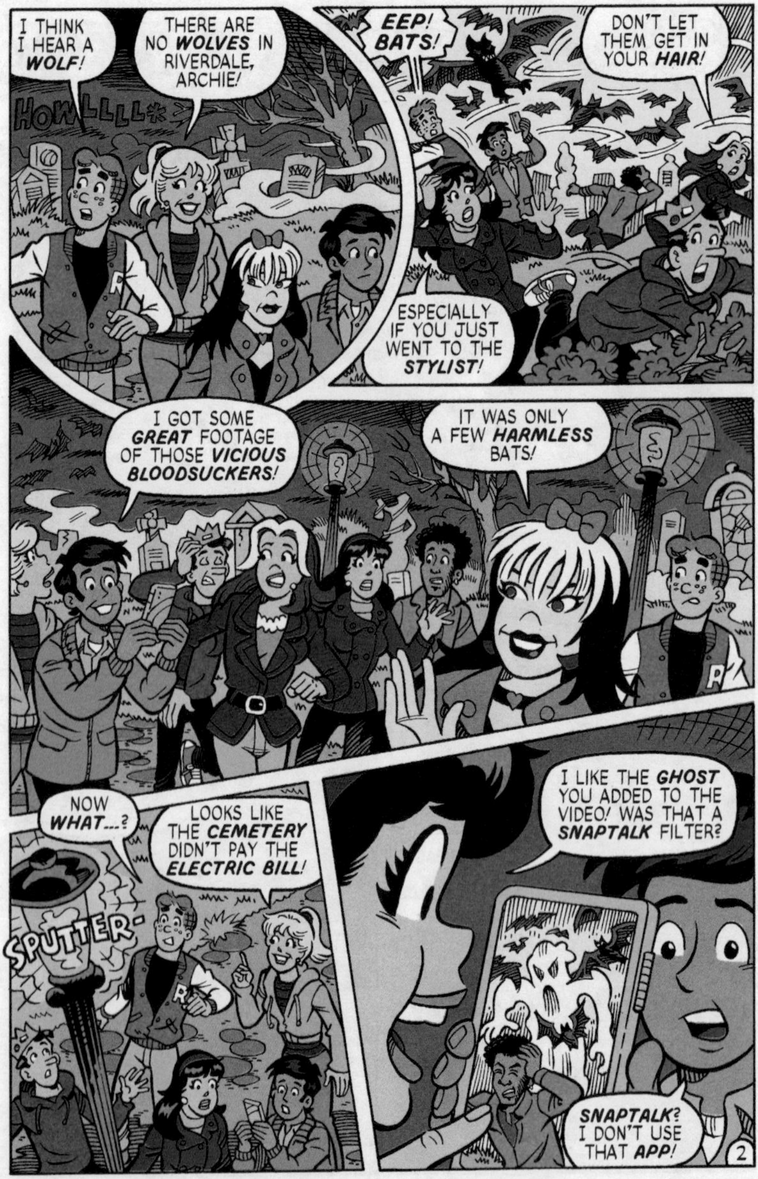
I THINK I HEAR A WOLF!
THERE ARE NO WOLVES IN RIVERDALE, ARCHIE!
HOWLLLLL*
EEP! BATS!
DON'T LET THEM GET IN YOUR HAIR!
ESPECIALLY IF YOU JUST WENT TO THE STYLIST!
I GOT SOME GREAT FOOTAGE OF THOSE VICIOUS BLOODSUCKERS!
IT WAS ONLY A FEW HARMLESS BATS!
NOW WHAT...?
LOOKS LIKE THE CEMETERY DIDN'T PAY THE ELECTRIC BILL!
SPUTTER-
I LIKE THE GHOST YOU ADDED TO THE VIDEO! WAS THAT A SNAPTALK FILTER?
SNAPTALK? I DON'T USE THAT APP!
2

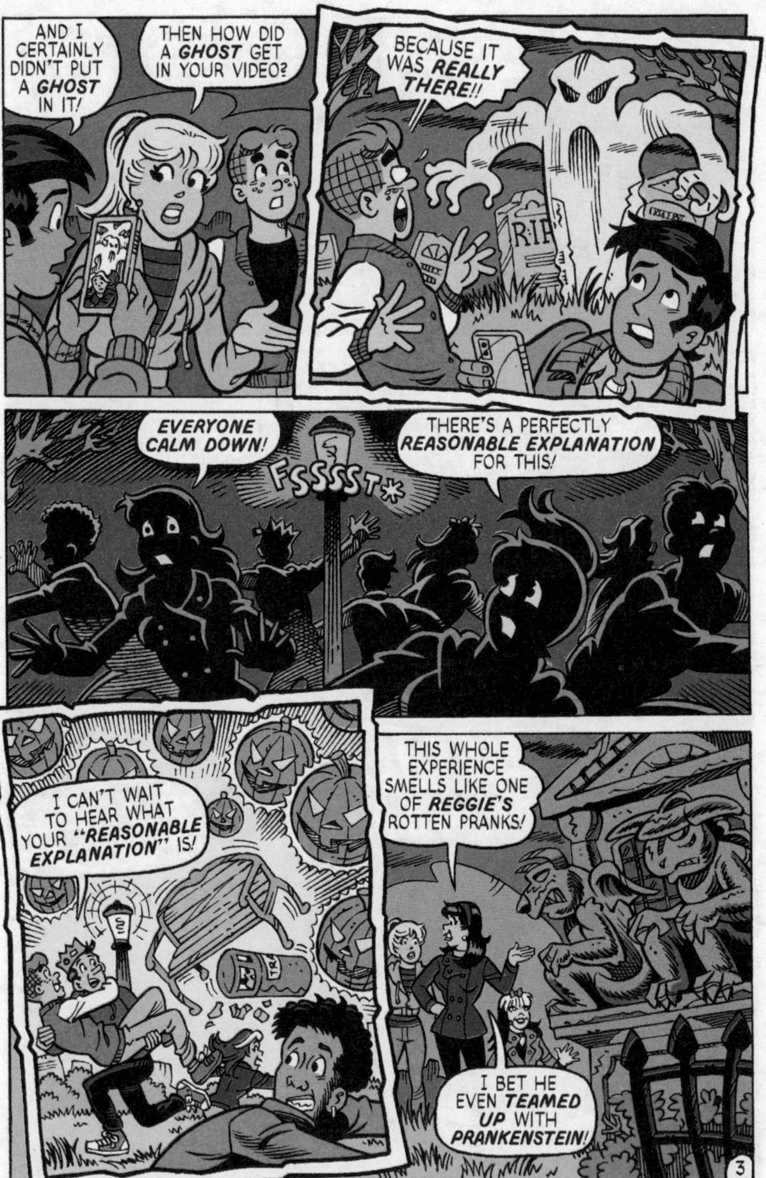
AND I CERTAINLY DIDN'T PUT A GHOST IN IT!
THEN HOW DID A GHOST GET IN YOUR VIDEO?
BECAUSE IT WAS REALLY THERE!!
R.I.P.
EVERYONE CALM DOWN!
FSSSST*
THERE'S A PERFECTLY REASONABLE EXPLANATION FOR THIS!
I CAN'T WAIT TO HEAR WHAT YOUR "REASONABLE EXPLANATION" IS!
THIS WHOLE EXPERIENCE SMELLS LIKE ONE OF REGGIE'S ROTTEN PRANKS!
I BET HE EVEN TEAMED UP WITH PRANKENSTEIN!
3

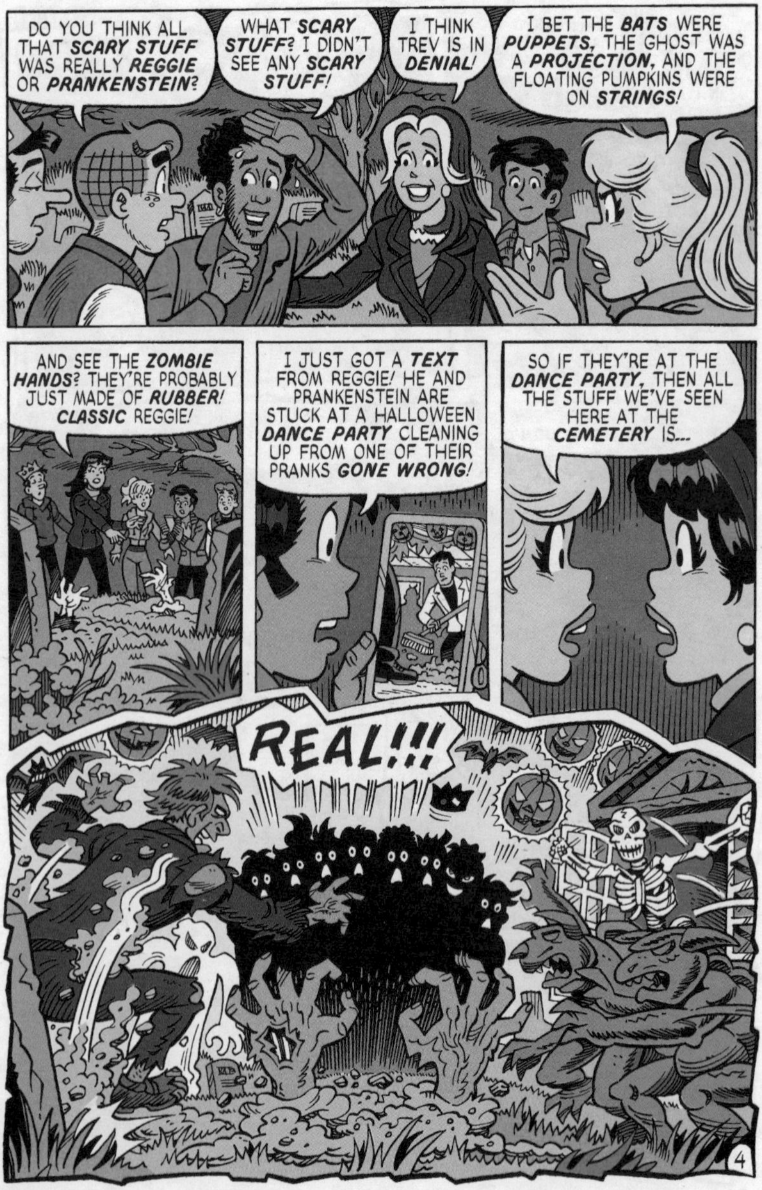
DO YOU THINK ALL THAT SCARY STUFF WAS REALLY REGGIE OR PRANKENSTEIN?
WHAT SCARY STUFF? I DIDN'T SEE ANY SCARY STUFF!
I THINK TREV IS IN DENIAL!
I BET THE BATS WERE PUPPETS, THE GHOST WAS A PROJECTION, AND THE FLOATING PUMPKINS WERE ON STRINGS!
AND SEE THE ZOMBIE HANDS? THEY'RE PROBABLY JUST MADE OF RUBBER! CLASSIC REGGIE!
I JUST GOT A TEXT FROM REGGIE! HE AND PRANKENSTEIN ARE STUCK AT A HALLOWEEN DANCE PARTY CLEANING UP FROM ONE OF THEIR PRANKS GONE WRONG!
SO IF THEY'RE AT THE DANCE PARTY, THEN ALL THE STUFF WE'VE SEEN HERE AT THE CEMETERY IS...
REAL!!!
4

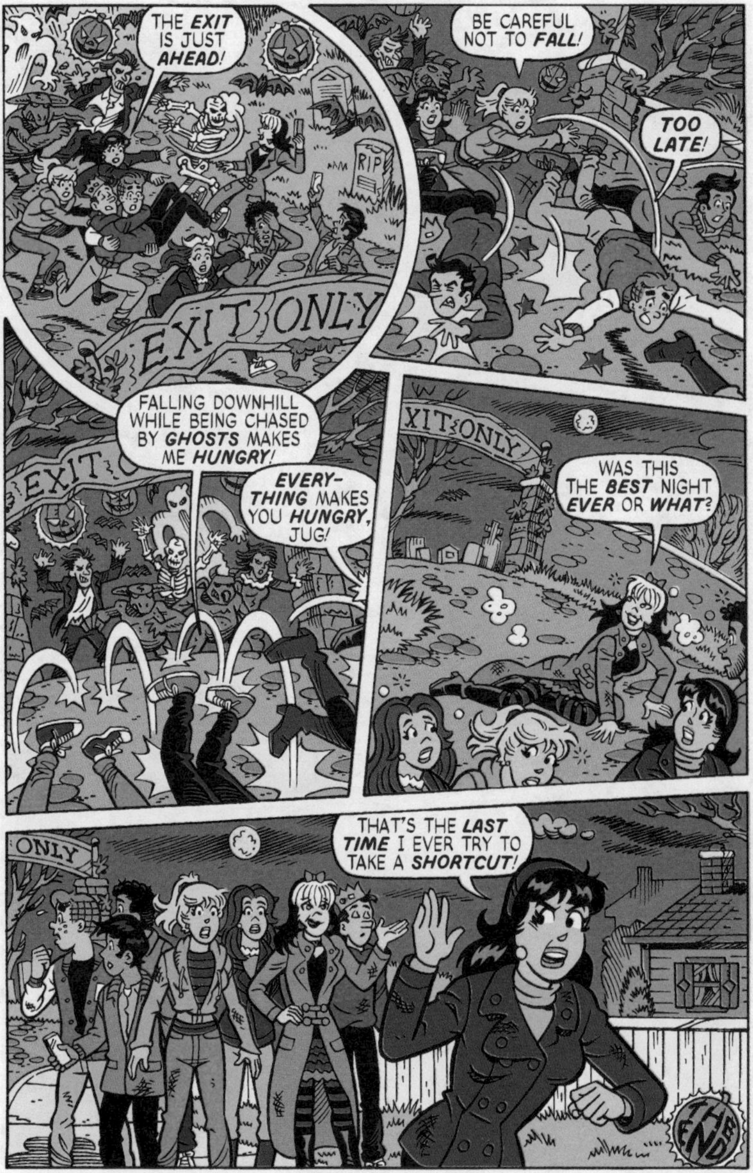
THE EXIT IS JUST AHEAD!
EXIT ONLY
RIP
BE CAREFUL NOT TO FALL!
TOO LATE!
FALLING DOWNHILL WHILE BEING CHASED BY GHOSTS MAKES ME HUNGRY!
EVERY-THING MAKES YOU HUNGRY, JUG!
WAS THIS THE BEST NIGHT EVER OR WHAT?
THAT'S THE LAST TIME I EVER TRY TO TAKE A SHORTCUT!
THE END

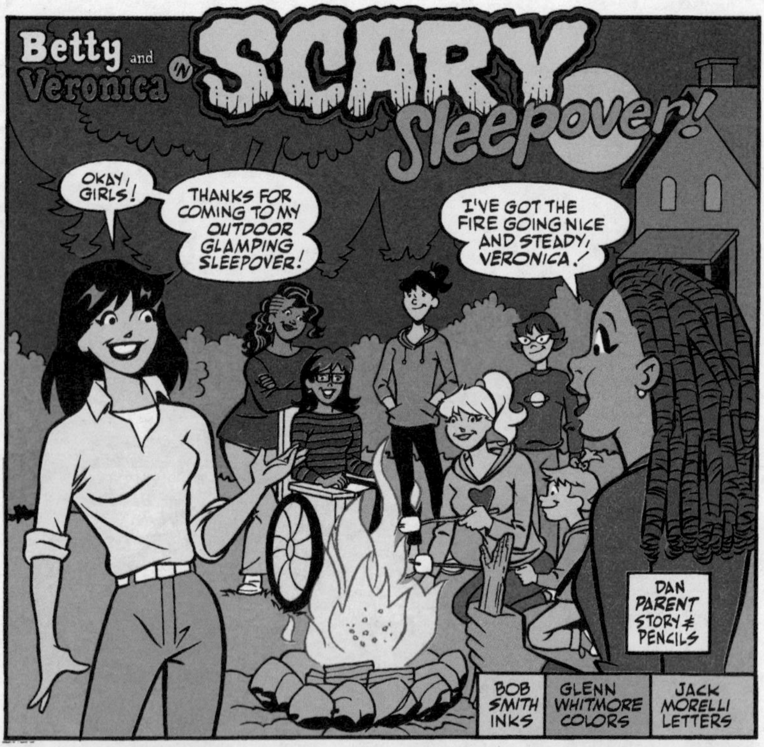
Betty and Veronica in
SCARY Sleepover!
OKAY, GIRLS!
THANKS FOR COMING TO MY OUTDOOR GLAMPING SLEEPOVER!
I'VE GOT THE FIRE GOING NICE AND STEADY, VERONICA!
DAN PARENT STORY & PENCILS
BOB SMITH INKS
GLENN WHITMORE COLORS
JACK MORELLI LETTERS

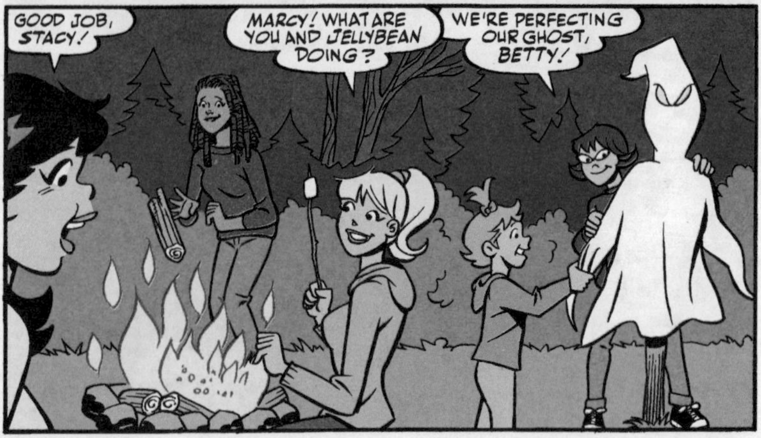
GOOD JOB, STACY!
MARCY! WHAT ARE YOU AND JELLYBEAN DOING?
WE'RE PERFECTING OUR GHOST, BETTY!

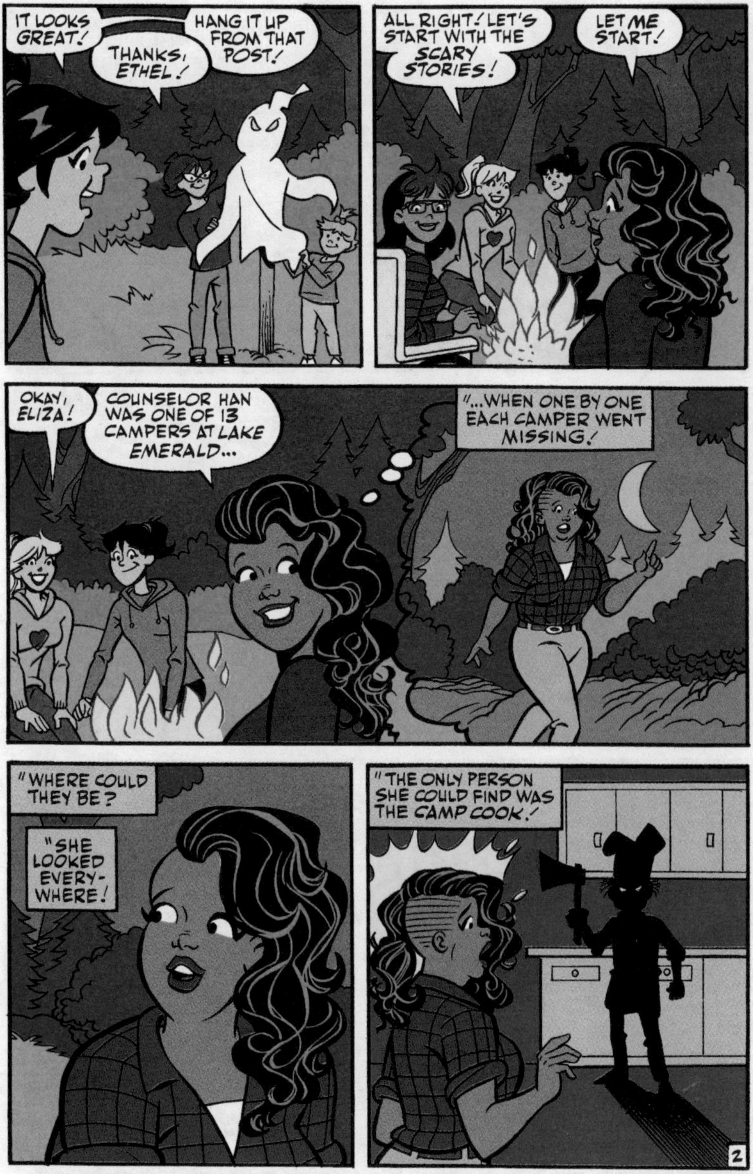
IT LOOKS GREAT!
THANKS, ETHEL!
HANG IT UP FROM THAT POST!
ALL RIGHT! LET'S START WITH THE SCARY STORIES!
LET ME START!
OKAY, ELIZA!
COUNSELOR HAN WAS ONE OF 13 CAMPERS AT LAKE EMERALD...
"...WHEN ONE BY ONE EACH CAMPER WENT MISSING!
"WHERE COULD THEY BE?
"SHE LOOKED EVERY-WHERE!
"THE ONLY PERSON SHE COULD FIND WAS THE CAMP COOK!
2

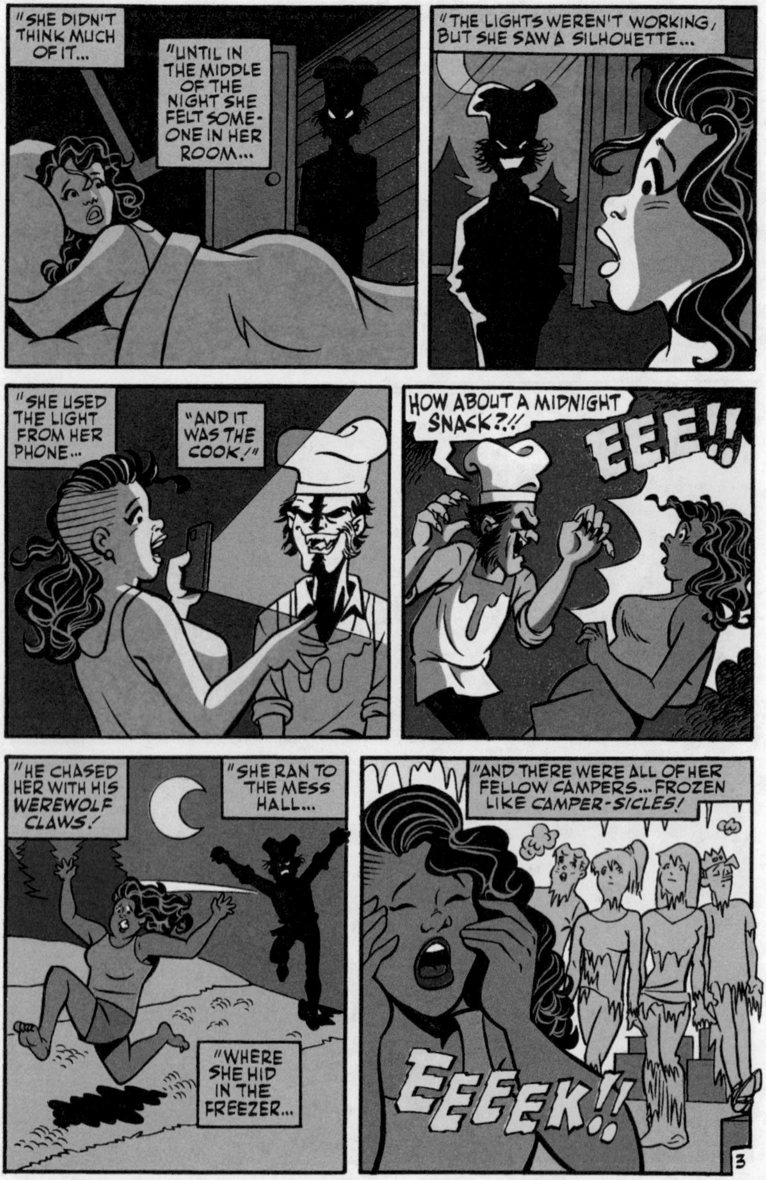
"SHE DIDN'T THINK MUCH OF IT...
"UNTIL IN THE MIDDLE OF THE NIGHT SHE FELT SOME-ONE IN HER ROOM...
"THE LIGHTS WEREN'T WORKING, BUT SHE SAW A SILHOUETTE...
"SHE USED THE LIGHT FROM HER PHONE...
"AND IT WAS THE COOK!"
HOW ABOUT A MIDNIGHT SNACK?!!
EEE!!
"HE CHASED HER WITH HIS *WEREWOLF CLAWS!*
"SHE RAN TO THE MESS HALL...
"WHERE SHE HID IN THE FREEZER...
"AND THERE WERE ALL OF HER FELLOW CAMPERS... FROZEN LIKE *CAMPER-SICLES!*
EEEEK!!
3

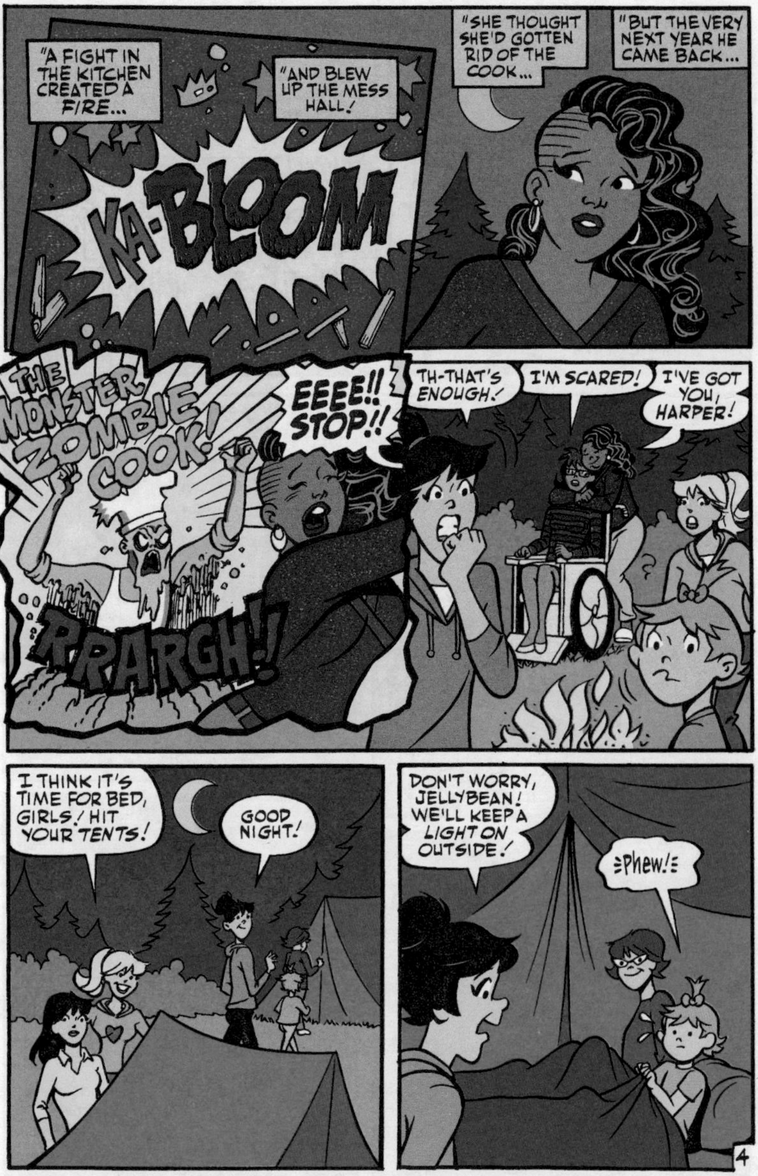
"A FIGHT IN THE KITCHEN CREATED A FIRE...
"AND BLEW UP THE MESS HALL!
KA-BLOOM
"SHE THOUGHT SHE'D GOTTEN RID OF THE COOK...
"BUT THE VERY NEXT YEAR HE CAME BACK...
THE MONSTER ZOMBIE COOK!
EEEE!! STOP!!
RRARGH!!
TH-THAT'S ENOUGH!
I'M SCARED!
I'VE GOT YOU, HARPER!
I THINK IT'S TIME FOR BED, GIRLS! HIT YOUR TENTS!
GOOD NIGHT!
DON'T WORRY, JELLYBEAN! WE'LL KEEP A LIGHT ON OUTSIDE!
Phew!
4

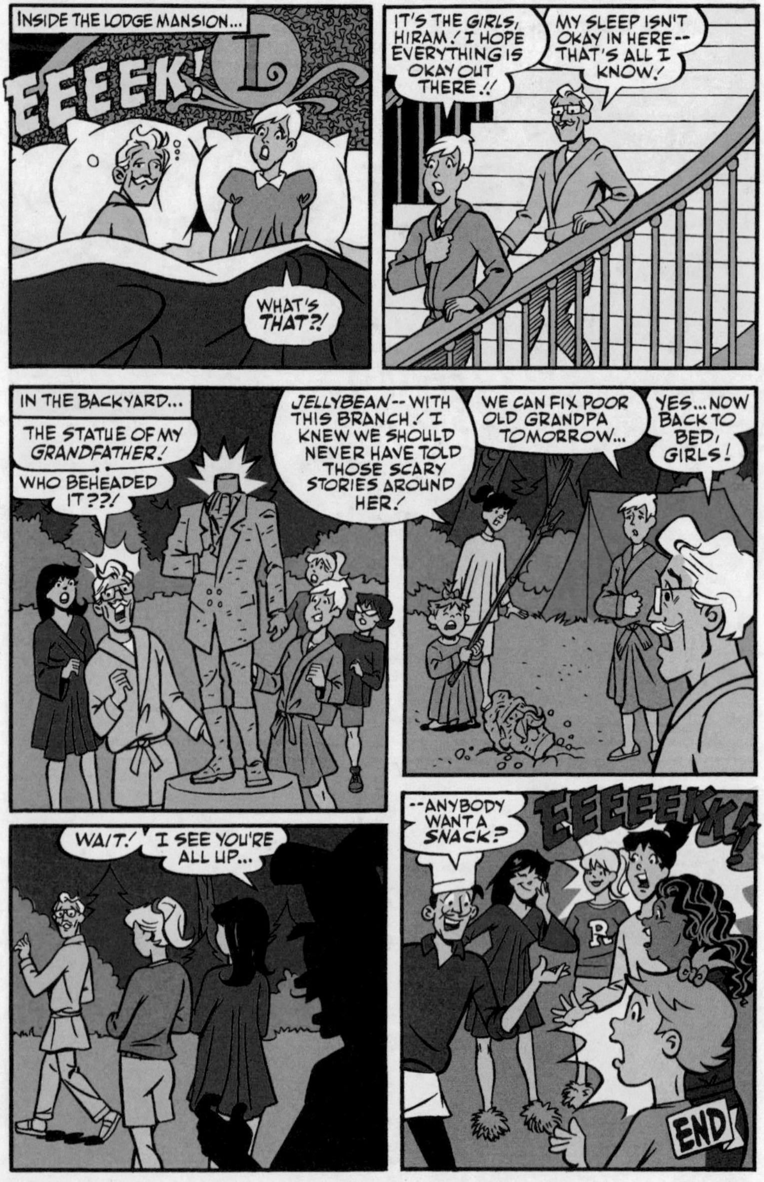
INSIDE THE LODGE MANSION...
EEEEK!
WHAT'S THAT?!
IT'S THE GIRLS, HIRAM! I HOPE EVERYTHING IS OKAY OUT THERE!!
MY SLEEP ISN'T OKAY IN HERE-- THAT'S ALL I KNOW!
IN THE BACKYARD...
THE STATUE OF MY GRANDFATHER!
WHO BEHEADED IT??!
JELLYBEAN-- WITH THIS BRANCH! I KNEW WE SHOULD NEVER HAVE TOLD THOSE SCARY STORIES AROUND HER!
WE CAN FIX POOR OLD GRANDPA TOMORROW...
YES... NOW BACK TO BED, GIRLS!
WAIT!
I SEE YOU'RE ALL UP...
--ANYBODY WANT A SNACK?
EEEEEKKK!!
END

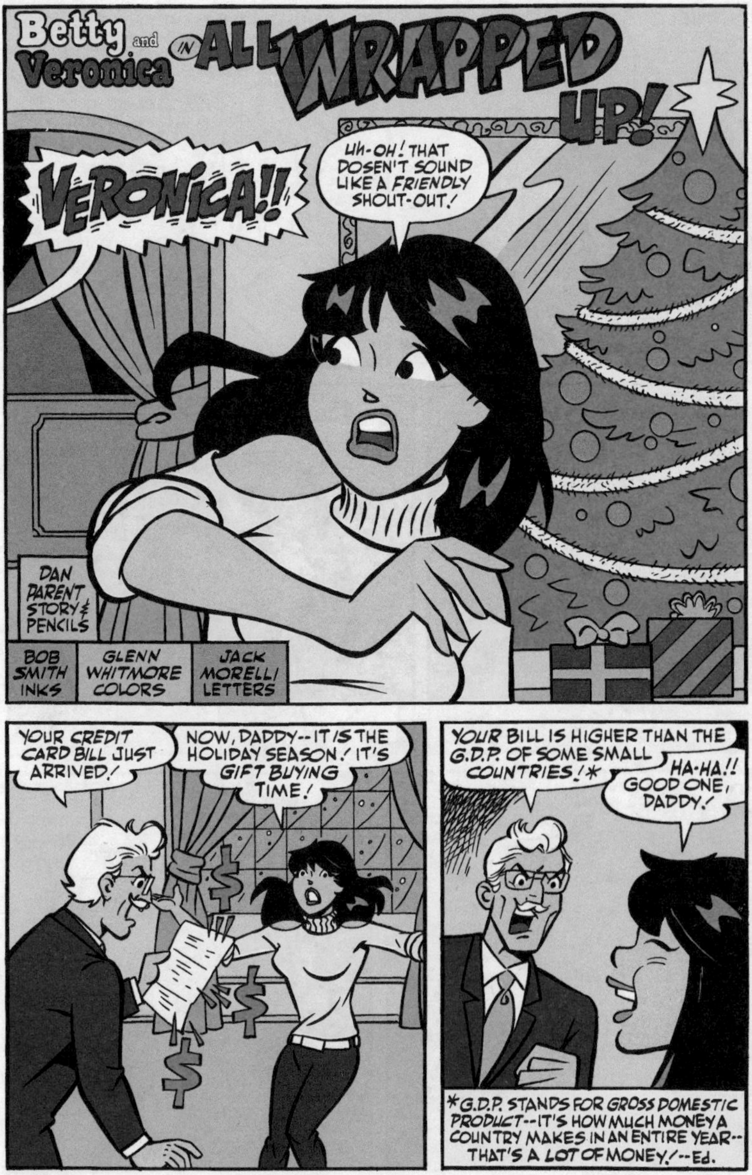
Betty and Veronica
IN ALL WRAPPED UP!
VERONICA!!
UH-OH! THAT DOSEN'T SOUND LIKE A FRIENDLY SHOUT-OUT!
DAN PARENT STORY & PENCILS
BOB SMITH INKS
GLENN WHITMORE COLORS
JACK MORELLI LETTERS
YOUR CREDIT CARD BILL JUST ARRIVED!
NOW, DADDY--IT IS THE HOLIDAY SEASON! IT'S GIFT BUYING TIME!
YOUR BILL IS HIGHER THAN THE G.D.P. OF SOME SMALL COUNTRIES!*
HA-HA!! GOOD ONE, DADDY!
*G.D.P. STANDS FOR GROSS DOMESTIC PRODUCT--IT'S HOW MUCH MONEY A COUNTRY MAKES IN AN ENTIRE YEAR--THAT'S A LOT OF MONEY!--Ed.

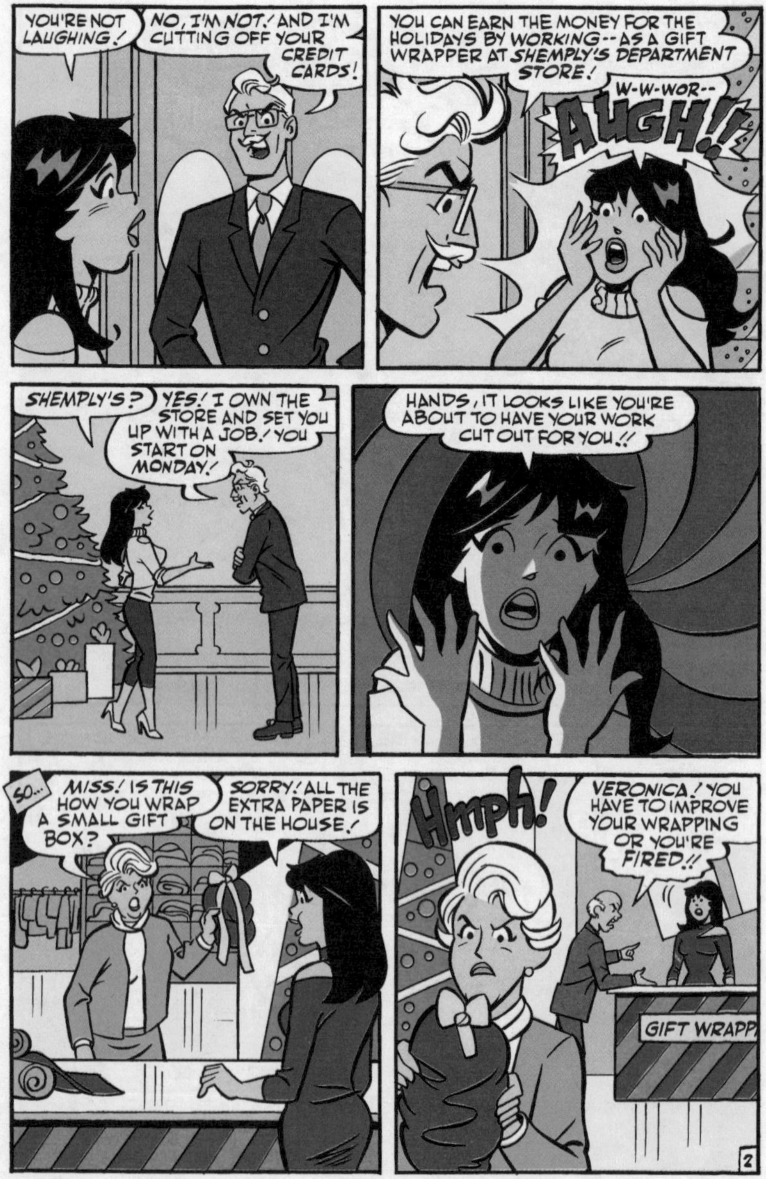
YOU'RE NOT LAUGHING!
NO, I'M NOT! AND I'M CUTTING OFF YOUR CREDIT CARDS!
YOU CAN EARN THE MONEY FOR THE HOLIDAYS BY WORKING-- AS A GIFT WRAPPER AT SHEMPLY'S DEPARTMENT STORE!
W-W-WOR-- AUGH!!
SHEMPLY'S?
YES! I OWN THE STORE AND SET YOU UP WITH A JOB! YOU START ON MONDAY!
HANDS, IT LOOKS LIKE YOU'RE ABOUT TO HAVE YOUR WORK CUT OUT FOR YOU!!
SO...
MISS! IS THIS HOW YOU WRAP A SMALL GIFT BOX?
SORRY! ALL THE EXTRA PAPER IS ON THE HOUSE!
Hmph!
VERONICA! YOU HAVE TO IMPROVE YOUR WRAPPING OR YOU'RE FIRED!!
GIFT WRAPP
2

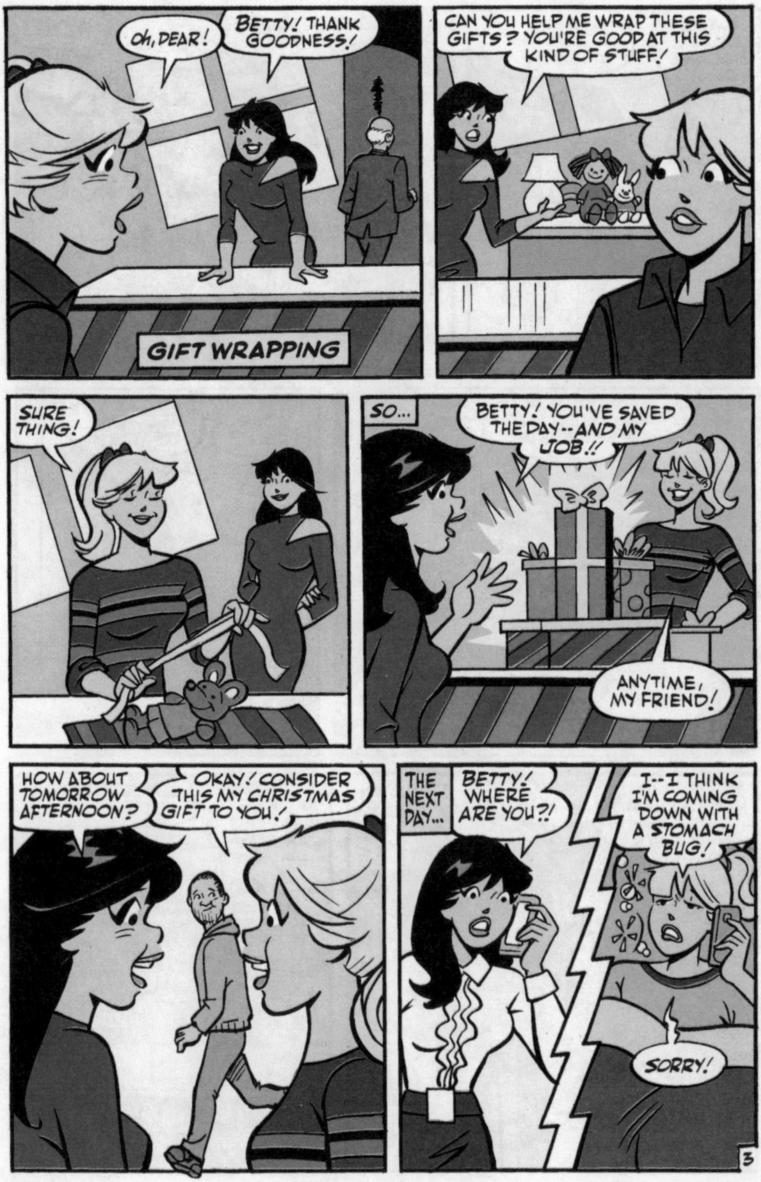
Oh, DEAR!
BETTY! THANK GOODNESS!
GIFT WRAPPING
CAN YOU HELP ME WRAP THESE GIFTS? YOU'RE GOOD AT THIS KIND OF STUFF!
SURE THING!
SO...
BETTY! YOU'VE SAVED THE DAY--AND MY JOB!!
ANYTIME, MY FRIEND!
HOW ABOUT TOMORROW AFTERNOON?
OKAY! CONSIDER THIS MY CHRISTMAS GIFT TO YOU!
THE NEXT DAY...
BETTY! WHERE ARE YOU?!
I--I THINK I'M COMING DOWN WITH A STOMACH BUG!
SORRY!
3

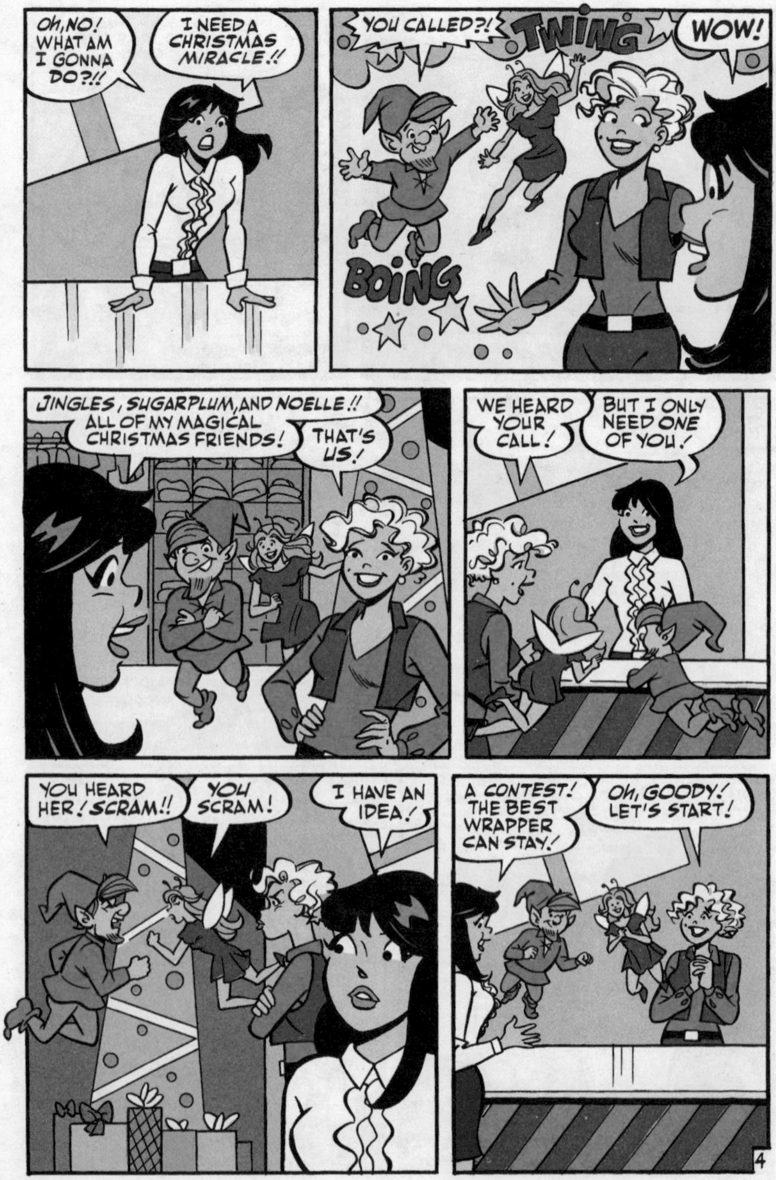
OH, NO! WHAT AM I GONNA DO?!!
I NEED A CHRISTMAS MIRACLE!!
YOU CALLED?!
TWING
WOW!
BOING
JINGLES, SUGARPLUM, AND NOELLE!! ALL OF MY MAGICAL CHRISTMAS FRIENDS!
THAT'S US!
WE HEARD YOUR CALL!
BUT I ONLY NEED ONE OF YOU!
YOU HEARD HER! SCRAM!!
YOU SCRAM!
I HAVE AN IDEA!
A CONTEST! THE BEST WRAPPER CAN STAY!
OH, GOODY! LET'S START!
4

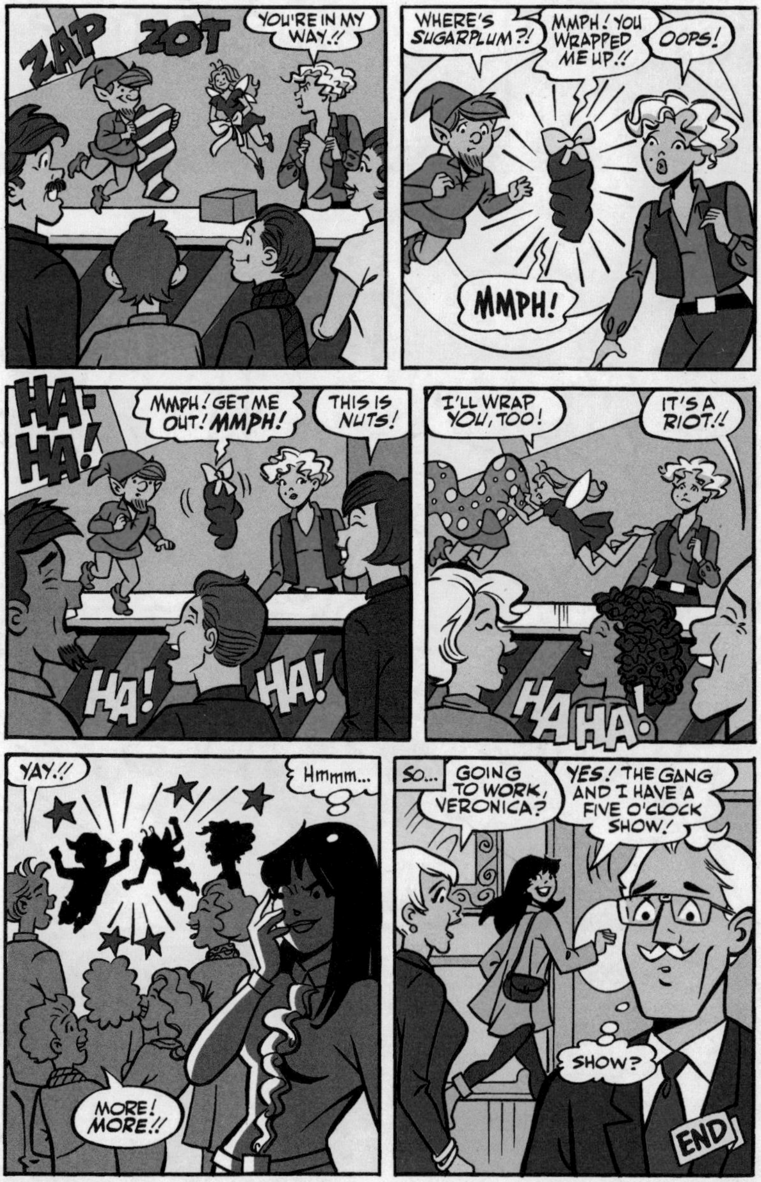
ZAP
ZOT
YOU'RE IN MY WAY.!!
WHERE'S SUGARPLUM?!
MMPH! YOU WRAPPED ME UP!!
OOPS!
MMPH!
HA-HA!
MMPH! GET ME OUT! MMPH!
THIS IS NUTS!
HA!
HA!
I'LL WRAP YOU, TOO!
IT'S A RIOT!!
HAHAHA!
YAY!!
Hmmm...
MORE! MORE!!
SO...
GOING TO WORK, VERONICA?
YES! THE GANG AND I HAVE A FIVE O'CLOCK SHOW!
SHOW?
END

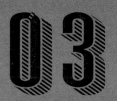

03 WORLD OF ARCHIE

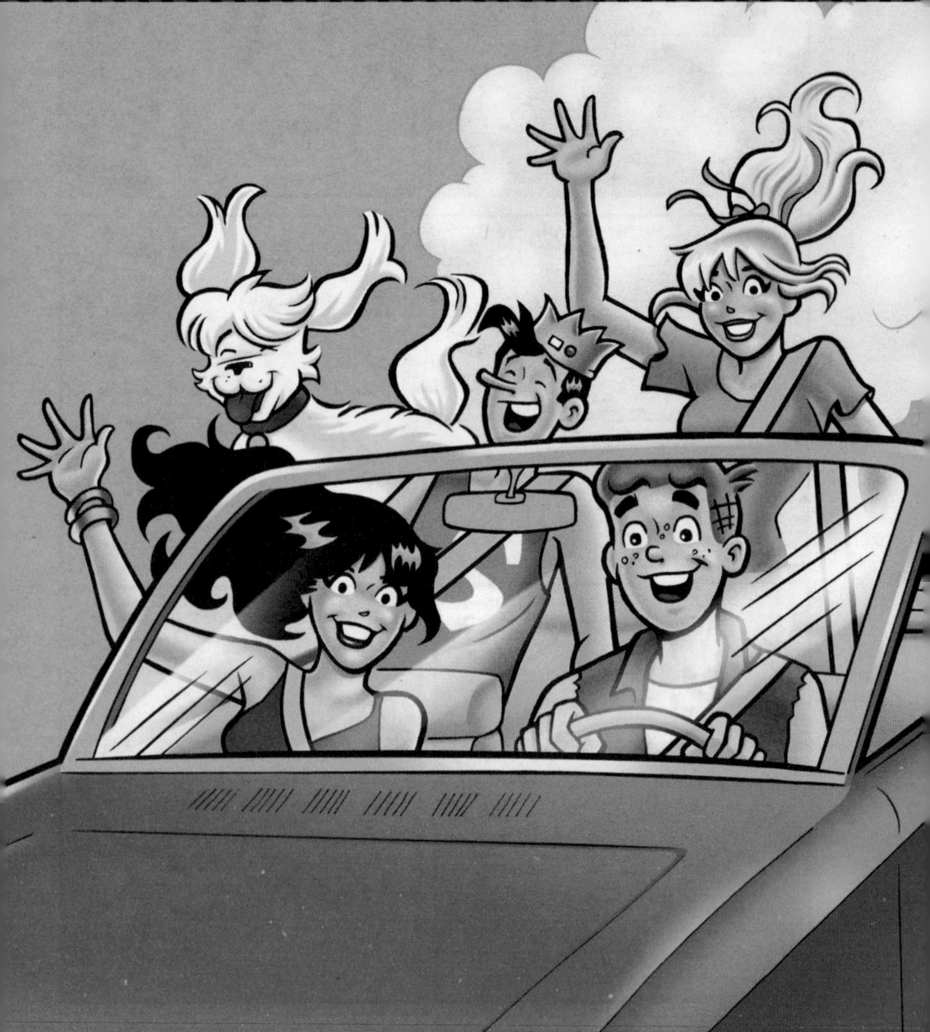

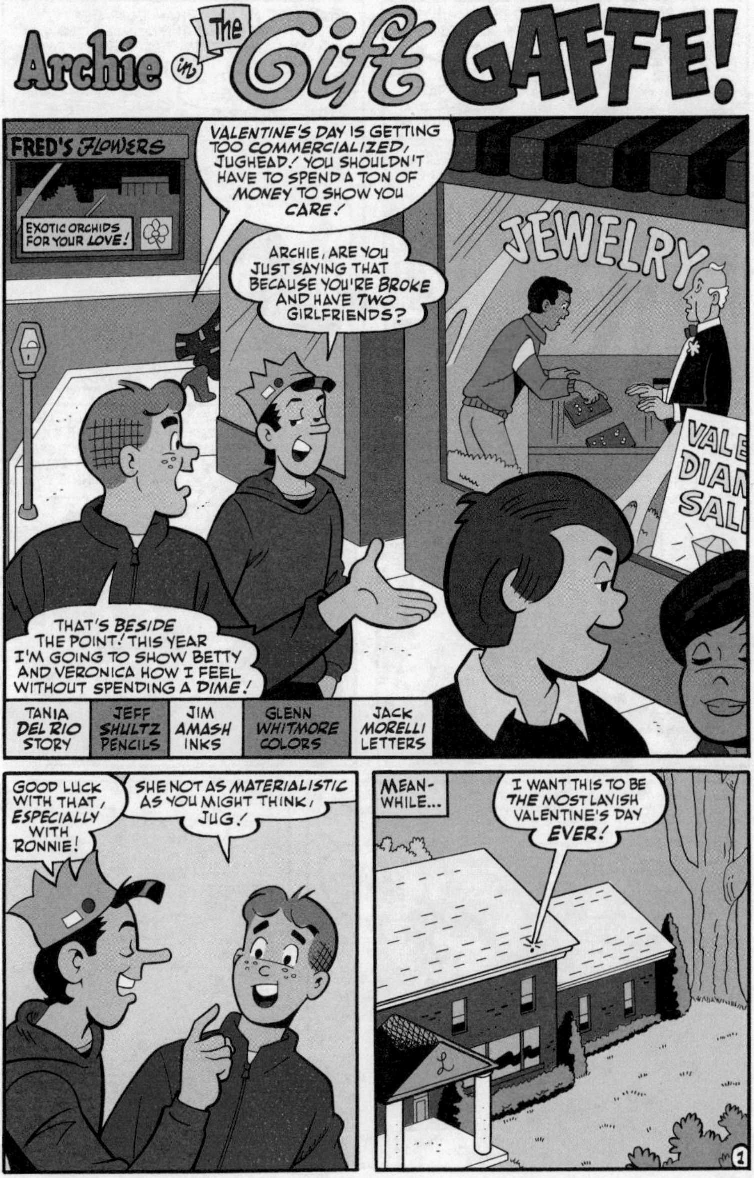
Archie in The Gift GAFFE!
FRED'S FLOWERS
EXOTIC ORCHIDS FOR YOUR LOVE!
JEWELRY
VALE DIAM SAL
VALENTINE'S DAY IS GETTING TOO COMMERCIALIZED, JUGHEAD! YOU SHOULDN'T HAVE TO SPEND A TON OF MONEY TO SHOW YOU CARE!
ARCHIE, ARE YOU JUST SAYING THAT BECAUSE YOU'RE BROKE AND HAVE TWO GIRLFRIENDS?
THAT'S BESIDE THE POINT! THIS YEAR I'M GOING TO SHOW BETTY AND VERONICA HOW I FEEL WITHOUT SPENDING A DIME!
TANIA DEL RIO STORY
JEFF SHULTZ PENCILS
JIM AMASH INKS
GLENN WHITMORE COLORS
JACK MORELLI LETTERS
GOOD LUCK WITH THAT, ESPECIALLY WITH RONNIE!
SHE NOT AS MATERIALISTIC AS YOU MIGHT THINK, JUG!
MEAN-WHILE...
I WANT THIS TO BE THE MOST LAVISH VALENTINE'S DAY EVER!
1

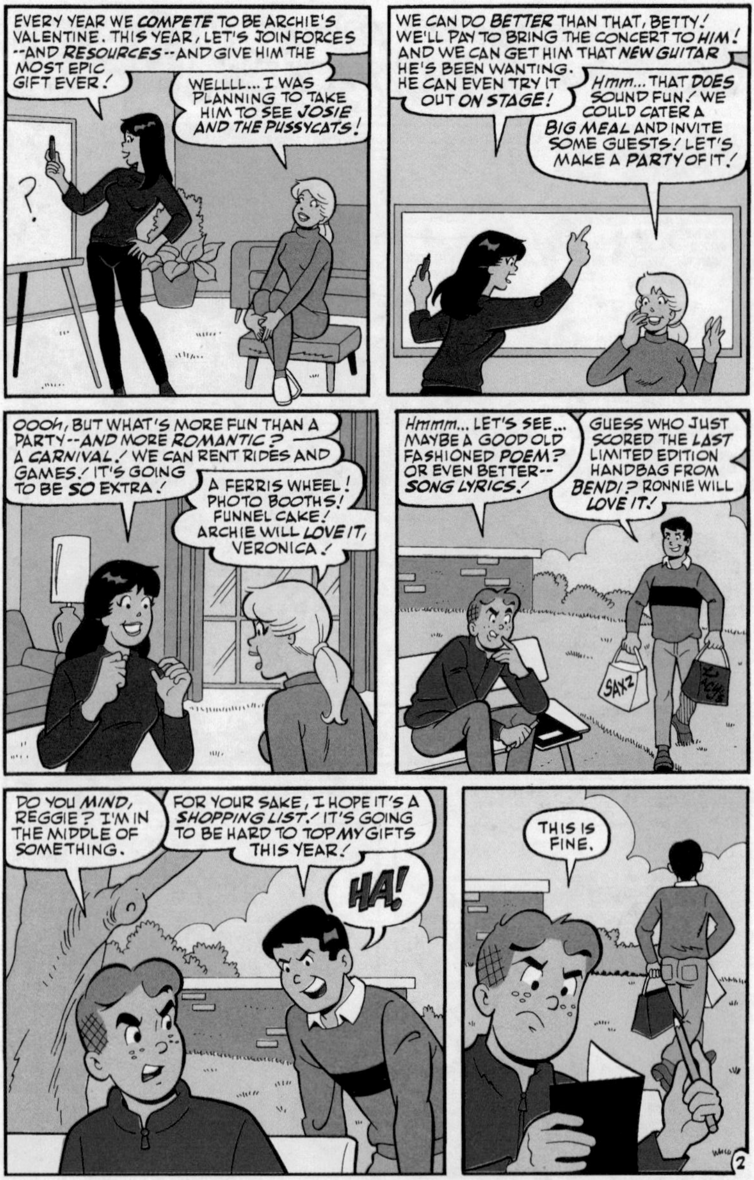
EVERY YEAR WE COMPETE TO BE ARCHIE'S VALENTINE. THIS YEAR, LET'S JOIN FORCES --AND RESOURCES--AND GIVE HIM THE MOST EPIC GIFT EVER!
WELLLL... I WAS PLANNING TO TAKE HIM TO SEE JOSIE AND THE PUSSYCATS!
WE CAN DO BETTER THAN THAT, BETTY! WE'LL PAY TO BRING THE CONCERT TO HIM! AND WE CAN GET HIM THAT NEW GUITAR HE'S BEEN WANTING. HE CAN EVEN TRY IT OUT ON STAGE!
Hmm... THAT DOES SOUND FUN! WE COULD CATER A BIG MEAL AND INVITE SOME GUESTS! LET'S MAKE A PARTY OF IT!
Oooh, BUT WHAT'S MORE FUN THAN A PARTY--AND MORE ROMANTIC? A CARNIVAL! WE CAN RENT RIDES AND GAMES! IT'S GOING TO BE SO EXTRA!
A FERRIS WHEEL! PHOTO BOOTHS! FUNNEL CAKE! ARCHIE WILL LOVE IT, VERONICA!
Hmmm... LET'S SEE... MAYBE A GOOD OLD FASHIONED POEM? OR EVEN BETTER-- SONG LYRICS!
GUESS WHO JUST SCORED THE LAST LIMITED EDITION HANDBAG FROM BENDI? RONNIE WILL LOVE IT!
DO YOU MIND, REGGIE? I'M IN THE MIDDLE OF SOMETHING.
FOR YOUR SAKE, I HOPE IT'S A SHOPPING LIST! IT'S GOING TO BE HARD TO TOP MY GIFTS THIS YEAR!
HA!
THIS IS FINE.
2

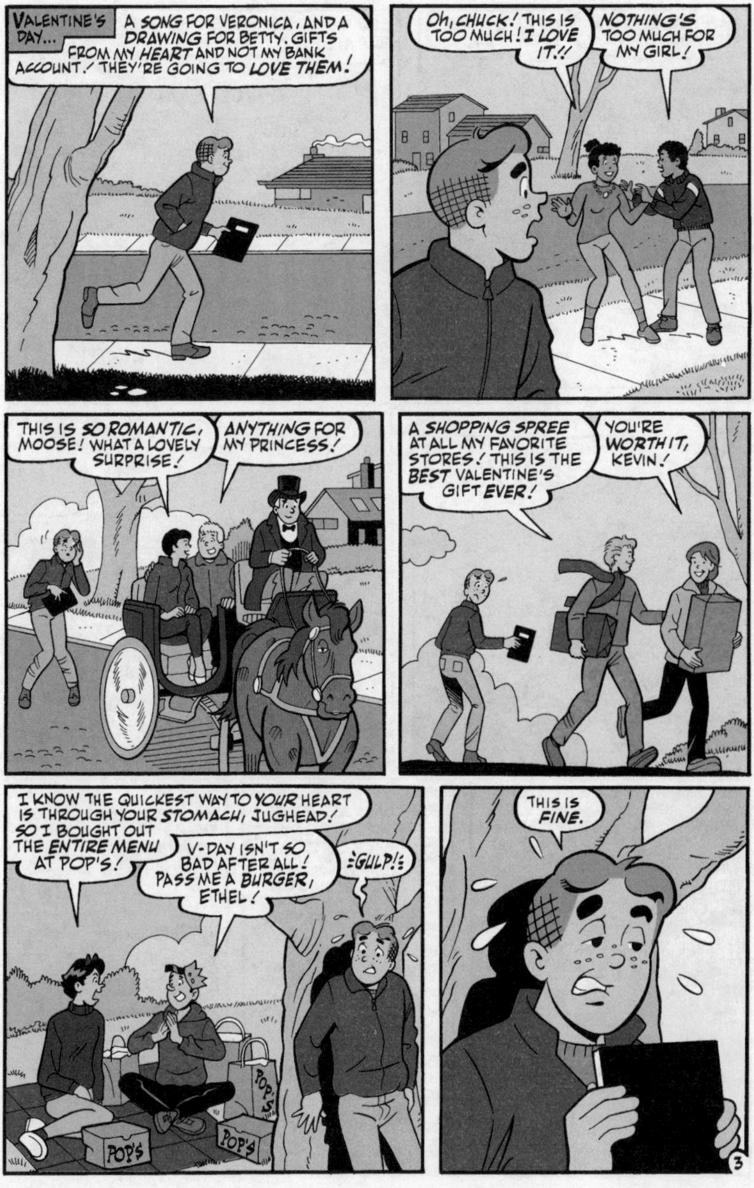
VALENTINE'S DAY...
A SONG FOR VERONICA, AND A DRAWING FOR BETTY. GIFTS FROM MY HEART AND NOT MY BANK ACCOUNT! THEY'RE GOING TO LOVE THEM!
OH, CHUCK! THIS IS TOO MUCH! I LOVE IT!!
NOTHING'S TOO MUCH FOR MY GIRL!
THIS IS SO ROMANTIC, MOOSE! WHAT A LOVELY SURPRISE!
ANYTHING FOR MY PRINCESS!
A SHOPPING SPREE AT ALL MY FAVORITE STORES! THIS IS THE BEST VALENTINE'S GIFT EVER!
YOU'RE WORTH IT, KEVIN!
I KNOW THE QUICKEST WAY TO YOUR HEART IS THROUGH YOUR STOMACH, JUGHEAD! SO I BOUGHT OUT THE ENTIRE MENU AT POP'S!
V-DAY ISN'T SO BAD AFTER ALL! PASS ME A BURGER, ETHEL!
GULP!
POP'S
POP'S
POP'S
POP'S
THIS IS FINE.
3

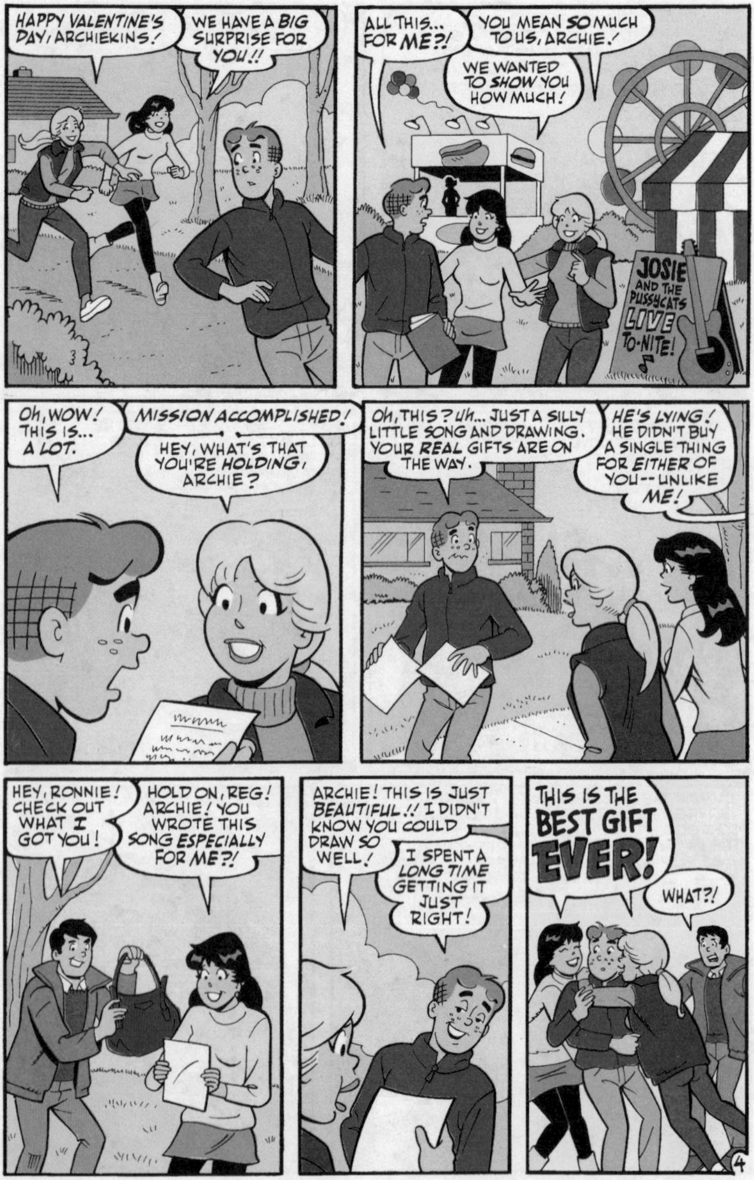
HAPPY VALENTINE'S DAY, ARCHIEKINS!
WE HAVE A BIG SURPRISE FOR YOU!!
ALL THIS... FOR ME?!
YOU MEAN SO MUCH TO US, ARCHIE!
WE WANTED TO SHOW YOU HOW MUCH!
JOSIE AND THE PUSSYCATS LIVE TO-NITE!
Oh, WOW! THIS IS... A LOT.
MISSION ACCOMPLISHED!
HEY, WHAT'S THAT YOU'RE HOLDING, ARCHIE?
Oh, THIS? uh... JUST A SILLY LITTLE SONG AND DRAWING. YOUR REAL GIFTS ARE ON THE WAY.
HE'S LYING! HE DIDN'T BUY A SINGLE THING FOR EITHER OF YOU-- UNLIKE ME!
HEY, RONNIE! CHECK OUT WHAT I GOT YOU!
HOLD ON, REG! ARCHIE! YOU WROTE THIS SONG ESPECIALLY FOR ME?!
ARCHIE! THIS IS JUST BEAUTIFUL!! I DIDN'T KNOW YOU COULD DRAW SO WELL!
I SPENT A LONG TIME GETTING IT JUST RIGHT!
THIS IS THE BEST GIFT EVER!
WHAT?!
4

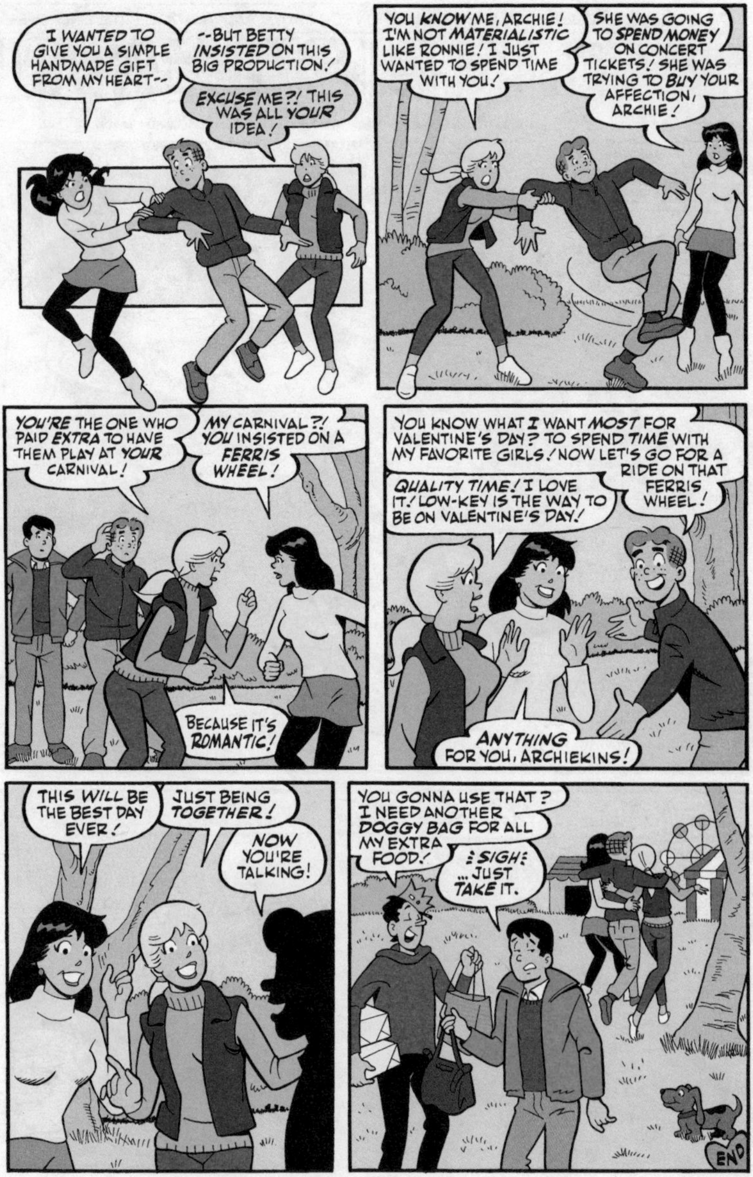
I WANTED TO GIVE YOU A SIMPLE HANDMADE GIFT FROM MY HEART--
--BUT BETTY INSISTED ON THIS BIG PRODUCTION!
EXCUSE ME?! THIS WAS ALL YOUR IDEA!
YOU KNOW ME, ARCHIE! I'M NOT MATERIALISTIC LIKE RONNIE! I JUST WANTED TO SPEND TIME WITH YOU!
SHE WAS GOING TO SPEND MONEY ON CONCERT TICKETS! SHE WAS TRYING TO BUY YOUR AFFECTION, ARCHIE!
YOU'RE THE ONE WHO PAID EXTRA TO HAVE THEM PLAY AT YOUR CARNIVAL!
MY CARNIVAL?! YOU INSISTED ON A FERRIS WHEEL!
BECAUSE IT'S ROMANTIC!
YOU KNOW WHAT I WANT MOST FOR VALENTINE'S DAY? TO SPEND TIME WITH MY FAVORITE GIRLS! NOW LET'S GO FOR A RIDE ON THAT FERRIS WHEEL!
QUALITY TIME! I LOVE IT! LOW-KEY IS THE WAY TO BE ON VALENTINE'S DAY!
ANYTHING FOR YOU, ARCHIEKINS!
THIS WILL BE THE BEST DAY EVER!
JUST BEING TOGETHER!
NOW YOU'RE TALKING!
YOU GONNA USE THAT? I NEED ANOTHER DOGGY BAG FOR ALL MY EXTRA FOOD!
SIGH ... JUST TAKE IT.
END

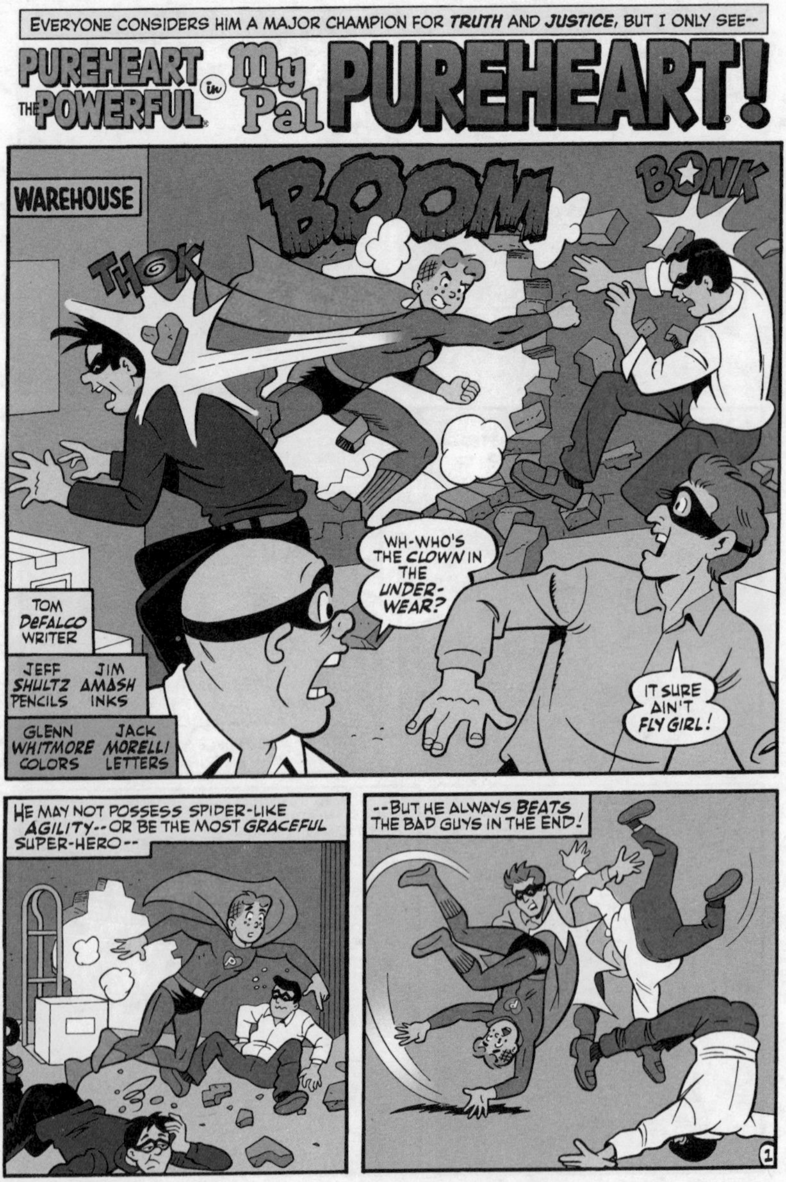
EVERYONE CONSIDERS HIM A MAJOR CHAMPION FOR TRUTH AND JUSTICE, BUT I ONLY SEE--
PUREHEART THE POWERFUL in My Pal PUREHEART!
WAREHOUSE
BOOM
BONK
THOK
WH-WHO'S THE CLOWN IN THE UNDER-WEAR?
IT SURE AIN'T FLY GIRL!
TOM DeFALCO WRITER
JEFF SHULTZ PENCILS
JIM AMASH INKS
GLENN WHITMORE COLORS
JACK MORELLI LETTERS
HE MAY NOT POSSESS SPIDER-LIKE AGILITY--OR BE THE MOST GRACEFUL SUPER-HERO--
--BUT HE ALWAYS BEATS THE BAD GUYS IN THE END!
1

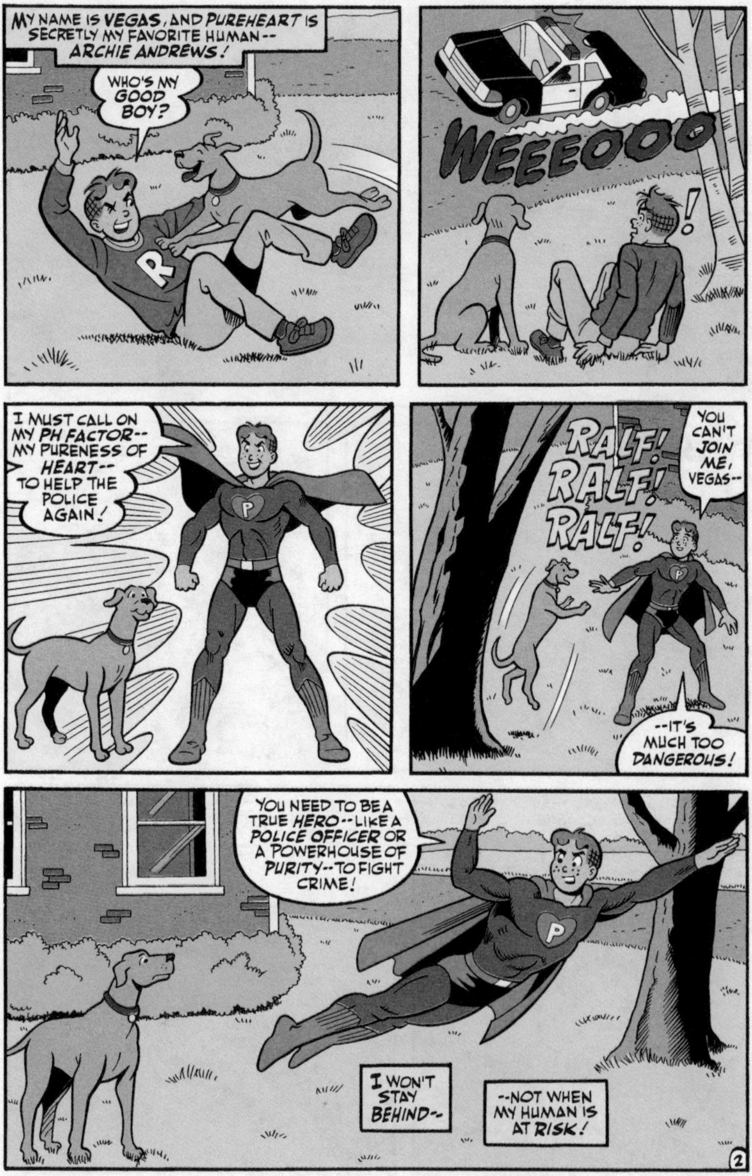
MY NAME IS VEGAS, AND PUREHEART IS SECRETLY MY FAVORITE HUMAN-- ARCHIE ANDREWS!
WHO'S MY GOOD BOY?
WEEEOOO
!
I MUST CALL ON MY PH FACTOR-- MY PURENESS OF HEART-- TO HELP THE POLICE AGAIN!
RALF! RALF! RALF!
YOU CAN'T JOIN ME, VEGAS--
--IT'S MUCH TOO DANGEROUS!
YOU NEED TO BE A TRUE HERO--LIKE A POLICE OFFICER OR A POWERHOUSE OF PURITY--TO FIGHT CRIME!
I WON'T STAY BEHIND--
--NOT WHEN MY HUMAN IS AT RISK!
2

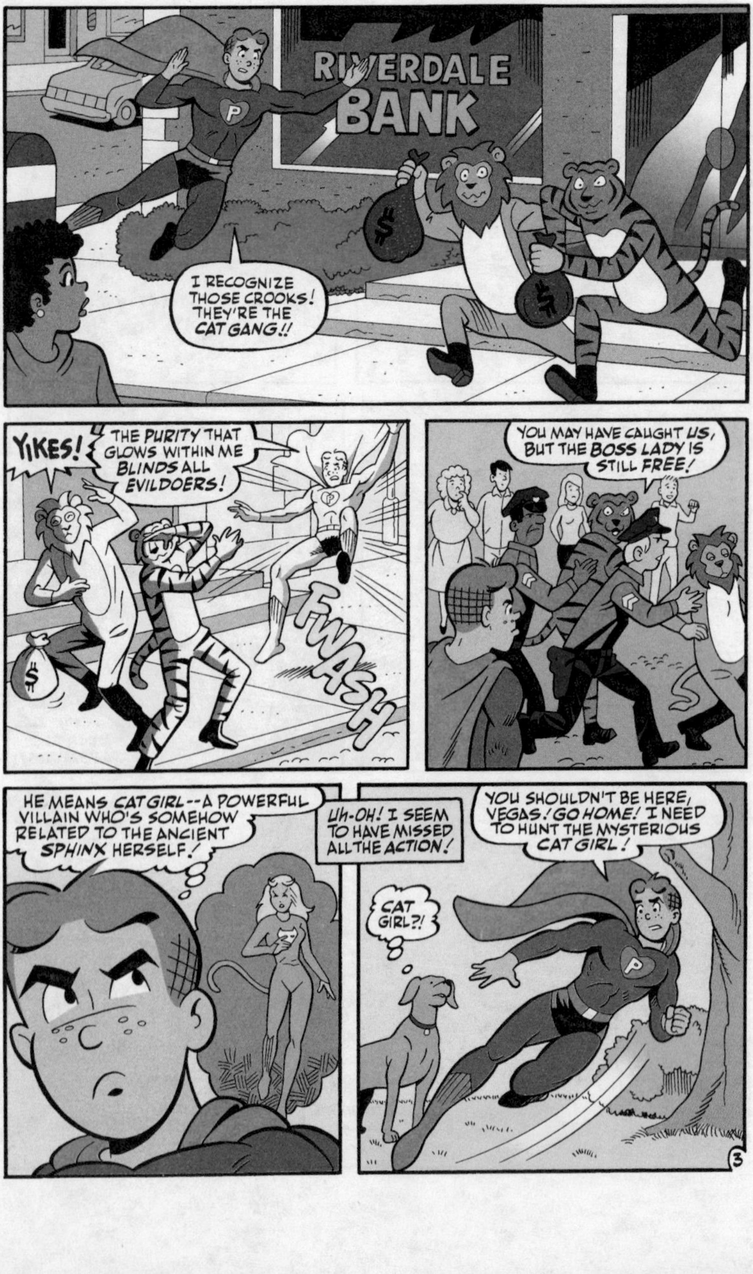
RIVERDALE BANK
I RECOGNIZE THOSE CROOKS! THEY'RE THE CAT GANG!!
YIKES!
THE PURITY THAT GLOWS WITHIN ME BLINDS ALL EVILDOERS!
FWASH
YOU MAY HAVE CAUGHT US, BUT THE BOSS LADY IS STILL FREE!
HE MEANS CAT GIRL--A POWERFUL VILLAIN WHO'S SOMEHOW RELATED TO THE ANCIENT SPHINX HERSELF!
UH-OH! I SEEM TO HAVE MISSED ALL THE ACTION!
YOU SHOULDN'T BE HERE, VEGAS! GO HOME! I NEED TO HUNT THE MYSTERIOUS CAT GIRL!
CAT GIRL?!
3

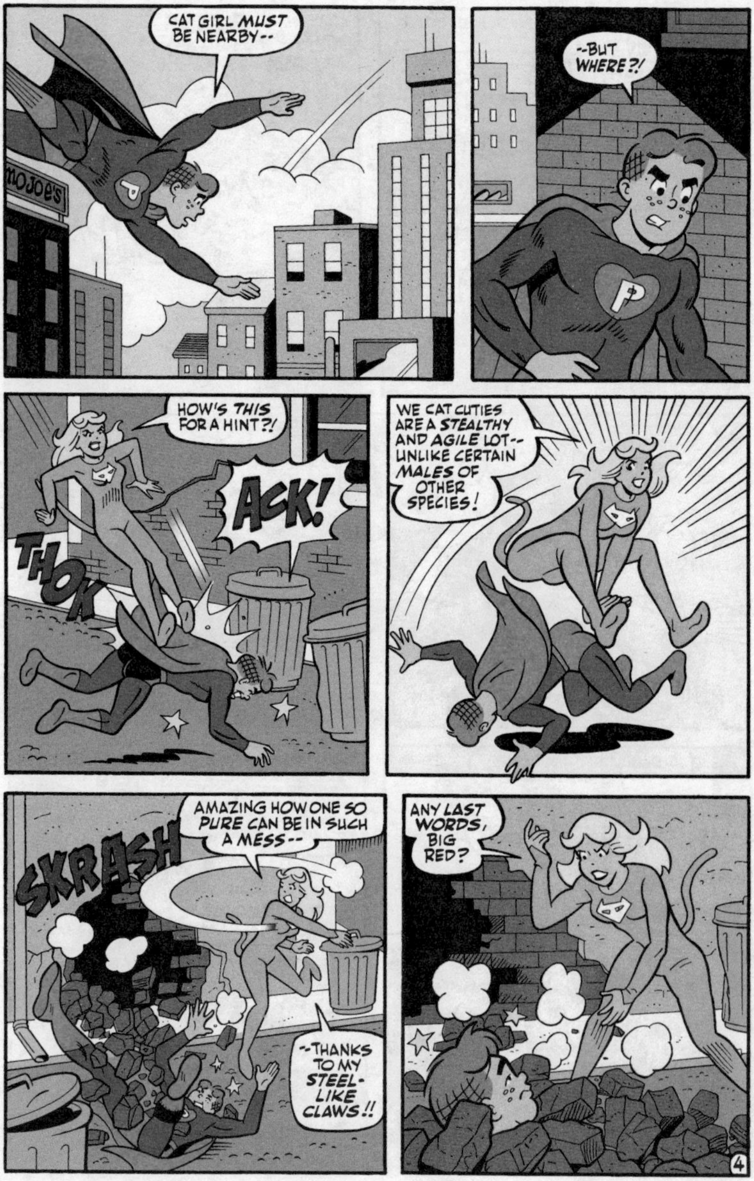
CAT GIRL MUST BE NEARBY--
MOJOE'S
--BUT WHERE?!
HOW'S THIS FOR A HINT?!
ACK!
THOK
WE CAT CUTIES ARE A STEALTHY AND AGILE LOT-- UNLIKE CERTAIN MALES OF OTHER SPECIES!
SKRASH
AMAZING HOW ONE SO PURE CAN BE IN SUCH A MESS--
--THANKS TO MY STEEL-LIKE CLAWS!!
ANY LAST WORDS, BIG RED?
4

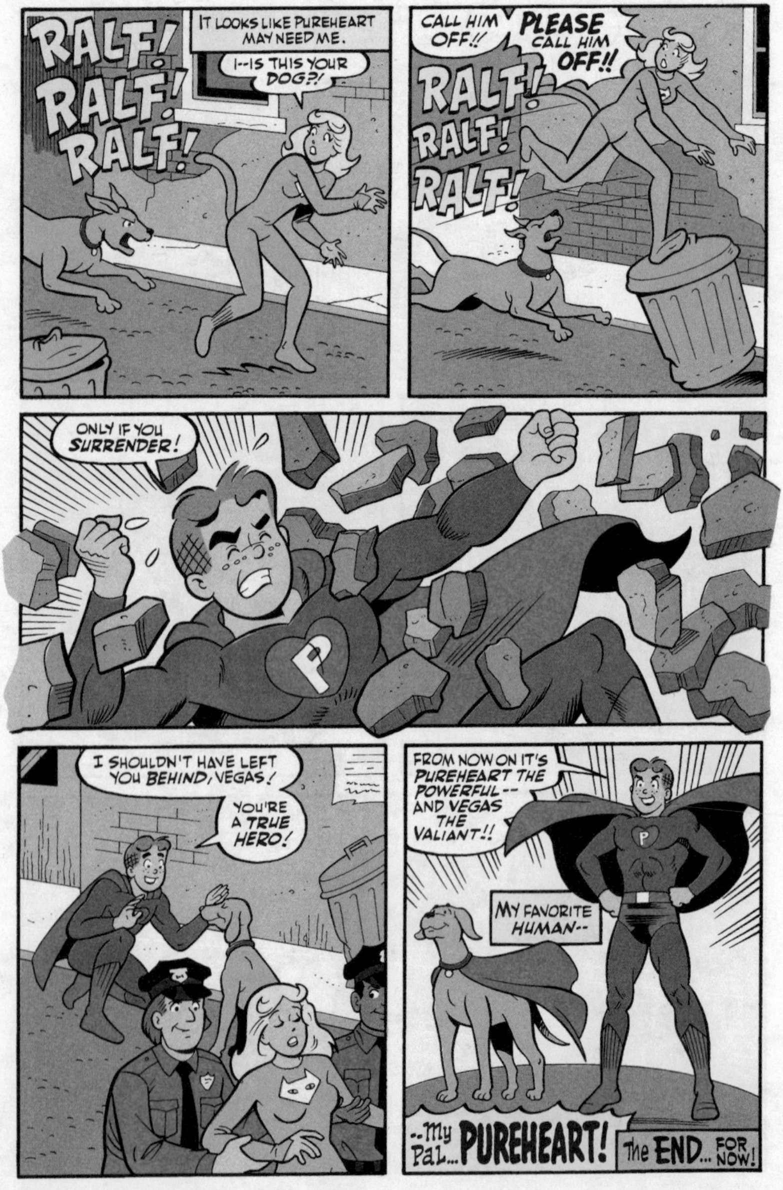
RALF! RALF! RALF!
IT LOOKS LIKE PUREHEART MAY NEED ME.
I--IS THIS YOUR DOG?!
CALL HIM OFF!!
PLEASE CALL HIM OFF!!
RALF! RALF! RALF!
ONLY IF YOU SURRENDER!
I SHOULDN'T HAVE LEFT YOU BEHIND, VEGAS!
YOU'RE A TRUE HERO!
FROM NOW ON IT'S PUREHEART THE POWERFUL-- AND VEGAS THE VALIANT!!
MY FAVORITE HUMAN--
--My Pal... PUREHEART!
The END... FOR NOW!

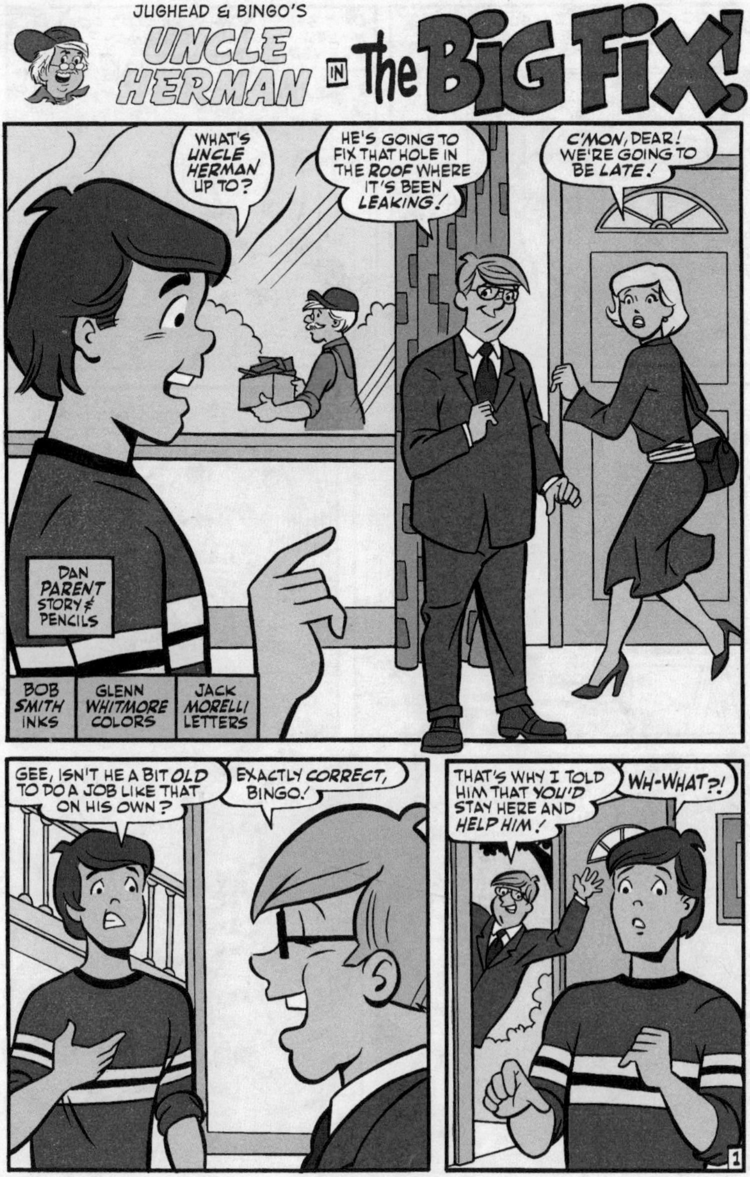
JUGHEAD & BINGO'S
UNCLE HERMAN
IN
The BIG FIX!
WHAT'S UNCLE HERMAN UP TO?
HE'S GOING TO FIX THAT HOLE IN THE ROOF WHERE IT'S BEEN LEAKING!
C'MON, DEAR! WE'RE GOING TO BE LATE!
DAN PARENT STORY & PENCILS
BOB SMITH INKS
GLENN WHITMORE COLORS
JACK MORELLI LETTERS
GEE, ISN'T HE A BIT OLD TO DO A JOB LIKE THAT ON HIS OWN?
EXACTLY CORRECT, BINGO!
THAT'S WHY I TOLD HIM THAT YOU'D STAY HERE AND HELP HIM!
WH-WHAT?!
1

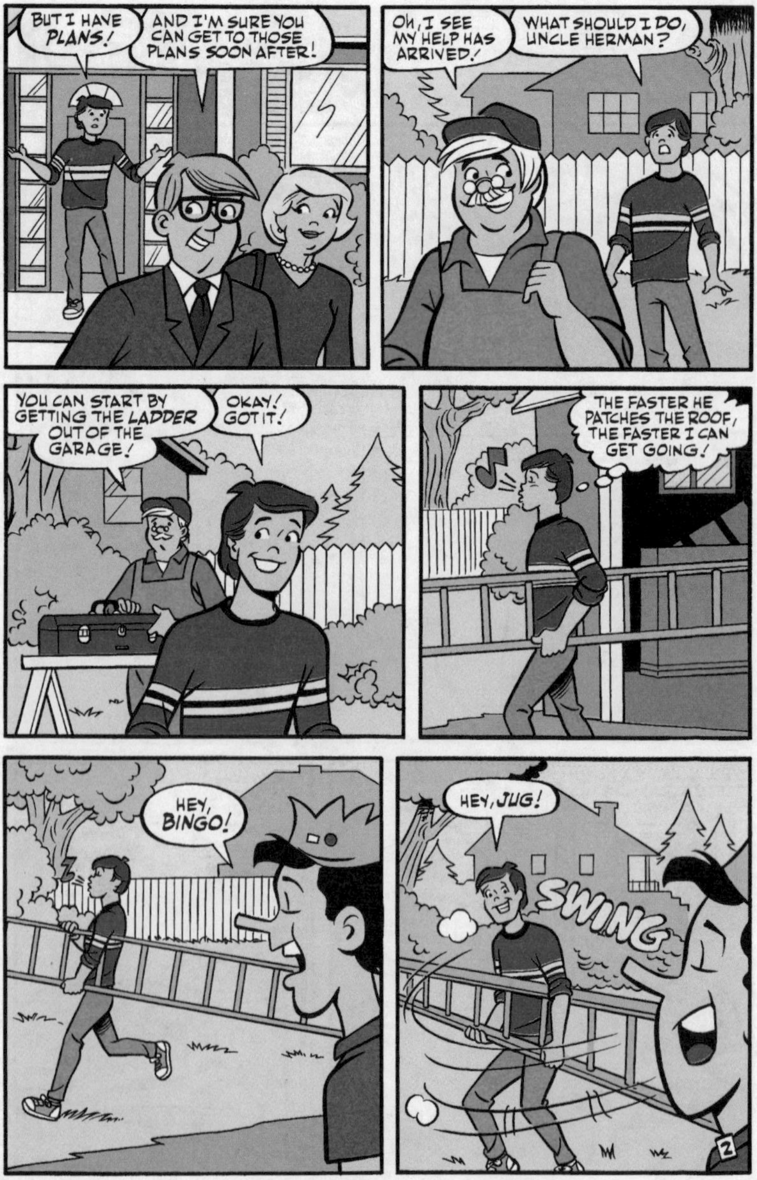
BUT I HAVE PLANS!
AND I'M SURE YOU CAN GET TO THOSE PLANS SOON AFTER!
OH, I SEE MY HELP HAS ARRIVED!
WHAT SHOULD I DO, UNCLE HERMAN?
YOU CAN START BY GETTING THE LADDER OUT OF THE GARAGE!
OKAY! GOT IT!
THE FASTER HE PATCHES THE ROOF, THE FASTER I CAN GET GOING!
HEY, BINGO!
HEY, JUG!
SWING
2

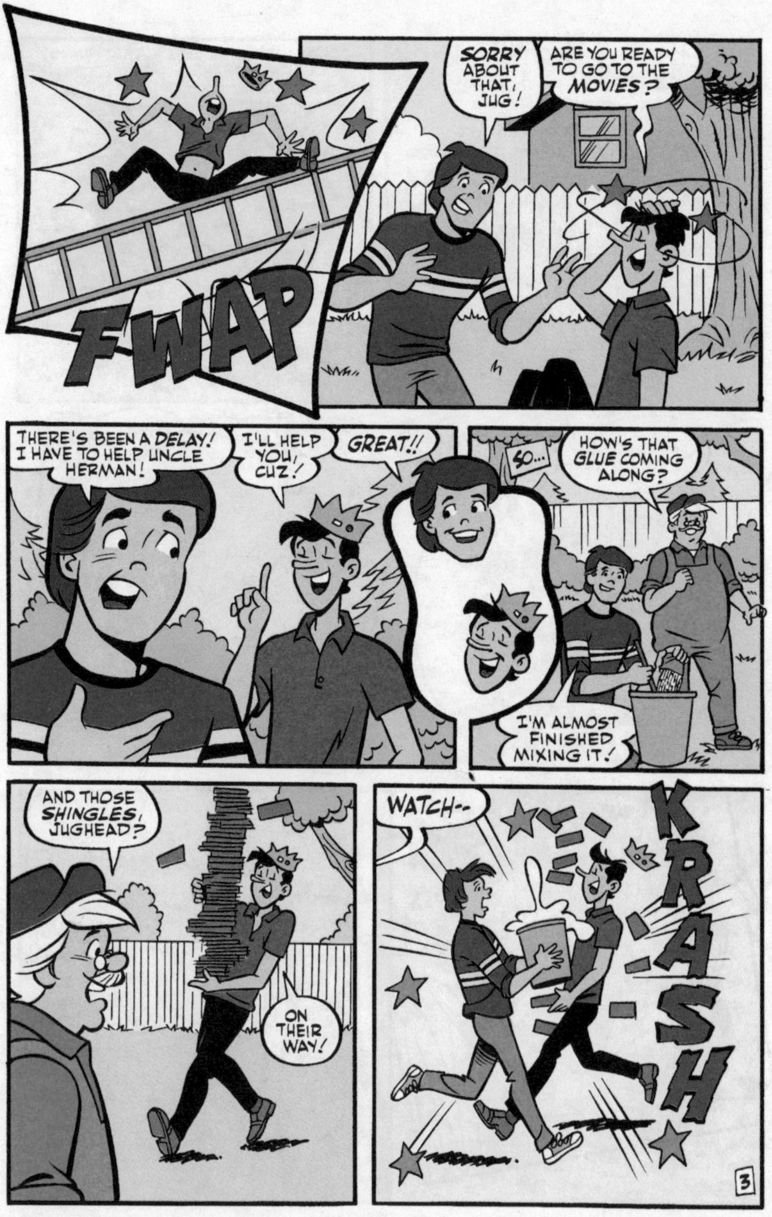
FWAP
SORRY ABOUT THAT, JUG!
ARE YOU READY TO GO TO THE MOVIES?
THERE'S BEEN A DELAY! I HAVE TO HELP UNCLE HERMAN!
I'LL HELP YOU, CUZ!
GREAT!!
SO...
HOW'S THAT GLUE COMING ALONG?
I'M ALMOST FINISHED MIXING IT!
AND THOSE SHINGLES, JUGHEAD?
ON THEIR WAY!
WATCH--
KRASH
3

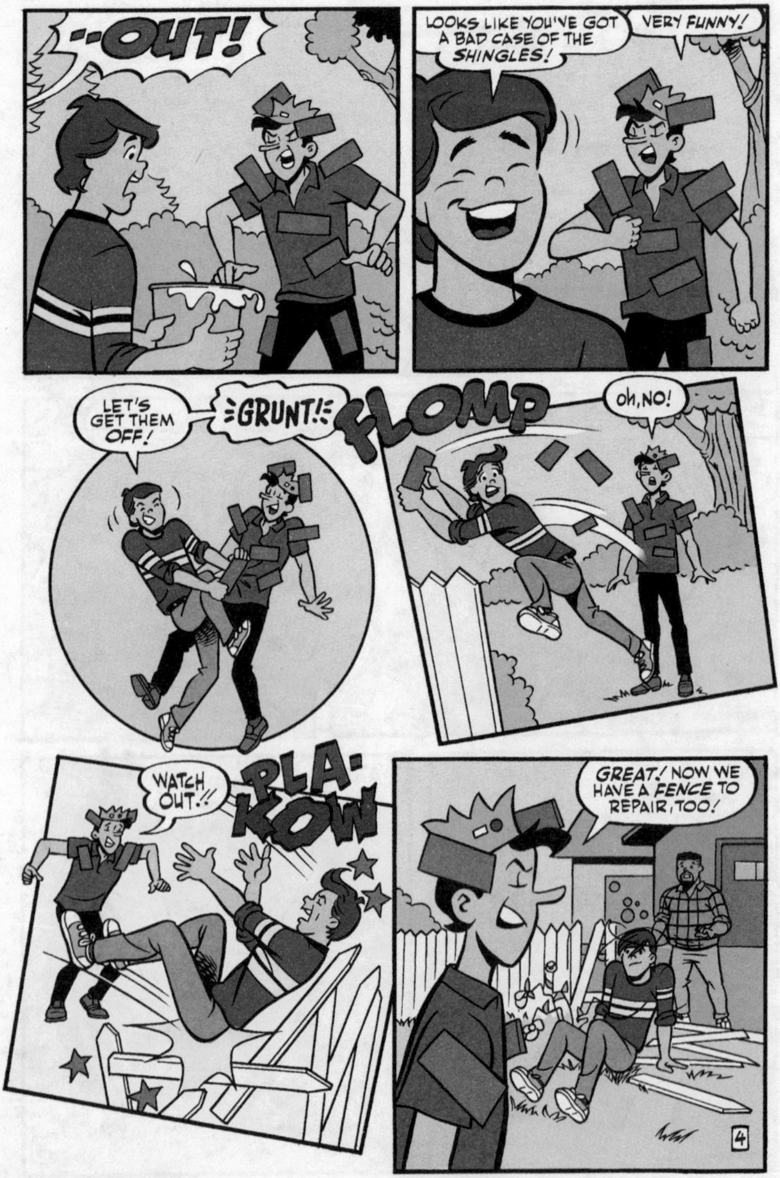
--OUT!
LOOKS LIKE YOU'VE GOT A BAD CASE OF THE SHINGLES!
VERY FUNNY!
LET'S GET THEM OFF!
GRUNT!
FLOMP
oh, NO!
WATCH OUT!!
PLA-KOW
GREAT! NOW WE HAVE A FENCE TO REPAIR, TOO!
4

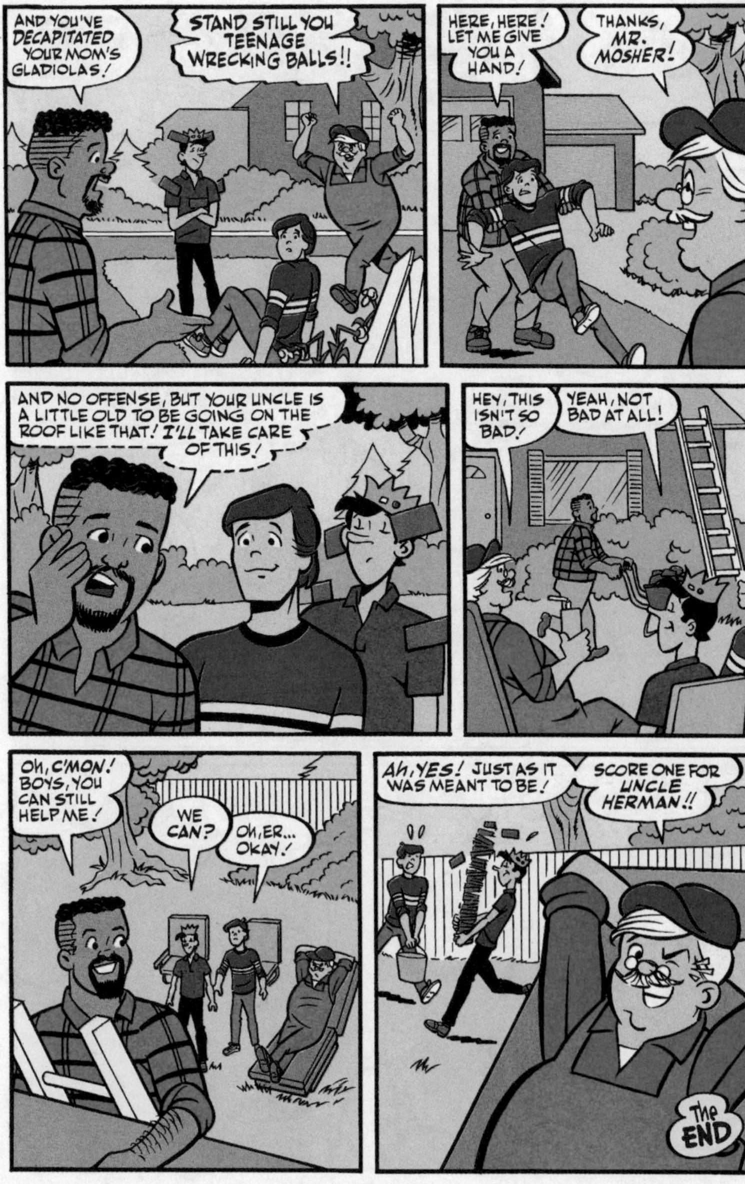
AND YOU'VE DECAPITATED YOUR MOM'S GLADIOLAS!
STAND STILL YOU TEENAGE WRECKING BALLS!!
HERE, HERE! LET ME GIVE YOU A HAND!
THANKS, MR. MOSHER!
AND NO OFFENSE, BUT YOUR UNCLE IS A LITTLE OLD TO BE GOING ON THE ROOF LIKE THAT! I'LL TAKE CARE OF THIS!
HEY, THIS ISN'T SO BAD!
YEAH, NOT BAD AT ALL!
OH, C'MON! BOYS, YOU CAN STILL HELP ME!
WE CAN?
OH, ER... OKAY!
AH, YES! JUST AS IT WAS MEANT TO BE!
SCORE ONE FOR UNCLE HERMAN!!
The END

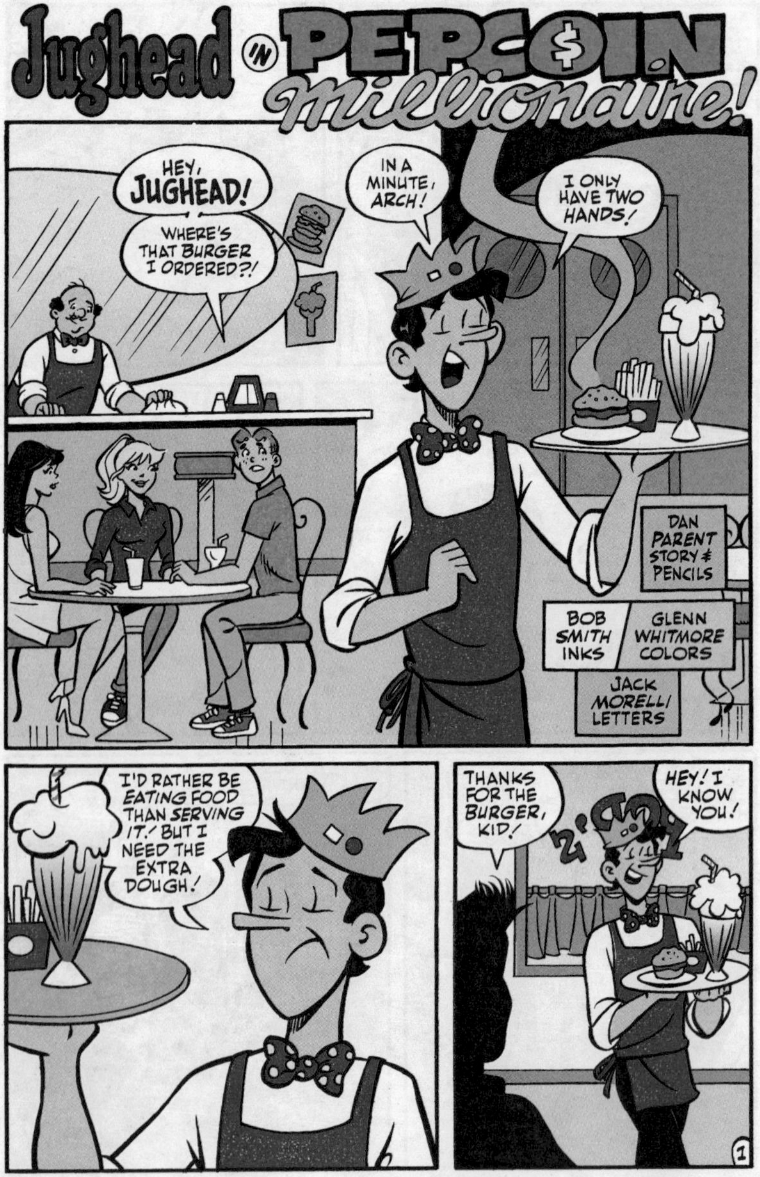
Jughead IN PEPCOIN Millionaire!
HEY, JUGHEAD!
WHERE'S THAT BURGER I ORDERED?!
IN A MINUTE, ARCH!
I ONLY HAVE TWO HANDS!
DAN PARENT STORY & PENCILS
BOB SMITH INKS
GLENN WHITMORE COLORS
JACK MORELLI LETTERS
I'D RATHER BE EATING FOOD THAN SERVING IT! BUT I NEED THE EXTRA DOUGH!
THANKS FOR THE BURGER, KID!
HEY! I KNOW YOU!
1

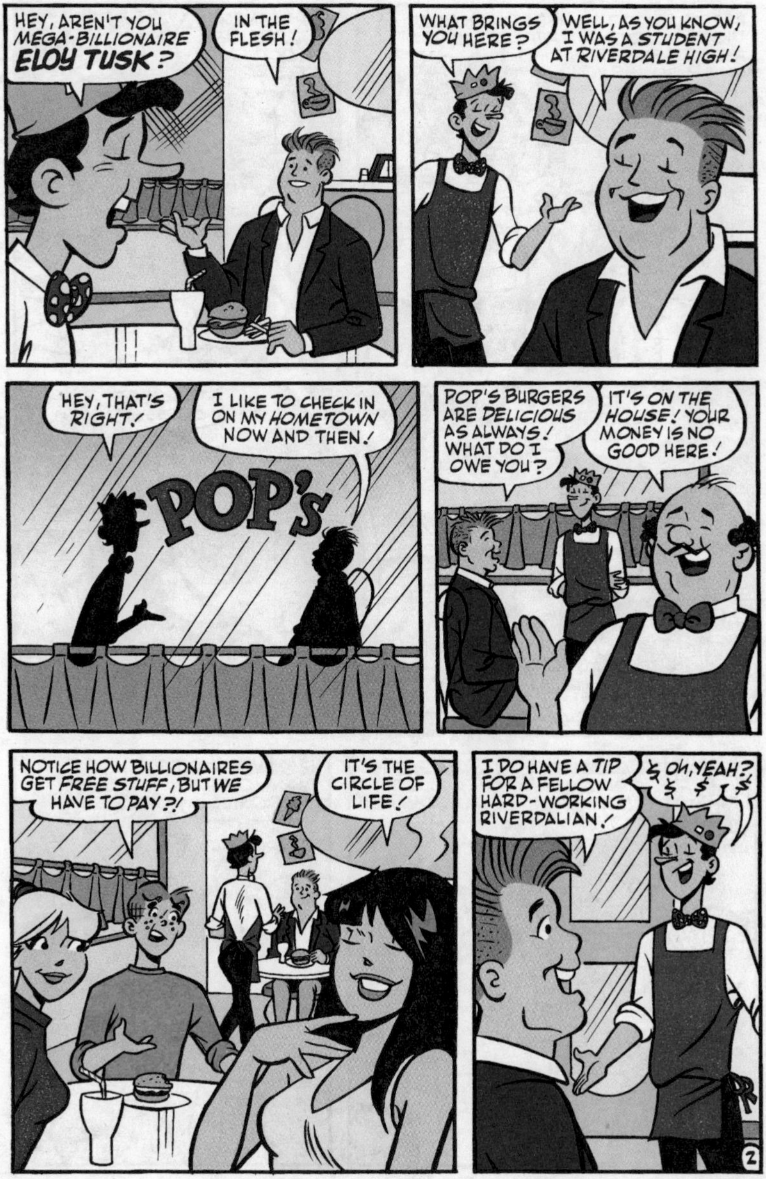
HEY, AREN'T YOU MEGA-BILLIONAIRE ELOY TUSK?
IN THE FLESH!
WHAT BRINGS YOU HERE?
WELL, AS YOU KNOW, I WAS A STUDENT AT RIVERDALE HIGH!
HEY, THAT'S RIGHT!
I LIKE TO CHECK IN ON MY HOMETOWN NOW AND THEN!
POP'S
POP'S BURGERS ARE DELICIOUS AS ALWAYS! WHAT DO I OWE YOU?
IT'S ON THE HOUSE! YOUR MONEY IS NO GOOD HERE!
NOTICE HOW BILLIONAIRES GET FREE STUFF, BUT WE HAVE TO PAY?!
IT'S THE CIRCLE OF LIFE!
I DO HAVE A TIP FOR A FELLOW HARD-WORKING RIVERDALIAN!
OH, YEAH?
2

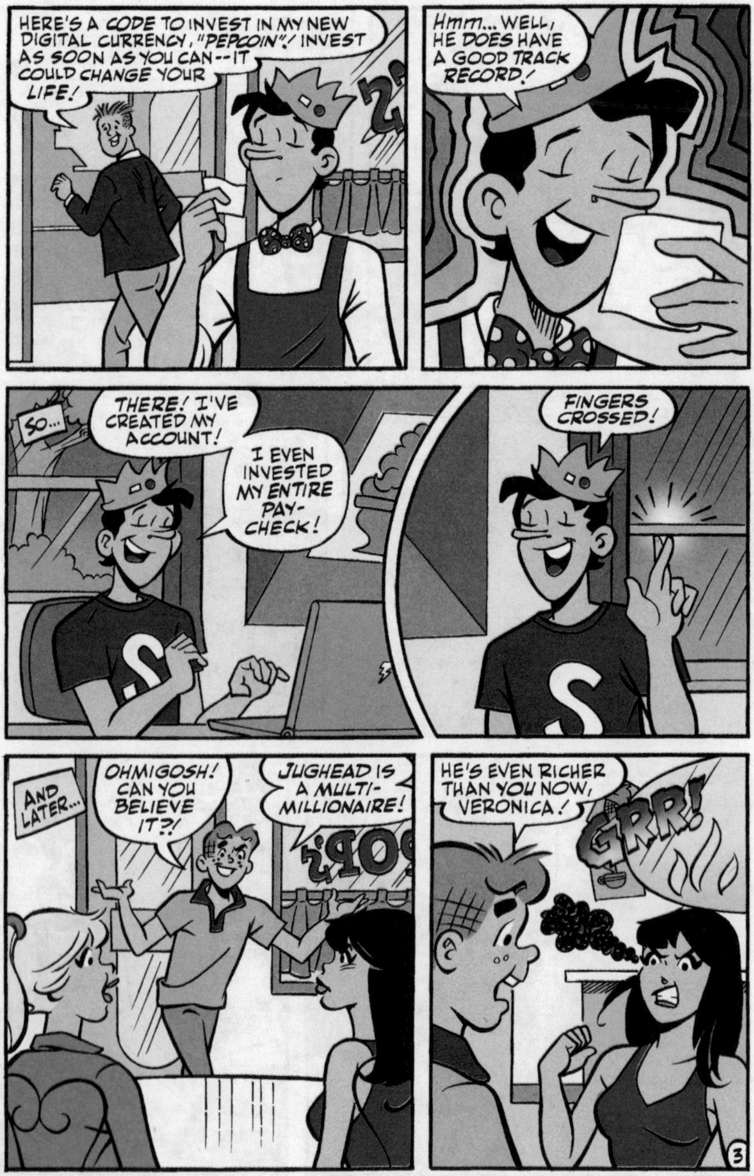
HERE'S A CODE TO INVEST IN MY NEW DIGITAL CURRENCY, "PEPCOIN"! INVEST AS SOON AS YOU CAN--IT COULD CHANGE YOUR LIFE!
Hmm... WELL, HE DOES HAVE A GOOD TRACK RECORD!
SO...
THERE! I'VE CREATED MY ACCOUNT!
I EVEN INVESTED MY ENTIRE PAY-CHECK!
FINGERS CROSSED!
AND LATER...
OHMIGOSH! CAN YOU BELIEVE IT?!
JUGHEAD IS A MULTI-MILLIONAIRE!
POP'S
HE'S EVEN RICHER THAN YOU NOW, VERONICA!
GRR!
3

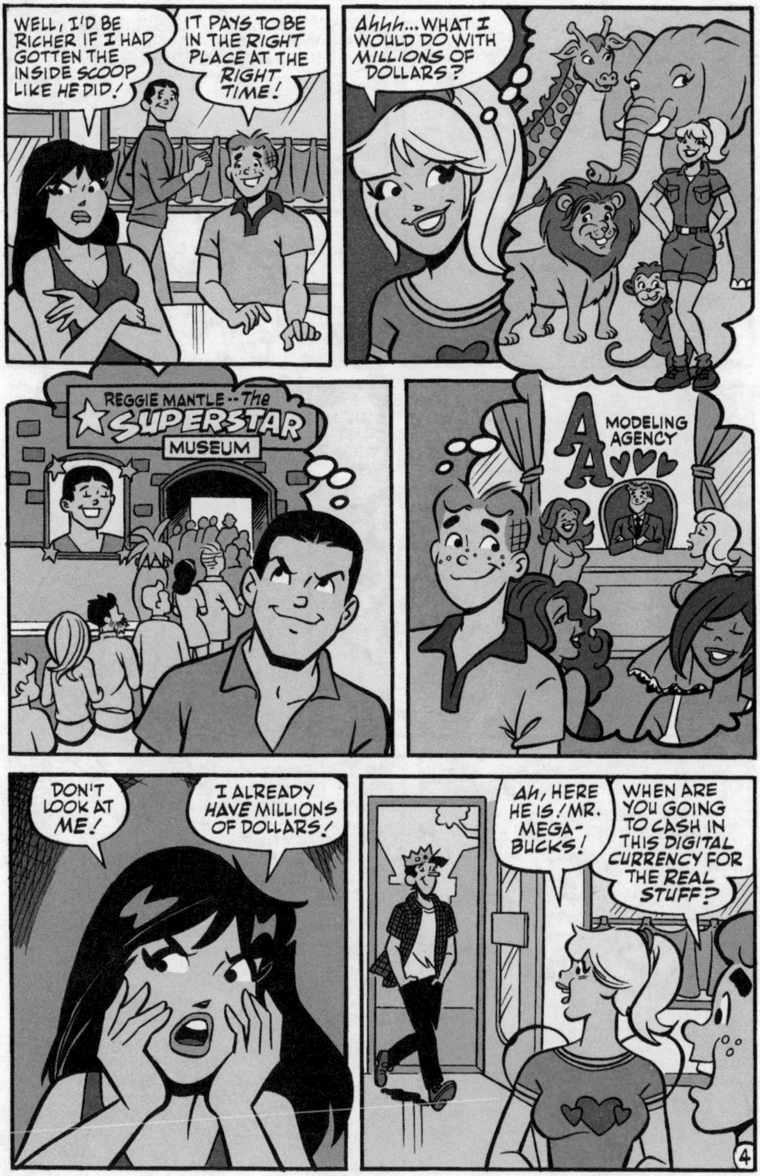
WELL, I'D BE RICHER IF I HAD GOTTEN THE INSIDE SCOOP LIKE HE DID!
IT PAYS TO BE IN THE RIGHT PLACE AT THE RIGHT TIME!
Ahhh... WHAT I WOULD DO WITH MILLIONS OF DOLLARS?
REGGIE MANTLE -- The SUPERSTAR MUSEUM
MODELING AGENCY
DON'T LOOK AT ME!
I ALREADY HAVE MILLIONS OF DOLLARS!
Ah, HERE HE IS! MR. MEGA-BUCKS!
WHEN ARE YOU GOING TO CASH IN THIS DIGITAL CURRENCY FOR THE REAL STUFF?
4

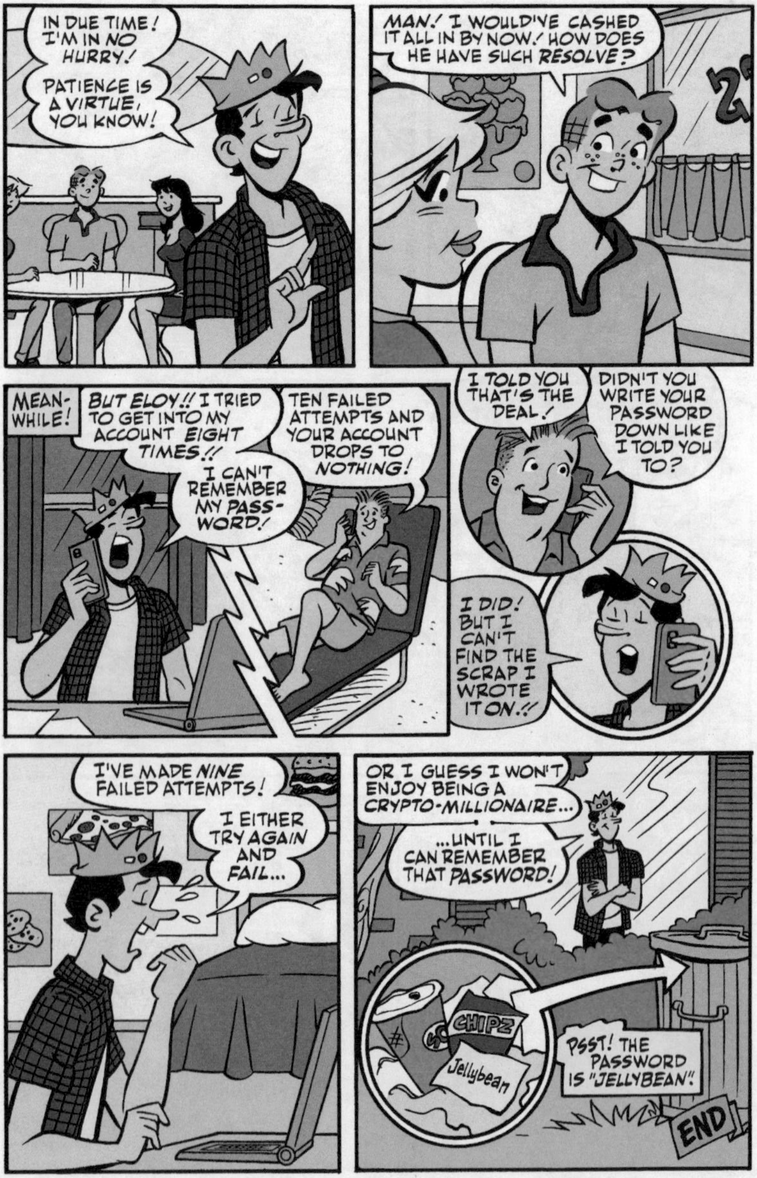

IN DUE TIME! I'M IN NO HURRY!
PATIENCE IS A VIRTUE, YOU KNOW!
MAN! I WOULD'VE CASHED IT ALL IN BY NOW! HOW DOES HE HAVE SUCH RESOLVE?
MEAN-WHILE!
BUT ELOY!! I TRIED TO GET INTO MY ACCOUNT EIGHT TIMES!!
I CAN'T REMEMBER MY PASS-WORD!
TEN FAILED ATTEMPTS AND YOUR ACCOUNT DROPS TO NOTHING!
I TOLD YOU THAT'S THE DEAL!
DIDN'T YOU WRITE YOUR PASSWORD DOWN LIKE I TOLD YOU TO?
I DID! BUT I CAN'T FIND THE SCRAP I WROTE IT ON!!
I'VE MADE NINE FAILED ATTEMPTS!
I EITHER TRY AGAIN AND FAIL...
OR I GUESS I WON'T ENJOY BEING A CRYPTO-MILLIONAIRE...
...UNTIL I CAN REMEMBER THAT PASSWORD!
CHIPZ
Jellybean
PSST! THE PASSWORD IS "JELLYBEAN"!
END

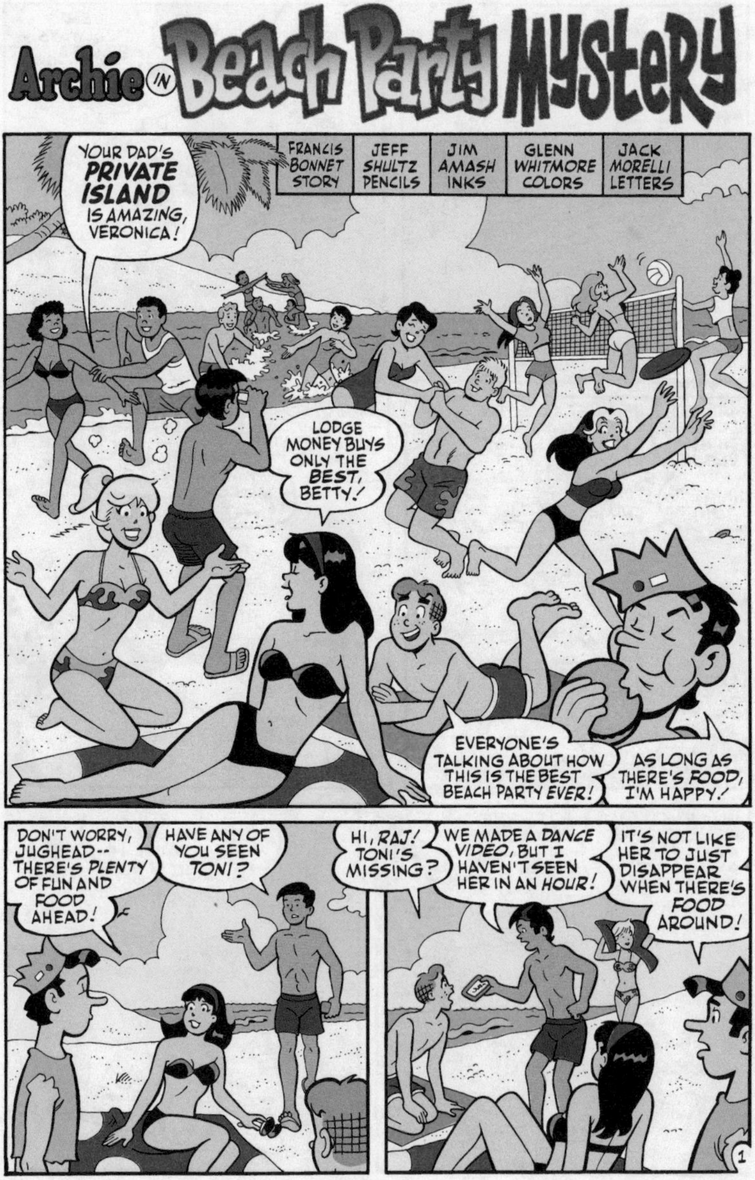
Archie IN Beach Party Mystery
YOUR DAD'S PRIVATE ISLAND IS AMAZING, VERONICA!
FRANCIS BONNET STORY
JEFF SHULTZ PENCILS
JIM AMASH INKS
GLENN WHITMORE COLORS
JACK MORELLI LETTERS
LODGE MONEY BUYS ONLY THE BEST, BETTY!
EVERYONE'S TALKING ABOUT HOW THIS IS THE BEST BEACH PARTY EVER!
AS LONG AS THERE'S FOOD, I'M HAPPY!
DON'T WORRY, JUGHEAD-- THERE'S PLENTY OF FUN AND FOOD AHEAD!
HAVE ANY OF YOU SEEN TONI?
HI, RAJ! TONI'S MISSING?
WE MADE A DANCE VIDEO, BUT I HAVEN'T SEEN HER IN AN HOUR!
IT'S NOT LIKE HER TO JUST DISAPPEAR WHEN THERE'S FOOD AROUND!
1

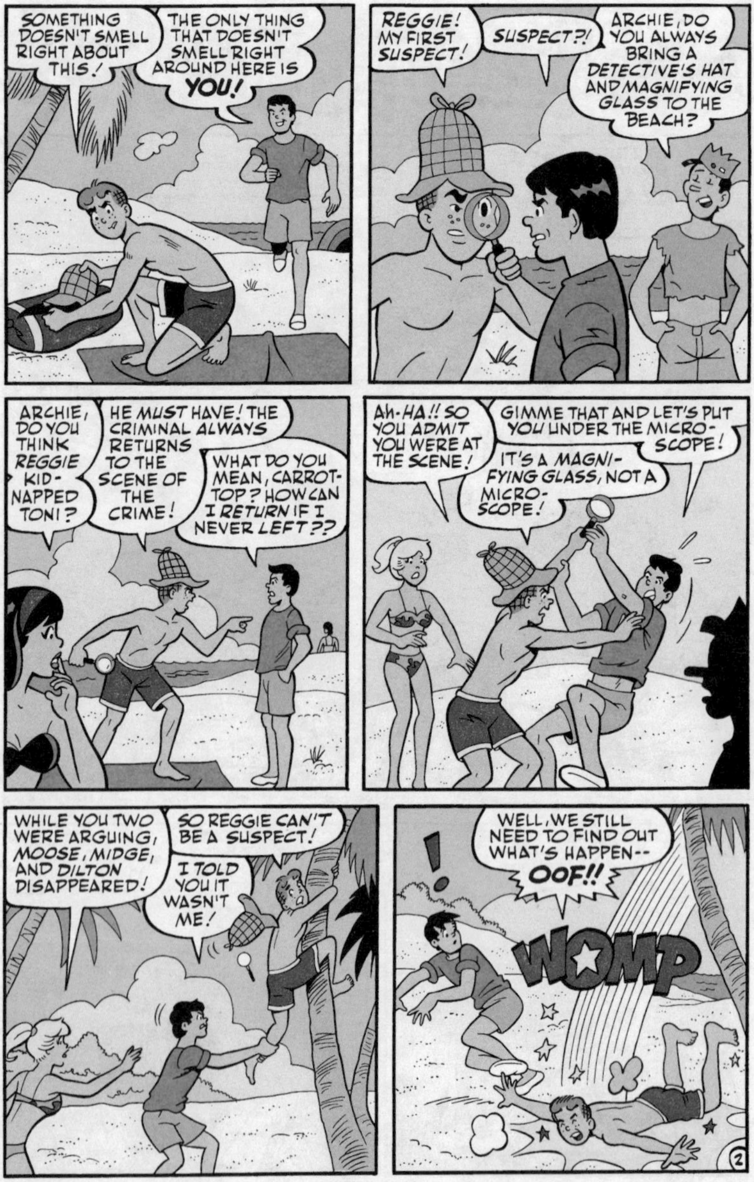
SOMETHING DOESN'T SMELL RIGHT ABOUT THIS!
THE ONLY THING THAT DOESN'T SMELL RIGHT AROUND HERE IS YOU!
REGGIE! MY FIRST SUSPECT!
SUSPECT?!
ARCHIE, DO YOU ALWAYS BRING A DETECTIVE'S HAT AND MAGNIFYING GLASS TO THE BEACH?
ARCHIE, DO YOU THINK REGGIE KID-NAPPED TONI?
HE MUST HAVE! THE CRIMINAL ALWAYS RETURNS TO THE SCENE OF THE CRIME!
WHAT DO YOU MEAN, CARROT-TOP? HOW CAN I RETURN IF I NEVER LEFT??
AH-HA!! SO YOU ADMIT YOU WERE AT THE SCENE!
GIMME THAT AND LET'S PUT YOU UNDER THE MICRO-SCOPE!
IT'S A MAGNI-FYING GLASS, NOT A MICRO-SCOPE!
WHILE YOU TWO WERE ARGUING, MOOSE, MIDGE, AND DILTON DISAPPEARED!
SO REGGIE CAN'T BE A SUSPECT!
I TOLD YOU IT WASN'T ME!
!
WELL, WE STILL NEED TO FIND OUT WHAT'S HAPPEN-- OOF!!
WOMP
2

I'LL SOLVE THIS MYSTERY AND SHOW BETTY AND VERONICA THAT I'M INTELLECTUALLY SUPERIOR TO YOU!
I'M THE DETECTIVE HERE! YOU CAN BE MY SIDEKICK-- LIKE WATSON!
I'M NO SIDEKICK!!
NOW NANCY, CHUCK, AND GINGER ARE MISSING!
Oh, NO! WE'D BETTER LOOK FOR CLUES!
AS USUAL, I'M ONE STEP AHEAD OF YOU!
THESE FOOTPRINTS LEAD INTO THE FOREST! THEY MUST BELONG TO THE CULPRIT!
REGGIE, THOSE ARE SEA-GULL'S PRINTS!
YOU'RE NOT A VERY GOOD SIDE-KICK, WATSON!
DON'T CALL ME WATSON!!
IT'S OBVIOUS THAT THESE ARE THE FOOTPRINTS BELONGING TO OUR SUSPECT!
ARCHIE, THOSE ARE YOUR FOOT-PRINTS!!
3

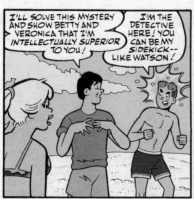

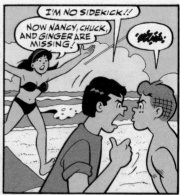

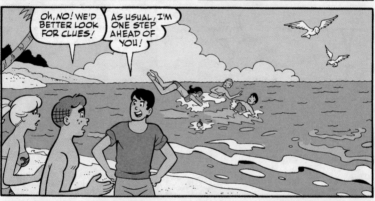

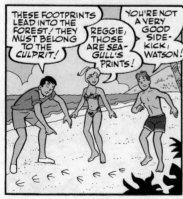

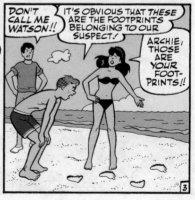

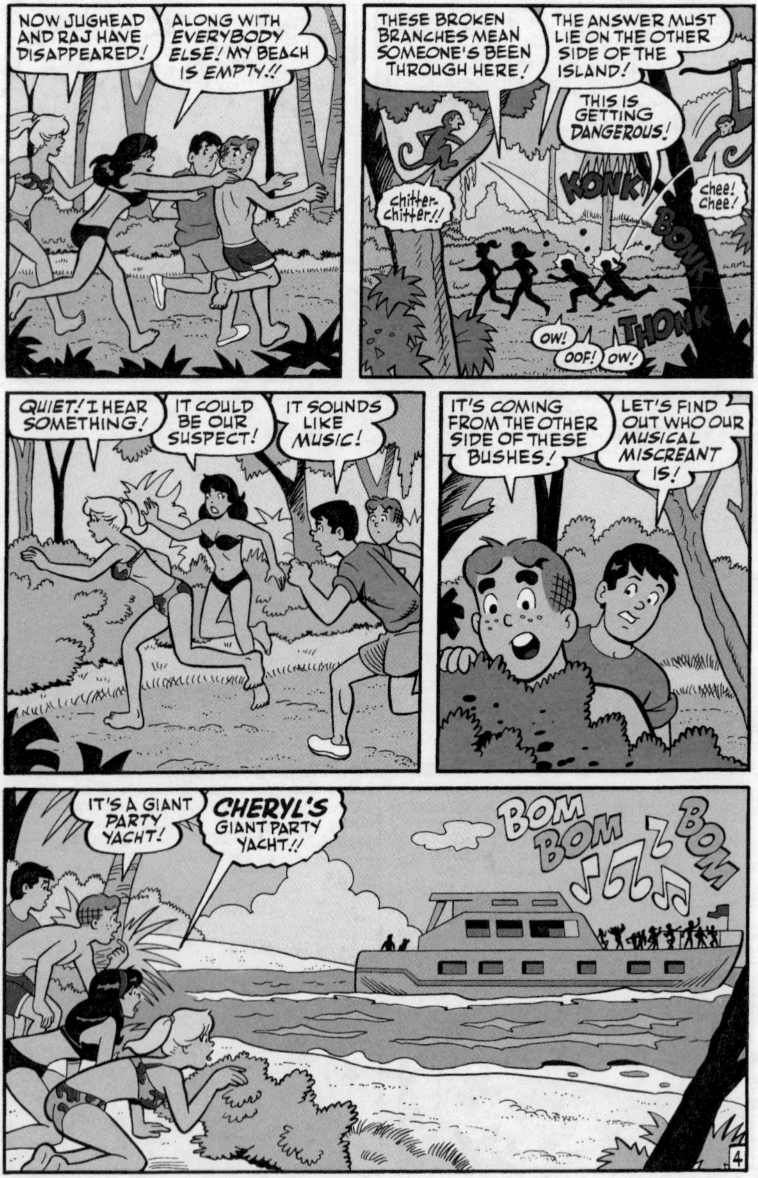
NOW JUGHEAD AND RAJ HAVE DISAPPEARED!
ALONG WITH EVERYBODY ELSE! MY BEACH IS EMPTY!!
THESE BROKEN BRANCHES MEAN SOMEONE'S BEEN THROUGH HERE!
THE ANSWER MUST LIE ON THE OTHER SIDE OF THE ISLAND!
THIS IS GETTING DANGEROUS!
chitter-chitter!!
KONK
chee! chee!
BONK
THONK
OW!
OOF!
OW!
QUIET! I HEAR SOMETHING!
IT COULD BE OUR SUSPECT!
IT SOUNDS LIKE MUSIC!
IT'S COMING FROM THE OTHER SIDE OF THESE BUSHES!
LET'S FIND OUT WHO OUR MUSICAL MISCREANT IS!
IT'S A GIANT PARTY YACHT!
CHERYL'S GIANT PARTY YACHT!!
BOM
BOM
BOM
4

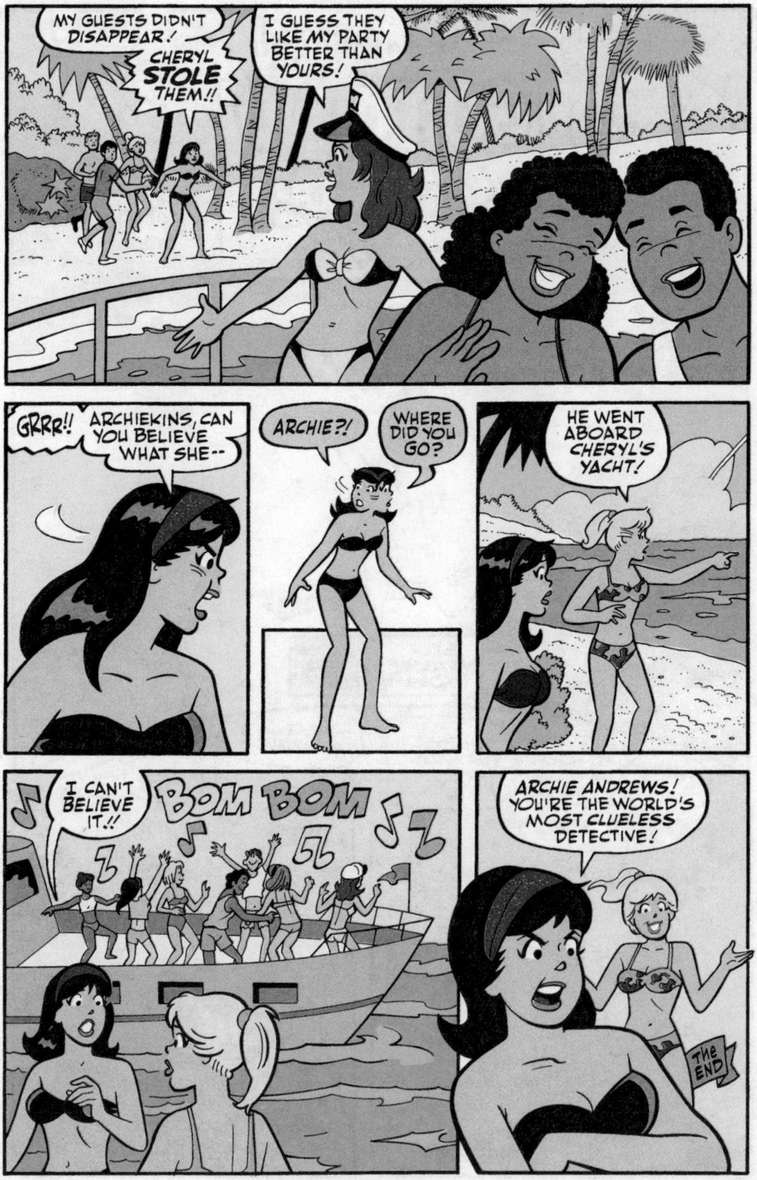
MY GUESTS DIDN'T DISAPPEAR!
CHERYL STOLE THEM!!
I GUESS THEY LIKE MY PARTY BETTER THAN YOURS!
GRRR!!
ARCHIEKINS, CAN YOU BELIEVE WHAT SHE--
ARCHIE?!
WHERE DID YOU GO?
HE WENT ABOARD CHERYL'S YACHT!
I CAN'T BELIEVE IT!!
BOM BOM
ARCHIE ANDREWS! YOU'RE THE WORLD'S MOST CLUELESS DETECTIVE!
THE END

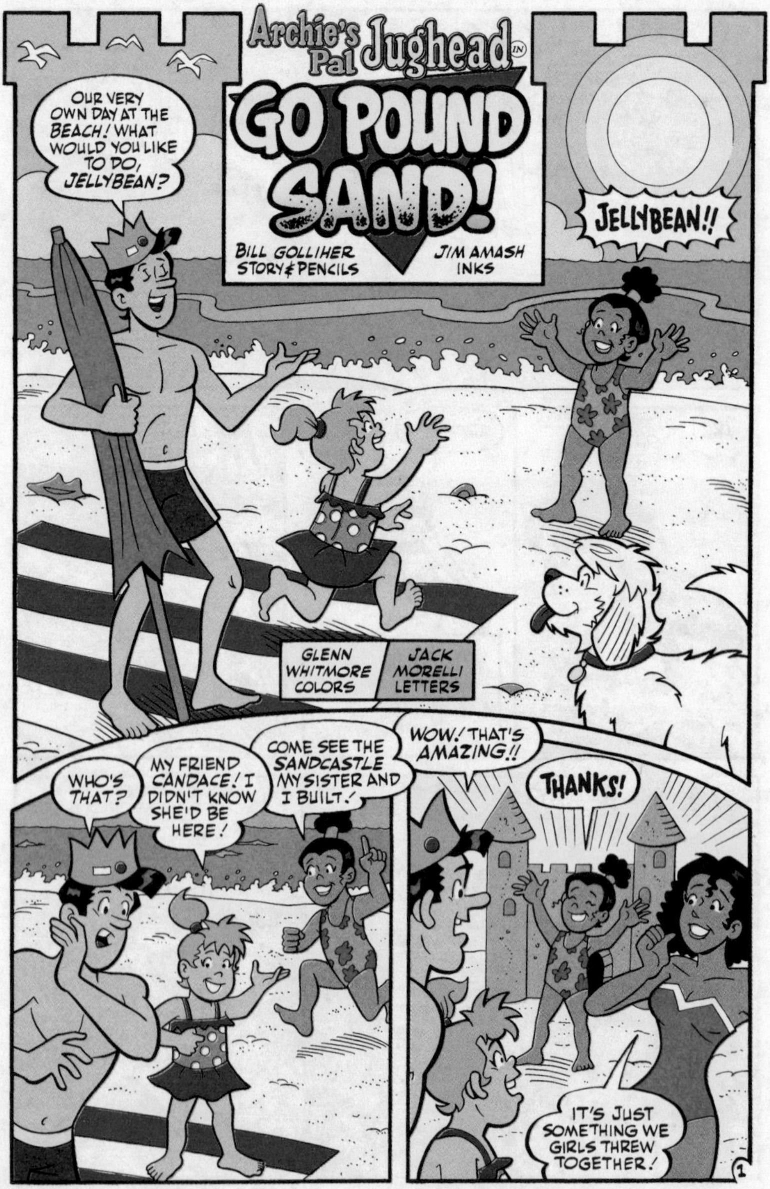
Archie's Pal Jughead
GO POUND SAND!
BILL GOLLIHER STORY & PENCILS
JIM AMASH INKS
OUR VERY OWN DAY AT THE BEACH! WHAT WOULD YOU LIKE TO DO, JELLYBEAN?
JELLYBEAN!!
GLENN WHITMORE COLORS
JACK MORELLI LETTERS
WHO'S THAT?
MY FRIEND CANDACE! I DIDN'T KNOW SHE'D BE HERE!
COME SEE THE SANDCASTLE MY SISTER AND I BUILT!
WOW! THAT'S AMAZING!!
THANKS!
IT'S JUST SOMETHING WE GIRLS THREW TOGETHER!
1

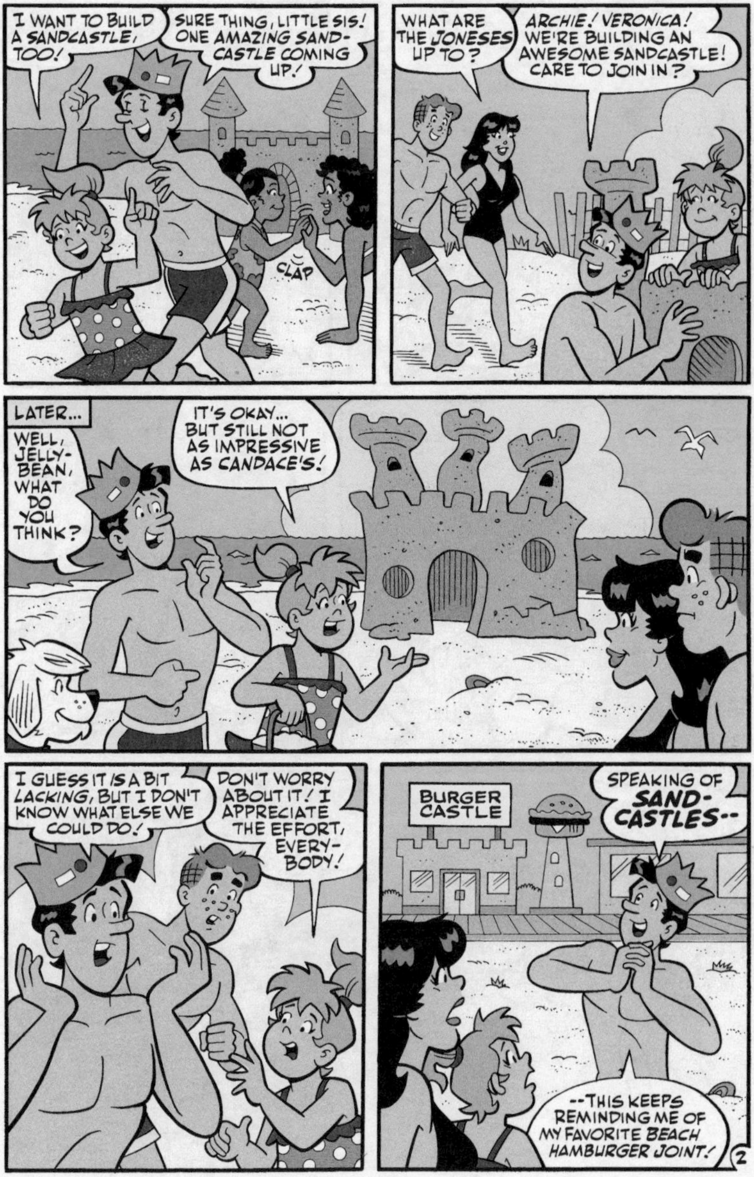
I WANT TO BUILD A SANDCASTLE, TOO!
SURE THING, LITTLE SIS! ONE AMAZING SAND-CASTLE COMING UP!
CLAP
WHAT ARE THE JONESES UP TO?
ARCHIE! VERONICA! WE'RE BUILDING AN AWESOME SANDCASTLE! CARE TO JOIN IN?
LATER...
WELL, JELLY-BEAN, WHAT DO YOU THINK?
IT'S OKAY... BUT STILL NOT AS IMPRESSIVE AS CANDACE'S!
I GUESS IT IS A BIT LACKING, BUT I DON'T KNOW WHAT ELSE WE COULD DO!
DON'T WORRY ABOUT IT! I APPRECIATE THE EFFORT, EVERY-BODY!
BURGER CASTLE
SPEAKING OF SAND-CASTLES--
--THIS KEEPS REMINDING ME OF MY FAVORITE BEACH HAMBURGER JOINT!
2

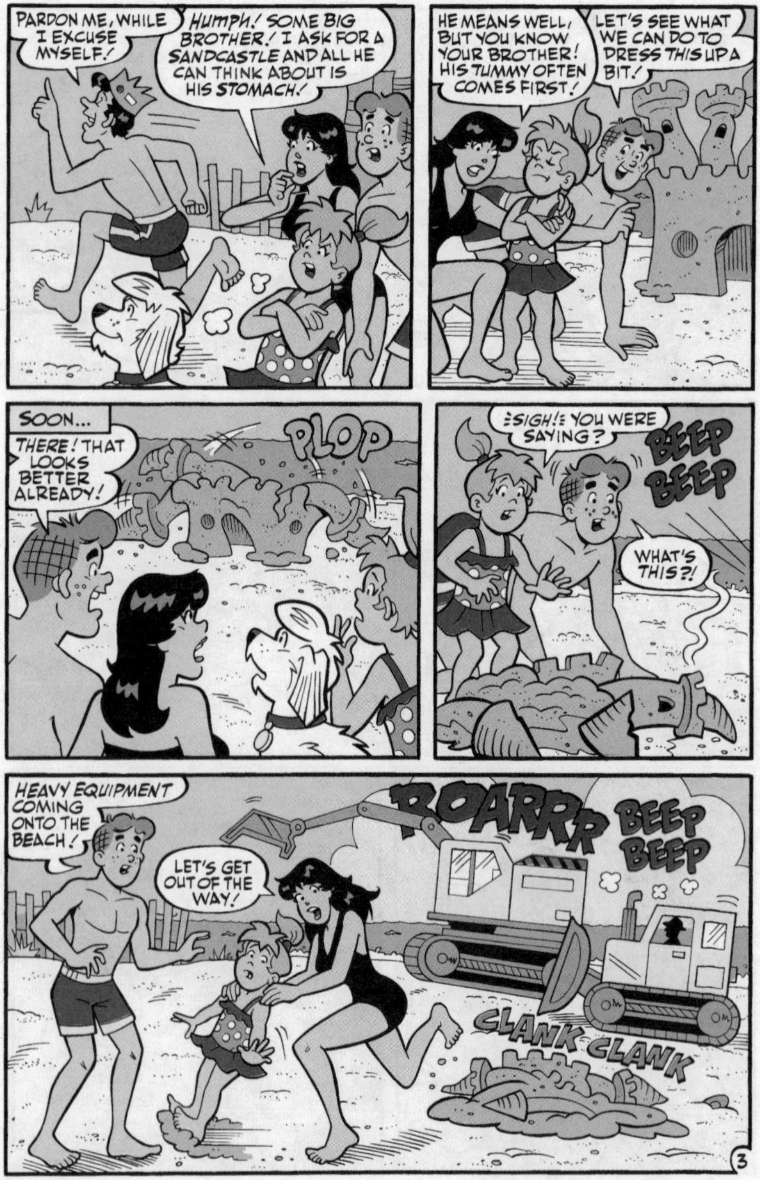
PARDON ME, WHILE I EXCUSE MYSELF!
Humph! SOME BIG BROTHER! I ASK FOR A SANDCASTLE AND ALL HE CAN THINK ABOUT IS HIS STOMACH!
HE MEANS WELL, BUT YOU KNOW YOUR BROTHER! HIS TUMMY OFTEN COMES FIRST!
LET'S SEE WHAT WE CAN DO TO DRESS THIS UP A BIT!
SOON...
THERE! THAT LOOKS BETTER ALREADY!
PLOP
SIGH! YOU WERE SAYING?
BEEP BEEP
WHAT'S THIS?!
HEAVY EQUIPMENT COMING ONTO THE BEACH!
LET'S GET OUT OF THE WAY!
ROARRR
BEEP BEEP
CLANK CLANK
3

LOOK AT THAT! I THINK THEY'RE FASHIONING AN ENORMOUS SANDCASTLE!
GLAD TO SEE THAT THEY TOOK MY ADVICE!
BEEP BEEP
VROARR
WHAT?!
I SUGGESTED TO BURGER CASTLE THAT A GIANT SANDCASTLE ON THE BEACH WOULD BE THE PERFECT WAY TO ADVERTISE!
THERE! THE CROWNING TOUCH-- BURGER CASTLE FLAGS ON EACH TURRET!
BURGER CASTLE
THAT'S WHY YOU WENT TO THE RESTAURANT-- TO ASK THEM TO DO THIS?
IT WASN'T TO EAT?!
OF COURSE NOT! NOTHING'S TOO GOOD FOR MY LITTLE SIS!
THIS IS AWESOME! CAN I PLAY IN YOUR SANDCASTLE, JELLYBEAN?!
SURE! COME ON IN!
4

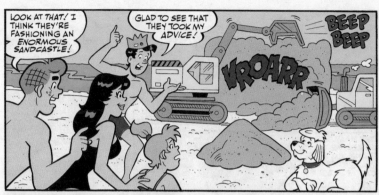

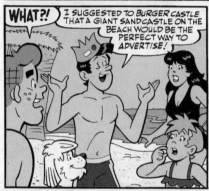

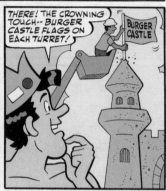

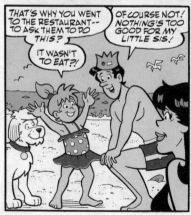

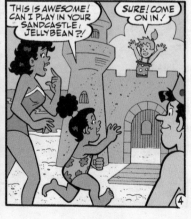

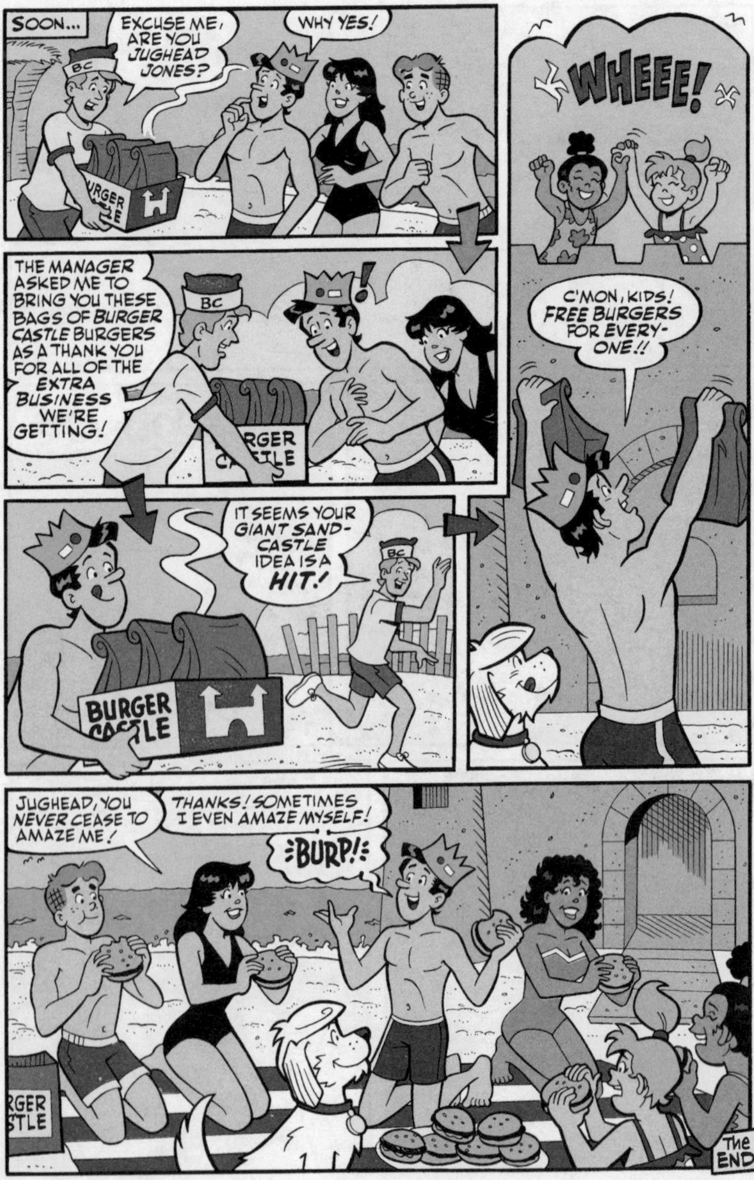
SOON...
EXCUSE ME, ARE YOU JUGHEAD JONES?
WHY YES!
BC
BURGER CASTLE
THE MANAGER ASKED ME TO BRING YOU THESE BAGS OF BURGER CASTLE BURGERS AS A THANK YOU FOR ALL OF THE EXTRA BUSINESS WE'RE GETTING!
BC
IT SEEMS YOUR GIANT SAND-CASTLE IDEA IS A HIT!
BURGER CASTLE
WHEEE!
C'MON, KIDS! FREE BURGERS FOR EVERY-ONE!!
JUGHEAD, YOU NEVER CEASE TO AMAZE ME!
THANKS! SOMETIMES I EVEN AMAZE MYSELF!
BURP!
THE END

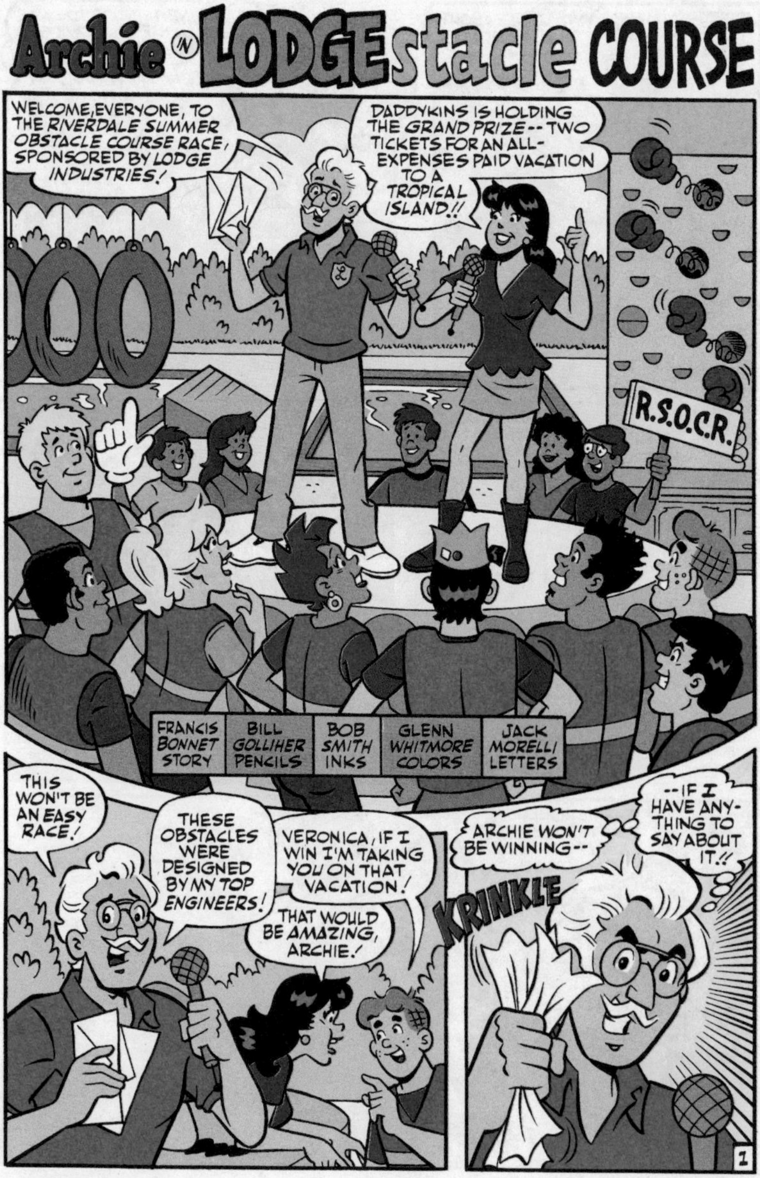
Archie in LODGEstacle COURSE
WELCOME, EVERYONE, TO THE RIVERDALE SUMMER OBSTACLE COURSE RACE, SPONSORED BY LODGE INDUSTRIES!
DADDYKINS IS HOLDING THE GRAND PRIZE -- TWO TICKETS FOR AN ALL-EXPENSES PAID VACATION TO A TROPICAL ISLAND!!
R.S.O.C.R.
FRANCIS BONNET STORY
BILL GOLLIHER PENCILS
BOB SMITH INKS
GLENN WHITMORE COLORS
JACK MORELLI LETTERS
THIS WON'T BE AN EASY RACE!
THESE OBSTACLES WERE DESIGNED BY MY TOP ENGINEERS!
VERONICA, IF I WIN I'M TAKING YOU ON THAT VACATION!
THAT WOULD BE AMAZING, ARCHIE!
KRINKLE
ARCHIE WON'T BE WINNING--
--IF I HAVE ANYTHING TO SAY ABOUT IT!!
1

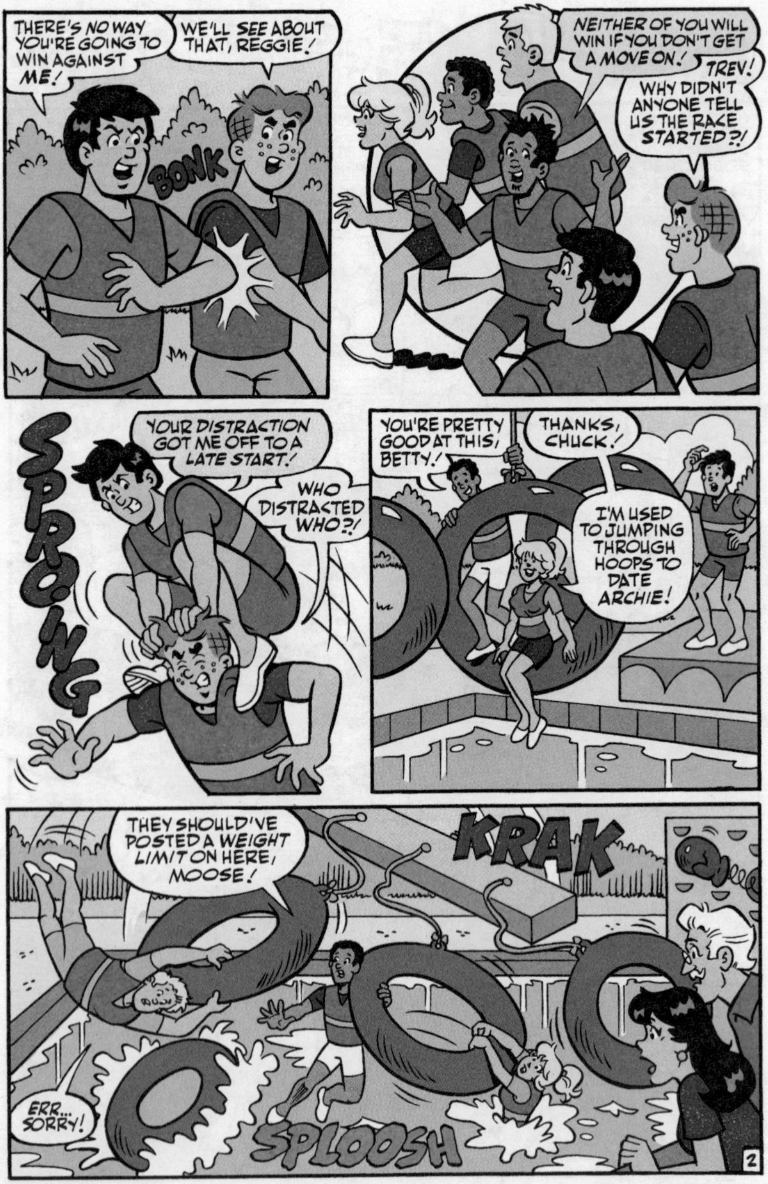
THERE'S NO WAY YOU'RE GOING TO WIN AGAINST ME!
WE'LL SEE ABOUT THAT, REGGIE!
BONK
NEITHER OF YOU WILL WIN IF YOU DON'T GET A MOVE ON!
TREV! WHY DIDN'T ANYONE TELL US THE RACE STARTED?!
SPROING
YOUR DISTRACTION GOT ME OFF TO A LATE START!
WHO DISTRACTED WHO?!
YOU'RE PRETTY GOOD AT THIS, BETTY!
THANKS, CHUCK!
I'M USED TO JUMPING THROUGH HOOPS TO DATE ARCHIE!
THEY SHOULD'VE POSTED A WEIGHT LIMIT ON HERE, MOOSE!
KRAK
ERR... SORRY!
SPLOOSH
2

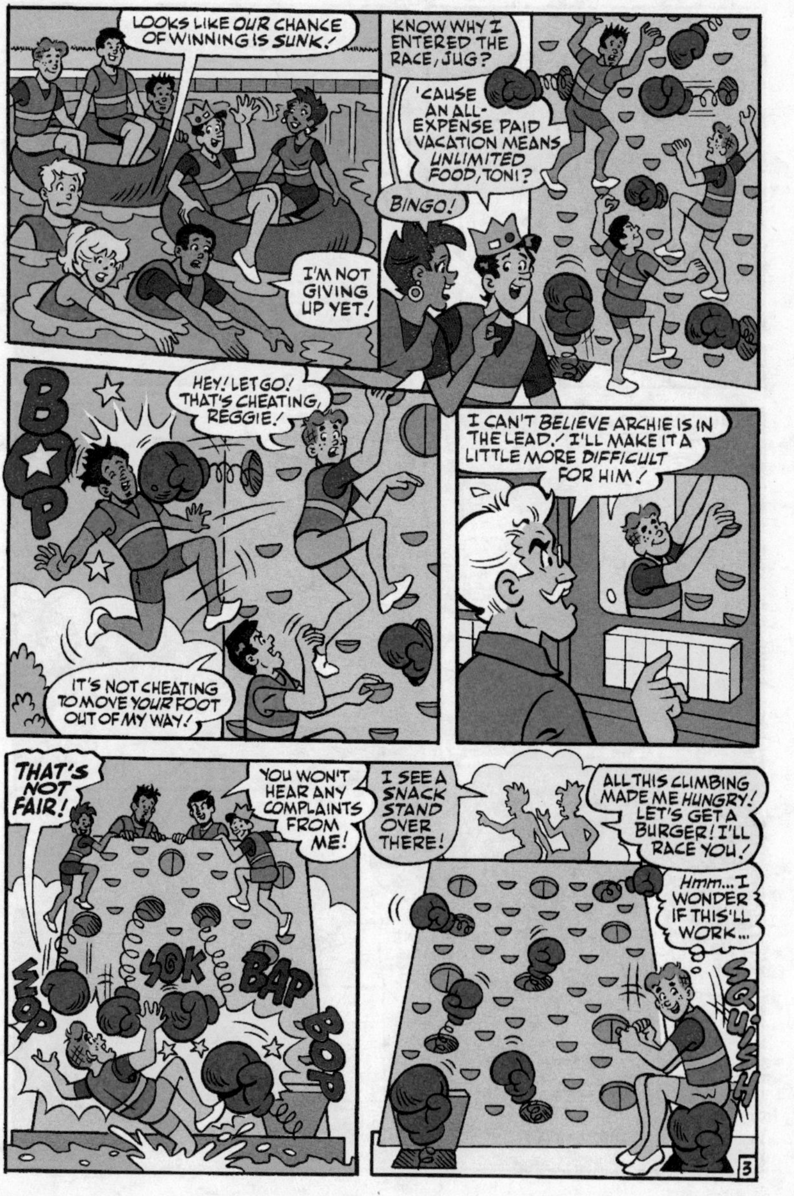
LOOKS LIKE OUR CHANCE OF WINNING IS SUNK!
I'M NOT GIVING UP YET!
KNOW WHY I ENTERED THE RACE, JUG?
'CAUSE AN ALL-EXPENSE PAID VACATION MEANS UNLIMITED FOOD, TONI?
BINGO!
HEY! LET GO! THAT'S CHEATING, REGGIE!
BOP
IT'S NOT CHEATING TO MOVE YOUR FOOT OUT OF MY WAY!
I CAN'T BELIEVE ARCHIE IS IN THE LEAD! I'LL MAKE IT A LITTLE MORE DIFFICULT FOR HIM!
THAT'S NOT FAIR!
YOU WON'T HEAR ANY COMPLAINTS FROM ME!
WOP
SOK
BAP
BOP
I SEE A SNACK STAND OVER THERE!
ALL THIS CLIMBING MADE ME HUNGRY! LET'S GET A BURGER! I'LL RACE YOU!
Hmm... I WONDER IF THIS'LL WORK...
SQUISH
3

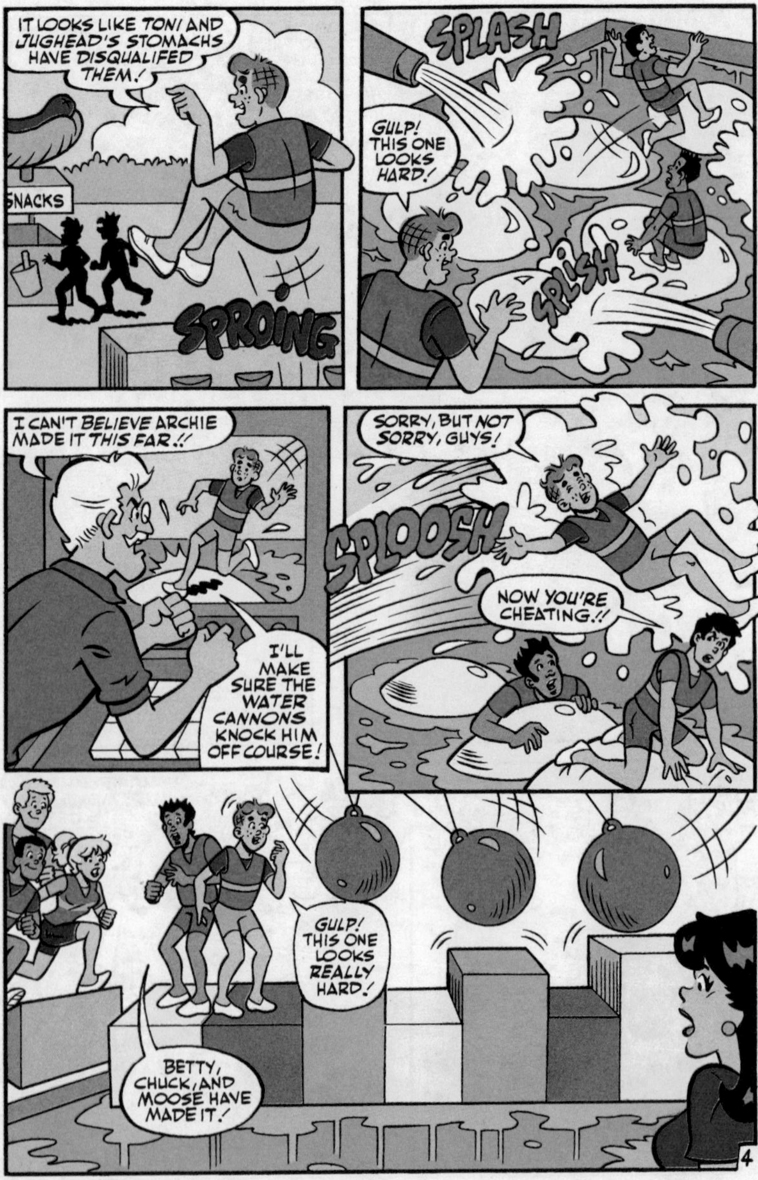
IT LOOKS LIKE TONI AND JUGHEAD'S STOMACHS HAVE DISQUALIFED THEM.!
SNACKS
SPROING
SPLASH
GULP! THIS ONE LOOKS HARD!
SPLISH
I CAN'T BELIEVE ARCHIE MADE IT THIS FAR.!!
I'LL MAKE SURE THE WATER CANNONS KNOCK HIM OFF COURSE!
SORRY, BUT NOT SORRY, GUYS!
SPLOOSH
NOW YOU'RE CHEATING.!!
GULP! THIS ONE LOOKS REALLY HARD!
BETTY, CHUCK, AND MOOSE HAVE MADE IT.!
4

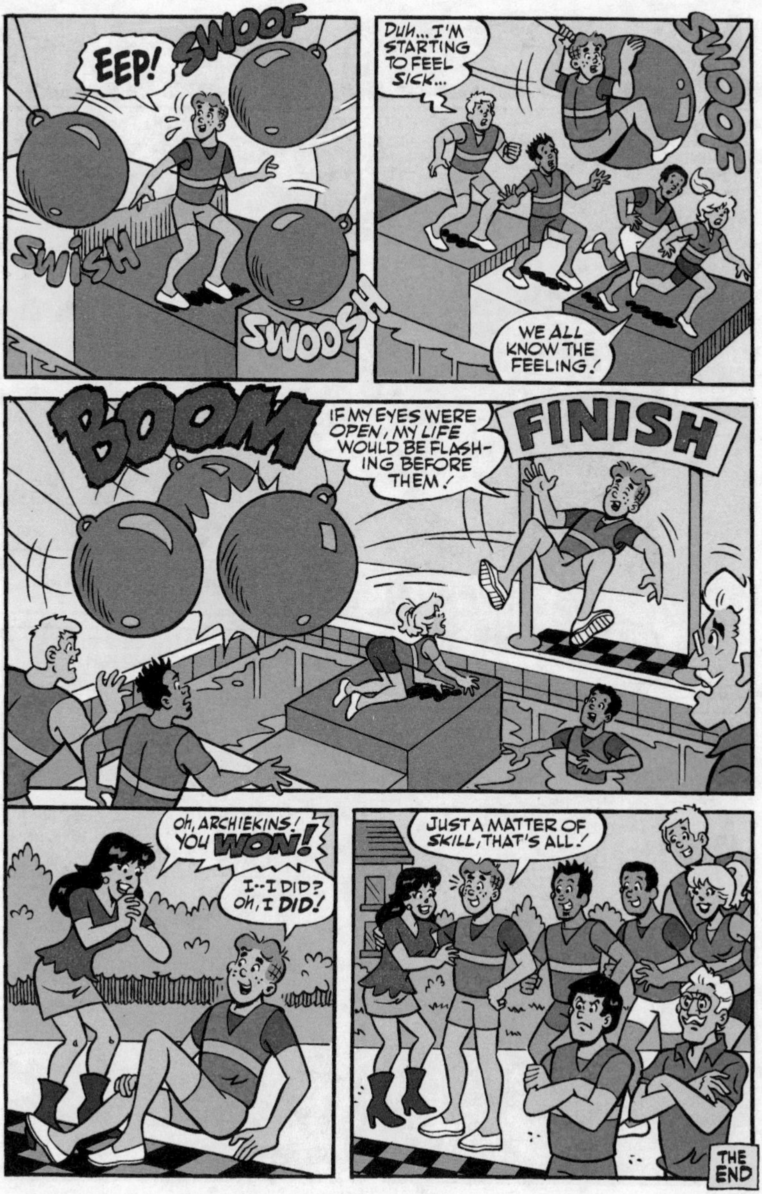
EEP!
SWOOF
SWISH
SWOOSH
DUH... I'M STARTING TO FEEL SICK...
SWOOF
WE ALL KNOW THE FEELING!
BOOM
IF MY EYES WERE OPEN, MY LIFE WOULD BE FLASHING BEFORE THEM!
FINISH
OH, ARCHIEKINS! YOU WON!
I--I DID? OH, I DID!
JUST A MATTER OF SKILL, THAT'S ALL!
THE END

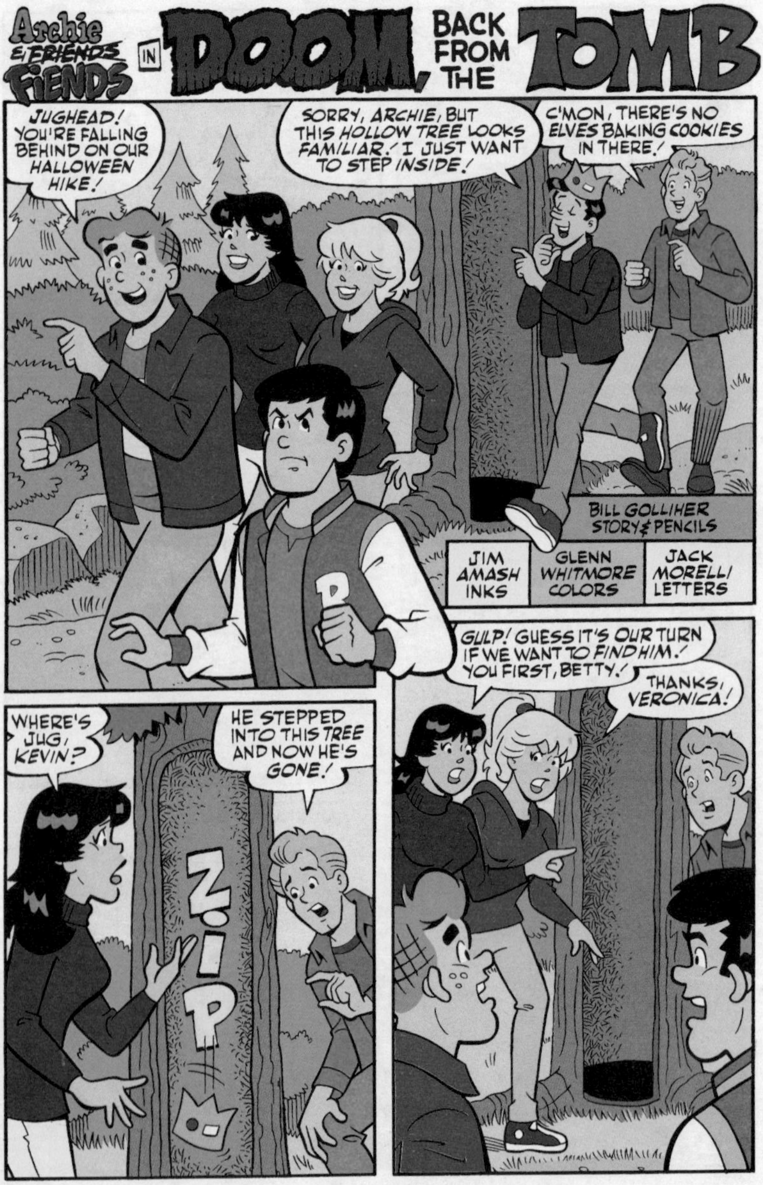
Archie & FRIENDS FIENDS
IN
DOOM, BACK FROM THE TOMB
JUGHEAD! YOU'RE FALLING BEHIND ON OUR HALLOWEEN HIKE!
SORRY, ARCHIE, BUT THIS HOLLOW TREE LOOKS FAMILIAR! I JUST WANT TO STEP INSIDE!
C'MON, THERE'S NO ELVES BAKING COOKIES IN THERE!
BILL GOLLIHER STORY & PENCILS
JIM AMASH INKS
GLENN WHITMORE COLORS
JACK MORELLI LETTERS
WHERE'S JUG, KEVIN?
HE STEPPED INTO THIS TREE AND NOW HE'S GONE!
ZIP
GULP! GUESS IT'S OUR TURN IF WE WANT TO FIND HIM! YOU FIRST, BETTY!
THANKS, VERONICA!

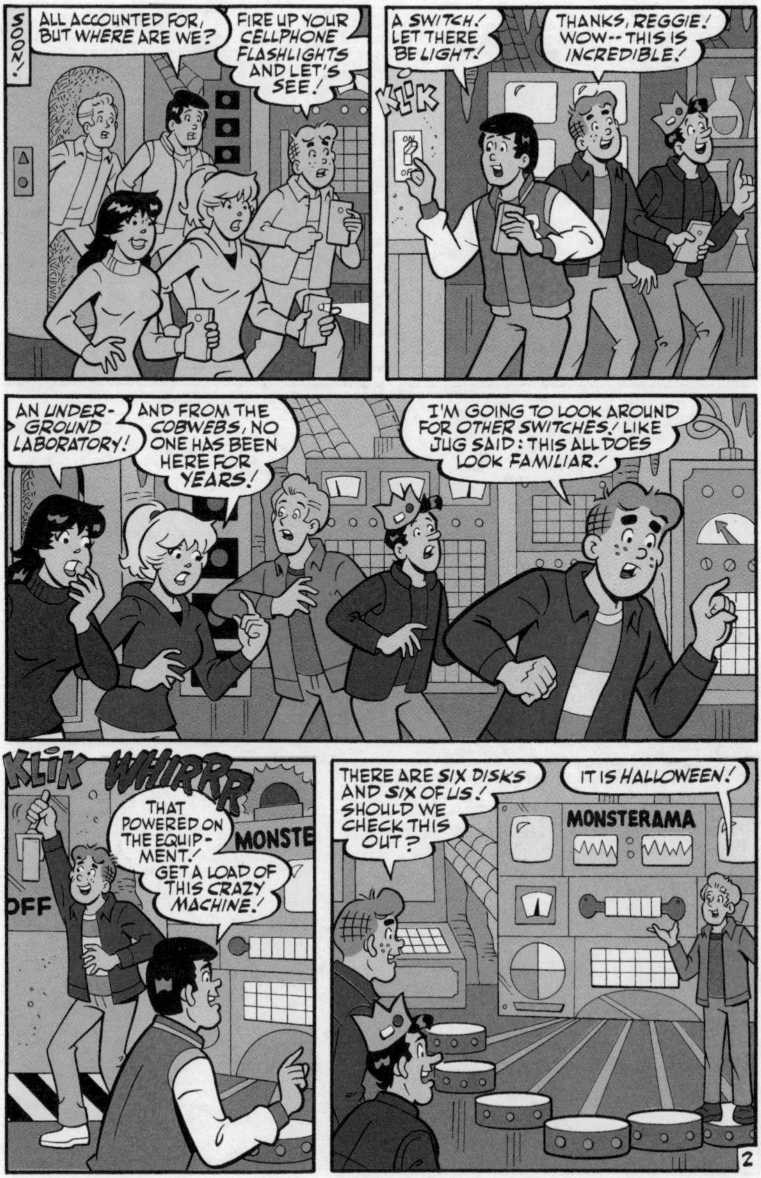
SOON!
ALL ACCOUNTED FOR, BUT WHERE ARE WE?
FIRE UP YOUR CELLPHONE FLASHLIGHTS AND LET'S SEE!
A SWITCH! LET THERE BE LIGHT!
KLIK
ON
OFF
THANKS, REGGIE! WOW-- THIS IS INCREDIBLE!
AN UNDER-GROUND LABORATORY!
AND FROM THE COBWEBS, NO ONE HAS BEEN HERE FOR YEARS!
I'M GOING TO LOOK AROUND FOR OTHER SWITCHES! LIKE JUG SAID: THIS ALL DOES LOOK FAMILIAR!
KLIK
WHIRRR
THAT POWERED ON THE EQUIP-MENT! GET A LOAD OF THIS CRAZY MACHINE!
MONSTE
OFF
THERE ARE SIX DISKS AND SIX OF US! SHOULD WE CHECK THIS OUT?
IT IS HALLOWEEN!
MONSTERAMA
2

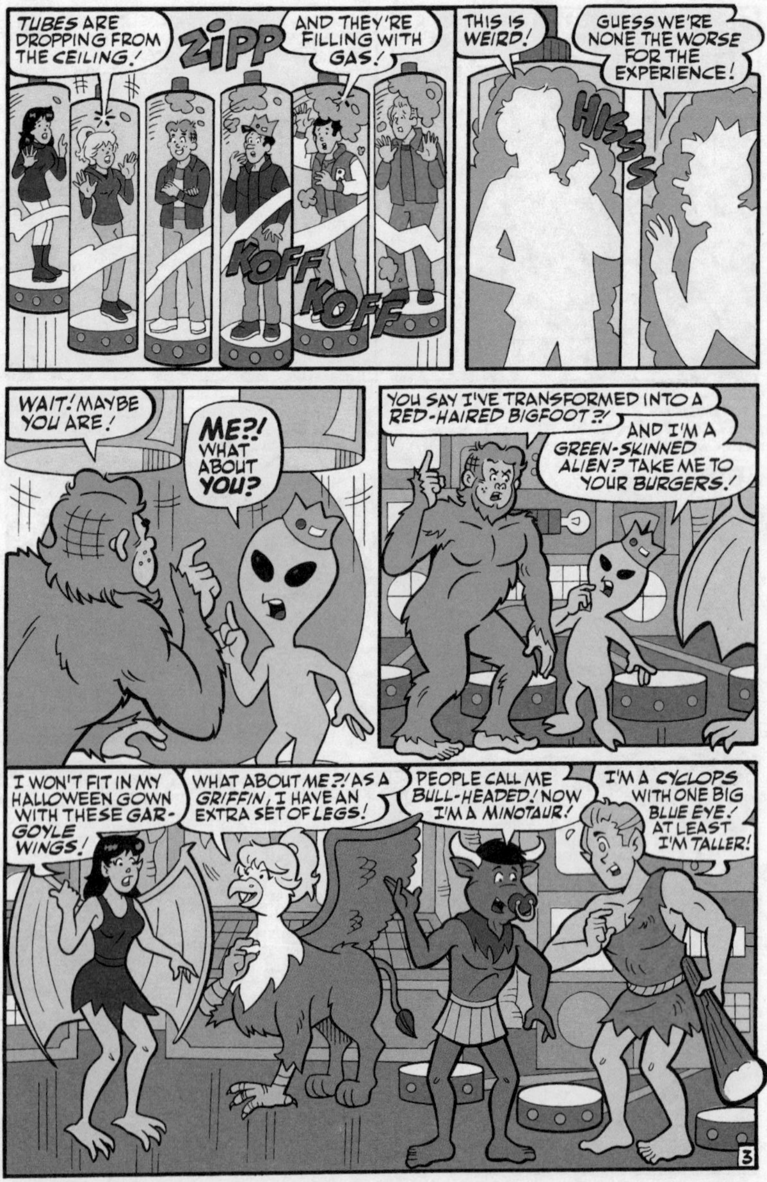
TUBES ARE DROPPING FROM THE CEILING!
ZIPP
AND THEY'RE FILLING WITH GAS!
KOFF KOFF
THIS IS WEIRD!
GUESS WE'RE NONE THE WORSE FOR THE EXPERIENCE!
HISSS
WAIT! MAYBE YOU ARE!
ME?! WHAT ABOUT YOU?
YOU SAY I'VE TRANSFORMED INTO A RED-HAIRED BIGFOOT?!
AND I'M A GREEN-SKINNED ALIEN? TAKE ME TO YOUR BURGERS!
I WON'T FIT IN MY HALLOWEEN GOWN WITH THESE GAR-GOYLE WINGS!
WHAT ABOUT ME?! AS A GRIFFIN, I HAVE AN EXTRA SET OF LEGS!
PEOPLE CALL ME BULL-HEADED! NOW I'M A MINOTAUR!
I'M A CYCLOPS WITH ONE BIG BLUE EYE! AT LEAST I'M TALLER!
3

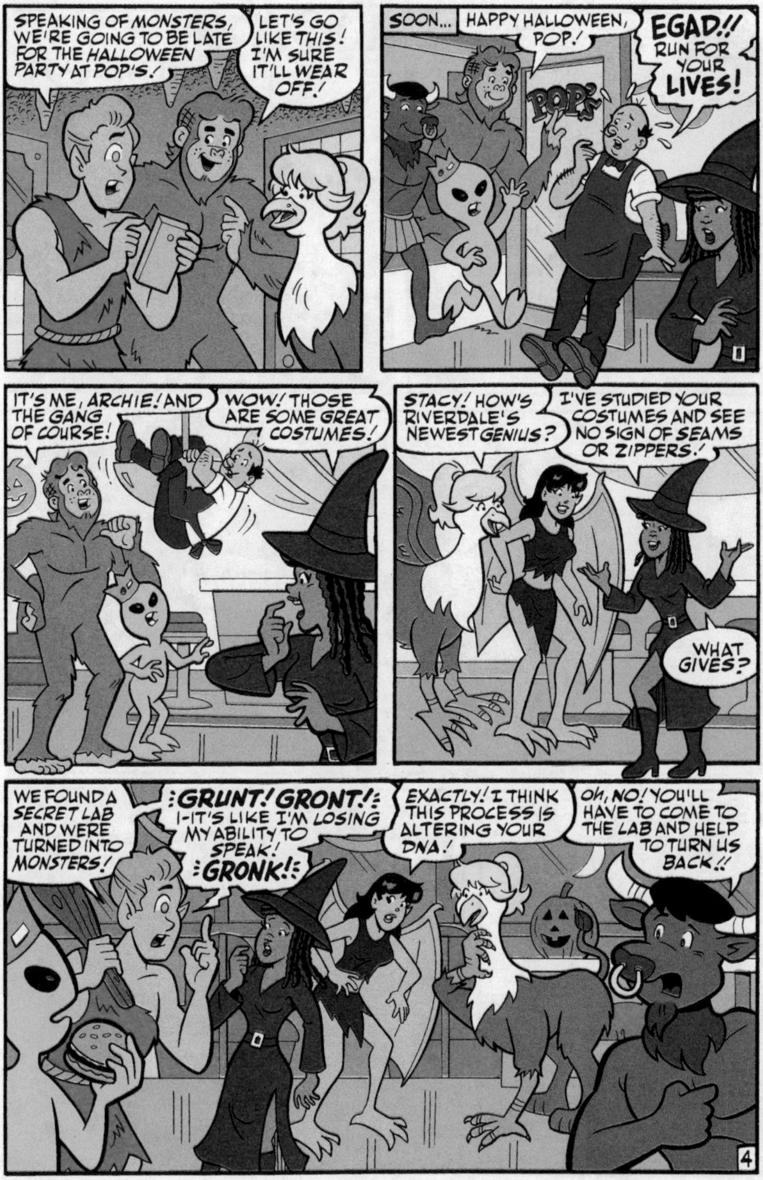
SPEAKING OF MONSTERS, WE'RE GOING TO BE LATE FOR THE HALLOWEEN PARTY AT POP'S!
LET'S GO LIKE THIS! I'M SURE IT'LL WEAR OFF!
SOON...
HAPPY HALLOWEEN, POP!
POP'S
EGAD!! RUN FOR YOUR LIVES!
IT'S ME, ARCHIE! AND THE GANG OF COURSE!
WOW! THOSE ARE SOME GREAT COSTUMES!
STACY! HOW'S RIVERDALE'S NEWEST GENIUS?
I'VE STUDIED YOUR COSTUMES AND SEE NO SIGN OF SEAMS OR ZIPPERS!
WHAT GIVES?
WE FOUND A SECRET LAB AND WERE TURNED INTO MONSTERS!
GRUNT! GRONT! I-IT'S LIKE I'M LOSING MY ABILITY TO SPEAK! GRONK!
EXACTLY! I THINK THIS PROCESS IS ALTERING YOUR DNA!
OH, NO! YOU'LL HAVE TO COME TO THE LAB AND HELP TO TURN US BACK!!
4

AND SO!

LUCKILY, THE MACHINE SEEMS TO HAVE KEPT YOUR ORIGINAL DNA INFO! STEP ON YOUR DISK, AND I'LL SEE WHAT I CAN DO!

CAUTION

BZZATT

WE'RE BACK TO OUR OLD SELVES! THANKS, STACY!

IT'S GETTING LATE! WE'D BETTER HURRY BACK TO THE PARTY AND SEE WHO WON THE COSTUME CONTEST!

WE'LL KEEP THIS PLACE OUR SECRET!

EXIT

KLIK

ZIP

SLEEP POD

:yawn!:

SOMETHING INTERRUPTED MY DECADE-LONG SLUMBER! IT'S TIME FOR DOCTOR DOOM TO GET BACK TO SOME EVIL!!

BWAH-HA-HA!

?

WHAT WAS THAT?!

OH, JUST SOME ANIMAL!

LET'S GET BACK TO POP'S PARTY!

THE END

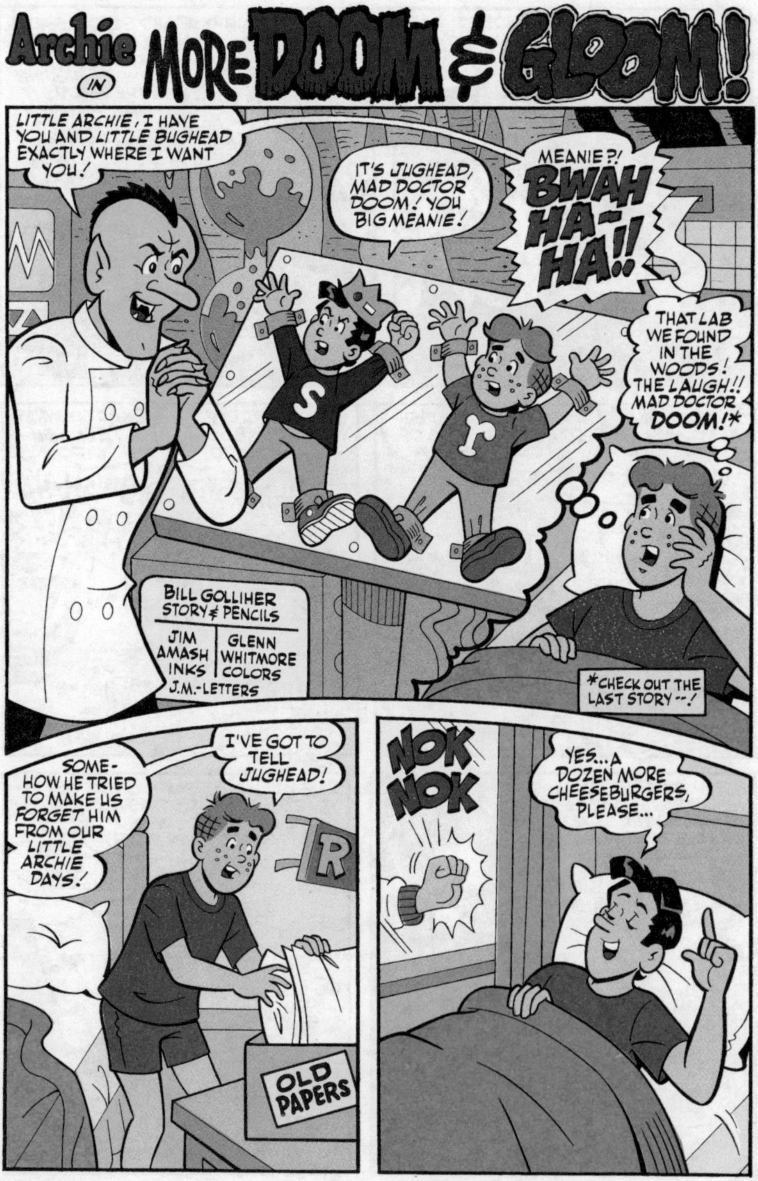
Archie
IN
MORE DOOM & GLOOM!
LITTLE ARCHIE, I HAVE YOU AND LITTLE BUGHEAD EXACTLY WHERE I WANT YOU!
IT'S JUGHEAD, MAD DOCTOR DOOM! YOU BIG MEANIE!
MEANIE?! BWAH HA-HA!!
THAT LAB WE FOUND IN THE WOODS! THE LAUGH!! MAD DOCTOR DOOM!*
BILL GOLLIHER STORY & PENCILS
JIM AMASH INKS
GLENN WHITMORE COLORS
J.M.-LETTERS
*CHECK OUT THE LAST STORY--!
I'VE GOT TO TELL JUGHEAD!
SOME-HOW HE TRIED TO MAKE US FORGET HIM FROM OUR LITTLE ARCHIE DAYS!
OLD PAPERS
NOK NOK
YES...A DOZEN MORE CHEESEBURGERS, PLEASE...

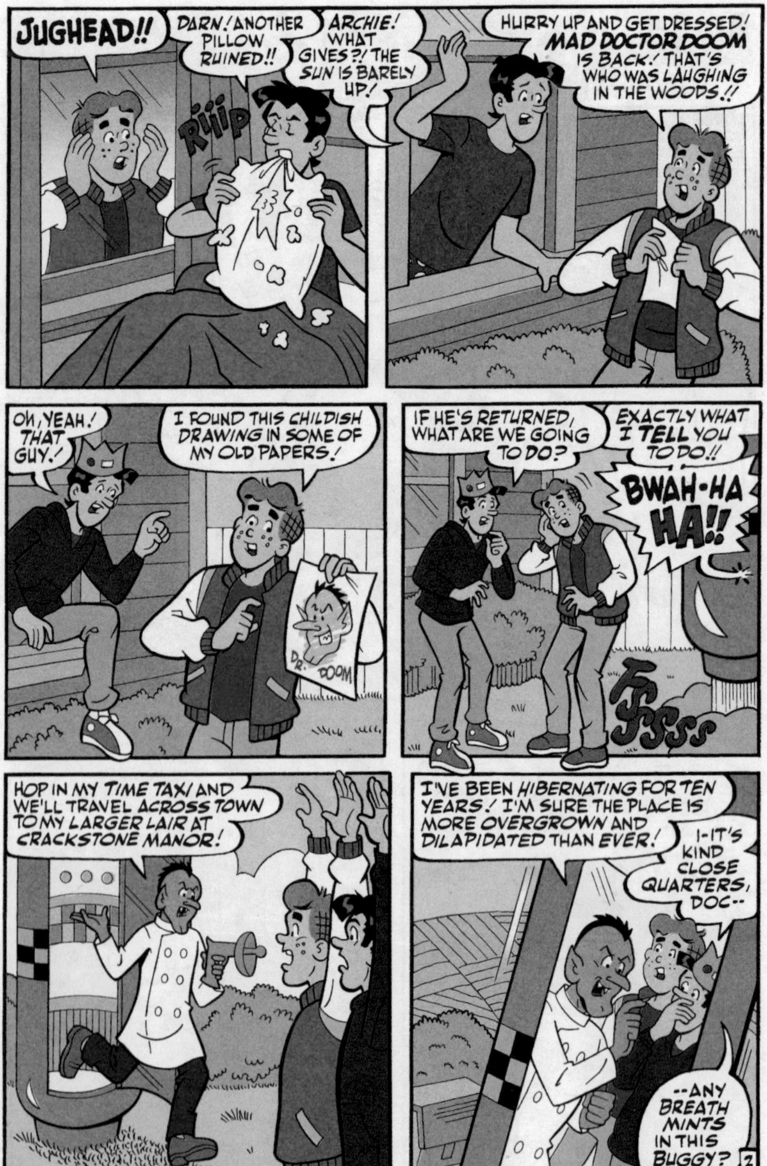
JUGHEAD!!
RIIIP
DARN! ANOTHER PILLOW RUINED!!
ARCHIE! WHAT GIVES?! THE SUN IS BARELY UP!
HURRY UP AND GET DRESSED! MAD DOCTOR DOOM IS BACK! THAT'S WHO WAS LAUGHING IN THE WOODS!!
OH, YEAH! THAT GUY!
I FOUND THIS CHILDISH DRAWING IN SOME OF MY OLD PAPERS!
DR. DOOM
IF HE'S RETURNED, WHAT ARE WE GOING TO DO?
EXACTLY WHAT I TELL YOU TO DO!!
BWAH-HA HA!!
FSSSSS
HOP IN MY TIME TAXI AND WE'LL TRAVEL ACROSS TOWN TO MY LARGER LAIR AT CRACKSTONE MANOR!
I'VE BEEN HIBERNATING FOR TEN YEARS! I'M SURE THE PLACE IS MORE OVERGROWN AND DILAPIDATED THAN EVER!
I-IT'S KIND CLOSE QUARTERS, DOC--
--ANY BREATH MINTS IN THIS BUGGY?
2

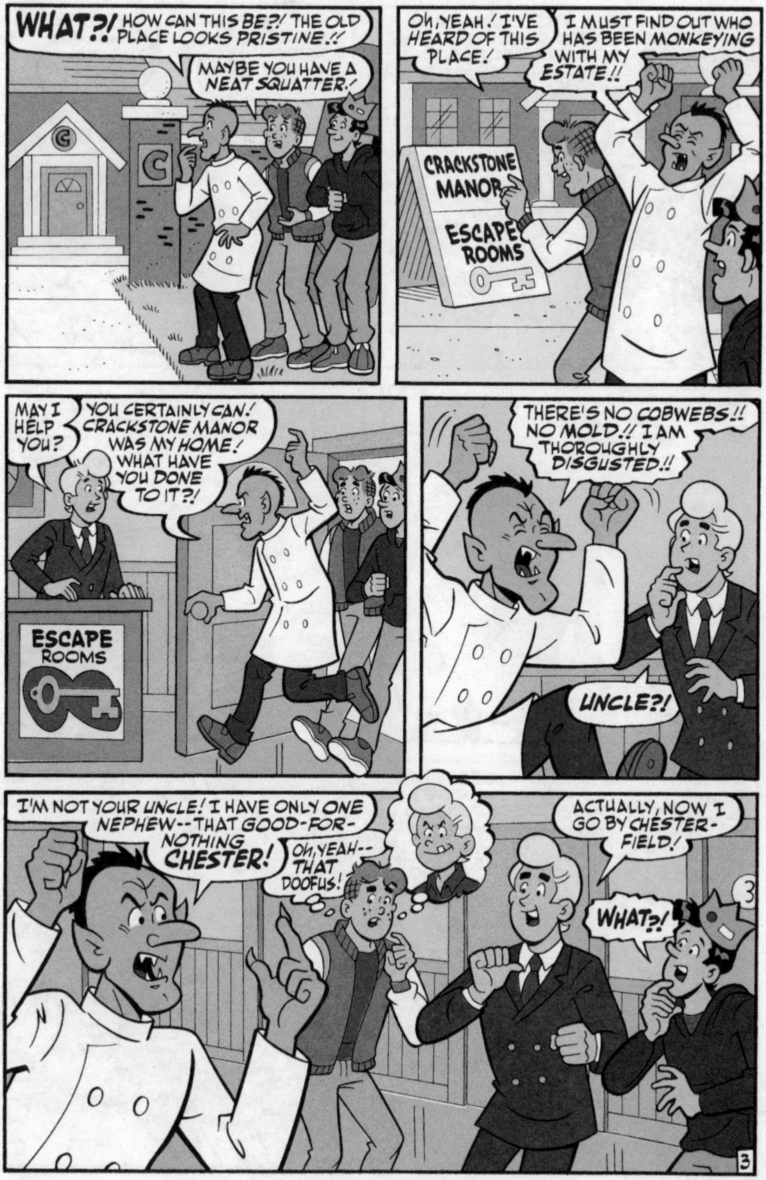
WHAT?! HOW CAN THIS BE?! THE OLD PLACE LOOKS PRISTINE.!!
MAYBE YOU HAVE A NEAT SQUATTER.!
CG
OH, YEAH! I'VE HEARD OF THIS PLACE!
I MUST FIND OUT WHO HAS BEEN MONKEYING WITH MY ESTATE!!
CRACKSTONE MANOR
ESCAPE ROOMS
MAY I HELP YOU?
YOU CERTAINLY CAN! CRACKSTONE MANOR WAS MY HOME! WHAT HAVE YOU DONE TO IT?!
ESCAPE ROOMS
THERE'S NO COBWEBS!! NO MOLD!! I AM THOROUGHLY DISGUSTED!!
UNCLE?!
I'M NOT YOUR UNCLE! I HAVE ONLY ONE NEPHEW--THAT GOOD-FOR-NOTHING CHESTER!
OH, YEAH-- THAT DOOFUS!
ACTUALLY, NOW I GO BY CHESTER-FIELD!
WHAT?!
3

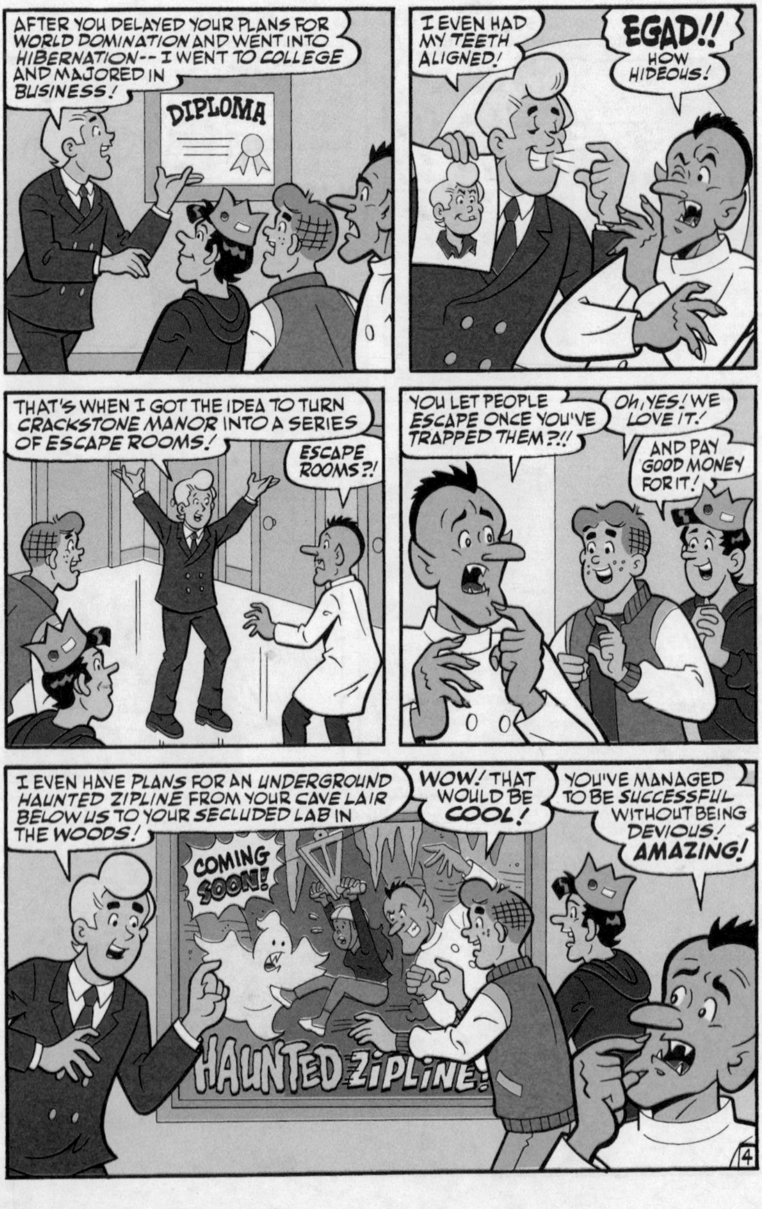
AFTER YOU DELAYED YOUR PLANS FOR WORLD DOMINATION AND WENT INTO HIBERNATION-- I WENT TO COLLEGE AND MAJORED IN BUSINESS!
DIPLOMA
I EVEN HAD MY TEETH ALIGNED!
EGAD!! HOW HIDEOUS!
THAT'S WHEN I GOT THE IDEA TO TURN CRACKSTONE MANOR INTO A SERIES OF ESCAPE ROOMS!
ESCAPE ROOMS?!
YOU LET PEOPLE ESCAPE ONCE YOU'VE TRAPPED THEM?!!
OH, YES! WE LOVE IT!
AND PAY GOOD MONEY FOR IT!
I EVEN HAVE PLANS FOR AN UNDERGROUND HAUNTED ZIPLINE FROM YOUR CAVE LAIR BELOW US TO YOUR SECLUDED LAB IN THE WOODS!
WOW! THAT WOULD BE COOL!
YOU'VE MANAGED TO BE SUCCESSFUL WITHOUT BEING DEVIOUS! AMAZING!
COMING SOON!
HAUNTED ZIPLINE!
4

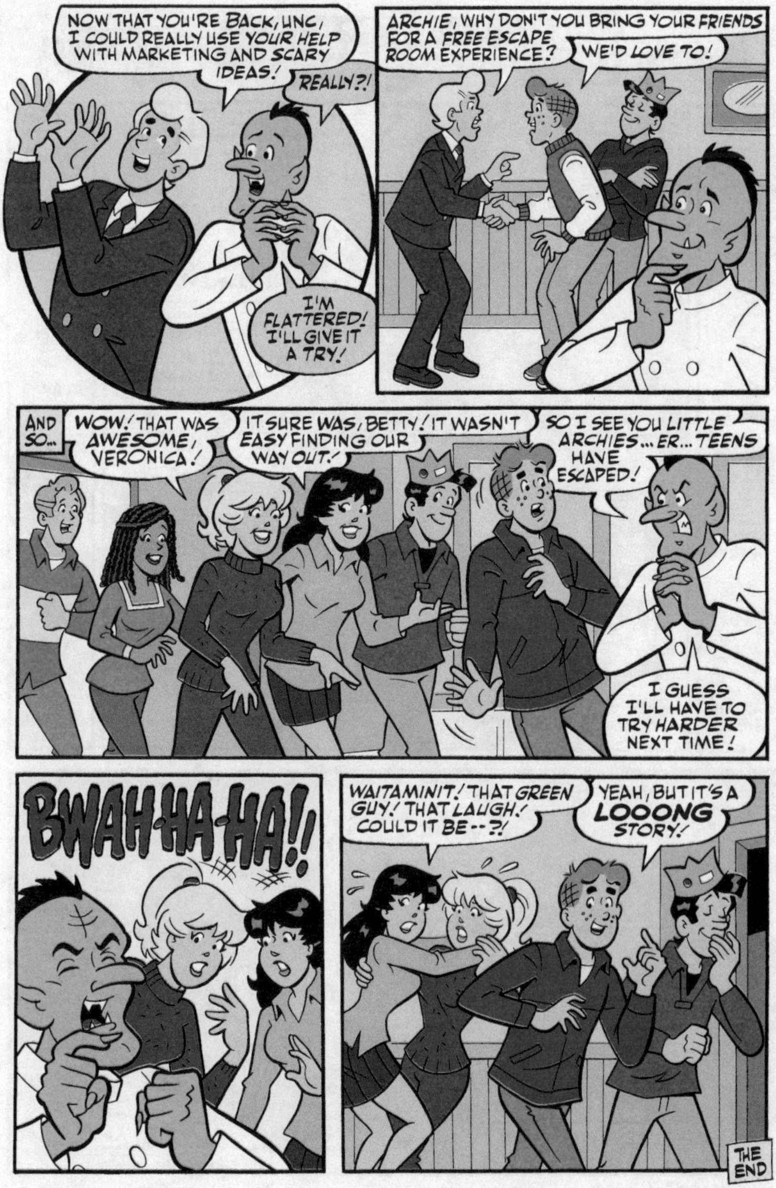
NOW THAT YOU'RE BACK, UNC, I COULD REALLY USE YOUR HELP WITH MARKETING AND SCARY IDEAS!
REALLY?!
I'M FLATTERED! I'LL GIVE IT A TRY!
ARCHIE, WHY DON'T YOU BRING YOUR FRIENDS FOR A FREE ESCAPE ROOM EXPERIENCE?
WE'D LOVE TO!
AND SO...
WOW! THAT WAS AWESOME, VERONICA!
IT SURE WAS, BETTY! IT WASN'T EASY FINDING OUR WAY OUT!
SO I SEE YOU LITTLE ARCHIES... ER... TEENS HAVE ESCAPED!
I GUESS I'LL HAVE TO TRY HARDER NEXT TIME!
BWAH-HA-HA!!
WAITAMINIT! THAT GREEN GUY! THAT LAUGH! COULD IT BE--?!
YEAH, BUT IT'S A LOOONG STORY!
THE END

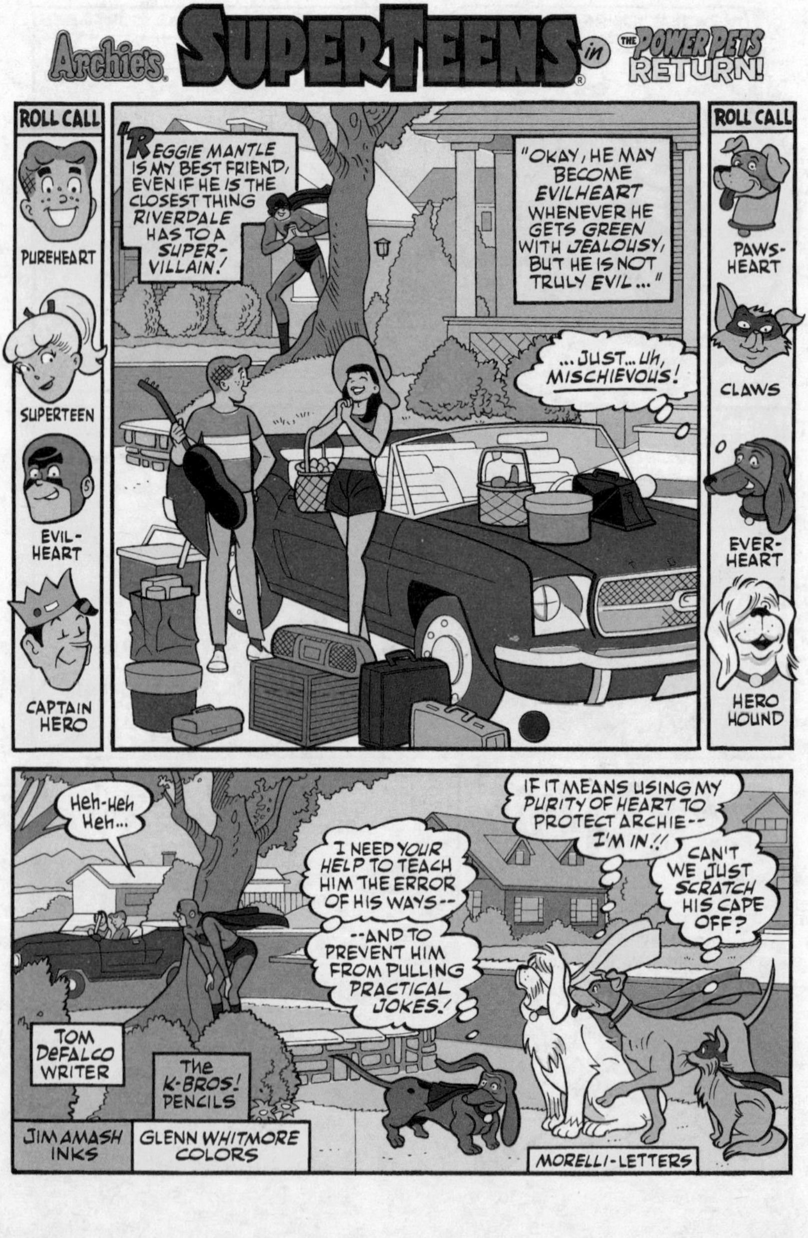
Archie's
SUPERTEENS
in
THE POWER PETS RETURN!
ROLL CALL
PUREHEART
SUPERTEEN
EVIL-HEART
CAPTAIN HERO
"REGGIE MANTLE IS MY BEST FRIEND, EVEN IF HE IS THE CLOSEST THING RIVERDALE HAS TO A SUPER-VILLAIN!
"OKAY, HE MAY BECOME EVILHEART WHENEVER HE GETS GREEN WITH JEALOUSY, BUT HE IS NOT TRULY EVIL..."
...JUST...uh, MISCHIEVOUS!
ROLL CALL
PAWS-HEART
CLAWS
EVER-HEART
HERO HOUND
Heh-heh Heh...
I NEED YOUR HELP TO TEACH HIM THE ERROR OF HIS WAYS--
--AND TO PREVENT HIM FROM PULLING PRACTICAL JOKES!
IF IT MEANS USING MY PURITY OF HEART TO PROTECT ARCHIE-- I'M IN!!
CAN'T WE JUST SCRATCH HIS CAPE OFF?
TOM DeFALCO WRITER
The K-BROS! PENCILS
JIM AMASH INKS
GLENN WHITMORE COLORS
MORELLI-LETTERS

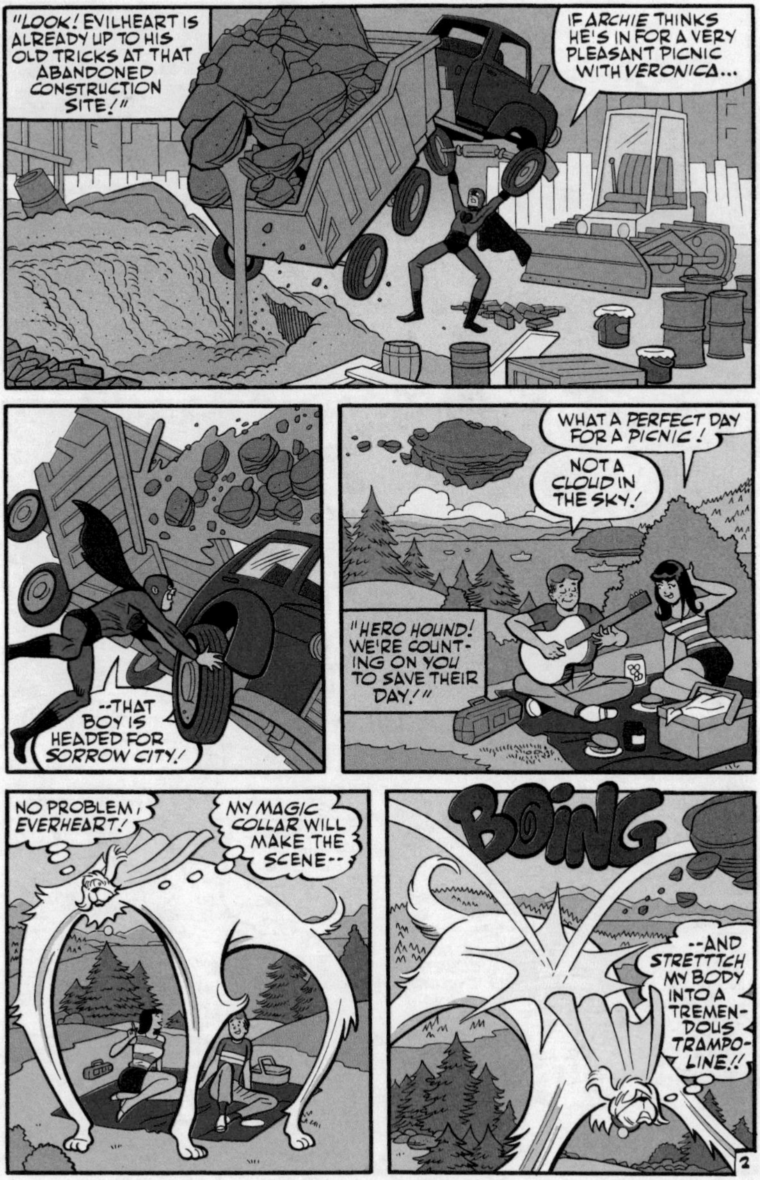
"LOOK! EVILHEART IS ALREADY UP TO HIS OLD TRICKS AT THAT ABANDONED CONSTRUCTION SITE!"
IF ARCHIE THINKS HE'S IN FOR A VERY PLEASANT PICNIC WITH VERONICA...
--THAT BOY IS HEADED FOR SORROW CITY!
WHAT A PERFECT DAY FOR A PICNIC!
NOT A CLOUD IN THE SKY!
"HERO HOUND! WE'RE COUNTING ON YOU TO SAVE THEIR DAY!"
NO PROBLEM, EVERHEART!
MY MAGIC COLLAR WILL MAKE THE SCENE--
BOING
--AND STRETTTCH MY BODY INTO A TREMENDOUS TRAMPOLINE!!
2

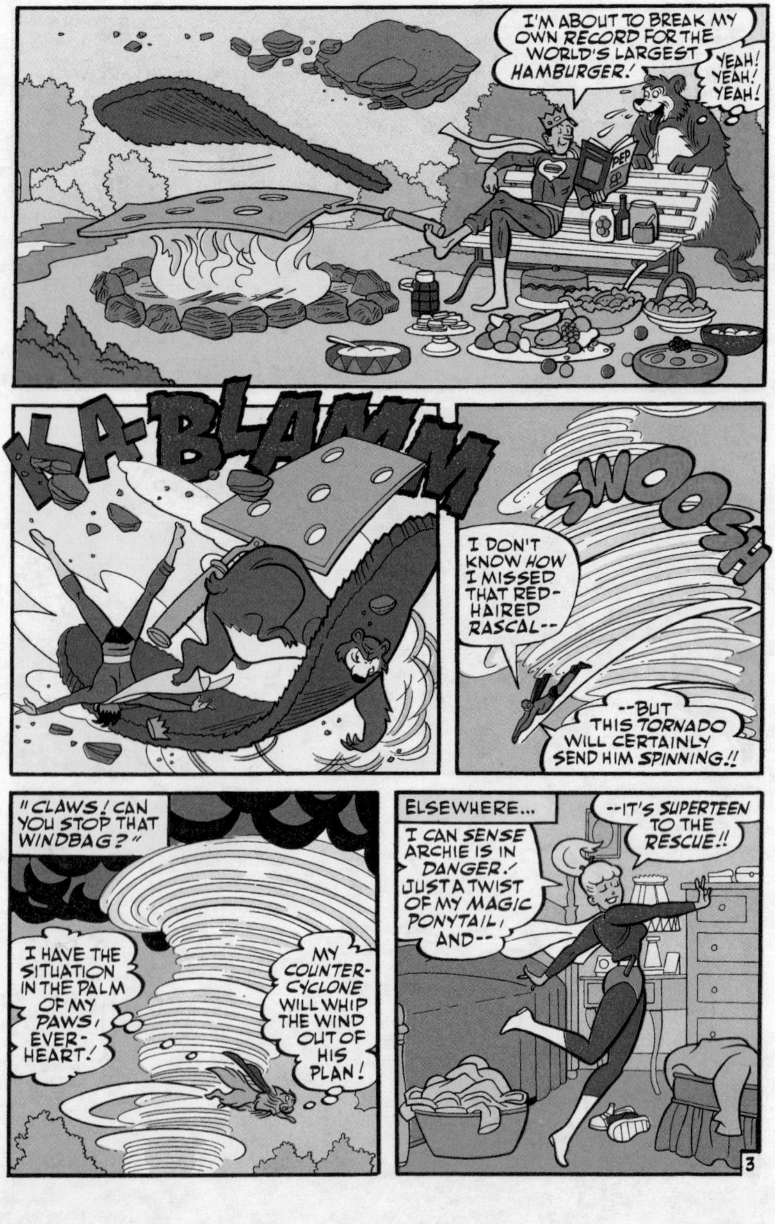
I'M ABOUT TO BREAK MY OWN RECORD FOR THE WORLD'S LARGEST HAMBURGER!
YEAH! YEAH! YEAH!
PEP
KA-BLAMM
SWOOSH
I DON'T KNOW HOW I MISSED THAT RED-HAIRED RASCAL--
--BUT THIS TORNADO WILL CERTAINLY SEND HIM SPINNING!!
"CLAWS! CAN YOU STOP THAT WINDBAG?"
I HAVE THE SITUATION IN THE PALM OF MY PAWS, EVERHEART!
MY COUNTER-CYCLONE WILL WHIP THE WIND OUT OF HIS PLAN!
ELSEWHERE...
I CAN SENSE ARCHIE IS IN DANGER! JUST A TWIST OF MY MAGIC PONYTAIL, AND--
--IT'S SUPERTEEN TO THE RESCUE!!
3

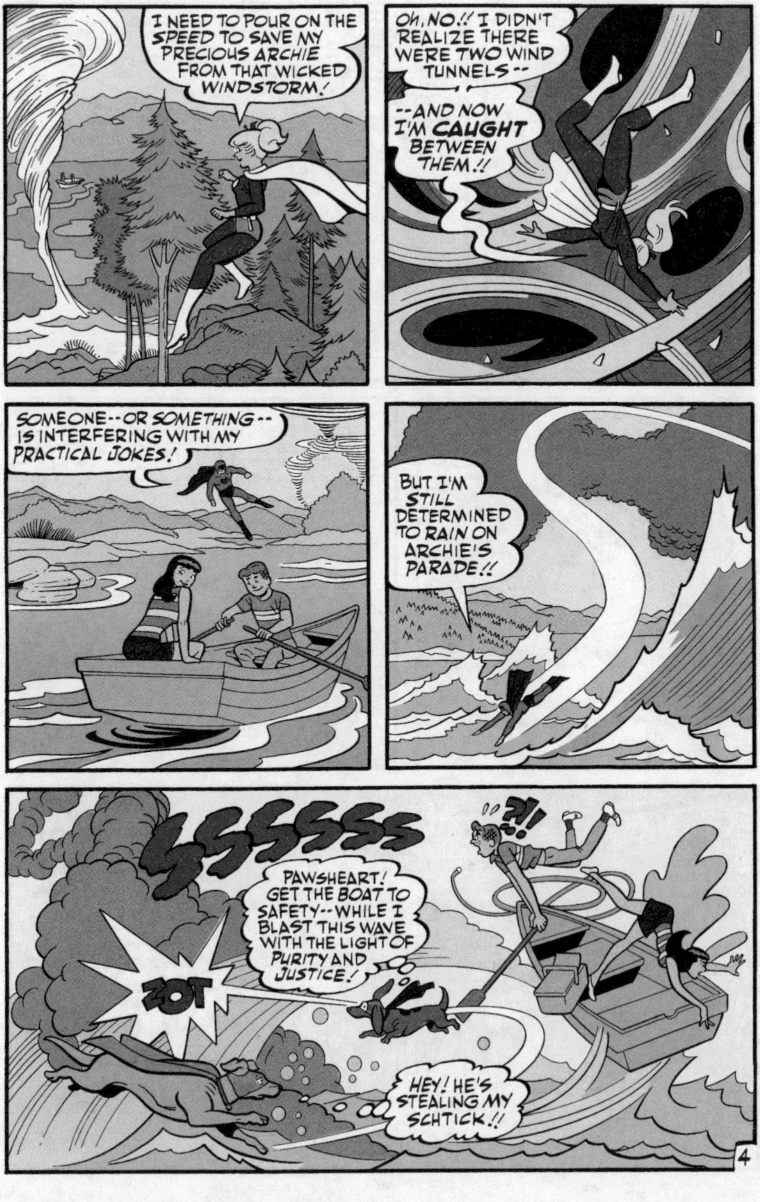
I NEED TO POUR ON THE SPEED TO SAVE MY PRECIOUS ARCHIE FROM THAT WICKED WINDSTORM!
OH, NO!! I DIDN'T REALIZE THERE WERE TWO WIND TUNNELS--
--AND NOW I'M CAUGHT BETWEEN THEM!!
SOMEONE--OR SOMETHING--IS INTERFERING WITH MY PRACTICAL JOKES!
BUT I'M STILL DETERMINED TO RAIN ON ARCHIE'S PARADE!!
SSSSSS
PAWSHEART! GET THE BOAT TO SAFETY--WHILE I BLAST THIS WAVE WITH THE LIGHT OF PURITY AND JUSTICE!
ZOT
?!
HEY! HE'S STEALING MY SCHTICK!!
4

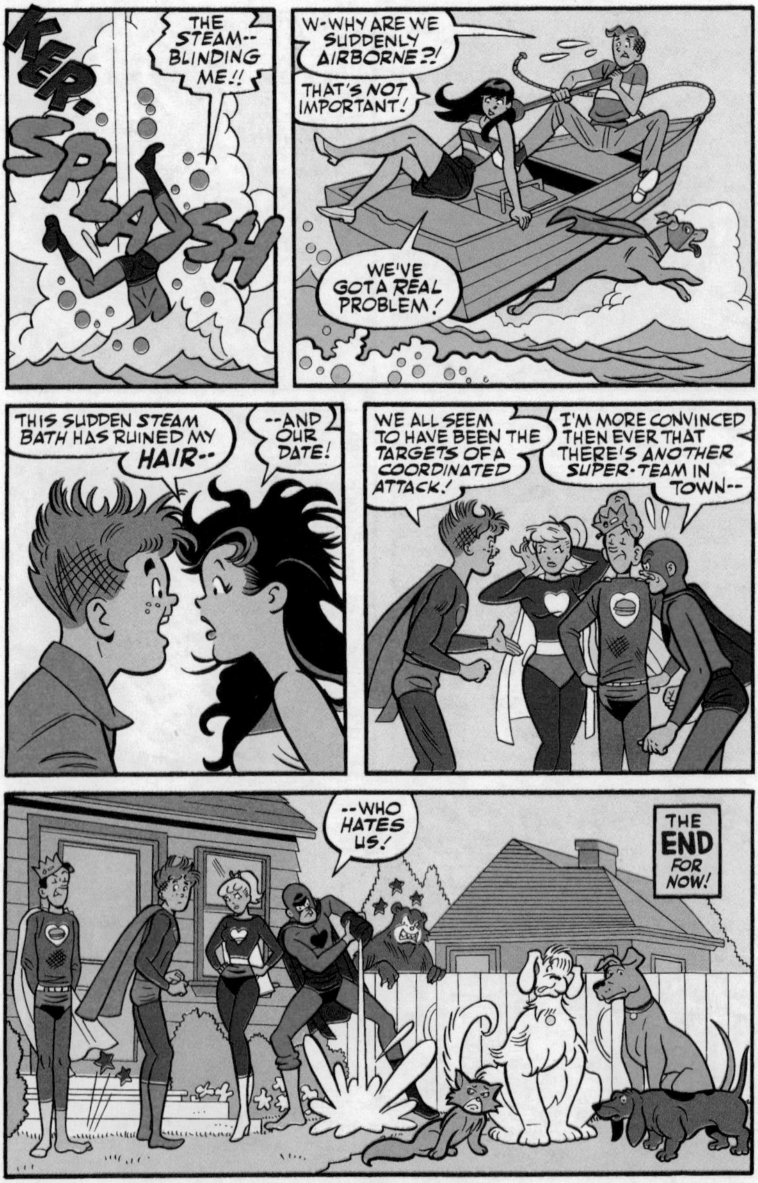
KER-SPLASH
THE STEAM-- BLINDING ME!!
W-WHY ARE WE SUDDENLY AIRBORNE?!
THAT'S NOT IMPORTANT!
WE'VE GOT A REAL PROBLEM!
THIS SUDDEN STEAM BATH HAS RUINED MY HAIR--
--AND OUR DATE!
WE ALL SEEM TO HAVE BEEN THE TARGETS OF A COORDINATED ATTACK!
I'M MORE CONVINCED THEN EVER THAT THERE'S ANOTHER SUPER-TEAM IN TOWN--
--WHO HATES US!
THE END FOR NOW!

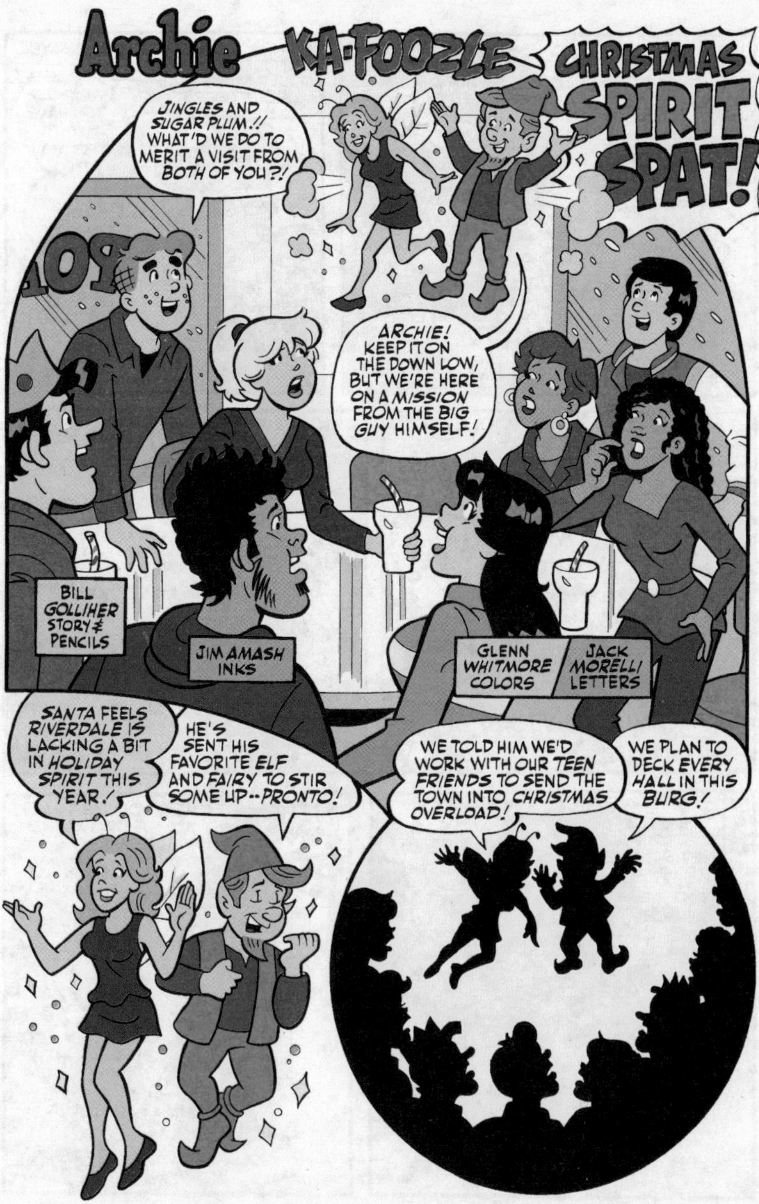
Archie
KA-FOOZLE
CHRISTMAS SPIRIT SPAT!
JINGLES AND SUGAR PLUM!! WHAT'D WE DO TO MERIT A VISIT FROM BOTH OF YOU?!
ARCHIE! KEEP IT ON THE DOWN LOW, BUT WE'RE HERE ON A MISSION FROM THE BIG GUY HIMSELF!
BILL GOLLIHER STORY & PENCILS
JIM AMASH INKS
GLENN WHITMORE COLORS
JACK MORELLI LETTERS
SANTA FEELS RIVERDALE IS LACKING A BIT IN HOLIDAY SPIRIT THIS YEAR!
HE'S SENT HIS FAVORITE ELF AND FAIRY TO STIR SOME UP--PRONTO!
WE TOLD HIM WE'D WORK WITH OUR TEEN FRIENDS TO SEND THE TOWN INTO CHRISTMAS OVERLOAD!
WE PLAN TO DECK EVERY HALL IN THIS BURG!

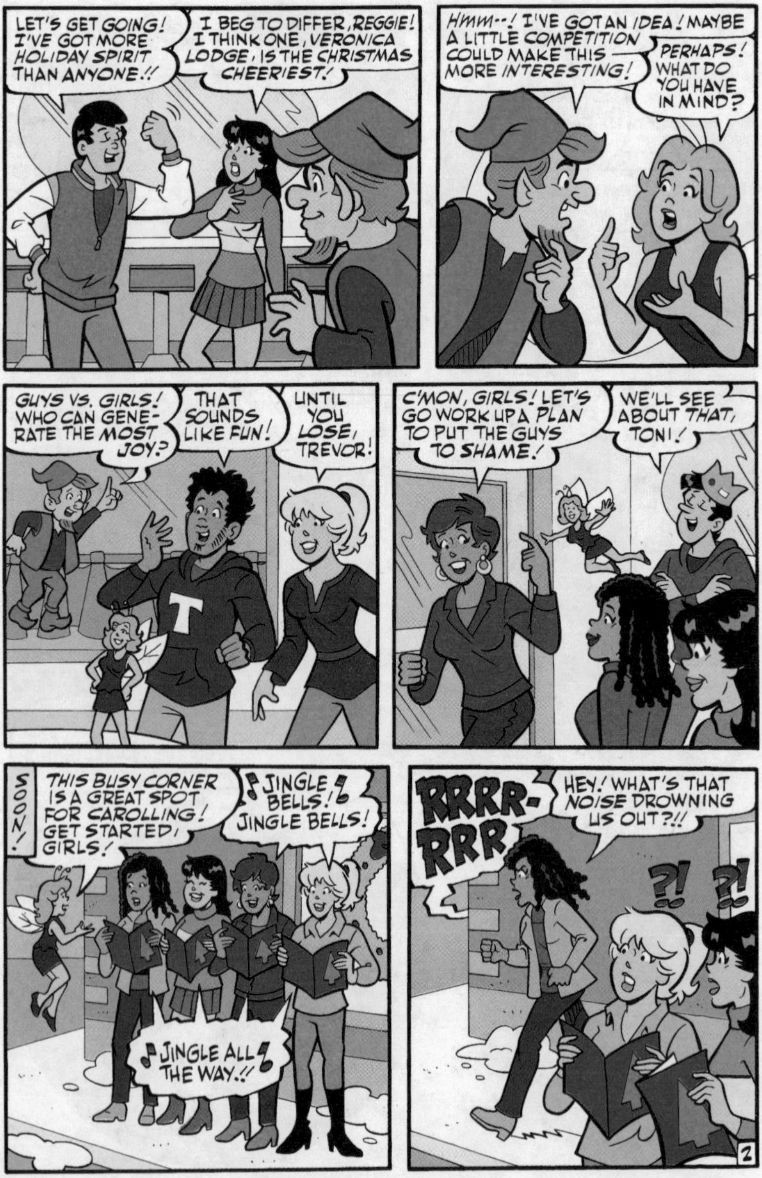
LET'S GET GOING! I'VE GOT MORE HOLIDAY SPIRIT THAN ANYONE!!
I BEG TO DIFFER, REGGIE! I THINK ONE, VERONICA LODGE, IS THE CHRISTMAS CHEERIEST!
HMM--! I'VE GOT AN IDEA! MAYBE A LITTLE COMPETITION COULD MAKE THIS MORE INTERESTING!
PERHAPS! WHAT DO YOU HAVE IN MIND?
GUYS VS. GIRLS! WHO CAN GENERATE THE MOST JOY?
THAT SOUNDS LIKE FUN!
UNTIL YOU LOSE, TREVOR!
C'MON, GIRLS! LET'S GO WORK UP A PLAN TO PUT THE GUYS TO SHAME!
WE'LL SEE ABOUT THAT, TONI!
SOON!
THIS BUSY CORNER IS A GREAT SPOT FOR CAROLLING! GET STARTED, GIRLS!
JINGLE BELLS! JINGLE BELLS!
JINGLE ALL THE WAY!!
RRRR-RRR
HEY! WHAT'S THAT NOISE DROWNING US OUT?!!
?!
?!
2

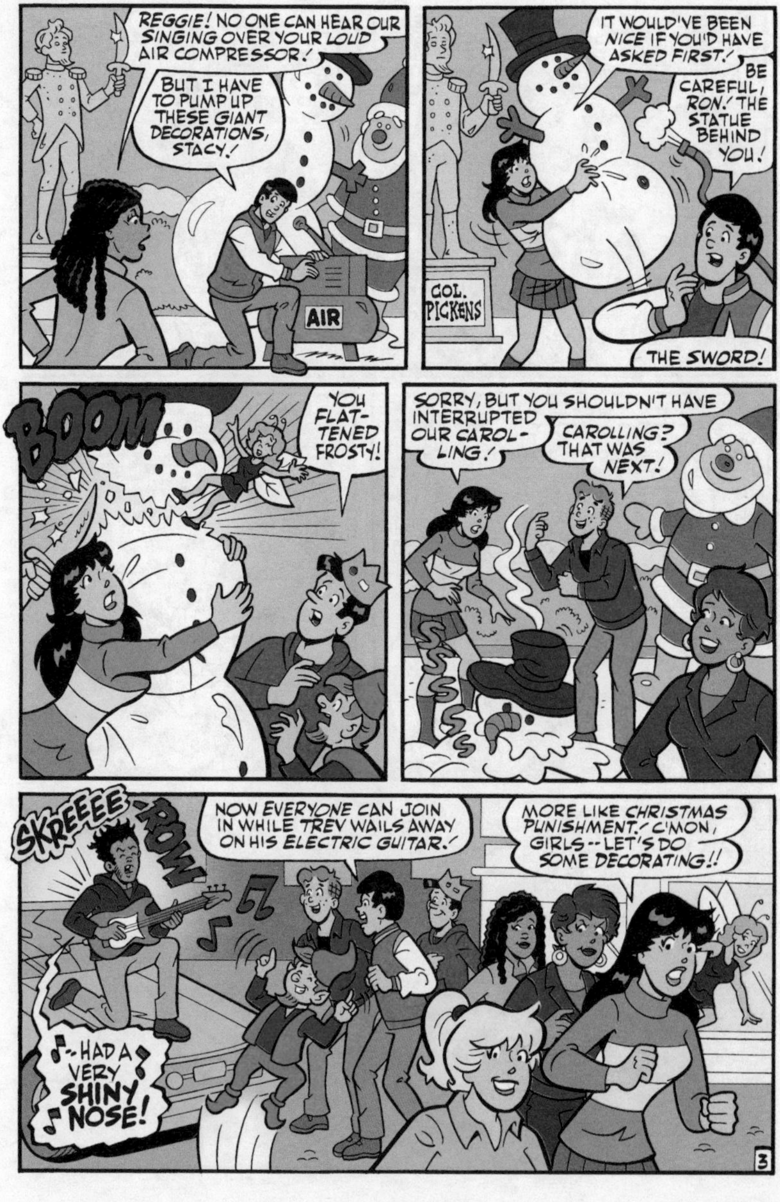
REGGIE! NO ONE CAN HEAR OUR SINGING OVER YOUR LOUD AIR COMPRESSOR!
BUT I HAVE TO PUMP UP THESE GIANT DECORATIONS, STACY!
AIR
IT WOULD'VE BEEN NICE IF YOU'D HAVE ASKED FIRST!
BE CAREFUL, RON! THE STATUE BEHIND YOU!
COL. PICKENS
THE SWORD!
BOOM
YOU FLATTENED FROSTY!
SORRY, BUT YOU SHOULDN'T HAVE INTERRUPTED OUR CAROLLING!
CAROLLING? THAT WAS NEXT!
SSSS
SKREEEE-ROW
NOW EVERYONE CAN JOIN IN WHILE TREV WAILS AWAY ON HIS ELECTRIC GUITAR!
MORE LIKE CHRISTMAS PUNISHMENT! C'MON, GIRLS -- LET'S DO SOME DECORATING!!
-HAD A VERY SHINY NOSE!
3

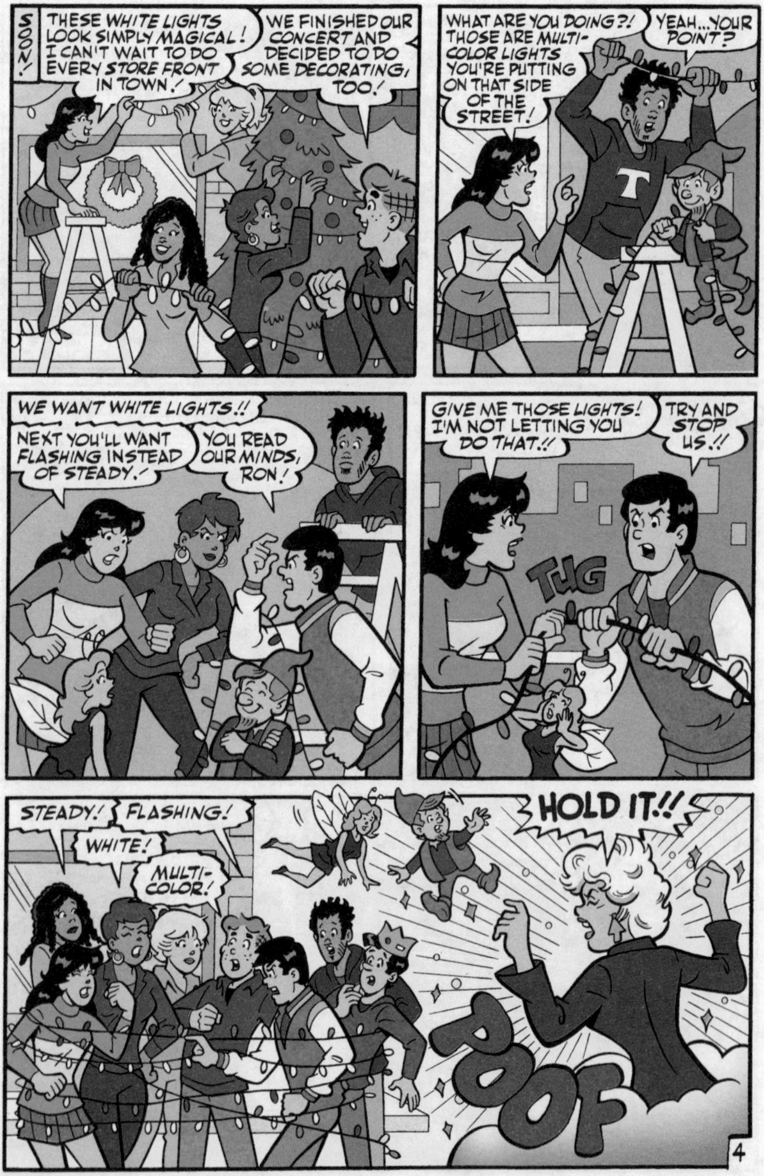
SOON!
THESE WHITE LIGHTS LOOK SIMPLY MAGICAL! I CAN'T WAIT TO DO EVERY STORE FRONT IN TOWN!
WE FINISHED OUR CONCERT AND DECIDED TO DO SOME DECORATING, TOO!
WHAT ARE YOU DOING?! THOSE ARE MULTI-COLOR LIGHTS YOU'RE PUTTING ON THAT SIDE OF THE STREET!
YEAH... YOUR POINT?
WE WANT WHITE LIGHTS!!
NEXT YOU'LL WANT FLASHING INSTEAD OF STEADY!
YOU READ OUR MINDS, RON!
GIVE ME THOSE LIGHTS! I'M NOT LETTING YOU DO THAT!!
TRY AND STOP US!!
TUG
STEADY!
FLASHING!
WHITE!
MULTI-COLOR!
HOLD IT!!
POOF
4

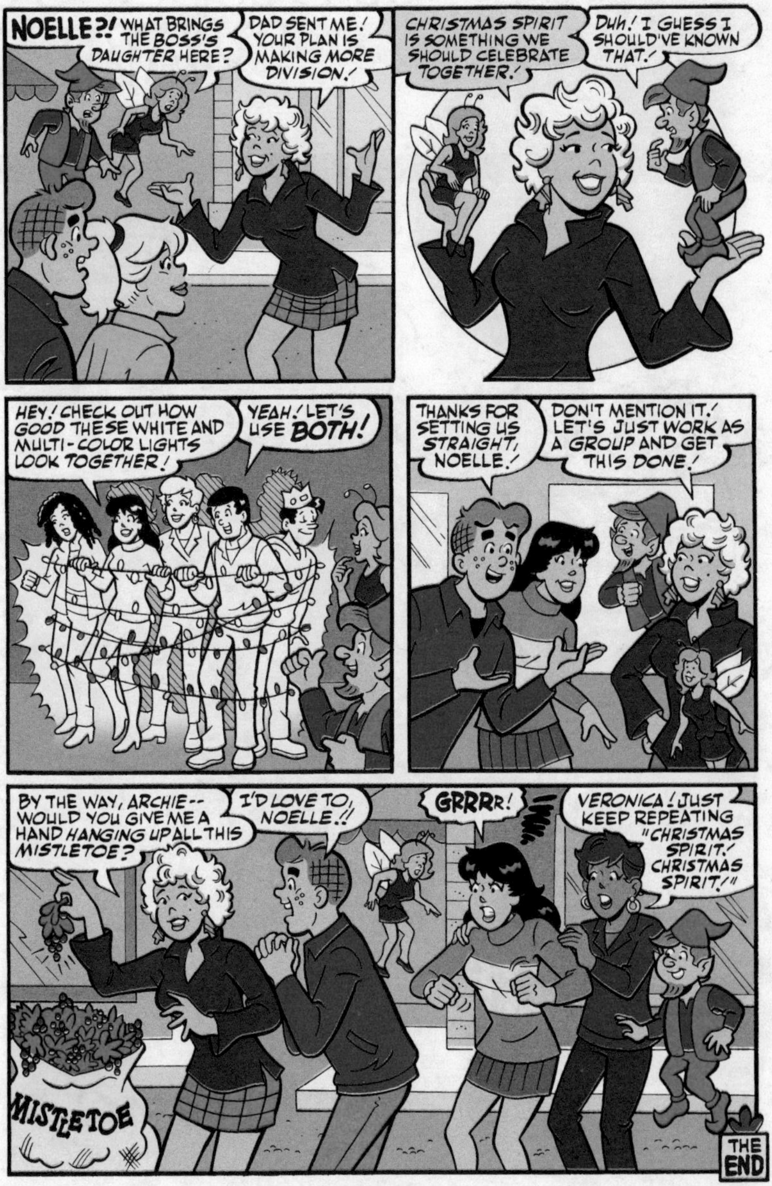
NOELLE?! WHAT BRINGS THE BOSS'S DAUGHTER HERE?
DAD SENT ME! YOUR PLAN IS MAKING MORE DIVISION!
CHRISTMAS SPIRIT IS SOMETHING WE SHOULD CELEBRATE TOGETHER!
DUH! I GUESS I SHOULD'VE KNOWN THAT!
HEY! CHECK OUT HOW GOOD THESE WHITE AND MULTI-COLOR LIGHTS LOOK TOGETHER!
YEAH! LET'S USE BOTH!
THANKS FOR SETTING US STRAIGHT, NOELLE!
DON'T MENTION IT! LET'S JUST WORK AS A GROUP AND GET THIS DONE!
BY THE WAY, ARCHIE-- WOULD YOU GIVE ME A HAND HANGING UP ALL THIS MISTLETOE?
I'D LOVE TO, NOELLE!!
GRRRR!
VERONICA! JUST KEEP REPEATING "CHRISTMAS SPIRIT! CHRISTMAS SPIRIT!"
MISTLETOE
THE END

04 WORLD OF B&V

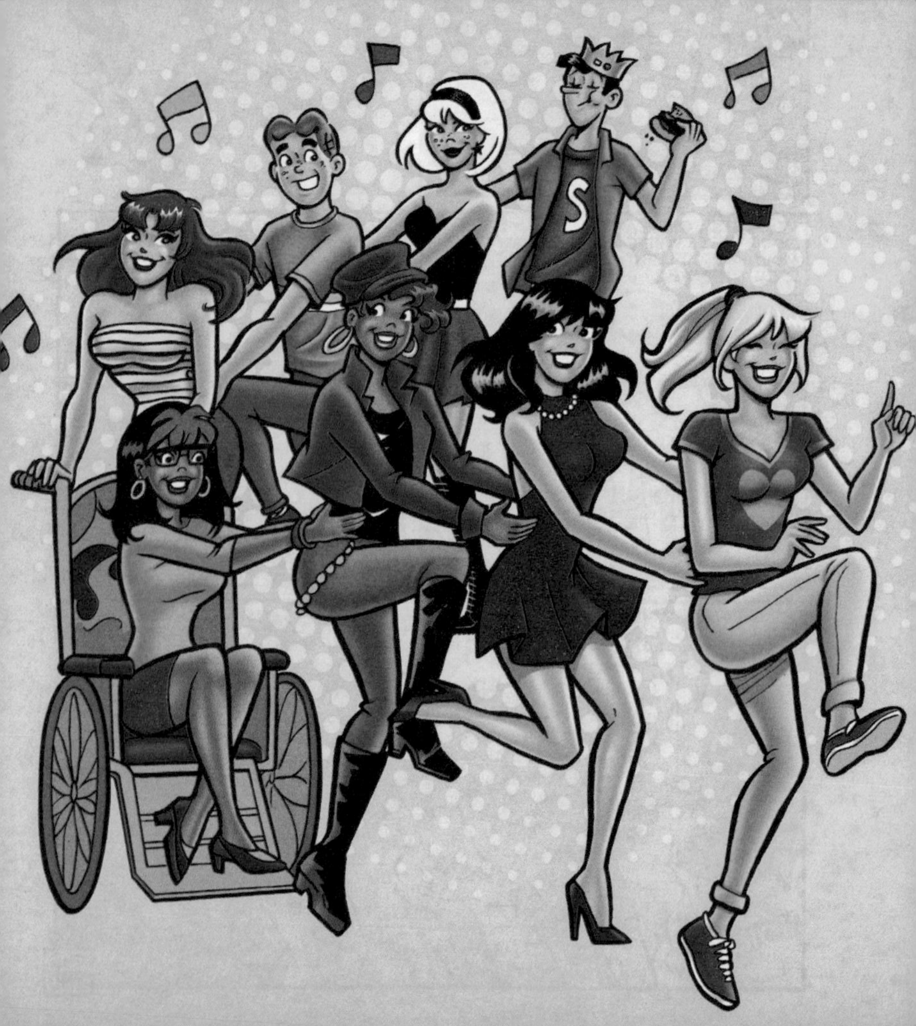

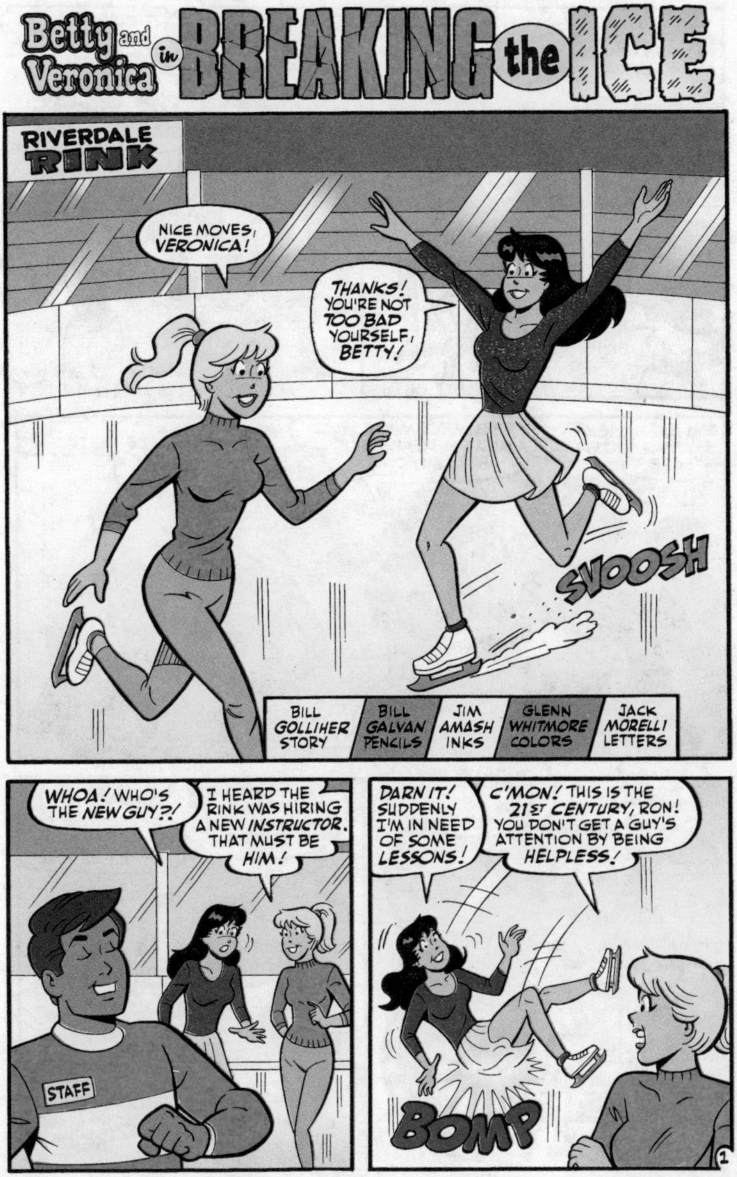
Betty and Veronica in BREAKING the ICE
RIVERDALE RINK
NICE MOVES, VERONICA!
THANKS! YOU'RE NOT TOO BAD YOURSELF, BETTY!
SVOOSH
BILL GOLLIHER STORY
BILL GALVAN PENCILS
JIM AMASH INKS
GLENN WHITMORE COLORS
JACK MORELLI LETTERS
WHOA! WHO'S THE NEW GUY?!
I HEARD THE RINK WAS HIRING A NEW INSTRUCTOR. THAT MUST BE HIM!
STAFF
DARN IT! SUDDENLY I'M IN NEED OF SOME LESSONS!
C'MON! THIS IS THE 21ST CENTURY, RON! YOU DON'T GET A GUY'S ATTENTION BY BEING HELPLESS!
BOMP
1

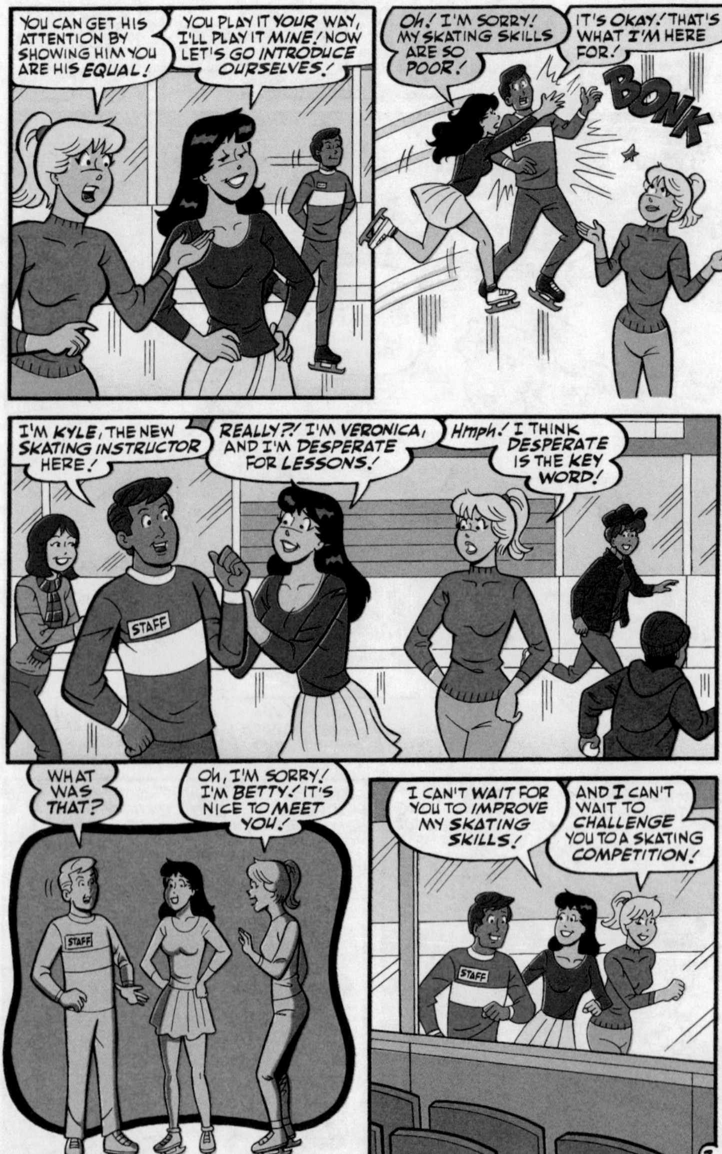
YOU CAN GET HIS ATTENTION BY SHOWING HIM YOU ARE HIS EQUAL!
YOU PLAY IT YOUR WAY, I'LL PLAY IT MINE! NOW LET'S GO INTRODUCE OURSELVES!
Oh! I'M SORRY! MY SKATING SKILLS ARE SO POOR!
IT'S OKAY! THAT'S WHAT I'M HERE FOR!
BONK
I'M KYLE, THE NEW SKATING INSTRUCTOR HERE!
REALLY?! I'M VERONICA, AND I'M DESPERATE FOR LESSONS!
Hmph! I THINK DESPERATE IS THE KEY WORD!
STAFF
WHAT WAS THAT?
Oh, I'M SORRY! I'M BETTY! IT'S NICE TO MEET YOU!
STAFF
I CAN'T WAIT FOR YOU TO IMPROVE MY SKATING SKILLS!
AND I CAN'T WAIT TO CHALLENGE YOU TO A SKATING COMPETITION!
STAFF
2

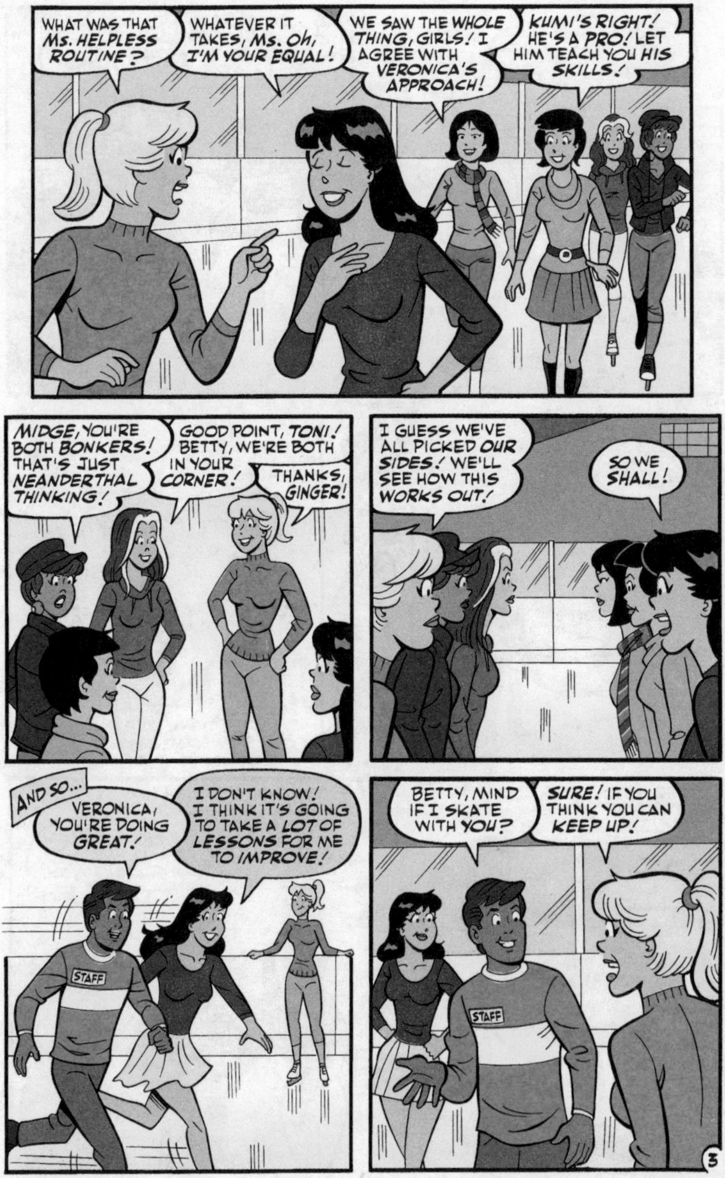
WHAT WAS THAT Ms. HELPLESS ROUTINE?
WHATEVER IT TAKES, Ms. Oh, I'M YOUR EQUAL!
WE SAW THE WHOLE THING, GIRLS! I AGREE WITH VERONICA'S APPROACH!
KUMI'S RIGHT! HE'S A PRO! LET HIM TEACH YOU HIS SKILLS!
MIDGE, YOU'RE BOTH BONKERS! THAT'S JUST NEANDERTHAL THINKING!
GOOD POINT, TONI! BETTY, WE'RE BOTH IN YOUR CORNER!
THANKS, GINGER!
I GUESS WE'VE ALL PICKED OUR SIDES! WE'LL SEE HOW THIS WORKS OUT!
SO WE SHALL!
AND SO...
VERONICA, YOU'RE DOING GREAT!
I DON'T KNOW! I THINK IT'S GOING TO TAKE A LOT OF LESSONS FOR ME TO IMPROVE!
STAFF
BETTY, MIND IF I SKATE WITH YOU?
SURE! IF YOU THINK YOU CAN KEEP UP!
STAFF
3

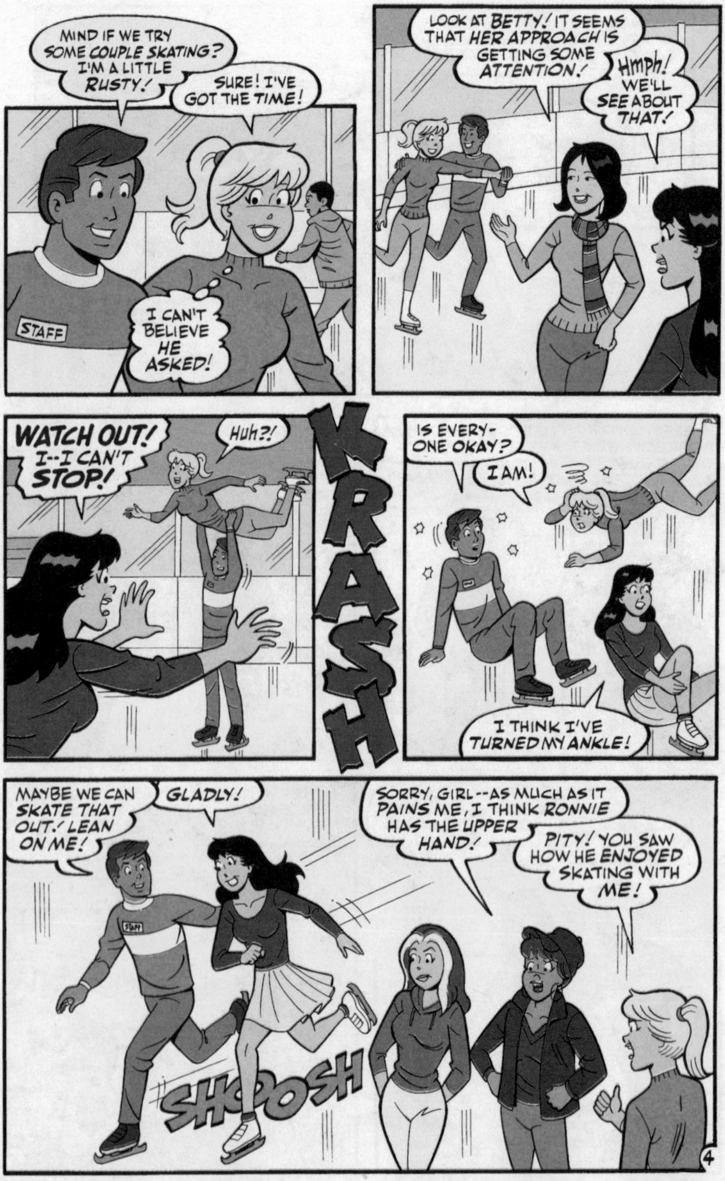
MIND IF WE TRY SOME COUPLE SKATING? I'M A LITTLE RUSTY!
SURE! I'VE GOT THE TIME!
I CAN'T BELIEVE HE ASKED!
STAFF
LOOK AT BETTY! IT SEEMS THAT HER APPROACH IS GETTING SOME ATTENTION!
Hmph! WE'LL SEE ABOUT THAT!
WATCH OUT! I--I CAN'T STOP!
Huh?!
KRASH
IS EVERY-ONE OKAY?
I AM!
I THINK I'VE TURNED MY ANKLE!
MAYBE WE CAN SKATE THAT OUT! LEAN ON ME!
GLADLY!
SORRY, GIRL--AS MUCH AS IT PAINS ME, I THINK RONNIE HAS THE UPPER HAND!
PITY! YOU SAW HOW HE ENJOYED SKATING WITH ME!
SHOOSH
4

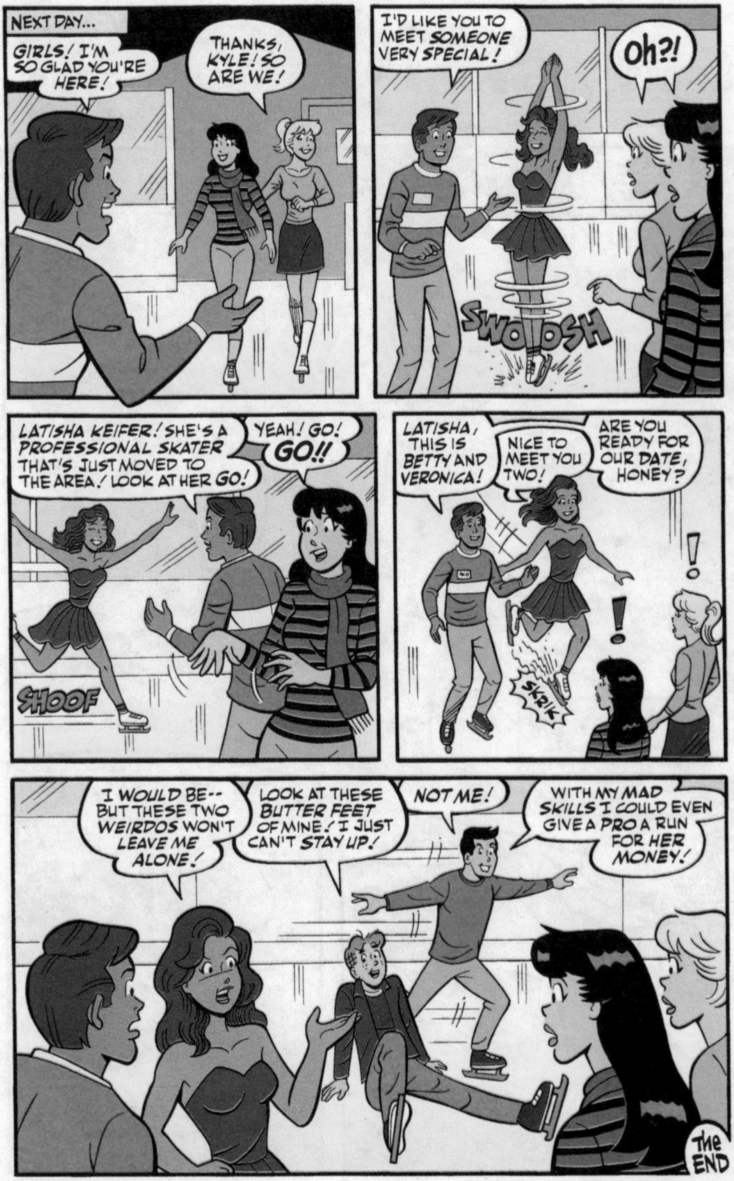
NEXT DAY...
GIRLS! I'M SO GLAD YOU'RE HERE!
THANKS, KYLE! SO ARE WE!
I'D LIKE YOU TO MEET SOMEONE VERY SPECIAL!
Oh?!
SWOOSH
LATISHA KEIFER! SHE'S A PROFESSIONAL SKATER THAT'S JUST MOVED TO THE AREA! LOOK AT HER GO!
YEAH! GO! GO!!
SHOOF
LATISHA, THIS IS BETTY AND VERONICA!
NICE TO MEET YOU TWO!
ARE YOU READY FOR OUR DATE, HONEY?
SKRIK
I WOULD BE-- BUT THESE TWO WEIRDOS WON'T LEAVE ME ALONE!
LOOK AT THESE BUTTER FEET OF MINE! I JUST CAN'T STAY UP!
NOT ME!
WITH MY MAD SKILLS I COULD EVEN GIVE A PRO A RUN FOR HER MONEY!
The END

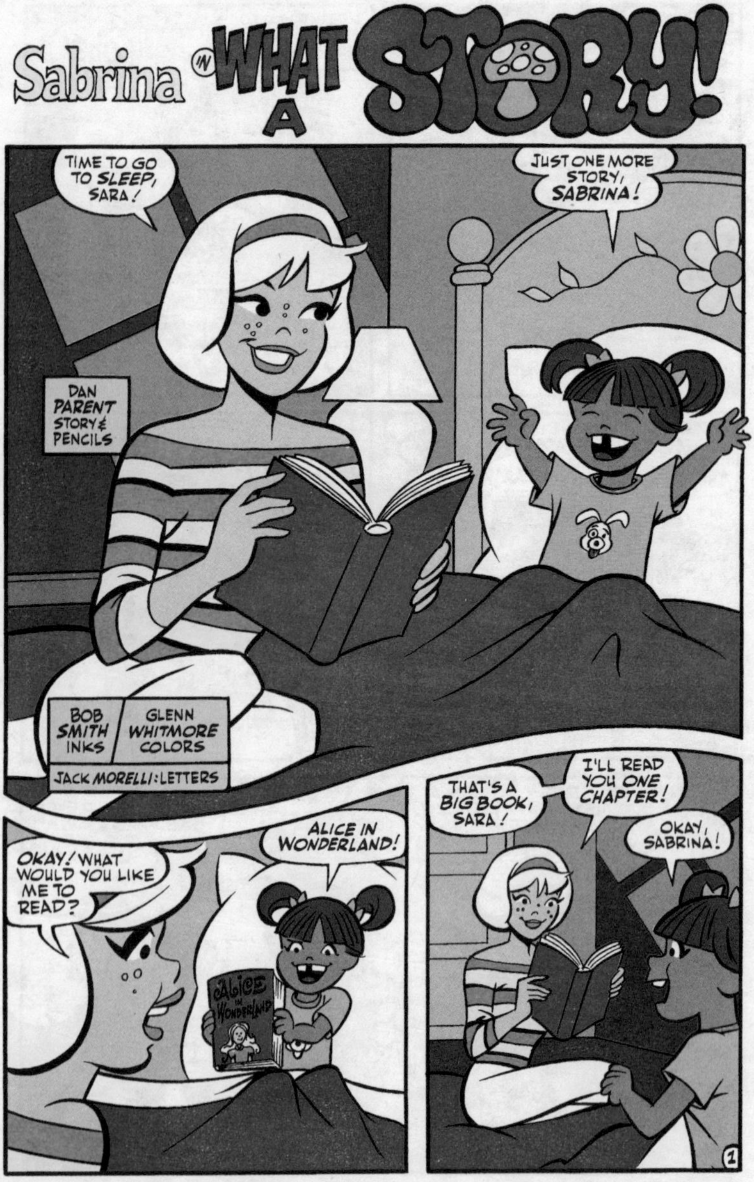
Sabrina in WHAT A STORY!
TIME TO GO TO SLEEP, SARA!
JUST ONE MORE STORY, SABRINA!
DAN PARENT STORY & PENCILS
BOB SMITH INKS
GLENN WHITMORE COLORS
JACK MORELLI: LETTERS
OKAY! WHAT WOULD YOU LIKE ME TO READ?
ALICE IN WONDERLAND!
ALICE IN WONDERLAND
THAT'S A BIG BOOK, SARA!
I'LL READ YOU ONE CHAPTER!
OKAY, SABRINA!
1

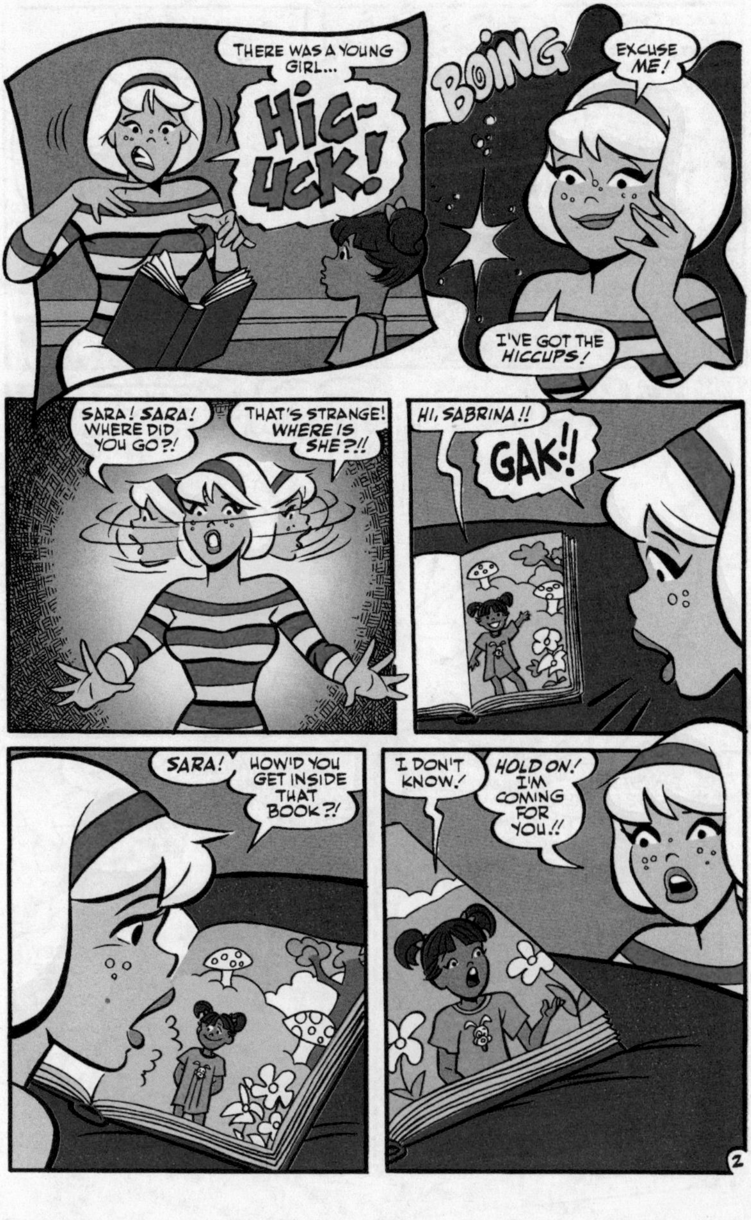
THERE WAS A YOUNG GIRL...
HIC-UCK!
BOING
EXCUSE ME!
I'VE GOT THE HICCUPS!
SARA! SARA! WHERE DID YOU GO?!
THAT'S STRANGE! WHERE IS SHE?!!
HI, SABRINA!!
GAK!!
SARA!
HOW'D YOU GET INSIDE THAT BOOK?!
I DON'T KNOW!
HOLD ON! I'M COMING FOR YOU!!
2

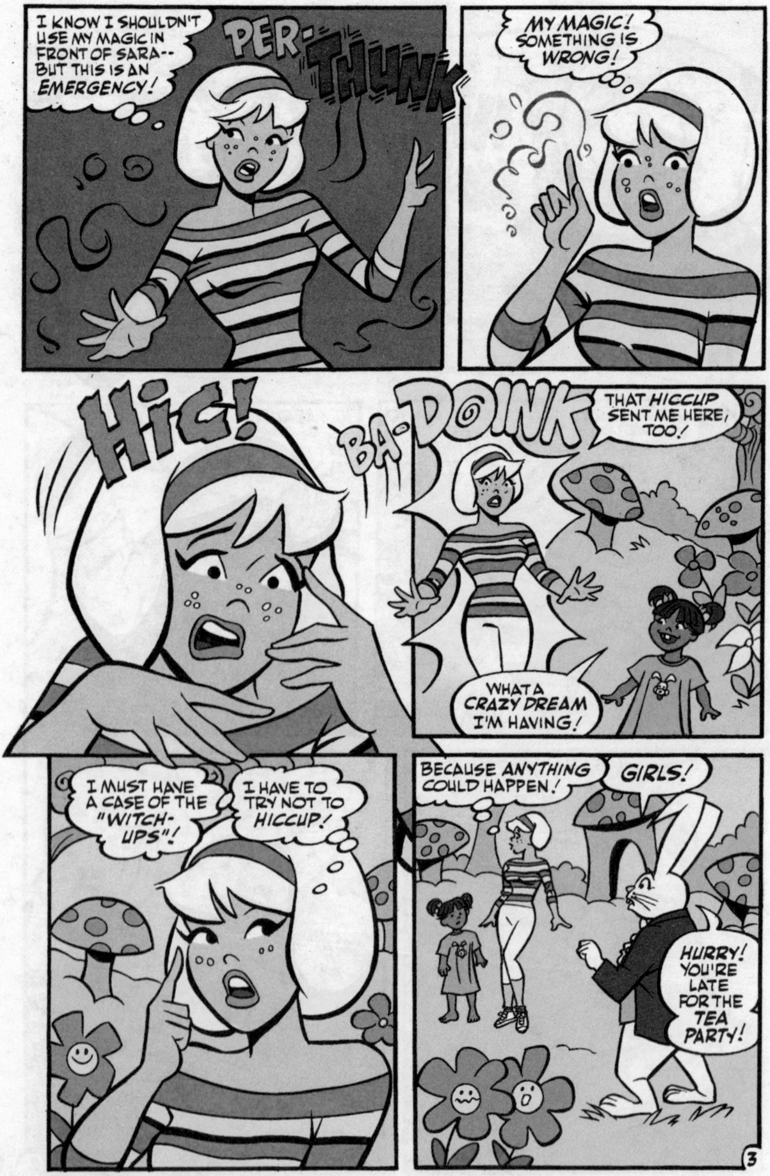
I KNOW I SHOULDN'T USE MY MAGIC IN FRONT OF SARA-- BUT THIS IS AN EMERGENCY!
PER-THUNK
MY MAGIC! SOMETHING IS WRONG!
HIC!
BA-DOINK
THAT HICCUP SENT ME HERE, TOO!
WHAT A CRAZY DREAM I'M HAVING!
I MUST HAVE A CASE OF THE "WITCH-UPS"!
I HAVE TO TRY NOT TO HICCUP!
BECAUSE ANYTHING COULD HAPPEN!
GIRLS!
HURRY! YOU'RE LATE FOR THE TEA PARTY!
3

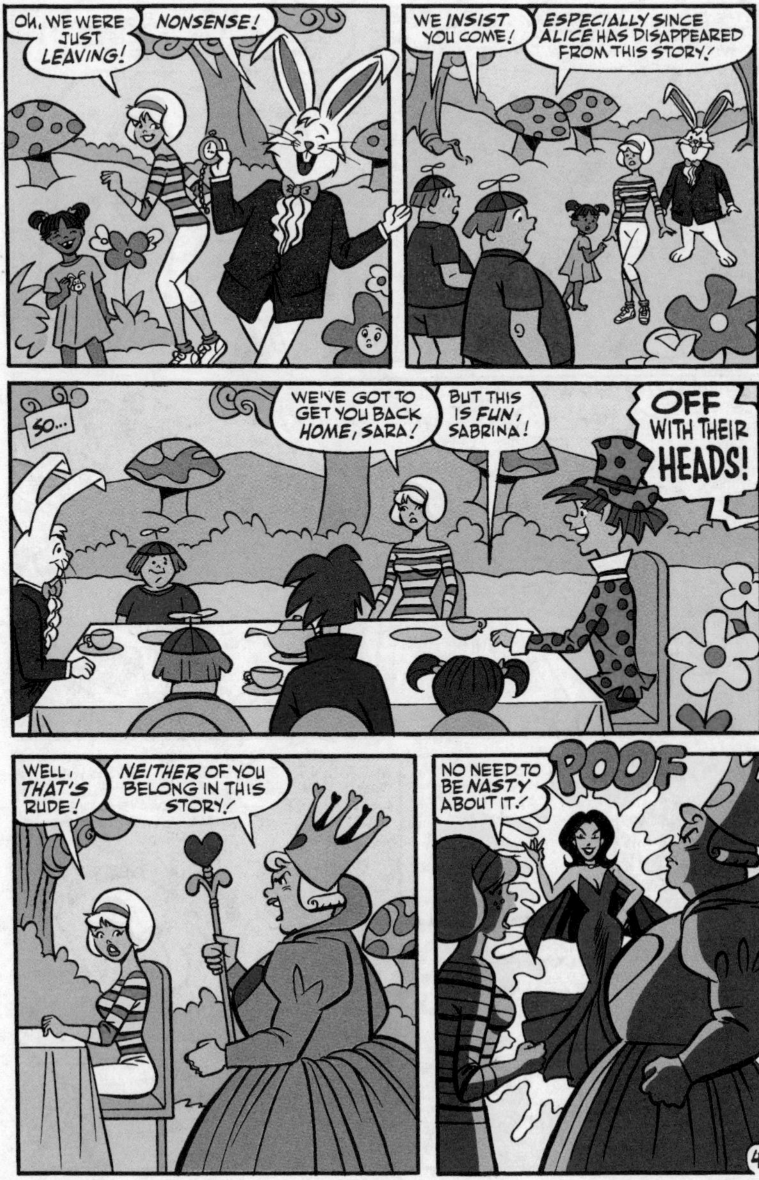
OH, WE WERE JUST LEAVING!
NONSENSE!
WE INSIST YOU COME!
ESPECIALLY SINCE ALICE HAS DISAPPEARED FROM THIS STORY!
SO...
WE'VE GOT TO GET YOU BACK HOME, SARA!
BUT THIS IS FUN, SABRINA!
OFF WITH THEIR HEADS!
WELL, THAT'S RUDE!
NEITHER OF YOU BELONG IN THIS STORY!
NO NEED TO BE NASTY ABOUT IT!
POOF
4

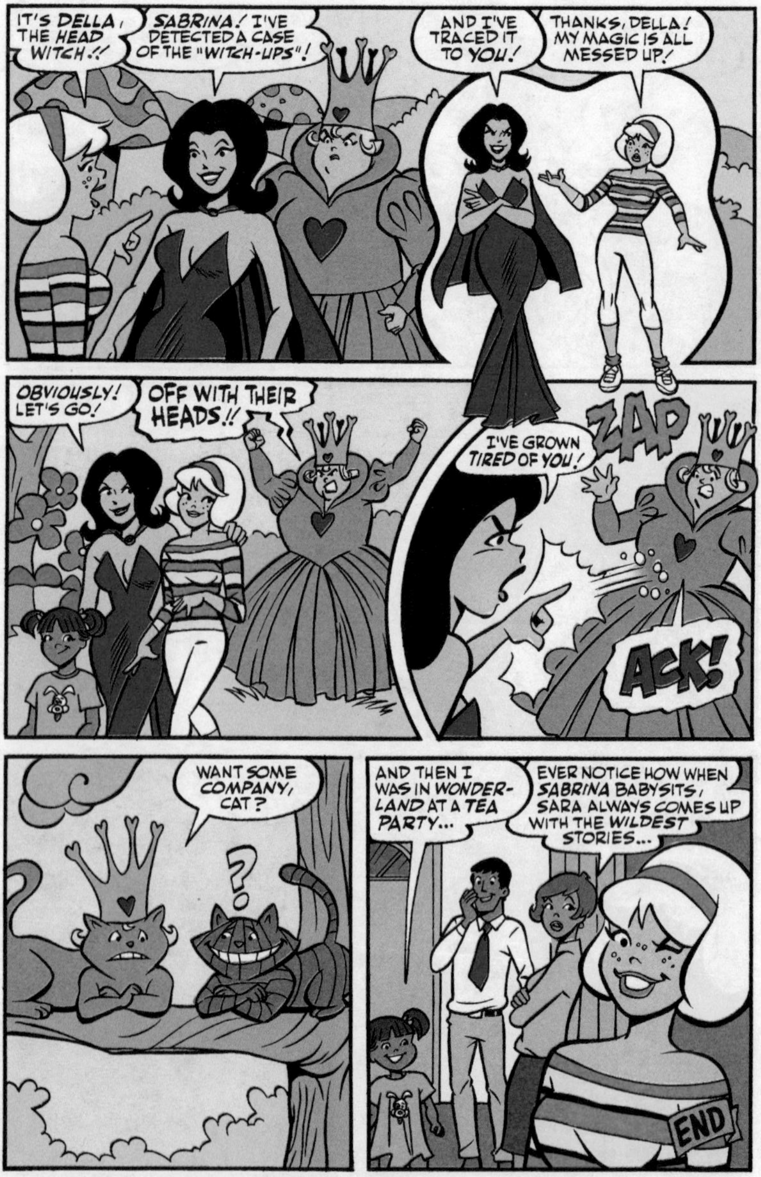
IT'S DELLA, THE HEAD WITCH!!
SABRINA! I'VE DETECTED A CASE OF THE "WITCH-UPS"!
AND I'VE TRACED IT TO YOU!
THANKS, DELLA! MY MAGIC IS ALL MESSED UP!
OBVIOUSLY! LET'S GO!
OFF WITH THEIR HEADS!!
I'VE GROWN TIRED OF YOU!
ZAP
ACK!
WANT SOME COMPANY, CAT?
?
AND THEN I WAS IN WONDER-LAND AT A TEA PARTY...
EVER NOTICE HOW WHEN SABRINA BABYSITS, SARA ALWAYS COMES UP WITH THE WILDEST STORIES...
END

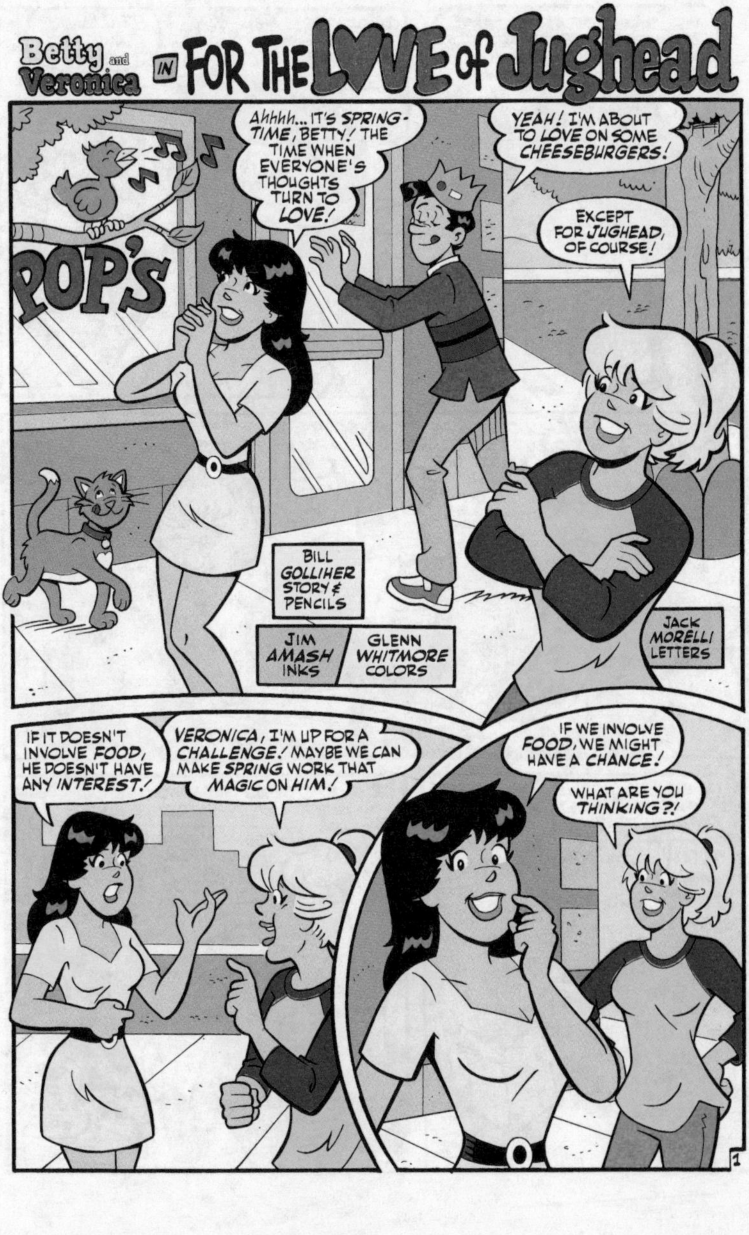
Betty and Veronica IN FOR THE LOVE of Jughead
POP'S
Ahhhh... IT'S SPRING-TIME, BETTY! THE TIME WHEN EVERYONE'S THOUGHTS TURN TO LOVE!
YEAH! I'M ABOUT TO LOVE ON SOME CHEESEBURGERS!
EXCEPT FOR JUGHEAD, OF COURSE!
BILL GOLLIHER STORY & PENCILS
JIM AMASH INKS
GLENN WHITMORE COLORS
JACK MORELLI LETTERS
IF IT DOESN'T INVOLVE FOOD, HE DOESN'T HAVE ANY INTEREST!
VERONICA, I'M UP FOR A CHALLENGE! MAYBE WE CAN MAKE SPRING WORK THAT MAGIC ON HIM!
IF WE INVOLVE FOOD, WE MIGHT HAVE A CHANCE!
WHAT ARE YOU THINKING?!
1

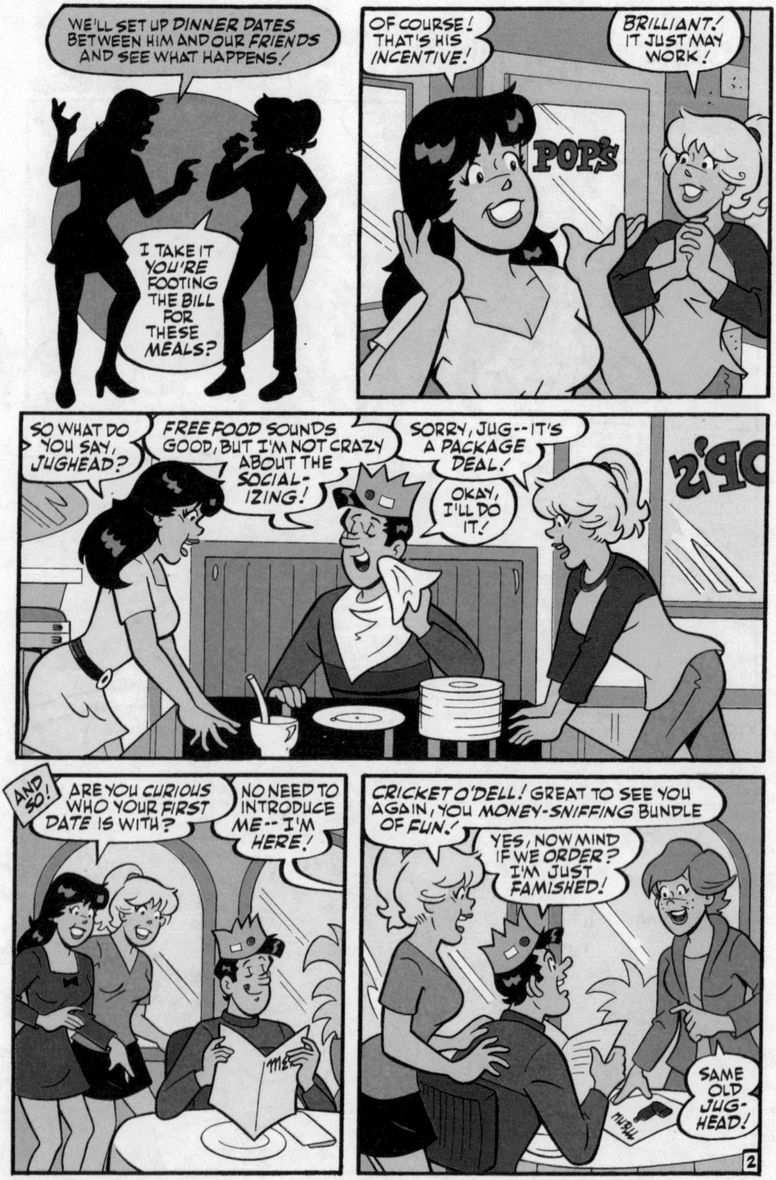
WE'LL SET UP DINNER DATES BETWEEN HIM AND OUR FRIENDS AND SEE WHAT HAPPENS!
I TAKE IT YOU'RE FOOTING THE BILL FOR THESE MEALS?
OF COURSE! THAT'S HIS INCENTIVE!
BRILLIANT! IT JUST MAY WORK!
POP'S
SO WHAT DO YOU SAY, JUGHEAD?
FREE FOOD SOUNDS GOOD, BUT I'M NOT CRAZY ABOUT THE SOCIAL-IZING!
SORRY, JUG-- IT'S A PACKAGE DEAL!
OKAY, I'LL DO IT!
AND SO!
ARE YOU CURIOUS WHO YOUR FIRST DATE IS WITH?
NO NEED TO INTRODUCE ME-- I'M HERE!
CRICKET O'DELL! GREAT TO SEE YOU AGAIN, YOU MONEY-SNIFFING BUNDLE OF FUN!
YES, NOW MIND IF WE ORDER? I'M JUST FAMISHED!
SAME OLD JUG-HEAD!
2

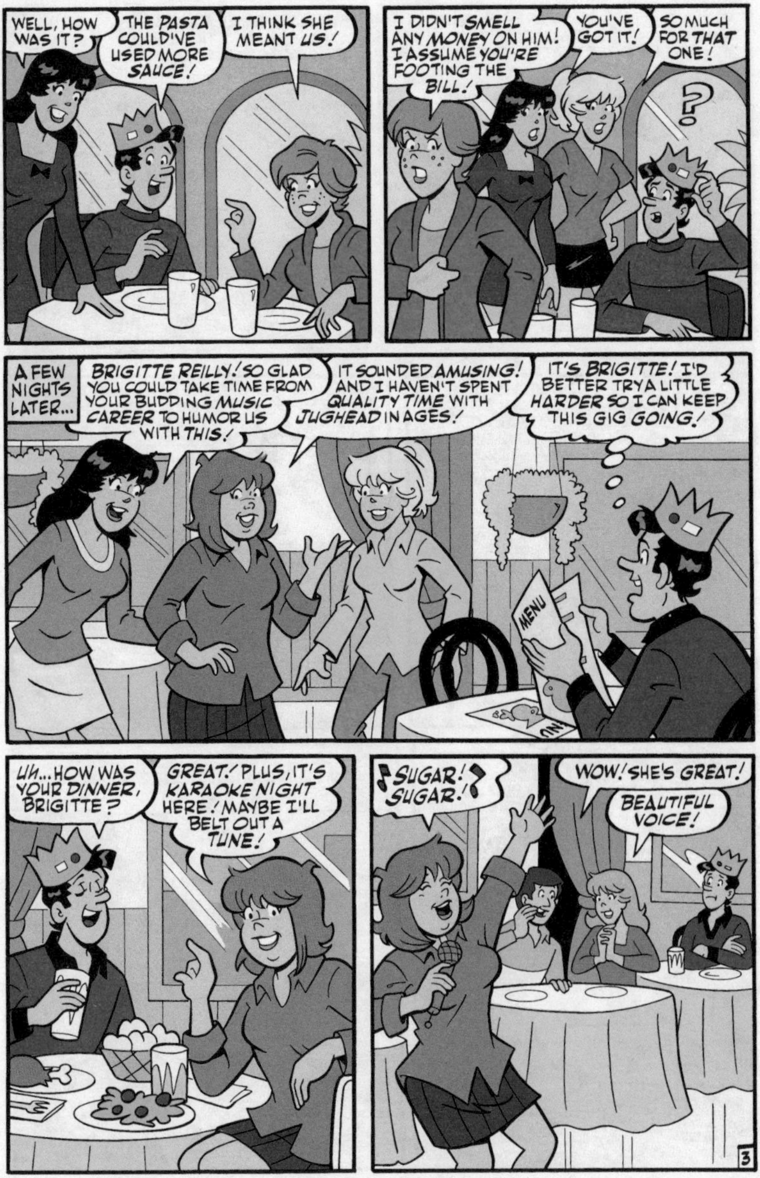
WELL, HOW WAS IT?
THE PASTA COULD'VE USED MORE SAUCE!
I THINK SHE MEANT US!
I DIDN'T SMELL ANY MONEY ON HIM! I ASSUME YOU'RE FOOTING THE BILL!
YOU'VE GOT IT!
SO MUCH FOR THAT ONE!
?
A FEW NIGHTS LATER...
BRIGITTE REILLY! SO GLAD YOU COULD TAKE TIME FROM YOUR BUDDING MUSIC CAREER TO HUMOR US WITH THIS!
IT SOUNDED AMUSING! AND I HAVEN'T SPENT QUALITY TIME WITH JUGHEAD IN AGES!
IT'S BRIGITTE! I'D BETTER TRY A LITTLE HARDER SO I CAN KEEP THIS GIG GOING!
MENU
UH... HOW WAS YOUR DINNER, BRIGITTE?
GREAT! PLUS, IT'S KARAOKE NIGHT HERE! MAYBE I'LL BELT OUT A TUNE!
SUGAR! SUGAR!
WOW! SHE'S GREAT!
BEAUTIFUL VOICE!
3

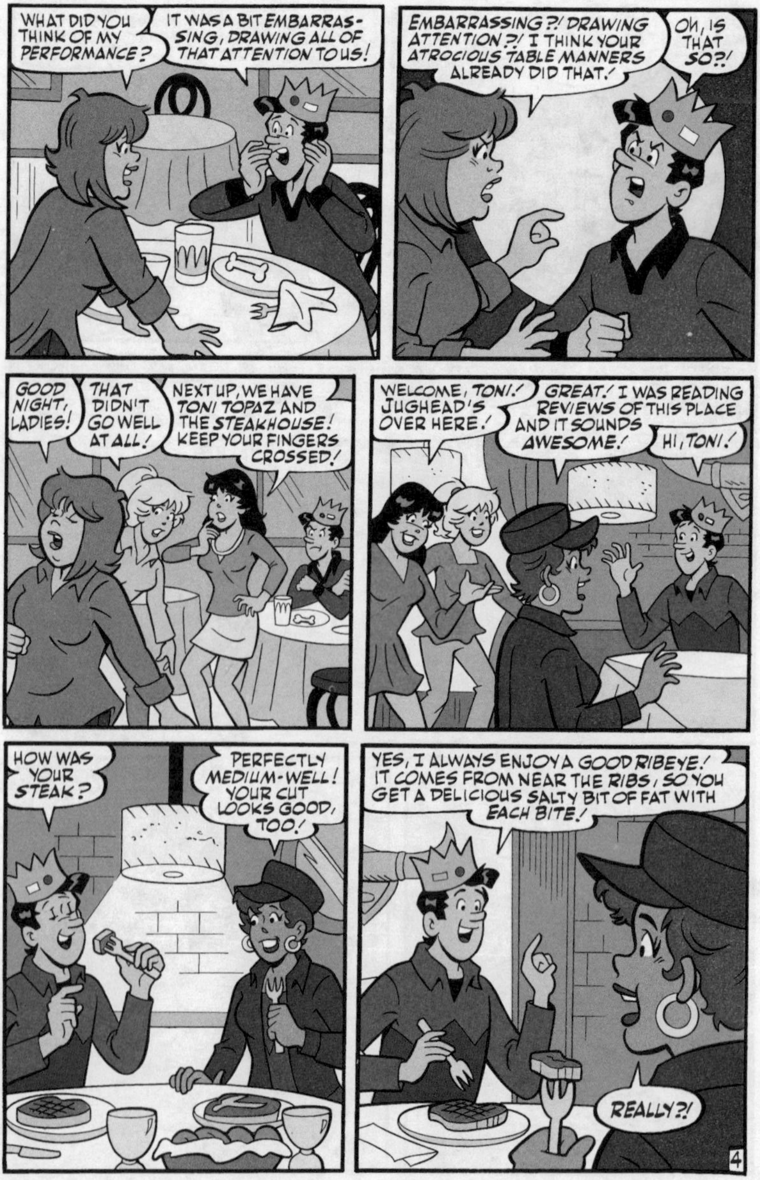
WHAT DID YOU THINK OF MY PERFORMANCE?
IT WAS A BIT EMBARRASSING, DRAWING ALL OF THAT ATTENTION TO US!
EMBARRASSING?! DRAWING ATTENTION?! I THINK YOUR ATROCIOUS TABLE MANNERS ALREADY DID THAT!
OH, IS THAT SO?!
GOOD NIGHT, LADIES!
THAT DIDN'T GO WELL AT ALL!
NEXT UP, WE HAVE TONI TOPAZ AND THE STEAKHOUSE! KEEP YOUR FINGERS CROSSED!
WELCOME, TONI! JUGHEAD'S OVER HERE!
GREAT! I WAS READING REVIEWS OF THIS PLACE AND IT SOUNDS AWESOME!
HI, TONI!
HOW WAS YOUR STEAK?
PERFECTLY MEDIUM-WELL! YOUR CUT LOOKS GOOD, TOO!
YES, I ALWAYS ENJOY A GOOD RIBEYE! IT COMES FROM NEAR THE RIBS, SO YOU GET A DELICIOUS SALTY BIT OF FAT WITH EACH BITE!
REALLY?!
4

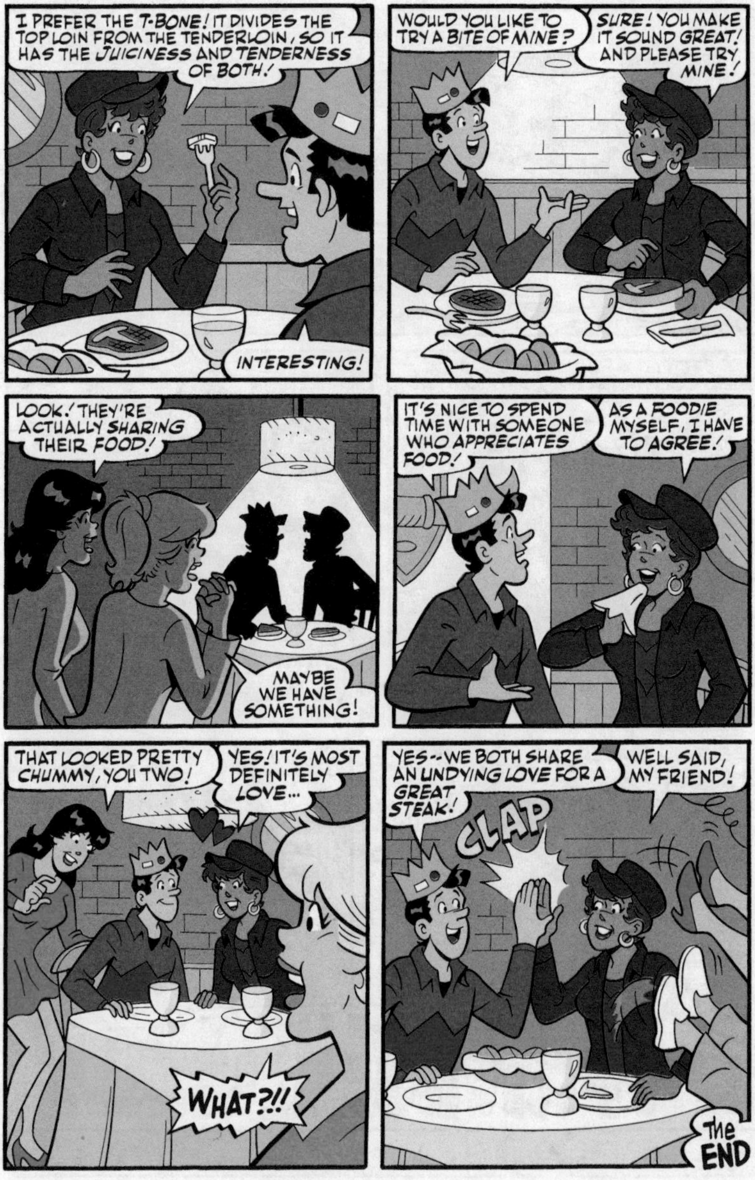
I PREFER THE T-BONE! IT DIVIDES THE TOP LOIN FROM THE TENDERLOIN, SO IT HAS THE JUICINESS AND TENDERNESS OF BOTH!
INTERESTING!
WOULD YOU LIKE TO TRY A BITE OF MINE?
SURE! YOU MAKE IT SOUND GREAT! AND PLEASE TRY MINE!
LOOK! THEY'RE ACTUALLY SHARING THEIR FOOD!
MAYBE WE HAVE SOMETHING!
IT'S NICE TO SPEND TIME WITH SOMEONE WHO APPRECIATES FOOD!
AS A FOODIE MYSELF, I HAVE TO AGREE!
THAT LOOKED PRETTY CHUMMY, YOU TWO!
YES! IT'S MOST DEFINITELY LOVE...
WHAT?!!
YES--WE BOTH SHARE AN UNDYING LOVE FOR A GREAT STEAK!
WELL SAID, MY FRIEND!
CLAP
The END

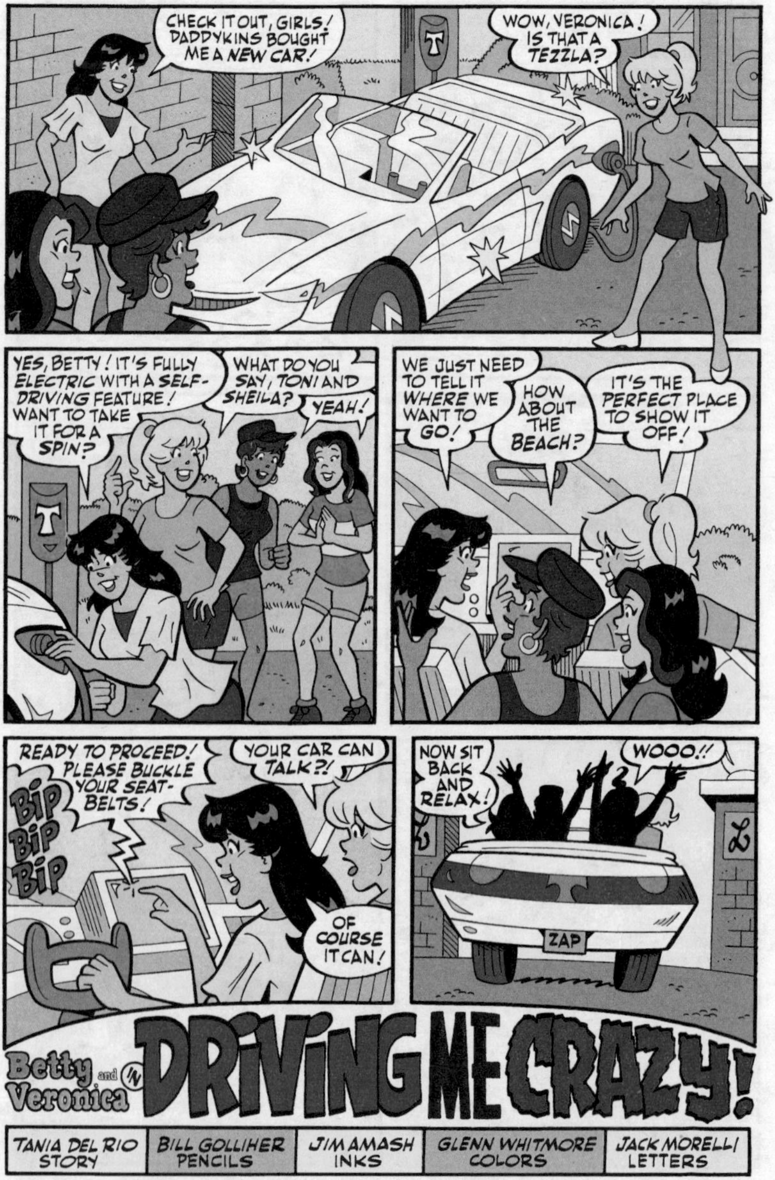
CHECK IT OUT, GIRLS! DADDYKINS BOUGHT ME A NEW CAR!
WOW, VERONICA! IS THAT A TEZZLA?
YES, BETTY! IT'S FULLY ELECTRIC WITH A SELF-DRIVING FEATURE! WANT TO TAKE IT FOR A SPIN?
WHAT DO YOU SAY, TONI AND SHEILA?
YEAH!
WE JUST NEED TO TELL IT WHERE WE WANT TO GO!
HOW ABOUT THE BEACH?
IT'S THE PERFECT PLACE TO SHOW IT OFF!
READY TO PROCEED! PLEASE BUCKLE YOUR SEAT-BELTS!
BIP BIP BIP
YOUR CAR CAN TALK?!
OF COURSE IT CAN!
NOW SIT BACK AND RELAX!
WOOO!!
ZAP
Betty and Veronica IN DRIVING ME CRAZY!
TANIA DEL RIO STORY
BILL GOLLIHER PENCILS
JIM AMASH INKS
GLENN WHITMORE COLORS
JACK MORELLI LETTERS

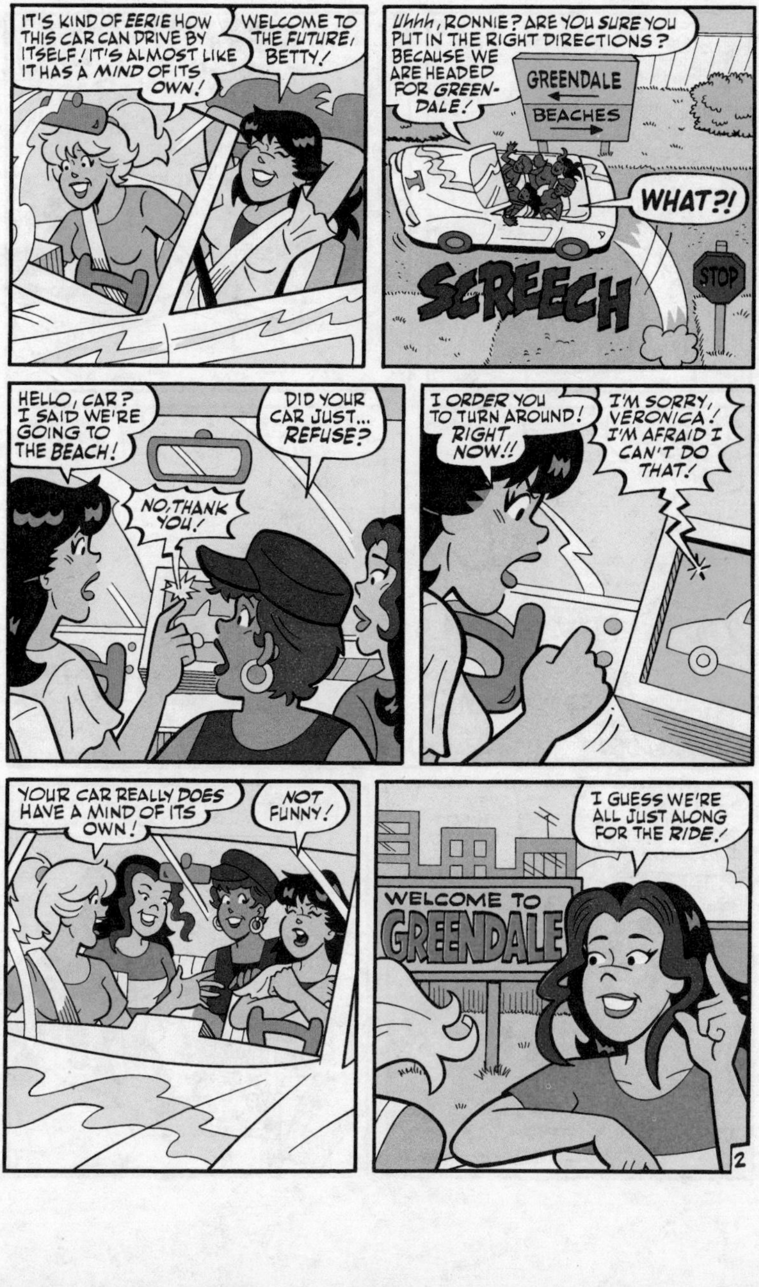
IT'S KIND OF EERIE HOW THIS CAR CAN DRIVE BY ITSELF! IT'S ALMOST LIKE IT HAS A MIND OF ITS OWN!
WELCOME TO THE FUTURE, BETTY!
Uhhh, RONNIE? ARE YOU SURE YOU PUT IN THE RIGHT DIRECTIONS? BECAUSE WE ARE HEADED FOR GREEN-DALE!
GREENDALE
BEACHES
WHAT?!
SCREECH
STOP
HELLO, CAR? I SAID WE'RE GOING TO THE BEACH!
DID YOUR CAR JUST... REFUSE?
NO, THANK YOU!
I ORDER YOU TO TURN AROUND! RIGHT NOW!!
I'M SORRY, VERONICA! I'M AFRAID I CAN'T DO THAT!
YOUR CAR REALLY DOES HAVE A MIND OF ITS OWN!
NOT FUNNY!
I GUESS WE'RE ALL JUST ALONG FOR THE RIDE!
WELCOME TO GREENDALE
2

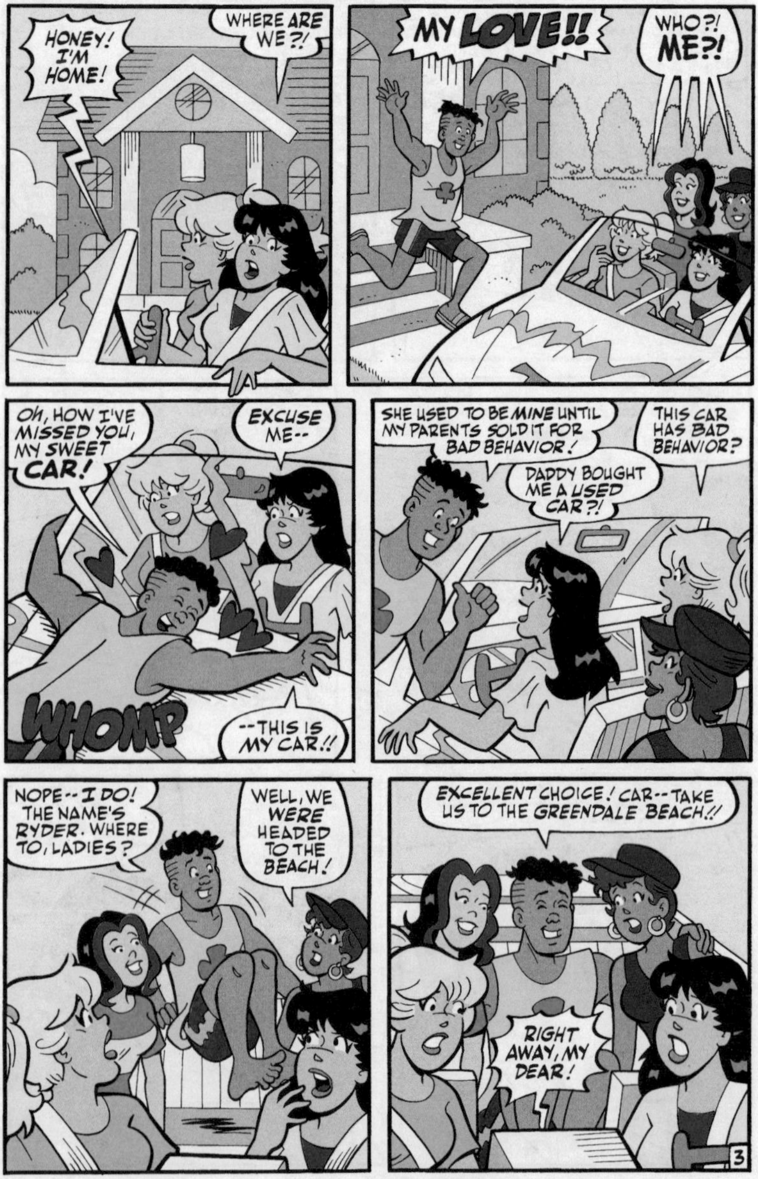
HONEY! I'M HOME!
WHERE ARE WE?!
MY LOVE!!
WHO?! ME?!
Oh, HOW I'VE MISSED YOU, MY SWEET CAR!
EXCUSE ME--
WHOMP
--THIS IS MY CAR!!
SHE USED TO BE MINE UNTIL MY PARENTS SOLD IT FOR BAD BEHAVIOR!
THIS CAR HAS BAD BEHAVIOR?
DADDY BOUGHT ME A USED CAR?!
NOPE--I DO! THE NAME'S RYDER. WHERE TO, LADIES?
WELL, WE WERE HEADED TO THE BEACH!
EXCELLENT CHOICE! CAR--TAKE US TO THE GREENDALE BEACH!!
RIGHT AWAY, MY DEAR!
3

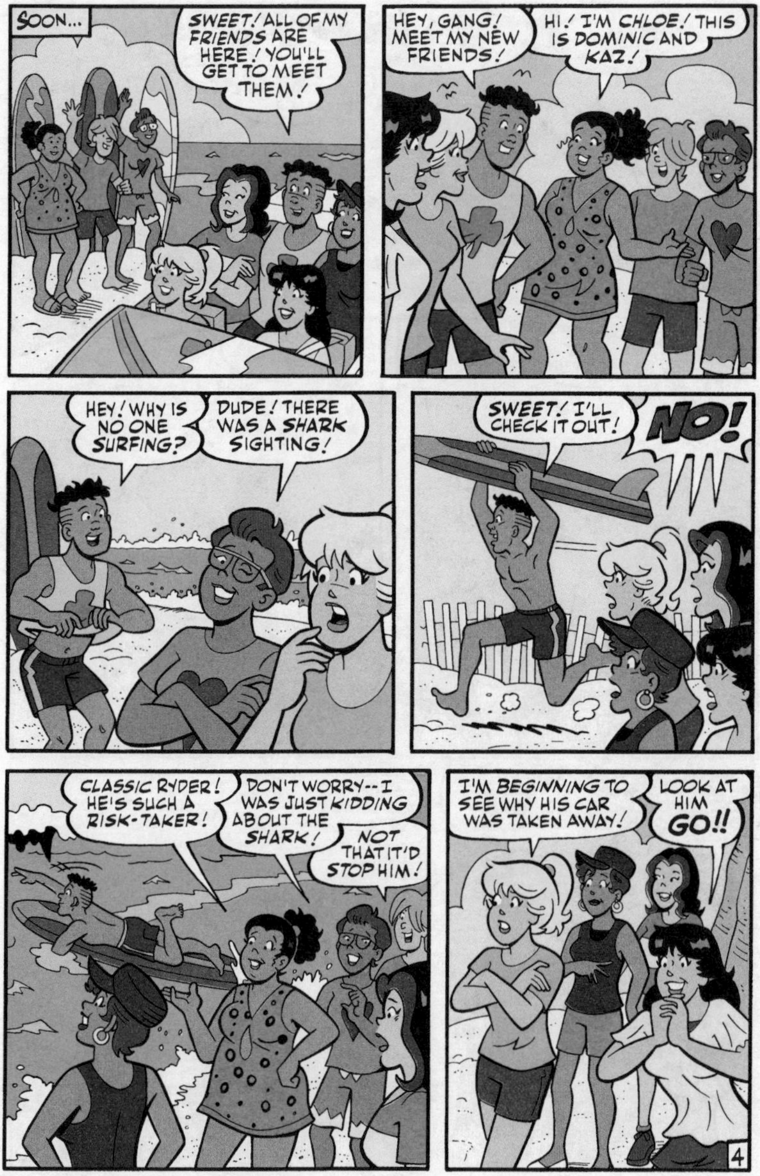
SOON...
SWEET! ALL OF MY FRIENDS ARE HERE! YOU'LL GET TO MEET THEM!
HEY, GANG! MEET MY NEW FRIENDS!
HI! I'M CHLOE! THIS IS DOMINIC AND KAZ!
HEY! WHY IS NO ONE SURFING?
DUDE! THERE WAS A SHARK SIGHTING!
SWEET! I'LL CHECK IT OUT!
NO!
CLASSIC RYDER! HE'S SUCH A RISK-TAKER!
DON'T WORRY-- I WAS JUST KIDDING ABOUT THE SHARK!
NOT THAT IT'D STOP HIM!
I'M BEGINNING TO SEE WHY HIS CAR WAS TAKEN AWAY!
LOOK AT HIM GO!!
4

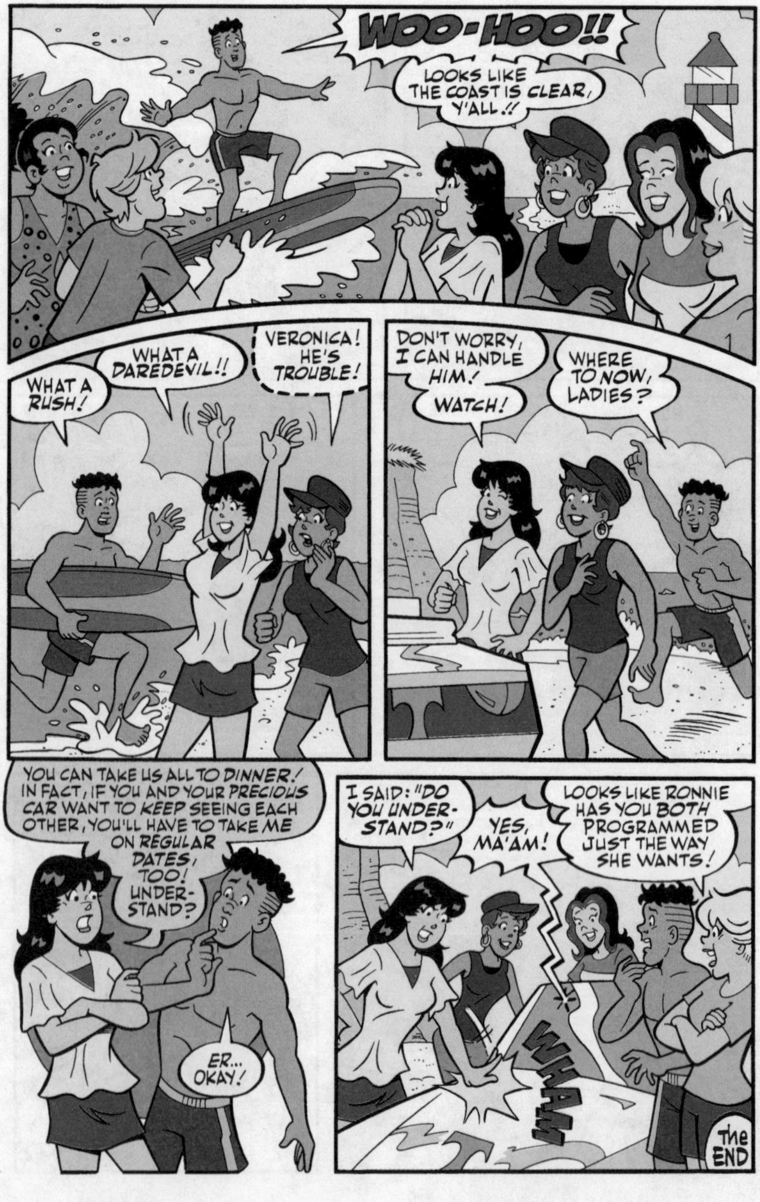
WOO-HOO!!
LOOKS LIKE THE COAST IS CLEAR, Y'ALL.!!
WHAT A RUSH!
WHAT A DAREDEVIL!!
VERONICA! HE'S TROUBLE!
DON'T WORRY, I CAN HANDLE HIM!
WATCH!
WHERE TO NOW, LADIES?
YOU CAN TAKE US ALL TO DINNER! IN FACT, IF YOU AND YOUR PRECIOUS CAR WANT TO KEEP SEEING EACH OTHER, YOU'LL HAVE TO TAKE ME ON REGULAR DATES, TOO! UNDER-STAND?
ER... OKAY!
I SAID: "DO YOU UNDER-STAND?"
YES, MA'AM!
WHAM
LOOKS LIKE RONNIE HAS YOU BOTH PROGRAMMED JUST THE WAY SHE WANTS!
THE END

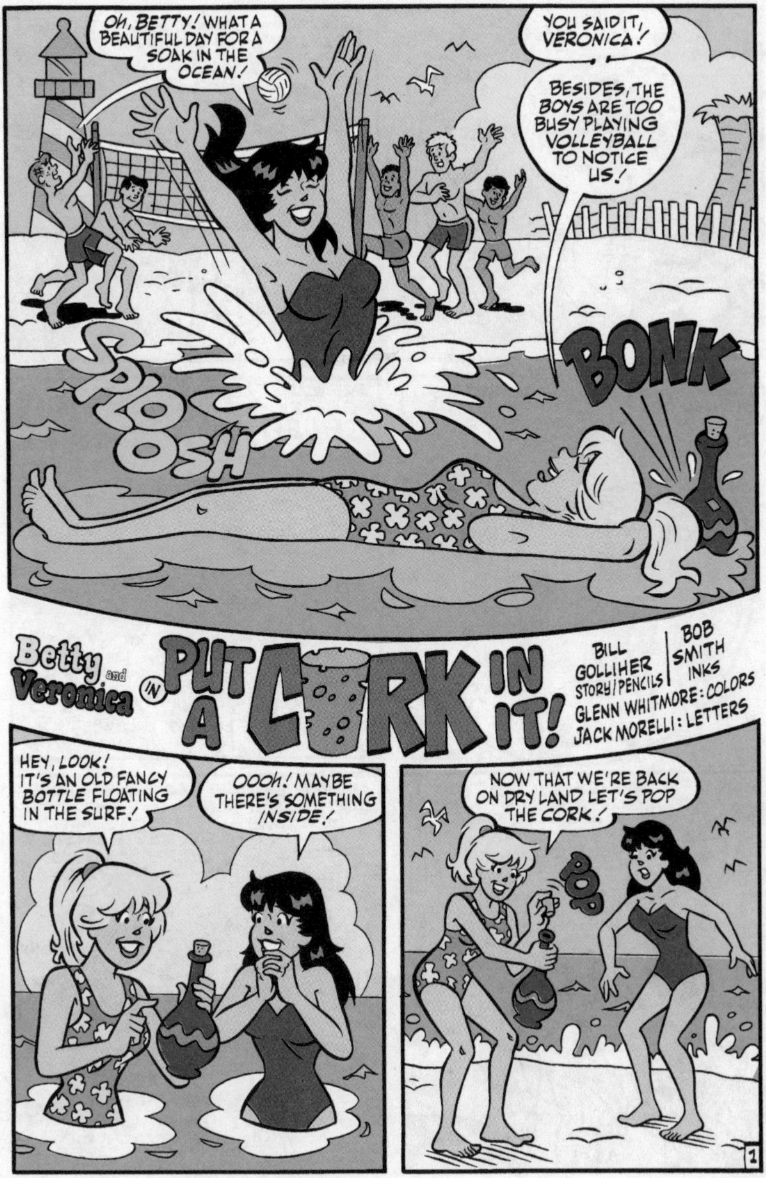
Oh, BETTY! WHAT A BEAUTIFUL DAY FOR A SOAK IN THE OCEAN!
YOU SAID IT, VERONICA!
BESIDES, THE BOYS ARE TOO BUSY PLAYING VOLLEYBALL TO NOTICE US!
SPLOSH
BONK
Betty and Veronica IN PUT A CORK IN IT!
BILL GOLLIHER STORY/PENCILS
BOB SMITH INKS
GLENN WHITMORE: COLORS
JACK MORELLI: LETTERS
HEY, LOOK! IT'S AN OLD FANCY BOTTLE FLOATING IN THE SURF!
OOOH! MAYBE THERE'S SOMETHING INSIDE!
NOW THAT WE'RE BACK ON DRY LAND LET'S POP THE CORK!
POP
1

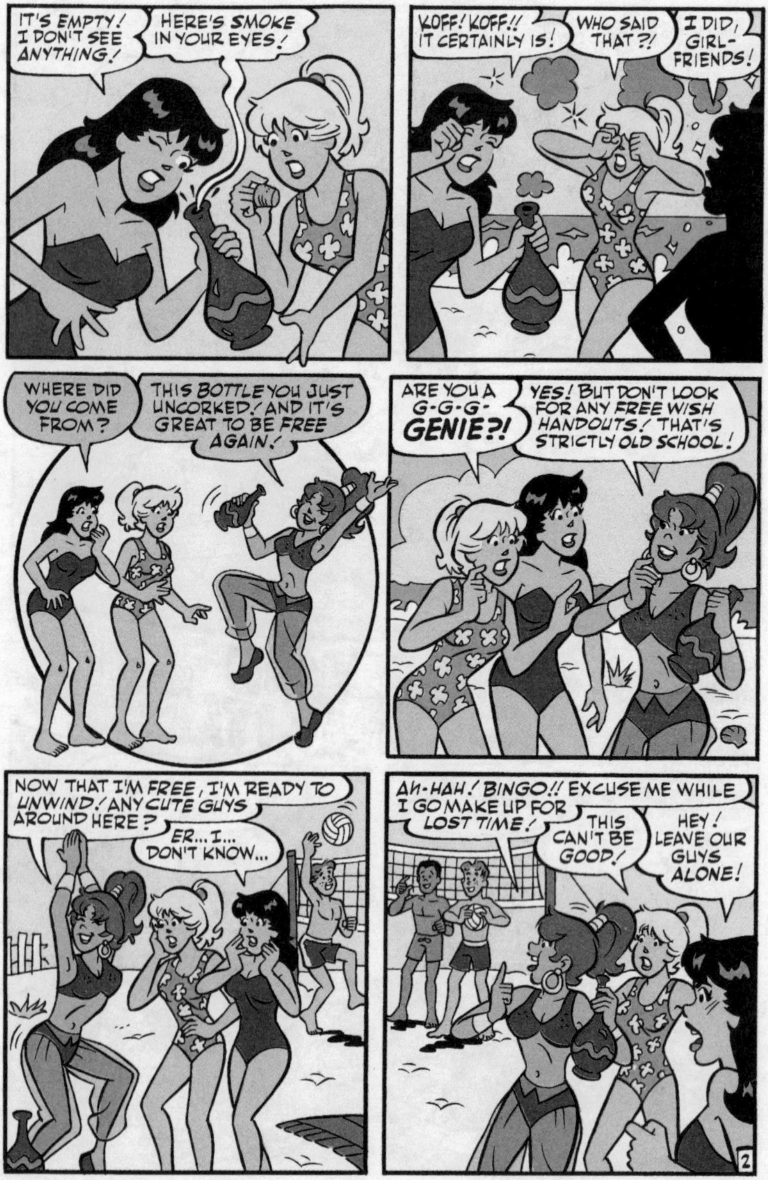
IT'S EMPTY! I DON'T SEE ANYTHING!
HERE'S SMOKE IN YOUR EYES!
KOFF! KOFF!! IT CERTAINLY IS!
WHO SAID THAT?!
I DID, GIRL-FRIENDS!
WHERE DID YOU COME FROM?
THIS BOTTLE YOU JUST UNCORKED! AND IT'S GREAT TO BE FREE AGAIN!
ARE YOU A G-G-G-GENIE?!
YES! BUT DON'T LOOK FOR ANY FREE WISH HANDOUTS! THAT'S STRICTLY OLD SCHOOL!
NOW THAT I'M FREE, I'M READY TO UNWIND! ANY CUTE GUYS AROUND HERE?
ER... I... DON'T KNOW...
AH-HAH! BINGO!! EXCUSE ME WHILE I GO MAKE UP FOR LOST TIME!
THIS CAN'T BE GOOD!
HEY! LEAVE OUR GUYS ALONE!
2

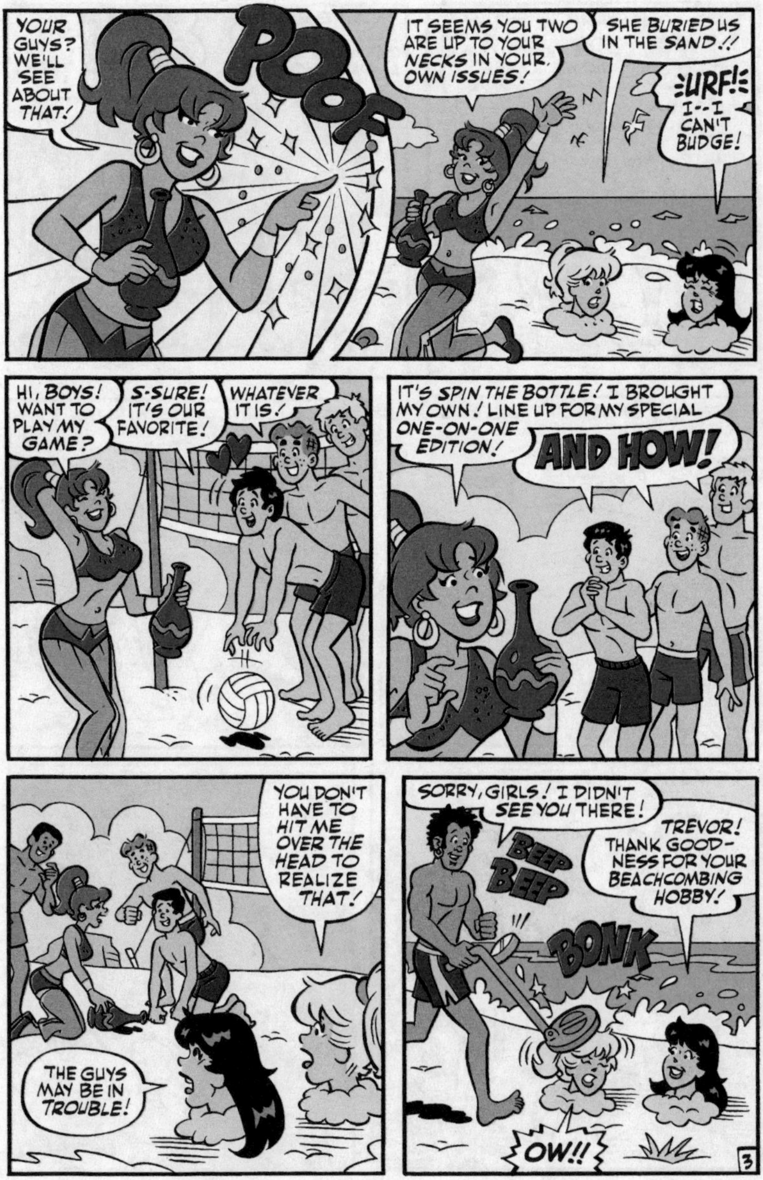
YOUR GUYS? WE'LL SEE ABOUT THAT!
POOF
IT SEEMS YOU TWO ARE UP TO YOUR NECKS IN YOUR OWN ISSUES!
SHE BURIED US IN THE SAND!!
URF! I--I CAN'T BUDGE!
HI, BOYS! WANT TO PLAY MY GAME?
S-SURE! IT'S OUR FAVORITE!
WHATEVER IT IS!
IT'S SPIN THE BOTTLE! I BROUGHT MY OWN! LINE UP FOR MY SPECIAL ONE-ON-ONE EDITION!
AND HOW!
YOU DON'T HAVE TO HIT ME OVER THE HEAD TO REALIZE THAT!
THE GUYS MAY BE IN TROUBLE!
SORRY, GIRLS! I DIDN'T SEE YOU THERE!
BEEP BEEP
TREVOR! THANK GOODNESS FOR YOUR BEACHCOMBING HOBBY!
BONK
OW!!
3

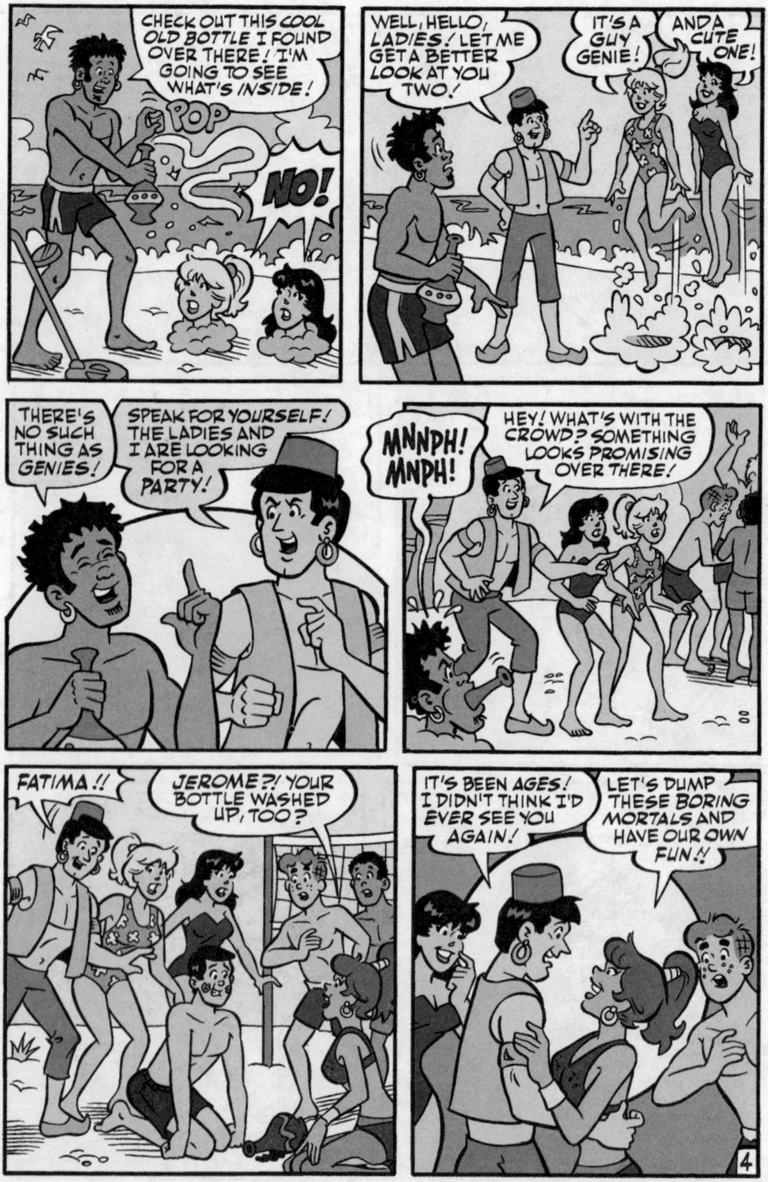
CHECK OUT THIS COOL OLD BOTTLE I FOUND OVER THERE! I'M GOING TO SEE WHAT'S INSIDE!
POP
NO!
WELL, HELLO, LADIES! LET ME GET A BETTER LOOK AT YOU TWO!
IT'S A GUY GENIE!
AND A CUTE ONE!
THERE'S NO SUCH THING AS GENIES!
SPEAK FOR YOURSELF! THE LADIES AND I ARE LOOKING FOR A PARTY!
MNNPH! MNPH!
HEY! WHAT'S WITH THE CROWD? SOMETHING LOOKS PROMISING OVER THERE!
FATIMA!!
JEROME?! YOUR BOTTLE WASHED UP, TOO?
IT'S BEEN AGES! I DIDN'T THINK I'D EVER SEE YOU AGAIN!
LET'S DUMP THESE BORING MORTALS AND HAVE OUR OWN FUN!!
4

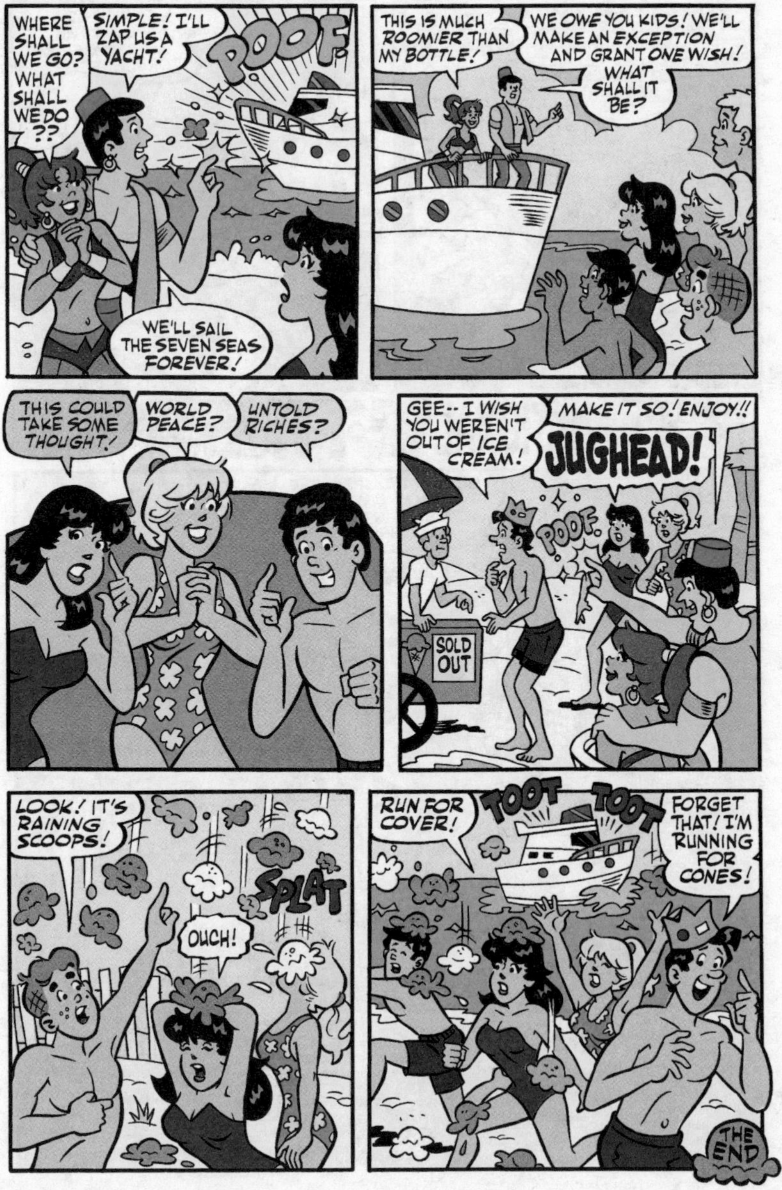
WHERE SHALL WE GO? WHAT SHALL WE DO ??
SIMPLE! I'LL ZAP US A YACHT!
POOF
WE'LL SAIL THE SEVEN SEAS FOREVER!
THIS IS MUCH ROOMIER THAN MY BOTTLE!
WE OWE YOU KIDS! WE'LL MAKE AN EXCEPTION AND GRANT ONE WISH!
WHAT SHALL IT BE?
THIS COULD TAKE SOME THOUGHT!
WORLD PEACE?
UNTOLD RICHES?
GEE-- I WISH YOU WEREN'T OUT OF ICE CREAM!
MAKE IT SO! ENJOY!!
JUGHEAD!
POOF
SOLD OUT
LOOK! IT'S RAINING SCOOPS!
SPLAT
OUCH!
RUN FOR COVER!
TOOT TOOT
FORGET THAT! I'M RUNNING FOR CONES!
THE END

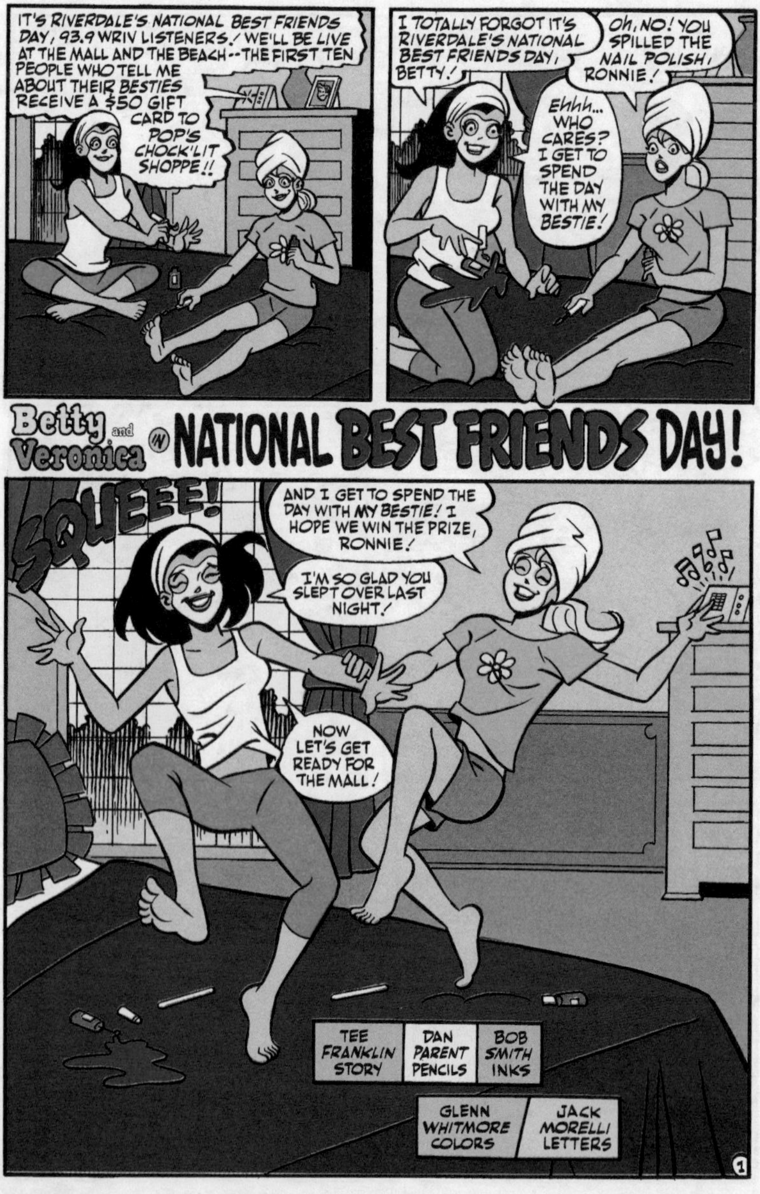
IT'S RIVERDALE'S NATIONAL BEST FRIENDS DAY, 93.9 WRIV LISTENERS! WE'LL BE LIVE AT THE MALL AND THE BEACH--THE FIRST TEN PEOPLE WHO TELL ME ABOUT THEIR BESTIES RECEIVE A $50 GIFT CARD TO POP'S CHOCK'LIT SHOPPE!!
I TOTALLY FORGOT IT'S RIVERDALE'S NATIONAL BEST FRIENDS DAY, BETTY!
OH, NO! YOU SPILLED THE NAIL POLISH, RONNIE!
EHHH... WHO CARES? I GET TO SPEND THE DAY WITH MY BESTIE!
Betty and Veronica IN NATIONAL BEST FRIENDS DAY!
SQUEEE!
AND I GET TO SPEND THE DAY WITH MY BESTIE! I HOPE WE WIN THE PRIZE, RONNIE!
I'M SO GLAD YOU SLEPT OVER LAST NIGHT!
NOW LET'S GET READY FOR THE MALL!
TEE FRANKLIN STORY
DAN PARENT PENCILS
BOB SMITH INKS
GLENN WHITMORE COLORS
JACK MORELLI LETTERS
1

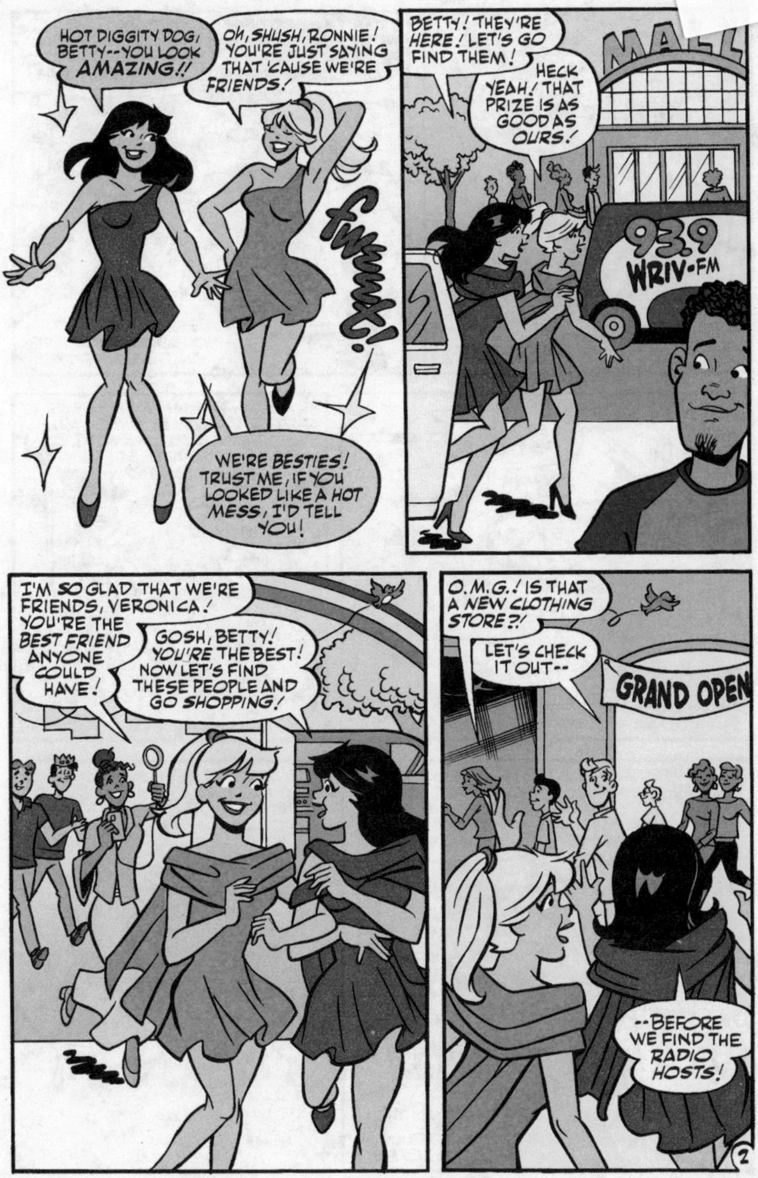
HOT DIGGITY DOG, BETTY--YOU LOOK AMAZING!!
OH, SHUSH, RONNIE! YOU'RE JUST SAYING THAT 'CAUSE WE'RE FRIENDS!
fweeet!
WE'RE BESTIES! TRUST ME, IF YOU LOOKED LIKE A HOT MESS, I'D TELL YOU!
MALL
BETTY! THEY'RE HERE! LET'S GO FIND THEM!
HECK YEAH! THAT PRIZE IS AS GOOD AS OURS!
93.9 WRIV-FM
I'M SO GLAD THAT WE'RE FRIENDS, VERONICA! YOU'RE THE BEST FRIEND ANYONE COULD HAVE!
GOSH, BETTY! YOU'RE THE BEST! NOW LET'S FIND THESE PEOPLE AND GO SHOPPING!
O.M.G.! IS THAT A NEW CLOTHING STORE?!
LET'S CHECK IT OUT--
GRAND OPEN
--BEFORE WE FIND THE RADIO HOSTS!
2

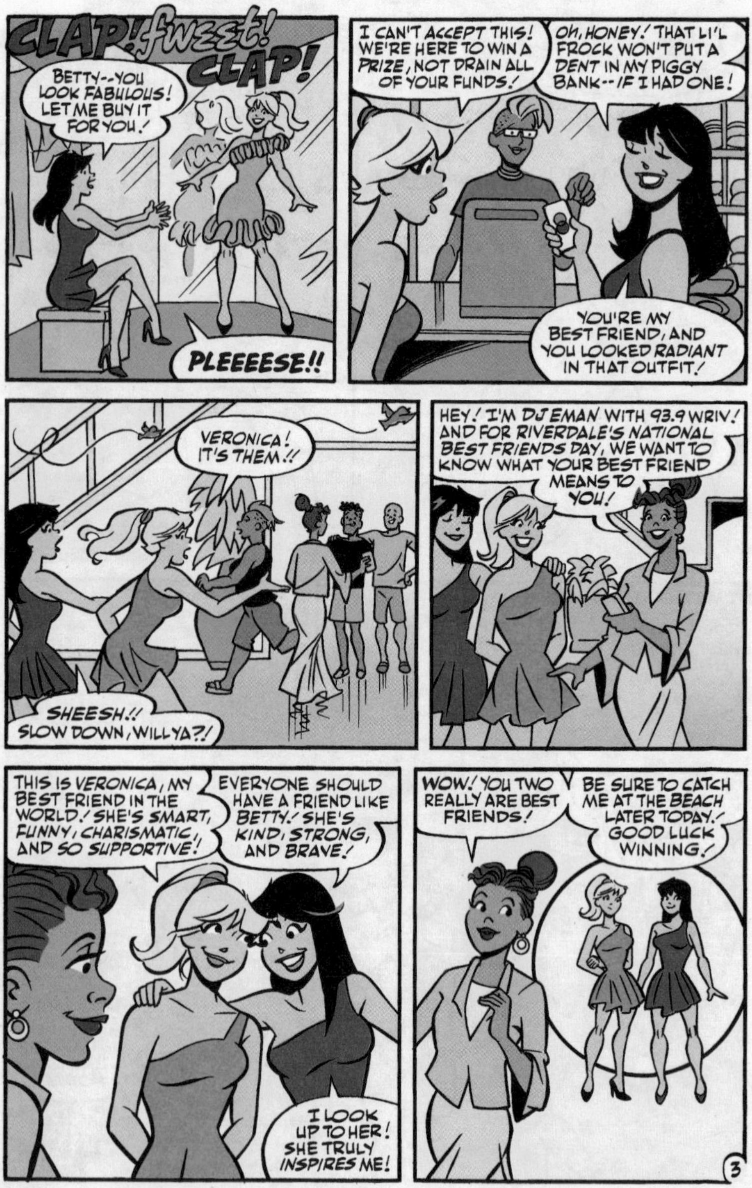
CLAP! fweet! CLAP!
BETTY--YOU LOOK FABULOUS! LET ME BUY IT FOR YOU!
PLEEEESE!!
I CAN'T ACCEPT THIS! WE'RE HERE TO WIN A PRIZE, NOT DRAIN ALL OF YOUR FUNDS!
OH, HONEY! THAT LI'L FROCK WON'T PUT A DENT IN MY PIGGY BANK--IF I HAD ONE!
YOU'RE MY BEST FRIEND, AND YOU LOOKED RADIANT IN THAT OUTFIT!
VERONICA! IT'S THEM!!
SHEESH!! SLOW DOWN, WILLYA?!
HEY! I'M DJ EMAN WITH 93.9 WRIV! AND FOR RIVERDALE'S NATIONAL BEST FRIENDS DAY, WE WANT TO KNOW WHAT YOUR BEST FRIEND MEANS TO YOU!
THIS IS VERONICA, MY BEST FRIEND IN THE WORLD! SHE'S SMART, FUNNY, CHARISMATIC, AND SO SUPPORTIVE!
EVERYONE SHOULD HAVE A FRIEND LIKE BETTY! SHE'S KIND, STRONG, AND BRAVE!
I LOOK UP TO HER! SHE TRULY INSPIRES ME!
WOW! YOU TWO REALLY ARE BEST FRIENDS!
BE SURE TO CATCH ME AT THE BEACH LATER TODAY! GOOD LUCK WINNING!
3

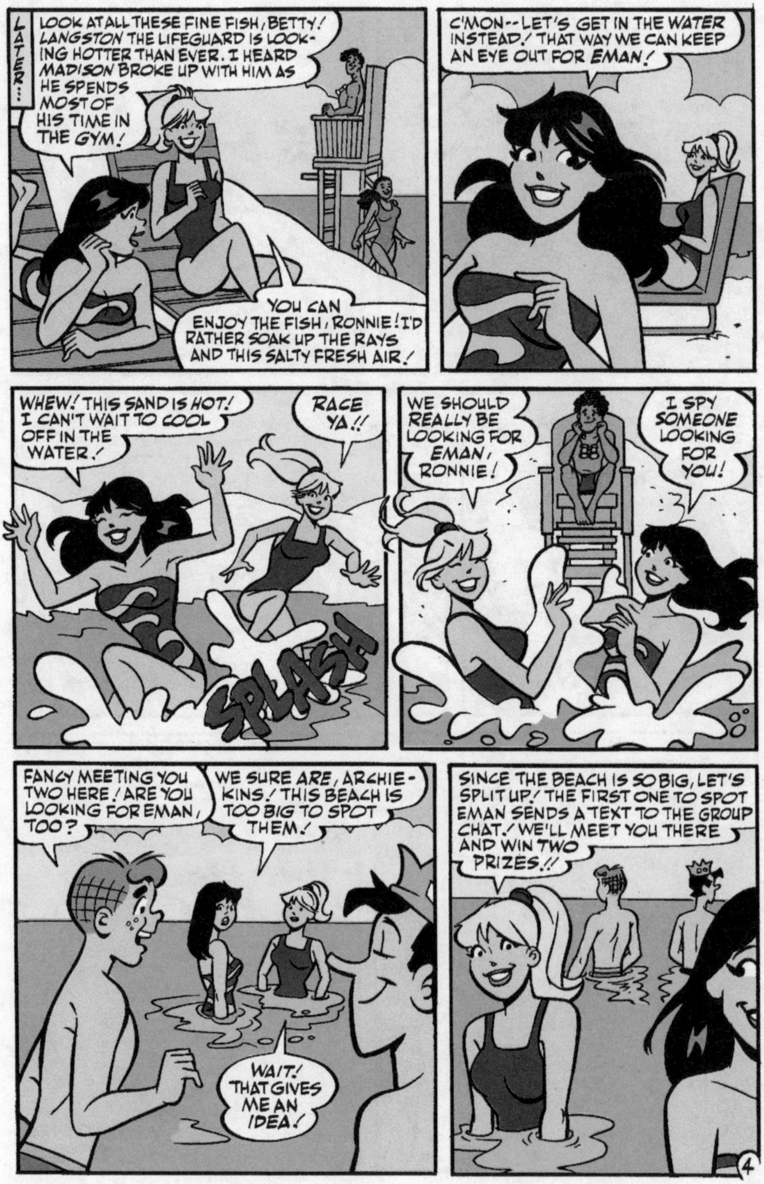
LATER...
LOOK AT ALL THESE FINE FISH, BETTY! LANGSTON THE LIFEGUARD IS LOOKING HOTTER THAN EVER. I HEARD MADISON BROKE UP WITH HIM AS HE SPENDS MOST OF HIS TIME IN THE GYM!
YOU CAN ENJOY THE FISH, RONNIE! I'D RATHER SOAK UP THE RAYS AND THIS SALTY FRESH AIR!
C'MON--LET'S GET IN THE WATER INSTEAD! THAT WAY WE CAN KEEP AN EYE OUT FOR EMAN!
WHEW! THIS SAND IS HOT! I CAN'T WAIT TO COOL OFF IN THE WATER!
RACE YA!!
SPLASH
WE SHOULD REALLY BE LOOKING FOR EMAN, RONNIE!
I SPY SOMEONE LOOKING FOR YOU!
FANCY MEETING YOU TWO HERE! ARE YOU LOOKING FOR EMAN, TOO?
WE SURE ARE, ARCHIE-KINS! THIS BEACH IS TOO BIG TO SPOT THEM!
WAIT! THAT GIVES ME AN IDEA!
SINCE THE BEACH IS SO BIG, LET'S SPLIT UP! THE FIRST ONE TO SPOT EMAN SENDS A TEXT TO THE GROUP CHAT! WE'LL MEET YOU THERE AND WIN TWO PRIZES!!
4

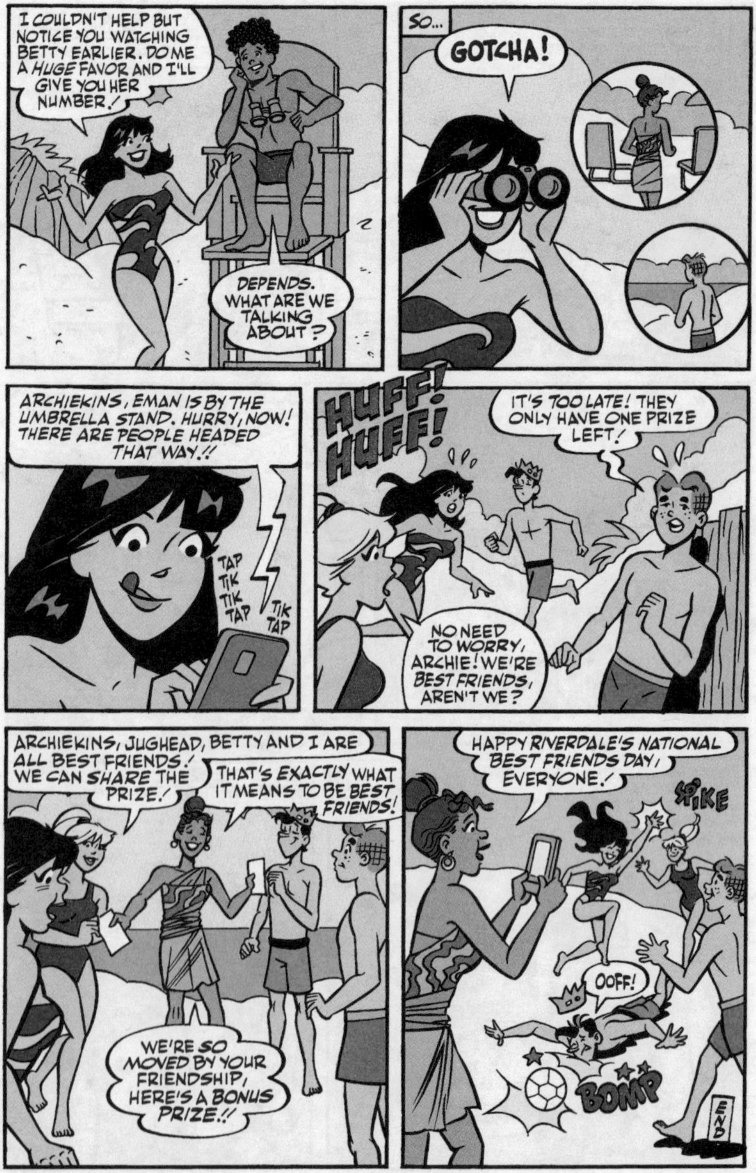
I COULDN'T HELP BUT NOTICE YOU WATCHING BETTY EARLIER. DO ME A HUGE FAVOR AND I'LL GIVE YOU HER NUMBER!
DEPENDS. WHAT ARE WE TALKING ABOUT?
SO...
GOTCHA!
ARCHIEKINS, EMAN IS BY THE UMBRELLA STAND. HURRY, NOW! THERE ARE PEOPLE HEADED THAT WAY!!
TAP TIK TIK TAP
TIK TAP
HUFF! HUFF!
IT'S TOO LATE! THEY ONLY HAVE ONE PRIZE LEFT!
NO NEED TO WORRY, ARCHIE! WE'RE BEST FRIENDS, AREN'T WE?
ARCHIEKINS, JUGHEAD, BETTY AND I ARE ALL BEST FRIENDS! WE CAN SHARE THE PRIZE!
THAT'S EXACTLY WHAT IT MEANS TO BE BEST FRIENDS!
WE'RE SO MOVED BY YOUR FRIENDSHIP, HERE'S A BONUS PRIZE!!
HAPPY RIVERDALE'S NATIONAL BEST FRIENDS DAY, EVERYONE!
SPIKE
OOFF!
BOMP
END

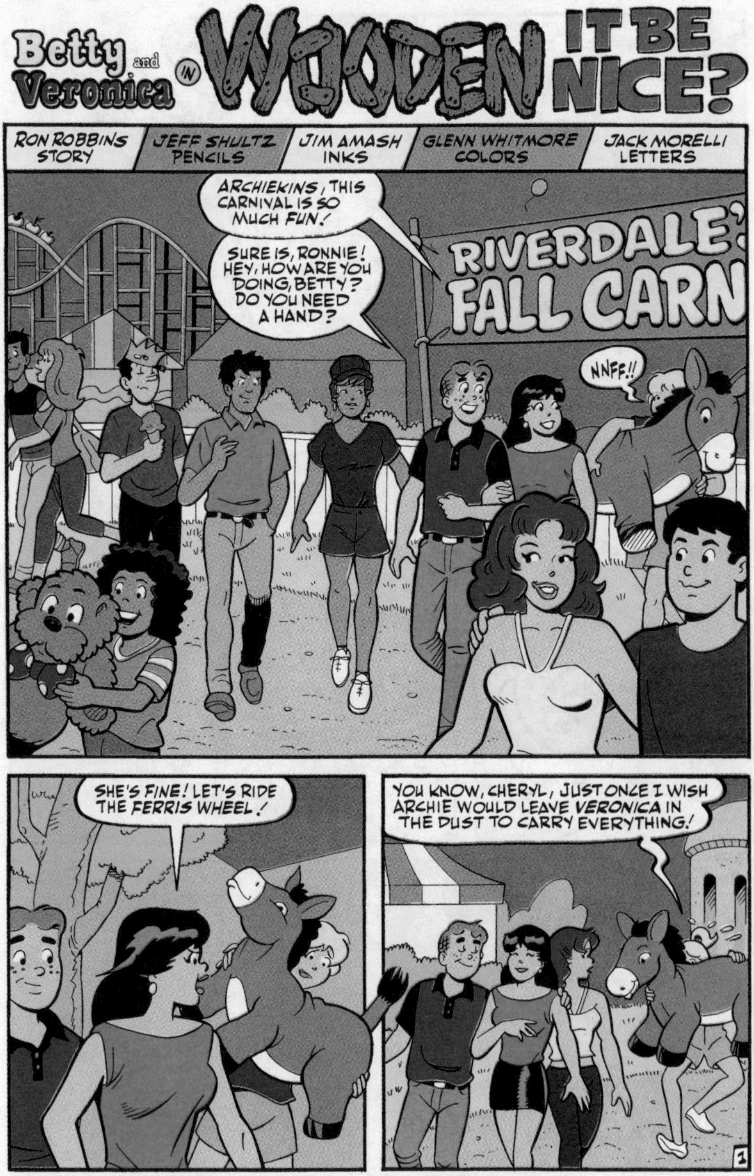
Betty and Veronica
IN
WOODEN IT BE NICE?
RON ROBBINS STORY
JEFF SHULTZ PENCILS
JIM AMASH INKS
GLENN WHITMORE COLORS
JACK MORELLI LETTERS
ARCHIEKINS, THIS CARNIVAL IS SO MUCH FUN!
SURE IS, RONNIE! HEY, HOW ARE YOU DOING, BETTY? DO YOU NEED A HAND?
RIVERDALE'S FALL CARN
NNFF!!
SHE'S FINE! LET'S RIDE THE FERRIS WHEEL!
YOU KNOW, CHERYL, JUST ONCE I WISH ARCHIE WOULD LEAVE VERONICA IN THE DUST TO CARRY EVERYTHING!
1

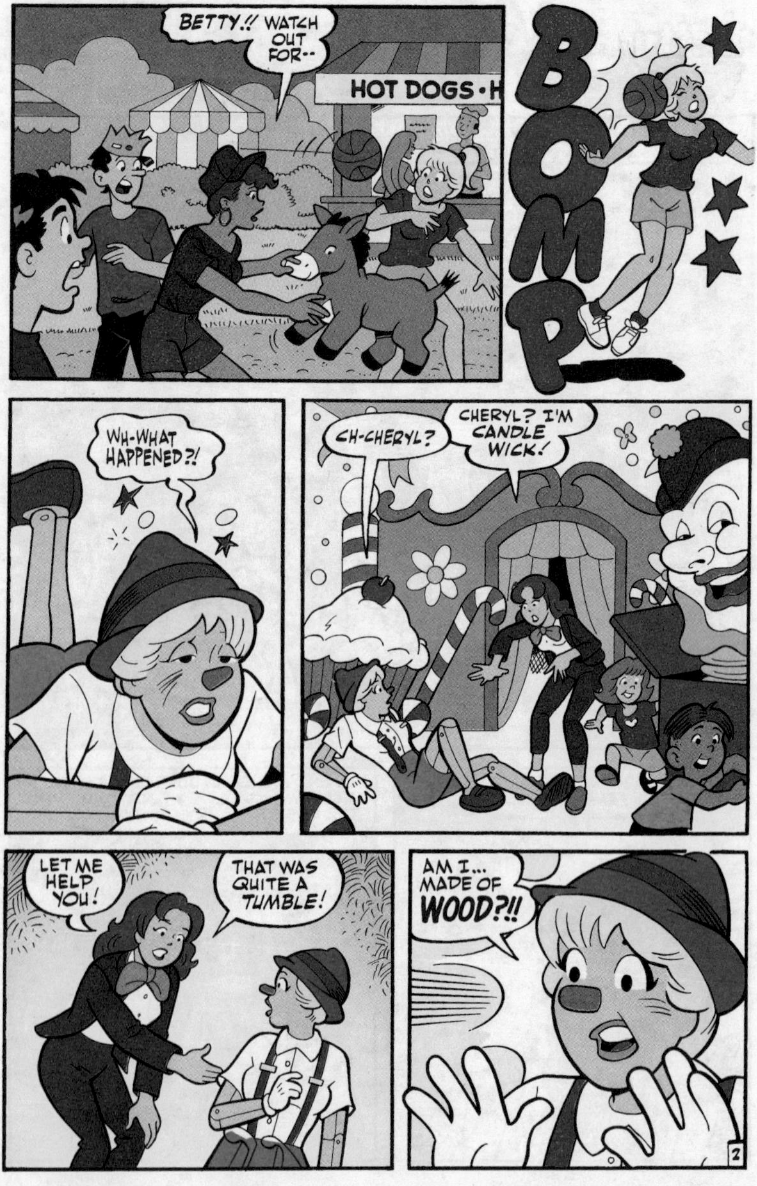
BETTY.!! WATCH OUT FOR--
HOT DOGS • H
BOMP
WH-WHAT HAPPENED?!
CH-CHERYL?
CHERYL? I'M CANDLE WICK!
LET ME HELP YOU!
THAT WAS QUITE A TUMBLE!
AM I... MADE OF WOOD?!!
2

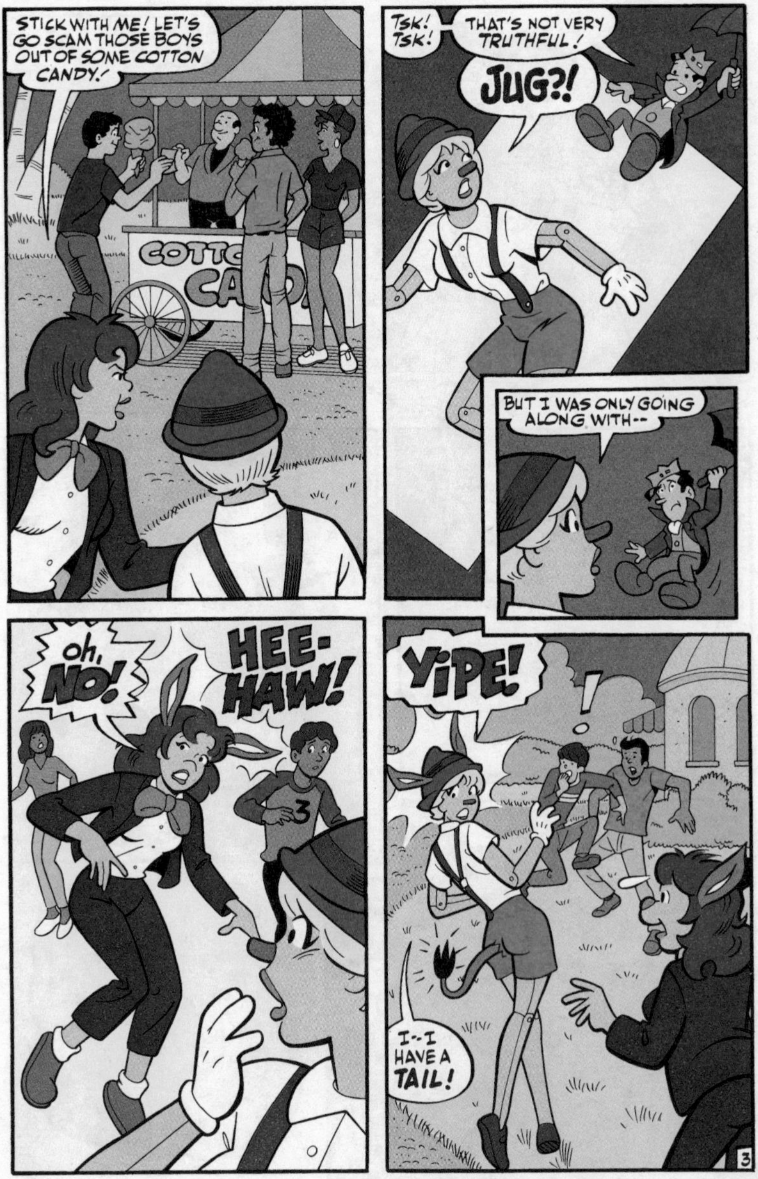
STICK WITH ME! LET'S GO SCAM THOSE BOYS OUT OF SOME COTTON CANDY!
COTTON CANDY
TSK! TSK!
THAT'S NOT VERY TRUTHFUL!
JUG?!
BUT I WAS ONLY GOING ALONG WITH--
oh, NO!
HEE-HAW!
YIPE!
!
I--I HAVE A TAIL!
3

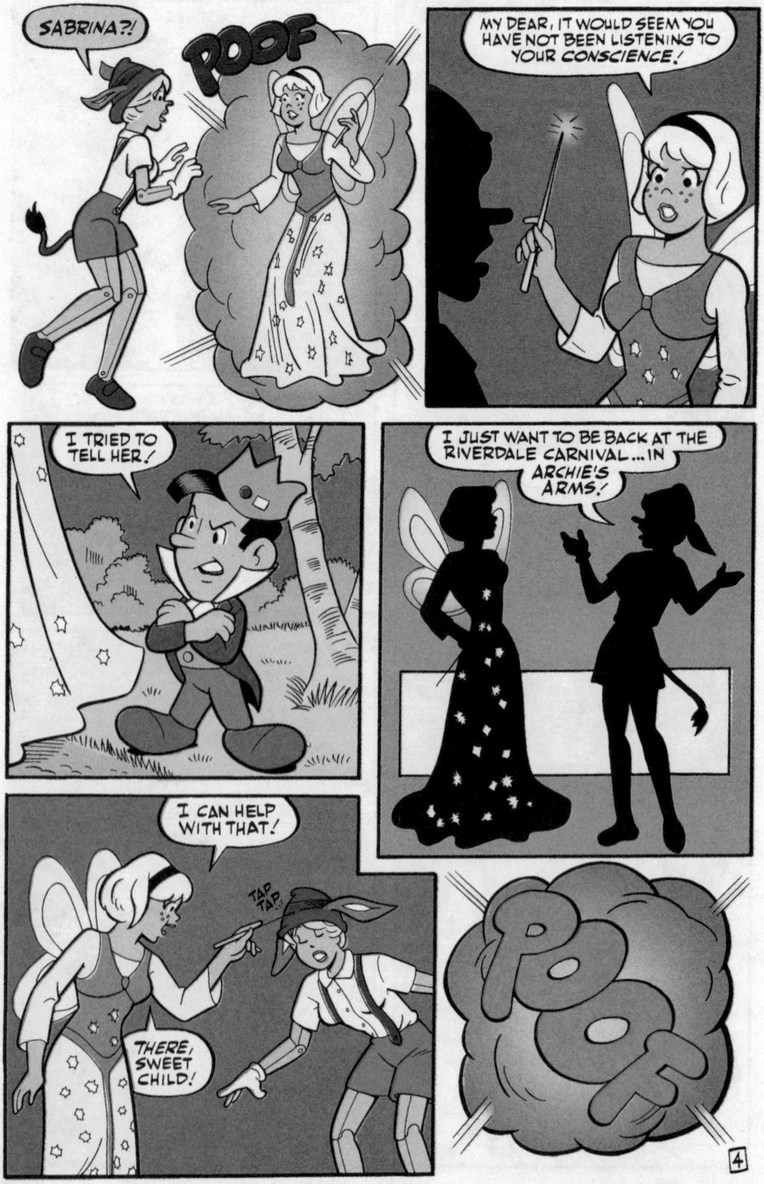
SABRINA?!
POOF
MY DEAR, IT WOULD SEEM YOU HAVE NOT BEEN LISTENING TO YOUR CONSCIENCE!
I TRIED TO TELL HER!
I JUST WANT TO BE BACK AT THE RIVERDALE CARNIVAL... IN ARCHIE'S ARMS!
I CAN HELP WITH THAT!
TAP TAP
THERE, SWEET CHILD!
POOF
4

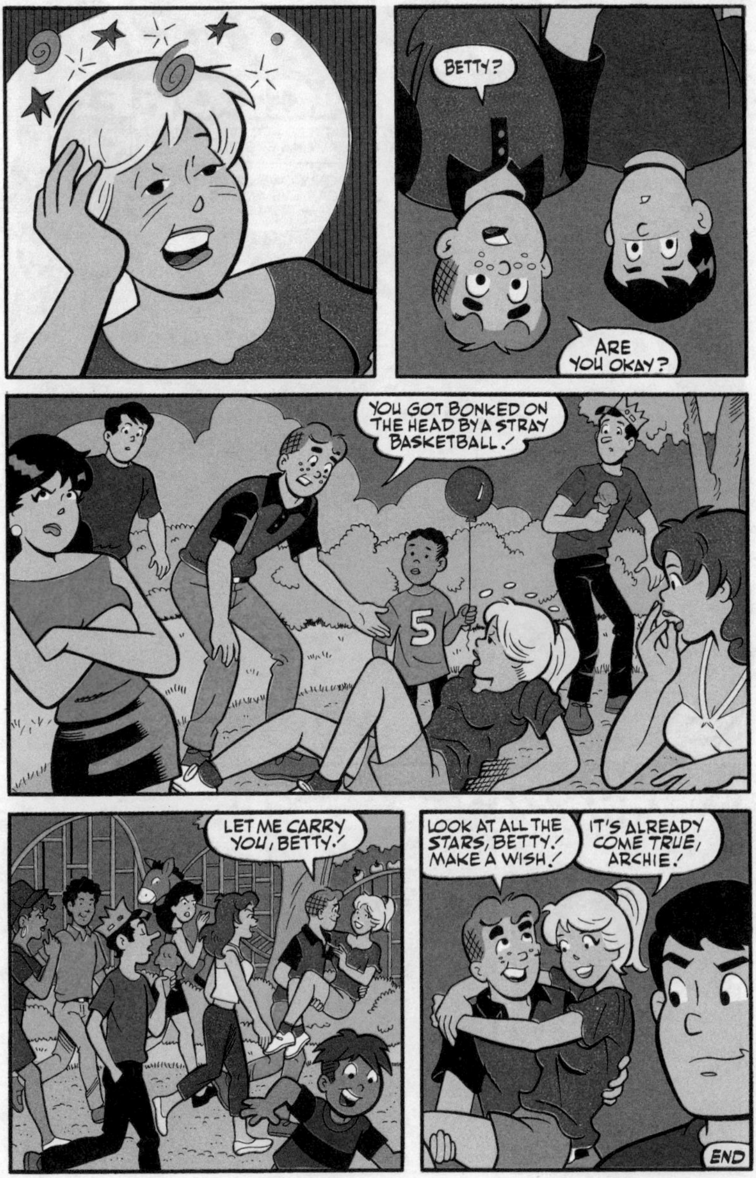
BETTY?
ARE YOU OKAY?
YOU GOT BONKED ON THE HEAD BY A STRAY BASKETBALL!
5
LET ME CARRY YOU, BETTY!
LOOK AT ALL THE STARS, BETTY! MAKE A WISH!
IT'S ALREADY COME TRUE, ARCHIE!
END

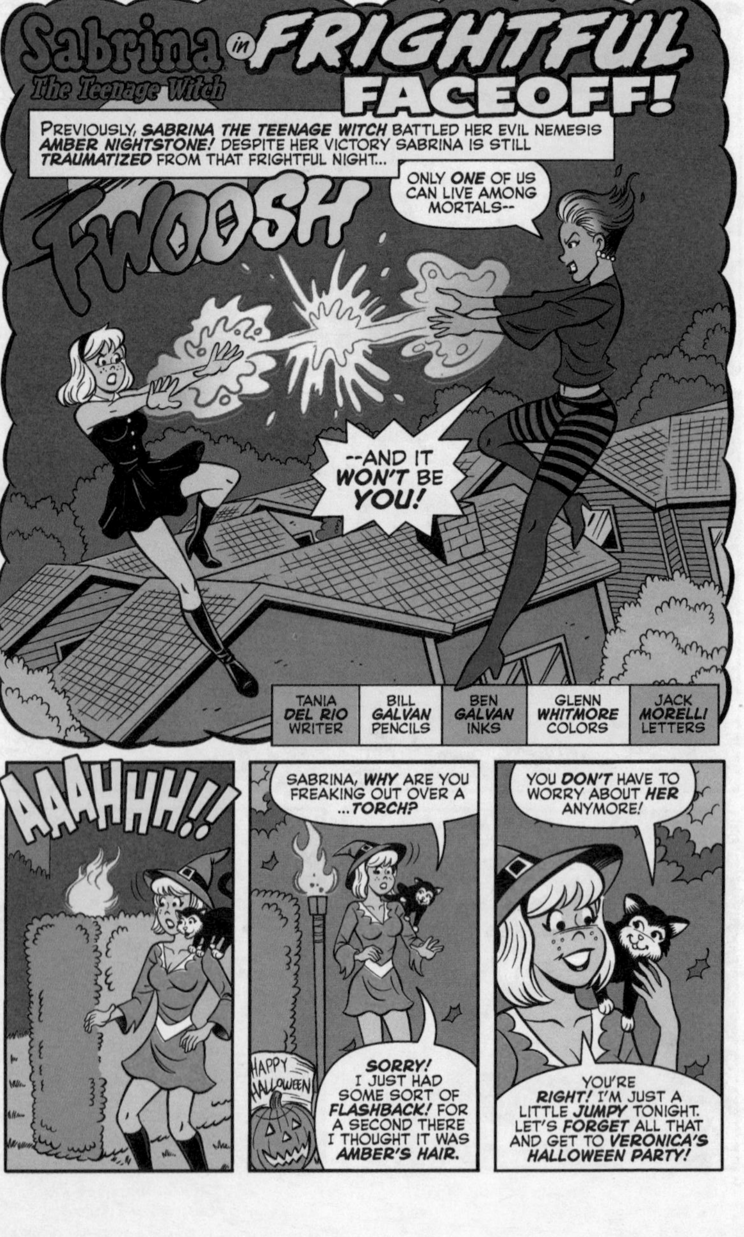
Sabrina The Teenage Witch in FRIGHTFUL FACEOFF!
PREVIOUSLY, SABRINA THE TEENAGE WITCH BATTLED HER EVIL NEMESIS AMBER NIGHTSTONE! DESPITE HER VICTORY SABRINA IS STILL TRAUMATIZED FROM THAT FRIGHTFUL NIGHT...
FWOOSH
ONLY ONE OF US CAN LIVE AMONG MORTALS--
--AND IT WON'T BE YOU!
TANIA DEL RIO WRITER
BILL GALVAN PENCILS
BEN GALVAN INKS
GLENN WHITMORE COLORS
JACK MORELLI LETTERS
AAAHHH!!
SABRINA, WHY ARE YOU FREAKING OUT OVER A ...TORCH?
HAPPY HALLOWEEN
SORRY! I JUST HAD SOME SORT OF FLASHBACK! FOR A SECOND THERE I THOUGHT IT WAS AMBER'S HAIR.
YOU DON'T HAVE TO WORRY ABOUT HER ANYMORE!
YOU'RE RIGHT! I'M JUST A LITTLE JUMPY TONIGHT. LET'S FORGET ALL THAT AND GET TO VERONICA'S HALLOWEEN PARTY!

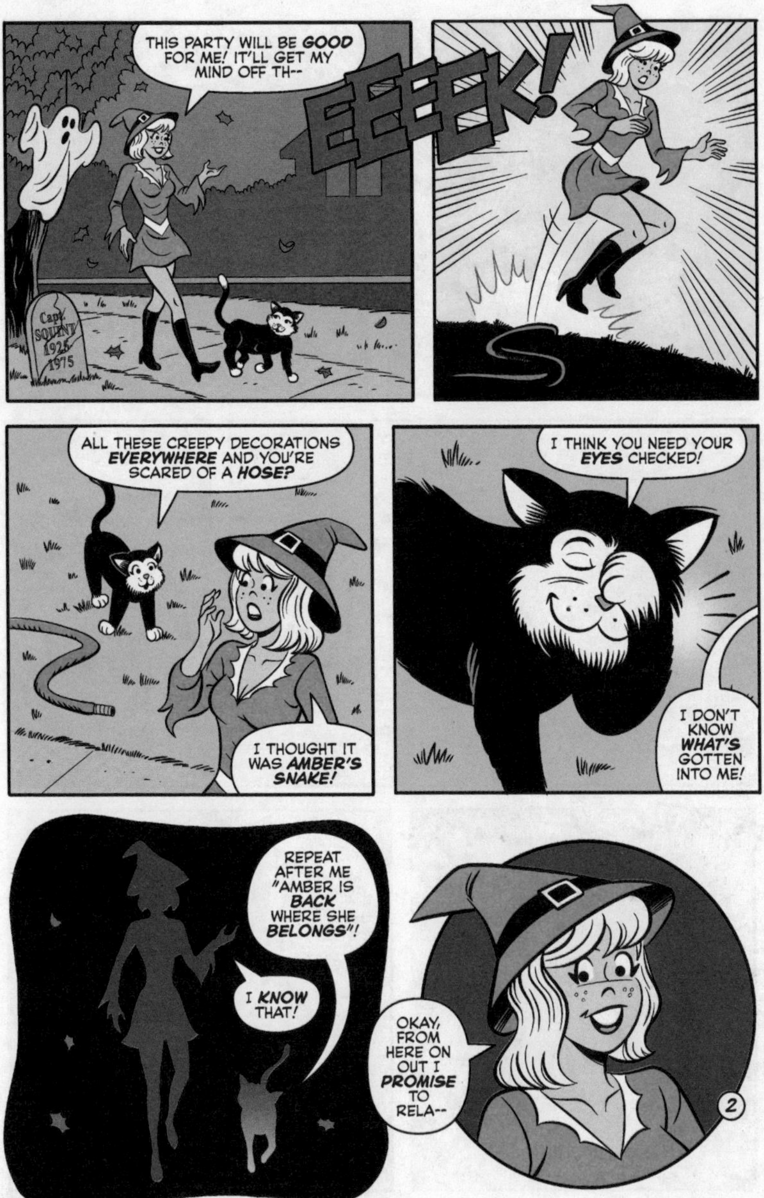
THIS PARTY WILL BE GOOD FOR ME! IT'LL GET MY MIND OFF TH--
Capt. SQUINT 1925 1975
EEEEK!
ALL THESE CREEPY DECORATIONS EVERYWHERE AND YOU'RE SCARED OF A HOSE?
I THOUGHT IT WAS AMBER'S SNAKE!
I THINK YOU NEED YOUR EYES CHECKED!
I DON'T KNOW WHAT'S GOTTEN INTO ME!
REPEAT AFTER ME "AMBER IS BACK WHERE SHE BELONGS"!
I KNOW THAT!
OKAY, FROM HERE ON OUT I PROMISE TO RELA--
2

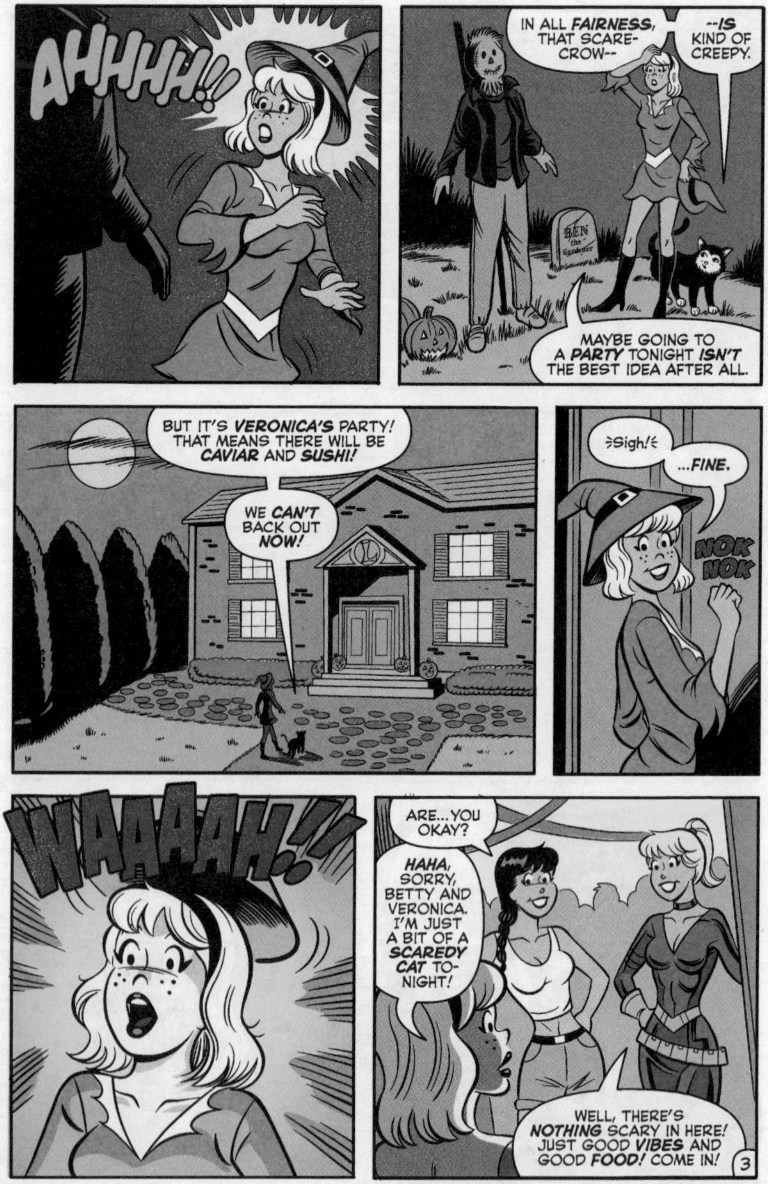
AHHHH!!
IN ALL FAIRNESS, THAT SCARE-CROW--
--IS KIND OF CREEPY.
BEN the Gardener
MAYBE GOING TO A PARTY TONIGHT ISN'T THE BEST IDEA AFTER ALL.
BUT IT'S VERONICA'S PARTY! THAT MEANS THERE WILL BE CAVIAR AND SUSHI!
WE CAN'T BACK OUT NOW!
Sigh!
...FINE.
NOK NOK
WAAAAH!!
ARE...YOU OKAY?
HAHA, SORRY, BETTY AND VERONICA. I'M JUST A BIT OF A SCAREDY CAT TO-NIGHT!
WELL, THERE'S NOTHING SCARY IN HERE! JUST GOOD VIBES AND GOOD FOOD! COME IN!
3

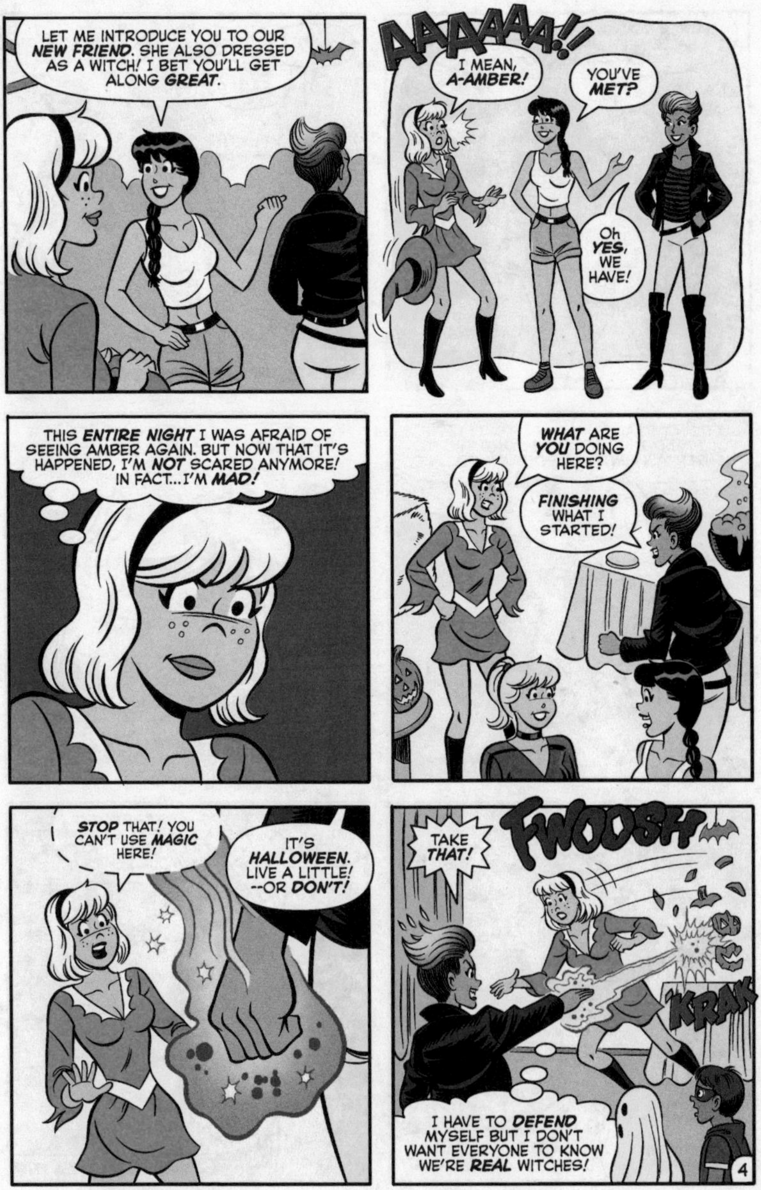
LET ME INTRODUCE YOU TO OUR NEW FRIEND. SHE ALSO DRESSED AS A WITCH! I BET YOU'LL GET ALONG GREAT.
AAAAAA!!
I MEAN, A-AMBER!
YOU'VE MET?
Oh YES, WE HAVE!
THIS ENTIRE NIGHT I WAS AFRAID OF SEEING AMBER AGAIN. BUT NOW THAT IT'S HAPPENED, I'M NOT SCARED ANYMORE! IN FACT...I'M MAD!
WHAT ARE YOU DOING HERE?
FINISHING WHAT I STARTED!
STOP THAT! YOU CAN'T USE MAGIC HERE!
IT'S HALLOWEEN. LIVE A LITTLE! --OR DON'T!
TAKE THAT!
FWOOSH
KRAK
I HAVE TO DEFEND MYSELF BUT I DON'T WANT EVERYONE TO KNOW WE'RE REAL WITCHES!
4

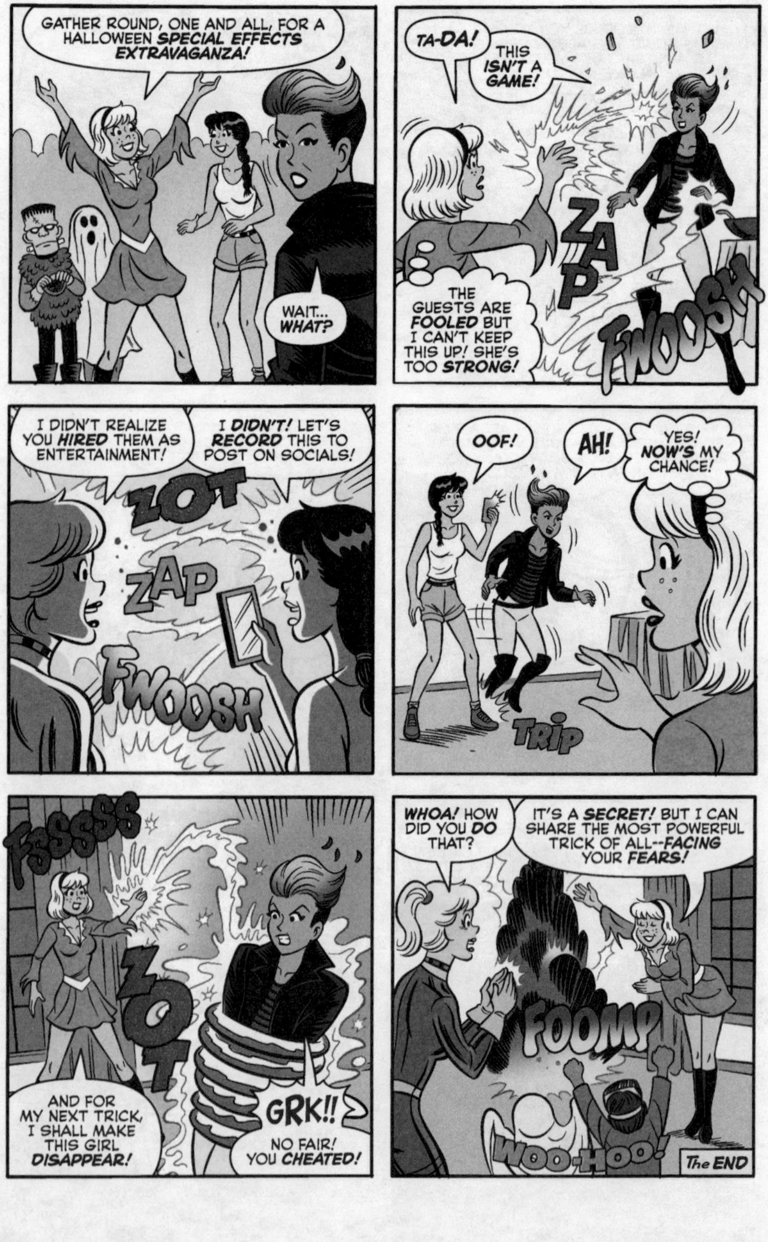
GATHER ROUND, ONE AND ALL, FOR A HALLOWEEN SPECIAL EFFECTS EXTRAVAGANZA!
WAIT... WHAT?
TA-DA!
THIS ISN'T A GAME!
THE GUESTS ARE FOOLED BUT I CAN'T KEEP THIS UP! SHE'S TOO STRONG!
ZAP
FWOOSH
I DIDN'T REALIZE YOU HIRED THEM AS ENTERTAINMENT!
I DIDN'T! LET'S RECORD THIS TO POST ON SOCIALS!
ZOT
ZAP
FWOOSH
OOF!
AH!
YES! NOW'S MY CHANCE!
TRIP
FSSSSS
ZOT
AND FOR MY NEXT TRICK, I SHALL MAKE THIS GIRL DISAPPEAR!
GRK!!
NO FAIR! YOU CHEATED!
WHOA! HOW DID YOU DO THAT?
IT'S A SECRET! BUT I CAN SHARE THE MOST POWERFUL TRICK OF ALL--FACING YOUR FEARS!
FOOMP
WOO-HOO!
The END

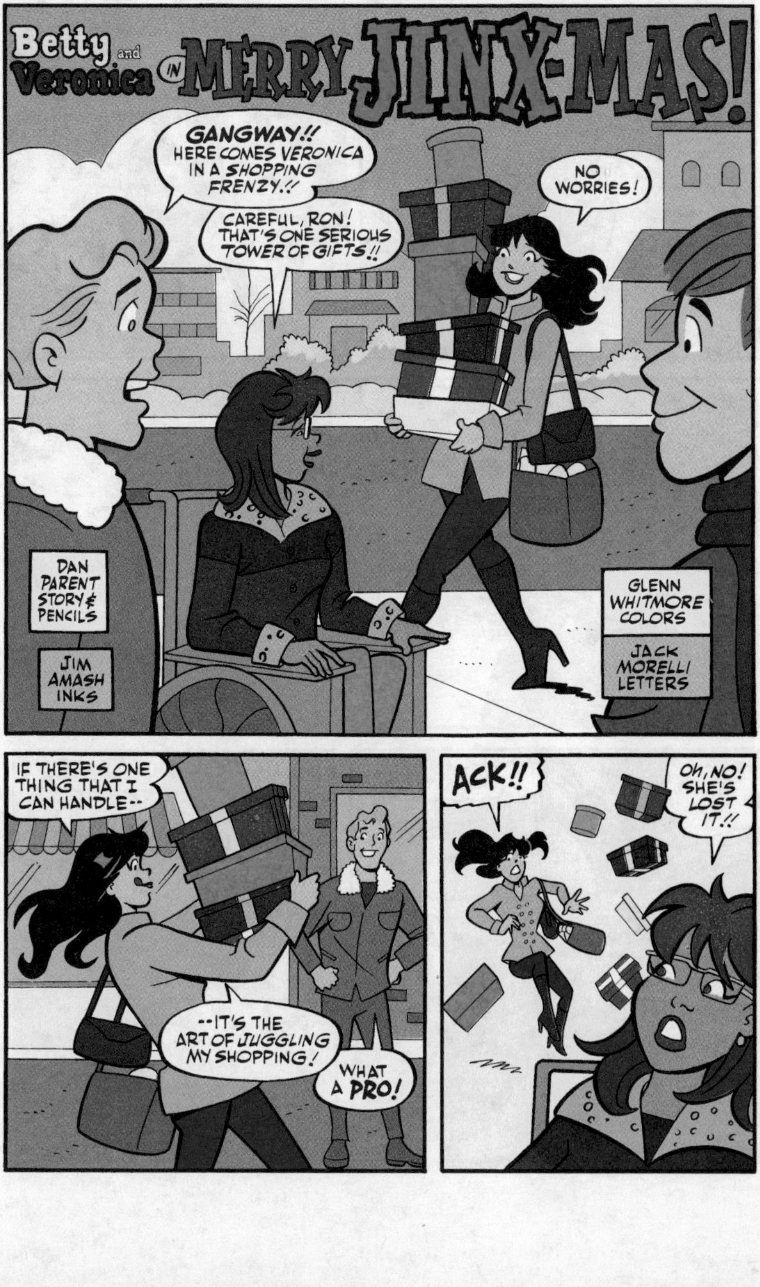
Betty and Veronica in MERRY JINX-MAS!
GANGWAY!! HERE COMES VERONICA IN A SHOPPING FRENZY!!
CAREFUL, RON! THAT'S ONE SERIOUS TOWER OF GIFTS!!
NO WORRIES!
DAN PARENT STORY & PENCILS
JIM AMASH INKS
GLENN WHITMORE COLORS
JACK MORELLI LETTERS
IF THERE'S ONE THING THAT I CAN HANDLE--
--IT'S THE ART OF JUGGLING MY SHOPPING!
WHAT A PRO!
ACK!!
Oh, NO! SHE'S LOST IT!!

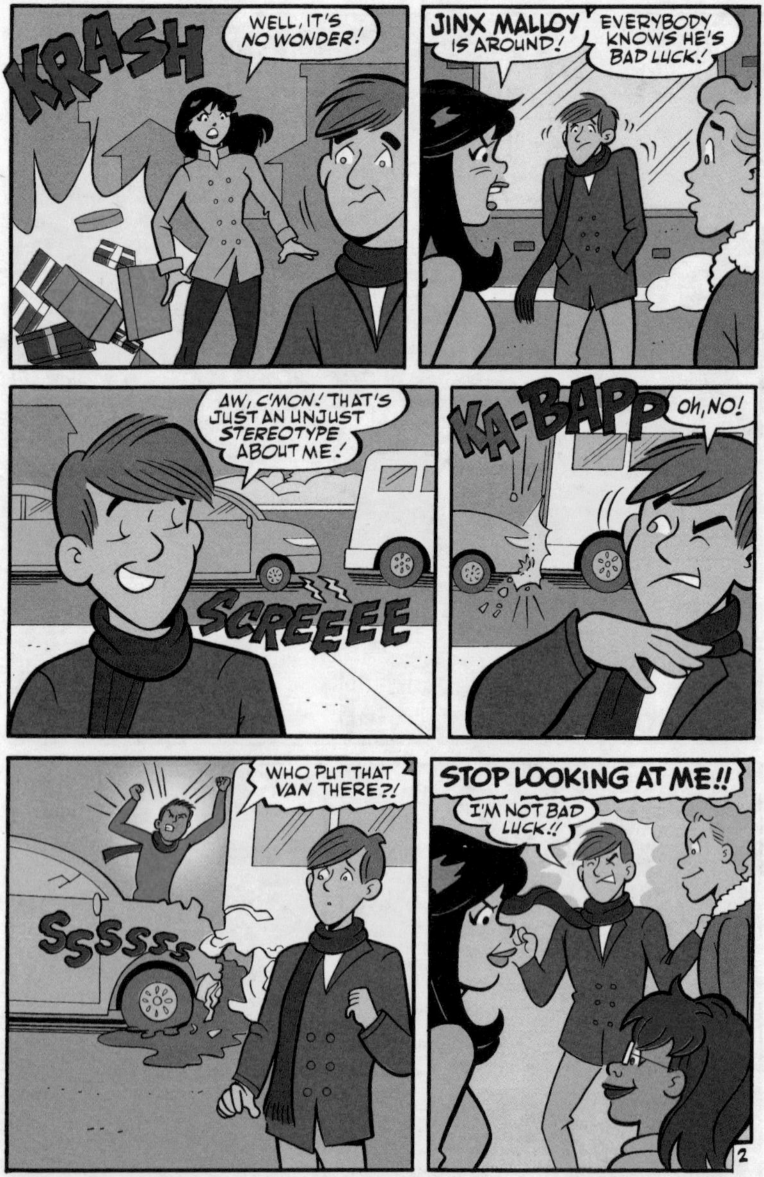
KRASH
WELL, IT'S NO WONDER!
JINX MALLOY IS AROUND!
EVERYBODY KNOWS HE'S BAD LUCK!
AW, C'MON! THAT'S JUST AN UNJUST STEREOTYPE ABOUT ME!
SCREEEEE
KA-BAPP
Oh, NO!
WHO PUT THAT VAN THERE?!
SSSSSS
STOP LOOKING AT ME!!
I'M NOT BAD LUCK!!
2

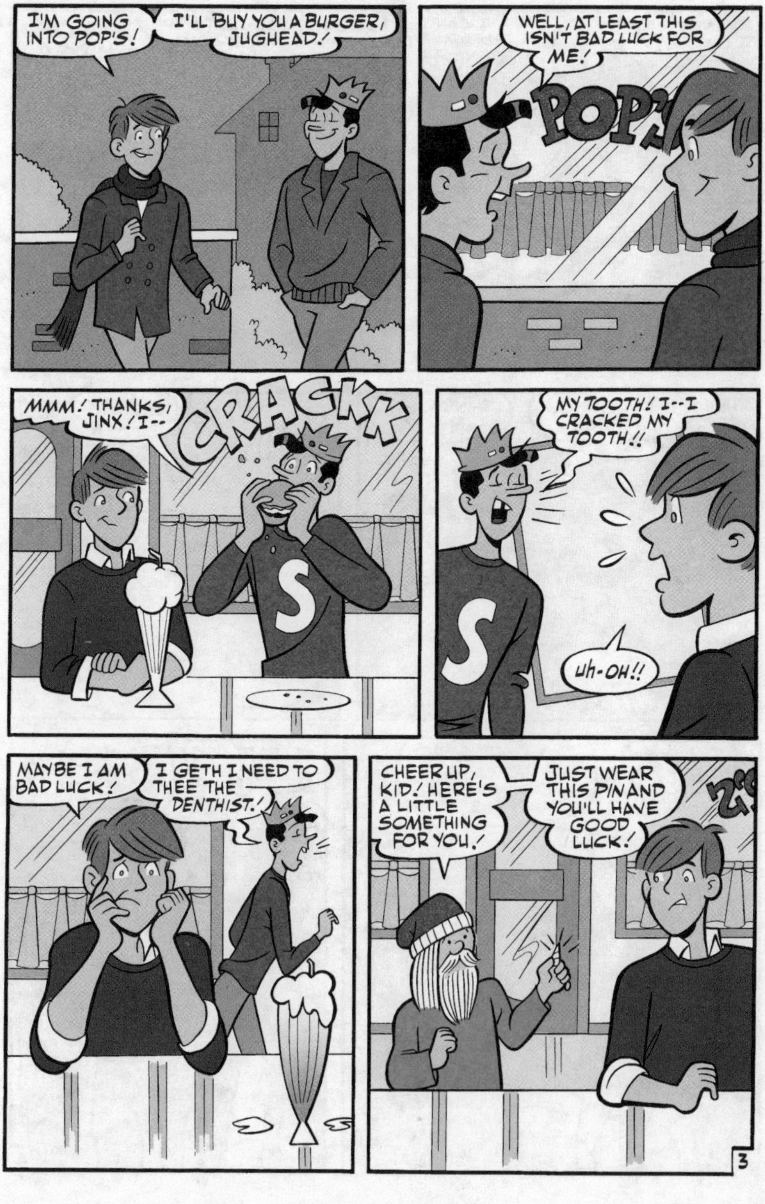
I'M GOING INTO POP'S!
I'LL BUY YOU A BURGER, JUGHEAD!
WELL, AT LEAST THIS ISN'T BAD LUCK FOR ME!
POP'S
MMM! THANKS, JINX! I--
CRACKK
MY TOOTH! I--I CRACKED MY TOOTH!!
uh-OH!!
MAYBE I AM BAD LUCK!
I GETH I NEED TO THEE THE DENTHIST!
CHEER UP, KID! HERE'S A LITTLE SOMETHING FOR YOU!
JUST WEAR THIS PIN AND YOU'LL HAVE GOOD LUCK!
3

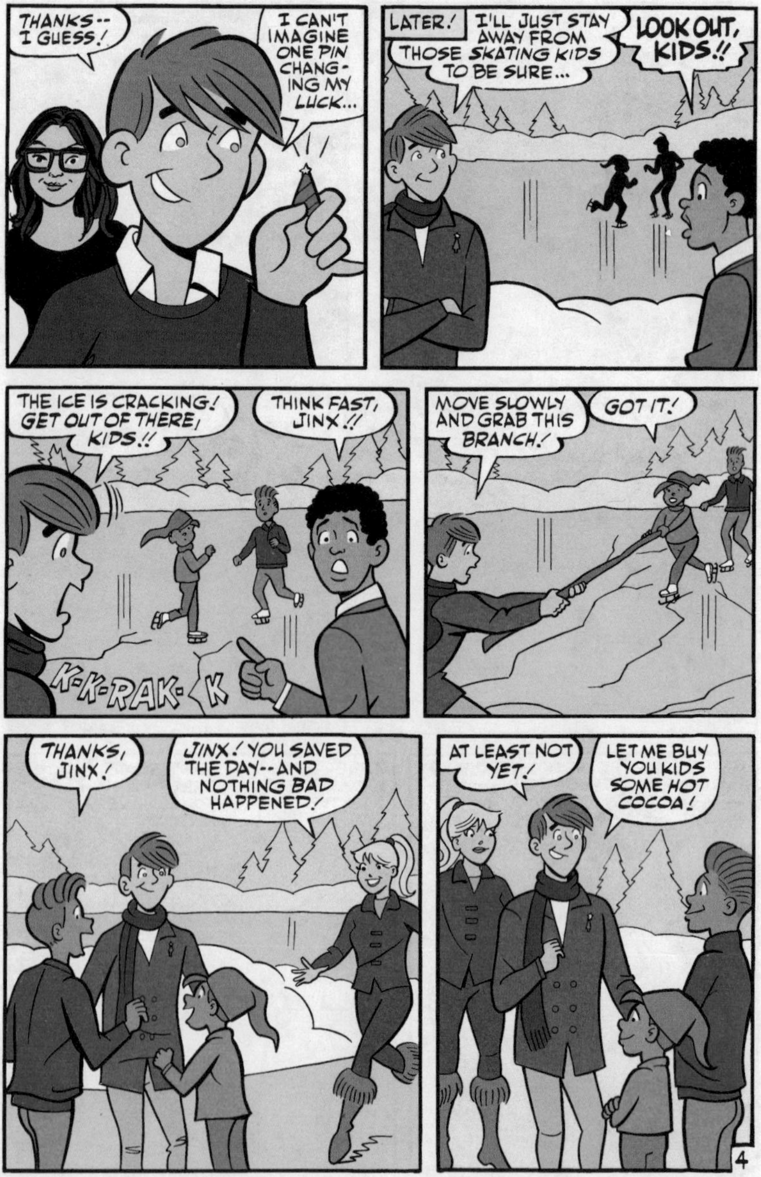
THANKS-- I GUESS!
I CAN'T IMAGINE ONE PIN CHANG-ING MY LUCK...
LATER!
I'LL JUST STAY AWAY FROM THOSE SKATING KIDS TO BE SURE...
LOOK OUT, KIDS!!
THE ICE IS CRACKING! GET OUT OF THERE, KIDS!!
THINK FAST, JINX!!
K-K-RAK-K
MOVE SLOWLY AND GRAB THIS BRANCH!
GOT IT!
THANKS, JINX!
JINX! YOU SAVED THE DAY--AND NOTHING BAD HAPPENED!
AT LEAST NOT YET!
LET ME BUY YOU KIDS SOME HOT COCOA!
4

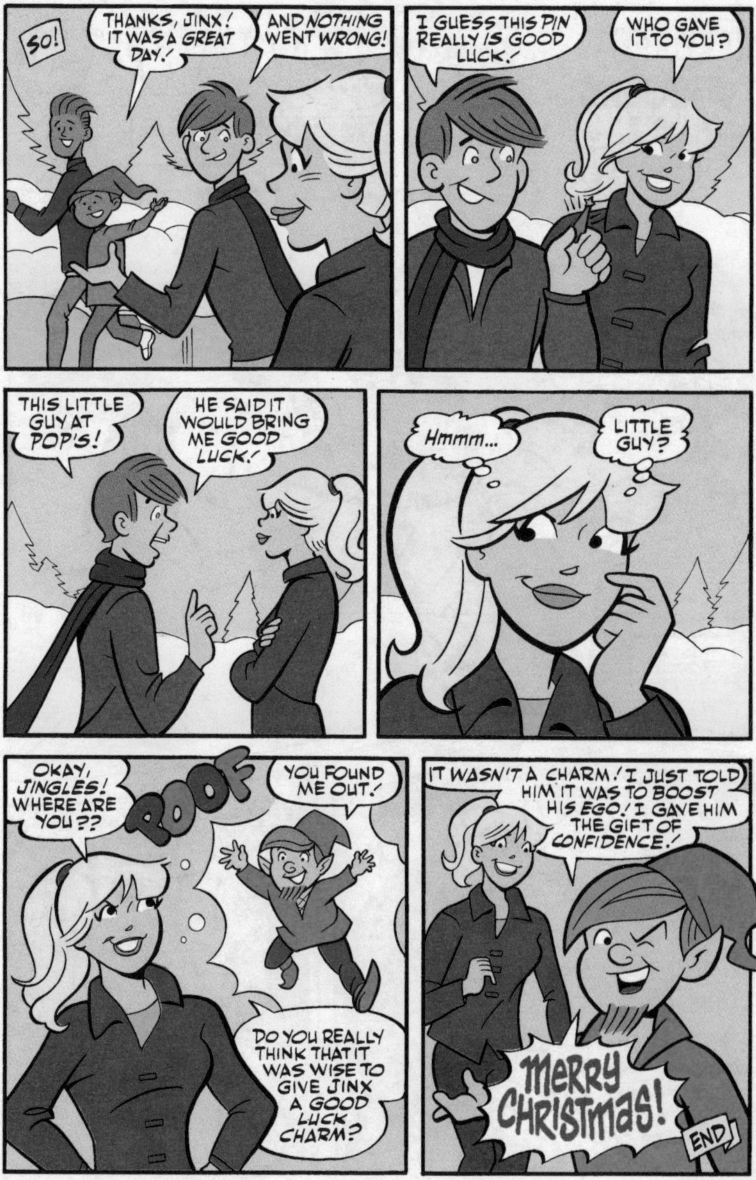
SO!
THANKS, JINX! IT WAS A GREAT DAY!
AND NOTHING WENT WRONG!
I GUESS THIS PIN REALLY IS GOOD LUCK!
WHO GAVE IT TO YOU?
THIS LITTLE GUY AT POP'S!
HE SAID IT WOULD BRING ME GOOD LUCK!
Hmmm...
LITTLE GUY?
OKAY, JINGLES! WHERE ARE YOU??
POOF
YOU FOUND ME OUT!
DO YOU REALLY THINK THAT IT WAS WISE TO GIVE JINX A GOOD LUCK CHARM?
IT WASN'T A CHARM! I JUST TOLD HIM IT WAS TO BOOST HIS EGO! I GAVE HIM THE GIFT OF CONFIDENCE!
MERRY CHRISTMAS!
END

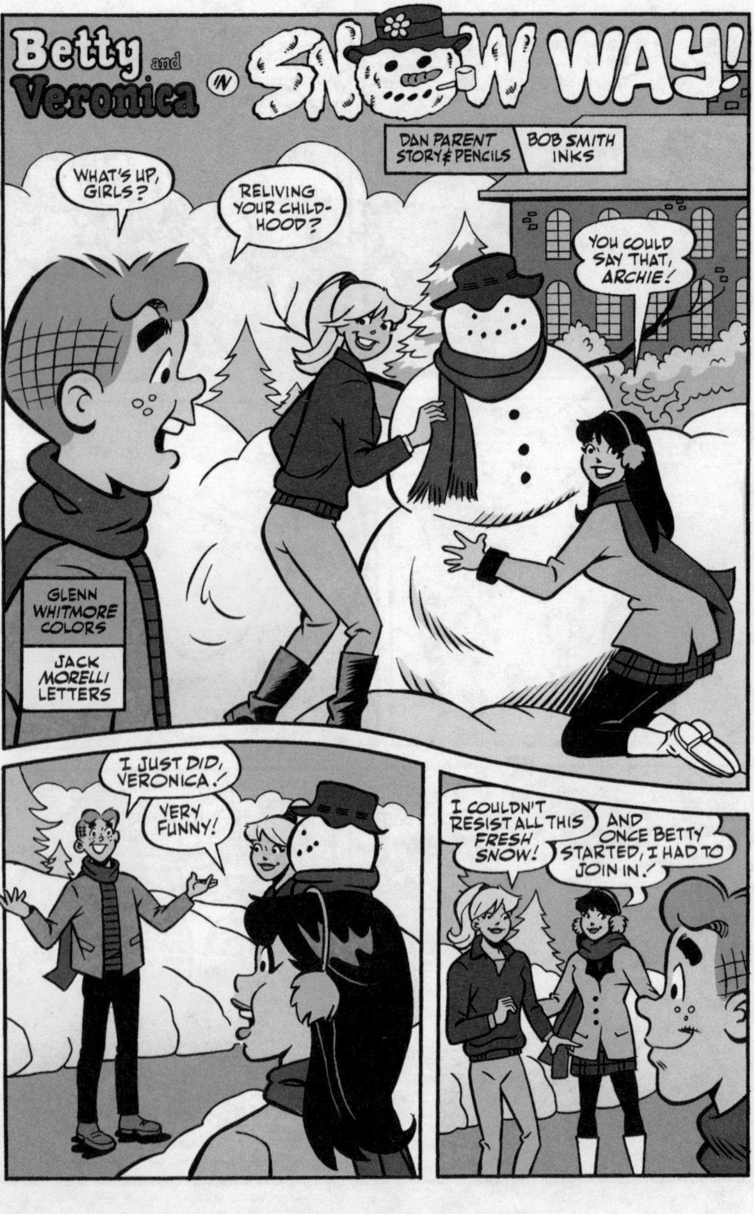
Betty and Veronica in SNOW WAY!
DAN PARENT STORY & PENCILS
BOB SMITH INKS
WHAT'S UP, GIRLS?
RELIVING YOUR CHILD-HOOD?
YOU COULD SAY THAT, ARCHIE!
GLENN WHITMORE COLORS
JACK MORELLI LETTERS
I JUST DID, VERONICA!
VERY FUNNY!
I COULDN'T RESIST ALL THIS FRESH SNOW!
AND ONCE BETTY STARTED, I HAD TO JOIN IN!

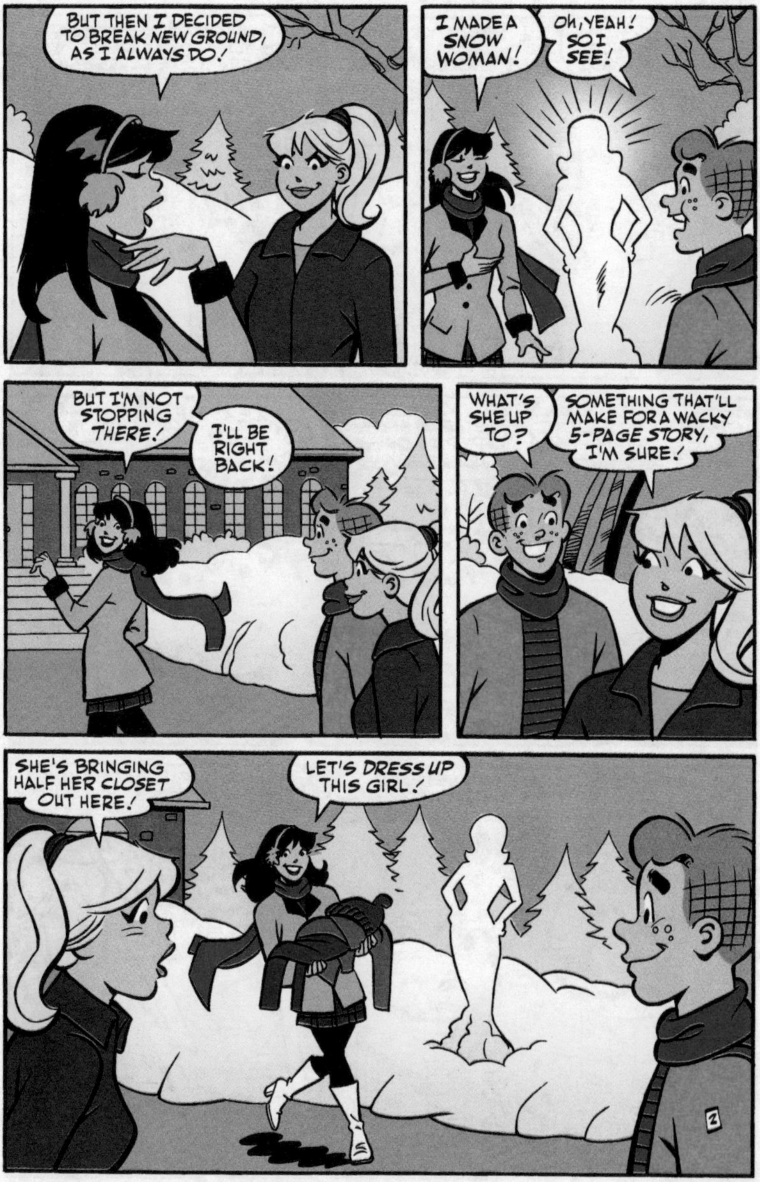
BUT THEN I DECIDED TO BREAK NEW GROUND, AS I ALWAYS DO!
I MADE A SNOW WOMAN!
Oh, YEAH! SO I SEE!
BUT I'M NOT STOPPING THERE!
I'LL BE RIGHT BACK!
WHAT'S SHE UP TO?
SOMETHING THAT'LL MAKE FOR A WACKY 5-PAGE STORY, I'M SURE!
SHE'S BRINGING HALF HER CLOSET OUT HERE!
LET'S DRESS UP THIS GIRL!
2

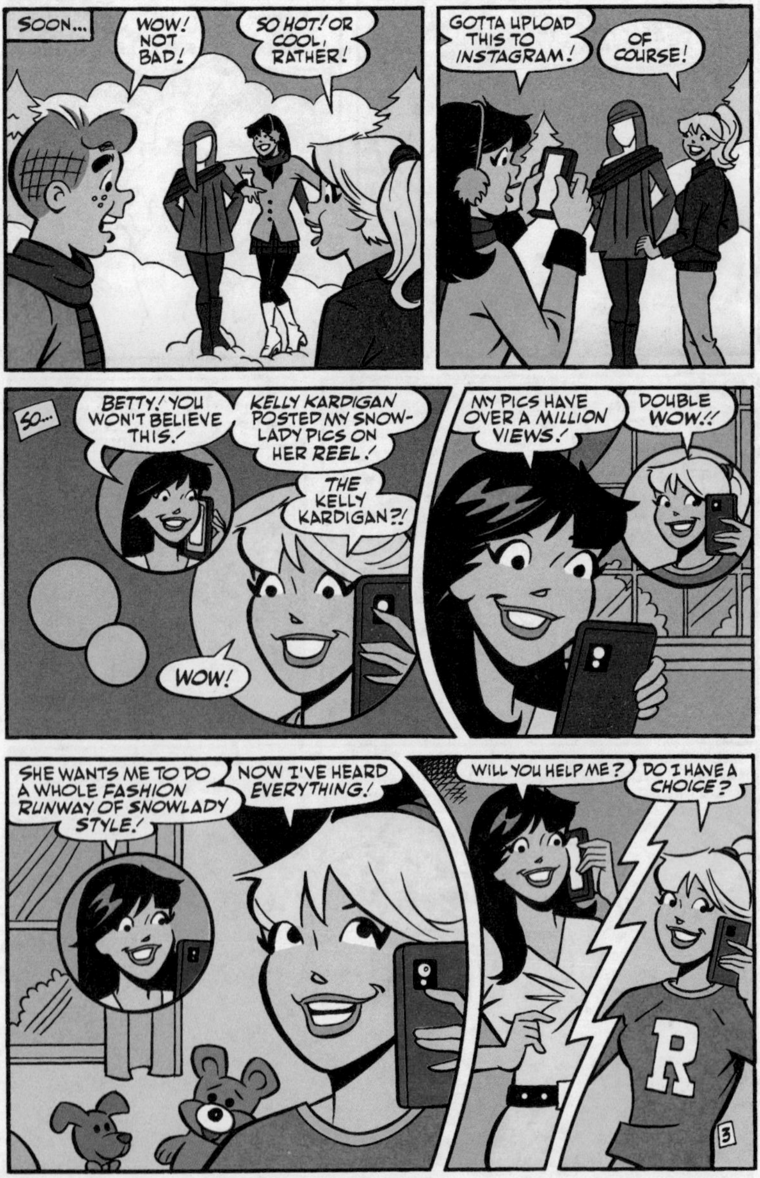
SOON...
WOW! NOT BAD!
SO HOT! OR COOL, RATHER!
GOTTA UPLOAD THIS TO INSTAGRAM!
OF COURSE!
SO...
BETTY! YOU WON'T BELIEVE THIS!
KELLY KARDIGAN POSTED MY SNOW-LADY PICS ON HER REEL!
THE KELLY KARDIGAN?!
WOW!
MY PICS HAVE OVER A MILLION VIEWS!
DOUBLE WOW!!
SHE WANTS ME TO DO A WHOLE FASHION RUNWAY OF SNOWLADY STYLE!
NOW I'VE HEARD EVERYTHING!
WILL YOU HELP ME?
DO I HAVE A CHOICE?
R
3

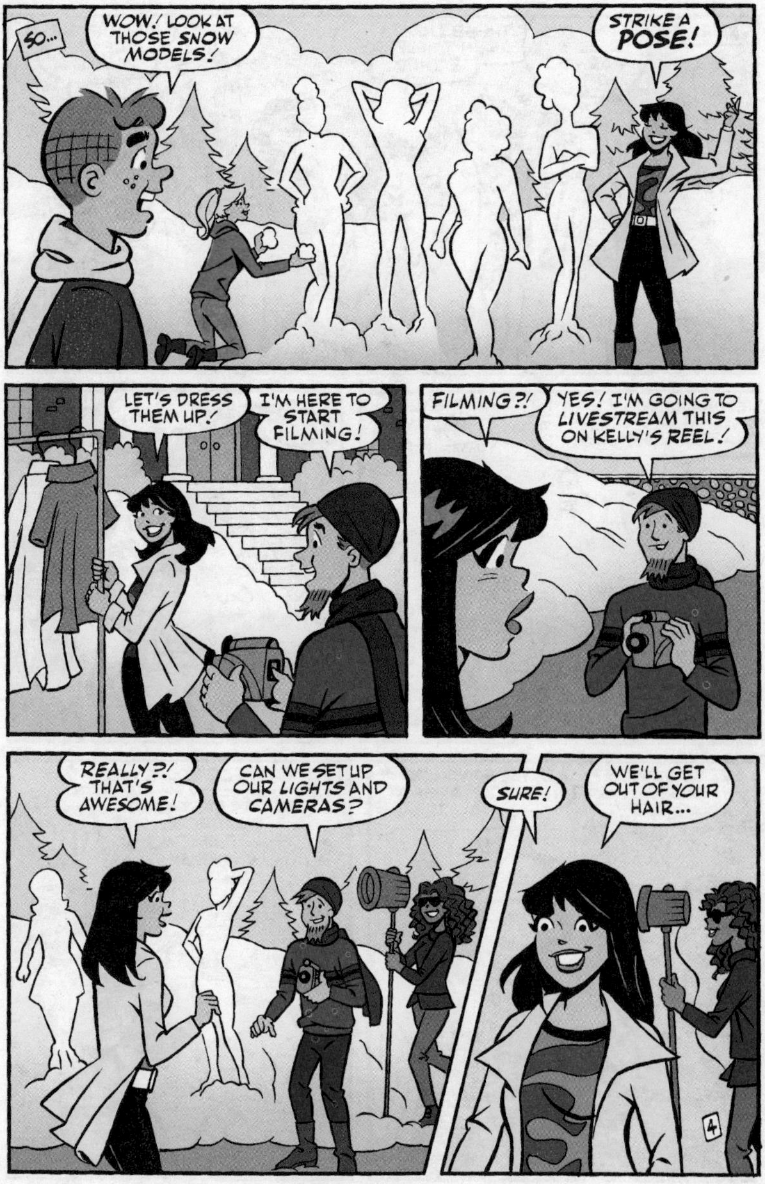
SO...
WOW! LOOK AT THOSE SNOW MODELS!
STRIKE A POSE!
LET'S DRESS THEM UP!
I'M HERE TO START FILMING!
FILMING?!
YES! I'M GOING TO LIVESTREAM THIS ON KELLY'S REEL!
REALLY?! THAT'S AWESOME!
CAN WE SET UP OUR LIGHTS AND CAMERAS?
SURE!
WE'LL GET OUT OF YOUR HAIR...
4

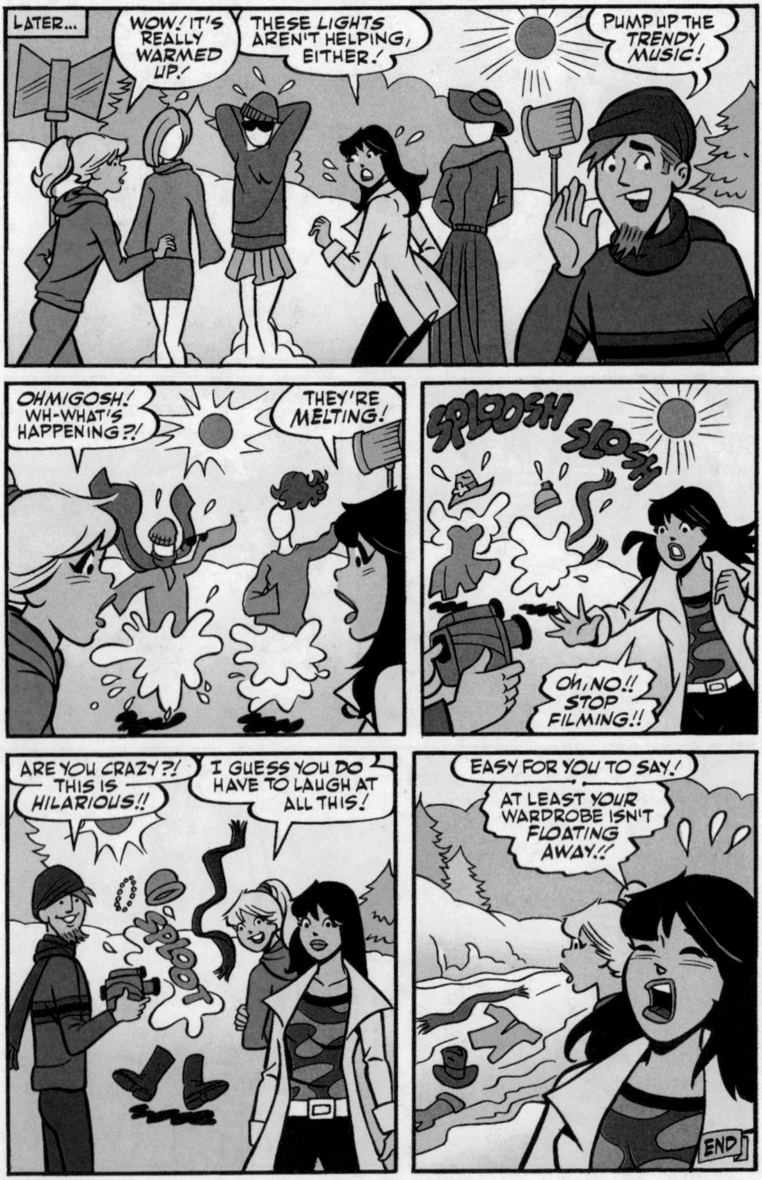
LATER...
WOW! IT'S REALLY WARMED UP!
THESE LIGHTS AREN'T HELPING, EITHER!
PUMP UP THE TRENDY MUSIC!
OHMIGOSH! WH-WHAT'S HAPPENING?!
THEY'RE MELTING!
SPLOOSH
SLOSH
OH, NO!! STOP FILMING!!
ARE YOU CRAZY?! THIS IS HILARIOUS!!
I GUESS YOU DO HAVE TO LAUGH AT ALL THIS!
SPLOOT
EASY FOR YOU TO SAY!
AT LEAST YOUR WARDROBE ISN'T FLOATING AWAY!!
END

05 ARCHIE MILESTONES

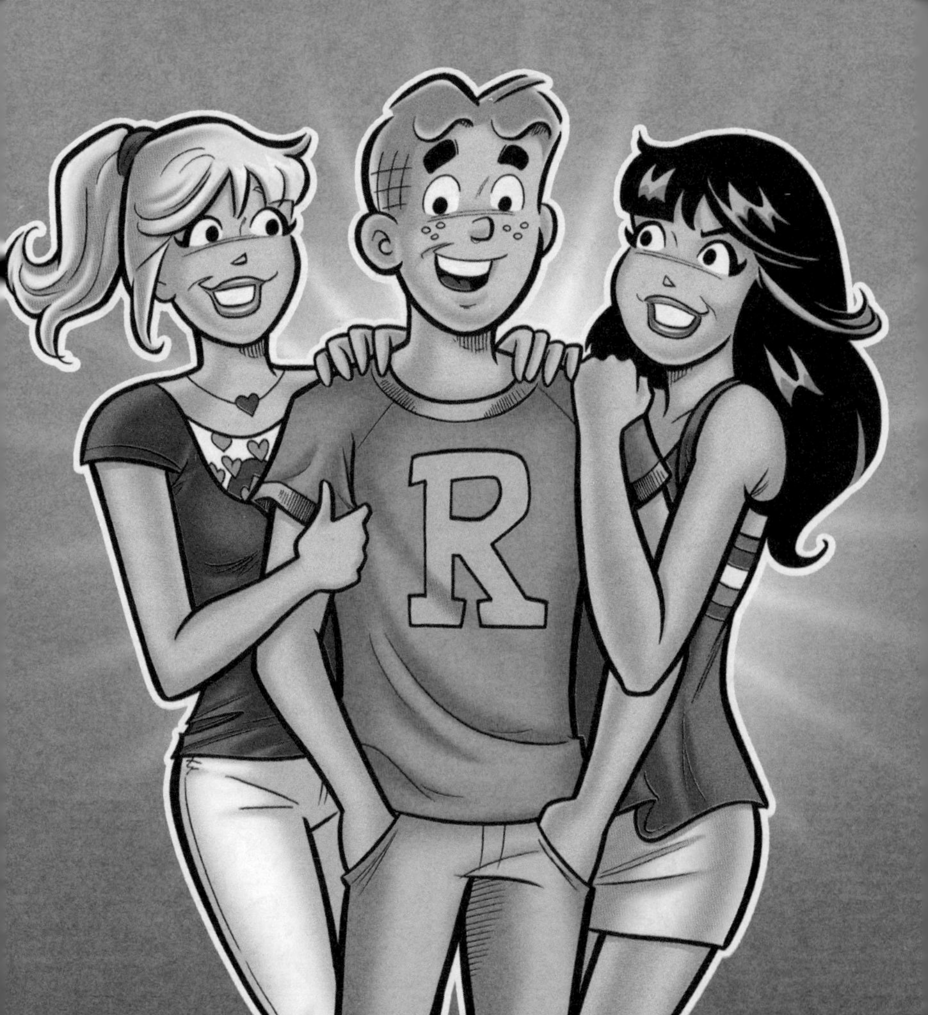

R

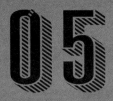

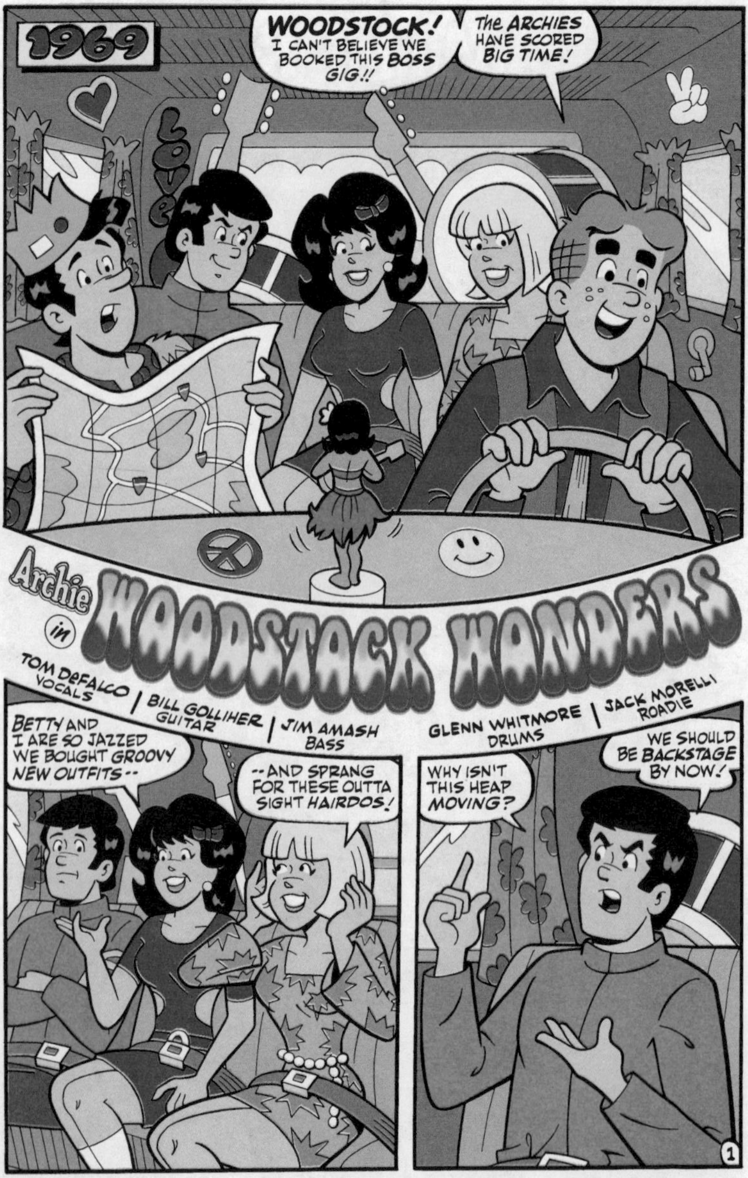
1969
WOODSTOCK! I CAN'T BELIEVE WE BOOKED THIS BOSS GIG!!
The ARCHIES HAVE SCORED BIG TIME!
LOVE
Archie in WOODSTOCK WONDERS
TOM DeFALCO VOCALS
BILL GOLLIHER GUITAR
JIM AMASH BASS
GLENN WHITMORE DRUMS
JACK MORELLI ROADIE
BETTY AND I ARE SO JAZZED WE BOUGHT GROOVY NEW OUTFITS--
--AND SPRANG FOR THESE OUTTA SIGHT HAIRDOS!
WHY ISN'T THIS HEAP MOVING?
WE SHOULD BE BACKSTAGE BY NOW!
1

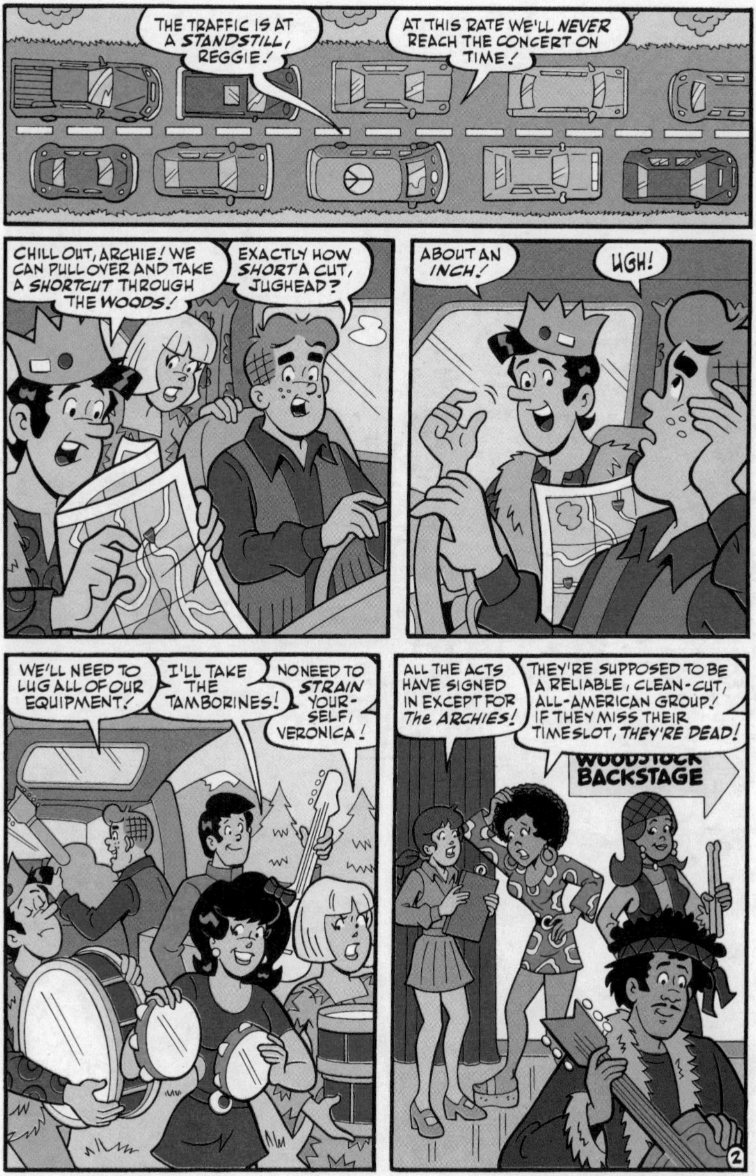
THE TRAFFIC IS AT A STANDSTILL, REGGIE!
AT THIS RATE WE'LL NEVER REACH THE CONCERT ON TIME!
CHILL OUT, ARCHIE! WE CAN PULL OVER AND TAKE A SHORTCUT THROUGH THE WOODS!
EXACTLY HOW SHORT A CUT, JUGHEAD?
ABOUT AN INCH!
UGH!
WE'LL NEED TO LUG ALL OF OUR EQUIPMENT!
I'LL TAKE THE TAMBORINES!
NO NEED TO STRAIN YOURSELF, VERONICA!
ALL THE ACTS HAVE SIGNED IN EXCEPT FOR The ARCHIES!
THEY'RE SUPPOSED TO BE A RELIABLE, CLEAN-CUT, ALL-AMERICAN GROUP! IF THEY MISS THEIR TIMESLOT, THEY'RE DEAD!
BACKSTAGE
2

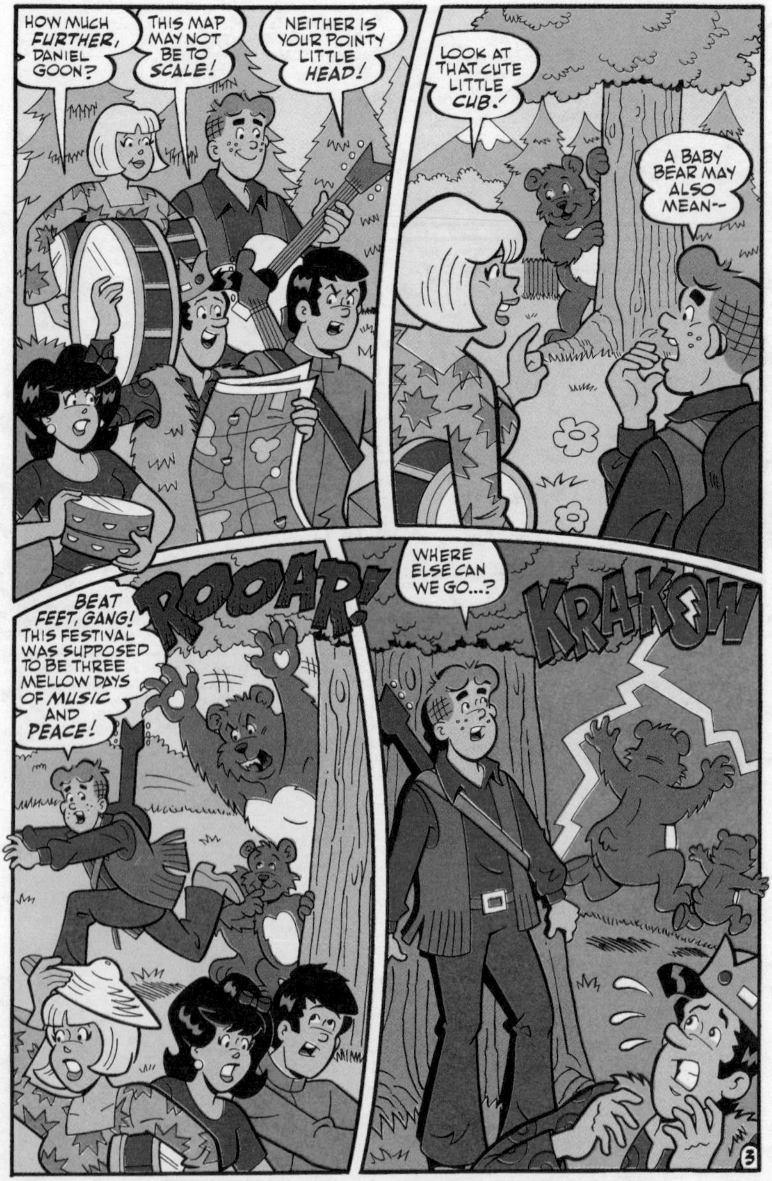
HOW MUCH FURTHER, DANIEL GOON?
THIS MAP MAY NOT BE TO SCALE!
NEITHER IS YOUR POINTY LITTLE HEAD!
LOOK AT THAT CUTE LITTLE CUB.!
A BABY BEAR MAY ALSO MEAN--
ROOAR!
BEAT FEET, GANG! THIS FESTIVAL WAS SUPPOSED TO BE THREE MELLOW DAYS OF MUSIC AND PEACE!
WHERE ELSE CAN WE GO...?
KRA-KOW
3

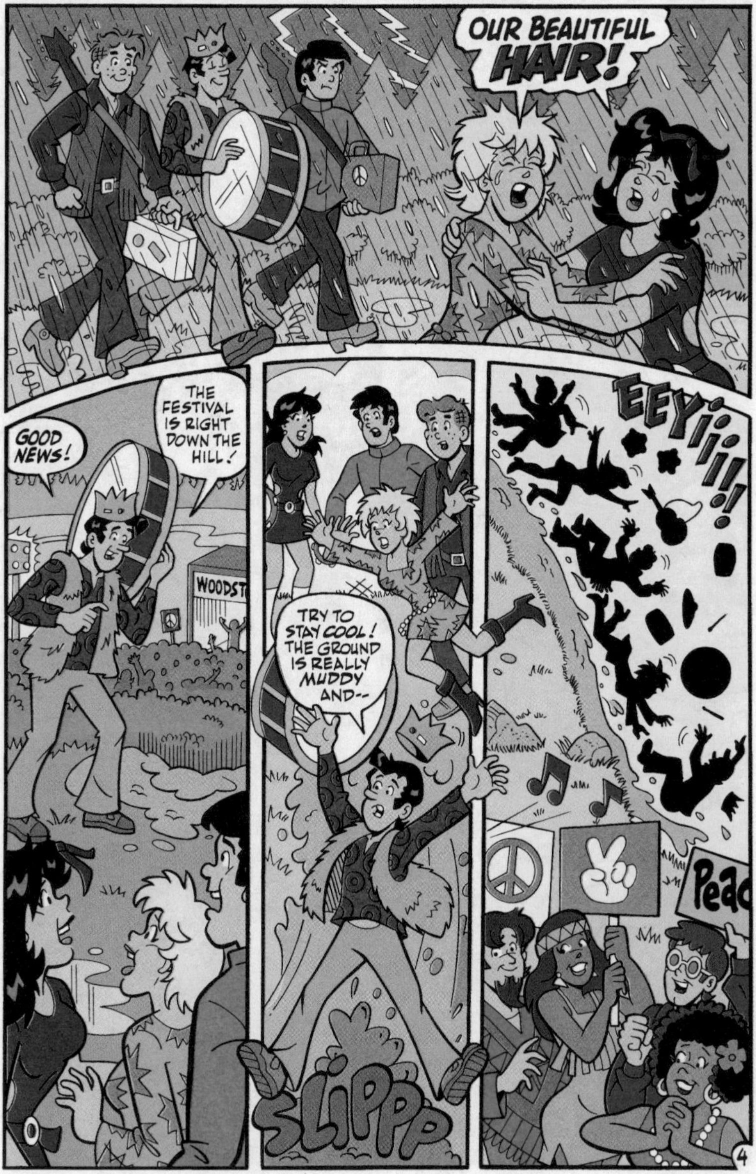
OUR BEAUTIFUL HAIR!
GOOD NEWS!
THE FESTIVAL IS RIGHT DOWN THE HILL!
WOODST
TRY TO STAY COOL! THE GROUND IS REALLY MUDDY AND--
SLIPPP
EEYIIII!!
Peac
4

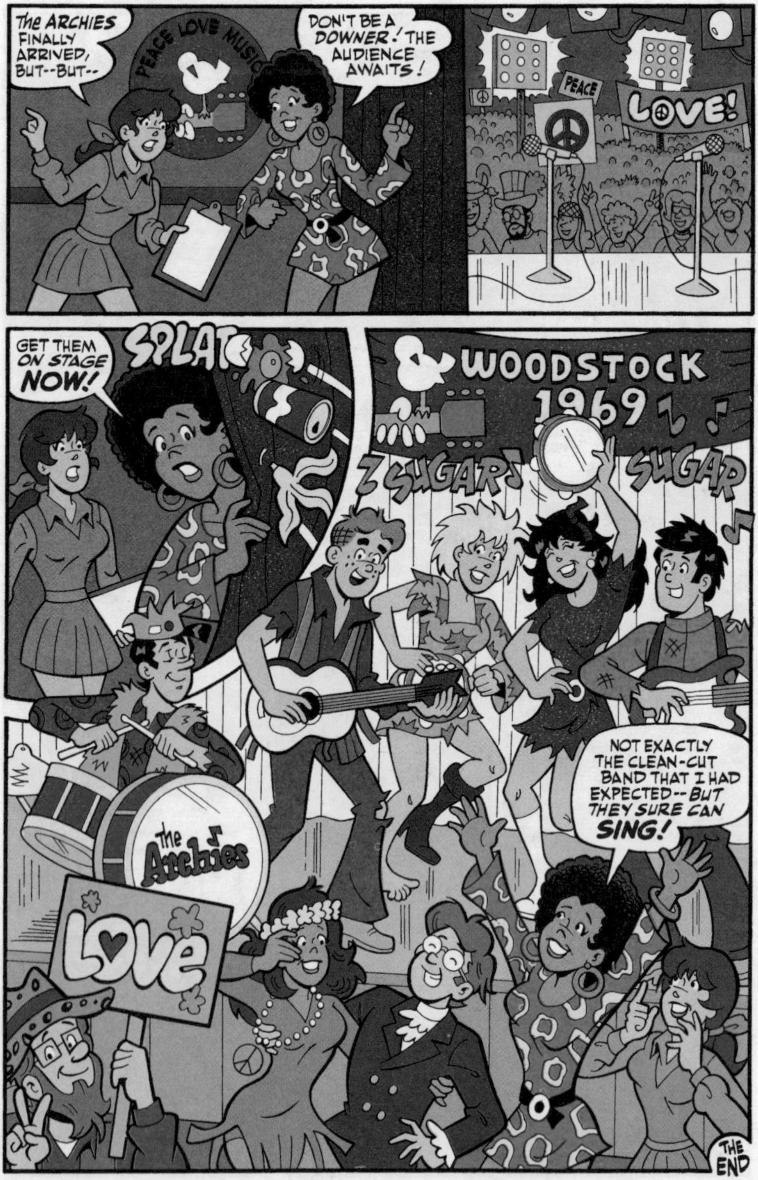
The ARCHIES FINALLY ARRIVED, BUT--BUT--
PEACE LOVE MUSIC
DON'T BE A DOWNER! THE AUDIENCE AWAITS!
PEACE
LOVE!
GET THEM ON STAGE NOW!
SPLAT
WOODSTOCK 1969
SUGAR SUGAR
the Archies
Love
NOT EXACTLY THE CLEAN-CUT BAND THAT I HAD EXPECTED--BUT THEY SURE CAN SING!
THE END

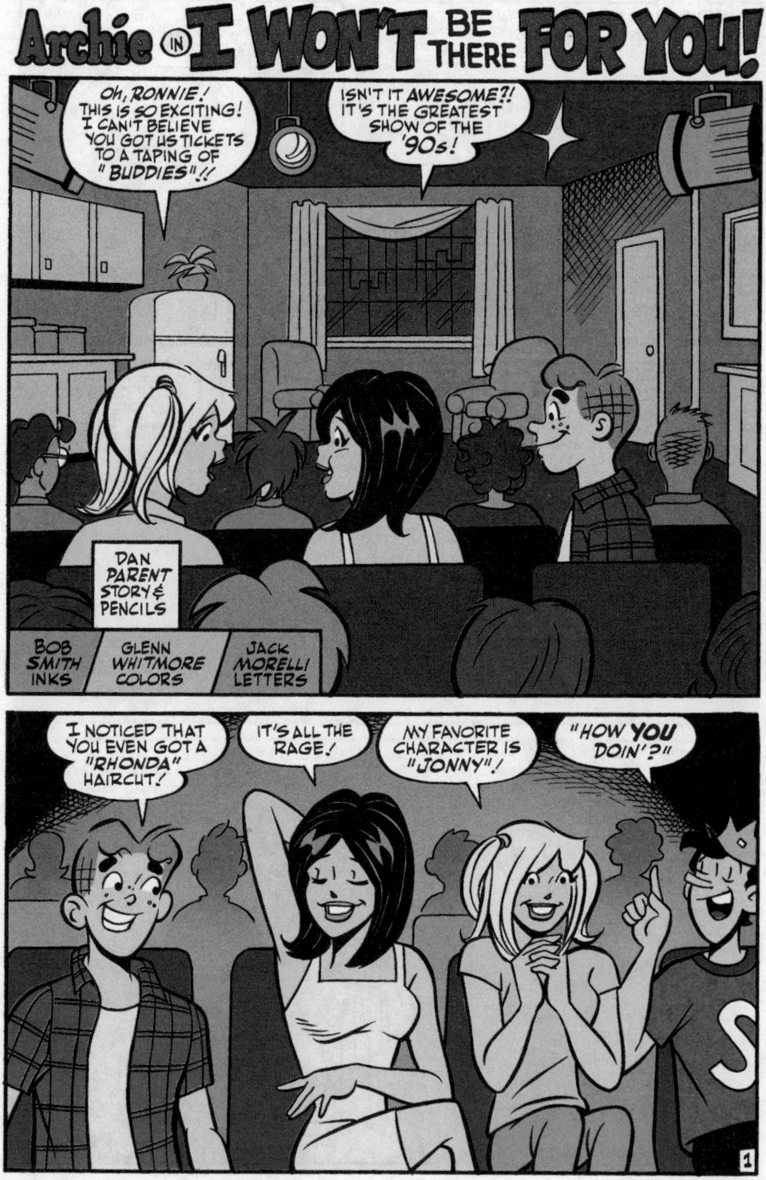
Archie IN I WON'T BE THERE FOR YOU!
Oh, RONNIE! THIS IS SO EXCITING! I CAN'T BELIEVE YOU GOT US TICKETS TO A TAPING OF "BUDDIES"!!
ISN'T IT AWESOME?! IT'S THE GREATEST SHOW OF THE '90s!
DAN PARENT STORY & PENCILS
BOB SMITH INKS
GLENN WHITMORE COLORS
JACK MORELLI LETTERS
I NOTICED THAT YOU EVEN GOT A "RHONDA" HAIRCUT!
IT'S ALL THE RAGE!
MY FAVORITE CHARACTER IS "JONNY"!
"HOW YOU DOIN'?"
1

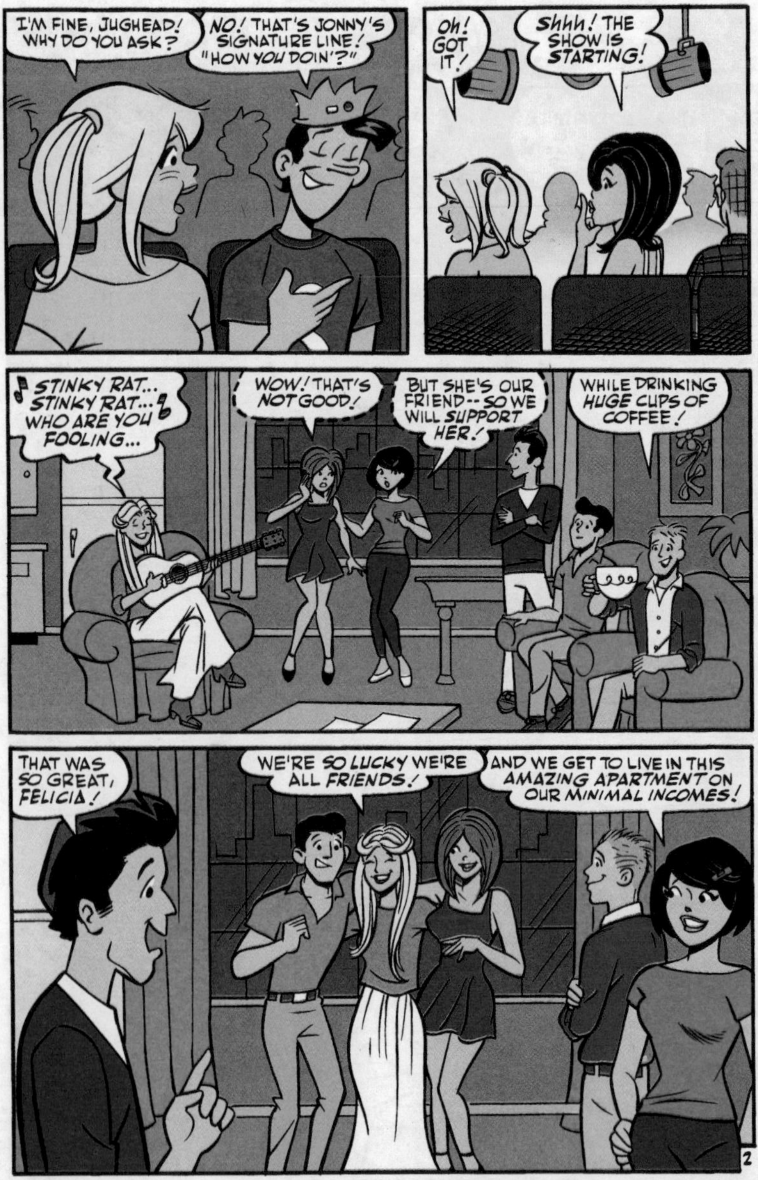
I'M FINE, JUGHEAD! WHY DO YOU ASK?
NO! THAT'S JONNY'S SIGNATURE LINE! "HOW YOU DOIN'?"
OH! GOT IT!
SHHH! THE SHOW IS STARTING!
STINKY RAT... STINKY RAT... WHO ARE YOU FOOLING...
WOW! THAT'S NOT GOOD!
BUT SHE'S OUR FRIEND-- SO WE WILL SUPPORT HER!
WHILE DRINKING HUGE CUPS OF COFFEE!
THAT WAS SO GREAT, FELICIA!
WE'RE SO LUCKY WE'RE ALL FRIENDS!
AND WE GET TO LIVE IN THIS AMAZING APARTMENT ON OUR MINIMAL INCOMES!
2

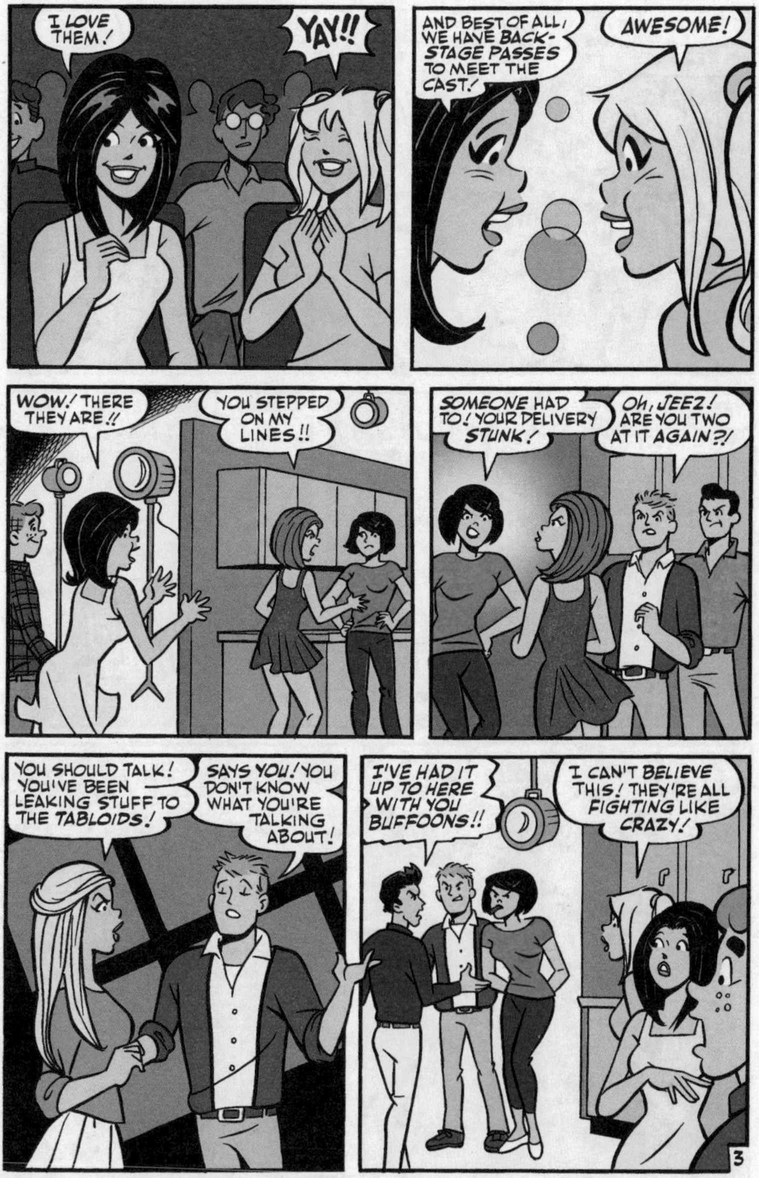
I LOVE THEM!
YAY!!
AND BEST OF ALL, WE HAVE BACK-STAGE PASSES TO MEET THE CAST!
AWESOME!
WOW! THERE THEY ARE!!
YOU STEPPED ON MY LINES!!
SOMEONE HAD TO! YOUR DELIVERY STUNK!
OH, JEEZ! ARE YOU TWO AT IT AGAIN?!
YOU SHOULD TALK! YOU'VE BEEN LEAKING STUFF TO THE TABLOIDS!
SAYS YOU! YOU DON'T KNOW WHAT YOU'RE TALKING ABOUT!
I'VE HAD IT UP TO HERE WITH YOU BUFFOONS!!
I CAN'T BELIEVE THIS! THEY'RE ALL FIGHTING LIKE CRAZY!
3

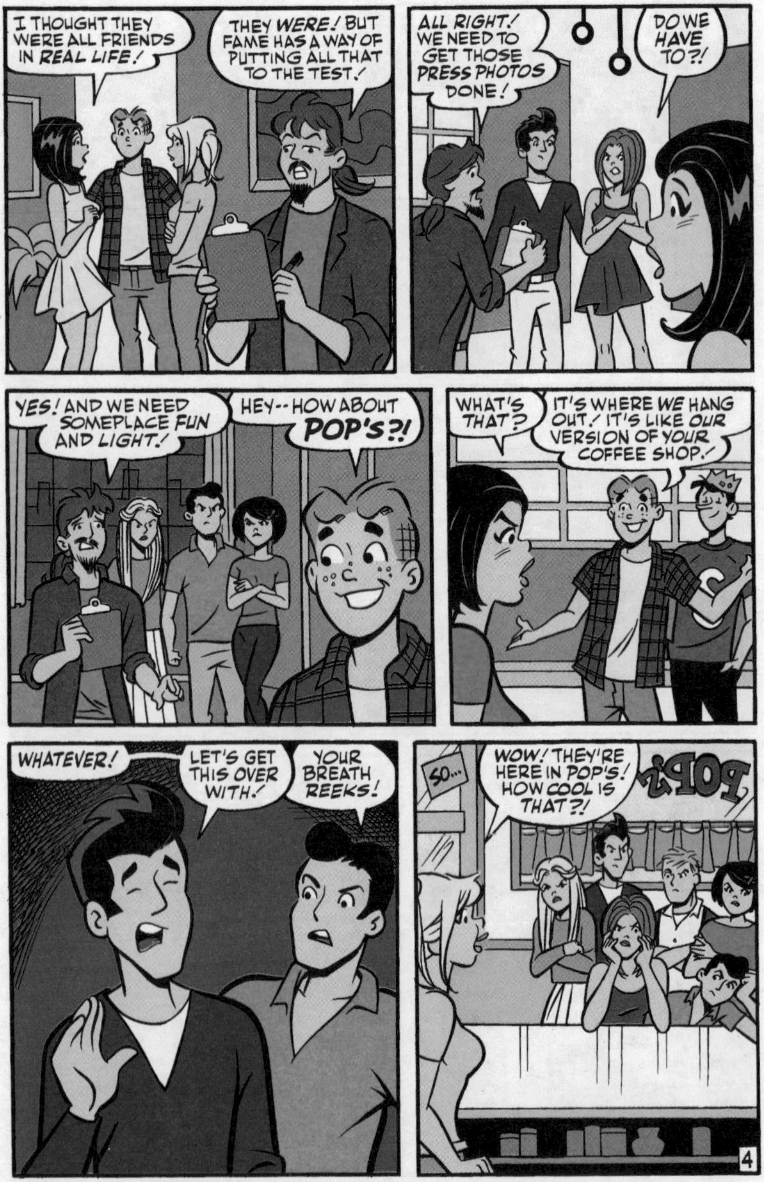

I THOUGHT THEY WERE ALL FRIENDS IN REAL LIFE!
THEY WERE! BUT FAME HAS A WAY OF PUTTING ALL THAT TO THE TEST!
ALL RIGHT! WE NEED TO GET THOSE PRESS PHOTOS DONE!
DO WE HAVE TO?!
YES! AND WE NEED SOMEPLACE FUN AND LIGHT!
HEY--HOW ABOUT POP'S?!
WHAT'S THAT?
IT'S WHERE WE HANG OUT! IT'S LIKE OUR VERSION OF YOUR COFFEE SHOP!
WHATEVER!
LET'S GET THIS OVER WITH!
YOUR BREATH REEKS!
SO...
WOW! THEY'RE HERE IN POP'S! HOW COOL IS THAT?!
POP'S
4

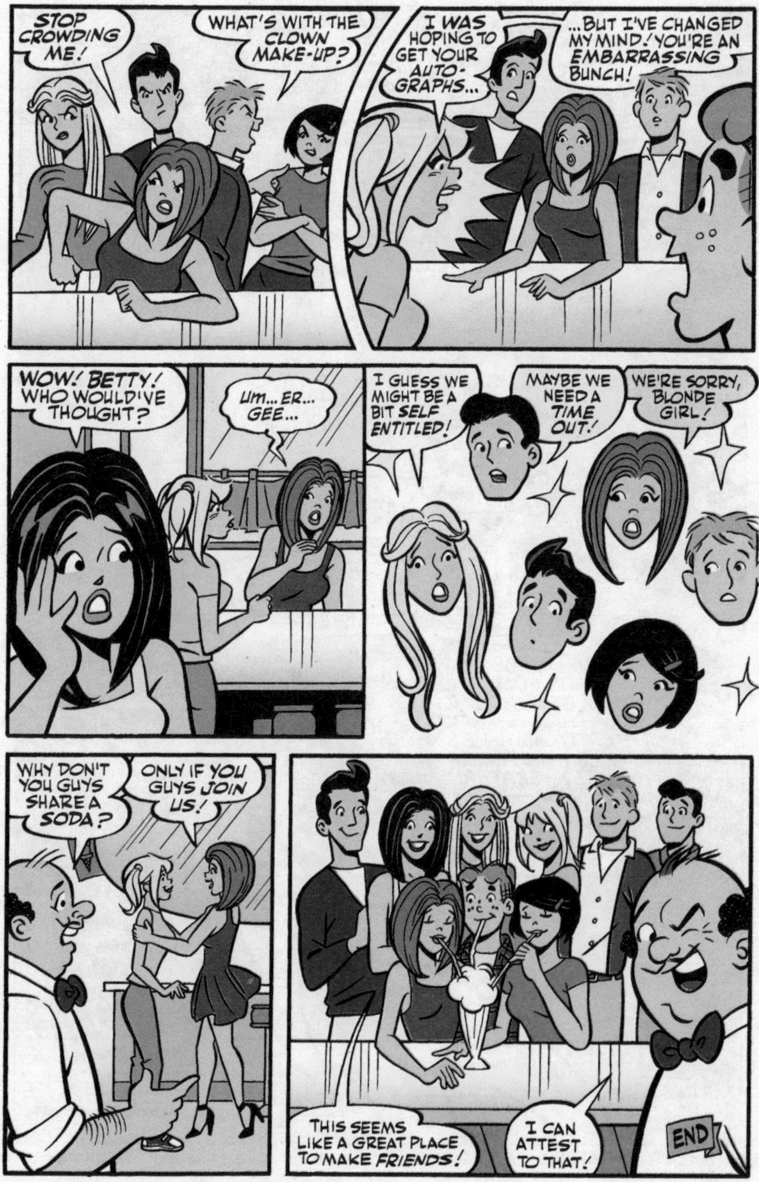
STOP CROWDING ME!
WHAT'S WITH THE CLOWN MAKE-UP?
I WAS HOPING TO GET YOUR AUTO-GRAPHS...
...BUT I'VE CHANGED MY MIND! YOU'RE AN EMBARRASSING BUNCH!
WOW! BETTY! WHO WOULD'VE THOUGHT?
UM...ER... GEE...
I GUESS WE MIGHT BE A BIT SELF ENTITLED!
MAYBE WE NEED A TIME OUT!
WE'RE SORRY, BLONDE GIRL!
WHY DON'T YOU GUYS SHARE A SODA?
ONLY IF YOU GUYS JOIN US!
THIS SEEMS LIKE A GREAT PLACE TO MAKE FRIENDS!
I CAN ATTEST TO THAT!
END

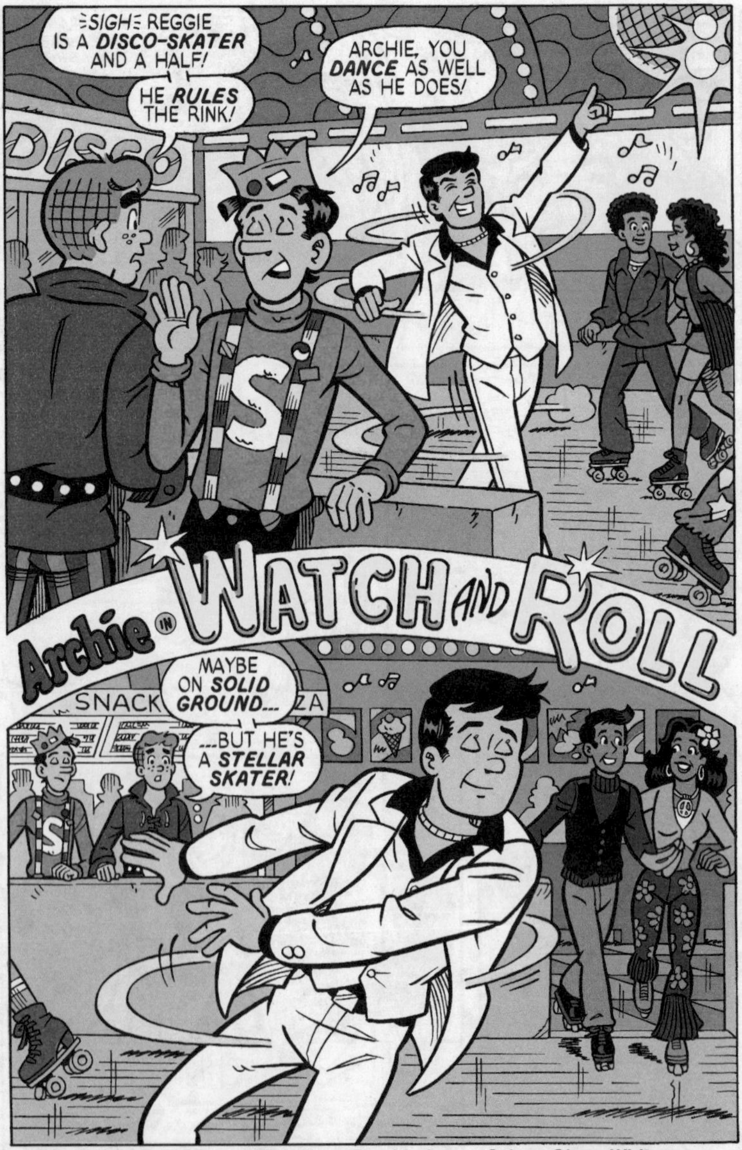
≡SIGH≡ REGGIE IS A DISCO-SKATER AND A HALF!
HE RULES THE RINK!
ARCHIE, YOU DANCE AS WELL AS HE DOES!
DISCO
Archie IN WATCH AND ROLL
SNACK
ZA
MAYBE ON SOLID GROUND...
...BUT HE'S A STELLAR SKATER!

Script: **Tom DeFalco** Art & Letters: **Rex Lindsey** Colors: **Glenn Whitmore**

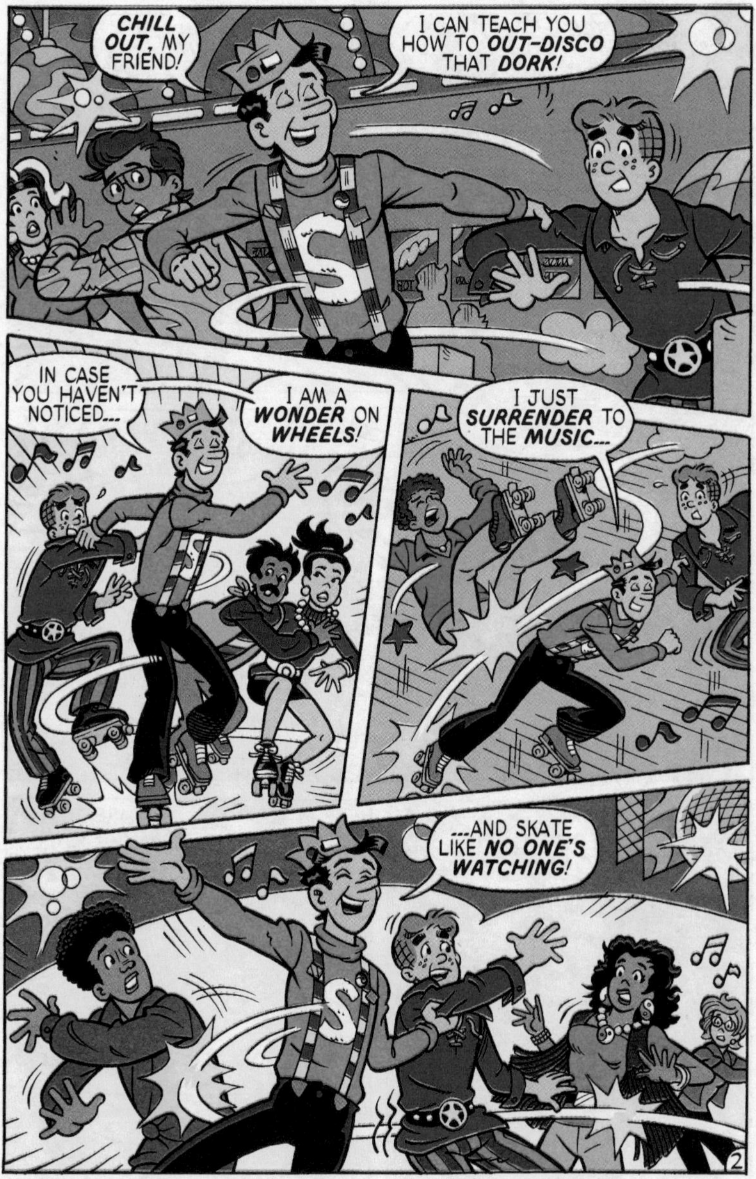
CHILL OUT, MY FRIEND!
I CAN TEACH YOU HOW TO OUT-DISCO THAT DORK!
IN CASE YOU HAVEN'T NOTICED...
I AM A WONDER ON WHEELS!
I JUST SURRENDER TO THE MUSIC...
...AND SKATE LIKE NO ONE'S WATCHING!
2

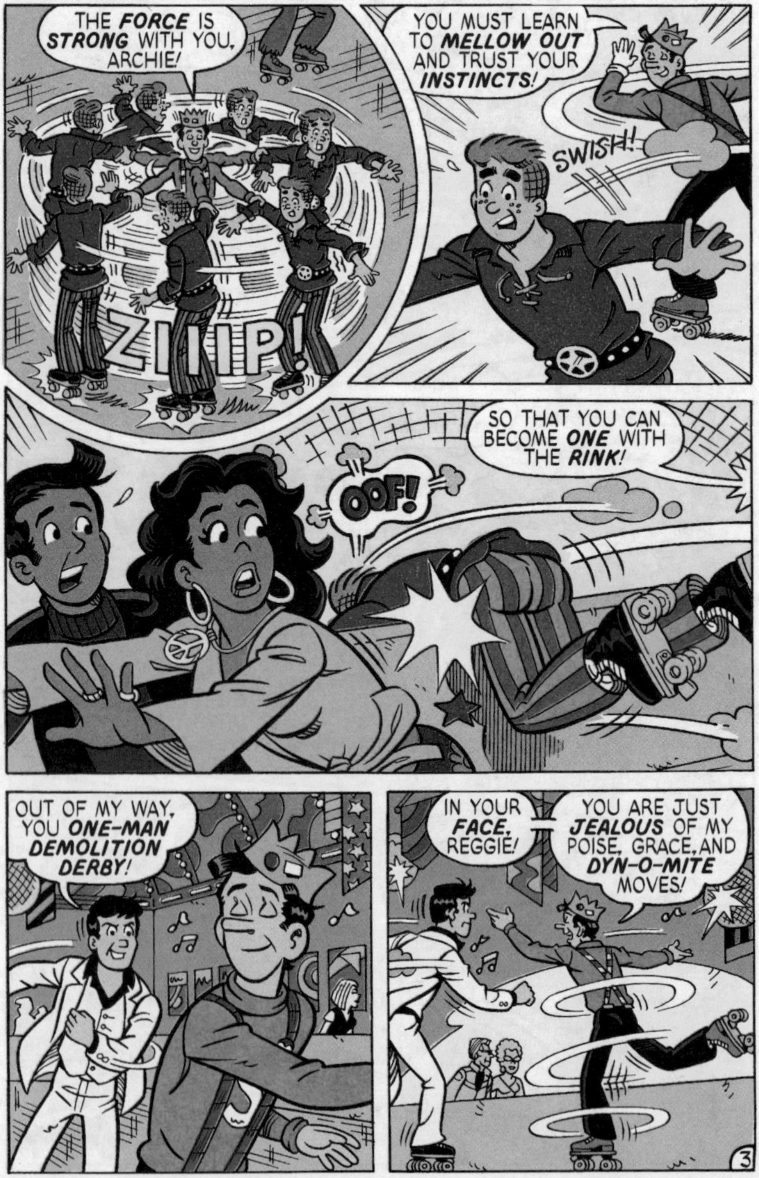
THE **FORCE** IS **STRONG** WITH YOU, ARCHIE!
ZIIIP!
YOU MUST LEARN TO **MELLOW OUT** AND TRUST YOUR **INSTINCTS**!
SWISH!
SO THAT YOU CAN BECOME **ONE** WITH THE **RINK**!
OOF!
OUT OF MY WAY, YOU **ONE-MAN DEMOLITION DERBY**!
IN YOUR **FACE**, REGGIE!
YOU ARE JUST **JEALOUS** OF MY POISE, GRACE, AND **DYN-O-MITE** MOVES!
3

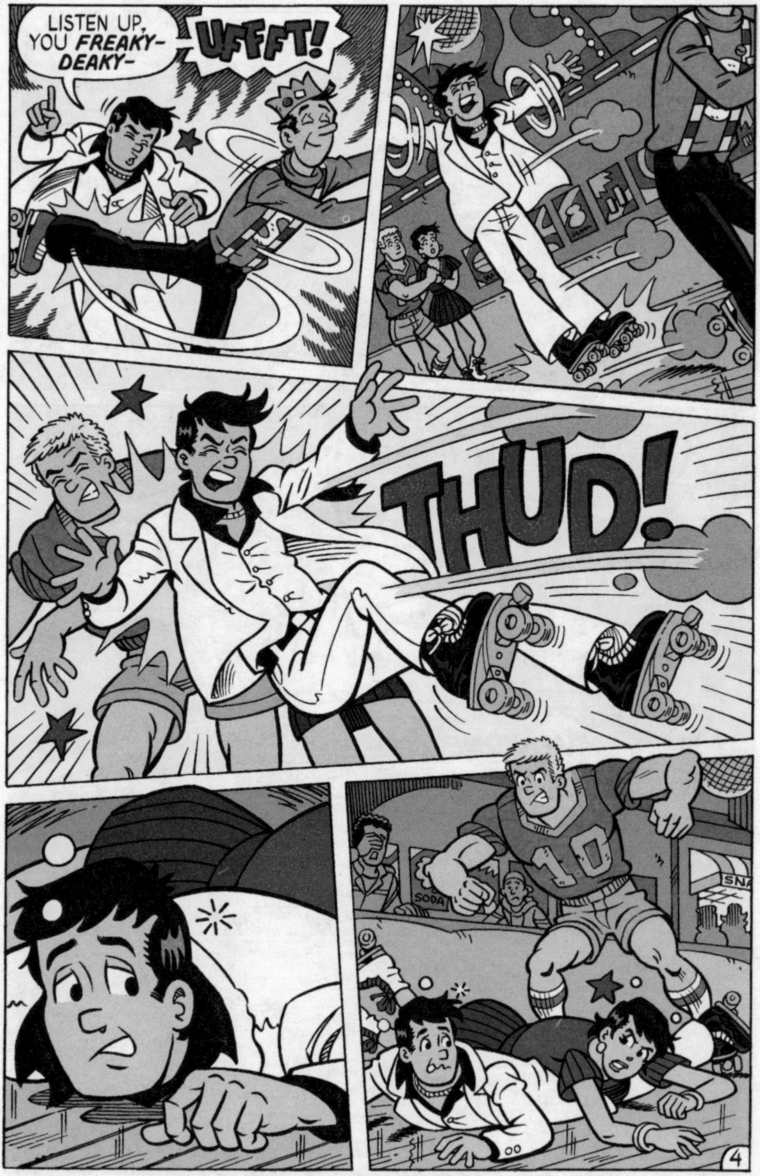
LISTEN UP, YOU FREAKY-DEAKY-
UFFFT!
THUD!
SODA
4

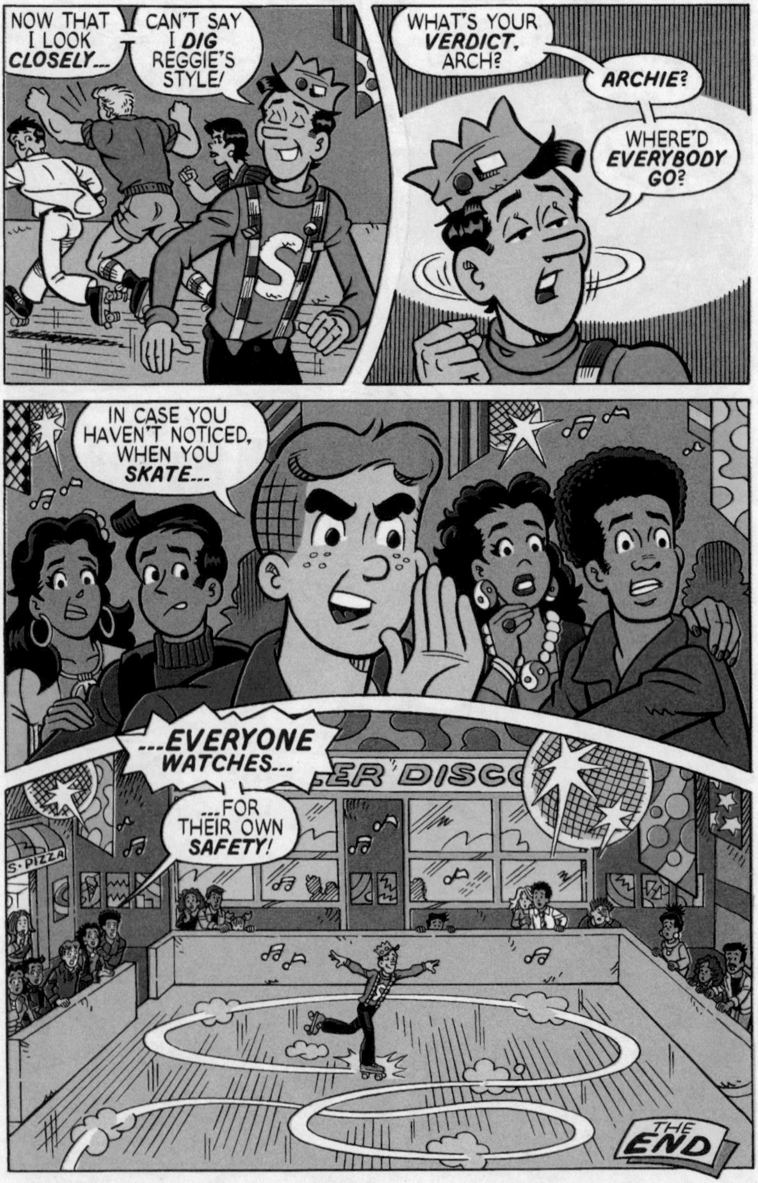
NOW THAT I LOOK CLOSELY...
CAN'T SAY I DIG REGGIE'S STYLE!
WHAT'S YOUR VERDICT, ARCH?
ARCHIE?
WHERE'D EVERYBODY GO?
IN CASE YOU HAVEN'T NOTICED, WHEN YOU SKATE...
...EVERYONE WATCHES...
...FOR THEIR OWN SAFETY!
ER DISCO
S·PIZZA
THE END

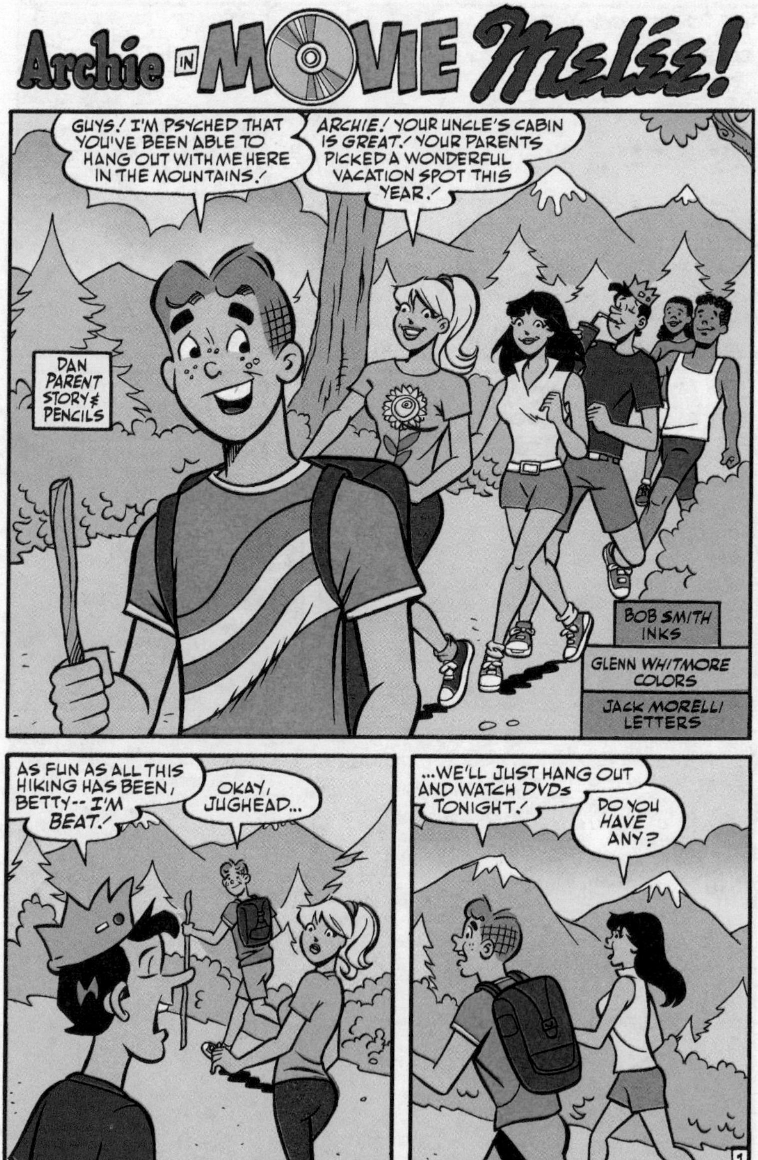
Archie IN MOVIE Melée!
GUYS! I'M PSYCHED THAT YOU'VE BEEN ABLE TO HANG OUT WITH ME HERE IN THE MOUNTAINS!
ARCHIE! YOUR UNCLE'S CABIN IS GREAT! YOUR PARENTS PICKED A WONDERFUL VACATION SPOT THIS YEAR!
DAN PARENT STORY & PENCILS
BOB SMITH INKS
GLENN WHITMORE COLORS
JACK MORELLI LETTERS
AS FUN AS ALL THIS HIKING HAS BEEN, BETTY-- I'M BEAT!
OKAY, JUGHEAD...
...WE'LL JUST HANG OUT AND WATCH DVDs TONIGHT!
DO YOU HAVE ANY?
1

YES, RONNIE! LOOK AT ALL OF THESE RED ENVELOPES!

THEY'RE MY "NETFILMS" DELIVERY!

NET FILMS

HOW DOES THAT WORK?

EVERY FEW DAYS I GET THESE DVDs SENT TO ME, BETTY!

THEN I WATCH THEM AND SEND THEM BACK--

--AND THEY SEND ME MORE!

WHAT A GREAT IDEA!

THIS'LL BE FUN, CHUCK!

ESPECIALLY SINCE WE HAVE NO CABLE TV OUT HERE IN THE BOONDOCKS, NANCY!

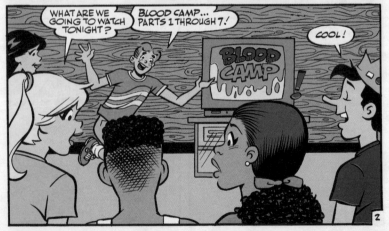

WHAT ARE WE GOING TO WATCH TONIGHT?

BLOOD CAMP... PARTS 1 THROUGH 7!

BLOOD CAMP

COOL!

2

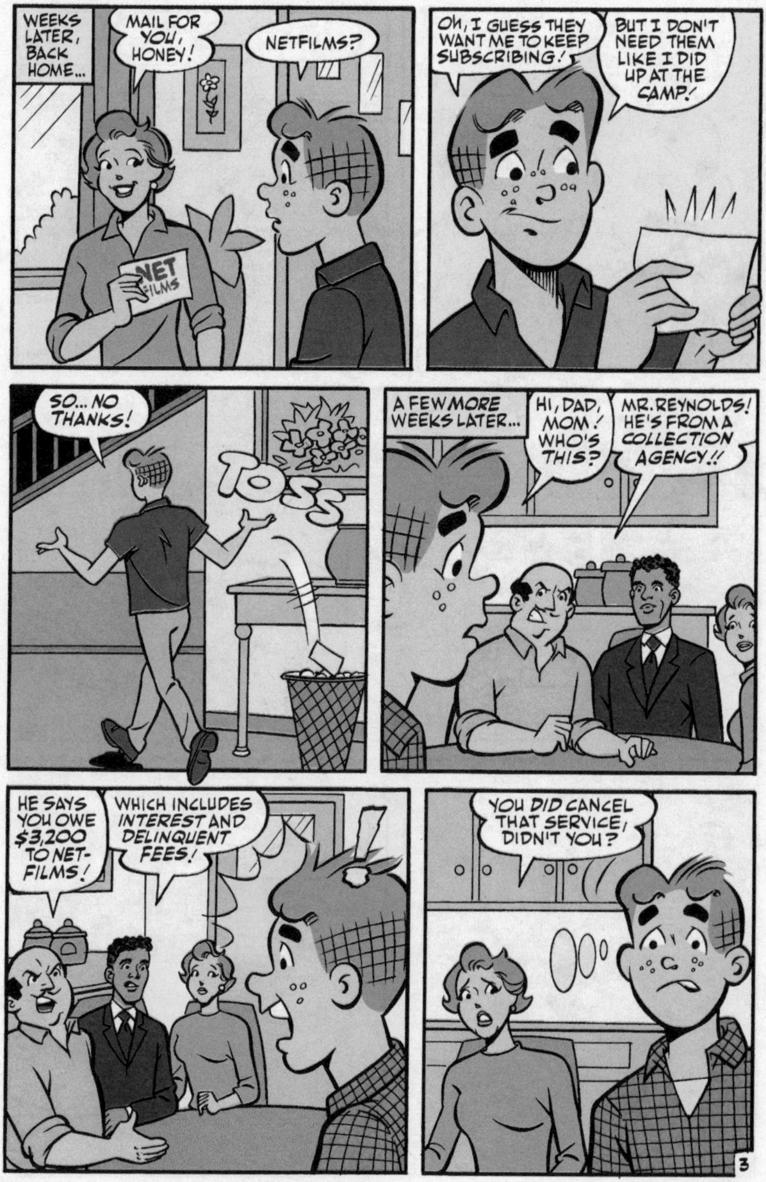
WEEKS LATER, BACK HOME...
MAIL FOR YOU, HONEY!
NETFILMS?
NET FILMS
OH, I GUESS THEY WANT ME TO KEEP SUBSCRIBING!
BUT I DON'T NEED THEM LIKE I DID UP AT THE CAMP!
SO... NO THANKS!
TOSS
A FEW MORE WEEKS LATER...
HI, DAD, MOM! WHO'S THIS?
MR. REYNOLDS! HE'S FROM A COLLECTION AGENCY!!
HE SAYS YOU OWE $3,200 TO NET-FILMS!
WHICH INCLUDES INTEREST AND DELINQUENT FEES!
YOU DID CANCEL THAT SERVICE, DIDN'T YOU?
3

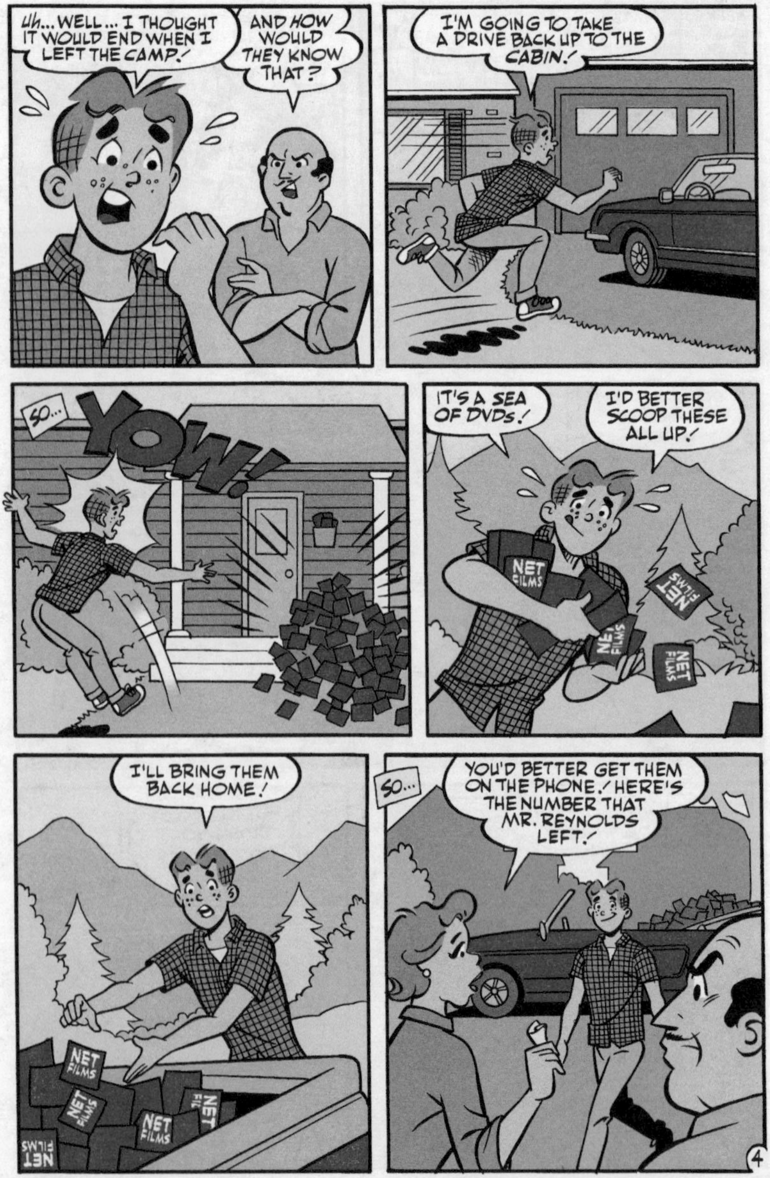
Uh... WELL... I THOUGHT IT WOULD END WHEN I LEFT THE CAMP!
AND HOW WOULD THEY KNOW THAT?
I'M GOING TO TAKE A DRIVE BACK UP TO THE CABIN!
SO...
YOW!
IT'S A SEA OF DVDs!
I'D BETTER SCOOP THESE ALL UP!
NET FILMS
I'LL BRING THEM BACK HOME!
NET FILMS
SO...
YOU'D BETTER GET THEM ON THE PHONE! HERE'S THE NUMBER THAT MR. REYNOLDS LEFT!
4

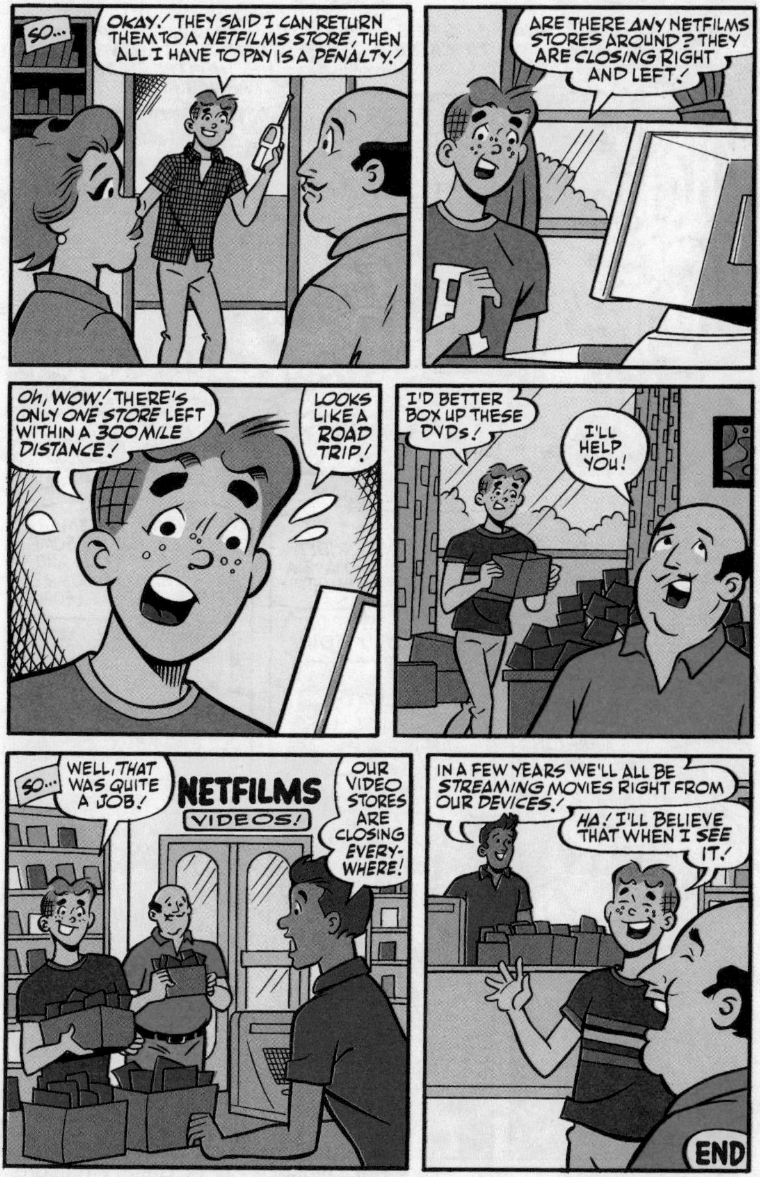

SO...
OKAY! THEY SAID I CAN RETURN THEM TO A NETFILMS STORE, THEN ALL I HAVE TO PAY IS A PENALTY!
ARE THERE ANY NETFILMS STORES AROUND? THEY ARE CLOSING RIGHT AND LEFT!
OH, WOW! THERE'S ONLY ONE STORE LEFT WITHIN A 300 MILE DISTANCE!
LOOKS LIKE A ROAD TRIP!
I'D BETTER BOX UP THESE DVDs!
I'LL HELP YOU!
SO...
WELL, THAT WAS QUITE A JOB!
NETFILMS
VIDEOS!
OUR VIDEO STORES ARE CLOSING EVERY-WHERE!
IN A FEW YEARS WE'LL ALL BE STREAMING MOVIES RIGHT FROM OUR DEVICES!
HA! I'LL BELIEVE THAT WHEN I SEE IT!
END

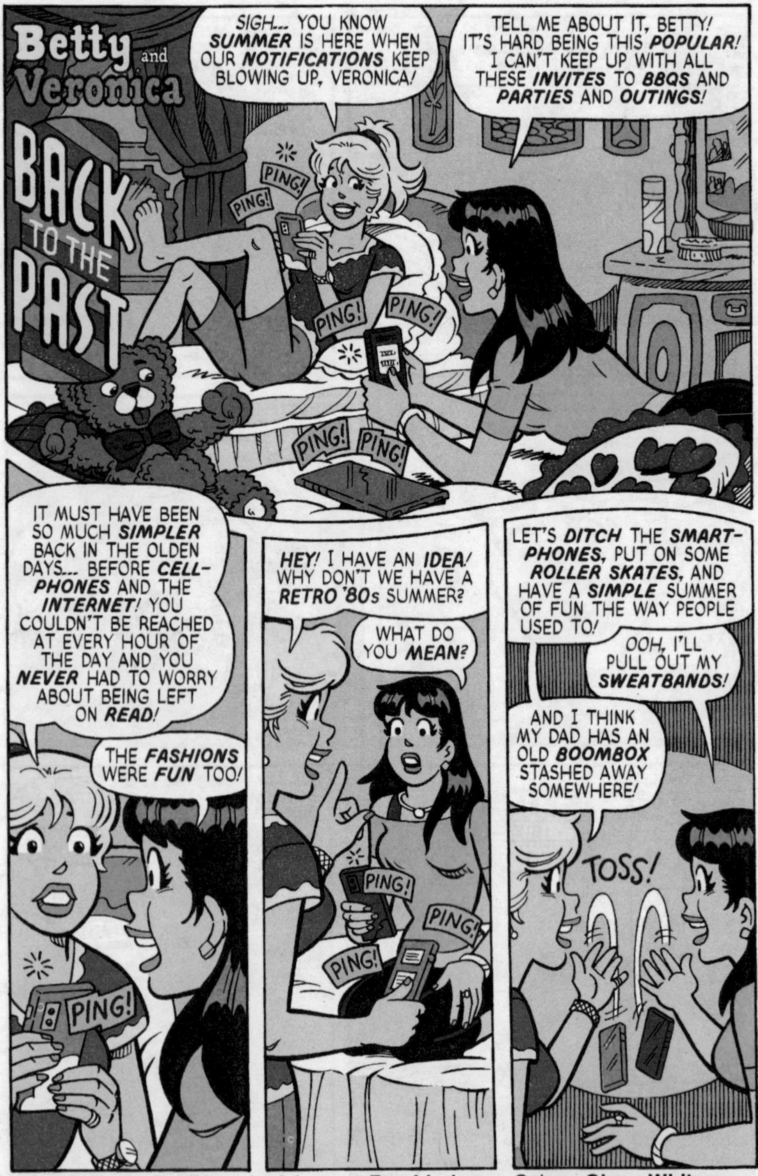
Betty and Veronica
BACK TO THE PAST
SIGH... YOU KNOW SUMMER IS HERE WHEN OUR NOTIFICATIONS KEEP BLOWING UP, VERONICA!
TELL ME ABOUT IT, BETTY! IT'S HARD BEING THIS POPULAR! I CAN'T KEEP UP WITH ALL THESE INVITES TO BBQS AND PARTIES AND OUTINGS!
PING!
PING!
PING!
PING!
PING!
PING!
IT MUST HAVE BEEN SO MUCH SIMPLER BACK IN THE OLDEN DAYS... BEFORE CELL-PHONES AND THE INTERNET! YOU COULDN'T BE REACHED AT EVERY HOUR OF THE DAY AND YOU NEVER HAD TO WORRY ABOUT BEING LEFT ON READ!
THE FASHIONS WERE FUN TOO!
PING!
HEY! I HAVE AN IDEA! WHY DON'T WE HAVE A RETRO '80s SUMMER?
WHAT DO YOU MEAN?
PING!
PING!
PING!
LET'S DITCH THE SMART-PHONES, PUT ON SOME ROLLER SKATES, AND HAVE A SIMPLE SUMMER OF FUN THE WAY PEOPLE USED TO!
OOH, I'LL PULL OUT MY SWEATBANDS!
AND I THINK MY DAD HAS AN OLD BOOMBOX STASHED AWAY SOMEWHERE!
TOSS!

Script: **Tania Del Rio** Art & Letters: **Rex Lindsey** Colors: **Glenn Whitmore**

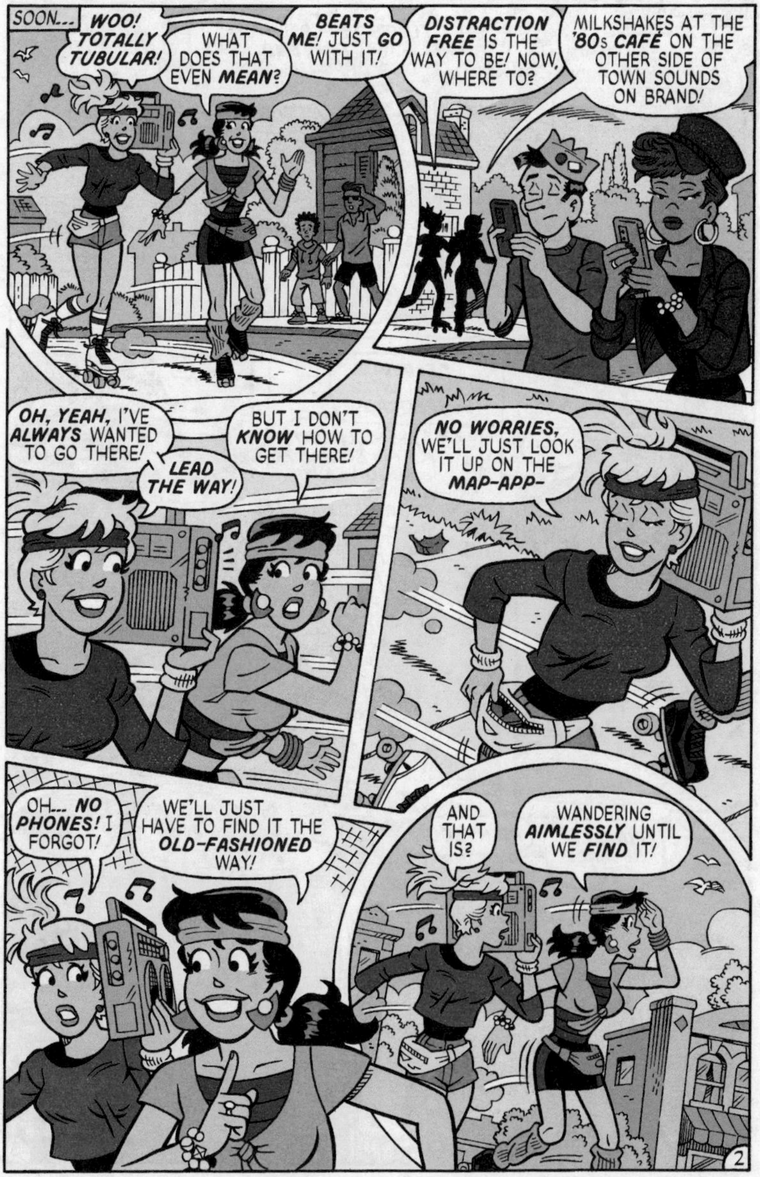
SOON...
WOO! TOTALLY TUBULAR!
WHAT DOES THAT EVEN MEAN?
BEATS ME! JUST GO WITH IT!
DISTRACTION FREE IS THE WAY TO BE! NOW, WHERE TO?
MILKSHAKES AT THE '80s CAFÉ ON THE OTHER SIDE OF TOWN SOUNDS ON BRAND!
OH, YEAH, I'VE ALWAYS WANTED TO GO THERE!
LEAD THE WAY!
BUT I DON'T KNOW HOW TO GET THERE!
NO WORRIES, WE'LL JUST LOOK IT UP ON THE MAP-APP-
OH... NO PHONES! I FORGOT!
WE'LL JUST HAVE TO FIND IT THE OLD-FASHIONED WAY!
AND THAT IS?
WANDERING AIMLESSLY UNTIL WE FIND IT!
2

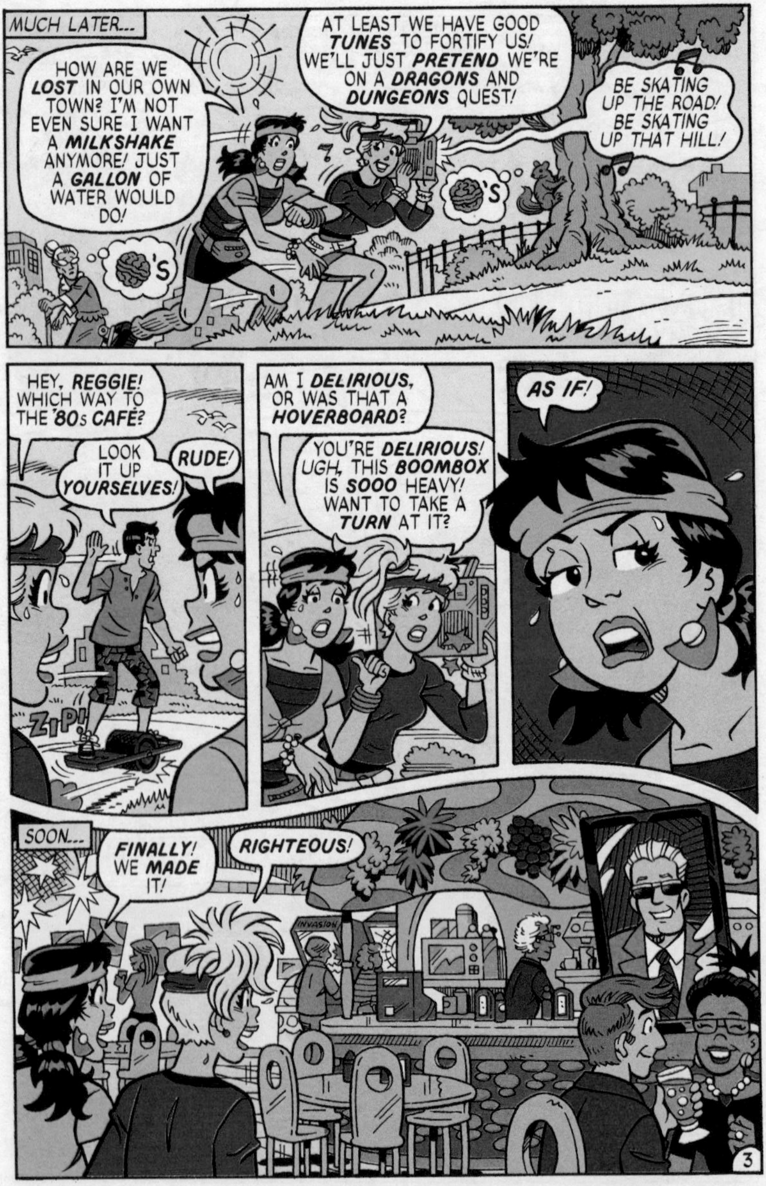
MUCH LATER...
HOW ARE WE LOST IN OUR OWN TOWN? I'M NOT EVEN SURE I WANT A MILKSHAKE ANYMORE! JUST A GALLON OF WATER WOULD DO!
AT LEAST WE HAVE GOOD TUNES TO FORTIFY US! WE'LL JUST PRETEND WE'RE ON A DRAGONS AND DUNGEONS QUEST!
BE SKATING UP THE ROAD! BE SKATING UP THAT HILL!
HEY, REGGIE! WHICH WAY TO THE '80s CAFÉ?
LOOK IT UP YOURSELVES!
RUDE!
ZIP!
AM I DELIRIOUS, OR WAS THAT A HOVERBOARD?
YOU'RE DELIRIOUS! UGH, THIS BOOMBOX IS SOOO HEAVY! WANT TO TAKE A TURN AT IT?
AS IF!
SOON...
FINALLY! WE MADE IT!
RIGHTEOUS!
INVASION
3

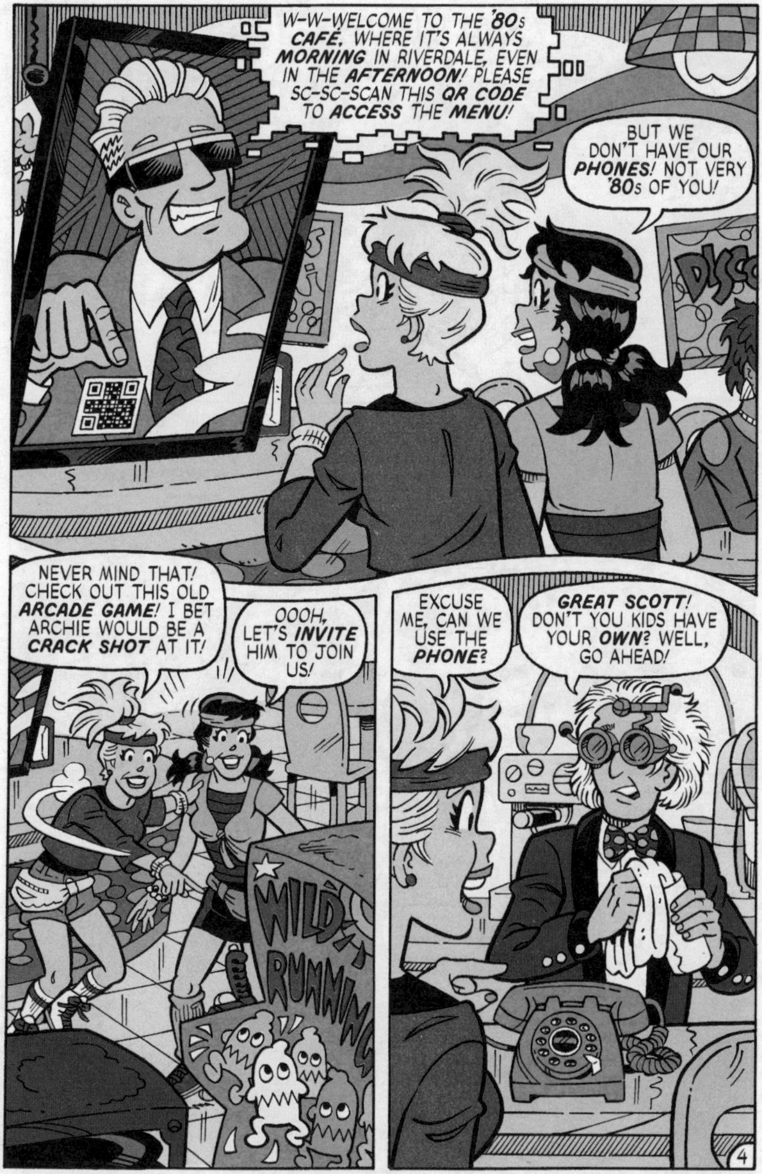
W-W-WELCOME TO THE '80s CAFÉ, WHERE IT'S ALWAYS MORNING IN RIVERDALE, EVEN IN THE AFTERNOON! PLEASE SC-SC-SCAN THIS QR CODE TO ACCESS THE MENU!
BUT WE DON'T HAVE OUR PHONES! NOT VERY '80s OF YOU!
DISCO
NEVER MIND THAT! CHECK OUT THIS OLD ARCADE GAME! I BET ARCHIE WOULD BE A CRACK SHOT AT IT!
OOOH, LET'S INVITE HIM TO JOIN US!
WILD RUNNIN
EXCUSE ME, CAN WE USE THE PHONE?
GREAT SCOTT! DON'T YOU KIDS HAVE YOUR OWN? WELL, GO AHEAD!
4

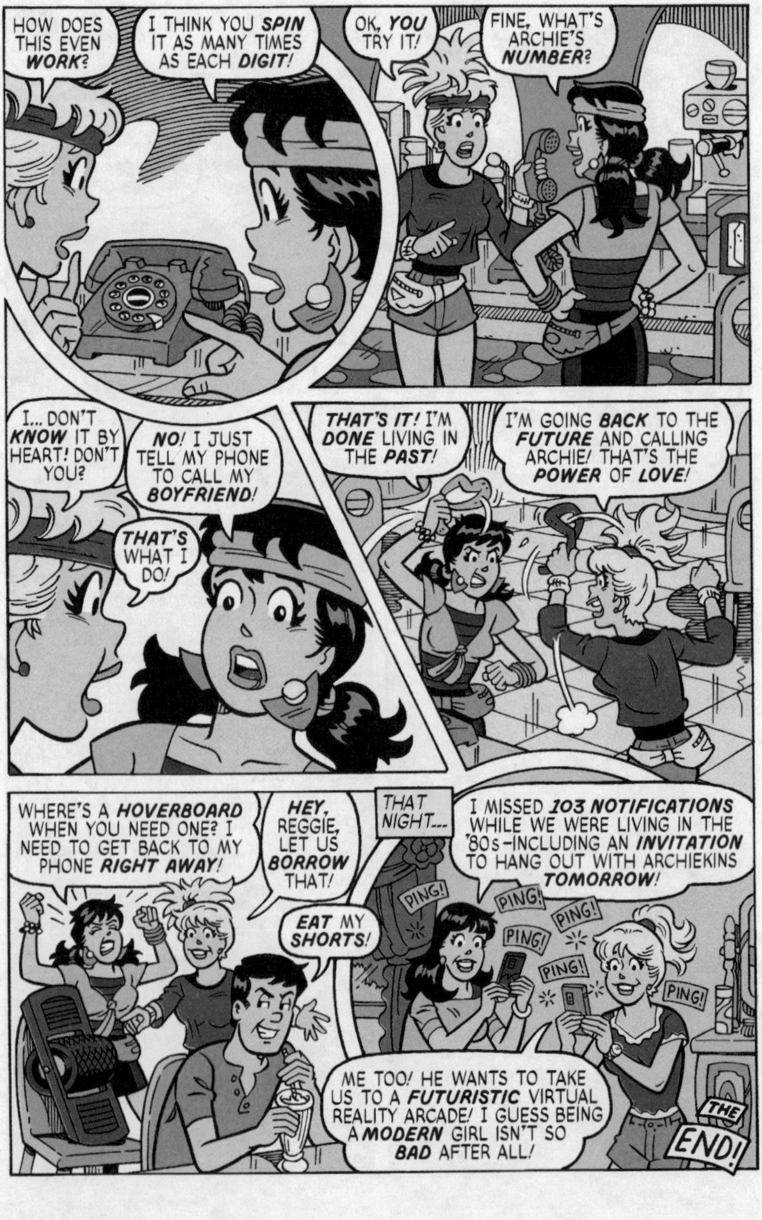
HOW DOES THIS EVEN WORK?
I THINK YOU SPIN IT AS MANY TIMES AS EACH DIGIT!
OK, YOU TRY IT!
FINE, WHAT'S ARCHIE'S NUMBER?
I... DON'T KNOW IT BY HEART! DON'T YOU?
NO! I JUST TELL MY PHONE TO CALL MY BOYFRIEND!
THAT'S WHAT I DO!
THAT'S IT! I'M DONE LIVING IN THE PAST!
I'M GOING BACK TO THE FUTURE AND CALLING ARCHIE! THAT'S THE POWER OF LOVE!
WHERE'S A HOVERBOARD WHEN YOU NEED ONE? I NEED TO GET BACK TO MY PHONE RIGHT AWAY!
HEY, REGGIE, LET US BORROW THAT!
EAT MY SHORTS!
THAT NIGHT...
I MISSED 103 NOTIFICATIONS WHILE WE WERE LIVING IN THE '80s–INCLUDING AN INVITATION TO HANG OUT WITH ARCHIEKINS TOMORROW!
PING!
PING!
PING!
PING!
PING!
PING!
ME TOO! HE WANTS TO TAKE US TO A FUTURISTIC VIRTUAL REALITY ARCADE! I GUESS BEING A MODERN GIRL ISN'T SO BAD AFTER ALL!
THE END!